Maxim Jakubowski is a London-based novelist and editor. He was born in the UK and educated in France. Following a career in book publishing, he opened the world-famous Murder One bookshop in London. He now writes full-time. He has edited over twenty bestselling erotic anthologies and books on erotic photography, as well as many acclaimed crime collections. His novels include *It's You That I Want to Kiss*, *Because She Thought She Loved Me* and *On Tenderness Express*, all three collected and reprinted in the USA as *Skin in Darkness*. Other books include *Life in the World of Women*, *The State of Montana*, *Kiss Me Sadly*, *Confessions of a Romantic Pornographer*, *I Was Waiting For You* and *Ekaterina and the Night*. In 2006 he published *American Casanova*, a major erotic novel, which he edited and on which fifteen of the top erotic writers in the world collaborated, and his collected erotic short stories as *Fools For Lust*. He compiles two annual acclaimed series for the Mammoth list: *Best New Erotica* and *Best British Crime*. He is a winner of the Anthony and the Karel Awards, a frequent TV and radio broadcaster, a past crime columnist for the *Guardian* newspaper and Literary Director of London's Crime Scene Festival. Over the past years, he has authored under a pen name a series of *Sunday Times* bestselling erotic romance novels which have sold over two million copies and been sold to twenty-two countries, and translated the acclaimed French erotic novel *Monsieur* by Emma Becker.

Recent Mammoth titles

The Mammoth Book of Hot Romance
The Mammoth Book of Historical Crime Fiction
The Mammoth Book of Best New SF 24
The Mammoth Book of Gorgeous Guys
The Mammoth Book of Really Silly Jokes
The Mammoth Book of Best New Horror 22
The Mammoth Book of Undercover Cops
The Mammoth Book of Weird News
The Mammoth Book of the Best of Best New Erotica
The Mammoth Book of Antarctic Journeys
The Mammoth Book of Muhammad Ali
The Mammoth Book of Best British Crime 9
The Mammoth Book of Conspiracies
The Mammoth Book of Lost Symbols
The Mammoth Book of Sex Scandals
The Mammoth Book of Body Horror
The Mammoth Book of Steampunk
The Mammoth Book of New CSI
The Mammoth Book of Gangs
The Mammoth Book of SF Wars
The Mammoth Book of One-Liners
The Mammoth Book of Ghost Romance
The Mammoth Book of Threesomes and Moresomes
The Mammoth Book of Best New SF 25
The Mammoth Book of Jokes 2
The Mammoth Book of Horror 23
The Mammoth Book of Slasher Movies
The Mammoth Book of Street Art
The Mammoth Book of Ghost Stories by Women
The Mammoth Book of Best New Erotica 12
The Mammoth Book of Urban Erotic Confessions
The Mammoth Book of Quick & Dirty Erotica

The Mammoth Book of Erotic Romance and Domination

Edited by Maxim Jakubowski

ROBINSON

First published in Great Britain by Robinson, an imprint of Constable & Robinson Ltd., 2014

Reprinted in 2019 by Robinson

5 7 9 10 8 6 4

A CIP catalogue record for this book is available from the British Library.

ISBN: 978-1-4721-1167-8

Robinson
An imprint of
Little, Brown Book Group
Carmelite House
50 Victoria Embankment
London EC4Y 0DZ

An Hachette UK Company
www.hachette.co.uk

www.littlebrown.co.uk

This is a work of fi ction. Names, characters, places and incidents are either the product of the author's imagination or are used fi ctitiously, and any resemblance to actual persons, living or dead, or to actual events or locales is entirely coincidental.

First Published in the United States in 2014 by Running Press Book Publishers
An Imprint of Perseus Books, LLC.
A Subsidiary of Hachette Book Group, Inc.
2300 Chestnut Street
Philadelphia, PA 19103-4371

Books published by Running Press are available at special discounts for bulk purchases in the United States by corporations, institutions and other organizations. For more information, please contact the Special Markets Department at the Perseus Books Group, 2300 Chestnut Street, Suite 200, Philadelphia, PA 19103, or call (800) 810-4145, ext. 5000, or email special.markets@perseusbooks.com.

US ISBN: 978-0-7624-5225-5
US Library of Congress Control Number: 2014931355

10 9 8 7 6 5 4
Digit on the right indicates the number of this printing
Visit us on the web!
www.runningpress.com

Printed and bound by CPI Group (UK) Ltd, Croydon, CR0 4YY

Papers used by Robinson are from well-managed forests and other responsible sources

Contents

Introduction

2012 was the year that erotica changed forever thanks to the success of a certain trilogy.

Not that the genre hadn't been around before as my own editing efforts in the field for the past two decades and the stories and novels of countless writers with a taste and talent for erotica can historically demonstrate. But it was the year when it moved from a relatively confidential corner of the bookstores and shelves to a wider and surprising appreciation and acceptance by the reading public, and in the process attracted the silly moniker of "mommy porn" when it was established that so many of it was being lapped up by women with young families. As an aside, I can certainly vouch for this curious segment of the public if only from the comments on the website and Facebook pages of the collaborative alter ego under which I have also committed much literate if commercial fare in the genre and adorned the bestseller lists to my great surprise in the wake of E. L. James.

What this means for the future of erotic writing is still unclear, as the inevitable flood of copycat books was promptly unleashed on readers by publishers and has quickly muddied the waters and a disorderly retreat is already in progress, but one can only hope that the fad will leave a lasting impression and that, in the future, the sales and popularity of erotica will have moved a few steps ahead from where they stood far back some years ago.

Of course, the determining factor in the success of *Fifty Shades of Grey* was the way it opened people's eyes and minds to the existence and importance of BDSM and its varied practices in the complicated world of sexual relationships and brought them into the open. Not a revelation for us grizzled veterans who had been writing around and about it for ages or the silent majority who had always indulged in real life, but a new world altogether for the average man and woman, it appeared! Where had they been hiding?

As is well reported, the Victorians freely indulged in the art of spanking and corporal punishment, a BDSM variation of sorts which still remains highly popular in deeds and words, but the genuine introduction of BDSM and its physical as well as psychological games of dominance and submission only fully came to light with the publication of the classic *Story of O* by Pauline Réage (a pen name for French academic and critic Dominique Aury) in the 1950s, a groundbreaking excursion into the byways of kink and sex which brought BDSM out from the under the counter territory it had long occupied and proudly into the open. Several generations later, and with all due respect to E. L. James's mega-selling phenomenon, I daresay that no one has bettered *Story of O* for its visceral and shattering impact and the way it thrust what had previously been taboo sexual practices and games of power into the limelight of the written word and paved the way for so many other, ever more explicit variations by the likes of Anne Rice, Molly Weatherfield, Laura Antoniou, Laura Reese, Michael Perkins, Alison Tyler, Kristina Lloyd, myself even and a whole palette of new erotica practitioners.

Hence the reason for this new collection: a wish to present to the reading public how varied and imaginative the influence of BDSM is in everyday life and how sexy (and scary) it can prove on the written page. Unlike my annual *Mammoth Book of Best New Erotica*, which mostly relies on previously published material, all the stories included between these covers were written specially for the volume by the absolute crème de la crème of contemporary writing as well as a handful of brand-new talents. Only a few authors I had hoped to include missed the deadline due to personal reasons or because of crowded deadlines, but overall I would venture that the line-up of contributors is one of the most prestigious that could be assembled today, and the contents are likewise challenging and so terribly exciting.

We open with a sensational new novella by *Sunday Times* Top 10 bestseller Vina Jackson, which ties in with her recent *Eighty Days* and *Mistress of Night and Dawn* novels. Another welcome newcomer to my anthologies is Stella Knightley, whose recent trilogy of sexy romances was one of the best post-*F.S.O.G.* efforts and who, like Vina Jackson, is also a ferociously colourful writer with a unique eye for kink and works far from the quasi-vanilla shores of the colour grey! Also on-board are Booker Prize-long-listed author Matt Thorne with a most unexpected take on a familiar theme, award-winning Science Fiction star Ian Watson, ebullient bonkbuster queen Rebecca Chance and the dazzling new star of Italian erotica, Ilaria Palomba as well as the very top ranks of British and American authors on their very best and worst behaviour . . .

Much to savour and make your eyes spin: imagination truly unbridled. But don't try any of this at home, please!

On a sad note, I would like to dedicate this anthology to the memory of Michael Hemmingson, who died shortly after delivering his story. He was a great friend, collaborator and writer who will be sadly missed.

Maxim Jakubowski

White is Not Just the Colour of Snow

Vina Jackson

As far back as she remembered Nelle had always dreamed in black and white. Colour never came into the equation. The illogical and haunting events that surged out of nowhere when she slept were also invariably soundless, like a silent movie although a touch more explicit than early days cinema would ever have allowed.

Even the blood that often gushed was white in this strange world of her perverse imagination.

There were moments when her conscious mind half realized she was moving through a dream and made a clumsy attempt to influence the plot or the outcome but it was, time and time again, to no avail. The dream kept to its inexorable path and she was carried by its tides to the ever-distant but fixed conclusion when she would wake, damp with sweat, her heart palpitating to the rhythm of a tango or pounding like death metal music. Breathless. Panicked. Lost.

She often tried to recall the strange course of events that had swept over her mind, and body, during the actual dream, but as soon as her soul found peace and she was able to orientate her consciousness, it all crumbled, vanished into a confused mass of faraway clouds, shards flying away to all corners of her memory, and the screen in her brain was just a Cinemascope landscape of white as far as the eye could see.

Lately, however neutral it was as a colour, black had been draining away from her dreams and all she could remember hours later was an immensity of white. Devouring both the land and the sky. Through which she fell, ran, stumbled, drowned. As you do in dreams.

That morning, she had rushed from the bed while it was still dark outside and made her way to the bathroom and stood for ages under the hot cascade of the shower, half dazed by the heavy sense of oppression and fear the dream had left her in the grip of. Water was dripping from her hair and shoulders as she slipped into her bathrobe without bothering to dry herself and walked downstairs to the kitchen. She had slept alone. Joseph had not joined her and had likely spent the night in his study.

He was sitting at the counter, absorbed by the eerie glow of his laptop screen, sipping a coffee. He didn't look up when she came in.

"Hi," Nelle said. "You didn't come to bed last night. Did you complete your research?"

He raised his eyes. "Your hair is still wet. You'll catch a cold," he replied, ignoring her question.

Nelle was unsure whether the remote prospect of her falling ill would pain or inconvenience him. His tone was so neutral. He was always like this when working on a new trick. But before she could protest, Joseph spoke again.

"You must take next week off work. We'll be going north."

Nelle shivered. "The Ball?" she asked.

"Yes."

"Where?"

"Far. It is to be a White Ball," Joseph said.

So this was it, she recognized. What she had been both fearing and expecting for some time now. The event that they had talked about for so long. That Joseph had attended in the past, but never with her. She hadn't been ready, he'd said. Maybe the reason why her dreams of the past weeks had gradually been morphing into something else, as if the unconscious part of her brain had already been preparing her for the days to come. She shuddered. Her body tingled with anticipation. They ate their breakfast in silence, lightly toasted bagels with a thick spread of cream cheese and then she noticed she was on the point of being late and rushed upstairs to dress and ran out of the house with just a wave goodbye to Joseph, who barely looked up, as she straddled her bike, and pedalled down the grey road, her wheels crunching the autumn leaves.

Even now, the memory of their first meeting was etched on her mind like writing on a stone tablet.

Nelle had been distracted. Living on autopilot, relying on her innate sense of grammar and punctuation to get her through the working days that she had previously relished, and barely awake the rest of the time. Still hungover on a past relationship that was leading nowhere slow and had eventually petered out with not even a sense of relief, leaving her wondering whether she had it in her to ever be happy. Or at any rate content.

Joseph was an up-and-coming magician. He had something of a cult reputation, she had read in a magazine article, compounded by his refusal to ever perform on television. He had been signed up by one of the small publishing houses she had worked for as a freelance copy editor for several years, and his manuscript had only recently been assigned to her. Nelle had received the commission with his copy attached out of the blue, and then been told by one of the publishing company's administrators that another copy editor had been offended by the contents of his work, stopped midway and had asked to be reassigned, slowing down the whole process.

Nelle had expected the book landing in her lap would be one explaining his tricks and the art of subterfuge and trickery, but it was, surprisingly, actually a novel.

Had Nelle been less distracted at the time, she probably would have been intrigued at the thought of reading whatever had left one of her colleagues so inflamed, but she merely added the script to her electronic to-do list and then continued with her work, barely registering the interruption to her schedule.

When she did finally click open the attachment and begin reading, it was the tone of his writing, even more than the content, that first began to waken the spark in her that she had not felt for so long she had nearly forgotten it had ever existed. His voice was strong and, to Nelle's mind, masculine. But the novel was not written from the point of view of a man, but rather that of a young woman. A dancer, who performed a series of erotic routines on stage in London's music halls and the homes of wealthy patrons in the twenties and thirties.

The heroine of Joseph's novel was not described as beautiful in any traditional sense of the word. Nor did she meet any of the other characteristics that were typical of the romance books that Nelle was now accustomed to trudging her way through, a genre that she was so often assigned to work on.

His heroine, Joan, was tall – too tall – and thin to the point of lankiness, flat-chested and with hair that was a perfectly ordinary shade of brown. Not unlike Nelle's own appearance.

Joan was not described in a more flattering light when filled with the heat of lust, or love, either, a state that possessed her often, as she was highly sexed. In fact, Joseph's writing was as cold as it was sparse and elegant, and his sex scenes verged on the anatomical.

There were many sex scenes. But none described lovemaking as Nelle had ever known it. She was not even sure that sex was the right word to use, as most of the erotic passages did not include penetration, but rather narrated the heroine's elaborate dance routines, which became more and more perverse under the tutorage of her mentor and lover, an older, stern Russian man, who by the end of it had Joan performing ballet naked, blindfolded and *en pointe* with knives affixed to her shoes.

It was animalistic, shocking, yet beautiful, and it wasn't until Nelle reached the end of the text that she realized she had stopped actually copy-editing by the third chapter and simply allowed herself to be carried along by the flow of the story until the early hours of the morning when she reached its final chapter and then had to start over again, this time with an eye to her work.

Joseph's story had continued to fill her thoughts when she

finally switched off her desk lamp and slid into bed. She had not been able to sleep until she had slipped her hand between her thighs and brought herself to orgasm with the artful movements of her fingertips playing over her clitoris, as his images played in her mind, only in her imagination it was not the heroine, Joan, who danced naked on knife blades in front of a faceless audience, but her, Nelle.

She had typed his name into her Google search bar the following morning with the guilty feeling of someone steaming the envelope of correspondence meant for another. Nelle heartily disapproved of nosiness, but she could not seem to assuage her curiosity. Besides, she told herself, it was research. Finding something about the man himself and his past career might help her to better understand his current work.

What she discovered surprised her at first. But the more she read, the more it made sense, in light of his novel.

Joseph had once been a chemist by education and trade. He had published a handful of academic articles in obscure journals, most related to the study of minerals, and had worked as a teacher for a time, before leaving to pursue a career as a magician. Albeit one of a different nature, where the illusions he unveiled in public had a touch of the supernatural and proved more subtle than pyrotechnic. In the rare interviews he had granted, he would talk of opening up the door to secret worlds, which could be accessed through abolishing one's sense of reality through a mastery of the senses.

The erotic nature of his story then, was a surprising as well as a logical departure. Try as Nelle might, she couldn't erase his lines and the tale remained painted across her mind, even days later.

With the return of her sexual urges, she regained some of her usual joy for life. The leaves on the trees seemed brighter. Her daily swims at the local lido in nearby London Fields again made her feel as though she was gliding through the water effortlessly, for pleasure alone, and not for the sake of scheduled exercise. Even her morning coffee tasted better. And she looked forward to crawling under the covers each night and letting her mind drift away into the world of her private imagination, where she replayed the words of Joseph's novel again and again as she brought herself to orgasm.

Sometimes she woke in the night, hot, sweating and desperately aroused to the point of discomfort, face down with her long limbs sprawled across the damp sheets, her pelvis grinding the mattress in an imitation of intercourse, her mind too carried away by the events reeling within to prevent her body from following suit. She felt compelled to seek out other erotic literature, hoping that she might find something else that struck the same chord in her, but it was no use. Other words aroused her, of course, but none engaged her mind as well as her cunt in quite the same way as the story of the ballerina on her knife blades, enduring pain for love.

Why it aroused her so, she couldn't say, though in her darker moments she wondered if there was something wrong with her for relishing the thought of discomfort so heartily, and worse, pain administered by another. So long as it was fiction, she supposed, it didn't matter what got her off.

But it would not stay fiction for long, as she came to meet him the very next day.

The pool was usually near empty when Nelle swam. She avoided the very early mornings when city workers ploughed ferocious laps before they scurried like ants to their office buildings, and the lunchtime aqua aerobics classes, which were full of expectant and new mothers, the elderly and the very overweight, who preferred to exercise beneath the sheet of invisibility and comfort that water brought.

She stood for a few moments and watched the only other swimmer in the pool, a man swimming laps in the fast lane. His singularity put him in the spotlight, a lone figure gliding through the water like a solitary ship in a vast sea, the swift movements of his arms creating a current that followed him like a rip tide.

Nelle lowered herself into the pool and began to swim in the lane alongside him, her mind and body quickly adjusting to the rhythm of her strokes, until it seemed as though the world around her had vanished entirely and there was nothing but her body and the vast cavern of her mind, as empty and weightless as the water that encased her like a shroud.

When she finally finished her allotted number of lengths and reached for the metal bar near the pool's edge to pull herself out, he was standing nearby with his back to her, wet shorts clinging to muscled thighs, his face half hidden in his towel as he vigorously dried his hair.

Again she caught herself staring, transfixed not just by the angles of his body but also by his solitude, his habits. The way he swam, moved, suggested that this man and Nelle shared whatever characteristic it was that drew them both to the lido at the quietest time of day to be as alone as it is possible to be in London, removing even the company of the earth beneath their feet, replacing the ever-bustling sounds of the world around them with the steady lapping of water.

Alerted by her presence, or perhaps the rushing noise the water made as she pulled her body from the pool, he turned, and their eyes met before Nelle could look away.

She recognized him immediately. Just that morning she had gazed at the photo on his website, the same close-up picture that appeared on the proof of the back cover of his book. Nelle had paused and stared at the face that watched benignly back at her from the screen, handsome, she supposed, but harmless. Academic yet approachable. The sort of face that looked as though it belonged to a science teacher. Not the sort of face that she imagined belonged to a magician with an undoubted flair for the erotic.

Nelle had quickly dismissed the thought as ridiculous. People rarely looked how you expected anyway, which was why she generally refused to turn the final page to find the author's picture on the inside or back covers of the books she enjoyed, preferring them to remain anonymous and not have reality intrude on the far more flattering light of her fantasy.

In the flesh though, she saw it as soon as he turned to face her. He possessed whatever it was that made a person appear sensual, as if the strength of his sexuality was such that it was apparent even in the lines on his face. His lips were much fuller and his mouth wider than it appeared in his photograph. His eyes were a darker shade of brown, so dark that they were nearly black, like pits of coal that she could fall into, but would surely burn up if she did. His hair, still wet, was thick and dark and clung in damp curls around his forehead.

"Joseph?" she said aloud, before she could stop herself.

His mouth dropped open slightly in shock.

"Yes?" he replied in the wary tone of someone who has been cornered by the dullest guest at a party or found themselves trapped in an elevator with a salesperson. His eyes darted over her face and then away again as if he was mentally running her features through his mind's eye, seeking out some detail that might remind him of where they had met, before he was forced to admit that he did not remember who she was.

They were trapped now. The unspoken laws of etiquette required that although they were both dressed only in their bathing suits, her feet still resting on the top step, half in the pool, she ought to explain herself, justify her intrusion into his privacy, put him out of the misery of wondering if he had committed a sin of terrible rudeness in forgetting her identity.

"Oh, no, you don't know me. I'm sorry. I recognized you. From your book cover."

He looked still more confused. And embarrassed.

"But the book hasn't yet been published," he protested. "Maybe you've seen my website. Are you a fan of magic?"

She realized her mistake, and felt her skin begin to redden despite the cold.

Joseph furrowed his brow, now seemingly wondering if she had mistaken him for somebody else.

Nelle explained. "I work with your publishers. Copy-editing. I finished reading your manuscript just last night."

Was he blushing, or was she imagining it?

"It's very good," she added. "I enjoyed reading it."

"I didn't think you copy editors actually read anything. Just scanned for all the infelicities." His eyes crinkled up at the corners in the beginnings of a smile.

"Your work was fine," she reassured. "I've seen much worse."

He laughed. "Well, that's a relief."

She stepped forward and extended her hand, remembering too late that she was still dripping wet, but he shook it anyway.

"I'm Nelle," she said. "Sorry about the wet hand. Not the most convenient place to meet, is it," she added, looking around at the harsh grey concrete of the poolside, broken by a long line of locker doors painted in bright primary colours but bereft of seats. The café at one end that opened in the summer serving cold drinks and ice creams was now closed.

"Here," he replied, offering her his towel. "It's mostly dry."

She took it, wrapping the fabric around her like a cape, grateful for the warmth and the opportunity to cover her body, although she had noted that Joseph had not cast so much as a glance below her neck. He was polite, in a very English sort of way. Nelle knew that, like her, he wore his social graces like a mask.

They paused, searching for something else to say, or some way to end this unplanned encounter between two strangers that had already gone on too long.

Nelle shifted her weight from one foot to the other. She licked her lips, embarrassed, wishing that she had never engaged him in conversation. The fantasies that his work had inspired in her had little bearing on the reality of meeting Joseph in person.

They spoke at the same time.

"Well," she said, "I should be . . ." as he asked, "Would you like to join me for . . ." "getting on," she finished, "coffee?" he said. "Yes of course," she replied, interrupting him again as he backtracked, "no problem."

They laughed uncomfortably, in unison.

"There's a Vietnamese coffee shop towards the market," he said. "They serve it with sweetened condensed milk. Very warming."

"That would be lovely," she replied, firmly this time, to counteract her initial rejection.

She handed back his towel.

"I'll change. Meet you out front in five?"

He nodded in agreement.

She turned away from him to fetch her change bag from her locker, conscious of the way that her bathing suit clung to her and crept up as she walked, exposing the tops of her thighs and the rounded edge of her backside. She tried to feign confidence, nonchalance, and did not stop to adjust herself. Was he watching? she wondered. Did he like what he saw?

Nelle looked good in a one-piece, and she knew it. Her slim legs sometimes appeared too thin to her eyes, in jeans, or a dress. Somehow the addition of clothes made her figure even more boyish. But her bathing suits accentuated what little she had in the way of curves, which was part of the reason why she owned so many of them but had relatively few other clothes. She'd never been particularly interested in shopping, or fashion.

She paused as she bent down to open the locker door, giving Joseph ample opportunity to let his gaze linger on her rear, but when she turned back again he had disappeared into the men's changing rooms.

When she emerged through the lido's glass double doors, he was already waiting for her, dressed in black running joggers and a grey jumper with the hood lying loose around his shoulders. It was an anonymous sort of outfit, the kind of clothing that advertised nothing at all about his economic status or sartorial taste.

Nelle had expected to return straight home after her swim, and hadn't even brought a bra with her, just a long-sleeved blouse, a skirt that hung down to her ankles and a pair of casual flat shoes. She'd hesitated over removing her bathing suit and left it on in the end, thinking that more modest than appearing braless, but by the time she had dried her hair and gathered her things her thin cotton shirt had begun to dampen and now clung to her like a second skin. The chill present in the air hit her as soon as she stepped out to meet him and her nipples immediately hardened.

"Sorry," she said to him, excusing her bedraggled appearance. "I wasn't expecting to meet anyone today."

"No need to apologize," he replied. "You look fine. And I'm hardly dressed for a lunch date, either."

He spoke as if he were cracking a whip, his tone brusque and his intonation clipped. She liked this quality in him. Joseph was honest, and his honesty relaxed her.

Nelle disliked meeting new people. She found it hard to be fake, a quality that, to her mind, almost all relationships required to begin with. Nelle simply didn't care much about people that she didn't know well enough to really like, and she resented pretending empathy for the sake of politeness, so spent a lot of time alone.

They fell into silence as they walked the length of the tree-lined footpath through London Fields to the Broadway Market. Nelle quickened her pace when she noticed that she was staring at Joseph's back. Almost without thinking about it, she had fallen into a gait slightly slower than his, so she was walking half a step behind him.

When they arrived, Joseph ordered two coffees without asking her how she took it, and raised his hand abruptly in a gesture of refusal as she fished in her purse for change.

They sat opposite one another at one of the worn red tables and sipped their drinks.

"I usually take it black," he said, almost apologizing for the thick, sickly sweetness of the drink. "But the sugar is nice after exercise." He paused. "I've seen you before, at the pool," he added. "You swim well."

Nelle nodded, unsure of how to reply. Until today, she hadn't noticed him.

"I swim every day," she replied. "Most days, at least," she added, and then swiftly gulped down another mouthful of coffee, fearing that she now sounded arrogant.

They finished their drinks and parted company uneasily.

Nelle hadn't been able to shake the feeling that he was laughing at her, somehow.

The following week, he was there again at the same time. Had he been there every week, and she just hadn't noticed him before? Or was he now following her? He was already swimming when she arrived, so she was able to observe him unnoticed for a time. He moved through the water with monotonous regularity, turning his head first to the right and then to the left. Nelle always breathed on the same side. She counted his strokes. One, two, three, four, five, six. He held his breath for an age before coming up for air and even then he did so with measured precision, not the startled gasp of someone who should have paused for air several strokes earlier.

He stopped suddenly at the end of the length and, placing his hands flat on the concrete of the poolside, he straightened his forearms and with one rapid motion pushed himself out of the water.

"Hello," he said, to her, smiling. "Are you swimming today? Or just waiting for me?"

Nelle was too embarrassed to reply. She simply pulled her goggles down as though she hadn't heard him and dived into the water with a soft splash.

She swam for twice as long as usual, until she felt as though she might dissolve if she carried on any longer, but still she couldn't shake the image of his wet body from her mind. He was older than she was. Probably in his early forties, to her early thirties, although she found it hard to guess the age of men, particularly fit men. He was tall, though not unusually so, and broad-shouldered, with just a light smattering of hair on his chest.

Images flashed into her mind unbidden. His pectoral muscles tightening beneath her hands. His dick hardening as she let her fingertips slide lower down.

When she was certain that he must by now have had ample time to grow bored of watching her swim, dry himself, change and leave, she ducked her head to cross under the lane rope and pulled herself up the metal rail on the side.

"Sixty-four laps," he said. "You always swim an even number."

He hadn't even bothered to wrap himself in a towel. Just sat there, drip-drying and watching her. She might have been spooked, had it not been for the undeniable fact that the sight of his still wet shorts clinging to his thighs and the undeniable presence of his cock and balls caused her breath to quicken and all of her muscles to tighten in immediate arousal.

She was aware that her own nipples were hard, and also that he had watched them harden, but this time she held his gaze impudently and did not look away.

"You must be cold," he added. "I live just a few blocks from here. And I have a coffee machine."

It hadn't even really been an invitation. Merely a statement. But the lack of a question had somehow made it more natural for her to go with him.

Joseph left her standing, waiting for a few moments, as he ducked into the outdoor showers and then emerged, still damp, but now wearing his tracksuit bottoms and, Nelle suspected, nothing underneath. She wondered how his cock would feel if she were to slip her hand beneath the waistband of his joggers and her fingers over his delicate skin, feel it jump to life in her hand.

He looked at her standing there, shivering in her bathing suit with usual long skirt and blouse hastily pulled overtop, and laughed.

"You'll catch your death of cold," he said. "Aren't you going to change properly?"

She felt rebellious, all of a sudden, and shook her head. "No," she replied, "I'll be fine."

"Come on then. Let's get you warmed up."

The suggestion in his words excited her. As they stepped through the metal exit gates and she turned away from the direction of her flat to follow Joseph to his, Nelle knew that she would have sex with him. At that moment, it seemed inevitable.

Nelle could see no sensible reason to follow Joseph now. She barely knew the man. They'd had one cup of coffee together, and even then, barely spoken. And yet her feet kept carrying her towards him, and with each step her heartbeat quickened and her already hard nipples became harder, until she felt as though she might drill holes through her bathing suit.

His mouth was on hers even before he had closed the door, and barely a moment after that, his hand had fastened around her throat. Nelle felt her feet leaving the ground as he picked her up as easily as a cat might pick up a kitten, and held her tightly against the door frame. He squeezed tighter, and she began to feel faint. Her mouth opened. She supposed she ought to scream, but with her airway restricted she could barely swallow and the only noise she could utter was half a gasp, half a moan.

Just as she thought she might pass out, his grip loosened a little. Enough so that her toes could touch the ground. She inhaled rapidly and coughed.

"Do you think I'm going to kill you?" he asked.

Nelle tried to speak but couldn't. There was no air in her lungs. She shook her head from side to side. "No."

"Good," he replied. "You're right. I'm not."

She sucked in a long breath and, as soon as she did so, his grip was around her throat again, and his hands grasping and lifting the hem of her skirt and then she felt his fingers brushing past the soft skin of her inner thighs to the crotch of her bathing suit, where he stopped, and began to rub. Softly at first, gauging her reactions, exploring, until he found the nub of her clitoris. His fingers travelled in slow circles clockwise, pressing against the damp fabric of her bathing suit until the muscles in her legs began to contract and spasm, her limbs stiffened and her crotch became wetter still.

Joseph increased the pressure on her clit. His fingers moved backward and forward, faster and faster, around and around. His breathing quickened as hers did. Nelle imagined that she could see the pulse in his neck beating in time with her own heartbeat. She felt acutely aware of his vulnerability at that moment. As if, despite the weight of his body looming over her, she could easily lean forward as soon as he released his hand from her neck and tear at his jugular with her teeth. The thought made her smile, but only briefly, as he began whispering in her ear again and the words that he spoke filled her with a rush of desire so strong she thought that her knees might give way and she would collapse onto the floor of his apartment.

"You're going to come, aren't you?"

Nelle moved her head awkwardly – "No." She didn't know him. She didn't want to give him the pleasure of being right. The victory.

"Liar," he hissed, increasing the pressure of his fingers on her mound until her hips began to grind, as if of their own accord.

Damn her body, she thought, why was she responding this way? Was she ill, sick? She must be. But the more that she tried to fight it, the more she told herself that the things he was saying to her and the things that he was doing were wrong, the more her nipples hardened and the nerve endings in her skin burned with the need to be touched. She was conscious of her own heat, and the wetness that continued to seep from her cunt even as she fought against it.

Then he dropped to his knees in front of her, as suddenly as a religious man catching a glimpse of God in a chapel. He pulled the fabric of her bathing suit aside so savagely that Nelle thought he might tear it right off her, not that she would have cared if he had. And then her mind went blank, as the sensation of his mouth on her pussy lips drove every other thought from her head.

He began slowly at first, dragging the flat of his tongue along the top crevice of her inner thighs and brushing his lips over her mound in a trail of soft kisses. Nelle gasped. His hand was no longer around her throat, but she had forgotten to breathe. Joseph paused for the briefest of moments, waiting for her to catch her breath, or perhaps for her to come back into herself so that she could fully concentrate on his ministrations. Then he began to lick, gradually moving closer to her nub, occasionally stopping to nip her labia between his teeth, careful to soften the sharp edges with his lips.

Nelle's legs began to tremble, as the pressure of his tongue flicking against her clit seemed to render all of the muscles in her body useless. She laid her hands on his head, first just resting them there and then, as he continued to lick, she threaded her fingers into his hair and pulled him against her, grinding her pussy against his face. He clasped each of her thighs in one of his hands, spreading her legs wider and using her body as leverage to keep his balance as he thrust his nose inside her. He stopped to inhale the same way that he did in the pool – rarely – but with far less precision. His breathing was laboured now, and he filled his lungs in short, swift bursts, keeping his lips on hers in an open-mouthed kiss and sucking the air in sideways, making a whistling sound with each breath as the air struggled to reach his lungs.

His hands travelled further up her thighs. He spread his fingers, brushing each of his thumbs against her hip bones and pushing up the fabric of her swimsuit so that her arse was exposed. He ran his hands over each of her cheeks, kneading her flesh beneath the soft pads of his fingertips, pulling her closer against him. Nelle let herself go. Joseph was strong. Strong enough to hold her weight and keep his balance as she thrust against him, fucking his face.

She came in juddering bursts, her whole body pulsing with the force of the orgasm that tore through her like a wildfire, leaving not destruction but renewed energy in its wake. Every one of her nerve endings felt as though it had been woken at once. She was buzzing.

Her limbs continued to twitch for a long while after she had reached her climax. She gasped with each successive aftershock until her body eventually relaxed. Nelle sank down onto Joseph, not caring in the slightest whether her weight, now unsupported by the door, would be a burden for him. It was not far to fall to the floor, anyway.

But Joseph had not finished, and did not allow her any respite. He lifted her up as if she weighed no more than a child and flipped her over onto her front. Nelle flailed, ungainly, but instinctively caught herself on her forearms before she hit the wooden floor. His floorboards smelled of lemon, she noticed, smiling to herself at the inanity of noticing such a thing at a time like that. Nelle had heard – and read – about people who made shopping lists in their head, or thought about all the chores on their to-do lists while they were having sex. She had never been one of those people. Sex consumed her whole being. There was nothing on earth so important that it couldn't wait for lovemaking.

She shuffled her knees closer to her chest so that most of her weight was leaning on her forearms and her arse was lifted in the air. "Doggy style" – a term she hated. It seemed to Nelle a crass and demeaning way to describe one of her favourite sexual positions. When positioned in that way, she thought of herself as offering a gift, not simply awaiting entry like a dumb animal.

She yelped when the flat of his hand connected with her backside. That was not what she had expected, and no one had ever spanked her before. The first slap left her arse cheek hot and stinging, but the pain quickly subsided as he held his hand against her flesh, as if he was absorbing some of the pain back into his body. She almost laughed with surprise. It was the sort of action that she might have considered silly if she had thought about it in advance, but Joseph was not a foolish man, and it was difficult to take him anything other than seriously.

She sucked in her stomach and bent her spine like a cat's, lifting her arse even higher into the air.

Slap.

His hand came down hard on the other side and Nelle whistled between her teeth.

It was a curious sensation. Both pleasant and unpleasant at the same time. Like walking a knife's edge between one feeling and another. She focused hard on the feeling, employing her logical, reasoning mind to decipher this new sense, and found that the more she focused her attention on the impact of Joseph's palm on her butt the more everything else disappeared until it seemed almost as though she was floating. It wasn't that she was disconnected or unaware of anything else but that other things disappeared, including the ache that had begun to develop in her forearms. She was flying above all of the trivial things, all of the banal thoughts and unimportant discomforts, balancing on that mysterious place that existed between good and bad, wanted and unwanted, desire and repulsion.

More than that, she was fiercely, fiercely aroused.

"You're dripping," Joseph said. The tone of his voice had changed. It was full of sex. Rich, deep, throaty, almost a growl. Something else too. Cold, mocking.

"You love it, don't you? You filthy bitch." He sounded pleased, but not surprised. Like someone who has finally affirmed a fact that they had all along believed to be true.

Nelle opened her mouth, but she could not find her voice to answer him.

She felt the pads of one of his fingers pressing a line firmly along the inside of her thigh. Scraping up the moisture that was now running down her leg. Then his finger was in her mouth. She sucked, instinctively, tasting both sweet and sour, the very particular sea salt tang of sex. He pushed his finger to the tip of her throat until she felt that she might begin to cough or choke and then rubbed his fingertips over her mouth, pulling at her lips, pressing his palm against her cheek in a rough caress.

Nelle could feel Joseph's excitement rising in tandem with hers. She knew, somehow, that it was not what he was doing but the way that she was reacting to it that aroused him so much. Toying with his senses pleased her, made her feel powerful. She shuffled her knees further apart and dipped her spine into an even more exaggerated position so that her legs were now spread wide, inviting.

He didn't utter a word in response. His breath came in short, ragged growls. She felt it then: his bare cock nudging at her opening, just resting against her lips. He was rock hard and large.

Nelle knew he wasn't wearing a condom. She hadn't heard the telltale rustling of a wrapper opening or noticed the awkward pause of him breaking out of the moment to find protection. She could feel the warmth and smoothness of his skin against hers, and the hesitation as he waited, prone, for her to give him some kind of sign that she wanted him inside her just as he was, without any barrier between them, no matter the health benefits.

She pushed back, taking his full length in one thrust. He let out a groan that emanated deep from his throat and half fell forward on top of her.

"Nelle," he said. The sound he made was like the cry of a bear caught in a trap. He grabbed hold of her hair and pulled. Her head snapped back, controlled by the grip of his hand wrapped around her long tresses.

He pushed harder into her and deeper with each thrust, ramming his cock inside her with such force that she could barely hold herself upright. Her hands, forearms, elbows all ached from resting on the wooden floor, but the discomfort was nothing, not even a pinprick in her consciousness, in comparison with the exquisite pleasure of Joseph's cock filling her so completely. She pushed back against him, meeting every one of his strokes with her own until they were moving back and forward with the precision of two metronomes meeting in sync and it was impossible to tell which of them was the driving force.

His movements became imperceptibly faster and faster, more desperate, until she felt the weight of him pushing her forward, flat on her stomach on the wooden floor and she collapsed under him, unable to hold herself up beneath the bulk of his body. He let go of her hair and his hand moved across her back, pressing her down and then wrapping around her mouth, preventing her breathing. He released his grip only at the point when she was frantic for air and even then only allowed her a brief, desperate gasp.

There was a rhythm to his movements. He was counting, Nelle realized. He knew how long she could hold her breath for. Perhaps he was guessing, or acutely aware of the signs that her body made, the difference between wanting to breathe and needing to. Perhaps he had counted the seconds between each breath she took when she swam.

She relaxed, feeling safe with this knowledge. Somehow this man she barely knew already knew her body well enough to take her beyond the edge of comfort but not into harm. She let go. Allowed him to carry her into that place where she was no longer in control, not even of the air that entered her lungs.

Nelle began to feel hazy. Again, everything fell away but the taste and the pressure of his fingers against her mouth and the sensation of his cock pumping inside her. She flicked her tongue out, began sucking at the flesh of his hand, and this simple act seemed to push him over the point of no return.

His hand clamped down over her mouth and he let out an almighty cry and thrust against her one more time, so deeply she felt he might split her in two. She felt his semen pumping out inside her. Hot, dangerous. He collapsed over her and pulled his hand away. They gasped for air together, filling their lungs in ragged bursts until the moment passed and reality began to creep back into focus.

Joseph lifted himself up, and Nelle felt his cock sliding out of her, leaving emptiness and a line of moisture across her buttock in its wake. He shuffled over so that they were lying almost side by side on the floor, one of his legs still draped over her thigh. She turned her head to face him.

"Are you okay?" he asked her softly.

She nuzzled against him as he stroked her hair. "Yeah," she replied softly, nodding. "That was . . . intense."

"I wasn't sure . . ." he said. "If it would be too much for you. If I'd read you wrong."

"How did you know?"

"The way you spoke about my book. The way you move. The way you respond to me. Everything."

Nelle was confused. She felt conflicted. He couldn't be sure, not without asking. Even if he had been right. If he'd stopped, and asked her if she enjoyed being choked, would she have said yes? she asked herself. The answer was no. Of course not. She had never considered such a thing.

"Come with me," he said, but it wasn't an invitation, or even an order that she might have refused, as he simply stood and then bent down and picked her up and carried her. Nelle let him. She draped her arms around his neck and let her head flop onto his chest. He laid her down on the bed and pulled a coverlet over her. It was a faux fur blanket, light and soft against her skin. He kissed her forehead and pulled her against him. They lay like that for hours. Until night fell and the sound of Nelle's growling stomach roused her enough to murmur that she ought to be making her way home.

"Stay," he said. "It's dark now. And cold. You only have your bathing suit," he chided.

"I'll get a taxi," she insisted, as she struggled to push herself up off the bed. But the fog that sex with Joseph seemed to induce in her mind had still not lifted. She felt sluggish, still drugged with pleasure, like a cat asleep under a sunbeam.

Finally, she submitted and lay back down again. The prospect of climbing back into wet clothes and making even a short trip home was not a pleasant one in comparison with staying where she was and enjoying the warmth of Joseph's body.

He left the room and returned a short while later carefully balancing a tray that held a bottle of red wine, glasses and a spread of cheese and bread.

Nelle ate as though she had been starved for days and then fell into a deep, dreamless sleep.

Somehow one night became two, and then three, and then a whole week. A week became month, and finally Nelle admitted to herself that she was living with him. She had moved in with a man after only meeting him twice, one date, a session of afternoon sex.

Nelle socialized so rarely outside of home and spoke to her family so infrequently that living with Joseph made little difference to her life. Still, on the odd occasion that she called her mother or communicated with one of her employers over the telephone she was careful not to mention him. The independent streak she had always had was still strong, somewhere deep inside her, and so she did not move her furniture, or rent out her flat in Hoxton. She let her mail continue to go there, piling up on the mat.

Initially, she popped back once every week or so to pick up new clothes, open the windows and check that nothing had gone wrong in her absence. Partly, she wanted to remind herself that she still existed as Nelle, as the person that she had been before Joseph. But as the weeks wore on, she visited her flat less and less and gradually she began to assimilate into a routine that revolved more and more around him. She still worked, of course, and despite continuing to pay her mortgage she even managed to save a little more than usual because Joseph insisted on paying all of the bills.

He often bought clothes for her too. Not just things to wear in the bedroom. He preferred structured, tailored shirts, crisp navy suit trousers that made her appear even taller and fragile somehow, despite their mannish cut. Her long, flowing skirts and light buttoned blouses hung in the wardrobe limply, unworn.

There was a simplicity in living with Joseph. Besides continuing her copy-editing assignments, she rarely needed to worry about anything. Many mornings she woke to find that he had already laid out what he wanted her to wear, had already prepared for her what he wanted her to eat. As if he had read her mind or instinctively knew what colour or fabric would suit her on a particular day. After all, he was a magician, Nelle reminded herself, although he hadn't performed for ages, she found out. Joseph explained this away, developing new tricks, new illusions in the converted attic he used as an office and which Nelle was only allowed to enter by invitation. Here, he would often disappear for hours on end or spend the night. Nothing sinister, he would say, promising that she would be his first spectator when everything was perfected.

"Your assistant?" Nelle asked, her head full of images from her childhood and twirling ladies in sequined outfits and extended arms dancing a graceful ballet around a stage full of props to the gasp of spectators in search of wonder.

"Maybe. One day."

Life had become like a moving meditation. In her waking moments, she never needed to think, only to be. Her dreams, though, became more and more vivid, filled with all the parts of her that she had begun to suppress since she met him. It was only in her dreams that she returned to the Nelle that she had been.

And that was when he told her about the Ball.

A black SUV awaited them as they walked out of the warm comfort of the airport arrivals hall. The air outside was cold but invigorating, just a soft breeze that brushed against her forehead and soothed her for the brief seconds she spent in the open. It was crisp, empty, pure. Many years ago, Nelle had once visited Sweden and remembered the crystal-like cleanliness of the air, but this was even more refined and precious. There was a grey-uniformed driver behind the steering wheel but he didn't exit the vehicle to open the doors for them. The engine was rumbling monotonously. Nelle couldn't see his face, just the back of his neck between the cap and the starched collar of his outfit. Joseph opened the car boot and dropped their luggage into it. Back in London, she hadn't known what to pack, as he had been unwilling to disclose their final destination or any details about the nature of the activities they would partake of. She had laid out half of her winter clothes across the bed and just stood there nonplussed, wondering what to pack or not and he had ended up banishing her from the room and filling her suitcase himself. Nelle wondered about the choices he had madc and what her luggage now actually contained. He was always particular about the way she dressed.

The hotel where the driver deposited them half an hour later reminded her of a cruise ship – not that she'd ever been on one, any temptation to do so defeated well in advance by her certitude she would end up being constantly seasick – in shape and appearance. Its sleek elongation alongside the city's docks and wilderness of porthole windows like a land Leviathan ready to pounce or swim away. Walking across the lobby, she was immersed in a babel of sounds and languages, half of which she couldn't understand, and experienced a sudden spell of dizziness. Joseph was briskly stepping ahead of her, reaching the dark smooth polished wood of the reception desk and declining the details of their reservation.

"Yes, just one night," he confirmed to the bland, vacant blonde receptionist. "We leave early in the morning."

This was news to Nelle, who had somehow been expecting they would spend at least a few days in the city. An acquaintance who had travelled here in the past had mentioned the existence of a wonderful spa outside of town. Maybe on the way back, Nelle speculated.

"The items you phoned us about were delivered yesterday and have been taken up to your room already, sir," the blonde said.

"Perfect," Joseph said.

The hotel room was also marine-themed, pale-blue roughly whitewashed walls with a green underwater tinge when a cold twilight sun squeezed its way through the porthole windows and bathed the narrow space in an approximation of light. The bed's chenille cover was a puddle of green and the heavy-framed paintings scattered haphazardly across the walls – or maybe they were prints? – depicted shipping vessels of earlier times, sturdy, ghostly shapes skipping along a criss-cross pattern of waves.

In a corner, three large shopping bags in shades of grey, with labels Nelle didn't recognize stood, bulky, dark with secrets. Sealed across their fragile handles with thin, silk lengths of string.

Curious, she stepped towards them, but was immediately called back by Joseph.

"No," he just said, with an ominous sense of finality in his voice and Nelle knew not to disobey.

She froze.

Looked him in the eyes. She'd experienced that imperious tone of voice before. He held her gaze.

The awkward silence was broken by a porter knocking at the door, bringing up their two pieces of luggage. Joseph opened and indicated to the unfeasibly tall, angular and cheekboned to high heaven black-clad young man to carry the suitcases towards the bed and tipped him.

Nelle stood waiting.

"Should I unpack?" she tentatively asked.

"No point,' Joseph answered. "We're only here for the night and move on in the morning. Unpacking would be a waste of time." He looked at her: she was still wearing the long green woollen coat she had travelled in and looked tired. "Maybe you should rest," he suggested. "Take a shower first. It will relax you. We have a lot ahead of us," he added.

"Sit down first." He indicated the bed and, when she did so, he got down to his knees and unzipped her ankle-length brown boots and pulled them off her feet. He then nodded and she rose.

He then helped her out of the coat and, with an arm around her waist, guided her to the bathroom door and closed it behind her once she had stepped over into its darkness.

Disorientated and puzzled by Joseph's sudden distance, Nelle fumbled for the light switch, found it and blinked as the recessed ceiling bulbs flickered into existence. The shower area was a glass sarcophagus fitted into a corner of the small space. A small porthole no larger than her hand and through which she could peer only on tiptoe unveiled a dark nearby sea where lights in the distance like remote stars betrayed boats in slow mo. It was already night. Joseph was right, she was tired. It couldn't have been the plane journey, which had been relatively short and uneventful. As she shed her clothing, she hoped the anxiety would fade. She adjusted the angle of attack of the showerhead and placed herself in its direct path. Then realized she had forgotten to take one of the complimentary miniature bars of blue soap dotted across the now out of reach sink. No matter, she reckoned; she wasn't actually dirty, encumbered by sweat.

The water alone would cleanse her.

She looked down at her body.

Out of the corner of her eyes, she could see her hair as it lay wet against her shoulders, rivulets of water pouring like wild cascades down her front, leaping across her nipples, streaming down the valley separating her breasts towards her navel before the downward journey towards her pubic curls.

She wiped her eyes free of water.

Closed them.

Wondered briefly whether Joseph would come in and interrupt her ablutions, join her in the shower, touch her, caress her, fuck her. She wanted him to. All of a sudden her whole body shook at the thought.

The warm water poured down, drip, drip, as Nelle felt her breath grow short.

Yes, how long had it been since he had held her under a shower, slipped his fingers inside her in the bath?

Too long.

She opened her eyes. Looked at the closed door. Which remained closed.

He did not touch her when she slid into the bed next to him either. She had been careful to dry herself properly so that she could curl her body up against his without wetting him with damp hair. And she had covered herself with the sweet-smelling body lotion that the hotel had provided, hoping that he would be aroused by the scent.

But it was no use. Joseph refused to even acknowledge her. She knew by the sound of his breathing that he was still awake.

"Get some sleep," he growled, when she reached out to caress his shoulder. Nelle pulled her arm back as though she had been stung and abruptly turned over.

If he did not want to fuck her, why had he even brought her all the way out here? Her muscles were tense with frustration. She wanted to yell, cry, stamp her feet, insist that he tell her what he was planning, but she knew that it would be useless.

And that no matter how much he insisted that she rest, she would not sleep tonight. Her mind was in too much of a whirl.

Despite his churlishness, Nelle still wanted him, and she still wanted to please him, no matter what that required of her. She still did not understand why her brain and her body worked this way but it was when he behaved coldly to her that she desired him most. He suited the north, she thought. The bleak, cold beauty of it resembled his nature, and his unwavering will, as hard as ice.

He turned towards her then and pulled her into his arms. Nelle moaned softly. Finally. He was touching her, at last. She arched her back, pressing her arse against his groin. He was not rock hard as she had hoped, but flaccid. The apparent absence of his desire for her left her feeling deflated. She was too upset to even masturbate, which she sometimes did after waiting for him to fall asleep. Instead she let her mind go as limp as her body had and travel into the world of her unconscious, the world of white that remained as cold and harsh as the man who lay alongside her.

The road endlessly kept on unfurling in front of them as they raced along a carpet of grey uninterrupted tarmac between a narrow corridor of black volcanic tongues. Their driver was the same, anonymous silent man who had picked them up from the airport and dropped them at the hotel.

Low, uneven hills dotted the landscape, broken geometrical shapes that somehow evoked the antechambers of hell for Nelle whose mind was still shaking topsy-turvy from the previous night's frustrations and a surfeit of tiredness. Somehow when Joseph had said they were travelling to the North, she had composed a false image in her mind, from shards of Philip Pullman and Jack London adventures.

"Is it still far?" she asked Joseph. He was sitting at the front next to the driver, his broad shoulders blocking most of the tarmac from view.

There was a long pause.

"It's up the road," Joseph finally said.

Two hours later or maybe more as Nelle had dozed off briefly she realized, they were still driving along the straight road, lullabied by the irregular rhythm of the darker volcanic flows indenting the rocky fields abutting the monotonous highway.

She wanted to ask Joseph again, but decided against it and reined in her impatience.

Could they have travelled beyond the Arctic Circle? she wondered.

Soon, the horizon faded in full sight and vertiginous mountains, like antediluvian mammoths, rose suddenly all around them, the thin ribbon of the road threading its way through steep passes and shadowy canyons.

Nelle shivered inside the warm cocoon of the fur coat with a sense of nervous anticipation.

Her nerve endings tingled.

In the space of a few miles, the heavy grey sky had turned blue and the shimmering, ragged mountain peaks dominating the land were now bordered with distant ice and snow, a sharp demarcation line between rock and pure air. Below the white scar zone a depth of green and brown forests hanging on to the steep slopes spread out like a coat cushioning the lower edges of the mountain's nudity.

The SUV was now having to slow as it took each turn at awkward angles as the road rose and grew narrower. Emerging from a sharp ascent and a full ninety-degree curve, the vehicle reached a junction, with an unsigned path to the right continuing straight into the wall of the mountain. It seemed almost impassable, not designed for cars and perilous even on foot.

Joseph turned his head. "We'll be there soon," he said. "Ready yourself, Nelle."

He looked away from her and nodded to the mute driver, who acknowledged his command with a movement of his chin and the car halted. Joseph opened his door and the cold air of the heights whooshed into the car's interior and she tightened the fur coat around her body to keep the cold at bay. Joseph stepped out, opened the back door for Nelle and extended his hand.

His touch was uncommonly warm, and she flashed back to all the occasions when she would seek the heat of his body under the covers, during winter nights when they invariably slept with the bedroom window open.

She shifted and slipped off the leather seat and tentatively set foot on the ground. Beyond Joseph, who stood still and silent, his face like stone, the narrow road disappeared abruptly and a chasm opened up below the mountain's sharp slope. Nelle caught her breath. She had always feared heights.

Joseph approached her, brushed her hands away where they'd been holding the heavy fur coat tight to her body.

He pulled on the garment.

Nelle didn't resist.

The fur coat opened. Unveiling her nakedness.

The freezing breath of the mountain air washed across her skin and she felt her nipples harden and her cunt tighten.

Her cheeks turned red as she noticed that the ever silent driver was watching, his steel-coloured eyes fixed on her, not betraying a single hint of emotion. A perfect spectator, or voyeur. But Nelle had long learned to lose any sense of self-consciousness in these sort of uncommon situations, although none had ever occurred on a dirt track by the side of a glacier before.

As the cold swept up her body, she felt momentarily grateful for the heavy leather boots he had asked her to wear; all that she now had on.

Joseph was clad in black from top to bottom, a multicoloured woollen scarf draped around his neck, blocking out the weather between his close-shaven features and the thick cashmere coat that reached below his knees. The razor-sharp crease of his dark slacks drawing a straight line all the way down to his ankle-high half boots.

"The car can't go any further. We continue on foot." He

indicated the dirt track on which they were standing, which just a few yards away appeared to merge with the mountain wall, leading nowhere.

He stepped ahead.

Nelle gritted her teeth and began to follow him.

The driver watched them move away, standing silently by his vehicle. Nelle wondered if he would wait for them, or whether they would be abandoned on the mountain. She took a deep breath. The air spread through her lungs, cold, bracing.

As the track narrowed into an ever unsteady path, unlike Joseph, whose progress along the track was assured, Nelle had to keep her hands against the rough rock walls to retain her balance. Out of the corner of her eyes, she couldn't avoid contemplating the abyss on her left, her naked body feeling even more fragile as the breeze rose. Her whole body was a landscape of goose bumps now.

For a second or so, Joseph disappeared around a bend and Nelle's heart stopped.

When she joined him on the other side of the perilous corner, her skin scraping against the ragged mountain's side, she saw they had reached a kind of natural platform where the track came to a halt.

Joseph looked towards her as she reached the natural end of the path.

"You look beautiful," he said, scanning her body with a smile full of kindness bathing his face.

He then gestured towards the mountain wall and Nelle saw where he was pointing to.

A roughly circular opening in the rock.

A cavern.

Or a passage of some sort.

Evidently their destination. Or a way station on the journey to it.

"Come," he said, bending his head and entering the darkness of the cave.

Why did her want her naked? Nelle speculated. Surely he could have stripped her on arrival.

How had he known there would be a passage through the mountain? Had he been here before? With other women?

As soon as she squirmed her own way through the opening in the mountain wall, Nelle felt the cold quickly fade away. Not that it was warm inside. Humid and dark was more like it. Sounds of dripping water echoed distantly through the hollow. She treaded carefully, attempting as best she could to follow Joseph's steps ahead of her, fearful of tripping or falling.

She had so many questions.

As her eyes adapted to the penumbra, her attention was caught by a spot of light some one hundred or more yards ahead in the direction they were heading.

All the while, as they made slow progress, the temperature was rising and the breath of cold air that had been curtaining her skin was melting away.

It was another opening. To the other side of the mountain?

Was Joseph leading her to just another dirt track which they would have to painfully negotiate on their way to this mythical event he had long spoken of, or would it actually turn out to be a valley? A modern Shangri-La.

Her steps now more confident, Nelle squinted and gazed ahead. The colour beyond the opening at the far end of the cave, which they were steadily approaching, was definitely blue. Sky blue. Unlike the monotonous grey on the opposing side of the mountain they had been journeying on.

Her attention increasingly captivated by the growing circle of light hanging like a motionless will-o'-the-wisp in the shadows of the cavern's passage far ahead of them, Nelle felt herself being drawn to the mystery that lay beyond, step by step, heartbeat after heartbeat. Even Joseph's presence faded as her mind fluttered in a frenzy of nervous expectation.

Sensing her agitation, Joseph said "Close your eyes now," and, as she obeyed, took her hands in his and guided her across the final distance of their subterranean journey through the heart of the mountain.

"Stop. There."

Nelle drew to a halt. She knew not to open her eyes until she was allowed. There was a subtle difference in the air now. It felt purer, crystalline, layered with subtle, clean odours she couldn't quite recognize. She felt the fur coat being drawn open by Joseph and brusquely pulled away from her body. She raised her arms in response and felt the warm material sliding across her skin until she was totally divested of it, and stood naked on the brink, in only her leather boots.

"Now," he said.

Nelle opened her eyes.

Drew her breath. Her body freezing in awe.

It wasn't Shangri-La and some verdant valley bordered by high mountains and dotted with shining pagodas, impossible gardens and a flurry of exotica.

It was better.

Majestic.

A path led from the exit of the cavern at her feet all the way down to a vast field of ice, maybe a frozen lake, as far as the eye could see, whiter than white, resplendent under the sharp rays of sunlight pouring down from the blue heavens, half circular and half rectangular, with rugged edges on its spread-out perimeter. Surrounding it was a wall of fierce snow-topped peaks, distant summits blurring into a wash of clouds. But, and even more so in view of her nudity, it felt improbably warm. A gentle and tepid breeze at distinct odds with the landscape. A whisper of wind flowing across her skin, caressing her nipples into hardness, buzzing at the gates of her cunt, triggering her desire and humidity.

The immense circle of ice was like the stage for a giant circus in the centre of this mighty glacier plateau, a modern Colosseum.

As she kept on gazing ahead at the dizzy spectacle of the ice plain, Nelle began to distinguish small, moving dots of black along its surface, like ants gathering and busying themselves into an organized frenzy at a frost fair. People. Vehicles. Poles. Flags. Yurts. Ropes. A growing vortex of movement.

"The building of the Ball . . ." Joseph whispered, as if the very thought of speaking loud here would cause the magic to cease.

Nelle remained silent.

Finally, Joseph indicated the narrow path down towards the ice plain and Nelle took a tentative step forward, her eyes looking up at him as if begging to be given the fur coat back, and some form of protection for her intimacy. It was on the ground, dishevelled, sprawled across the soft grass like a melting puddle, too beautiful and expensive to be abandoned.

Joseph shook his head. "No."

They walked down towards the valley of ice, he a sharp, straight silhouette in black from head to toe, she a wraith in white, her skin like milk offered to the improbable sunlight, the fire between her thighs raging along with a symphony of nerve endings buzzing like electricity in her gut. A sensation, Nelle knew from past experience, she was unable to control. Never wished to control.

As they neared the throng of people, Nelle realized that she was not the only one naked, and her self-consciousness began to ebb away. Even if she were the only example of nudity, the sights and smells that invaded her senses were so remarkable that the shock of it all would have made her forget her sense of modesty.

A sweetness lingered in the air.

"Do you recognize it?" asked Joseph.

Nelle breathed in. Had she been able to see herself through Joseph's eyes at that moment she would have noticed the child-like wonder that swept across her face, softening her features and lifting the edges of her eyes and mouth in a wide smile.

"Toffee apples," she said. "And candy floss."

"Yes," he replied. "Come on, quickly. The show will begin soon."

Joseph strode ahead and Nelle struggled to keep up with him as each step brought her closer to the myriad of visual delights that surrounded them. In every direction that she glanced there was something wonderful that caught her eye.

"Joseph! Look!" she cried, pointing to the sheet of blue sky above them that was now decorated with a dozen gulls free-wheeling overhead. Each bird was larger than she was and had the body of a woman and wings that must have been twelve feet across. As if the creatures sensed Nelle's gaze, they put on a show, gliding and diving and somersaulting in the air in unison. One after the other, they wrapped their feathers around their naked bodies as though donning a cloak and then dropped down like thunderbolts from the sky until they were almost level with Nelle and like flashers they spread their wings wide so she could view them in their entirety.

The youngest of the bird-women was in her fifties or sixties, Nelle reckoned. Their age showed in the lines on their skin, stomachs that had lost their flatness – if they had ever had it – breasts that hung when they were stationary or swung like pendulums when they moved. But age had not taken away the suppleness of their limbs or the speed and grace in their movements, as they shifted their bodies through the air, twisting, turning and balancing on the mildest gusts of wind. There was a power and a vitality and sureness in the bird-women. They were like witches of the air.

Nelle stared, straining her eyes to find what trick of the light or what invisible mechanism allowed these creatures to appear to be flying but she could see none.

"They're really . . . they're really flying," she breathed in wonder.

"They're the Women of the Wind," Joseph replied. "When it grows dark, later, they bring the light for the performances. It's easier than setting up stage lighting, you see," he added, as if that made the presence of women with wings less fantastical. He looked up. "And until they are needed," he said, "they play."

Nelle turned back again, following the line of Joseph's gaze. The winged women were now hovering above a troupe of young men. Dancers, Nelle guessed, or acrobats perhaps, who were warming up for a routine. Their flesh was as taut and firm as the women's was soft and each of them was as muscled as any Adonis. Their skin was the improbable tan colour of caramel, as if they had recently arrived in the North from a beach holiday some place tropical. They were like carbon copies of one another. The same height and sturdiness, the same dirty blond short hair.

The bird-women circled the men like carrion fowl at a feast. One by one, they darted down with arms outstretched and swept one of the young men into their arms until the entire troupe was borne aloft. Some of the men cried out in surprise as they were taken, but most simply allowed themselves to be carried away. Their sturdiness was no match for the strength of the women, who carried the boys in their arms as easily as if they were scraps of meat ready to be devoured. Again the women seemed to be aware of their small audience, as Nelle watched their antics in wonder, and they flew down low and near enough that she could make sense of their strange dance. Despite, or perhaps because of the age difference between them, the men were obviously aroused by the attentions of the bird-women. They each sported prominent erections, which the women took turns to either make fun of or pleasure themselves with. One would hold a man upright as another woman dived down to take his stiff cock into her mouth and tease him to the point of explosion, before darting away again, laughing at his frustration.

Another promptly let go of her hostage, letting him plummet almost to his death before swooping beneath him, and catching him with her body directly beneath his so that he penetrated her as he fell. The young man stiffened and shuddered the moment that he entered her, as if the marriage of his cock into her cunt at the moment of his almost certain death had aroused him so much that he ejaculated immediately. She then lowered him carefully to the ground in an apparent faint and took to the air again in search of another. Droplets of ejaculate ran down her thighs as she sprung into the air and sizzled when they hit the earth, not more than two feet from where Nelle stood.

Nelle's mouth gaped open. She dropped to her knees to check that her eyes had not deceived her, but, sure enough, the droplets that she had just witnessed falling down from the bird-woman's cunt had sprung into miniscule white lilies. She crawled through the grass, careful not to knock or trudge on any of the new blooms and found more and more of them, springing up instantly as the juices of the airborne men and women hit the ground and sprouted into delicately petalled flowers. She bent her head to breathe in the heady scent that emanated from the blooms. It was rich and floral but also undeniably musky, like no flower Nelle had ever known.

"But . . . but this is impossible," she said to Joseph. "It's impossible," she repeated firmly, as if saying the words a second time would make everything in front of her eyes disappear.

"Nothing is impossible," he replied. Joseph bent down alongside her on the grass. He perched on flat feet, with his knees bent up like a grasshopper's to avoid staining his trousers on the damp earth, then leant forward and began to pluck a handful of the white flowers. Nelle hissed as he pulled them up at the roots. They seemed so alive to her that the act of him tearing at the stems with hands that were gigantic in comparison to the tiny buds was an unnecessary violence. Then she gasped as she saw the flowers he had plucked change shape and join together in the palm of his hand. Instead of a handful of dead flowers, he now held a glittering pearl necklace.

He pushed himself to his feet, pulled her up, and stood behind her to fasten the luminescent strand around her throat. Nelle shivered as his knuckles brushed her chin. His hands felt as cold as the ice that surrounded them. The pearls, though, were as warm as any living creature. She ran her fingertips along the smooth beads. She could have sworn that they had a pulse that beat in time with her own, as if she now carried a part of the bird-women with her. Nelle raised her hand to them in an awkward wave of acknowledgement but they had gone already and were now gliding towards the arena.

"We're late," Joseph said. He raised his hand into the air and twisted his fingertips as if he was turning an invisible doorknob and, for a brief moment, Nelle felt as though all the air had been knocked from her body. Her eyes watered and she stumbled as the ground seemed to be shifting beneath her. Then the world was still again.

Nelle blinked. They had moved somehow without taking a single step and were now standing right at the edge of the icy stage. Behind them stood row upon row of seating. They were at the front of an enormous stadium without a single empty pew. All of the people that had seemed like brightly coloured ants from a distance had now gathered here. Up close they were totally unlike ants, and there was nothing uniform about them unless variety could be considered a uniform. Some were laced tightly into corsets, others were totally nude or painted with stripes or spots like animals, and some were adorned in elaborate couture gowns. The gender norms that Nelle was accustomed to did not apply here. She saw women with shapely hips accentuated by latex jodhpurs and square jaws covered with neatly clipped beards, men with long, lustrous hair and pert breasts. Many wore masks, but not the ordinary sort favoured by guests at masquerade parties. These were decorated with large curled horns or elongated cat-like noses or even gnarled bark, giving the wearer the appearance of a forest nymph.

Joseph wiped his brow. The colour had drained from his face entirely. He took hold of Nelle's elbow. Not, she thought, to support her but rather to support himself. She had not previously noticed how much each of his tricks drained him. Perhaps that was why he hadn't performed publicly for so long – it simply sapped too much of his energy. Nelle, on the other hand, felt stronger, more alive and more invigorated than ever before. The pearls around her neck pulsed with life, which permeated her skin and seeped into her bones until she felt as though she was glowing, as luminescent as the beads that encircled her throat.

The whole landscape suddenly turned pitch black, as if they were in a windowless room with the lights suddenly switched off. Devoid of sight, Nelle's other senses became keener. She could hear the rustle of fabrics as the crowd behind them shifted in their seats and smell the odour of sex, sweat and rising excitement mixed with perfumes and the dry cold Nordic air.

A light burst into flame, but to Nelle's surprise it did not come from atop or above the large, blank circle of ice that spread out like a skating rink in front of them, but rather below. She looked down at her feet in wonder. The sheet of ice that they were standing on had turned transparent, like very thin glass. Beneath it the winged-women dived and glided, each of them holding torches that brightened and dimmed on cue, like stage lights. Their feathered wings remained completely dry, and no current swept out behind them. They were not holding their breath and were not attached to oxygen tanks.

"There's no water," Nelle whispered. She shrugged. Considering all the other impossible things she had witnessed, she supposed that seeing a dry world under the ice rather than a watery one was no stranger than anything else she had seen that day.

The winged-women gathered into formation, creating a ring of light, about the size of a football pitch. Their torches dimmed, and for a moment they were again cast into darkness. The crowd fell silent. Then the light burst forth again, this time into a column, like a sunbeam. Within the sunbeam stood an enormous woman. Whether it was a trick of perspective, or she really was a giant, Nelle wasn't sure, but she made even the winged-women seem Lilliputian. Each of her limbs was as thick as the trunk of a tree and her breasts were like mountains, but she was perfectly proportioned and moved with effortless grace. Her hair was pitch black and swam over her shoulders like a waterfall. The woman raised her arms overhead and, as she did so, a dozen invisible television screens burst into life so that her image was projected in every direction that Nelle looked. Instead of one giantess, it seemed as though they were surrounded by a dozen, all nude besides their flesh-coloured ballet shoes.

Piano music broke the silence and, as the first notes filled the air, the woman beneath the ice tensed her calves, lifted her heels into a perfect *en pointe* and took a short step to the right. As she did so, Nelle realized that the shining surface the woman was standing upon was in fact the flat end of a knife blade. In contrast to the gentle lullaby of sound emanating from a seemingly invisible instrument, the expression on the dancer's face grew more and more pained with each turn on the points of her blades. Every muscle in her body was as taut as a drawn bowstring and her nipples had frozen into points as long as Nelle's fingers. The moisture gathering at her cunt was apparent on the apparitions projected on the screens around them. Her thighs glistened as the juices of her arousal ran down between her legs. Like the heroine of Joseph's novel, it seemed that pain aroused her.

The lullaby rose to a crescendo and, as it did so, the woman's face shifted further from pain and closer to pleasure. She spread her arms out like a crucifixion, raised one leg into a standing split and spun on the point of the blade that supported her until Nelle began to feel dizzy just watching. The dancer's body tensed and then shuddered as if she was experiencing her own private earthquake beneath the ceiling of ice that enclosed her. The moisture that had previously seeped onto her thighs now poured from her cunt like rain in a thunderstorm, but each droplet took the form of a falling star that lit up the dark night with an unearthly glow.

Gradually her body stilled.

As the image of the graceful dancer incomprehensibly faded into thin air to the final accompanying, dying notes of the music, Nelle blinked as if the rapid movement of her eyelashes might miraculously fix the image and make it return, render it whole again. But as she opened her eyes, full of hope, all she could now see was a canvas which was whiter than white, a glacial sun that consumed the valley's landscape, feeding on the memories of the dancer on the knives.

She took a deep breath and, as she did so, felt the warm touch of Joseph's hand on hers.

"That was beautiful," she said. "It seemed so real."

"It was just an illusion," Joseph said.

"But how . . . ?"

He interrupted her. "Everything is an illusion. Tricks, misdirection, make-believe . . ."

A wave of disappointment coursed through her, as if he was actually revealing the secrets of his trade, denying her the succour of actual magic. His hand left hers and he traced a circle in the air and, for a brief moment, it looked as if he was somehow grabbing a distant snowcapped mountain peak inside the hollow of his hand. Only to open his fist and pull out of nowhere a whole series of brightly coloured handkerchiefs, which he draped across her shoulders and perilously balanced on the hard tips of her nipples.

He smiled.

Her nerve endings stirred, like will-o'-the-wisps inside her fluttering wildly.

"Would you have liked it to have been real?" he asked Nelle.

"I want magic to be real," she said.

"There'd be no coming back," Joseph stated, his features an unsettling blend of severity and irony. She was about to retort jokingly that it was a bad magician who lost his assistants when it dawned on her.

She didn't want to come back.

"Show me the real magic," Nelle said.

Nothing made sense any longer. The central tower, from which sturdy ropes flowed weightlessly around the whole perimeter of the citadel of ice, emerged from a widening crack in the ground peppered with snow where its thick mast was surrounded by a bed of wildly coloured orchids in contrasting shades of bright blue, ivory white and deep purple. The flowers were impossible, could in no way survive in this environment. And then Nelle was reminded of the ambient warmth in the air, the soft and soothing breeze caressing her naked skin even though they were just miles from the Arctic Circle. She looked to the sky above and the white explosion of the sun that had now relegated the blue of the day to another dimension.

Joseph led her down an invisible path that only he could decipher along the glass surface of the artificial glacier lake. As they moved across its canvas, she could follow the razor-sharp lines, the thin, sinewy indentations the dancer's knives had carved across its skin. Like hieroglyphs, a language she couldn't decipher properly, but which held the power to disturb her senses until her mind was drowning.

They stopped and she felt the feather-light touch of his breath down the back of her neck.

Ahead of them, the banks of canopies scattered across the valley floor appeared to have multiplied, like a chain reaction spreading out in concentric circles. At the entrance of each, like watchful guards posted either side of the thresholds to protect the treasures or the secrets concealed within, stood darkened silhouettes, their bodies lost in a cloud of black gauze. The whole landscape kept feeling unreal to Nelle.

By the nearest tent they had reached, a tall Medusa-blonde-haired woman detached herself from the group standing at attention, their collective gaze inquisitively examining the two arrivals.

She nodded at Joseph in recognition.

At first, Nelle assumed the woman approaching her was wearing a billowing dress full of motifs, weird shapes and random, almost cabalistic, illustrations from the neck downwards. But it was yet another illusion. As her eyes became further accustomed to the brilliant whiteness that suffused the scene, she realized the woman was as naked as she was. Her whole body was covered in tattoos. Dragons, snakes, trees, lips, faces. Nelle's mind was struck with an unsettling form of dizziness.

The illustrated woman extended her arm towards them. Captivated, Nelle walked closer to her, sensing Joseph had stayed back and was no longer following her.

The woman's smile was limpid, all kindness and expectation as she watched Nelle's movements. Behind her the small crowd was growing, all eyes on Nelle.

She recognized the dancer on knives, from both the earlier spectacle and Joseph's book. Men and women in flimsy attire, masked, partly dressed, a carnival of fabrics and flamboyance, men who were half-animals, women who were half-birds, and even, it was just a brief glimpse, unholy beautiful creatures who exhibited the sexual characteristics of both men and women. Nelle didn't know where to look next. She told herself that it was just another magician's trick, what Joseph had been leading up to ever since their fateful encounter, a masterpiece of illusion, of misdirection and that there would be a logical, simple explanation for it all.

Lost in her frantic speculations, Nelle was now merely a few feet away from the Ball's participants, when her progress was halted by a wall of glass, which her toes hit before she could bang her nose or forehead against the invisible rampart.

Instinctively, she raised a hand and felt the smooth surface of the barrier separating her from the others and her soul was overcome with a terrible disappointment, as if she had travelled all this way only to fail at the final stage of the adventure. A wave of frustration swept across her and she was unable to hold back a solitary tear, which pearled down her left cheek.

She heard the soft tone of Joseph's voice whispering in her ear. "The magic is part of you," he said. "Use it."

Clumsily, Nelle wiped the tear away and raised the wet tip of her finger to the invisible barrier and spread what was left of the tear across it. The wall shimmered and disappeared.

Nelle stepped forward.

Stopped. A final hesitation. Looked back.

The glass wall had reconstituted itself and Joseph was now out of reach. He waved at her. A farewell.

"Welcome to the Ball," the woman said. "I am the Mistress. My name is Aurelia. You must be Nelle, our magician's offering."

"Offering?" Nelle queried.

But the woman didn't answer, just took her by the hand and led her inside the tent as all the spectators brushed aside to let them pass.

Once inside, the flimsy construction had inexplicably grown in dimensions, now extending high and wide, a Tardis-like cave of thick drapes, quilts, carpets, and a geometry of tables laden with food and jewels and, to one side, a gallery of exotic attires – dresses, sheaths, uniforms, silk wraps – hanging as if in thin air, waiting to be plundered, worn.

It felt like a dream.

Aurelia led her to a vast oak table, full of gold and silver platters, on which exotic cuts of meat and fish sat, piled on each other, alongside deep bowls of ripe fruit.

"Eat," Nelle was told. And realized how long ago she had eaten last. She grabbed a pomegranate and greedily separated the fruit from the skin and bit hard into the individual grains to extract the heady juice. A curly-haired man in his mid-twenties, naked to the waist, and wearing tight white leggings through which the shape of his genitalia was unavoidably and prominently outlined, rushed to her side, holding out a small porcelain recipient for her to spit the crushed remains of the pomegranate out onto it. Nelle could smell a spicy kind of warmth radiating from his body. The faint sugar rush sharpened her senses. Her appetite revived, she helped herself to a slice of rye bread over which she spread some slices of smoked fish.

Nelle allowed herself to relax and took in her surroundings. The vast, cavernous, endless interior of the tent was like an enclave out of time, its pleated materials hanging from a central pole where they unfolded like a night sky glimmering with a thousand tiny stars (or were they electric bulbs?). Again, the outside temperature had miraculously been kept at bay, and her naked body was caressed by a summer-like warmth despite the close proximity to the snow, ice and northern mountains around.

Nelle turned to the Mistress and the waiting crowd of Ball revellers.

"I'm ready now," she said.

She was no longer the magician's apprentice.

* * *

It could have been Joseph, or it could have been another man altogether. The man in the sharply creased tuxedo, black silk shirt, scarlet-red bow tie, dark bandanna and velvet mask obscuring even his eyes, was of similar height, although his posture was more regal and demonstrative. Although Nelle had never actually witnessed Joseph perform, and had only seen photographs of his act.

He raised his right hand and opened his closed fist and a small ball of fire surged forth and then changed into a bouquet of flowers. The audience obediently gasped as if following a script. It was hours following her arrival, and Nelle had been bathed and scrubbed and she knew her body smelled of lavender and incense, both fragrances swirling around her skin, in unseen waves.

A broad cape appeared out of nowhere, which he then waved theatrically in front of him and, when he pulled it back with an exaggerated flourish, a tall mirror stood, in which she caught a reflection of herself against a background of stars from the tent's artificial sky. Her breasts appeared fuller than she remembered them, her hair more lustrous, her limbs more supple. Maybe it was a trick mirror? One conceived to flatter.

From afar, she could hear the plaintive sound of a violin playing a tune she was unfamiliar with until it burst aloud into a devilish pizzicatto and the audience surrounding her began clapping to its beat.

The master of ceremonies waved to Nelle and she stepped towards the mirror, peered into its depths and in one swift movement walked into and through it, emerging on the other side, with the insistent sound of the music still accompanying her.

She was in a field of snow, which extended to infinity. There was no horizon. Even the surrounding mountains had vanished.

She looked down at her feet. She no longer wore the leather boots and under her toes the snow crunched like cotton candy, although it felt like wool to her nerve endings. It wasn't cold.

A drop of rain splashed against her bare shoulder blade. Another landed on the slope of her breasts, swimming down towards her nipple, where it then cascaded down towards her belly and, its flow never diminishing, reached the slit of her cunt and melted into her wetness. Another raindrop brushed against her nose and Nelle extended her hands out to catch the falling drops in her palms.

She caught one. The music ceased.

She gazed at the hollow of her palm and watched in fascination as the raindrop slowly began to grow in size until it was as large as a Christmas bauble and could no longer be held there. She let it go but it did not fall to the ground. It just floated in the air, still expanding, like a transparent and tenuous bubble growing exponentially, its crystal-like walls a whirl of colours, all in shades of white. Finally, as she stood there with her mouth open in amazement, the bubble, having reached the size of a giant sphere, settled down onto the snow's surface, facing her.

Nelle put her foot forward and, taking a deep breath, she entered the transparent sphere. It did not burst and closed up behind her. She was now inside it. Within seconds, the giant bubble began moving, floating above the bed of snow with grace and alacrity. Nelle extended her arms towards the bubble's seemingly thin walls in order to keep her balance. The consistency felt like rubber but helped her maintain her equilibrium when the ball began gaining momentum and rolling across the endless snow plain.

On and on, she floated along the white tundra, surfing the ever-stretching plain on unseen thermals. Until she felt she had almost circumnavigated the globe, or at any rate the valley where Joseph had led her.

A sense of detachment crawled across her thoughts.

A woman's voice cut through the silence.

"Let them in."

Nelle realized her eyes had been closed, a side effect of her floating in space and her consciousness not wishing to take a geographical bearing.

She opened them.

The giant transparent bubble in which she was standing, legs firmly apart to keep her balance and arms stretched out like a Da Vinci geometrical figure, was now motionless and back in the vast tent from where she had begun her journey of sorts. It was now more like an arena, with tiers of seats surrounding the sphere in which she hovered, a sea of masks gazing out at her.

The faintest of touches grazed her right cheek. Nelle turned her head. A palm tenderly caressing her bare buttocks. Then, another hand, invisible but firm, teasing a nipple and then another contact, skin gliding against skin, a nail drawing across the back of her knee. The white light streaming in from the roof of the structure blinded her to what was happening. She could be seen by the audience, but was unable to observe her spectators inside the sphere, caught as she was in the unnatural glare.

Nelle surrendered.

Soon the avalanche of touches multiplied. A single hand became a flurry of hands, fingers dancing across her bare skin, caresses drawing out her juices, a symphony of subtle contacts causing her heart to beat faster, orchestrating the palette of her senses, electrifying her, clever hands and fingers ingeniously waking her body, each personal erogenous zone in turn, warm, soft alien lips now moving across hers, a tongue that tasted of chocolate and delicate spices sliding past the barrier of her teeth and entwining itself with hers, clever digits delving between her thighs, warm breath lullabying her body.

Her mind in total disarray, Nelle lost her footing and her arms retreated from the resistance of the bubble's opaque walls, allowing herself to float in turn, suspended in the heart of the sphere surrounded by the countless invisible folk who had somehow been conjured out of nowhere to play with her.

She was unable to see any of them – men? women? both? – but every contact was exquisite, both a torture and a delight.

Far away, the music resumed. An exotic melody, sinuous, hypnotic. More than a violin now, the darker notes of a cello stirring deep feelings in her soul, as the ocean of pleasure flooded across her senses.

Impervious to gravity, Nelle felt her body being moved, transported, arranged in a Christ-on-the-cross posture on a cushion of warm air, her arms extended, a stray finger sliding across her cheekbone like burning wax, her thighs being parted, her intimacy fully revealed to the onlookers on the other side of the bubble's thin wall. She sighed.

The heat inside the sphere was rising. Her eyes grew more accustomed to the white light in which she was bathing and Nelle increasingly began to distinguish the shapes of the bodies sharing her space, dispensing their abominable caresses, toying terribly with her.

There were four men and a woman, she realized, as her sight returned. Perfect specimens, buffed, oiled, delicately proportioned and lithe, acting as one, hard, determined, but all faceless, as their movements were too swift or their configuration too clever for her to catch a sight of their features. They fed on her from all angles, touching, sliding, biting exquisitely, licking, caressing, like one single body or organism.

Nelle didn't know where they had arrived from or how or who they were. They just existed to make her feel more alive than she had ever felt before. Wonderful sylphs, apparitions, entities of the night, creatures of the white from whence they had come from and would no doubt return. All to provide a sense to her wantonness, to turn her into what she had always fundamentally been but had never had the courage to openly express.

She pressed herself against hard flesh, invited their tongues and fingers, rubbed against silken skin. Her body was now bathed in sweat, as she became a mermaid overloaded with desire, seeking out pleasures untold, squirming, welcoming their assault.

The jigsaw took shape. The woman gently bit on the lobe of one of Nelle's ears, just as a hard cock pressed against her opening and effortlessly made its way inside her, stretching her wide and grazing against her inner walls. Someone grabbed her shoulders and manoeuvred her extremities at an impossible angle and she felt a second penis joining the first in her depths, while a finger massaged her anal breach, soon to be replaced by yet another man's cock.

Nelle's senses moved into overdrive. Her heart jumped and her mind rebelled briefly: she had never taken three men, let alone two . . . But before she could offer any resistance, the woman's lips reached hers and kissed her with an infinite kindness that just made all her reluctance fade away and allowed her body to relax and willingly succumb to the rising tide of excitement coursing through her.

She knew that all of Joseph's sometimes extreme lovemaking had been calibrated to take her to this stage. There was no longer any shame or morality involved. She had become a creature of pleasure.

The woman retreated from her face, her sweet intoxicating taste still lingering on Nelle's tongue and the final penis travelled gently beyond her lips. It was ruthlessly straight and thick and Nelle instinctively thrust towards it and impaled herself on its hard softness, feeling the woman's fingers gripping her hair and guiding her forward movements until the penis had ploughed her throat and she was fully speared and the gag reflex evaporated.

If she had willingly surrendered earlier to the inevitability of this multiple violation, now Nelle retreated totally from reality and allowed the savage fucking to reach its ultimate conclusion. Yes, she was being invaded in all her openings by four men, with a woman providing further assistance and guidance, and this was being witnessed by a crowd of total strangers just yards away in the arena seating of the Ball's tent, but it no longer mattered.

All that mattered was the moment and the way emotions and feelings flowed in a frenzy inside her mind. But, at the same time, she was blanketed by a surreal form of peace.

Nelle was unaware how long the fucking continued. Minutes or centuries? She had let go. Become just cunt, arse, mouth, orifices, electrical synapses.

The music rose to a crescendo, the frantic movements tearing her apart ever accelerating, the tangle of bodies morphing into an infernal engine running out of control and fuelled by breath-deprived lungs, every thrust conjugated to the power of *n*. The pleasure was equal to the pain. Intense. Annihilating. For a moment, her heart felt like it had stopped and Nelle gasped for air, for something to hold on to for fear of plunging into a deep tunnel that would inevitably end with a blinding splash of white. Death.

And then the whole world exploded.

Nelle's body shook with epileptic animation. Her bare, wet skin traversed by wave after wave of tremors.

Air rushed into the sphere where she was lying. She gasped. Through half-closed eyes she saw the other men and the woman disentangle themselves from her and rise groggily and, in shadows, exit the sphere.

She was unable to move. Starved of energy, drained.

She lay motionless, still spreadeagled, juices leaking from everywhere, snot blocking her nose, her heart imbued with wonderful lightness, her body at peace, still basking in the aftershocks of desire.

As the Mistress of the Ball leaned over her to wipe the sweat away from her forehead, Nelle smiled.

"You did good. The magician was right," the older Medusa-haired woman said in a soothing tone of voice. "Never have I seen a woman harness the powers of pleasure the way you did. It was a beautiful sight to behold . . ."

"Did I?" Nelle weakly answered.

"This will be a Ball to remember," Aurelia said.

Nelle had difficulty keeping her eyes open as the adrenaline deserted her veins.

"Sleep, Nelle," the Mistress said and pulled a large fur blanket over her body. "Sleep . . ."

And, as Nelle fell into the embrace of sleep, she knew that all the days before the arctic valley had just been mere stages on her journey to the Ball, and that the failures, the experiments, the wrong men, the wrong sex, the bondage, the ropes, the doubts, the disappointments and the ultimate acceptance of her submission to sex itself rather than men, had all been necessary.

Joseph had been good for her, but he was not enough. She belonged to the Ball.

She would not see him again and would remain here. Forever.

How to Help a Writer

Teresa Noelle Roberts

Rob tugged on the back of Valerie's hair, not an obnoxious schoolboy yank, but a firm, dominant pull designed to force her head back, transferring her focus from the computer screen to him. Valerie arched back in her chair, following the pressure of Rob's hands so she was looking back at his bearded face. She smiled for the first time in several hours, and a weight of frustration lifted. Then it fell back again, heavier than ever, because even when she was looking away from the screen and at Rob's hazel eyes and his narrow, wicked smile, she was visualizing the first few lines of the scene she just couldn't write.

He released her hair, ran his hands over her breasts. She gasped and arched further, seeking more contact. He obliged, pinching her nipples firmly through the soft, worn grey cotton of her "Caution: Novel Under Construction" T-shirt. The sensation zinged through her body, but it didn't manage to cut through the fog in her brain. "Shut down, lover," he whispered, his voice a tiger's growling purr. "You've been staring at the same page for hours – when you weren't venting on Twitter or surfing the Net. Writing's obviously not working. So it's time to play."

"Nailed. I didn't know you'd been checking up on me."

"I always check up on you when you're writing. There are benefits to dating an erotic romance writer." He cupped her breasts now, rolling the nipples between thumb and forefinger. Now the pleasure was working its way through the tangled mess of her thoughts, both giving her delicious ideas about things she and Rob might do to each other and underlying her lack of clarity about what her characters should be doing, and more importantly, *why*.

She sighed, half pleasure at Rob's touch, half anxiety. "Not when I'm writing against my will. The editor insisted I need two more sex scenes, including one to close the book."

Rob pulled his hands back and nodded, then spun her chair around so she was facing him. Valerie couldn't help smiling. After a few years of living with a writer, he knew when she needed to talk something through – or just rant for a while. "The first scene wasn't a problem – the editor had suggested a logical place to add one and I got that written by early afternoon – but at the end of the book the hero and heroine are both exhausted and he's injured. She's had to shape-shift a few times to find where the villains were holding the hero, and they've had to kill bad guys, including one they didn't realize was a bad guy until the end and had liked. Even my perpetually horny, kinky werewolves aren't going to fuck under those circumstances." She snorted. "And the editor wants it back by Monday, which means by Sunday since I have to be at the damn day job by eight on Monday for a stupid team meeting. Said she knew I wouldn't have any trouble writing a couple of quick scenes over a weekend. Which usually I wouldn't, but a whole new end for the book isn't just a quick scene."

"Ouch." Yeah, Rob knew the right things to say after all this time.

"Ouch indeed. It was a great, dramatic ending, with them covered in blood and finally admitting they loved each other. But it's a stupid time for them to have sex. So I figure I'll write a chapter or two that take place a few days later when they're semi-recovered. She thinks she should leave and give him space so he can figure out if he was just talking about love because of the adrenaline rush. I've managed a few paragraphs of that scene, and I know where it has to go, but I can't get it moving in a way that's going to be sexy instead of talky. The hero's not so good with words, and the heroine will yammer forever if I don't watch myself. The whole thing's making me cranky, and cranky makes it hard to think sexy."

"How about he ties her to the bed so she doesn't bolt, maybe gags her so she'll have to listen – you said the characters were kinky – and then proves how he feels? Very slowly and sensually, all night long."

"That would just piss her off."

Rob raised one eyebrow and grinned. "It's worked on you before."

That brought Valerie up short, all her self-defeating mental chatter silenced by the memory of that night. It was early in the relationship, before they were living together, and they'd been trying to figure out if they could afford takeout that night or should piece dinner together out of the pantry. She'd been having a crappy day, though – another day of writing frustration, in fact, though the pre-publication kind of writing frustration when you despair because you're working your ass off and still not getting anywhere – and she'd ended up crying and ranting and picking a fight for no good reason. At a certain point, Rob had scooped her into his arms, carried her into the bedroom, and done just what he described. She'd struggled for about three seconds, then realized that her arguments had no weight that compared to the weight of Rob's love and lust.

Or maybe she simply decided that kinky sex was fun and fighting and crying weren't, but eventually, by a come-drenched, blissfully exhausted dawn, it led her to accept that Rob loved her and would even if she never saw her name on the cover of a book.

She saw the scene play out in her memory. Then she saw how the scene would play out with her characters. Rougher than she and Rob had been, because they were werewolves, after all, and even their non-kinky sex was rough and intense. And because they were werewolves, her heroine would be able to *smell* her guy's truth, once he'd stopped her from arguing and shut down the over-analytical parts of her brain. "That'll work!" Valerie exclaimed. She slid out of her chair and engulfed Rob in a hug.

A hug that swiftly shifted from the exuberant to the sexual. Valerie slid her hands inside the waistband of his sweatpants, cupping a firm butt cheek with one and letting the other flirt with his cock and balls, lightly brushing them as they quickened to life. He bent to kiss her, devouring, fierce, full of need. All thought of the book fled Valerie's mind, replaced by urgent desire. She moved her hand out of the way so she could grind against him, and he gripped her ass tight and moved her methodically. He was getting hard, and her yoga pants were damp, and she wanted, she wanted . . .

"How about you tie me to the bed and fuck me? For inspiration, you know," she whispered, during a pause in the kissing.

In response, he grabbed her wrist, and for a second she thought he was thinking about it. Then he growled, "Sit down," and plopped her into the chair.

She blinked at him, bewildered and bereft of contact. But she couldn't be annoyed, not when Rob looked at her the way he did, loving and possessive and wicked. He had a plan, she could tell, a very dirty plan. A plan that she'd enjoy, once she found out what the hell it was.

He put one big hand on her ribcage, just above her breasts. "Stay put," he said, in a commanding tone he usually reserved for special occasions in the bedroom. She opened her mouth, not sure which question she was going to ask of the many running through her mind – all of which boiled down to *when will there be sex?* – but he gently shut her mouth with the index finger of his other hand on her jaw. "You'll know soon enough," he said. "I'll be right back."

He was out of the room before she could translate her disobedient thoughts into action.

By the time he came back, Valerie had managed to write a paragraph of setting and a few lines of dialogue. It wasn't a lot, but it felt less like drilling into concrete with a teaspoon than her previous hours of painful effort. And unlike the laboured result of those hours, these few snippets sounded good. Fresh. In character.

"Give me a sec." She saved her work. "I had to get that down. The words just started flowing."

"Good girl," Rob said, surprising her. "I thought they might. Give me your hands."

She turned the chair around, puzzled.

Rob was holding several short lengths of their thinner bondage rope and a longer one of hemp.

Her cunt jumped, and she held out her hands out of boneless instinct. Part of her brain screamed that she had to keep working on the scene now that she'd finally gotten it started, but the rest of it slowed to a trickle, utterly focused on the magical combination of Rob and rope.

He made a simple cuff tie on first one wrist, then the other. Valerie focused on the cool, smooth softness of the rope on her skin, on the deft movements of Rob's hands, on the way the rope transported her to a different place. A better place, both sexy and serene, as if the act of being bound was an erotic meditation, and perhaps it was.

When the cuffs were complete, he made a simple loop in the end of each rope and lassoed them loosely around the arms of her desk chair. "Test that," he said. "Make sure you can type and use your mouse."

Heart racing, pussy throbbing, she did. The bonds didn't interfere with her ability to type. In fact, before she gave it any thought, she wrote a few more lines of dialogue, fraught with erotic and romantic tension.

She felt rather than saw Rob smile, felt it because she didn't turn away from her keyboard.

Not even when he looped the hemp rope around her ankle and attached the end to the leg of the desk. "This is long enough so you can reach the bathroom if you need to," he said. "Make sure you can slide the loops off the chair arms." She tested that too, suspecting where he was going next before he said it. Part of her was pissed. Being tied up and bossed around in the bedroom was one delicious, dirty, hot thing, but this was her career, dammit. He couldn't just tie her to her chair and force her to write. It was . . . unprofessional. High-handed. Crossing all kinds of lines.

On the other hand, it was sexy as hell.

And words were racing through her brain, when they'd been racing the other way all afternoon.

"I'll be in the other room. Yell when you're ready for dinner, or if you need something to drink. Otherwise, I expect you to stay in that chair and write until you're done."

She gulped. Clenched.

And realized that the combination of arousal and annoyance was just what she needed to fuel the scene. Parts of her were thoroughly, delightfully distracted by the rope, by Rob's commanding tone, by all sorts of wonderful, wicked things she hoped would happen soon. At the same time, all those delightfully depraved notions and sensual promptings – and the touch of annoyance that spiced them – gave her the imagery she needed to finish her writing.

And finish it quickly.

"Damn, you're good."

Rob preened. "I know." Then, all seriousness, "But not as good as you. You'll make your deadline and the book will rock even more with the new scene than it already does."

"I still can't decide if I'm glad I opened my email this morning or sorry." What she really meant, she realized as she said it, was *I'm sorry that I end up writing all the time instead of being able to goof off. Sorry I don't have more time for you.* But she didn't say it out loud, because he'd scoff and say he knew what he'd signed on for when he started dating a writer.

And while she was sorry, sometimes, that between the writing and the still-needed day job, she didn't have more time to just be with Rob, she couldn't be any other way.

And he knew it and wanted her just the way she was.

"You'll get it done in no time now that you know what you need to say. You always do. And then we'll celebrate."

He kissed the top of her head and whispered, "I love you, crazy writer lady."

Valerie was already writing.

It had taken her more than two hours to write the first awkward paragraphs setting up the new scene. It took her just over twice that long, not counting a short dinner break, to write two new chapters that took her characters from angst and doubt to bondage-induced ecstasy.

Every time she started to slow down, every time she considered saying she'd finish later and go play with Rob instead, she brushed her hand over the rope on her other wrist.

Rob loved her. Rob wanted her to make her deadline.

And the sooner she made her deadline, the sooner she could say thank you to Rob for his inspiration. Writing the intense final sex scene allowed her to channel her pent-up desire, but she was wet, her nipples tight, oversensitive points against her T-shirt, a mass of need that writing about bondage and sex could blunt, but only bondage and sex in the flesh could sate.

Sometime around 11 p.m., Valerie saved for the last time and shut the computer down. She'd review it tomorrow and send it out, and she'd probably even have time to work a bit on her new book.

But first things first.

She could have untied herself, but instead she called Rob's name. She didn't need to try for a sultry voice. Undistracted now by her work, Valerie could focus on the rope binding wrists and ankle, on the desire now raging through her, and a breathy, sex-drenched voice came naturally.

Rob was there in a heartbeat, a twinkle in his eyes and an impressive bulge in his crotch.

"I'm done! Thank you so much. I'll let it rest until tomorrow and tweak anything that needs tweaking but basically I'm done." Sheer glee overcame her and she laughed.

"I knew you could do it." Rob kissed her, and for the duration of the kiss, Valerie couldn't even think of a complete sentence.

But when he released her lips, words returned. "All it took was the right inspiration, which you provided. But now I think you should untie me from the desk chair—" her voice slipped back to the sultry, breathy place it had been before "—and tie me up again in the bedroom."

Rob smiled. "I thought you'd never ask."

Among the Trees

Matt Thorne

June

"She knows I don't mean no harm when I call her the Elephant," the taxi driver says as he looks for the entry road to Richard's parents' estate. "She is a very large girl, and, in my book, that's something to celebrate. Especially as both her parents are so skinny. It's like she puts in special effort, and I respect that. They say being fat is bad for you, but there's plenty of fat people who live to a decent age. I read about a man who was so fat that when he got cancer, the cancer couldn't kill him because there was too much of him to fight through. Oh, she moans that she can't find a boyfriend, but there's plenty of men who like fat women. There's some men who even try to get thin women fat. Feeders, they call them. Mind you, with the best will in the world, I would feel happier if she found someone her own size. It's always a bit creepy when you see a fat man with a thin wife, steering her from behind like a cow—"

"This is it, isn't it?" interrupts Claire, looking up from the directions. "This road ahead?"

The driver turns onto a muddy track. "Do you want me to drop you here?"

"No," says John, "it's a huge estate. We need to take a left up ahead to get us to the guest accommodation."

"OK," says the driver. "I had no idea all this land was owned by one family."

The track is harder to navigate and the taxi driver stops talking. Claire shows John the directions. There isn't much light in the back of the car and it's hard to see. The journey has taken far longer than she anticipated. Two cancelled trains and then this unhelpful taxi driver – who'd initially refused to drive from Kemble and only relented when John offered him five pounds on top of the meter – has added three hours to their journey. It is now nearly nine o'clock and Claire worries they won't be able to get the keys to the house where they are staying.

"Someone's following us," says the taxi driver. "Maybe they think we're trespassing. I'll pull over."

Claire looks through the rear window. She'd assumed it was the groundskeeper but couldn't understand why he was in an anonymous old car instead of a Land Rover. After they pull over, he stops, opens the door and walks across. The taxi driver lowers the window and the groundskeeper pokes his head in, shining his torch at the back seat.

"Hello, Claire," he says, "good to see you again. I wondered if you'd be coming."

She feels embarrassed to be recognized in front of John. She wants to tell him that she's only been here three times before and there's no reason why the man should know her name. Then she remembers the time he came across them in the grounds at night, the moment of humiliation as his torch-light reared over her naked back and buttocks before Richard noticed and shouted at him to leave.

"You know where you're staying, I take it?"

"Number seven."

"Lucky you. Do you remember where it is?"

"No."

"OK, I'll go ahead and you follow me up."

They wait while the groundskeeper drives round them and then the taxi driver starts the engine. "I'd be happy with just one of these houses," he says. "How many rooms do you think are in each one? At least a dozen by the look of it." He continues driving past the six large farmhouses, talking to himself as much as to them. "We do have a nice house. But we're nowhere near paying off the mortgage. It's my own fault, I've never been sensible with money."

The groundskeeper stops by the seventh house and they drive past him and onto the forecourt. Three cars are already poorly parked outside the house. John takes out his wallet and pays the driver, who gets out and helps them with their bags. The groundskeeper shouts from his car, "The door's on a code. Three-oh-nine. Just tap it in."

None of the doors inside the house have locks. Claire and John find the biggest room and put their bags in the wardrobe. Then John comes up behind Claire and shoves her down onto the bed.

"John," she protests, but he is already turning her over and unbuckling her belt. She wants to warn him that she has her period, but knows if she speaks now she'll spoil it. She tells herself not to be frightened of his lust; his passion is not unexpected.

John pulls her entire belt out from her waistband, and she wonders whether he is going to tie her wrists or whip her cheeks. He doesn't do either, instead throwing the belt onto the floor. She gets up onto her knees and he roughly yanks her jeans over her butt as if skinning a rabbit. Oh, she thinks, this could be good.

He removes her flimsy blue striped knickers with a similar motion, pulling so hard the material tears at the side and they are ruined. He is too impatient to undress her further, turning her round in her arms until her legs are open in front of him. She is impressed when he tugs out her tampon and puts his mouth straight to her vagina without squeamishness or ceremony. He takes his time with his tongue, progressing slow enough to ensure the whole of her sex is alive. This is the type of fucking she fantasizes about: being *taken* by someone big enough to hurt her if he wasn't so tender. It is a year since she last had sex. And it has been a while since she last masturbated. When she was younger she did it almost every night, but recently she has felt her body drift away from her and when she does it now it is mainly to ensure that she can still climax.

The only reward for her recent chastity is that she has started to have powerful sex-dreams, sometimes ending in a nocturnal orgasm. Her first orgasm ever was a nocturnal one, and when she researched this she discovered that it was unusual for girls to have nocturnal orgasms unless they've come by other means first, which made her feel special. She likes that her brain can do this to her body. It seems almost noble. After these dreams, Claire feels like she's had sex – so much so that if it wasn't for her vivid memory of her dream's content, and her delight at possessing herself, she could believe in incubi.

She is surprised at how gratifying it feels to have her genitals exposed; for her vagina to be the focus of someone else's dedicated attention. She closes her eyes and feels embarrassed at how quickly she comes. Claire hopes John understands, is gratified rather than angry. He definitely noticed, which pleases her, as it was a small orgasm, and might have been missed by a less observant man.

Claire is also pleased that he stops for a moment, clearly able to control himself, no matter how eager he feels. They lie there for a moment, then she decides to undress him, unbuckling his belt and tugging down his jeans. She wonders whether he is circumcised. As she slips her fingers under his waistband, she discovers the pleasing ruffle of a foreskin. She strokes his prick a couple of times and then – in a slightly awkward, wordless manner – indicates to John that she wants him to sit on the edge of the bed.

John seems taken aback by her attempt at even minor control and she feels giddy when she sees the flash of anger that passes over his face. Still, after a moment, he responds to her dragging hands and shuffles across the bed to sit where she wants him. She gets down on the floor and her fingers quickly cover her vagina in shame as she feels blood dribble onto the carpet.

She tries not to think about it as she wipes her red fingers against her white thighs and removes John's shoes and socks. She pulls his jeans and underpants down the rest of the way and over his feet, then drops them alongside her own clothes. Then she gets up on her knees and takes John into her mouth as deeply as she can, bunching her fingers against the bed and using the mattress's spring to get a steady, even rhythm as she sucks his prick.

It feels so reassuring to be doing this, and she moves her hips in a gentle curl as she does so, no longer worried about ruining the carpet. She plans to take him all the way with her tongue, but before long he puts his hands around her head and tries to stop her. She moves her head in a minute shake of defiance but he struggles until she has no choice but to stop.

"I want to come inside you."

"You can't."

"Why not?"

"I'm not on the pill."

"It doesn't matter. Not when you're . . . like this." He inserts his finger inside her vagina and draws a line of blood across her left breast.

"I can still get pregnant."

"I don't care."

He lifts her onto his prick. She is astonished by the sound that comes out of her, from deep inside her throat, a noise completely different from the small mewling that she normally makes during sex. Is this what she's wanted? She is on top but he is completely in control; so much so that she can barely stay upright. Sex has never been like this. One second she's lost in dreamy detachment; the next more connected to the world than she's ever been before. It doesn't feel like pain, but is too intense and uncontrollable to be called pleasure. Moments after he comes, she does too, as if in sympathy, knuckles wedged into her mouth.

Alone in the shower afterwards, she examines the bloody fingerprints on her thigh and the stripe on her breast and is proud of the markings. For the first time in her life she feels as if someone has taken her and used her and satisfied himself and her too. It shouldn't be such a rare sensation, she's sure, but it has been for her. When Richard made love to her, it was all about how he controlled his desire. Her brain is racing. There is still sperm inside her, but instead of feeling worried, she feels happy. She hasn't started the water yet, and is just standing, alone in this private space, recovering. A trickle of sperm runs down her left thigh and she halts it with her finger and rubs it against the blood smears, watching as the red and white turn pink. All of her previous squeamishness, and lifelong fastidiousness, is temporarily absent, replaced with a new fascination with the workings of her body. She wonders if she is prepared to start taking the pill again. She'd grown so used to – and fond of – her natural rhythms that she'd promised herself she never would, but now she's worried. It isn't so much that she's frightened John doesn't want to use condoms, but she's anxious that if they have to negotiate their sex life, the magic will be gone. She doesn't want to be a fantasy woman for John; she wants him to appreciate the corporeality of her, but given that he wasn't worried about her menses, it seems wrong that she's the one who wants to stop their lovemaking being natural. Sex is spunk and blood and love and mess.

Suddenly, the shower door opens and John is standing there. She feels silly and embarrassed, naked with no water.

"I thought you should know," he says, "there's no danger of you getting pregnant."

"It is possible, John," she replies, knowing she sounds petulant.

"No, it's not. I had a vasectomy."

"But why did you pretend?"

He looks at her legs. "I wanted you to feel scared."

Amazed at how much she has changed in the last hour, Claire whispers, "Thank you," and kisses him so hard he breaks away and steps backwards, rubbing his face and looking almost as spent as she feels.

The next day, they get to the church at three o'clock. The ceremony has already started and they have to sneak into a pew at the back. Claire's irritation with John diminishes when she notices another couple of latecomers following them, smiling across the aisle in a spirit of shared mischief. She now feels silly for getting so worked up, but the way John shouted at her when she tried to hurry him made her feel like he was punishing her, and she resented this so soon after giving him her body.

Claire scans the congregation, looking for her friend Harriet. There's a fluttery ache in her stomach. She feels tired, the physical exertion of last night's lovemaking still shadowing her body. Although she's not as afraid as she expected, she is still troubled by a strange sense of exposure. This is the first wedding she's attended, but she's struck by the conviction that all church weddings must be like this: the negative past purged through healing ritual. Now she understands why Jane was so keen for her to be here. In spite of everything, there is something holy about the sanctity of marriage. She feels naked here, a fragile, sweating mess, in a state of defilement, convinced the bloodstains she washed from her thighs the night before are still there.

Later, large space heaters billow the canvas of the marquee as the dance floor fills. Richard comes to her on the fourth song. He guides her out into an almost empty corner and leans in close so he can hear her speak. "Will Jane mind you dancing with me?" she asks.

Richard smiles and shakes his head. "We trust each other. The most important thing for both of us today is that all our ghosts are laid to rest."

"Is that how you think of me? As a ghost?"

"I think of you," he whispers directly into her ear, "as a missed opportunity."

The song comes to an end and Claire walks back to John, wiping her cheeks.

"Are you OK?" he asks.

She nods.

"What did he say to you?"

"Nothing."

"Tell me."

"I don't want to talk about it."

He grabs her arm. "Either you tell me what you were talking about, or I'm going to leave you here."

Claire doesn't reply. He shoves her arm back at her and turns away. He's outside before she comes after him.

"I'm sorry I upset you," she says. "I didn't mean to do anything wrong."

"Just tell me what he said."

"It's not important."

"It was important enough to humiliate me."

Claire looks at him, her voice trembling. "How did I humiliate you?"

"Every single person in that marquee was staring at me while you were dancing with Richard."

"I could hardly refuse, John. It's his wedding day."

"I know. But you're protecting him."

"I'm not protecting him. I'm trying to protect myself."

She drops his hand and runs on ahead. He chases after her. "Who are you protecting yourself from, Claire?"

"You," she shouts, "you, you, you, you, you, you . . ."

"Claire," he calls after her, "come back."

She stops running and looks up at the moon. She slowly walks back to him, her shoes crunching the dirt. The two of them stand there together, staring into each other's eyes. Claire is crying again. He holds her as hard as he can, only breaking away as a car slowly rumbles up the dirt road towards them.

July

It's 1 a.m. Only now does Claire feel frightened. She trusts John, but is also aware that he no longer has the same barriers other men do. Maybe it had been a mistake to confide in him. Some of things she's said to him would have encouraged any man, no matter how normal, to become sadistic.

He's hardly said a thing since they got into the car. It was a game at first. And when he placed the long length of rope on the back seat, she worried that to speak would break the spell. Now she simply wants reassurance, but knows it would be a mistake to ask for it.

Unable to question John, Claire tells herself to relax. When he invited her to climb into the car she'd initially been disappointed he hadn't told her to wear a blindfold, but now she realizes that this isn't necessary. Although Claire has lived in this area her whole life, and if you questioned her she would insist she knew all the surrounding neighbourhoods, after twenty minutes she already feels lost. She supposes it's because her usual journey is towards the centre of the city instead of away from it. She has forgotten how close they were to so many fields, how little she knows about these hidden areas fenced off by trees.

Not real forests, not yet, but close enough.

Unpoliced areas.

The true England.

John continues driving, the radio silent. Claire is still now, having decided she's going to trust him. Let those who don't understand ask questions later. She knows what she is doing.

He parks the car near a densely wooded area, protected by a broken fence. He holds back the wire meshing so it won't scratch the flesh of her thighs as she steps inside. He's carrying a torch and a length of rope, and once she's safely at the foot of the path leading into the woods, he flicks the beam at her and says, "You're a good girl, Claire . . ."

"Thank you."

". . . But now it's time to take off your clothes."

Claire has no real sense of how long she's been in the woods when the magic potion starts to take effect. For some time she is only slightly cold, sleepy, and a little afraid. At first, she believes he is going to come back. Surely he doesn't expect her to sleep in her bonds? Then, almost imperceptibly at first, Claire begins to feel a series of slow changes in her body. She senses her heartbeat speeding up. She wants to put her hand to her chest and see if she can slow it down by trying to squeeze it through her chest, but as her hands are restrained she cannot do so. Her mouth and sinuses feel dried out, in the same way they do when her mother puts on the central heating before she has arisen. At the same time, she feels a strong urge to urinate.

But then the panic subsides in declining waves, and is replaced by a return of the previous sleepiness. This time, it's richer, more narcotic. She is under the spell of Morpheus. She spends a long time in this intoxicated state, unaware of everything apart from the forest, which she now experiences as a tangible force of darkness against her skin.

Claire starts when a woman comes out of this darkness and stops a short distance in front of her. The woman looks at her for a long time, staring at her feet, then her legs, vagina and breasts. Claire closes her eyes, seeing red pulses and feeling lost. She thinks if she keeps her eyes closed long enough then when she opens them again the woman will have disappeared. But when she does so, the woman is still standing there. She's silently watching Claire, who realizes she's seen the woman before. She wonders who she is, what time in her life she has come from, and how John persuaded her to take part in tonight's events.

"Hello, Sleeping Beauty," says the woman, and Claire thinks she hears the voice inside her head instead of through her ears, but is still so disorientated that it's hard to tell. The woman walks closer to her and places her hand on Claire's belly. Her fingers are cold and Claire flinches. The woman removes her hand and says in a tone that sounds sympathetic and mocking at the same time, "What a state you've got yourself in."

Claire feels ashamed. She has never understood how people who she's not even sure actually exist can make her feel like this. She is convinced that this woman must be someone significant from her past life who she's subsequently forgotten. But who is she? A teacher from one of her schools? That doesn't seem quite right, but she's pretty sure this woman is some forgotten authority figure.

"Can you help me?" Claire asks.

"Help you how? Would you like me to make you come?"

"No. Untie me."

"I can't do that. Let me make you come."

"No. Where do I know you from?"

"You don't remember?"

"No."

The woman purses her lips, but doesn't say anything. Claire has a strong sense that she's going to disappear in front of her eyes, and closes them again, willing this to happen. When she opens them again, the woman is gone.

Early August

They both stare down at Claire's body. She hears herself asking John, "Do you like my breasts?"

He doesn't reply.

"It's OK if you don't. I don't like them. It's just that . . . you touch them differently."

"Differently?"

"Properly," she says quickly. "As if you care about them. As if they're beautiful to you."

"They are beautiful."

"No, they're not. My nipples are too big. It's like my breast is all nipple."

He laughs. "Don't be ridiculous. They're beautiful. Seriously. And not just because they're yours."

"Thank you," she replies, and then, emboldened, asks, "What's your favourite part of my body?"

"Your legs."

"By which you mean my fanny?"

"What?"

"You're saying my legs so you can touch and stroke them to show me how much you like them, but the whole time you'll be looking at my fanny."

John takes his hand from her breast. He goes through to the bedroom and comes back with her underwear.

"Put these on," he says, handing them to her.

"Why?" she asks, doing so.

"I want to show you how much I like your legs."

He unzips his trousers and she feels illicitly thrilled as he begins rubbing his prick along the smooth inside of her thighs.

At first he grips her legs and holds them open, but then he begins hammering his prick into her inner thigh, gripping himself in a hold that she knows would only hurt him if she tried to emulate it. It seems cruel that she can't work out what he likes just from watching him do it to himself. It's something she has to learn through trial and error. He is staring at her thighs so intently that she feels relieved when he comes, the sperm trapped for a moment before it runs down her inside leg and curves round the arch of her left buttock.

"Believe me now?" he asks, and she nods, pulling him to her.

Late August

John leaves the flat at seven o'clock, hoping to get to the restaurant before the evening crowd trickle in. It's oddly located, this restaurant, not on the main drag of Pentonville Road where it might catch the trade heading from King's Cross to Islington but hidden down a side street, and this prevents it from being as popular as John believes it deserves to be. John's idea of a good meal is one that doesn't squat in his stomach after he's finished it and this restaurant excels in such fare. He hasn't been here since Claire's moved in and he's very pleased to see his waitress is working tonight, as she usually was in the days when he came here every night, even on Sundays, and she looks over at him as he comes through the door.

"Hey," she says, "where have you been hiding?"

"Nowhere special," he replies, and walks across to where he used to sit by the window. He looks back to his waitress. She often wore the same outfit she has on tonight: an orange T-shirt with a faded silver stencil of Mickey Mouse in his classic pose and a pair of almost white faded jeans that remind him of a similar pair he'd seen Claire wearing before. He could never tell whether the waitress was trying to grow out a blonde dye or if she liked her hair like this, but she's had it in this style for so long now he assumes it must be deliberate: certainly her two-tone hair fits with the tattered silver Mickey. She comes over and places a bottle of Peroni on his table. He smiles, pleased that there's somewhere he gets this treatment. He thanks her and she walks away.

It always takes too long for his food to arrive, even when the restaurant is empty. He should've brought a newspaper or a book. Every time he comes here he thinks this, and the next time he always forgets. He gets up and goes to the toilet, killing time. When he returns, the waitress is approaching his table with his dinner. He decides he's ready to ask her. "Excuse me," he says, as she walks away.

"Yeah?"

"This place closes at midnight on Saturdays, doesn't it?"

"Yeah. Why?"

"Do you have any plans for afterwards?"

"No."

"Good. Listen, I live near here. Would you like to come back with me?"

"Why?"

"I just like the way you . . ."

"The way I what?"

"I don't know. Look. Dress. I like your hair. And your eyes."

"My hair's dyed."

"I know. That's what I like."

This isn't the first time John has chatted someone up, but it's been a while, and he's never approached a waitress in a restaurant before. He wonders why he feels he can do it now; he never could when he was in the flat alone. He supposes it's because he wanted Claire so much, and worried that to sleep with another woman would take the edge off his hunger. He knew it didn't really work like that, though, and if he had been sleeping with another woman, it would only have made Claire want him more.

The waitress still seems to be considering the possibility. "Look," she says, "I don't even know your name."

"John."

"I'm Cassie," she says, and laughs. "I'll be your waitress for the evening."

* * *

She doesn't arrive till past one, and though he's stayed awake, John had almost given up on her. As he opens the door, he kisses her, concerned that she might have changed her mind. She kisses him back and then comes inside. "I like your flat," she says, reaching down to slip off her tattered, dirty blue Converse. John notices that she has a small tattoo of a heart just above the toes of her left foot.

"Would you like some whisky?" he asks.

"Sure," she replies.

John's flat is dingy and he wonders if Cassie really does like it. He's also curious to know if Cassie has ever seen him walk past the restaurant with Claire. He's hidden away as much of Claire's stuff as he could find, but he knows that women can sense even the slightest female influence on male decor. He hands her the whisky and wonders whether they should talk more or if he should make a move on her. He's so used to being forceful with Claire that seductive conversation feels beyond him.

"Hey," she says, "you have a record player."

It's Claire's record player. All the records are Claire's too. He's surprised at how much younger women seem to like record players now: he thought their generation only listened to music on their phones. She's gone across and is looking through the records. She stops and pulls out a record with what looks like a large phallus on the cover but is actually a guitar. "This looks fun."

There is red horror-movie style writing on the sleeve saying *Hair and Thangs*. John has never heard this record, as far as he knows, though he doesn't keep track of what Claire plays. He takes the record from Cassie and puts it on the turntable. The first track is instrumental – guitar, organ and drums – though John would be hard pressed to define what genre it is or what period it is from. Cassie seems to like it though, smiling and muttering, "Groovy" in a jokey voice.

They go through to the bedroom. Cassie takes off her jeans and lies on the mattress. He lies next to her and runs his hand over her face. They kiss for a while and then he turns her round so she has her back to him. "Do you know what my favourite thing is?" she says. "When a man takes all my clothes off but doesn't get undressed himself."

"You want me to strip you?"

"Yeah, but slowly . . ."

John is so unused to someone making a sexual request of him that he is uncertain how to respond. He decides he will do as she asks and slowly pulls her orange Mickey Mouse T-shirt over her head. She is wearing a light cream bra. He unclasps this too and holds her tight as he caresses the upper half of her body. Her breasts are bigger than Claire's, with very small nipples. He kisses her neck and breathes in her hair, which smells like cigarettes. He reaches around her and undoes the belt of her jeans. Someone has starting singing on the record, and he can hear a voice saying "sunshine" repeatedly but can't discern the rest of the lyric.

Her jeans have tack buttons instead of a zip and he undoes them one at a time. Cassie raises herself up so he can pull them down over her buttocks and legs. Her knickers are black. He likes her mismatched underwear; it fits with his idea of her. He also likes that when he pulls down her pants he finds short black stubble. He knew she was really a brunette, like Claire. He wonders what Claire would look like with blonde hair. He can't imagine it.

"Make me stand up," she whispers.

John isn't used to being directed like this, but swallows his irritation and tells her, "Stand up."

She doesn't move. He grabs her arm and hoists her up. He pushes her against a wall and she says, "Tease me with your cock."

"What?" he replies.

"And after you've teased me, fuck me with just the tip. Do it until I can't bear it."

John's tempted to fuck her hard as punishment for trying to control him, but says instead, "I want to give you head."

"No," she says, "I don't know you well enough."

This strikes him as so surprising John almost laughs. Instead he stands behind her and strokes her breasts, before reaching down to touch her between the legs. He wonders whether she'll stop him doing this too, but she doesn't resist. John has never felt quite as certain with his fingers as with his tongue, but after a few minutes she is breathing shallowly enough for him to start rubbing the head of his prick over her buttocks and down to her vagina. He does as she instructed, teasing her as gently as he can. This feels very different to the sex he has with Claire, or anyone before her.

For the next twenty minutes, he touches her breast (she has informed him that her left nipple is incredibly sensitive while she has hardly any feeling in the right one at all), strokes her clitoris and fucks her with just the head of his prick. Then she whispers, "Have you got any KY?"

"Are you getting dry?"

"No," she says, "I want it . . . well, you know where I want it."

"You don't know me well enough for me to give you head but you're happy for me to do that to you?"

"I need it sometimes. It's like I have a G-spot there or something. Please . . . can we stop talking about it?"

John nods and goes to the bedside table and gets the lubricant. Cassie is no longer facing the wall but is kneeling by the bed. He squeezes it onto his fingers and lowers himself down so he is facing Cassie's buttocks. He gently pulls them open and starts to smear the jelly. He pushes a finger inside her, moving it back and forth gently before replacing it with the head of his prick. He fucks her there in the same way, only entering her with the tip. But she seems to want more of him inside her and soon starts to bear down on him. After a few minutes, he is deep inside. She's stroking her own clitoris now so he starts touching her breast again. "Hold me tight around the hip," she tells him, and he does, as he feels her start to orgasm. He has never made a woman come this way before – when he tried this with Claire, he could tell he was causing her pain – and he feels a strong affection for this waitress and pride at what they have achieved. She is still coming, her groans changing to little shrieks. To his astonishment, even though he usually needs far more stimulation than this, he feels the throb he usually experiences when his own orgasm is near, and he starts fucking her faster, riding through her climax until he is upon his own, amazed that this has happened during a one-night stand.

"Is it OK if I sleep here?" she asks afterwards, and John is touched by the request. The two of them cuddle up together in bed and though it feels more natural than it ever does with Claire, he knows it is wrong. His journey with Claire is far from over; tonight was some kind of terrible temptation to deviate from his path. In the morning he will ask the waitress to leave, and will not think of her again. It was not wrong to betray Claire tonight: he was getting weak and she only loves him when he is strong. He could not do what he experienced tonight with Claire; it is clear the waitress is a far stronger woman who knows exactly what she wants. It should be compelling to him, but it isn't. For all of Claire's apparent submissiveness, he knows when he is pleasing her and when he isn't, and he knows better than to abandon their journey together now. It would be like leaving her among the trees that night he took her there, rather than going back and rescuing her and bringing her home. They are both in the woods now, and it seems dark, but they can still find their way back into the light.

September

At eleven o'clock, Claire hears the door buzzer. She is sitting in the lounge, watching television in her blue silk robe. She goes to the intercom and says, "Hello?"

"Claire? It's Tony."

"Tony? This isn't a great time."

"I'm sorry. But I wouldn't come here if I didn't have a good reason. It's to do with your payment. It'll only take a minute. It's very simple."

"OK," she says, "I suppose you'll have to come up."

Claire ducks into the bedroom and takes off her blue silk robe. She grabs a light pink T-shirt from the laundry basket and, finding nothing else, pulls on a pair of grey tracksuit bottoms.

"So what's the problem?" she asks, unembarrassed about revealing her impatience.

"Can I come in?"

"Of course."

They walk through to the lounge. He sits down opposite her and says, "I lied about needing to see you about your payment. I just wanted to see you."

"Why?"

"Jeena's really pissed off with me. She thinks it's my fault you left."

"I told her it was nothing to do with you. I can call her if you want."

"I'm not bothered about the job." He looks away. "I know you think I'm an idiot . . ."

"Tony, why do you care what I think of you? It doesn't matter."

"It does to me. That's why I'm here. To apologize."

"For what?"

"Making life difficult for you." He sighs. "Look, Claire, I don't want to give you the wrong idea. I understand that you're deeply in love with John and I'm not going to criticize your relationship. I've been in this situation before and . . ."

"What situation?"

"Falling in love with someone who . . ."

"Someone who what?" she asks, before realizing what else Tony had said. "You're in love with me?"

Claire had suspected Tony might fancy her, but was astonished to hear him use the word "love". She feels a small blush of pleasure. Her smile is enough of a prompt for Tony to come over and sit beside her, and before she can say anything more, he's kissing her face. Claire doesn't know how to respond. She knows she could stop him, but it feels so gratifying and she finds herself thinking maybe if she doesn't do anything, if she lets him make love to her and is as passive as can be, she can't be held responsible for what happens. John can never know, of course, but maybe it wouldn't even count for her.

"Force me," she whispers.

"What?"

"Don't be violent, but . . . make me do it. I mean, make me let you do it to me."

She doesn't know if what she's said makes any sense to him – she hopes it isn't off-putting – but Tony nods and gently pulls her T-shirt over her head. He holds her down against the couch as he kisses her neck and breasts, his messy hair tickling her skin. It takes all Claire's willpower not to laugh at this and soon she stops noticing it and feels aroused again. She is amazed both by how pleasurable it feels and that she's able to disregard the person doing it to her. He could be anyone. It doesn't matter that it is Tony and not John and it doesn't matter that it is Tony at all. All Claire cares about is that someone is paying loving attention to her body, and the parts of her body that she sometimes enjoys having touched the most. He takes off his shirt but Claire keeps her hands at her side, not wanting to touch his body, which is more defined than she'd expected from his somewhat puffy face, partly because it will break the deal she's made with herself, but also because she worries that doing so will make this real. She resists as he tries to tug down her tracksuit bottoms, softly saying, "No", and he understands what he's supposed to do and becomes more forceful. She feels embarrassed that she isn't wearing underwear and wants to explain to him how he'd surprised her, but doesn't let herself do that either. Let him think what he wants of her. He loves her. He pulls up her legs and turns her so she is horizontal on the couch and she worries for a moment that sex with Tony might be like sex with John has become recently. Although their first few couplings had been extraordinary, the best sex she's ever had, lately they only make love in an uncomfortable stop-start fashion, as if John lacks the energy or desire and constantly needs to change position or rhythm or sometimes stop altogether and just stare at her. Other times, he's forced her into being active, into participating fully when sometimes she simply wanted the freedom to drift away from what was being done to her body. Tony doesn't go down on her for long, but it doesn't matter today: it's easy for him to enter her, and she feels glad as John always makes such a big deal out of cunnilingus, like he's the world expert.

She can't tell if Tony genuinely doesn't care about her pleasure or is obediently following her instructions, but soon he is fucking her like all he cares about is his own orgasm. And she has a sudden worry about him coming inside of her. Claire is so used to not having to fear getting pregnant because of John's vasectomy that it hasn't even occurred to ask Tony to wear a condom until now. She'd hoped he'd pull out before climaxing inside her, but realizes now she can't trust him to do this and says, "Tony," but he shushes her and puts his hand over her mouth and starts fucking her harder, gasping as he does so. He fucks her until he comes and then collapses on top of her.

October

Claire bought her white boots after spending a weekend in Prague with Richard. A troop of American drum majorettes were staying in the same no-frills hotel that she was, and they'd all left their boots outside the doors of their rooms as if expecting a shoe-shine while they slept. Claire had never been a thief – she'd shoplifted only once, just to see if her conscience would allow her to do it, and she'd spent the next week trying to return the purloined lipstick without getting caught – but was so desperate for a pair of these boots that she'd promised herself if she resisted stealing them, she'd buy herself some when she returned home. The pair she found in Dolcis weren't majorette boots, but close enough. Once she had them she found she didn't need to wear them – mere ownership was enough – and they'd sat in her wardrobe for several years unloved. But John has become obsessed with them. The first time he made her wear them for sex she hadn't realized how much he liked them. They'd been playing a game, instigated by John, where he went through her wardrobe and chose what he wanted her to wear, and she'd been so disappointed by the other items he'd chosen, almost all unwanted presents from Trevor, her boyfriend before Richard – including a scratchy black satin teddy, that didn't fit properly and which she'd only kept for nostalgic reasons – that she almost welcomed him seizing on the boots. But since then he'd made her wear them so often that she wondered if he'd even be able to get an erection if she refused.

Tonight when she gets home, he urges the boots on her the moment she opens the door. "Put these on and take everything else off."

"John . . ."

"I'm not going to fuck you. Take off your clothes and put the boots on."

"Look, please, let me give you a blowjob instead."

"Don't talk like that."

She can't help laughing. "It's a bit late to expect me to blush."

His voice becomes stern. "I know about Tony."

She looks up at him, startled.

"I won't be angry. Not if you do something for me."

"What?"

"Take your clothes off."

She does as he asks. Sometimes he'd start masturbating when she undressed, but today he sits down in a chair, sipping a glass of whisky and watching her. Is there any possibility this will turn out OK?

Claire zips up her boots and asks, "Where do you want me?"

"Out on the balcony."

He smiles at her. Claire remembers the night when he fed her a magic potion and abandoned her in the woods and realizes somewhere deep inside, no matter how wrong it is, she is still excited by this. It is as if he sent Tony here himself purely so he could punish her for her transgression. That isn't possible, is it?

It isn't that cold an October day, and there are no windows in the wall opposite, and if anyone could see her from

Pentonville Road she doubted they'd know she was naked. She takes her glass from him, finishes the whisky left there, walks across the room and opens the door to the balcony. He follows her and as soon as she is outside he tells her, "Press your body against the glass."

She does so, waiting to see if this will excite him. She wants him to get his prick out, start masturbating, anything to prove this is turning him on. He doesn't say anything for a moment, then comes out onto the balcony with her. Claire expects him to embrace her or touch her body, but instead he simply stands there, his expression impossible to read. Between John's flat and the building opposite there is a narrow brick wall that runs all the way down to the ground. It's two bricks wide and eighteen feet long. The wall has often puzzled Claire. There is nothing behind it and it blocks off a small muddy area that no one can access. The blocked-off area is filled with rubbish inhabitants have thrown from their windows. It can't have been designed to be used as a walkway as it is so high up no one would risk climbing out onto it and she can't see how it serves any architectural purpose. Now John tells her, "Get up there."

"What?"

"Walk to the wall and back."

"You're joking."

"Get up there, Claire."

"My boots. They're so hard to walk in anyway. What if I trip?"

He moves towards her. She puts her hand on his shoulder and climbs up onto the narrow support. Claire wants to know how long he has been planning to make her do this. Is it something he's been contemplating for months? Did he want her to do it so badly that he was even prepared to arrange for her to be unfaithful simply so she could not refuse (she keeps clinging to this possibility because it seems so reassuring; if he did arrange for Tony to seduce her then it wasn't her fault that she gave in). Or is he improvising? She takes two steps, feeling the wind against her skin and telling herself that she can get to the wall and back and that once she has done so, he will love her again.

She manages the first ten steps looking downward only slightly, just enough to see her boots and the bricks, but tricking herself into not recognizing the distance below, but then it all shifts into focus and she feels a sickening lunge in her stomach, as if she's already fallen, and freezes for a moment, closing her eyes and then immediately opening them again, scared this alone might make her topple over.

Claire is over halfway towards the wall. She realizes she can't walk any further and quickly crouches down, and when one of her boot-heels slips slightly and is even less safe, Claire sits directly on the brick, with her legs straddling either side, gripping the wall. It occurs to her that if he was being truly sadistic he might have gone back inside. The brick scratches the flesh of her inner things as she inches backwards. "John, if you're still there, please say something."

"I love you," he says.

His voice sounds calm, and she has no idea whether he is still angry or not, whether this is just a trick. She needs to feel his body to feel sure.

"How far is it?"

"Not far."

She continues backwards, feeling more alive than she ever has. Every time she thinks she's got back to the balcony, she realizes she has further to go. Finally, she feels his palms against her back and then his fingers in her slippery armpits as he pulls her to safety. Her legs are unsteady and she collapses on the floor.

"I'm so sorry, John," she says.

"It doesn't matter," he tells her. "I don't care."

He curls up behind her and holds her for a moment and then she feels him push his prick inside her and in that instant she knows that everything is OK. He has found her again; she has come home.

How to Get Sex When You're Dead

Kristina Lloyd

I never considered myself a voyeur but there's not much else to do when you're dead. We hang out at cloud level, shooting the breeze and watching what's going on down below. I wish I could talk to Gabe. He might sleep better if he knew I hadn't cashed in my chips and there was still some residue hanging around, or "soul" if you want to be romantic. Then again, if Gabe knew how frustrating it was to be incorporeal and horny, he'd be desperately sad for me, so it's probably best I keep schtum.

Oh, but I have heaps to tell him, like: Dying really hurts! But trust me, Gabe, the pain's gone in a flash. Your pain memory gets wiped and nothing lingers. Losing your body is the weirdest sensation. Oh Gabe, I hope you get to keep yours till you're old and grey. Look after it, won't you? Mine's gone for good and, like I say, the transition's so weird. One moment I'm being ripped apart from the inside, my mouth filling with blood, the next I'm totally spaced out, seeping into the ether and rising on a high no drugs could match.

As I slipped away, I gazed down at the Honda, upright but crushed, and at the mess I'd made of my face. Behind the shattered glass, I was as still as a mannequin, looking so peaceful despite the violence done to my body. Bizarrely, at the moment of impact I had a flashback of standing before the bathroom mirror that morning, choosing a lipstick I didn't often wear. I'd tipped the tube to check the shade: Fast Ride. Later, I wondered if I'd chosen the lipstick thanks to my sassy mood or if reading the name had subliminally affected me, causing me to keep my foot on the pedal as I rounded the bend. This might sound shallow but, either way, I'm pleased I went toes up with a plum-dark pout.

I didn't think this at the time, oh no! I wasn't pleased about anything. My main thought before bliss engulfed me, was: *Shit, shit, shit! Why so fast, Emily?*

I begged to have those last few seconds back, promising whoever was up there I'd get it right this time. But no fucker was listening. You don't get it back. Life's not a rehearsal, as they say.

I also want to tell Gabe I'm sorry about that night in Antigua when I said things I shouldn't after my seventh caipirinha. Plus, I have – *I have? I had?* Grammar's so hard when you're a ghost – I had a secret bank account with £18,000 in. The statements go to my sister's but I'd like Gabe and the kids to have the money. That was my running-away fund. I had no plans to run away, I swear, but my mother used to say every woman should have a running-away fund. Oh, and there's another thing. I'd like to apologize to my mum for dying before her. That's not the correct order of events, I know. I fucked up. Fast Ride.

But I can't do any of this. I'm voiceless and I'm bodiless. I can see them but they can't see me. I'm not omniscient but it's close. I can see everyone I ever knew, and, by Christ, but there's a lot of you, too many to keep up with. I follow those who meant the most to me, or (and this is my guilty pleasure) those who are pure entertainment. It's like Twitter but for dead people. No one follows me.

And that's the awful part because I'm following a guy I dated in my twenties, Ash Akbari. I doubt he remembers me but I never forgot him. Hey, Ash! I was the annoying brunette who liked to make a drama out of a crisis out of nothing much at all. I was a tad screwy back then, and I'm sorry. Then again, you weren't exactly Mr Sane, were you? Oh, but wow, haven't you grown? If I had the ability to be moist, I'd be soaked and swollen, my body opening in readiness for your cock. However, as things stand, I have desire and it swirls most intensely somewhere below my seat of consciousness. Damned if I can relieve the itch though. I have no hands, see?

Oh, let me tell you about Ash. (I'm sorry, Gabe! I love you madly but I don't think this counts as cheating, and I'm sure you'd understand.) Ash was stunning. He was Anglo-Iranian, and had inky, collar-length curls he would tuck behind his ears. His cheekbones hung on a perfect slant, and his intense, Persian eyes were teal-green ringed with black. He looked as if he could read minds with those eyes. Maybe he could. I used to imagine he was someone who could get under my skin. But I was young. I didn't want him under my skin. Or rather I did, but didn't want to admit that. I was trying to be cool and invulnerable. Besides, if I'd let him under my skin, he most likely would have stayed a while and tried to destroy me. Ash liked to cause suffering, which was part of the attraction. I was needy and attention-seeking. I liked to suffer. I liked to blame. I liked to fight.

He ran me a bath. We'd been arguing and fucking all afternoon at his place and, in the evening, I said I fancied a soak. The water was too hot. I dipped my toe in and yelped. I reached for the cold tap but he stopped me by grabbing hold of my hair. His fist was by the nape of my neck and he tilted my head back. His voice was by my ear. "I don't care if it's too fucking hot," he said. His words were so close I might have been making them up myself, hearing voices inside my head. "Get in."

I was knocked by a rush of arousal so acute my legs nearly buckled. The threatening tone in his voice, not to mention the nastiness of his order, got me right where it shouldn't. My lust confused the hell out of me. I didn't like that I liked it, and I don't think Ash liked that he liked it either.

"You serious?" I said.

He released me. "Nah, just messing." He ran the cold tap then waggled his fingers in the water. "It's fine now."

I was disappointed. I'd wanted him to respond to my reticence by continuing with his bossiness. I'd wanted him to force me to take pain for his pleasure. Maybe not a hot bath but, you know, a sexy thing. We had another row later that night, something and nothing. I do know it was my fault though. I pushed it, baiting him to get angry because I wanted to be subjected to his aggression again. I was an emotional masochist, re-routing an unexplored taste for pain into a more acceptable outlet, that of being a pain-in-the-butt girlfriend. But as I say, Ash wasn't comfortable with his dark side either. We were young, too scared of revealing ourselves in case we got rejected.

But hey, not any more! I'm dead, I'm twisted and I'm horny! What have I got to lose?

Ash has aged well. His hair's in a similar style, a wavy Byronic bob now threaded with silver, and his face, as well as acquiring a few lines, has hollowed out a smidge. It suits him. He looks refined and cruel, like a fairy-tale prince gone wrong.

From what I can glean, Ash is single but has a sexual relationship with a freckled redhead called Elena who enjoys being hit and tormented. I enjoy watching Elena being hit and tormented. She squeals and cries, her face scorched with tears, her pale body trembling as she waits for more pain. It turns me on enormously and I wish I were her, wish I'd been braver when I was alive and had voiced my wants.

A couple of days ago, I was complaining about this to my best dead friend, Carol. "Ah well, too late now," I said. If I had any shoulders, I would have shrugged them.

"You kidding me?" said Carol.

Turns out, she's quite the expert in how to haunt your exes and how to get sex when you're dead. Carol can't haunt in the traditional way: you know, appearing in the middle of night, going "wooo" and scaring the bejeezus out of people. That's advanced level, and I'm told breaking through to the other side hurts like hell. Plus, you don't get laid at advanced level. (Hey, enough already. We've heard all the jokes about laying ghosts.) Carol's technique is to haunt her exes by getting inside their dreams. She does it mainly for revenge. That's not my style but the idea of hopping into Ash's dreams for kinky kicks was right up my alley.

Carol warned me it would hurt. Apparently, it's not as harrowing as the pain encountered in advanced-level haunting but it's still a bitch. And no wonder. When you break through and enter someone's dreams, you become embodied again. Seriously, it's true. I couldn't believe it either. You get your insides and your outsides back; you get your arms, legs and skin back; you get to feel pain and pleasure, just as you did in life.

Trouble is, when you're ethereal you're massive. No, not massive. You're infinite, that's the word. I am infinite. I have Saturn's rings on my fingers and hell's bells on my toes. I am the wind in your hair and the grass beneath your feet. And breaking through is like funnelling that lot down into a teeny-tiny, body-shaped vessel. "Squeeze" would be an understatement. But the prospect was beyond tempting.

"So, say me and the dreamer are having incredible sex," I began, "I get to feel it? I get the sensation of him on me and in me?"

"Absolutely," said Carol. "It feels as real as reality."

I wasn't sure how real that was but thought it wise not to go there. Besides, the big question was: "Can I come?"

"No probs, so long as the dreamer dreams of you coming."

And there's the rub, as it were. Once you're inside someone's dreams, you're at their mercy, or more accurately, at the mercy of their subconscious. Sure, said Carol, you can attempt to take the wheel and steer but the subconscious is a slippery old devil. You never know what it's going to spring on you.

The thought of tangling with Ash's subconscious made me nervous. My money was on his brain being a mighty exciting jumble of perversion and passion. Oh, but the poor guy. He didn't even know I was married, let alone dead. He'd wake up in the morning and think, *Wow, I just had an amazing sex-dream about an ex from years ago. Wonder where she is now.*

At least I hoped he'd think that rather than, *Holy guacamole, may I never have a nightmare about that crazy bitch again.*

Carol was right about the pain. Breaking through was like crashing the car a second time but worse. Screaming sheets of metal tore through my veins, slicing me open from the inside, even though I didn't yet have any veins or viscera. If I hadn't been so frustratingly, incorporeally horny, I'd have quit and resigned myself to being a randy vapour in a world without wanking.

But thoughts of Ash, beautiful, experienced and debauched, and of a dreamscape where I could feel myself once more, bolstered my stamina. I craved embodiment. With hindsight, I can see I wasted my matter when I had it. Skin and nerves are these astonishing pathways to joy, and I didn't exploit that enough. Oh, and the things I miss now. I long to be touched, I long to have another's flesh pressed sweatily against mine.

Until you discover breaking through, being dead's like being single but without the hope. Other stuff I miss too. A piece of grit in a shoe, a bra fastening that rubs, a tickle in your ear, all these irritations to remind you you're still alive. I'd give anything to know them again. But as the song goes: you don't know what you've got till it's gone. Pah pah pah, they put up a parking lot.

And then, as the song doesn't go: but you can damn well try to grab it back when you're a goner.

I kept on pushing and, within minutes, I was past the agony and flying through a derelict asylum with endless corridors, graffiti-scrawled walls and rusting beds. In a room where weeds poked through broken windows and ivy crawled across the ceiling, Ash was adjusting what appeared to be a dentist's chair, a patch of dappled sunlight forming a dry, shimmering puddle at his feet. He was on one knee and frowning, his dark bob falling across those high, angular cheekbones while his slender fingers twiddled with a knob on the base of the chair.

My heart rate shot up and, boy, what a feeling that was! Having grown accustomed to the nothingness of being uncarnate, I found the sensation so overwhelming I briefly wondered if I'd turned into an actual pulse. The beat roared and hammered in my chest, in my ears and my groin. I could feel my limbs and I was as heavy as ten mountains. Parts of my body rested against other parts, and I gained a shocking awareness of the intricacies of a mass I'd been oblivious to in flesh-life. The insides of my cheeks were damp against my molars; my neck and shoulders ached from the weight of my head; my nostrils were chilly from the air I inhaled. My knees seemed unfairly burdened and, with every blink, a thick shutter rolled over the curve of each eyeball. I was me again, and I had 206 bones, nearly eight pints of blood, six and a half square feet of skin and around 100,000 hairs on my head.

Ash glanced up at me. "Are you wet?" he asked matter-of-factly.

Wet? With his question, I was an ocean. Moisture slid from my folds and, between my thighs (between my strong, hefty, weighty thighs!), a liquid heartbeat pumped, slicking my skin with heat.

Ash wasn't surprised to see me but I guess nothing surprises in dreams.

"Are you?" he repeated. "Because if not, I'll make you wet." He stood.

"I'm dripping," I replied. I was tense and embarrassed. I'd expected my voice to emerge as a meek little whisper but instead it bellowed inside my ears, its vibrations strumming my throat and making my head hum.

Ash crossed to me, smirking. He looked me up and down. Under his scrutiny, I felt both deliriously alive and deliciously insignificant. I was my body. I was made of meat. As far as I was concerned, Ash could use that body however he saw fit.

When he reached me, he clasped both my wrists and pinned them lightly behind my back. "Elena," he said.

That wasn't me, I'm Emily, or I was. But the name made sense as wrongness often does in dreams. He pressed my wrists together then released them. I kept them behind my back as surely as if he'd bound me that way. I barely even moved when he leaned close to kiss me, although my knees weakened and either I swayed or the room did. My senses sang to know the scent of his skin, the brush of his hair and the rasp of stubble on my chin. Our noses knocked, but he didn't kiss me. Instead, he took my bottom lip between his teeth and pulled, stretching me out and holding me in a steady bite. It seemed like a test. I was motionless, though my heart was going nineteen to the dozen and my clit grew quickly fat. Ash squeezed, his teeth nipping into the wet membrane of my mouth. Saliva pooled under my tongue as our breath mingled in warm, sweet humidity.

When he cupped his hand to my groin, his touch crude and hard, I groaned awkwardly, flooded with lust. My lip slipped from Ash's grip. I saw the whole of his face again, the glossy, black hair, pale-toffee skin and eyes coloured like the streaks of green in petrol.

"Dirty little whore," he said. "Aren't you?" There was something new to him, a suppressed fervour making his eyes sharp and his mouth loose. Like a child at play, he was absorbed in what we were doing, quite without self-consciousness.

"Whore." He raised his hand. It soared in my peripheral vision then came swooping down as fast and furious as a giant bird of prey. My left cheek exploded under a stinging crack and the room lurched. A blur of red and blue graffiti whizzed past, the rotten floorboards spinning to the ceiling, light blaring as if the sun had burst in through the weedy window. The impact left me startled, my senses turning fuzzy. I began sinking into a deep, comfortable space of my own, the world about me receding into meaningless. When my vision righted itself, I gazed at Ash with dumb, muted contentment. He seemed far off, hazy, so extraordinarily beautiful. He slapped me again.

My cheek burned. I felt quelled.

We were the only people in existence.

Stepping closer, Ash bunched my hair at the nape of my neck, tipping my head backwards. I remembered this from the bath incident. My follicles stabbed like needles, my scalp tightening. My cunt throbbed in answer.

"Welcome to the Asylum of Pain," said Ash. It sounds funny now but at the time, it didn't. "I'm your doctor for the evening," he continued. "My remit is to find your limit and break it. Understood?"

My voice was thin and scratchy. I tried to speak but no words came.

"Understood?" barked Ash.

I wanted to nod but his grip was too firm. I felt so strange, my world enriched with a hyper-real lucidity, and yet I was remote from it, cocooned in a balmy glow. Time appeared to be unfolding in a linear fashion, much as Carol had promised. But Ash – the real Ash, not Ash the man Ash was dreaming of – would, said Carol, understand it differently, his recall on waking distorting the sequence of events, warping its logic and erasing huge chunks. I wondered how puzzled he'd be by his dreams of me and concluded not much. After all, the subconscious often reunites us with lost loves in our sleep.

"I'm going to take you higher and higher," said Ash, "until you're made of pain and made for me." He released my hair and stepped back. "Get undressed. Show me your skin, my canvas."

My clothes melted away as I used to wish they would in life when I was eager to get it on. This time though, I'd have preferred a slow, shared undressing, leaving me with some wisps of clothing for protection. But in the dream, realism faltered and I was instantly vulnerable and exposed, standing naked before Ash, not knowing where to put my hands and wondering if I'd shaved my legs. After all, when I'd set out on this date, I didn't have any legs so it never occurred to me to shave them.

Ash prowled in a wide circle around me, practically licking me with his eyes. I shivered and it was like an avalanche of goosebumps. "Firstly," he said, "I want to make something clear to you." He stood before me. In his hand was a dress-maker's pin, its silver length glinting in the half-light. I held my breath as he pressed the pin to my belly. Slowly, he scratched a line upwards. Sensation scored my flesh. He drew another line angling down.

"This is what you are," he said. He was writing on me, using my pain as his ink. Pink, puffy weals surfaced on my skin, but from what I could tell, he wasn't drawing blood. I gritted my teeth as he continued, each pin-line a narrowly focused scrape, leaving heat expanding in its wake.

I was unable to decipher the letters from his touch. I waited until he'd finished before looking down: MINE.

"That's what you are," said Ash.

Fear clutched. Only a dream, I told myself. But the reassurance made no sense. Here, I was more alive than I ought to be. My senses were responsive. I sought pain, but if Ash took the administration of that too far, there were no consequences. I was already dead. I ended when the dream did, a figment of his imagination. And who could say what the moral order of Ash's sleeping world was? If the subconscious of a sadist was given free rein, what would it inflict upon its victims?

That Ash had used only a pin to mark me was, I hoped, a good sign. My hopes vanished when he raised the pin to my face, touching its tip to my cheekbone. Oh dear God, he was going to mark my face. I'd destroyed half my head in the accident. In the dream, I'd returned to being whole and pretty. I desperately wanted to stay that way. Wouldn't anyone?

I stood stock still, immobilized by panic. If I moved, would he punish me? Would his hand slip and damage me? Ash smiled, his eyes locked on mine, feasting on my reactions. I pressed my lids shut, trying to regain a sense of calm against the surge of my adrenaline. My pulses thundered and pressure swelled in my head, hurting my skull.

"Look at me," said Ash.

I opened my eyes.

"Do you trust me?"

I considered it. Did I? Nah. Ash laughed then flung the pin aside. On hitting the ground, the pin burst into silver flames before dimming to mercurial blobs. The broken puddle shifted, fragments of quicksilver merging and separating as if the floorboards were undulating beneath it. When I looked at my belly, the word "MINE" was soldered in silver. I stared at the lettering in shame and excitement. But I'm married, I thought. I can't be yours.

Then Ash's hands moved towards my breasts and they were silver too, a pair of elaborate robot-pincers opening to chomp on my nipples. They latched on to me, squeezing my tips to sore, angry points. I gasped for breath. When Ash removed his hands, his fingers returned to flesh and bone. A clamp hung from each of my nipples, two freaky, sci-fi fish biting into my softness. I bleated as the pain rose then I quietened as it plateaued out. Within a minute or so, I'd accommodated the clamps. They might not have been there at all.

Ash flicked the left clamp, reigniting my pain. It was back, a futuristic fish with jaws of steel. Ouch, ouch, ouch! Then the right clamp. Ow! Left again. And again and ow!

Oh, what a clever bastard he was, intensifying my suffering with minimal effort. Ash smiled as he played, watching me with brazen delight. Laughing, he tugged and twisted one of the clamps, stretching my breast out to a scrawny point. I hissed and cursed but I wanted him to continue because my cunt was throbbing like there was no tomorrow which, let's face it, there wasn't. And he did continue, toying with me for several, pitiless minutes until, leaving the clamps dangling, he announced, "Level two."

That was one? Oh boy, I hoped it didn't go up to eleven. "Ash," I said. "Ash, I'm new to this, don't forget. Go easy on me."

"Oh, Elena," he mocked. "Don't play the virgin with me."

"I'm Emily," I said, but my words fell on deaf ears.

"Get on all fours," said Ash. "Like a dog."

I obeyed, the pain in my nipples soaring as the clamps dragged with a new weight, my cunt opening to emptiness. The soldered MINE burned like ice on my belly. Ash squatted by my head. In one hand, he held a black candle, a silver-blue flame darting around its wick. Odd, I thought, that the desires of Ash's snoozing psyche are in sync with my own. But then, hadn't I watched with envy as he'd dripped wax onto Elena? Hadn't I ached to be her when I'd seen hot liquid hardening over her freckles? That's why I was here, visiting Ash instead of my husband, bringing my unlived fantasies to life and eager to risk mistakes I'd once avoided.

But, wow, a silver flame? What if the materials of Ash's dream were too extreme for my body? At what temperature did metals become liquid around here? Were the laws constant? No, of course they weren't. Ash was asleep. This was a lawless world. And too late for me to worry whether I should have been more upfront about my motives so Carol could have warned me of potential dangers. "Just dropping in on an ex and hoping for a jump," I'd said, preferring to keep my private life private.

"I'm going to hurt you," said Ash. He wafted the candle under my chin, warming my skin. I remembered a game my sisters and I would play in childhood with flowers picked from the meadow. "Do you like butter?" we'd ask, holding a golden buttercup under another's chin and looking for a yellow reflection.

"Do you like flame?" asked Ash.

Again, strange that the two of us were so in tune. I could only conclude I was able to influence his dreams more than I'd anticipated, although how my thoughts got into his head was beyond me. Or was it vice versa? Were his thoughts getting into my head, even though my head was inside his. Gah, it was far too complicated. I'd ask Carol when I was home.

"I reckon she does," said Ash, standing.

"'Course she does," said another male voice. My heart went boom. Still on my hands and knees, I looked up. Gabe! How the hell did he get here? And why was he naked with his cock stiff and springy?

I felt guilty and ashamed but more that that, lust-struck. My husband had one hell of a physique. I'd grown used to it over the years, what with taking him and bodies in general for granted. But there he was, glorious and tall, his athletic thighs cloaked in soft hair, his belly taut from regular Wii Fit exercises. Shining by his hip was that pale scar from the time he had his appendix out, age eleven. I gazed up at him through the grateful eyes of a dead person, craving his touch, his love, and wanting to relive all those tender, late-night moments when the house was quiet and we were most ourselves.

"Stick your dick in her mouth," said Ash from behind me. "It'll keep her quiet."

A splash of molten wax landed on my back. The burn was quick and vicious. I squealed, those evil clamps swinging on my tits. As soon as I yelped, Gabe filled my mouth with his cock. The shape and weight of him was perfect. I moulded my mouth to him and he tasted like home.

"There you go, hon," he said kindly. He slid in deep, nudging at my throat. After several strokes, I was struggling for breath. Wax pattered onto my buttocks. I couldn't scream. I gave a muffled howl around Gabe's cock, then pulled away, gasping for air and mercy. Wax kept on falling. Ash laughed when I cried. The pain was unlike any I'd known, hits of liquid fire plunging steeply into benign warmth. With the shock of every droplet, I had a split second of thinking I couldn't take any more and must beg him to stop. Then the intensity subsided, and I yearned for its return.

Gabe thrust into me, clutching a handful of hair and moving my head on his cock. "Take it, go on, honey."

For a small moment, I slipped out of my perspective. I saw Gabe lunging into my mouth with easy arrogance, his buttocks hollowing as he pumped. I saw myself on all fours, my back and ass stippled with black wax, my face flushed and hectic. And there was Ash at my rear, naked, lithe and erect, candle in his left hand, cock in his right. His fist jerked on his swollen shaft, the muscles in his shoulder dancing with the play of candlelight on his smooth, caramel skin.

"Take it," he said, echoing my husband. He angled his cock at my entrance, waggling my lips apart with his end. "Go on." Stout and hard, he butted at my opening then sank into my wetness, tilting the candle as his length invaded. Black droplets fell like the devil's tears. I wailed around Gabe's cock, the pain on my flesh hooking up with the pleasure in my cunt. *Burn! Burn!* went the wax and *Fuck her! Fuck her!* went the guys.

Agony and ecstasy merged, carrying me on a tide of bliss. With a few nudges on my clit, my orgasm hurried close, nearness clustering at my centre. Gabe removed the clamps. Hot, brutal pain surged to my nipples as the blood returned. My tips throbbed with an escalating soreness. My face tightened, temples pulling at my eyebrows. My inner thighs quivered then I was coming hard, all fireworks and stars and ohsweetJesus, am I dying again?

Transported by rapture but bound by my body, I wailed wetly around the meat in my mouth. I wasn't dying, no, because my cunt was shimmering inside me, mini bombs of wax were dropping on my skin, my nipples were aflame and I could hardly breathe for cock. I remembered the joy of warm summer rain and I remembered too that Ash didn't know Gabe so why was he here? How the hell could Ash have dreamt him?

"Look at her loving it," said Ash.

"Slut," hissed Gabe, which was most unlike him.

"Keep fucking her mouth, bro."

I tried to untangle the situation through the fog of my euphoria. It had to be me. I'd brought Gabe into Ash's dream, hadn't I? So I had more control and power than I knew. Gabe thrust into my groans as my climax ebbed, nearing his own peak and making quite a racket. In life, I'd always wanted him to be noisier. So in death, my wishes and fantasies could be fulfilled, was that it? Well, if my memories and desires could steer Ash's dreams, there was more fun to be had if I could handle the pain of re-embodiment. Maybe the afterlife wouldn't be so bad, after all.

"Oh, man, yes!" Gabe roared, as he came into my mouth, his tangy jets rushing over my tongue. Ash picked up his pace, the candle abandoned as he gripped my hips, hammering relentlessly. I was outside myself once more, and I saw his mouth gape, watched him throw back his head and come on a series of heavy, incredulous grunts, his cries echoing in the empty, broken room.

Their breath still ragged, their chests heaving, the two men grinned and high-fived each other above my back. I thought to myself: *Ash meet Gabe, Gabe meet Ash.*

My perspective shifted again. Gabe's face was inches from my own.

Gabe's face is inches . . .

Impossibly, his head is on a pillow. He gives me a smudgy look. We smell of bedclothes and skin. I'm beginning to forget.

"Mm," he murmurs. He drapes a lazy arm across my waist. The blur of waking holds me between two worlds.

I'm about to speak then I stop, thinking, *Some things are best kept to yourself.* And a perfect example would be, *Wow, I just had an amazing sex-dream about an ex from years ago. Wonder where he is now?*

I nuzzle closer to Gabe and print a kiss on his warm, familiar lips. He gives a soft grunt of acknowledgement and I think, *Well, I guess we could spice it up a little but thank heavens I found the right man in the end.*

The Slave's Revolt

Ilaria Palomba

(translated by Maxim Jakubowski)

That Saturday was one of the best in my life. The phone call. The train. The sudden change of plans. The encounter. The smell of aftershave on his skin. That steady and penetrating gaze. Muse on the stereo. Eyes closed. My corset. His hands. Goosebumps across my skin. Endless sharp shivers flowing through me. Not a single word. No greeting.

We park in a small alley. We get out. We walk along the road, our steps in parallel as if following a target. The key in the lock. His jeans stained with lust. My heart beating like clockwork, on the verge of exploding. His lips. The door closes. A thud. Between the look in his eyes and my body, art. The art of lying, acting, concealing.

There is a white rope on the floor. Eight metres or more in length. A pair of black leather gloves. A glance down at the floor, my eyes looking down at the floor.

"Undress," he says.

He stares at me. The promise of kink. The instructions. The games. The challenge. My naked body. Warmth.

"Touch yourself!" An order.

My fingers linger below my navel. Reach my sex. I skim across my lower lips. Then my clit.

"Put the gloves on."

I slip them on. My black leather fingers across my skin. His eyes are like sharks' appraising meat, cutting through me.

This particular moment enchants me. This act of total submission. He pulls his zip down and his dick approaches my lips.

"Get down!"

I obey. I bow to his will. The extreme manifestation of his subconscious. The vertiginous downhill path of his desires.

He wets his glans with spit. He presses hard against me. His cock forces my lips wide open. I press them closed again.

"Ah!" he says. "Won't you try it?"

I could take him between my teeth and bite him until he bleeds profusely. But I don't do so. Total obedience acts as a rein to my impulses.

I delicately move my lips around his sex. I can feel his glans pulse, his foreskin stretch. I can feel my mouth fill and my throat rebel. I shudder. My stomach clenches. I feel like puking.

I want to be more than just an empty body, a receptacle with no soul. For me to become totally myself, from head to toe, with no hint of reservation.

He grasps my hair and pushes his midriff towards me. I choke. Am almost sick. I try to free myself from his grip. He then pinches my cheeks with his hands and immobilizes me. I look up at him. His unforgiving eyes of ice. A tear trickles down my cheek and pearls across his hand. He pushes my face away. He licks the back of his hand and tastes me. I am kneeling on the floor, my breath heavy. He takes hold of me. His forefinger penetrates my sex. Checking out how wet I am. In his grip. Makes me rise to my feet. Juices flowing from my sex and tears from my eyes. My voice sounds like a child's lament. There are two, three, four fingers delving inside my cunt. I scream. He glares at me.

"Shut up," he says.

His whole hand slides inside me. I can feel the skin of my outer labia scream in pain. I close my eyes. He places his hand against my lips. Continues to masturbate me. I am reaching a peak of pain and about to reach and breach a sharp wall of pleasure when it will all flow out of me. He rubs his fingers against my clit and then deeper inside. Every single finger. I am his goddess and his whore. I am everything and nothing. Attaining the emptiness I have always been seeking. Just a body, no ties, no thoughts. A soul sundered from my body. As if the soul could detach itself from the body through the pain and float up into the transparency of the sky. Beyond things. Like a mote of dust impervious to notions of good and evil.

He is licking my neck. I cling on to him. I kiss his jugular and savour the soft skin of his ear lobe.

"Get up," he orders me.

He pushes me against the glass of the window. Moving his right hand across my back. I am oblivious to the heat. The pressure. I try to squirm away, leaving the mark of my fingers against the glass. I turn my head, begging him.

"Not here . . . Everyone can see me."

He grabs me by the hair and turns my face back towards the window. My forehead is pressing against the glass.

"I want them to see it all," he says. "It excites me."

It's only then that he takes the rope and positions it around my stomach. It's coarse and cold. He tightens it. Then passes it round my neck. I shudder. He ties my wrists behind my back and presses me against the glass of the window. He penetrates me. I can feel his pelvis thrusting towards me. I can feel his cock grow inside me. I can feel my juices spreading across his member. He is spanking me. Slowly at first. Then increasingly faster and harder. My mouth is wide open. I scream.

In the apartment across the street I notice a man. The man is opening his curtains. Looks across at us. I clench my legs tight.

"Good girl. Squeeze hard."

The man facing us brings a hand down to his trousers. I see lust invade his features. I close my eyes.

"Open your eyes," my master says.

I can feel my joints held in place by the rope. My mind is floating in space again. In a void. I no longer have a soul, a body, desires or will. I am insignificant magma. An emptiness filled. My body contracting into a spasm. Held tight by the rope, I am a puppet, drunk on pleasure.

This unspoken consent that shatters you inside. This voice, the very sound of perversion. And then, utter silence. Once at least he told me I was fantastic, that I made him crazy. You're beautiful, he said. But this time, all he says is:

"I'm coming."

He holds my head, lays his hands on my face, keeps the pressure on and comes in my mouth. I can taste the bitter flavour of his orgasm in my throat. I swallow every last drop. As if it isn't really his body, but just an alien object through which he can transmute all the anxiety of everyday life.

And then his cruel glance of contempt and hatred to make me understand yet again what my true station in life is: on my knees, my head bowed, merely there to service his cock.

He unties me. As we are getting dressed, he says he has to go somewhere. He throws me out of the house. I would have to run to the railway station. It's five in the morning and there is no soul around. I look back towards his window. I feel like smashing the glass. But I don't. I stand quietly, observing. The man in the apartment across the street is now inside his house with him. Handing him money. A silent scream grows from deep inside my body. Rage is boiling across my brain. I clench my fists, grip the lace of my dress and mechanically stamp my feet against the pavement's asphalt. I walk back to the entrance of his house, hide out of sight, and wait for the neighbour to come down the stairs and leave and I then press the button on the entryphone.

"I need to use the bathroom," I say.

He urges me to hurry. The door opens. I go in. He doesn't see me. He's busy at his computer. I step into the bathroom and lock it. Once again I slip on the black gloves. I open a drawer beneath the sink. The rope is there. Teasing me. He knocks on the door.

"What are you doing? Can you open up?"

"I've just finished," I say in a childlike voice.

He knocks again. I pick up a large iron pot that was sitting in front of the window. It's heavy. Should do the business.

"Right away," I answer.

The key turns three times inside the lock. His prick face stares me in the eyes. I hit him on the side of the head with the pot. He cries out. I hit him again. He sways unsteadily. He holds on to my wrists. I give him another blow on his hands. His grip weakens. I hit him twice again and he falls to the ground. Almost unconscious. Now it gets better: I twist the white rope four times across his neck. I pull hard. His eyes open wide. He attempts to speak. I don't release my hold, refusing any possible compromise. I twist again. He blinks. I watch as his gaze grows distant. His light is going out. My lips begin to smile. My tongue slides between the wall of my teeth. I put the rope away where it was being kept. I repair my make-up and am on my way.

Brushed

Kay Jaybee

"Brushes?"

Leah stared down at the expensive gift wrap she'd just carefully undone.

This was the first birthday she'd celebrated with Callum, and Leah had expected something special. In fact, he'd promised her something special – something personal. The way in which he'd said it had made Leah assume she was going to receive some lingerie or maybe some sort of sex toy; a gift they could definitely enjoy together.

In her lap, however, placed neatly side by side in a red silk-lined wooden box lay, not the latest high-tech vibrator or a set of lacy underwear, but three different-sized brushes. Backed with polished oak wood, one looked like a posh scrubbing brush, one was a pincushion-style hairbrush, and the last was rather like a toothbrush, but was just a little too thin for that function. With its long slim wooden handle, the only use Leah could think of for it was to clean the spout of a teapot.

"Yes. I really have bought you some brushes for your twenty-eighth birthday." Gazing over the hotel's breakfast table into his girlfriend's eyes, Callum saw a frisson of confused desire flicker across her face as he added, "They are however, *very* special brushes."

Callum's dark eyes had taken on an even deeper chestnut than they had done last night, when he'd made love to Leah with a thorough mind-blowing fuck that had screamed professionalism, and left her gasping with the type of blissful body shock that she'd never experienced before. "I promise that these brushes will turn out to be the best birthday present you have ever received – ever."

Leah hadn't expected a diamond ring or anything ridiculously expensive as a gift, but brushes?

As Callum's eyes dipped from Leah's face to the brushes, and back again, her pussy clenched with yearning, but she wasn't sure why.

Reaching across the table, Callum took the scrubbing brush from her box and stroked its stiff bristles with the pads of his fingers.

Leah watched, as if hypnotized, as each individual bristle bounced back into place, and her pulse quickened. She couldn't believe this. She was getting turned on by the sight of her lover playing with a brush.

As Callum swapped the handle-free brush for the hairbrush, he said, "You have beautiful hair, you deserve a beautiful brush to stroke it with."

Automatically, Leah reached out a hand to pat her shoulder-length ginger curls. She knew Callum liked her hair. He'd confessed early on in their relationship that it was her orange locks which had attracted him to her in the first place.

Leah had always loved people playing with her hair, but until she'd met Callum six months ago, she'd never found anyone who was willing to caress it for her without it becoming a chore. When they snuggled up together on her sofa of an evening, Callum would spend hours winding her hair through his fingers.

"Tell me," Callum whispered across their empty breakfast plates, "how would you like me to brush your hair for your birthday. All of your hair. For as long as you want?"

Leah didn't know what to say. She'd never been offered such a bizarre way to spend any day before, let alone her birthday. Now and again, she worried that he only wanted to be with her because he loved her hair, but something about the way Callum spoke to her now, not to mention the increasingly dangerous sheen to his eyes, sent shots of salacious curiosity through her and cancelled out that fear.

"Do you want any more breakfast?" Callum's voice had become husky. He was looking at her new brushes with the kind of expression that other men reserved for pictures of naked women, and Leah knew she had to experience whatever it was he was planning – and the sooner the better.

The second they crossed the threshold into their bedroom, Callum took Leah by the hand, and sat her on the edge of the bed. Then, after reverently taking the wooden container from her hands, he placed it on a nearby dressing table. Looking his girlfriend straight in the eye, Callum stroked her hair as he spoke, "Leah, I want this to be the best birthday you've ever had. Ever. Will you trust me? Will you let me use your brushes on you?"

The intensity of Callum's words made Leah's spine tingle. "Yes please." Her words sounded feeble, but she really didn't know what else to say. She knew she trusted him, and wanted to discover what he'd planned with almost as much urgency as he obviously wanted to show her.

As Callum pulled off her shoes and socks, Leah suddenly found she couldn't catch her breath properly. All that had happened was that her feet had been freed, and yet every part of Leah already felt intensely sensitive, as if her flesh was primed and poised to react to each forthcoming touch.

Cursing her imagination, which had morphed visions of a nude Callum brushing out her hair into a wide variety of more interesting uses for her new possessions, Leah sighed with pleasure as he pulled off his shirt. She'd never been into men with six-packs before, but Callum had somehow managed to become mouth-wateringly toned without becoming a gym slave, and Leah had recently become a convert to the gorgeous view that was the toned male chest.

"Stay there babe." Snatching up the "Do not Disturb" sign from the bedside table, Callum dived to the bedroom door, placed the notice on the external handle, before double locking the door just in case the maid should choose an inappropriate moment to come and redo the linen.

Teasing his hands through her hair, Callum peered down at Leah's up-tilted face, "Now I can do what I like to that delicious body of yours without anyone else coming in and getting an eyeful!"

Leah blushed as he ran approving glances over her frequently fucked body. She had expected Callum to return to the bed and jump on top of her, ripping her jumper and jeans from her flesh, smothering her with his body. Instead, he took the scrubbing brush from the wooden box and, with an expression of total concentration, began to tickle it over her toes.

Leah jumped; she couldn't help it. The contact was like nothing she'd ever known. The pressure Callum was applying was firm but light, and it neither prickled nor hurt. Leah tried to calm her breathing and relax into the feelings that were grouping in the base of her feet, and travelling northwards on a beeline for her crotch. She found her hands were gripping the edge of the bed, and her knickers were growing moist. Leah couldn't believe Callum was starting his attention below the neckline, and not with her hair as he usually did.

"Just relax, baby." Callum moved the brush up to her ankles, circling one and then the other, causing the mini sparks of electricity he was creating to knock together as they waltzed towards her pussy.

"Lay back for me, and lift those hips a little." Callum was talking to her as if she was a client going to see a masseuse and, as Leah complied, she felt his fingers deftly undo her belt and zip fly, before tugging down her jeans.

Although Callum had removed her outer clothing very quickly, it still felt like a lifetime before the brush came to her lower legs. Leah couldn't believe how cruelly abandoned she'd felt for the few seconds she hadn't been stroked. Her muscles spasmed with relief as contact was resumed, and Leah's brain nudged her with a reminder that this was just the first of three brushes. *What on earth was he going to do with the other two?*

Edging the scrubbing brush over the front of her legs, Callum began to exfoliate her knees. Over and over, around and around, he repeated the same strokes again and again, until Leah began squirming against the bed. Her increasing impatience at Callum's snail's pace was equalled by the erotic fluttering that every single swipe ricocheted through her, leaving Leah wishing for this strange new experience to never end, as much as she wanted it to speed up.

Currently, the only unpleasant factor in the room was Leah's bottle-green satin underwear. Her knickers were sodden with wasted juices, and she longed for them to be taken off, to feel the brush directly on her nub, to . . . *No!* Leah stopped her thoughts in their tracks. If she kept thinking about that, she'd come before he'd even reached her thighs.

It was difficult to take her mind off it though, especially as her breasts were heavy, swollen and hot beneath her bra, T-shirt and sweater.

"Did you know—" Callum held Leah's left ankle firmly as he worked the brush up her leg, stopping its quivering from diverting the course of his careful grooming of her bare skin "—that human beings have more hairs on their bodies than gorillas do?"

Brought out of her kinky musings by this unexpected piece of trivia, Leah licked some moisture back into her lips. 'Really? But gorillas are really hairy.'

"Visibly yes, but just you think about how many tiny hairs cover the human body."

"I suppose so." Leah couldn't say any more. Callum was now stroking the bristles of the brush over the cap of her knee, and an extra potent zip of stimulation forced out an involuntary struggle against his grasp.

Lifting his lover's leg a fraction, Callum smiled, as he glided the bristles across the underside of the knee, and Leah shivered afresh at the unexpected sensitivity of the move.

"Nice?"

Leah gulped. She couldn't begin to describe the feelings cruising through her system at each touch of the brush, and, more peculiarly, the sense of loss she felt each time the brush was temporarily removed from her flesh altogether. "Uh huh."

Callum laughed. "I'm going to brush all the hair on your body, visible or invisible."

Leah moaned softly. Her arms felt fidgety, but at the same time she didn't want to take them from her sides and distract Callum from his work. "I would never have thought that a scrubbing brush could make me so turned on"'

"It's not exactly a scrubbing brush, baby, it's a masseur's brush or body brush. They use them for stimulating the blood flow. Not only does it feel amazing, but it's doing you good as well."

"I've . . . never . . . heard . . . of . . . those . . . before." Every word that escaped from Leah's lips was an effort now, as Callum swapped legs, giving her right knee the same nerve-tingling treatment as the left had received.

"Well, maybe I'll sort you out a masseur's body-brushing session for your Christmas present."

Hugging the knowledge that Callum was thinking four months ahead to Christmas with her still as a fixture in his life, Leah couldn't help but squeak as the brush progressed another inch north. Playing it with alternate light and firm pressures over her thighs, Callum broke up the polishing action by starting to flick the bristles briefly on and off her skin.

Her breath snagged in her throat as this new stinging sensation merged with the contrasting soothing tingling engendered by the rubbing of the brush. Leah, unable to keep her hands still any longer, brought them to her chest, and pinched her breasts through the jumper. "Please, Callum, let me take my top off, I'm sweltering here."

"Not only sweltering, but as horny as fuck by the look of you." He put down the brush, and Leah groaned. She hadn't expected him to stop his careful buffing, but simply let her sit up and remove her upper garments while he carried on working.

"Take off your tops, but leave on your bra; I'm not ready for you to be naked yet."

Leah groaned for a second time, "But I'm so hot."

"You most certainly are!"

Leah smiled as, with her chest taut, and her nipples at full attention beneath their satin prison, Callum added, "Besides, if you were totally naked there is no way I'd be able to contain myself. I would have to leap on you."

Thinking that would be no bad thing, but also wanting the bizarrely frustrating but arousing brushing to begin again, Leah collapsed back onto the bed, but not before noting how much the cock beneath Callum's jeans was tenting. She marvelled at his self-control as, avoiding contact with her knicker-covered crotch, Callum landed the brush onto her stomach, making her insides lurch all over again.

Leah shut her eyes as her exposed flesh was polished and scoured. Lost in a sea of sensation, she didn't hear Callum as he asked her to turn onto her stomach, and Leah found his large palms rolling her over on the bed before her brain caught up on events.

Tensing as the masseur's brush began rotating across her again, Leah found she was flinching in anticipation, even before the backs of her knees were retouched.

Fighting to relax, Leah buried her face into the soft bed linen. She'd just regulated her breathing, when abruptly the bristling of her back stopped, and with a sharp thwack, the flat of Callum's hand came down hard onto Leah's butt.

Screeching with surprise, Leah lifted her head and tried to turn herself round, but Callum had pinned her in place with his free hand in the small of her back, just as his other palm landed against her other satin-covered butt cheek. She yelled out again, but this time the yell died, as the stinging burn in her butt was instantly cleared away by the stroking of the handleless brush.

Twisting her head to look at Callum, Leah saw that his face was flushed, and his eyes were dilated wider than she'd ever seen them before. He wasn't looking back at her though. All his focus lay on the triangle of fabric that covered her arse.

Keeping the masseur's brush moving, Callum took his hand from Leah, as if sensing she wasn't going to try to escape, and swung it back.

This time Leah was ready for the smack. His palm

connected sharply with each butt cheek twice in quick succession, but the burn was then tenderly dissolved by the contrasting light sweep of Callum's brushing.

Leah swallowed hard, bracing herself for it to happen again, eager for another spank to her arse. Squeezing her eyes shut, she could feel the heat rush through her butt. She badly wanted to feel the flat of his hand again. It was a struggle not to raise her arse up towards the next slap as it flew across the crack of her arse, making her yelp for a split second before, once again, any pain was deliciously tidied way.

Her mind raced. It had been years since anyone had spanked her. How could she have forgotten how much she loved it?

Her fists tangled in the sheets as she waited.

The brush moved.

And no smack came.

Callum began to soothe the mildly ticklish bristles over her hips and sides. It was as if he'd already forgotten about her palm-singed butt.

Leah couldn't believe how robbed she felt as, without a word about what he'd just done to her, Callum teased the brush over and around her bra strap. With excruciating stealth, Callum applied the brush again and again to the same square inch of skin. Then, shuffling up to sit on the back of Leah's legs, Callum bent his head to her ear, sweeping her hair from the side of her face. "I don't think I've ever met anyone who has smelt so utterly and completely wanton." He slid three fingers over the gusset of her knickers. "Or so wet. You liked that, didn't you? You liked me spanking your butt?"

Whimpering into the sheets beneath her head, Leah nodded, wishing her boyfriend's fingertips weren't being denied the direct contact she longed for at her clit by the barrier of her panties.

"Have you been wondering what the other two brushes are for?"

Leah's pulse drummed out a faster beat.

"Maybe." She couldn't manage any further words as the bristles travelled up her neck, turning another area of her being into an erogenous zone.

"Roll back over and tell me." Without faltering in his attention to Leah's throat, Callum stretched one hand behind him, took the hairbrush from the box, and began to stroke it through the ends of the curls that weren't trapped beneath her head.

"I can't, I . . ." Leah blushed bright pink, her embarrassment at being asked to share her kinky dreams a total contradiction to the increasingly wanton arousal the twin application of the brushes was providing.

"I think you *should* tell me." Callum trailed the head of the masseur's brush down to the cleft of Leah's cleavage. He hovered it there suggestively, not moving, the only stimulation it gave coming from the rise and fall of Leah's chest. "If you share your fantasy, I might make it come true for you."

Closing her eyes, Leah saw flashes of red and orange flame and swirl beneath her closed lids. She knew she was near to climaxing whatever happened next. "Please Callum, I can't, I . . ."

"Tell me." Callum, his hands still clasping both brushes, kissed Leah's dry panting lips. "I can see you're close. What would it take to tip you over? The tap of my fingers over your panties? A kiss to your clit? A rub of my brush over the tips of your nipples? A spank of your tits with the back of this hairbrush?"

Leah's body jerked at his last remark, betraying her secret thoughts. Callum smiled. "Your wish, my beautiful birthday girl, is my command."

She'd hardly had time to register all of the tempting options Callum had laid before her, before her body had reacted of its own accord.

"Put your hands under your head." All the softness to Callum's tone had gone as he barked out the order.

As Leah obeyed, not wanting to risk wasting time in which she might change her mind, Callum swung his right arm back, the hairbrush aloft, but this time its wooden side was on a collision course for Leah's flesh.

All the time his left hand kept the scrubbing brush rotating over her panties. Leah's eyes fixated themselves on the hairbrush, trying hard not to flinch, half grateful, half terrified that Callum had her legs trapped beneath his so that she couldn't roll away.

Suddenly, everything happened very fast.

With a precision aim, Callum brought the brush down on Leah's right tit, hard and firm. Her scream as she was struck sent an agonizing pleasure through her chest, which triggered tears to stream down her face, as Callum swiftly evened up the attention on her left breast.

She felt as though she'd been hot-wired from her nipples to her toes as Callum dropped the hairbrush and brought his mouth to the cups of the satin, sucking them with his cool mouth, making Leah's pussy twitch and her back begin to arch beneath him.

Leah's mind was a blur of nothing but desire. She could picture the body brush scouring over her tits. The brushing had felt so good over the rest of her skin. It had turned her from an aroused girl keen for a fuck, into a desperate coiled spring of physical craving. She *had* to experience her birthday gifts' bristles over her tits. Only that would stop their unbearable ache of neglect beneath her underwear.

Crouching over Leah's legs, Callum was working faster still.

Holding the body brush so tightly that it was beginning to leave an impression in the skin of his palm, Callum grasped the head of the hairbrush in the other, and dragged the bristles of both brushes simultaneously over Leah's satin protected breasts.

The sound that shot from Leah's throat was more squeal than moan, and more moan than mewl. It was a high-pitched sigh of bodily relief, which coincided with her hips almost bucking Callum from his position across her legs, and made Leah throw her hands to her chest.

Tugging roughly at the cups of her bra in her impatience to feel her breasts being wiped, Leah flipped up the fabric, exposing her tits just as a well-aimed arc of Callum's brush zipped across her nipples.

An instant contraction deep within Leah's pussy catapulted tears of shock to her eyes, and froze her body for a split second, before she finally came with a juddering yelp of ecstasy between her lover's legs and the hotel's bed sheets.

"Oh wow, baby." Callum's hushed words were full of awe as he watched his girlfriend's reaction to his skilful application of her birthday present.

Lying still, Leah felt the glow of Callum's urgent lust radiate into her. She revelled in the line of his gaze, which was devouring the sight of her fingers, which had already returned to playing with her nipples. Nipples that shone a satisfyingly startling scarlet after their brief encounter with the brush.

Breathing slowly, her stomach buzzing with the comedown from her orgasm, Leah beamed. "That was wonderful, I've never felt like that before."

"It looked bloody incredible." Getting up carefully, his erection obviously cramped and uncomfortable in his boxers, Callum's face glowed red as Leah's did. Freeing himself from the remains of his clothes, his penis saluted his lover. "Tell me. Tell me *precisely* what else your dirty little imagination was picturing me doing with the other brush."

Knocking Leah's knees up and outwards, Callum wrenched her knickers from her body, relishing the sticky sound the fabric made as he suctioned them away from her soaked mound.

Emboldened by the devilish gleam to Callum's eyes, which told her exactly how badly he wanted her to tell him what she was thinking, Leah banished all inhibitions and embarrassment from her mind.

Pulling Callum towards her, so his dick knocked against her stomach, Leah kissed him as she spoke into his lips. "In my head, I was perched on the edge of the bed, my legs were stretched out to the sides, and . . ."

Callum jumped up. "Show me. Show me as you tell me."

Moving to the edge of the bed, Leah continued to describe

her fantasy. "You were right behind me, naked, your legs next to mine, your cock nudging my back."

In less than a second, Leah felt the presence of Callum's solid shaft against her spine, and his hands had reached round to gently smooth the undersides of her breasts. Murmuring with delight at his touch, Leah continued to speak, her voice becoming almost as gravelly as her partner's in her excitement. She couldn't believe Callum was doing this for her; actually carrying out the scenario she'd conjured in her mind while he'd brushed her to climax. Leah was almost afraid to go on. Could she physically handle what she had imagined? It was bound to be more intense than what had gone before.

As if sensing her sudden uncertainty, Callum spoke softly. "It'll be all right, I promise. I think I can guess what you're going to say. If we try and you can't take it, we'll stop. Go on, baby, tell me what to do next?" Stopping his manipulation of her globes, Callum began to work out the knots of Leah's ringlets with her new hairbrush.

"Well, that was part of it. You'd be brushing my hair with one hand. With strong strokes, just like you're doing now. So I can feel each bristle against my scalp. That's it—" Leah broke off; Callum's dick was poking against her. She knew he must want some attention to his shaft as badly as she wanted him to use the final brush against her.

"And then . . ." Callum's tone was growing more urgent, and Leah began to speak faster.

"In my mind, you took the thin brush. You brushed it carefully over my pussy, and then . . ."

Leah's throat closed in on itself. She couldn't finish her sentence, but then she didn't need to. Callum had sprung to his feet again, seized the last brush, and was already manoeuvring its small rectangular soft-bristled end over her mound. As he investigated her neat triangle of pussy hair, speech from either of them became impossible. The sound of their combined breathing drowned out everything except the rhythmical graze of the two brushes.

Leaning back against Callum's toned torso, Leah opened her legs wider as he coordinated his strokes. First Leah's pussy was swept, and then her hair was teased, in an alternating but continuous tango of attention.

Dizzy, overdosing on desire, Leah clenched her fingernails into her palms in an attempt to delay her fast-building climax, but it was no good. She needed to come, and she needed to come now.

"Please Callum. Do it—do it *now*!'

She didn't need to tell him what "it" was.

Standing before her, with his dick pointing at Leah as if accusing her of causing the rock-solid state it was in, Callum ran the hairbrush through her fringe while scraping the end of the slim-handled brush's bristles over her clit. Then, with just enough of a pause to add to the tension that hung tangibly in the air around them, Callum wrenched his arm backwards, and brought the back of the brush down hard against Leah's exposed nub.

Her victorious cry of "Yes!" hadn't finished echoing around the room before Callum twisted the brush around and pushed its head all the way up inside her slick channel.

The effect was explosive. Leah's hips jacked forward, engulfing more of the handle up inside herself, so she was internally brushing herself.

Almost coming merely from the sight of the exotic tableau he'd created, the lust that had been bunching in Callum's stomach for the past half an hour finally got the better of him, as he tried to imagine how it might feel to be fucked by brush.

After dropping the hairbrush to his side, Callum grabbed his cock and began pumping himself off in time to his easing of the slim brush in and out of his lover. He felt goose pimples bump his own skin, as he grazed the soft bristles up inside Leah's tender channel.

As dots of red blotched across his chest, Callum sped up his dedicated cleaning of Leah's pussy.

Then abruptly, unable to wait another second, he let go of the thin brush, leaving it wedged within Leah, picked the hairbrush back up, threw his arm back, and brought it bristle side down onto her right nipple.

Her cries of almost delicious pleasure sent Callum's creamy spunk showering across Leah's totally brushed body.

Leah collapsed back against the bed. The slim brush was wrenched free from her slit as she fell backwards, her frame convulsing while her eyes watered, and her head spun.

Lying down next to Leah on the tangled sheets, Callum wiped away the perspiration from her forehead, and untangled the knots that had formed in her hair. Cradling her against his shoulder, Callum said nothing as she came down from her high, and her quivering body stilled.

When she finally opened her eyes, Leah found herself peering straight into Callum's dazzling smile.

"Happy birthday Leah."

She kissed him gently. Words simply didn't feel an adequate enough way to thank him for the present he'd just given her. It was time to show Callum her appreciation with actions instead. To prove that it was as good to receive as it was to give.

Sitting up, Leah scooped up the brush that had just cleansed her channel so intimately. Her smile curled into a wicked grin.

"I think it's time we had a shower to clean ourselves up." She ran a finger through the come that clung to her chest, licking it suggestively off her fingertips. Then, with a mischievous wiggle of her hips, she pulled Callum by the hand towards the en suite. "I can't help thinking that certain bits of your anatomy could do with a little brushing off of their own . . ."

[Title Forgotten]

M. Christian

Intelligence is the wife, imagination is the mistress, memory is the servant.

Victor Hugo

A second cup of tea, that had been extraordinarily rich and flavourful, a pungent cascade of scent and taste too much not to give him at least a few long, smiling, moments to savour, combined with a fascinating article on *ericoid mycorrhiza* meant that by the time he called for a car he was already twelve minutes and some seconds late.

No worries, no concern, nothing to dull the intrigue of the article, the mouthy resonance still remaining from the brew: he knew he was twelve minutes and some seconds late by the peripherally wagging icon in his iGlasses. No worries, no concern because he knew, without even thinking about it, that the Lodge had already been told of his late arrival.

There were other options, of course, but for some reason he always hired a car, travelled to that particular Lodge instead of just having a Counsellor coming to his house; maybe, he half thought, it was just to watch the ocean so far and blue below on the right, the dusty red of redwoods flashing by on his right, as the car took him there. Or, perhaps, he wanted a touch of the familiar on his way to experience something slightly unfamiliar.

The car arrived, gentle crunching of fine gravel under its small tyres loud enough to penetrate the interior. After it had come to a complete stop – its thankfulness and hopefulness at a job well done another merrily dancing icon at the bare periphery of his vision – he stepped out onto the gravel driveway, the sound of his steps equal in their remarkable loudness.

The Counsellor he knew would be waiting for him, stood standing relaxedly in front of the coarse wooden structure of the door – a brass fitted and perhaps hand-blown-glass windowed entrance melding contemplatively with the rest of the lodge that rose from the drive and meandered back into the redwoods.

He didn't need to tell her who he was, just as he hadn't needed to tell her that he was running late. What she wanted to say, for others to know, lethargically rolled around the top of her head – a halo of iconic information fed from her shared information to his iGlasses. Parallel she knew who he was, and everything he wanted to tell her about himself, revealed in whatever style of information she wanted in her cast into her own periphery of vision by her own style of eyewear.

"Greetings," she said, with a gentle bow, even though she already knew his name just as he knew hers. The formality was actually speaking, especially when it wasn't necessary, and felt warm and inviting. "Welcome back to Meliora."

Claire's hair was grey, long, captured – against what looked to him to be quite stubborn and strong hair – by an ornate brass, or maybe gold, pin in the back, and from it a complex high and low sparkle that left blinded him – if just for the time of a reflexive blink – and ignorant of the icons of her life that were still orbiting her head. It spoke of nurturing and kindness, of a woman who would hold you in her arms, rock you back and forth, while whispering *It's all going to be okay . . .*

Her dress was so simple that all he could say of it was that it was that: a dress that covered her from wrists to sandal-covered feet. It was colours on drugs mixed in bathtubs: tie-dye was a kind of fashion statement for all the Counsellors. Even though he already knew what it was called, the focusing of his pupils were noted, recognized as possible curiosity by his glasses, and a brief commentary on sixties fashions trickled by in his iGlasses.

"Thank you," he replied, returning the bow. Behind him, the car closed its door, gently rolling rolled away after it did – accompanied again with that too-loud gravel crunch. "I . . . I can't say I'm happy to be back."

Claire laughed, a very pleasant sound he could hear a lot more of. "I understand." Turning, she opened the door, beckoning him with the movement to step inside. "But you do come back," she said. "And – as we like to say here – being willing to look back is the first step of looking forward." And, door closing behind her, her laughter again chimed again. "Maybe we should have it carved on a little rock; a souvenir to take home?"

His own laugh, he knew, could not compare but hers drew his out anyway. "I actually think I'd like that . . . something to hold on to. A little bit of the ambience to put in my pocket."

"That's sweet. I like the idea of you taking us with you – a little stone in your pocket. I know coming here can be . . . difficult, and a whole lot more convenient: drop in, walk out. No fuss, no muss. But you like to come here and – at the risk of sounding like I'm talking out of a rock again – that does say something."

It did, and that it did made him stop for a brief second. He had choices . . lots of choices: many lodges to go to, hospitals he could simply walk into, even ones that would come to him: the whole procedure with him comfy in bed. But he always came to Meliora. The view? The trees on one side, the ocean on the other, the idea of getting away . . .

Maybe under there, hidden in the memories he'd had grafted over those two years, was why he always came back to Meliora?

Things like that happened, of course; they were *supposed* to be there: a craving for a food you hadn't liked before – midnight raids for pickles or ice cream – or a tune that you knew, with certainty, you'd never heard before miraculously appearing, tone for tone, in your mind. You *had* to know that none of it was real – that it was crafted, created, manufactured to explain the time of what had been taken out.

What was odd was that he hadn't considered Meliora part of that: Meliora had always felt . . . *his*, rather than part of what he'd been given.

Just like the atrium: a warm wood skeleton arching in all kinds of organic directions, between the lattices bubbles of what again could have been handmade, hand-blown coloured glass . . . though, as always, there was more than a bit of doubt there: handmade was rare, precious, valued . . . more than likely there were other Meliora's, or variations on a theme, stamped out, prefabricated and assembled where wanted.

Even though he knew the way, and his glasses could have guided him as well, Serkis followed Claire as she began to walk down one of those wood-warm, glass-sparkling rooty corridors.

This time it would be room number six, a hovering, ghostly arrow just above her head when she stopped in front of it.

It was always a bit difficult to do, but he took his iGlasses off. He didn't have to, he actually could have left them on during the whole process, but there was a . . . reality he always liked to feel when he went into one of the rooms. The flatness, the boredom of ignorance at not being able to instantly know whatever he looked at as much a part of coming to Meliora. Smiling, Claire carefully accepted his glasses – recognizing his new state of total informational blindness.

The room was basically the same as any other in Meliora: its motherly comforts and details so embracing, so restful, so soothing that the mystery of it – and everything in it – didn't bother him, was a plush cushion against ignorance.

There was the plush bed, swollen with quilts; a tiny sideboard so perfectly scuffed and worn that he guessed (guessed!) it must have been manufactured – but then there was also a small wooden table so dark it looked like a show of what could have (could have!) been its former, newer self. It whispered a story of hands working it, even though the stained-glass shaded lamp on top of it – that cast a light that he instantly compared with the flash from her hairpin, but on a much softer, lower, intensity – again felt (felt!) stamped out.

And there, on the floor, the black case. He didn't need to have his glasses to know about the case: no decoration, no attempt at warmth or welcoming. No matter where you went – home, clinic, or theme park of comfort like Meliora – there would always be that same ubiquitous form of instrumentality.

He got undressed, she taking his clothes in a motherly little ritual, and neatly piling them on the sideboard.

As she bent over the case, he closed his eyes and breathed in and out, in and out, in and out. Then the first of the contacts went on, the coolness of the metal making him open his eyes, but only for a second. Even blind – and not just from information – he sensed Claire's movements like part of a tea ceremony: the precise and intricate dance of preparation.

Meliora . . . he always came to Meliora. There was something about the place. Was it his? Some down-deep tangle of desire and experience, or was it an accident? A leak of what should have been stopped up . . . ?

Not the time. In and out, in and out, in and out. "I know you've heard them before . . . but do you want me to say them again?"

He shook his head. He didn't need to hear her say it. A switch inside his mind would be thrown, what had been pushed aside would be brought out into the light of his mind, the fakes would fade. Many lived with happily, cheerfully, without a question or stray thought that parts of their lives were not what they appeared to be: that they were cinematic patches covering up darkness.

But others, like Serkis, came back to places like Meliora every once and a while, the itch of curiosity becoming too much to stand. They lay – like he laid – with those neurons flipped from *off* to *on*, and see what they'd asked to have hidden.

Because one day they might be able to look at what they'd asked to have hidden . . . and then not ask that it be forgotten all over again.

"I'm going to count down from three, Mr Serkis. Ready?"

He nodded, feeling the fine wires leading from the contacts to the box on the floor gently slide against his suddenly damp forehead.

"One . . . two . . . three—"

With them gone, the layers – the shade, the tone, the flavour – of what had been overlaid were obvious: the reality of . . . reality so sharp, so clear, so contrasted that – still lying on the bed in that little room in Meliora – Serkis squeezed his already closed eyes tighter, pushing down for a moment with the muscles around his eyes, giving himself an aching strain there for a moment.

It came all at once, a cresting threat and then a breaking reality of those too sharp, too clear, too contrasted four months of his life – four months of his life, from three years ago.

Those years had been there, in his mind, before, of course, but lifted, unveiled, there was *more* . . . and with it he winced again, but this time not at the brightness of their reality – but, instead, the *more* of the reality itself. A detail was now remembered: a part of the greater whole revealed.

"Look out below!" Billings had said, spitting over the side of the raft, performed like a ritual he'd thought long and hard about, a spittle celebration that the dirigible had deposited them safely on the canopy.

He hadn't felt like doing the same, or sipping from the champagne Paddy brought in a small plastic bladder bag. Billings, however, had no reservations, and accepted a squeezed stream of it – most of it splashing around his already-bearded face.

They all had a reason to celebrate: two years of grant proposals, committee meetings, and research, research, research. Broadly there had been nothing new, special, rare in what they were doing – teams had shared their gentle descent onto the Amazonian canopy for decades – but theirs would be a voyage of detail, of focusing on the ecology on a scale no one had ever tried before.

He hadn't spit, hadn't drunk champagne, but Serkis had allowed himself his own congratulations with a glance towards Laura, who was celebrating even less: her head and hands had been already deep in their equipment bags ... intern Laura Butler. The fourth in their four-person team, her head and hands would, of course, have been where they were: she had a lot to do – and, more importantly, a lot to prove to the three professors on the raft.

Billings, Paddy and Serkis were veterans, but only of virtual voyages, digital lectures, so they had proving to do as well: the spit, the booze, all of it had been done with a slight tension of apprehension: a lot hung – by a very thin string – on those three months.

"I claim this corner!" Billings had said, crawling to a corner of the inflated structure. It hadn't mattered at all which corner was which. It was like his spit, a tightly delivered gesture: his way of dealing with dangling at the end of that string.

Four months had been perfectly, ideally, long enough for them all to slip into roles: Billings, for instance, had become the joker in the deck: if a joke could be pulled from anything, anywhere he would pull it. For the first week, they'd joined in, but after the first two weeks his was the only laughter that popped out, then drifted off across the treetops.

Paddy, meanwhile, had become the unwavering, incessant, and more than a little irritating voice of caution: as the raft settled onto its perch high above the rainforest it . . . complained a bit: sudden unexpected tops, the buzzing rift of the fabric dragging across a particularly strong part of the usually delicate canopy, an unusual dip in the power it pulled from the high, hot sun above, or the gentle undulations it performed when the winds came, were all reasons for him to tense.

"Don't you think we should—?" had begun to begin almost every sentence that wasn't directly related to their research. But then, sometime in month two, even that world began to him to show signs of imminent and total failure: "The resolution on this scope is a little off, don't you think?" "I'm sure we didn't bring enough crystal violet or safranin—" "The picric acid doesn't seem up be working as fast as it should—" It didn't take very long for them to only half listen to anything he'd said.

Serkis, he liked to think, had been the moderator, the diplomat, the captain of their little ship on a cracking and groaning sea of rainforest canopy: he'd smile – even when they were never funny – at whatever Billings said; he'd pat Paddy on the back – especially when there really wasn't anything to worry about – when he was tight and tense.

He'd been the one to make coffee in the morning, run quick diagnostics on the little, but powerful network, to make sure Paddy would have nothing to worry about. He'd become the schedule keeper, dancing his fingers in real space, to send the gestures into digital space through his iGlasses, to program in what the day would be, what their goals were.

Laura had been . . . on the raft, a sweet-faced figure, who'd also giggle when Billings cracked his jokes, who'd also make sure – sometimes for the thousandth time – that they actually, really, honestly had enough crystal violet, safranin, or that the picric acid was up to snuff.

Laura had been . . . on the raft; Minnesota shoulders rising and falling as she worked; blue Midwest eyes bright and clear, red hair, a forest fire of curls, the freckles on her high, wide cheekbones becoming higher and wider with each easy smile – at a hollow joke from Billings or as a way of lightening the tightness in Paddy.

Laura had been . . . That was what he'd had in his mind: overlaid, colourized, smoothed and, most of all, edited – but lifted, revealed, he felt the sobs begin as a spasm in his chest, the pressure of tears around his eyes.

"It's okay, Mr Serkis . . . it's okay," he heard the Counsellor say; her throaty kindness coming to him from a distance he couldn't measure, but the touch of her hand on his forehead – neatly avoiding the leads – was there, with him, in the room.

Laura had been . . . it had been in the first month, a night like every other night, the warm familiarity of instant meals chemically heated – or cooled, depending – chatter about what they'd seen that day, a laugh at something Billings would say, reassurance at something Paddy would say, and then they'd move to their selected corners of the raft to sleep.

But that night the sky changed everything: they went to bed with it over their heads shy of skies: invisible clouds high above making the stars just as invisible.

Around midnight, tough, the sky changed again: they went to be with the night air, still and warm, humid as it always was, but then it began to move – and with the sudden winds their inflatable raft began to move as well.

The storm came. Not as bad as they could be in that part of the world, that high above the ground, but it was bad enough to jostle their sanctuary. The designers of the raft had been at their craft for a long time, and the network woven into the fabric was very smart, so there was little danger, but the ride was still quite rough.

No doubt, in his corner of the raft, Billings was trying to think of something funny to say in the morning, when the storm had abated. No doubt, in his corner of the raft Paddy had put on his iGlasses and was nervously looking over the digital shoulder of that network, making sure with fast-beating heart that it was inflating and deflating, tensing and relaxing, their home to ride out the gale.

Wrapped in his own cocoon, Serkis was somewhere between the two: amused by the ride, slightly concerned whether those designers were as good as they were supposed to be.

The rough ride was unexpected, and he had been ashamed that it had made him start – if just a little. Behind that ghostly interface, he saw her face, glowing like another kind of spirit from the soft projections coming from his iGlasses. Her Minnesota shoulders were barely visible, but he could tell that they were bound up tight, her blue Midwest eyes were still bright, but at that moment they were too large, too bright, her blaze of hair was feral from the winds, and those high, wide cheekbones were pulled down and in with an expression he hadn't seen on her face before.

Without any real thought, he unsealed his bag and she slid inside. Her head, with those eyes, those cheekbones, that red hair, curled into his own shoulder, while her strong arms wrapped around his naked chest, pulling him close and tight.

The storm continued, pushing and shoving at their treetop raft, the trees below and around them hushing and groaning in answer.

Laura had been . . . in one their monofibre suits, the ones they all wore under their normal clothes: ultimate protection against heat, cold, impact . . . while remaining easy to get on and off.

Serkis had been naked, having easily removed his own suit before crawling into his bag. At first they were simply *there*, the two of them: Laura gently quivering with fear, he holding her, trying to take in her fear, smooth her anxiety.

Then her hands began to move, and to his shame (in recalling it) and shocked desire (then) he did not stop her – and as her hands moved her head left the sanctuary of his shoulder. So close together, breaths mixing in the stale air of the confines of the sleeping bag, a kiss was the only thing they could do.

At first it was almost a chaste one, like the way he held her against the gale, but then their kiss had grown hotter more feral and hungry: tongues playing, teeth gently biting, the stale air grew hot then hotter.

There was something about her, despite their cocooning, the ridiculous confines of their safety: she bowed her head, shrunk back a bit into herself, becoming smaller, more fragile, more reserved.

Despite the winds, the gentle bucking of the raft, he felt himself pull back and into the bag with her – his mind meeting that new *something* about her with a ferocity that was as exciting as it was frightening: "You want to touch it, don't you?" he whispered to her.

She nodded, her head brushing his chest.

"Do you deserve to touch it?"

Her voice was soft, almost too low to hear: "I—I don't know."

He was a teacher, a professor; she was a student. This was the way of the things, as real as the storm pushing against the raft – but they were more than just that; they were even stronger than that.

"You do want it, don't you? You hunger for it. You need it. Tell me you want it."

"I—I want it."

"What do you want to do?"

"I—I want to touch it."

"Touch what?"

A gust lifted the raft, rolled under and over it – her hands, moving of their own accord, splayed and flattened against his chest.

"I'm sorry, sir," she said, her voice loud even against the moan and roar of the winds.

"You should be," he found himself saying, the words forming and escaping his lips without his mind being aware of them. "Apologize."

"I—I'm sorry for touching you."

"That's good." He pulled her closer, kissed the top of her head – smelling and tasting the simple shampoo/conditioner she used. "Now you may touch me. You deserve it."

One of her hands found his erection; he was amazed at the strength and determination of her grip, the hunger that was there, the need that was there.

"Now you may kiss me," he said. As they did, lips sliding and tongues pushing and shoving at each other, their breathing mixed into matching inhale and exhales. She began to stroke him.

It was . . . what it was, but there was a more to it, and he knew it almost instantly: the times he'd watched her, the ways she'd looked at him. The storm was frightening, but what had been building up between them had been even more so. She belonged to him. He owned her.

"You have been very good. You deserve my cock."

The raft shook, and with it she stroked him, using the tiny bit of moisture that softly leaked from the head to add lubrication. Soon he was moaning, and – with a return of the gesture – his head was on her shoulder, biting down through the resilient fabric of her suit.

Which, it turned out, was quite a puzzle to remove, but they managed it. But then it was solved, and he pulled the crumpled emptiness of it out of the sleeping bag.

His hand found one of her plump breasts. "You like that, don't you?"

With the contact, he had a flash of watching her, thinking without really thinking of what was under the utility of her clothing, beneath the close embrace of the undersuit. The touch was electric, a sexual shock that ran up his body from hand to body to his erect cock and back down to his hand. Beneath his fingers, her nipple grew harder and harder still, going from a soft nub to a firmness that drew his mouth and lips from their kiss to it like the pull of some fundamental force.

Their sex was ferocious, animalistic: after some more sleeping bag acrobatics, she was looking down at him: the red curls of her hair black in the night. Her expression was real, hungry – the face of the submissive woman who'd been hiding all this time under the face of an intern named Laura.

Entering her was calm, an eye in the storm: a shift of her hips, a shift of his hips and his cock was pushing into the right moisture of her. At first, she didn't move. At first, she just looked down at him and smiled with that reality, that hunger. Even with the memories lifted, restored, he couldn't remember who began to move first. It didn't really matter; what did was that they began it: he sliding in and out of her, she pushing herself up and down on him.

He smiled, at the time, and a new maxim for the universe came into his mind – *wonders make clichés of us all*: a really hot day actually does feel like walking into an oven, a beautiful work of art honestly takes your breath away . . .

And time, occasionally, does stand still. They could have

been moving together – he sliding in and out of her, she pushing herself up and down on him, again and again and again – time really did come to a complete halt.

And through it all, her moans that sometimes became words: "Thank you, sir; thank you, sir; thank you, sir; thank you, sir . . ."

The storm was just a shoving, pulling against the bag, a background he didn't feel – and he doubted she felt.

Wonders really do make clichés of all: when the orgasm began it was slow, easy, coming up from somewhere deep down, a more-than-just-sex place – and when he did, her breathing changed, her rhythm changed, her eyes half-closed and her mouth half-opened – and the cliché came for both of them at the same time: they came together.

"Good . . . you did very good. You pleased me." He kissed the top of her head again. "Take pride in that."

In answer she pulled him closed, nuzzled his neck and whispered in answer: "Thank you, sir."

The storm continued its job of making their raft roll and flap, as the two of them drifted away, half exhaustion, half sleep, both still connected – and not just cock in cunt.

During the night, the gale gave up, dawn warming and lighting a welcoming panoramic veldt of rainforest treetops. Laura and Serkis didn't try – or think of trying – to hide what had happened between them. Serkis, Billings and Paddy had been on expeditions before and so knew, and even accepted, that when you mix the chemicals of men and women together for a certain amount of time the result was always the same.

The days went on as they had before: Billings's jokes continuing to elicit polite half-laughs, Paddy's nervousness continuing to pull reassurances from them all. They studied the world beyond the raft, the one they'd come all that distance, put aside all that time to do.

And the work went well: the champagne was brought out again when Paddy found the evidence he'd been looking for; and came out again when Billings found a new spider species – and they all laughed when he said he'd name it

Peter Parkarest – but the nights, when Billings went to his corner of the raft, and Paddy went to his, Laura and Serkis went to theirs: transitioning from professor and student to lovers.

That was there, the times they crawled into Serkis's sleeping bag: the memories vivid and clear and obviously true. But woven through their days on the raft, the nights of *her begging for his cock, he playing with her, teasing her, pulling and tugging at her nipple until she could stand no more, he sliding in and out of her, she pushing herself up and down on him*, was a softness, a lack of focus, like Vaseline smeared over his mind. He cared for his pet that was Laura, cared for her a lot, but the volume of that caring had been turned down.

Then, cresting on the fourth month, Paddy had slid along the fabric of the raft – a movement they'd all become expert at, as standing was pretty much impossible – and said, in a conspiratorial whisper, "We need to talk."

For a flash, Serkis thought that it would be about he and Laura – that, maybe, they'd become too obvious, violated some intimate researcher's rule of volume, or too many public displays of what had to stay private.

But it wasn't: when Paddy had worried it was always at full voice, a regular, predictable background – like the hushing of the canopy's leaves or the backing laughter of Billings – so his whisper in Serkis's ear pulled the world down to just the two of them, one speaking to the other.

That moment, in his mind, was direct and present: he could very well be there, at the moment, all over again. "We're out of safranin."

He'd wanted to laugh, thinking that – somehow – the raft had flipped over and their roles reversed: Billings would now start to tell bad jokes at every opportunity . . . and he and Laura . . .

But the raft was upright – and Laura was looking back over her shoulder at him, a loving look of concern on her face, visible even behind the plastic of her icon fuzzy iGlasses, as Billings, sitting next to her and, even though fixated on some instrument or preparation Serkis couldn't see was, was saying something – another joke, more than likely.

And Paddy was still worried, but this time he had a good reason to: without safranin their work was pretty much over, their time on the raft – with many more weeks to go – would have to be called off. They could go on, of course: improvising and making do, but they knew their work would suffer – and work that suffered equals doubt, and doubt could, too easily, equal a descent in career. Findings would be reviewed more thoroughly, publications would review more carefully. Respect would be much harder to earn.

That afternoon, they had a meeting: the four of them sitting near the centre of their raft, the combined weight of their bodies – and their worry – denting the fabric: they conferred and discussed at the bottom of a bright yellow cone of high-test nylon. Their iGlasses were all pushed up onto foreheads, the seriousness of the conversation not suitable for distractions of instant information.

But even before they descended down there, they all knew what the outcome would be: a call would have to be made.

An aereon would have to be dispatched. They could, simply, have the preservative shipped to them directly – Paddy, in fact, already having ordered a new supply once he realized they were actually, honestly, really running low, but that would mean time – but, again, the ticks of the clocks on their expedition would be counting down to resorting to doubt.

One of them would have to go, to intercept the package at the aereon base, to check its quality, and hop right back on the airship to bring it back. It was a difference of only a few days, certainly, but two days could be mean the difference between the certainty they'd meticulously been maintaining, the observations they made, the theories that were already forming, *Peter Parkarest,* and . . . everything.

Lying in the lodge, on the softness of the bed, Serkis touched the edge: it was there, clear and crisp – no doubt there, pure certainty: this was where those neurons had been tricked, switched off, superimposed, rewritten. The intensity of he and Laura were the same, of course, but that had been a pulling-back of emotion, a cushion that had been placed between what he'd really felt and the hot, joyous, giddy, pleasure of reality.

There'd been no question of who was to go. Serkis, Paddy and Billings were professors, those days were theirs to worry over, to lose.

It wouldn't be a risky trip: the aereon was as computationally elegant and careful as their raft – whatever happened the ship would be able to handle it. The aereon though, would have to be a smaller one – information they received as a tiny video of apology from the aereon base manager on their iGlasses – but it would get Laura to the base to intercept and inspect their delivery in less that a day, with another to get back.

There: right there. He knew it was there, because it was again intentionally obvious, but tripping into it, falling down into the unlocked hole of what actually happened, made him, stretched out on the bed in the lodge, squeeze his eyes tightly shut once again – so tight that when the tears came they were thick and slow, pushed out from between his aching lids.

What was behind lock and key wasn't much: just a moment – no more than maybe five words spoken over five minutes.

The aereon arrived, its cooling shadow rolling across their raft, the octave rising and falling of its ducted fans making them have to raise their voices to be heard.

Serkis, looking up at the white, swollen aerodynamically perfect shape of it, the blue and yellow logo of its maker distorted, so distorted by its proximity, that it was so very, very small. The lifter that had brought them and the raft had been a greater machine, an immense artificial cloud of smart materials that had cast a much larger shadow over the canopy of the Amazon. The one that, then, hovered over them had a transparent teardrop underneath, clear enough that he could see the orange survival suit of the pilot, and the empty spare seat directly behind him.

Dressed in her own survival suit, red rather than one-part

corporate shade yellow, Laura had looked comical: but Billings did nothing but give her a hug – and if Paddy shared Serkis's fleeting worry over the smallness of the aereon he didn't add it to his own, "Thank you," to her.

The memory was there, smoothed over, edited out, but now he heard himself say it, saw her face when he said it: "I order you to go."

It had been a joke, worse than anything Billings ever said – or would ever say – and he immediately wished he could swallow the words: but still something like those words. He wished he could have said that he did love her, that she had brought him a gift he never would have ever expected, a gift that no one else had ever given him.

Instead he'd said, "I order you to go." Then she was rising into the sky, the thin cable connecting her to the aereon winding her into the sky. Dangling at the end of the line, she waved back down at them, her hands in the orange survival suit looking like they belonged on a crudely made doll.

They all watched as the tone of the aereon's lifters changed, as it elegantly danced away from them – the icons and information in their iGlasses telling them more than they needed to know about the machine, its proposed flight path, the pilot's last performance review (exemplary), and a last message from Laura.

A last message pinged through all this flowing data directly into Serkis's: *Love you, sir.*

The rest of what had happened was there – untampered with, unmodified, exactly as what had happened—

They'd gone back to work, the men on the raft: Billings, studious and serious in a thick blanket of dedicated professionalism; Paddy, meticulously checking and rechecking and re-rechecking their remaining supplies; and Serkis looked over his notes, flicking them up and down in his projected vision.

Laura was still with them, in brief messages of fondness and clumsy observations of how the canopy looked from so much farther up. The course of her travel was a silver-white line that wove and undulated off into the distance.

They awoke in the depths of the night to the sound of an emergency communication: a strident howl telling them that something was wrong.

It didn't happen often, but it did happen: the best computers running the best software, carefully built and maintained machinery, weather observed and plotted with exacting detail.

They sat on the raft that had been their home for four months, Paddy, Billings, and Serkis, as the information streamed to their own network, and from that network to them.

They all took the news hard: Paddy had retreated to a far corner of the raft, beginning to pack up his equipment; Billings began to do the same, but after sitting and staring out across the darkness of the Amazon.

Serkis became a machine: poorly maintained, running fragments of thought and waves of agonizing guilt. It was over, it was done. There was nothing left to do but go home.

And when they did get home, there'd been a memorial, a dedication in papers that still managed to get written and even published.

It took Sertis a week – just a week – to realize that he couldn't go on, that what he'd said, and what he'd felt, were burning him up, tearing at his sleep, and crushing his mind when he was awake.

He opened his eyes, looking up at a hand-hewn wooden ceiling and then, slowly entering his vision, Claire. "How are you feeling?" she said, her voice warm, embracing, and clearly – wonderfully – sincere.

The tears wouldn't stop, they came and came and came, and with them the punches to his stomach, the fisting ache throughout his entire body.

She gave him a glass of water, and he sipped at it while also trying to catch his breath.

"Can you make a decision?" she said, as he handed her back the empty glass.

Serkis nodded and, without doubt, hesitation, pause, he looked down at his still quivering hands and said: "Take it away . . . take it away again."

The Counsellor helped Serkis sit up from the warm comfort of the bed, stroking his clenched back with firm, clearly professionally adept hands.

Eventually, the tightness began to leave his body and he turned, slowly, to look at her – offering a weakly vulnerable smile. In steady, unrushed stages, she got him up from the bed, picked up his iGlasses – but did not offer them to him – and led him off to an intimate corner of the lodge's main room: a curvature of a seating that arced from near the huge stone-hearthed fireplace – the heat from which came and went with each flicker of flame – to one of the uniquely shaped windows and the too-blue distant sky of the Pacific.

Leaving him for a moment, she brought him tea in a handmade, almost lumpy, white mug. As he hesitantly sipped, she smiled – both at the pleasure of his recovery and in memory of the flavour: a side effect of the neurotransmitters mixed into the brew, designed to aid the recovery even more.

"I . . . I guess I didn't want to keep it," he said after a moment, beginning with rough hesitation, ending his long silence.

Claire shook her head.

"Then . . . that's for the best."

She nodded. "I think you made the right decision for yourself."

He nodded back and carefully, ritualistically finished the tea – handing her back the cup when he was done.

When he was ready, which wasn't too many minutes after, she led him back towards the front door. The lodge's system, always aware and with digitally precise knowledge, had already called him a car, which was waiting with infinite mechanical patience on the gravel drive.

"Thank you," he said, kissing her on her offered cheek.

"You've . . . helped me a lot. I think." The last added with another weak smile.

"Be well," she said, as she handed him his iGlasses.

And, without putting them on, leaving the too vibrant augmented view of the world behind, if just for a few minutes, he got into the waiting car.

Claire stood on at the door of the lodge for a moment, watching the smooth efficiency of the car as it crunched its way down the drive and then, with a perfectly executed turn, vanish down the highway.

She took the cup back to the kitchen, placing it on the mosaic of the counter next to the sink: the action keying a ghostly reminder in her own digital vision that it would be her turn to do the dishes in two days.

From the undulating dark woods of the kitchen she walked back through the nurturing comfort of the main room – designed with intelligence and care by software, but carefully built by hand – and down a softly undulating corridor towards the back of the lodge. As she walked – as she always walked through it – the little handmade irregularities that came from human labour, even guided by expert software tickled at the edges of her perception: a mis-stitch in the wandering rug at her feet, a hand-hewn board that had not been nailed perfectly and so leaving the faintest of dark gaps.

It was comforting, relaxing, intimate – which was why she lived as well as worked at the lodge. Distantly, she was aware of the value of it all: the near pricelessness of human craftsmanship over laser-cut mass production, but – again, as always – it didn't really matter to her: the lodge may have been software designed but it was a place for men and women to be – especially when they were dealing with very human pain and trauma.

A door on the right side of the wandering hall, somewhere between the crackling logs and comfort of the main room, just beyond the warm embrace of the bed in the counselling room, was an extra-whimsical, more-than-irregularly shaped door, like a polished wooden half of a shell. Glancing at it, she saw – projected into her vision from the own augmented view of reality – a symbol of welcome, and not of privacy.

But, still, she knocked – even knowing that as she approached the person inside would know that she would: a lodge formed by software, built by hand

. . . human, but actually unneeded gestures were common in the lodge.

"Come in," came a voice from inside – again unnecessary, but done the same.

The room beyond was larger than any other room – aside from the solarium, the greenhouse forest of organically elegant, hand-blown glass where they sometimes had to take clients who'd had particularly difficult experiences. She walked into a geodesic space – the panels of which were made of reclaimed flotsam and jetsam: a washed-out billboard with only a few cryptic, peeling letters still visible; the metal side of some once-massive truck now just a triangle of corrugated blue. No matter how many times she'd knocked, when it was okay to enter, of course, the room felt to Claire like she was walking into the higher function of the living, breathing shape of the lodge.

The floor was a crazy quilt of reclaimed rugs, no pattern matching any other pattern: an undulating sea of frayed and thinly worn fabrics. And, sitting in the middle of the room, on an almost-perfectly round pillow of pale cerulean silk, was a young woman: naked except for her own pair of augmented reality eyewear.

"Morning, sweetness," Nora said from her straight-spined position. "The morning treating you right?" Even though the words were to Claire, Nora never moved her head from what she was seeing through her iGlasses.

Again, she didn't need to answer – the information of what kind of day Claire had been having, at least observed by the lodge's system, could very easily be right in front of Nora's eyes. But, yet once more, a simple human question:

the politeness of actually opening a mouth and asking with words.

"Just finished with Serkis," Claire said, shutting the door behind her. Nothing in the room was unusual, striking: she'd been there many times before – so many that the sun-baked skin of Nora, her tightly uplifted breasts with their remarkably large nipples, as much a part of the humanity of the house as a mis-stitched rug or a misaligned board.

Nora didn't look at her, instead focused on something only she could see and, as she didn't look, her boyishly slight yet still strong hands wove and darted in front of her: knitting and forming and weaving and manipulating a virtual structure only she could see. "He came back again, didn't he?"

Claire nodded, not needing to say anything: Nora already knew that Serkis had come back, and how many times he'd come back, and even the details of the overlay of his memories that were working to keep the pain of his loss away.

A tightness caught in Claire's throat. "No more than usual."

Nora turned to actually look at the other woman, a grin on her pixie face, her narrow, dark eyes peering out from under her precisely cut hair: "It's okay," she said. "I'm not worried – and neither should you be."

"Thanks, sweetie," Claire said, the tightness in her own shoulders not realized until she released it. "You know I just . . . worry about you."

One of Nora's hands dropped from a moment of programming ballet to give Claire a friendly wave of dismissal. "I'm tougher than you think – though if his visit numbers got worse then . . . well, then maybe you would be holding my hand."

"Anytime," the Counsellor said, fondness a musical chime in her voice, even though she and Nora had never been intimate – not because there was an unwritten, not-programmed little tradition in Meliora prohibiting such a thing, but because the two of them had simply never felt like taking a step in that direction. "You do know you're the best."

Nora, perhaps distracted or perhaps uncomfortable hearing the praise, repeated "Thanks, sweetie."

Claire shuffled her feet, a question clearly squirming around inside her.

Nora smiled again, her eyes remaining turned away from whatever she'd been working on. "I—I really could do with a bit of help." She flicked her gaze towards another part of the domed room, meaning whatever she was working on. "It's for Sears . . . and, well, I just can't get it to overlay right. I want to do a good job . . . especially for her."

Nora flicked her hand, a tiny gesture – a miniscule near-twitch of her finger-dancing ballet of programming – and the room exploded for Claire into sweeping, multi-shaded arcs; cracks – or leafless trees – of rainbows, bursts of geometric fireworks; and gardens of programming blooms. Then it was gone, whisked back into Nora's solitary vision.

Even though she knew what the answer would be, Claire still felt herself say it: "You sure?"

Nora nodded again – and with a great sweep of her hand more than likely dismissed for herself as well the program she'd been working on. "Yeah, I know it bothers you. But . . . for her, I want to do the best job I can."

It was Claire's turn to nod. It did bother her: what Nora was asking her to do. But the whole Lodge knew about Sears, about what had happened to her son. A flash of memory came, then, without invitation, and Claire fought back the same kind of tears that had come when everyone at Meliora had heard about her.

Claire crossed the dome, ending at a small teak chest. Without looking up from it, opening it, seeing what was inside, she said: "I just don't like . . . seeing what it does to you."

The moment she said it she wished she hadn't, but was still, somehow, grateful that she'd finally released the words.

"Sweetie . . . Claire . . ." Nora began to say, but then stopped.

Nora's words came from behind her as the Counsellor carefully pulled the black-plastic cased unit from the chest, but when she turned she saw that Nora's dark eyes were shimmering, light dancing from tears barely held back.

"I know . . . but it's how I do my best work. She deserves my best, right?"

Claire scooted across the undulating sea of mismatched rugs, the fabric of her sundress making a strange sound. "I guess so," she began, but she shook her head to change the channel of her mind. "No, you're right – she does deserve the best."

The room was quiet for a brief time as Claire opened the case, removed and carefully placed the dermal patches on key spots of Nora's head.

As the last one went on, adhering as they always did with almost-magnetic attachment of complex polymers to skin, Nora said: "I want to tell you."

"You don't have to."

Nora laughed. "I know I don't have to, silly. But I want to. Is that okay?"

Claire nodded, not knowing what to say. No, she and Nora had never been intimate, but hearing her say those words, Claire knew that it wasn't because they simply hadn't taken that step – but because that step would be a very big one, a too important one to take lightly.

Nora took a breath. "Flip the switch, sweetie," she said through a tight smile, "and I'll get to work . . . and you'll get to see."

Claire did, and – after a few moments – Nora took a very slow, very deep, very calming breath. Then, slowed, deepened and calmed, she twisted away from the other woman. Away, her arms, hands and fingers began another dance through the air; coding, programming, creation visible only to her.

Coding, programming, creation . . . but between her and Claire a recorded appearance: a semi-transparent version of the Pixie sitting cross-legged on the floor.

This Nora, the recorded version that Claire saw, was naked: her smooth, lithe and boyish body somehow smaller, shrunken. The recorded woman was the same size as the living one behind, but the ghostly version's posture, the architecture of her body, was pulled inward, compacted.

"Hey . . . sweetie," the smaller Nora said, the endearment interrupted by a cough, a throat clearing. A pause, an echo of the same kind of very slow, very deep, very calming breath, then she began again: "I made this for you – the last time you pulled back my curtain. I—I'm not too sure why I did it. I mean . . . I mean, you must know by now how I feel about you, and I know the expression on your face when you put those certain memories back in their box . . . so I thought . . . I thought that maybe you'd like to know what its about. "But if you don't, just turn me off." The semi-transparent woman waved a faint arm across her chest, a gesture anyone who viewed the world through augmented vision knew as the sign language for stop.

But Claire didn't. "Okay then," the recording said with an even slower, deeper, calming breath. "I—I haven't been here all that long, but – well, it feels right, you know? It just feels good to be here. The work it part of it, sure, being able to help all these people but . . . there's you, as well."

Claire felt her face warm with a blush.

"But I haven't always been like this, like the person you know. A few years ago, I was . . . involved with someone. We were at school, in San Jose. We met in Confabulation Programming. Her name was . . . Beth. I know, I know, everyone meets someone in college. But Beth was different . . . or at least I felt she was.

"Things with her were . . . hot. Nah, hotter than hot: sex-on-the-first-date hot – that kind of thing. We both felt it. Yeah, everyone says that as well, but it was . . . it really was. We moved in together a week after we . . . slept together. It was good – so good – that time we had together: sleeping till noon when we didn't have classes. My friends never even asked what had happened to me – guess they could see it in my face.

"But . . . the thing was . . . Beth was good. Really good. Not just in Confabulation but everywhere else. She was a star pupil, the one that everyone else in whatever class she was in just hated." The last with a laugh, but not a deep one.

"School was hard for me. I had the skill, I knew that, but

the details – I tried my best but I just couldn't get it. Beth, though, she got it. She could do it better than anyone, especially better than me. She was a real artist: when she laid it all out the memories she made were . . . elegant, beautiful. You could see the seams, of course, but she didn't just trowel over the rough parts – no, she took what was there and used it to make the patient better.

"During her internship, I heard that she had the lowest recall rate in the State, maybe in a few years the whole country. The patients she worked on . . . they didn't want to see what was missing, and if they did they put them back – but when they did they didn't cry: they smiled. They fucking smiled, sweetie. They saw what she'd done with them and saw that it was so good, to elegant, so caring.

"I . . . I was bad to her. I was jealous. I can say that now; for the longest time I couldn't say that, but that's what I was.

"I was *very* bad to her." Even through the transparency of the recording, Claire could see the tightness around Nora's eyes and, when she spoke next, the throaty tones of trying to hold back tears. "I put her down; I stood in her way. I questioned everything she did. I even liked it when I saw her start to doubt herself, when she began to hesitate.

"She was up for an . . . an award. Pretty big thing, actually – came with all kinds of perks: internship, advanced training. That kind of thing. I knew it was important to her – so I did everything I could to make sure she didn't get it. And, guess what, she didn't.

"I think she figured it out, about then. I was too obvious, I guess. My fangs really out and all. She left me then, moved out. A week later she transferred to Phoenix – and I thought that was that. The end.

"Then, years later, I was at Confab – the big conference they have every year. I knew she would be there, she'd become bright and brilliant, the shining star not just at events like that but everywhere else. She was writing the science of memory modification just about every day.

"I went to one of her lectures and . . . she told a story. It was—" the ghostly Nora sniffled, the sound ringing oddly as it came from Claire's iGlasses and not the image before her "—it was about how she'd actually operated on herself, trying out a whole new technique: a way of not just suppressing but actually using trauma as a positive emotional tool.

"Afterward I walked up to her and . . . and I knew, the moment I saw her and she saw me, that what she'd done had worked very well – and I also knew what memories she'd worked on. She didn't know me – I was just another face in the crowd to her."

For a minute, maybe two, Claire thought the recording had frozen, but then she saw subtle silver-white risings and falls of breaths and knew that the digital memory of Nora had simply stopped.

When she spoke again her voice was stronger, but still crackling with broken, smashed, sharp-edged emotion. "I put that away. I put it in a box . . . all of it: Beth, what I had done to her, the way I'd felt, the way she'd looked at me. I put it all away, just like so many other people do.

"But I take it out of the box, sweetie – or I ask you to. I do it because . . . well, because it makes me understand how important all of this is. What we do, how we help people. I take it out when I work because when I do . . . I hurt, oh, Lord, it hurts, but it also is there, right in front of me, in big letters: do a good job – do a great job – as good a job as I can do."

Then the ghost died, flickering away with a soft sweet smile. When it did, when Claire's vision was cleared of it, she could finally see through it, at what had laid beyond.

Nora was looking at her; thin hands done with work and now folded in her thin lap – and on her face was a soft, fragile expression.

The tears on Claire's face felt burning hot, their salt mixing with the heated rose of her cheeks. She got down herself and wrapped her meatier arms around the other woman, held her tight.

"Thank you," she whispered in Nora's ear.

"I wanted you to know, sweetie," was the other woman's also whispered reply. "Now . . . you know."

Claire nodded and, moving, as little as she could, towards the device next to Nora . . .

. . . but just before she touched it, pushing Nora's memories back down, the other woman whispered, almost too soft for Claire to hear: "Keep it if you like but . . . if it changes anything . . . between us. Please, forget all about it."

"It doesn't," Claire said in a soft voice back. "I won't."

Then a switch was thrown, Nora's eyes blurred for a second as her memories were shuffled, and – after it was done – Claire took the other woman's face in her hands and kissed her, once, gently on the lips.

The Locked Room

Rose de Fer

I close my eyes and listen to the music. A harpsichord is playing something mournfully erotic, the soundtrack from an old Italian film. One of those starring Edwige Fenech, whose impossibly glamorous eye make-up I can never reproduce no matter how hard I try.

But my eyes don't matter because George is fastening a blindfold around my face. The sheer black silk presses against my eyes, a veil that permits me visual gasps of shadow but nothing of substance. Nothing to remind me of reality. We could be in any time or place. I picture Venice out of season, cold and bereft of tourists. Just the two of us, lost in the maze of canals and bridges and winding alleys until we find our hotel and can hide away from the world. Safe and warm, like this room. We could be there now.

Slowly, George undresses me. First he slips off my shoes, then my stockings, one by one. My skin tingles, every inch of flesh anticipating his touch. My skirt is next, then my top. I imagine him folding everything neatly on a chair, taking his time, making me wait. He unhooks my bra and eases the cups away from my breasts. My nipples stiffen and a nervous little shudder courses through me. But I stand still, moving only as he positions me. Finally, he slips my knickers down and I sense his smile as he sees how damp the gusset is. I blush.

Now, I stand on the threshold, naked and trembling. I have some idea of what's about to happen because I was allowed to see what was beyond the door before being blindfolded. I saw the strange devices and customized furniture, the purpose of each piece unmistakable. Just a glimpse, but it was more than enough. Now I know why he's brought me here.

A surprise, he'd said. Something to take me away. Far away from reality and deep into fantasy. I hadn't understood at the time, hadn't fully processed what that could mean. I'd taken his words literally and, throughout the long drive, I'd thought of fairies, of magic and the realm of dreams.

But no. George had something else in mind entirely.

He takes me by the hand and I go where he leads me. The floor inside is cold against my bare feet and I place them carefully, moving slowly, frightened and uncertain. It's true what they say about being robbed of one sense; the others do become more powerful. I can smell leather, its rich musky scent overpowering the delicate aroma of the candles burning somewhere nearby. The door closes behind us and I jump, frightened by every little sound.

My heart is fluttering like a trapped bird, my breathing fast and shallow. Although the room is warm I can feel my skin prickling. I have the crazy sense that I'm in a haunted place, a place stained with blood and tears, the walls imprinted with sights both frightening and wildly exciting. How many gasps and cries have they absorbed? How many screams? If the walls were a tape I could play back, what would I hear? For a moment I imagine the echoes of past encounters. I can almost hear the meek submissive voices begging for mercy, for pleasure, declaring love and obedience. I can feel the hot fervent whispers, taste the salty tears.

The music plays on, the notes delicate and precise. I let it wash over me.

When we reach the centre of the room, my knees touch something smooth and cool. One of the specialized pieces of furniture I'd seen from the doorway. A padded leather bench. I keep my eyes tightly closed behind the blindfold, comforted by the darkness, as George places my knees on the supports. He eases me into a kneeling position before helping me stretch out across the centre. I remember the shape of the bench and I can picture how I must look lying across it.

There is no question of trust, no flicker of fear, other than the delicious anticipation of the unknown. He might do anything at all to me, but I know I am safe. All I have to fear is the pain I know is coming.

He has never whipped me before. It's a fantasy I shared with him one evening some time ago after an indulgent meal and a bottle of wine. We'd seen a film. One of those dreamy soft-focus European ones with a little light BDSM.

"Mmm," I'd said, my voice muffled in his warm chest. "What if you did that to me?"

He hadn't said anything at the time, had given me no clue to suggest that the thought appealed to him in any way. But he fucked me with an almost frightening passion that night. I could barely walk afterwards. I cried like a child when we said goodbye at the airport the next day and when I got home I told my husband it was just female problems that had put me in such a funny mood. He believed me, accepting my feeble excuse with a shrug. His indifference only reinforced how little I meant to him, how much was lost between us. I was married to a complete stranger.

But now. The bench.

I tremble, not knowing what to expect. Never knowing what to expect, only knowing that it will be intense.

I am never the same after one of our trysts. Each one transforms me, kills off one more bland part of me and reawakens something hidden. Something beautiful.

George is like sweet poison for my soul, like a wound I never want to heal. I am a locked room no one else can enter. No one but him. It's not a question of having the key; no one else even knows the room is there.

I am on all fours now, my body bent forward over the leather padding, a trembling figure composed of right angles. George gently spreads my legs and I sigh, wanting to be touched. He draws a finger down between my cheeks, making me shiver, but he doesn't go any further. Instead, he arranges my legs how he wants them and I feel something cold and smooth against my right ankle. A strap. I hear the creak of leather as he pulls it tight and buckles it. He does the same to my left ankle and then both thighs, just above the knees. A wide thick strap goes across my lower back, holding me firmly in place. It sets my heart pounding even more. Lastly, he guides my arms down by my sides and buckles them into the cuffs dangling from the sides of the bench. I strain against my bonds, testing their strength, confirming that I am well and truly helpless. My heart is racing.

I try to calm myself, but my breathing only comes in short panting gasps. I'm afraid, but I also want to please him.

"Good girl," he says, as though reading my mind, sensing my need for reassurance. "You will make me proud, won't you?"

All I can do is nod. I don't know the rules of the game. All I know is that I trust him. I love him madly and I trust him absolutely. He knew more about my body in one night than my husband did after ten years. He awakened things in me. He brought me to life. I am his, completely.

"I'm going to whip you now, Julie."

A bright flash of panic leaps in my chest and I feel light-headed. His voice is low and cultured, as soothing as it is exciting. I feel my sex responding as it always does to his words and his touch. Tingling, dampening, hungering.

I am helpless. I have allowed myself to be helpless. A single word from me could stop all this. He would release me and I could relax. No more dread, no more anxiety, no more edge.

And there it is. The edge. I don't want to call it off, don't want to be back in control of myself. I don't want to be reminded of reality with all its sorrows and regrets. It's terrifying, but I want to be terrified. I need to feel alive. A freezing wave of fear surges through my mind, plunging me into the unknown.

I am vaguely aware of a tickling sensation as George trails something over my back. I know immediately that it is a whip. The softness of the tails belies the severity I suspect they are capable of, the pain they will produce, the cries they will wrench from my throat. But this is pain I have chosen, pain I've wanted. It's the kind of pain only a lover can give. The kind of pain that heals and cleanses, that washes away the stains.

"What do we say, Julie?"

His voice is even softer than the velvety tails of the whip. And although I have never spoken the words before, I know exactly what he wants me to say.

"Please whip me."

He doesn't say anything in response, but I sense he is nodding to himself, pleased at my total surrender, proud of me for my absolute trust. I hear the swish of the tails as he draws back and I hold my breath, waiting. When the whip falls lightly across my upper back I utter a little squeak of surprise but not pain. It was just a kiss. The feeling is an alien sensuality, scary but exquisite.

Another stroke falls, this one a little harder. This time there is the promise of more. A deep glow infuses me and I imagine I am being painted with warmth. The haunting music continues and I let it flow over and around me like water, seducing me away from unwelcome thoughts just as George seduced me away from my unhappy life, my dead marriage. Cool air caresses me as he draws back his arm for another stroke. I brace myself, sensing it will be harder this time. It is.

This time the whip lands with considerable force. The slap of the soft tails against my back is almost deafening in the little room. I writhe in my bonds, both frightened and exhilarated by my inability to escape. I cannot move in any way. I can flex my fingers and toes, tense my muscles, move my head from side to side . . . But I cannot escape. I am completely at his mercy. He is my master and I am his slave. An obedient little pet he will reward afterwards if I am good.

The loss of power, of responsibility, even of self, is nearly as intoxicating as the fear. It makes me weak with desire and I shudder as he drags the tails along my body again, teasing me, awakening me.

The air stirs as he raises the whip and brings it down again, this time across my bottom. I cry out, writhing over the bench. The pain flares brightly, spreading out along the sensitive nerves, becoming a hot steady pulse before fading to a warm glow. It is like being nipped by the sun.

Gradually, the pain dissolves into pleasure and I hear myself moaning, sighing, as though in the throes of fantastic sex, lost in this new way to fuck.

Another stroke. Another gasp. Another wave of strange bliss. If I weren't strapped down I might float away.

The tails of the whip explore every inch of my body, slapping me, licking me. Some of the strokes are gentle flicks, enough to make me whimper softly and wriggle. Others are laid on with a will, striking me sharply and forcing cries of pain from me. One particularly hard stroke makes me scream and I thrash in my bonds for several seconds, unable to absorb the sensation. He follows it with a volley of playful swishes, tickling my legs and feet with the ends of the tails until I am calmer. My sex throbs in concert with my burning flesh, my pounding heart.

And then he begins the process again, teaching me the limits of my own body. Each time I reach a level I think is more than I can take, he shows me that I can take more, that I want more.

He plays the whip over my legs, my arse and my back, building the intensity gradually until each stroke sounds like a pistol shot in the small room. He focuses on my upper back, delivering a barrage of hard strokes, each more severe than the one before it. At last I begin to scream in earnest. The pain is both terrible and exquisite and I find myself relishing the freedom to cry out, as though my only responsibility is to suffer.

Each stroke hits me like a wave, drenching me, drowning me in sensation. The music sounds as though it is reaching me through vast depths of water. At some point the lines begin to blur and I can no longer distinguish pain from pleasure. Both are equally stimulating, equally welcome. My entire being feels alive in a way I've never even imagined before. Tears stream down my face and time seems to be slowing down. I am weightless, drifting. No, I am flying.

It seems a long time before I register that I am no longer restrained, that George has unfastened the straps. I lie limply over the bench, breathing hard, my head buzzing with delirious bliss.

"My darling," George says.

His voice is my tether to sanity, to reality. Immediately, I dissolve into great gulping sobs once more, unable to speak, unable even to move.

I hear him laugh softly, a fond, affectionate sound, as he gathers me in his arms and lifts me up. I curl into his chest as he carries me across the room. I feel so small and fragile, as though I've shrunk to the size of a doll. Then there is the cool softness of silk sheets beneath me and I sink into the comfort of a bed, curling into a ball as my tears at last begin to subside. The blindfold is soaked with tears.

"Am I good?" I ask meekly.

I can hear the smile in his voice as he tells me that I am. "Such a good girl," he murmurs, kissing my tear-stained face. "Such a very good girl for your master."

Master. The word sends a jolt of excitement through me and I press my thighs together, feeling dizzy. If he doesn't take me soon I'll burst.

I feel his fingers behind my head and soon the blindfold slips away. I open my eyes and shut them again immediately, dazzled by the blazing light. Even the warm candlelight is too much. It takes a while for my eyes to adjust enough to let me look again and the love I see in his eyes makes me feel weightless all over again. I gaze at him as though at an apparition, a fantasy come to life.

"Are you real?" I ask, only half joking.

"I'm every bit as real as you," he tells me. He strokes my face, caressing my lips with his thumb. My tongue darts out to lick it and then I close my mouth over it, sucking and licking it as I would his cock.

He shuts his eyes with a little sigh and I feel him stiffen against me. In moments he is undressed and lying naked beside me. He turns me over onto my front and his hands stroke and caress my punished flesh, reawakening the sting of the whip. I writhe beneath his touch, part of me greedily craving more pain. But right now I want something else. I spread my legs for him, moving my hips to encourage his touch lower.

He runs a finger down the line of my spine and over the curve of my bottom, before finally slipping it down between my legs. I gasp at the contact. It's electric after so much torment and teasing. Gently, he caresses my sex, sliding his hand up and down along my dewy slit before finally pushing one finger inside. Then another. He pushes them deep, pressing the flat of his palm up against me and grinding it against my clit. I moan, thrilling to the stimulation. It won't take much to make me come.

He senses this and withdraws. I feel his weight shift on the bed and then he lifts me by the hips with one hand, shoving a pillow underneath me with the other. The position always makes me blush; it forces my back into an arch, my bottom raised and on display. I spread my legs wide for him, knowing he likes to see everything.

"Good girl," he says.

At last I feel the warm pressure of his cock against my sex and I push back against him, urging him in fast and deep. I'm more aroused than I have ever been in my life. His cock fills me, sending a powerful jolt of pleasure through my entire body. And he fucks me with savage passion, every hungry thrust intensifying the sweet pain of the whipping. My throat is raw but I cry out again, overwhelmed at last by the chance to scream his name without worrying who might hear. This moment belongs completely to us.

Again and again, he pounds into me, exciting me past reason, past caring. At this moment we are the only two people in the world and we exist only for each other. I tense myself around his cock and hear him sigh with pleasure. I writhe against him, twisting my hips the way he likes, grinding against him as his thrusts become ever more urgent and frantic.

My cries turn to wild animal sounds as I come, shuddering and gasping with release. His own climax follows fast behind mine and he empties himself into me with sharp hot jets that prolong the spasms and twinges battering me from inside. I collapse in a sweaty heap, gasping for breath, lost in the moment.

I barely notice when he rises and dresses. I lie exhausted and peaceful, listening to the music, watching the shadows leap on the wall, forming fantastic shapes. They might be the ghosts of our passion, enacting a spectral dance just for us.

After a while I turn onto my side, wincing a little at the pain.

George is sitting on the edge of the bed, watching me intently, studying me. After a little while his sombre gaze begins to unnerve me and suddenly I worry that something is wrong. Then he speaks.

"I've left my wife."

His words are unexpected and at the same time they are no surprise at all. They are the words all women in my position yearn to hear but never actually believe they will. Tears well in my eyes as new vistas open before me. Free. We could both be free, be together. No more furtive trysts, no more lies, no more guilt. No more secrets.

He smiles, a wistful, rueful little grin. I kiss him and he crushes himself to me, reawakening the pain from the whipping. I feel both purged and strengthened. I know now what today has been about. George pulls away to meet my eyes.

"I haven't hurt you too much, have I?" he asks.

"No, of course not. I feel . . . euphoric. I never knew it was possible to feel like this."

"Neither did I. I never imagined I could do that to anyone, especially not to you. I'm afraid you have quite a few marks."

No doubt my back is criss-crossed with welts and bruises. The thought only excites me more. "I'll cherish every one," I say.

"No, I meant – they won't be easy to hide."

I smile. His courage has inspired my own and the experience of suffering at the hands of my lover has actually made me stronger. I feel invincible, immortal. "I'm not hiding anything any more. I want to be with you. We belong together."

"Really?"

My heart begins to pound with a strange mixture of fear and excitement. I love who I am with George. I love my openness, my trust, my submission. I cherish the vibrant and passionate woman I become in his arms. I can't condemn myself – and my husband – to a lifetime of misery. I can't face the thought of looking back on my life when I'm old, my heart filled with regrets, my soul rotten with resentment. Sometimes pain is necessary for the comfort that lies beyond it.

I nod. "Tonight," I say. "I'll tell him it's over."

The words are terrifying. But the idea that we can both have a new life, our own life, fills me with hope. I feel as though I'm emerging from a tomb, realizing that I'm not dead after all, despite being walled up for so many lonely years. My body begins to tremble as George gathers me in his arms and holds me tight. With him I can be completely vulnerable. I can let go and fall and know I'll be caught. I can be the centre of his world, just as he is the centre of mine.

I start to cry again, tears of joy and tears of release. He kisses them away, murmuring words of love and comfort. And I listen with my soul as he tells me all about how our life is going to be. Together.

Cities of Water

Maxim Jakubowski

This is the story of how I became a slave. The story of a man who loved women too much and in the process learned the art of disappearing.

It is a true story.

It is a figment of my imagination.

It is a fairy tale, even.

It all happened in the cities of water.

AMSTERDAM

"Hold my hands down," she said, a hint of desperation in the thin stream of her voice.

Her body was under mine, a cushion of unbearable softness.

My cock was inside her, slipping and sliding pleasingly within her hot voluptuousness. Feeling the beginning of cramp in my left leg, I had just adjusted my position and accidentally pinned her down as I altered my stance, fearful of crushing her. I was overweight. She was so deliciously slim.

I froze.

"Harder," she said.

I was unsure, taken aback by her reaction, my concentration disturbed, worried I might lose my hardness.

We were both married to others and had arrived separately in late evening in Amsterdam from London on separate planes, meeting up as arranged in the Schipol arrivals bookstore. The hotel bordered a large canal a stone's throw from the Central Train Station. Barges were moored on either side of it, and bicycles parked in studied disarray along its cobbled banks. The breakfast room, that morning, had offered a buffet of assorted cheeses, cold cuts of charcuterie and thin slices of *saucisson sec*, alongside white fake porcelain jars full of orange – red as blood – and opaque grapefruit juices. The smell of the coffee simmering away in the Pyrex dish in the downstairs breakfast lounge had percolated through to our first-floor bedroom and woken us earlier than we'd wished. So, we'd gone and grabbed a quick bite and then returned to bed, as the morning sounds of the city began sweeping across the canal's dirty green waters.

Her name was Eddie.

And no, it isn't her real name. But she will recognize herself when she reads these lines.

My open palms pressed against hers and her long-fingered hands sunk further into the fabric of the bed.

Eddie moaned quietly.

We kept on fucking.

A sheen of sweat washed over her forehead, her eyes retreating into an ocean of thoughts I could hardly fathom.

Her throat pulsed.

I shifted my weight and her hands escaped from my uncertain grip. Instinctively, I moved to control them again and pushed them back behind her head and applied further pressure.

On our arrival in the hotel room the previous evening, we had frantically undressed each other as if catching up for lost time. Eddie had quickly fallen to her knees and taken me into her mouth and impaled herself furiously on my cock, greedily inviting me to thrust as fiercely as I wanted into the back of her throat. Once or twice she had gagged and I'd had to moderate my thrusts only to see her voluntarily throw herself against my midriff in an attempt to swallow me to the hilt notwithstanding the possibility of puking. There was a desperation about her. In me too. Releasing all the tension of the past weeks, the plans, the lies, the wanting.

I had come too early, unable to control the stirrings of lust overcoming my cock, spilling inside her mouth and, due to tiredness, had then been unable to get hard again and we had quickly both fallen asleep.

"Tie me down," Eddie rasped.

In thrall to the moment, the sheer wilful power of her desire surged across me and no further words proved necessary. I magically understood what she craved for. On the occasion of our previous encounters, the questioning, beckoning and unexpressed look in her eyes had so often hinted at invisible yearnings I had until now been unable to interpret properly.

I briefly withdrew from her and rolled over to the side of the bed where I had dropped my clothes and pulled the black leather belt from my trousers, returned to my earlier position, straddling her, took hold of her hands and tightened the belt around them as tight as I could. Eddie remained silent, spread below me, open, hungry.

I entered her again with barely a pang of guilt. I had never done this to a woman before, even if right now it felt so natural, arousing some primeval instinct inside me and unholy scenarios ran uncontrolled through my mind.

Sure, I had seen my share of hardcore movies and clips, but had always found the periphery of BDSM more comical than serious. And, as for spanking, one of its mildest if most common characteristics, it had always seemed to me to verge on the ridiculous. Deep down, I just couldn't see the attraction of spanking or being spanked.

For just a second, I realized I was venturing into new territory. Crossing a bridge with no way back, as if a new me was being born . . . And Eddie was actively encouraging me, demanding that I treat her this way.

Later, I would ask her why, in an attempt to rationalize the proceedings and the way it affected our nascent relationship.

"Being out of control and powerless makes me love you even more. It's a question of trust," she said.

Only now do I understand her fully.

On that Amsterdam morning as the quiet flow of a hundred and more canals lullabied our dark embraces and of no doubt a thousand further fucks happening all across the city, we abandoned rationality and followed the call of pleasure as we had never done before. Eddie no longer had to suggest the next steps in our wonderful escalation or even locate the right words, as basic instinct took over and I began running down that slippery slope, guessing, doing, dominating her and finding all the right buttons to push.

Even now, my whole body sings electric as I recall the way my fingers wrapped themselves against the soft velvet of her throat in the semblance of a choke and the way her eyes shone as a gentle, measured form of pressure was applied against her carotid and the implicit trust she gifted me as I controlled her breath and her whole body bucked wildly against mine as we shared the danger and the lust.

Inserting finger after finger inside the juicy wetness of her cunt until my whole fist was luxuriating inside the intoxicating warm cavern of her innards, and each successive movement of my wrist launched terrible tremors throughout her body, turning her into an epileptic but happy mess, sighs and moans orchestrating a grateful song of abandon, deep orgasmic calls taking birth in the deepest part of her lungs and escaping like perfumed breath through her thin lips.

Brutally turning her round on the bed, forcing her onto all fours and taking aim with my cock and diving into her with a hand around her hair, pulling, riding her like a wild west stallion, observing as I did so the thin golden down at the outset of the valley of her buttocks grow damp with perspiration, golden corn illuminated by the sun of my lust.

The pink imprint of my fingers against the white alabaster of her rump, not a spanking comedy but a rough serenade, where every blow fell against her soft skin like the rhythm of wind breath, the melody of our lovemaking, the sounds rising from her throat, the metallic haziness bathing her eyes, the limpness of her limbs, the surrender, the life.

The dampness of the bed sheets as we tangled with them,

pulling them, tearing them, staining them, the smell of our conjoined bodies, the agony of knowing this couldn't last forever and that it somehow could never get better, the joy.

Minutes and hours that will stay with me forever, and that changed me into what I have now become.

We only spent two further days in Amsterdam and, when not fighting our Holy War in the hotel bedroom, followed all the obligatory tourist footsteps: visits to museums, canal boat excursions, *rijsttafels*, shopping, the flower market, the Atheneum Bookshop, Rembrandtplein, wanders through the Red Light District with wide open eyes, Vondelpark, where we stole a quick fuck under cover of growing darkness and convenient bushes, encouraged by the sounds of other lovers in close proximity, excited by the fear of discovery, one of the many Argentinian steak houses, the Nieuwe Zijd, but all that is now a blur. What I do remember is that outside the room, we barely spoke, as if our actions now spoke for us and we had no need for further communication and certain things were now unspoken. We'd arrived in Amsterdam as adulterers and left it as lovers.

Within a month, we had broken up, after Eddie's husband found out about our affair in curious circumstances and applied understandable pressure for her to give their marriage a further chance. Maybe they should even try for a baby? To cut a long story short, they had to resort to IVF and some years later finally had twin girls and maybe even lived happily ever after for all I know.

Having fortuitously unveiled and witnessed her deep sense of submission at such intimate range and experiencing how strong it was, I can't help wondering if there are days when she now feels she is living a lie?

NEW ORLEANS

God only knows the time I spent, after losing Eddie, speculating about her character and attempting to understand why the latent submissiveness I had triggered within her had had such a strong effect on me. I knew I was no dominant and felt no compulsion to experiment and try the same things I had done with Eddie in the heat of ardour with other women. Nor was I tempted to explore BDSM and its dubious world. Leather, latex, handcuffs and ropes didn't attract me in the slightest, or the theatrical make-believe of its more formal activities.

What had moved me so much about Eddie was the total trust she had shown when encouraging me, prompting me to move into this new – for me – realm of dominance and submission. It was a form of love and it just damn broke my heart.

I knew I was made of the same raw material.

Throughout my life I had so often fallen in love with love itself and opened myself a hundred per cent to its grip, even when all the warning signs had been flashing.

It nagged me.

On and on.

I met other women. We made love. Parted. But it was not the same as with Eddie. I became more of an expert at detecting the essence of submission in the women I came across. There was the American intern journalist at the *Sunday Times* whose body, when I undressed her, on the stone garden back steps of an Islington semi-detached, was covered in bruises from a previous encounter with her dom when he had visited her from home the weekend before. The opera singer in New York who wanted me to share her with other men. The Asian chemistry student who was ashamed of the stretch marks on her stomach and would only let me fuck her from behind. The Essex middle-aged bank assistant manager who participated in gangbangs in a hotel close to Victoria Station and invited me to watch. I did. Each new woman was different, singularly unique, and I wanted so hard to understand them, as if understanding what drove them would be a way of owning them once and for all. I was mixed-up and unhappy.

The imagination is a terrible tool. I began to speculate what it would be like to be on my knees in front of a relative stranger and take his cock in my mouth. What it would taste like. What sensation being penetrated felt, both at the point of entry and in my gut, my heart. As if I wanted to be a woman myself in order to understand women, submissives, experience that feeling of both abandon and trust they explored each time they gave in to a man.

It became an obsession.

I was in New Orleans on business and the heady atmosphere of dissipation of the city was getting to me.

I was lonely. I missed Eddie. Like hell.

Walking down Bourbon Street, I was serenaded by the sounds of duelling guitars and bass from either side of the road, the rotten smell of stale beer blending with the spices from nearby vats of gumbo or crawfish stewing in restaurant kitchens. People were drunk and merry. Beyond Jackson Square the Mississippi ran, mud churning in its wake, a calliope piping out a mechanical tune on one of the tourist wheeled steamboats, the *Natchez* or the *Cajun Queen*. My mind was held in a vice of memories and longing.

Escaping from the crowds, I darted into the nearest door. An oyster bar called Desire, which was attached to the Royal Sonesta Hotel. I'd normally go to the Pearl, but had no desire to fight my way through the joviality all the way to Canal Street.

There was a young woman at a nearby table. She was in her early twenties and accompanied by two tall, clean-cut guys in Abercrombie & Fitch shirts and beige slacks. She appeared bored, sucking her ice-drowned soda through a straw. Her hair fell to her shoulders, dark blonde and silky. She wore a white pleated shirt. She caught me gazing at her and smiled back. They were all eating jambalaya, yellow hillocks of rice spilling from their plates.

It was difficult to read her smile, though I sensed loneliness. But I also knew there was no way of making her acquaintance. New Orleans was a friendly place, but not one where a middle-aged man could steal her away under the nose of two companions in the heart of Vieux Carré; one a boyfriend and the other her brother maybe? Or both her lovers? My mind briefly ran amok.

It didn't take me long to finish my oyster platter and there was no point waiting for the trio to end their meal. What was I going to do – follow them, stalk her? I slowly walked back to my hotel on Toulouse Street.

My laptop was, as ever, in sleep mode. I opened the lid.

I felt desperate for . . . something.

The odds were high that the young woman full of sadness in the oyster bar had a core of submissiveness at her centre. But I would never know her. Understand her. Be like her.

It was an adult chat room.

An hour later, there was a knock at my hotel room door.

He was in his late forties and had light brown hair and a small Mephisto-like beard and moustache set, was average height and wore a grey suit. He held a shapeless attaché case by his side.

As instructed earlier, I looked down at the floor and avoided his eyes, as he looked me up and down in a stern fashion.

He slammed the door shut behind him and I knew another metaphorical bridge had been crossed and there was no turning back.

There was a moment of heavy silence.

"Undress," the dom said. There was a harshness to his voice that chilled me. I began to unbutton my shirt and, as I was doing so, partly turned and was quickly corrected.

"Facing me."

I adjusted my position.

Bending over to slide out of my pants, I saw his hands moving to the attaché case and open it. He pulled out what appeared like a variation on a ping-pong bat. A paddle, I recognized.

"You will always address me as 'Sir', and never speak unless spoken to," he ordered.

I nodded silently, straightening, naked in his presence, my cock limp and minimal, almost retreating into my balls as he cast a critical eye on me, appraising me like a piece of meat.

"So, you're the one who wants to be a sub?" he said.

"Yes," I quickly said, obediently.

He struck me on the thigh with the paddle. It stung. "Yes what, cunt?"

I realized my mistake. "Yes, Sir."

His hand reached down and cupped my testicles, as if weighing them. I shuddered.

"Turn round and display your fat arse."

I did so. His nimble fingers traced patterns on my now cold buttocks. He was still fully dressed. He gave me a gentle pat on the left side, as if satisfied by my docility.

"Bend over. Leaning above the bed." I followed his instructions, self-consciously holding my stomach in. The sounds of revellers roaming the French Quarter spilt into the room. The window was half open. I waited.

The paddle made contact with my buttocks and I flinched.

Then the dom struck me again. And again. I bit my lip. It hurt. More than I thought it would. Online, as he'd warned me what to expect from our encounter, I had briefly protested that I was not into pain and had no wish to be spanked or punished and he had summarily dismissed my protests. "You don't choose, boy," he had typed, the words flashing across my laptop screen. "It's all or nothing. Either you're a sub or you're not." Reluctantly, I had agreed to his non-negotiable terms. I wanted to know how it would feel to submit to a man. The way Eddie and other women had to me, albeit in more natural circumstances and a tender, laid-back, relaxed way in which emotions and affection came to the fore.

I gritted my teeth. My whole backside stung, a sensation that gradually settled down, unpleasant, annoying, but as the pain spread evenly across my skin, diminishing in intensity.

"Nice," the grey-bearded dom said, perusing the redness of my arse cheeks and admiring his handicraft and I absurdly pictured him in a badly lit lecture hall in an obscure regional university pontificating on some arcane and quite irrelevant academic subject.

"Stand."

I rose. Once again, he cupped my balls as I faced him, with a smirk of self-satisfaction, as if he owned them, me and had ulterior motives that were soon about to be unveiled. They would.

"On your knees, boy."

I lowered myself to the hotel room floor.

"Worship me," he ordered.

I was nonplussed.

Irritated by my open-mouthed passiveness, he swatted me across the cheek with the back of his hand.

"Suck my cock." He raised his voice.

And just stood there, waiting.

I raised my hands towards his trousers and busied myself undoing his belt and then pulling the zip down, revealing a pair of blue-striped boxer shorts, beneath which the substantial mound of his cock and balls lay nested. I was about to hesitantly slip a finger in the opening in order to extract his penis when he halted me.

"Lick it first. Through the material. Carefully."

My lips approached, taking the thin cotton of the boxer shorts between them and then reaching for the genitalia underneath it and began licking. The texture felt rough to my tongue and I could feel the growing firmness of his penis as my oral ministrations grew in confidence. Until I knew he was rock hard inside the tent of his shorts. I was unsure what to do next and continued licking the cotton and sensing the pulse of his cock beneath it.

"Now. Suck."

The hard, straight cock had buried itself in the folds of the boxer shorts and it took me two fingers to pull it free.

He was not circumcised, his glans peering fiercely through a thin corridor of wrinkled skin. A wild palette of colours, moving from pink to light brown to red, purple and beyond. Another man's cock. Up close.

Slowly, I moved my lips towards it.

It was both firm and soft, velvet-hued, scarred and heavy-veined to the touch of my tongue.

Oh, Eddie, was this the way it felt to you? Tasted. Hardening further under the wet tip of your teasing tongue?

The dom took hold of my head and patiently guided my movements until I had most of him inside my mouth. I panicked, hoping my gag reflex would not be triggered too early, if at all.

I sucked a man for the first time. Relying on the sweet memories of all the women who had sucked me before. Taking care to distribute my caresses equally, my licks even-handedly roaming across the round mushroom-head tip, the ridge, the trunk, the birth of the pole, even halting briefly to lick and then swallowing his heaving shaven balls. I'd had good teachers, I knew.

I was hoping he wouldn't come in my mouth. Felt I wasn't quite ready for that yet.

Finally, he tired of my sucking him and gave me a tap on the top of the head.

"Enough," he said. "Stand now." I did. "Turn round and face the bed and bend over."

My heart jumped.

But I meekly obeyed his instructions.

"Spread your legs."

I heard him fetching something from his bag and then felt his breath on my neck.

He kicked my legs further apart and shackled my left ankle to a contraption he had just retrieved from his sack of treasures, and pulled on the connecting stick and I recognized a spreader bar as he attached my other ankle to its opposite end. The angle between my legs was now permanent. I hoped I wouldn't cramp.

One of the dom's fingers glided across my arsehole and probed. My sphincter muscles clinched in automatic reaction.

"Relax," he said.

"I hope you're clean." he continued. I had been ordered, prior to his arrival, to wash my anus, inside and out, which for lack of the right implements in the hotel room I had attempted to do with limited chances of optimum cleanliness. "I'm going to fuck the shit out of you, boy," he had written, "but not literally. LOL

. . . So prepare yourself well. Or else . . ."

The shard of a calliope tune, skimming across the streams of the Mississippi, reached the room, distant, triumphant, journeying across the surrounding waters of the Gulf of Mexico, Lake Ponchartrain and the flimsy levees, which uncertainly protected the city. A melody to accompany my being sodomized for the first time.

Another finger, or maybe it was the dom's cock, pressed against my reluctant opening, evaluating my natural resistance to its thrust.

"Damn, you're tight, boy," he said. "Let's see to that."

Behind my back, I heard him foraging again in the bag he had brought along. Out of the corner of my eye, I saw him holding a small jar, which he unscrewed and liberally dipped his fingers inside. It wasn't lubricating oil but a thick white cream.

Before I could utter a word, he began spreading the cold cream around my anus and continued swiftly massaging it into my ball sac and the root of my cock and my perineum.

Within seconds, I was screaming. It had only taken an instant for the cold cream to turn red hot and I felt like the whole lower half of my body was on fire, burning like hell. I shook but was unable to move, my legs held tight apart by the spreader bar.

"Quiet, boy," he said. And stuffed a red handkerchief in my mouth to muzzle my sounds of pain. It felt as if lit matches were being paraded under my balls and the flames were reaching out and dousing my cock and arse. It was excruciating. A tear rolled down my cheek. This was not what I had signed up for. No way.

I bit hard against my tongue.

And then he forced himself inside me. As I was unceremoniously breached the dimension of pain doubled. I closed my eyes and tried to detach myself from my own body and survive the scene, observing the sheer pornography of what was taking place, the thrust of a hard cock through the puckered, stretched, reddened hole of what the dom now called my cunt, the shades of white of my bent-over middle-aged body and the humiliating stance I was obliged to hold, my head buried into the bedcover, my arse raised, my legs obscenely held apart.

The pain began to fade, and I became increasingly aware of the piston-like movement of another man's penis in my entrails.

And, to my immense shame, my own cock began to harden.

I had crossed the frontier.

As Eddie had once done.

Later, after he had sated his lust, the dom unshackled my ankles and led me, stumbling, to the adjoining bathroom, opened the shower and pushed me into the bathtub, and, accusing me of having been unclean and soiled his cock, peed over me. Again, an unsettling feeling. Liquid heat. Being marked. Then he left me lying there, the water washing across me, stealing my sins and my confusion away.

I needed fresh air. That night, rather than lingering in bars, savouring more oysters and listening to music, I took a slow stroll down to the river and walked all the way from the Café du Monde to the Algiers Ferry terminal, listening to the night sounds of the quiet waters.

And thought of Eddie and wondered if now I understood her better.

VENICE

Over several years, I had encounters with other tops, doms, Masters. I got little pleasure or satisfaction from the sex but was drawn to the submission, the ritualized humiliation and even when I so often decided right after a particular scene that this would once and for all be the last I got myself involved in, I would then suffer an odd form of nostalgia and craving and would venture out into the demi-world of BDSM again at some stage.

My mind yearned for the rituals of submission, even when my body proved indifferent to its scars.

I had given up attempting to understand my nature. Was I just seeking taboo thrills or was I punishing myself for all the women I had failed to know, to understand, to love properly?

In the gay area of a Spanish nude beach, thirty minutes south of Barcelona, where many of the men wore cock rings and displayed piercings, I allowed myself to be picked up by another dom. He was a cruel man, but he was clever enough to see me for what I was.

One night in the nearby dunes, he fixed a dog collar around my neck and connected it to a thin red leather leash and guided me naked through the sands in his wake and displayed me publicly and had me service other men. I was scared throughout the happening, sexually indifferent to their cocks and varied penetrations, but excited by the level of submission I had willingly reached. I travelled back to England after the vacation, separated from my wife and one day Ivan rang me and ordered me to join him in Venice the following month where he would be celebrating the Carnival.

"You will become my slave," he said. "I think you are ready."

I thought so too.

The Grand Canal shimmered in the sun, triangulated by embarkations in all sizes and shapes navigating their way up and down its stream, gondolas, vaporettos, barges, private motorboats, as the countless historical Palazzi bordering the Canal glittered like gold in the shadows of the bridges.

Beyond the Canal and St Mark's lay the lagoon, deep, majestic like an inner sea, pockmarked with small islands, a world of ancient fishing shores, mental asylums, cemeteries and abandoned churches.

It is to one of these islands almost forgotten by the maps, that I will be taken tonight as my Master's slave.

I was picked up by his Russian chauffeur at Marco Polo Airport and led to a motorboat moored nearby. We crossed the lagoon at dusk, until we reached a smaller, narrow canal into which we floated with the engine now switched off, after which we drifted towards a nearby set of stone steps that led up to a crumbling Palazzo which had no doubt witnessed better days.

Up a set of stairs to a cavernous hall, where my luggage was taken from me and I was stripped naked. Ordered to stand still, I waited for my Master to join or greet me. But it was the bulky uniformed chauffeur who returned and placed his massive hands around my neck and measured the circumference of my neck before escorting me to a nearby alcove where a camp bed had been placed. Then he locked me in.

My sleep was uneasy.

I was woken early in the morning. Dirty white clouds hovered over the canal outside my window, a restricted panorama of wet stones and stagnant waters.

The chauffeur handed me a plate with two thin slices of rye bread and a jug of water. There were also a couple of pills next to the food. When I enquired about their nature, I was informed they were extra vitamins to strengthen me for the trials ahead.

"Is that all?" I reacted.

"The Master wants you to slim down and be in better shape. A slave's sloppiness reflects badly on its owner," he remarked in a pronounced Eastern European accent and left me to my own devices, locking the door to the miniscule room behind him as he departed.

Maybe the water had been spiked as I quickly fell asleep again shortly after I had taken a sip from it.

This continued for several days and yes, I did lose weight and slept a lot. Questions were visibly unwelcome when the bulky chauffeur visited with the bread and water and to take the chamber pot in which I had no choice but to pee and shit.

My mind was blank.

The Master had warned me that it would take a few weeks to have me trained properly.

I was finally led out of the room after eight days of loneliness with only my own thoughts and the pitiful spectacle of my own thinning body for company. The room I was escorted to was draped with lush Persian carpets on walls and floor.

At the centre of the room stood a small oak circular table on which a couple of sheets of A4 white paper lay. My Master was standing by the table, fierce, imposing. He looked me over.

"This is your slave contract," he said, without a word of greeting. "Please sign it." He handed me a silver Parker ball-point pen.

I quickly glanced at the text, then signed at the bottom of the second page.

"You didn't read it," the Master remarked.

"I didn't, Sir," I replied. "There is no need. I trust you."

"Good," he said. "I do think you'll work out," he remarked, with a satisfied smile. "Come."

I sucked his cock. He came in my mouth. I obediently swallowed. Somehow his taste changed in subtle ways every time.

The chauffeur returned to the room, spread my legs, and plugged my arsehole with a stone object, and I was led back to my alcove. I was being stretched for further use by the Master or others of his choice, I knew.

The following day, I returned to the carpeted room and a young woman, with cascading blonde hair who reminded me a little of Eddie, awaited me.

The oak table on which I had signed away my life was no longer present and a large, elongated copper bathtub on art deco claw-like feet was now the room's centrepiece. She nodded to me and I stepped into the bathtub and she washed me with water from a tall jug standing by the bathtub. Throughout she remained mute. The smell of her so close to me, and the way her hands moved like quick-fire across my bare skin, soaping me, cleansing me, caressing me even, invading my private creases, was intoxicating and I was unable to prevent an erection, my first in ages. She ignored it, with not a hint of emotion crossing her face.

As she wiped the final soapsuds away from my body, the Master walked into the room, his dark presence eclipsing the warmth of her nearby body.

"Proceed," he said to the young woman, as I stood there still, my feet bathing in now tepid water, naked, blushing, my hard cock standing proud at an angle from my body like a flag attached to a flagpole.

I looked away from him and saw that the young woman was now holding an elongated old-fashioned barber's razor in her outstretched hand. She took hold of my cock in her left fist and raised the implement. I swallowed hard. Should I have read the damn contract?

My blood ran cold.

But before I had a chance to speak or draw back, the blade fell and, holding my rapidly shrinking cock away from its edge, the attractive blonde began clearing my nearby pubic hair away. Her hand was steady. Experienced. Had she done this before? After she had scraped away my thatch, she then calmly proceeded to take my ball sac between her fingers and, similarly, shave it clean. Small clumps of dark curls floated down into the bathtub in which I stood, glued to the spot. When the time came to eliminate the remaining stray hairs around my genitalia from the epicentre of my anus, she deftly pulled out the plug that was obstructing her swift movements and carefully navigated the ridges and bumps of the area with the blade. It only took her a few seconds and then she expertly reinserted the butt plug in its appointed place.

By now I was uncomfortably soft again.

The girl's face showed absolutely no emotion.

My midriff was now totally smooth and hairless.

But her work was far from over and she cleaned the blade on a cloth she held by her side and brought the blade back towards my body and began forcibly scraping the hair from my chest.

Half an hour later, she had completed shaving my whole body. Chest. Back. Shoulders. Legs. I was well on the way to becoming a living doll.

But the task was far from over.

With a simple gesture, under the watchful eyes of the Master, she applied gentle pressure to my shoulders and wordlessly communicated to me that I now had to get down on my knees. Where she shaved away all the hair from my head. I felt bereft. Never had I been so totally naked, having always sported a full head of hair and unruly curls. I ached to see myself in the mirror now, although the idea of gazing at myself hairless and totally bald gave my heart a sinking, terrible feeling.

But still she continued.

And even eliminated my eyebrows.

She was fast, professional, an angel of follicle devastation. I remained on my knees, feeling despair and utter vulnerability and she stepped away and exited the room, leaving me alone with the Master.

"Stand," he ordered.

I did.

I had become a grown-up, helpless doll of flesh.

He moved behind me and pulled out the plug blocking my rear entrance.

And then he fucked me relentlessly, every movement inside my churning guts a reminder of what I now was.

The following day, the chauffeur awoke me in the heart of the night with his rough hands around my neck and pulled me up from the rudimentary bed I had been allowed. He then fixed a black leather studded dog collar around my neck; it fitted perfectly, no doubt crafted from his initial measurements on my arrival in Venice. There was no buckle to close it, just two metal bars, which he proceeded to solder together, the heat of his appliance grazing my skin.

Later, he and the young silent woman entered my cell and I was ordered to lie on my stomach, my hands were bound and my right buttock was tattooed, a procedure which caused little pain. On completion, I was allowed to briefly view the result in a small mirror the young woman pulled out from the side pocket of her curve-hugging green skirt.

It was a bar code. Black on white.

I was now owned.

I wanted badly to see the rest of myself – the living doll,

smooth all over, almost sexless bar the stain of my limp, hairless cock, I had become, but this was denied to me.

Tonight I will be taken to the island where my Master says I will begin my life as a slave.

It will be dark and the moon will reflect deceptively like a light in shadows across the surface of the lagoon, and the domed skyline silhouette of La Serenissima will fade behind us in the distance.

Tonight I will become a part of the cities of water.

I will be water.

And I will miss you so, Eddie.

Money

Clarice Clique

I laid the money out on the old wooden kitchen table between us, taking time, licking my fingers as I separated the wad of notes and placed them down for him to see. Ben gazed over his glass of cheap red wine at me; one eyebrow raised, his dark eyes teasing, a half-smile playing over his lips but never quite settling into a definite expression.

He'd been the same since our school days; most of the girls that flocked around him thought his coolness came from his classic movie star good looks and athletic build. But even then I'd seen his real attraction was in the easiness of his bearing. He flowed along with life as if he had no care what direction he went. No, it was more like whichever direction he went was inherently the right one. Even now, with his modelling career mysteriously dried up (however, hard I pushed him, bribed him, for an answer all he'd do was shrug), and his acting career yet to materialize, he seemed completely relaxed with his life.

In keeping with that part of his character, he liked to appear casual at these times, unconcerned, as if the cash had nothing to do with him. But I knew from experience he was counting it all with more skill than any savant, making quick calculations in his head concerning what combination of things I might ask him to do tonight.

If he counted correctly, and he always did, he would have worked out I could ask him to repeat anything we'd done so far, and more. A whole lot more. As I continued producing more money, his eyes widened for a clear moment before his expression settled back to its usual mask of casualness. When I placed the last note down, there was two thousand and fifty-five pounds on the table.

He took a deep breath, only a hint of excitement and surprise audible in his voice. "Someone has had a good week. You been flashing your tits at old men, promising a blowjob with every car they test drive?"

It amused him to pretend that he didn't understand my job as an executive for a very successful car manufacturer. He preferred to visualize me as some sort of seedy second-hand car dealer. And some days it amused me too. I played along with him, telling stories of me displaying myself on the forecourt in a barely there bikini, being everyone's favourite whore. Soaping cars down, covering my body with suds, pressing my breasts against the windows of shocked strangers' cars.

But not today.

I took ten notes off the table and screwed them back into my handbag.

"Like that today, is it? One of the old men spank your fat titties too hard, bite down on your nipples and leave his dentures behind?"

I ripped a note in half and let the pieces fall to the floor. "We've been playing this game long enough for you to know how to behave."

He leant back in his chair and gazed at me. "You're right we've been playing this game for long enough. How about we try a new one? I take you out for dinner, you wear a nice little black dress, I wear a smart suit. We exchange pleasantries, interact like people out on a date, get to know each other. You know, be a normal couple for once."

"I've been part of a normal couple. You know what a divorce costs. You're a much healthier economic option." I bit down on my lower lip, keeping my eyes on the stack of cash.

He gave a slight movement of his shoulders, so small that it didn't even qualify as his habitual indolent shrug.

"I'm in control. I decide what we do. What you do." I may have sounded like I was trying to convince myself. But it wasn't like that. This was a business transaction, like any other. I had the money; he gave me the goods. "You mentioned a dress, so why don't you be a good boy for once and go and put one on."

He rose from his chair and gave me a mock bow. "Is there any particular dress madam wishes me to adorn for her viewing pleasure?"

"You choose."

"Does my beloved Mistress desire me to wear stockings?"

"You should be capable of making such decisions for yourself by now."

"And what about panties? Would it please you to see me wearing your favourite panties?"

I deliberately looked away from him.

My "favourite panties" had cost over a hundred pounds. They were black lace strips fashioned into a garment that revealed more than it covered, the glossy catalogue had described them as "featuring an alluring derrière aperture". I'd pretended that I'd bought them especially for Ben. I'd made a ceremony out of gifting them to him, demanding his humble gratitude.

In reality, I had purchased them months before Ben and I had come to our particular arrangement. The panties dated back to the lost time when I still believed that some new lingerie could save my marriage.

Somehow I sensed that Ben knew my lie. There was no reason he should. But the way he smiled, the light mocking tone to his voice, made me blush as if I'd been caught out in a serious misdemeanour.

I dismissed him with a wave of my hand and he retreated without another word.

I didn't know why I put up with Ben. There were pages and pages of men on the internet who advertised themselves as escorts. I had tried several of them out:

Easy-going early twenties Danny, whose stated hobbies were socializing and car racing.

Cheeky Chris, who looked like a young Robert Redford

and kept his mind and body stimulated as a keen martial artist (both training and teaching).

Down-to-earth Neil, who was proud of serving his country and wanted a lady to feel safe and protected with him.

Silver fox Craig, interested in travelling, able to converse on an eclectic range of subjects, also a qualified tennis coach.

And tall Max, with a goofy smile and impeccable manners, who charged double what the others did.

Those were the ones I could still remember.

I tried to pretend that I didn't know why I put up with Ben.

With all the others, the situation had been the same: paying a man for sex. I always had the power, I put ten pound notes into their sweating hands, empty pockets, filled G-strings; I left crinkled notes on their bedside cabinet, thrown on the floor, dropped on the bed. I ordered them to do things that almost all of them would have done for free:

Massage.

Tongue-fucking.

Licking my toes.

Resting over my knee while I spanked them.

Lying naked, bound hand and foot on the floor, as I walked over their bare flesh in four-inch stiletto heels.

But it was never the same as with Ben.

Sometimes I came, other times I didn't. Always with the others though, even with the best of them, there was something mechanical, almost anaesthetic about the whole experience. It was kind of like that old Paul Newman quote – why go out for hamburgers when you have steak at home. Except it was more like wolfing down a cheap burger because your body's screaming out hunger and you don't have the time to invest in searching out a better meal. Instead of going out for an evening and having nothing to do but enjoy all the delicacies that a Michelin star chef places before you.

Occasionally, amongst the lies about being some sort of desperate masochistic whore who loved rubbing my tits around the cocks of customers, I told Ben the truth about being some sort of desperate sadistic nymphomaniac who needed to regularly nipple-clamp gigolos in order to get through the long lonely nights.

If Ben believed anything I said he never showed the slightest sign of jealousy.

I listened to Ben above me now in his spare bedroom. He took longer to get ready than any woman I'd ever met. I closed my eyes and imagined him squeezing his muscled body into a tight dress. I thought of him carefully colouring his chiselled, handsome face, with delicate pastel powders and rudely scarlet lipsticks and blushers.

It was with effort I resisted going upstairs to watch his preparations. I reminded myself of the thrill I got when he appeared before me in full costume and make-up.

When I heard his step on the stairs, the thump of my heart told me that I'd been right to wait. I swivelled the chair around so I faced the door.

He was dressed in a slinky black dress matched with knee-high red PVC boots. He wore no jewellery, apart from a pearl necklace. The necklace had once belonged to my mother. I tried not to think about that.

I gazed up and down his body and motioned for him to twirl around. It was a show of power, but it also enabled me to gain control of myself before I spoke. When he faced away from me though, and I could see the material clinging to his ass, the breath caught in my throat and my heart thumped even harder.

I'd had sex with many men who would have been considered as attractive as Ben, but every time I saw him like this, every single time, I felt like a young virgin yearning to see her first naked man.

Ben completed his turn and smiled at me. I never seemed to succeed in hiding the effect he had on me.

"Dance for me, bitch," I ordered in a voice more commanding than the whirl of hormones inside me should have allowed.

He moved his hips in small delicate motions. His hands were more expressive, telling stories of wonder and lust. And love.

I don't know why you haven't succeeded at everything you've ever done. You are the best amongst us, you are the one for whom dreams are supposed to come true. You are beautiful. You are wonderful. You always were.

Out loud my voice was harsh, all tenderness and awe suppressed. "I didn't come here for some prissy acting, I'm here for fucking. Dance like the bitch you are."

He laughed at me, not mocking, simply merriment. "Pardon me, Mistress, but you're too screwed up to be serious with. Your soul absolutely yearns for art, but you're so scared of real emotions, you'll pay a couple of quid and ride a roller coaster to get some fake thrills and pretend you're satisfied."

"Don't presume to know what I want. Or feel. Or do," I said. "And if you genuinely think someone is screwed up, it's all a joke to you, is it?"

"Laugh or cry. That's our choice." He shrugged his shoulders as if neither response truly mattered.

I swept a wad of cash back into my bag; most of it fell onto his floor. Probably where it would stick and stay until he got desperate. Despite his precision and care with some areas of cleanliness, there were places he never seemed to touch. Below my feet, on this lino, there were probably still traces of the last time I allowed him to spunk in this room. Such thoughts would disgust me with another person, but with him, it made me burn for his touch.

"I don't judge you, Mistress. I say what I see," he said.

"You are not a good slave. I'll take you to a party and let women who are not as generous as me use you."

"As you wish, whatever you wish." His voice was soft and I could almost believe his words were true.

"I will. One day I really will watch you get beaten." I was surprised by the fact that I was breathless, panting. "But now, dance like the bitch you are. That's what I commanded you to do and that's what you'll do."

He parted his lips in a mock glamour kitten pout and ground against the door frame with exaggerated hip thrusts.

It was always at moments, moments when he was both most like himself and least like himself, that I saw him as the schoolboy who winked at me whenever I walked past. The boy, who being fifteen months older than me, I'd viewed as the epitome of manliness. I gathered facts about him like they were rare treasures; he played in a local football team, never missing a match, but skived every PE lesson. His brother wore silver nail varnish and his sister was a slut or frigid depending who you asked. He won a national essay competition, writing about the elusiveness of nocturnal animals and walked his mongrel dog at 7 a.m. every morning. He spent lunch-times with the groups outside the chippie, but rarely ate anything himself. The clothes he wore were either just about to come into fashion, or were just falling out of fashion, and they always looked perfect on him.

When he saw Holly Baker and her friends tugging my bag away from me and throwing my books in the mud, he stopped and smiled his half-smile.

"Leave her alone, she's all right," he said. He picked my French textbook out of a puddle, wiped it on his shirt, passed it to me and walked on past.

And I fell in love.

I fell into the swirl of the one true romantic love, the love that has nothing to do with paying bills, ticking lists, compatibility, similar life goals, dinner parties, petty jealousies, arguing over washing up, or any of the crap that a marriage evolves into. I fell into the love where all you need is to smell the animal warmth of their body, feel their breath on your neck, and to gaze on the eternity of their smile.

"Is this what you want?" Ben bent backwards with fluid flexibility. "Is this what my Mistress desires?"

Yes.

No.

Yes.

I got up from my chair so quickly that it fell backwards onto the floor. I stepped over to him and grabbed his wrist. I pulled him to the table and pushed him backwards onto it. As if it was my physical strength that dictated what happened, as if I was the one in control. Wine spilt, staining the wood like blood. Notes of various denominations pressed against the sweat of his body. I ripped the front of his dress open, clawing my nails over his nipples. I pushed my body between his legs and rumpled the fabric up his firm thighs. My fists clamped around the heels of his boots and I forced his knees into his chest. My hips humped against his groin, every nerve in my cunt was alive. I imagined my clit growing and penetrating him through our clothes, through our skin.

My left hand had moved to his arse before I'd made any conscious decision about what I wanted to do. He was wearing my favourite panties, of course. If there was any chance left that I'd be gentle tonight, it vanished when he chose to adorn that tiny piece of lace. The material strained around the hardness of his cock. My fingers curled into a fist, I pounded between his ass cheeks as if there was no resistance. There was no resistance. He couldn't resist me. I was too many years of love, too many nights of yearning, too many times alone remembering his boyish smile.

The grip of his body around my fist made me believe that he wanted me as much as I wanted to be part of him. I scrambled onto the table, scraping my shoes against his bare skin, and sat on his face. The heat of his tongue, his mouth, searched for me. But I didn't need anything from him but his presence. I ground against the hard bone of his nose. I let my juices drip into his eyes. I rubbed myself over his hair.

My first fervent orgasm a nuclear bomb of destruction.

Except it was nothing like that. It was the first wave of a tsunami. The wind rattling the shutters before the hurricane breaks.

Without being fully aware that I'd moved away from him, I was emptying his cupboards out. I poured honey-hinted Greek yoghurt over his face, smeared smooth peanut butter over his chest, squeezed mayonnaise over his groin. I cracked eggs onto his nipples and splattered custard down his thighs. I threw fruit, bits of meat at him, at the walls. I broke bottles, cups, plates. Then, when I had the visual mess and chaos that I craved, I took his hand and led him up to his own bedroom.

Here he'd prepared for me correctly. All the tools were laid out neatly. I picked up the biggest dildo and he bent over without waiting for my command. It was tempting to fist him again, but I tried to keep to my initial decisions when I was with him. I pushed the toy into him without pausing for lube. Then he lay on his back as I cuffed his wrists to the metal bed frame. Then I pulled the boots off him, revealing clean skin in stark contrast to the rest of his body. He had put the heavy iron manacles out – at different times he'd told me that he'd got them off an ex, from a film set, or scavenged from a scrap yard. I didn't care. I relished putting the rusting metal against his beautiful skin.

I leant my forehead against the wall and, for a moment, I just breathed deeply, imagining an endless circle as my chest rose and fell.

Another moment's pause as I looked at the thin whip and spanking paddle he'd left out, before I rejected both of them and clambered astride him. I lowered my sex onto him, I enveloped him, I encompassed him, I squeezed him inside me.

He moaned gently.

I pressed my body against his, all the food and mess entangling my hair, dirtying my own skin. I could still smell the natural warmth of his body beneath the peanuts, wine, meat, fruit, yoghurt, everything else I'd covered him in; beneath the spice of his chosen aftershave and the citrus scent of his shower gel, I could still find him.

"Fuck me," he whispered. "Fuck me hard."

I sat upright and I fucked him.

I love you I love you I love you I love you I love you I love you I love you I love you I love you I love you I love you I love you I love you I love you I love you, I fucked him, *i love You, i love You, i love YOU.*

When his balls tensed and his face blanked in near ecstasy, I pulled away from him.

"Let me come, baby, Mistress, darling, baby. Let me come today. Please."

The "please" weakened me. With one hand, I straightened my appearance as best as I could, which was next to nothing, with the other hand I wanked him off. I barely needed to touch him, less than a dozen strokes, and he jetted over his stomach.

I wiped my fingers over his lips.

"This is for my pleasure, not yours," I said as he licked his come off my skin. "Understand?"

He nodded.

"Next time you'll get paid less and I expect more."

He nodded.

I undid the cuffs and manacles and walked out of the room before he recovered and started a conversation. Maybe asking me if I wanted to go on a normal date with him again. Maybe explaining that he didn't need the money any more, that he didn't need a "next time" to pay his bills.

I fetched my car keys out of my handbag, but left the bag itself and all the money it contained in his wrecked kitchen.

Vaniglia

Stella Knightley

Most of the time, I wasn't that enthusiastic about my job, but for one week in September last year, I was very excited about it indeed. The company I worked for was holding its annual international conference and I was going to be there. In Rome.

Well, not exactly in Rome, as it turned out, but in a fairly hideous conference hotel close to the airport, where we spent three days doing the sort of bonding exercises that make sticking pins in your eyes seem like fun. Outside, the Italian sun shone down its late summer blessings. Meanwhile, we were trapped inside a beige-walled room, with the kind of carpet that gives you electric shocks, where the air conditioning had been turned to "fast freeze" to spare the blushes of the fat execs whose shirts were stained with sweat patches the moment they were expected to do anything more strenuous than walk from the buffet to the breakfast table.

So, I shivered through three days of brainstorming, fire-starting and blue-sky thinking. I counted my goosebumps while the international head of marketing delivered the sort of exhortative speeches that, had he been a First World War general, would make you ready to go over the top only because death was preferable to the boredom. The only thing that kept me from impaling myself on a pencil was the thought of the weekend ahead.

I had persuaded the girl who was booking the conference travel to extend my plane ticket by two days. It wouldn't cost the company any more. In fact, I pointed out, because I would be staying a Saturday night, it would cost them slightly less.

'But we won't pay for your accommodation,' she reminded me.

I didn't want them to. I wanted to stay somewhere special and that was not an adjective that sprang to mind when looking at any of the hotels on the company's approved list. I couldn't wait to get out of the sterile box with a trouser press that passed for an "executive double". I was going to stay at the Hotel De Russie, just a short walk from the Spanish Steps, right in the heart of the Eternal City.

On Saturday morning, my colleagues dawdled over breakfast. I could tell they were reluctant for the conference to be over. They were flying back to Stansted and thence to their horrible homes, their hideous husbands and long-suffering wives. I was the only one who had no ties and no reason to hurry back to England. I was the only one who would not be dodging horizontal rain later that afternoon. While they climbed on-board the minibus to the airport, I caught a taxi in the opposite direction. I was going into Rome.

I had never been to the city before and so I was not sure what to expect. I did not expect the Colosseum to be so large, despite its name, or for it to be effectively the middle of a traffic island. I did not expect such ancient history to be right there, on every corner. Three centuries BC butting up against breeze blocks, as though a child had taken two boxes of themed Lego – gladiators and astronauts – and mixed them up with glee. And the noise and the light and the crazy driving. A Vespa squeezed by as we waited at a red signal. The girl on the back was wearing only a wisp of summer dress that left her slim brown legs completely exposed every time the moped got over five miles an hour. I envied her daredevil nature. I envied her legs.

My hotel was reached via a narrow cobbled street. Instinctively, I held my breath as the taxi driver forced his way through crowds of shoppers loaded down with the best of

Italy: Dolce and Gabbana, Cavalli, Valentino. The entrance to the hotel was discreet. If you didn't know what you were looking for, you'd miss it. Only the liveried doorman spoke of the luxury inside. While I waited at the check-in desk, I glanced through into the courtyard garden, which crept up the hill behind the hotel towards the park. The courtyard was already busy with people having lunch. Elegant locals mingled with international travellers of the more sophisticated kind.

I had treated myself to a weekend at this wonderful hotel for a special reason. What my colleagues at the conference did not know was that on Sunday I would be turning forty. Lately I had been feeling it and so I wanted to celebrate and remind myself that forty was really no age at all and getting there was far better than the alternative. There was good stuff still to come.

But of course I still wished I could be spending my landmark weekend with someone else. Someone I wanted to fuck.

The receptionist handed back my credit card and arranged for me to be shown to my room by one of her colleagues. I followed the young girl to the lift and listened with an expression of quiet interest while she explained the hotel's facilities. As she told me how to work the Jacuzzi bath in my suite, my mind drifted to a story I'd once read, in which a solo female traveller invites a bellboy to help her settle in. The first thing she had him do was run a bath for her. As I was thinking about it, a bellboy duly arrived with the case I had left in reception.

The bellboy was good-looking and fit, but he wasn't my type. He was handsome, but he was young. I'd never been that interested in the young ones, even when I was young myself. I wanted the experience that only came with age. Youth may have more stamina but there is nothing more off-putting than the tentative touch of someone who isn't sure if he's getting it right. I didn't want to be anyone's teacher. I wanted someone else to take control.

Right then, however, that wasn't on the agenda. I gave the hostess and the bellhop five euros apiece and shooed them out of the room as quickly as I was able, brushing away their repeated efforts to tell me how the air conditioning worked. I'd figure it out, I told them. In truth, I wouldn't bother. I hate air conditioning. I just wanted to be alone in the room. I wanted to change out of the clothes I had been wearing for the benefit of my colleagues and into something more fitting for my birthday treat.

Having showered, I slipped into the little red sundress I'd bought in Harvey Nichols before leaving London. It was possibly a little over the top for the day but as its feather-light hem settled around my knees, I could feel the Dolce Vita enveloping me at the same time. I was going to have a good weekend.

I had no real agenda. Though I wanted to see the "sights", I wasn't going to set myself any timetable in which to do it. I just wanted to wander and get to know the city by osmosis. The moment I stepped out of the hotel's front door, I was sucked into the stream of Roman life. Chattering, preening, laughing, flirting. Old and young, beautiful, ugly and noisy. So very very loud. I went with the flow as far as the Spanish Steps. I took in the school trip parties, the new lovers on their first mini-break, the golden anniversary celebrants. I patted the nose of one of the weary horses that trod the same cobbled path every day, not understanding or caring how their relentless labour would make a treasured memory for the passengers they brought along.

And there! My first nun. The young woman in grey scuttled down the Via Frattina with a carrier bag held close to her chest. What had she been buying? Had she visited La Perla? The mind boggled. But then, wasn't the Vatican supposed to be one of the hottest places on earth to party?

I wandered as far as the Trevi Fountain and duly threw in my three coins, though the scammers were there too with their nets, fishing out the treasure before the tourists had finished making their wishes. A policeman appeared. The scammers took off.

I followed the crowd along another narrow street. According to TripAdvisor, here was the best ice cream in the city. I had to have some. I joined the queue, listening with amusement and slight alarm as a pair of British tourists ahead of me complained about the prices.

"We could have had a whole dinner for that back home."

The ice cream was arrayed in plastic tubs beneath an arch of perspex. In the bad strip lighting, it didn't look like the sublime experience it was supposed to be. It looked as though it was brimming with additives. Even the hazelnuts artfully arranged on top of the *nocciola* looked as though they had been oozed out of a tube in a Chinese plastic novelty factory.

Having got close enough to see what was on offer, I made up my mind that I didn't want any of it, but before I could turn away and leave the shop, one of the guys behind the counter was asking me what I wanted and my English urge to be polite overcame my better instincts. I couldn't tell him "nothing" and so I chose vanilla.

"*Vaniglia*," I said.

He piled three scoops into a cone.

I handed over a twenty-euro note and got alarmingly little change. I left the kiosk feeling cheated and slightly stupid. My mood didn't improve when I tasted the teetering boules of frozen milk. Just as I had expected, it tasted artificial. No better than the supermarket ice cream I'd eaten as a child.

And suddenly the street seemed much busier than before. I didn't feel so much that I was going with the flow now, more that I was battling my way through human rapids. My posture was crabbed as I tried to protect that stupid gelato. I didn't want it, but I couldn't find anywhere to dump it. And then, I suppose, the inevitable happened. My ice cream met somebody's chest.

Of all the people in that street right then. Why he should be wearing a suit on a Saturday, I did not know. And why it had to be one of those suits that cost more than a car. I could tell with the most cursory of glances at its sharp seams that it was expensive. Bespoke. My own dress was not spared the fallout. When we bounced back off each other, we each bore a heart-shaped splat.

"*Cazzo!*" the suited man swore.

He flicked at the ice cream on his chest with elegant fingers. I stood in front of him, waiting for the shouting to begin. Indeed, his eyes were burning with fury when he finally looked at me. Then something strange happened. His face softened. While I remained frozen to the spot, unsure what would happen next, the man dipped a finger into the blob of ice cream that remained on his lapel and tasted it in a gesture that seemed faintly inappropriate. He pulled a face. Then he pulled a handkerchief from his breast pocket and handed it to me.

I went into apologetic overdrive. I couldn't use his handkerchief. I tried to hand it back to him.

"No," he said. "You must."

He caught my wrist and directed my hand to the ice cream, which was still dripping down my front. In that moment, when his fingers curled around the narrow bones of my forearm, I knew that he was going to take charge.

"Come here."

He guided me out of the main flow of human traffic. We stood in a doorway while I mopped myself down. I continued to apologize. He told me it was just an accident. He had been in a hurry. He hadn't noticed me. He didn't know how he could have failed to notice me.

"In that beautiful dress."

I was blushing already, having taken all the blame for the accident upon myself, but his compliment made me flush even harder.

"I need to pay to have your suit cleaned," I said.

"On the contrary," he told me, "it is I who should pay for your dress."

We both looked down at the sad stain on my bodice. I'd been wearing it for less than two hours. It was ruined.

"I know the perfect place," he said. "I'll take you there now."

I demurred but he insisted and I was soon following him down the Via Condotti. I asked about his suit as we walked. He said it was an old one. Turned out he was far more concerned about his tie.

"My favourite."

He waved the end of it towards me. It was garish red. The kind of red that only a bronzed Italian man of means could pull off.

"It's Marinella," he said. "Handmade, of course. They make just a handful in each fabric. I won't be able to get another one."

"Is it salvageable?" I asked.

"It will still have its uses," he told me.

I thought he was taking me to Rome's best dry cleaner, but instead he took me to a boutique.

"We'll find you something here," he said.

"Oh no."

But he insisted and I followed him inside. Of course it crossed my mind that this could be a terrible mistake. He had yet to tell me his name. But it was daylight. We were in a public place. The shop assistants greeted him like an old friend. An old customer? How had he come to be in a dress shop before? I was suddenly strangely, ridiculously jealous at the thought that this experience was not so unusual for him as for me.

He gestured towards me and one of the shop assistants quickly stepped forward to help. She regarded me with an expert eye and pulled three dresses from the racks with the confident air of someone who knows she's got the answer. She wasn't wrong.

I knew which one would be mine right away. It was similar in shape to the spoiled dress I was wearing, but it was blue. A deep gentian that would go with my eyes. The fabric was a heavy silk jersey that I knew would be flattering to my curves. When I put it on, I couldn't help but smile at my reflection. But the price tag was insane. Was the fabric woven by virgins who used only silk collected by the light of the new moon? My smile faded. I couldn't afford this frock.

Neither could I accept it as a gift, which was what my new friend was suggesting now.

"You lost your ice cream," he said.

"I ruined your suit," I replied. "And your tie."

"For that you will pay," he assured me. "In kind. But for now . . ."

He took out his credit card.

Standing in that tiny boutique, while the sales assistant wrapped my red dress so that I could wear the blue one right away, I took a proper look at my new friend for the first time. I guessed that he was five or maybe ten years older than I. His wavy dark hair was threaded with silver at the temples. He had the kind of lines you get from growing up in the sunshine. Laughing-in-the-summer lines. Not the kind of wrinkles you see on the grey faces in a London office such as the one I had left behind. He had a warm smile. Wide and inclusive. Somehow trustworthy but naughty too. Very naughty indeed.

"In kind?" I repeated.

"Oh yes.'

"In that case," I said. "I'd at least like to know to whom I am so indebted."

"My name is Ilario," he told me.

"Christine."

I gave him my hand. He lifted it to his lips and held my gaze as he kissed it.

Ilario paid for the dress and we stepped back out into the sunshine. The ice cream on his breast had dried into the shape of India. He asked me where I was staying and arranged to pick me up there at eight o'clock. As we parted, he kissed my hand again. It was a courtly gesture and yet it sent a shiver through me such as I hadn't experienced in years. An erotic sort of shiver. One that left me sure everyone I passed on the way back to the hotel must be able to see my most wicked thoughts plastered across my forehead like a tattoo.

Ilario arrived to take me to dinner exactly on time. He had changed his suit but I was amused to see that he was still wearing the red Marinella tie, with the ice cream dried upon it. He saw me looking at it.

"It's my lucky tie," he explained.

We had dinner not far from my hotel on the terrace of a traditional Roman trattoria. I was pleased to hear Italian voices on every side. I felt absurdly proud of myself that I wasn't eating alongside all the other tourists. There was no English menu. Ilario toasted me in prosecco and insisted I try the *carciofi*. Both were delicious.

Possibly, I drank too much wine. I was nervous. I was excited too. But this was what I had dreamed of, wasn't it? An adventure. There was romance, but there was also danger. I was out to dinner with a handsome *stranger*. Sure, the waiters at the restaurant had recognized him. The women in the shop too. But should I really be taking that acquaintance as a reference?

When we had finished eating, I let my left hand rest on the table as I sipped the last of my wine. When he lay his hand upon mine, to emphasize some point in a conversation about *La Grande Bellazza* – the one Italian film I had seen – I felt the heat rise between us again. The message was simple. Life is short. Shouldn't we take advantage of the beautiful opportunities that come our way?

All the same, when we got to the door of my hotel, I was certain that I would call it a night and send Ilario home. Indeed, it seemed that was what he was expecting too. But when he kissed me goodnight, I knew it couldn't be over. The warmth of his lips spread through my whole body like a drop of red ink in a glass of cool water. I had never wanted anyone so much.

"Come up to my room," I said to him.

He grinned his naughty boy grin.

'I knew you'd say that," he said.

We squeezed into the lift with two other couples. We were pressed against the wall. As the lift climbed, I felt Ilario's fingers creeping up the inside of my arm, electrifying a path from my wrist to my elbow. He was only touching my arm but it was all I could do not to groan. My skin seemed suddenly to be so thin and alive with tingling nerves.

The other passengers got out a floor below us, leaving us

just enough time to fall into another deep kiss before we reached the top.

Ilario started to kiss my neck as I searched for my room key. I paused to savour the feeling of his hands upon my breasts. I got the door open just as he tucked his fingers inside the bodice of my dress and made contact with my nipples.

The housekeepers had tidied my room in my absence. There was a single chocolate on one pillow. A single chocolate for a single woman. That would soon be brushed to the floor. For once I wouldn't need that kind of consolation.

Ilario shrugged off his jacket and danced me backwards towards the edge of the bed. At the same time he unclipped the barrette that was holding my hair off my neck, so that it fanned out around me on the pillow when I fell onto the mattress.

"*Bellissima*," he said.

I certainly felt *bellissima* with Ilario's eyes upon me. He pushed the spaghetti straps of my new dress from my shoulders and placed kisses in the tender dents to the sides of my breastbone. I directed his face back up to mine and kissed him hard. The taste of him was causing an actual chemical reaction inside me, like a match dropped onto a puddle of oil.

The new blue dress was soon discarded. It billowed briefly like a sail in the wind before falling to the floor. I was naked now but for a small pair of knickers. They were nude coloured, lace, cut high on the leg. Ilario dipped his head and traced the edges of the knickers with his tongue.

I picked up a pillow and held it to my mouth, biting down on the fabric to stop from laughing out loud. Ilario was tickling me with his gentle attentions. My belly was covered in tiny goosebumps, though I was far from being cold.

Ilario lifted his head and looked at me. He moved the pillow out of the way and swayed back to take in the whole of me spread out on the mattress before him.

I felt so alive beneath his gaze. He ran his hands up my waist, across my ribcage to my breasts. He circled my nipples with his thumbs. They were already puckering with anticipation.

"Sit up," he said. "Take a look at yourself. You should see how sexy you are."

He pulled me up so that I could see myself in the mirror above the dressing table. He moved to sit behind me, holding me briefly by the shoulders. Then he traced the outline of me as he gave a commentary of what he saw.

"You have such a beautiful shape," he said. "You are like a fine cello. Your shoulders are elegant and absolutely balanced. Your breasts are swollen perfection. Your waist is so small. Your hips are made for holding."

Seeing myself through his eyes, I felt a surge of confidence. I pulled my long hair to one side so that he could kiss and nibble at my bare neck. When I opened my eyes, they seemed darker than usual. My pupils were huge and deep. It was as though, like a vampire, he had filled me with a strange nocturnal spirit without having broken my skin.

I turned to kiss him again. My hands roamed all over his chest and his back, though he was still almost fully dressed. I loved the feeling of his crisp cotton shirt against my bare skin. My nakedness, contrasted with the fact that he still wore that silly tie, made me feel at once wild and vulnerable.

Ilario pushed me back down onto the mattress. His hand sought out the space between my legs. He moved my knickers to one side and gently felt the contours of my most private place. Twenty-four hours earlier, I had not known he existed. Now I was ready to let him see everything and touch every part of me, outside and in.

The fabric of my knickers bit into the soft crease of flesh where the top of my thigh met my pubis. The slight discomfort only increased my pleasure, reminding me that I was all but naked with a stranger who could just as easily hurt me as bring me pleasure. I was ready to do whatever I shouldn't do.

Ilario massaged my clitoris as he sucked on each of my nipples in turn. I writhed against the pure white bed sheets. I threw the pillows aside and reached up to the headboard, bracing myself against it. I pressed my feet down into the mattress. Somehow, increasing the tension in my muscles in this way always increased my pleasure.

Glancing up at me and smiling when he saw the effect he had, Ilario removed my knickers, which were wet through with the proof of my arousal. He threw the knickers to one side in a slightly comical gesture of abandon. They draped themselves over the shade of a standard lamp, as if that was where he had aimed.

With the knickers out of the way, Ilario got back to work. He parted my thighs. I gave a small show of resistance, but only a small one. His head moved to the space at the top of my legs.

His tongue, which had already given me such pleasure, made contact with my clit, while he tucked two fingers inside me. I felt my body close around those fingers greedily. I couldn't get enough of him. I was vibrating with desire.

Ilario licked and sucked as he finger-fucked me. I twisted above him, grabbing for a pillow again so that I could stuff it into my mouth. Biting down hard, I reached for his head and knotted my fingers in his thick dark hair. I wanted to pull him into me and push him away, all at the same time.

"You have to stop moving," he told me.

"I can't," I insisted. "It's all too too

. . . much."

"Stop."

He put his hands on my thighs and held them still, but the moment his tongue touched me, I was thrashing again.

Ilario sat up. His expression was one of exasperation. "How can I make you come if you won't stop wriggling and give in?"

"I've already given in," I told him.

Ilario shook his head. "No, you haven't. Nowhere near."

He got up from the bed and walked to the window.

I sat up against the headboard and picked up one of the pillows. Not to bite this time, but to use as a shield. I was afraid that I had ruined everything. I was so unused to being made love to these days that I had somehow got it wrong. Now my Latin lover was going to leave me and I hadn't even come.

Ilario picked up the phone and barked something at the guy on room service that night. I asked him what he'd ordered.

"Wait and see," he said and at last he took off his tie.

"So you are staying," I said.

"I am. And so are you."

He came back to the bed. Gently taking my hands, he looped the silk tie around the wrists and pulled so that they were pressed tightly together. Not too tight but with a delicious firmness of well-intentioned restraint. Once my wrists were tied together, he took the loose ends of the tie and used them to fasten me to the bedhead.

"Ilario!" I protested. "What are you doing?"

"I am making sure you enjoy yourself," he told me. "You'll give in when you have no choice."

I decided I would have to believe him. A little tug on my bonds suggested that they wouldn't be too difficult to escape. If I wanted to.

Now that he had taken off his tie, Ilario pulled off his shirt.

My eyes took in the shape of his chest with delight. He was a man who took care of himself. His torso was as well carved as any of the statues I'd seen in Rome that day. His chest was covered with the perfect amount of hair.

The doorbell rang. I looked at Ilario desperately. It was room service and, in my experience, they never just handed over what you'd asked for at the door. In a hotel like this, they would want to come in, lay a little table with a tiny tablecloth. The whole performance.

"Ilario," I whispered desperately, as though he wasn't perfectly aware of my nakedness. He just smiled.

He went to the door. Thankfully, he opened it just a crack. I squirmed in embarrassment as he passed the time of day with the room service boy. Could he see into the bedroom? Could he see me reflected in the hallway mirror? Was Ilario letting him see me? It seemed like an age before Ilario stepped back into the room with a tray in his hands.

"You bastard," I said. "He could see everything."

"I expect so. But it's one of very few perks to his job."

I kicked out at Ilario. He moved out of reach. I continued to flail ineffectually, somehow tightening the bonds around my wrist. I had been kidding myself they would be easy to wriggle out of.

"The more you move, the tighter they get," Ilario warned me.

"Undo me," I said. "I hate feeling this helpless."

"But it suits you rather well."

Ilario put the tray down on the bedside table. There was a small dish in the middle of it, covered by one of those silver domes. As I watched, Ilario removed the dome with a flourish. Beneath the dome was a small white dish containing two scoops of soft vanilla ice cream.

"With luck, this will be better than the crap you were eating earlier on."

"I didn't get a chance to eat any of it," I reminded him.

"And you're not going to be eating any of this," he said, as he helped himself to a mouthful. "Open your legs."

I kept them firmly clamped together.

"Open your legs."

"Make me."

"I will."

Ilario pulled my thighs apart and, to keep them there, he used the cord of the dressing gown he found in the bathroom. That went around my right ankle. My left ankle was tethered with one of the curtain ties. Ilario had a Boy Scout's knack for inspiration.

So, I was tied down. A limb towards each point of the compass. Ilario went back to his ice cream. Of course I knew what was coming but he was in no hurry. He sat in the chair by the side of the bed and studied me as though he were planning a sculpture. I was starting to get a little uncomfortable, both from the position I was holding and the intensity of his gaze.

At last, Ilario moved. He dipped his spoon into the bowl once more. And this mouthful was for me.

Not for me to eat, however. Ilario carefully tipped the spoonful of ice cream into the hollow of my belly button.

"*Bastardo*," I said.

"Good Italian," Ilario commented.

"Come on, Ilario. This is ridiculous. It's cruel."

Ilario's mouth twitched into a smile. "I suppose I shouldn't let the ice cream go to waste."

He leaned over and sucked the ice cream into his mouth, making sure afterwards that my belly button was completely clean with his expert tongue. Then he placed another spoonful a little lower. And a little lower. And a little lower still.

Held as I was in place by the ruined tie and those other makeshift tethers, all I could do was shiver and complain and wish, as Ilario cleaned up each spoonful with his tongue, that I had stayed still when his mouth was on my pussy. I had not truly known the meaning of agony until then. And Ilario meant me to know agony now. Each spoonful brought fresh goosebumps to my skin. Then the perfect contrast of his warm lips and tongue, which made me want more and more and more.

"Ilario," I begged him.

He reached up and put his hand on my mouth. Gently. I could smell my own flesh on his fingers, mingled with the scent of creamy vanilla. Ilario took his hand away and went back to tracing a wiggling line from one of my hip bones to the other. The tip of his tongue followed the line of my pubic hair, trimmed into a triangle.

"An arrow," Ilario called it. "In case I miss the spot."

He was missing the spot. He wasn't going anywhere near. Half an hour earlier, I had been so close to having an orgasm. Now he was teasing me towards the very edges of my endurance.

"There's just one spoonful left," he told me. "Would you like to have it?"

He held it towards my mouth.

"Or?"

He snatched it away and, with great mirth playing across his handsome features, he dripped the last of the vanilla straight onto my mound of Venus. As it melted, it began to ooze towards the cleft of my labia. The sensation as the ice cream crept was not unlike a thousand tiny tongues, licking and flickering, but never with quite enough intensity. I pulled against my restraints, trying and failing to reposition my body to turn the tickle into a turn-on. Ilario watched me. His amusement was clear.

"You're still resisting," he told me. "You're not ready to stop moving."

"How can I?"

"You have to try harder."

I did try. I tried to lie still in the middle of the bed with the tension on each of my bonds exactly equal. I tried not to move a muscle as the ice cream continued to melt and the sticky trickle between my legs grew more and more difficult to ignore.

"For God's sake, just lick me!" I yelled.

At last Ilario's head between my legs was the most wonderful sight.

When I woke in the morning, Ilario had already gone. I was disappointed, of course, but I wasn't especially surprised. Our evening together was just one of those moments that soon take on the quality of a dream. I might never see him again but I would certainly never forget him.

But there was a note scribbled on the pad by the telephone, accompanying a number.

"I have an especially nice tie by Charvet," wrote Ilario. "Perhaps you'd like to help me knot it. In Paris."

The Four-poster Bed

Rebecca Chance

(Due to writing novels back to back and not having time to write a standalone short story, this piece is actually an extract from my upcoming bonkbuster novel, Bad Brides, *out later in 2014. All you need to know to read it is that Tamra, our sexy American cougar heroine, during a very lively house party in a stately home, has an assignation with Dominic, a hot young boytoy, who was supposed to sneak into her room at bedtime. Dominic, however, hasn't shown up, and a frustrated and angry Tamra has decided to visit his room instead – only, through a series of comic coincidences, she finds an entirely different young man in the four-poster bed, a young man who naturally assumes that she's his fiancée popping in for a booty call . . .)*

The room was almost completely dark, just a few glowing embers in the fire by which she could make out the shapes of the furniture, the drawn curtains of the four-poster bed. For a moment, she thought that Dominic wasn't here at all, and then she heard slow, steady breathing from behind the heavy brocade curtains, and she realized that the bastard had, instead of sneaking into her room, come back to his and gone to sleep.

How dare he? Well, if he thinks he can turn me on and leave me hanging, he's got a second thought coming! I'm going to ride him like a bronco for this!

The cashmere dressing gown fell from Tamra's perfect, silky shoulders and puddled on the carpet. She kicked off the slippers and, naked and angry, condoms in hand, stalked to the four-poster bed, pulled open the curtains and climbed up onto the mattress beside the man she thought was Dominic.

Edmund, who had been fast asleep, stirred into semi-consciousness at the brief glimmer of light as the curtains parted. They fell closed behind Tamra, and the next thing he knew was the covers being pulled off his recumbent body, and a warm hand reaching decisively into the slit of his pyjama bottoms and taking hold of his cock in a way that meant business.

"Christ!" he mumbled sleepily, feeling himself respond instantly. "Oh, God . . ."

She was tickling his balls now with the fingers of her other hand, working them expertly, making him moan even as he managed to say: "I thought you went to bed . . ."

Tamra straddled him, bending down to kiss him, a kiss which she deliberately turned into a sharp, punishing bite, which for some reason had his cock springing up, rock hard now.

"I don't care what you thought, you fucker," she whispered against his lips. "Stop thinking and get ready. I'm going to start fucking your brains out in about thirty seconds, so you better brace yourself and hang on for dear life."

His fiancée had never, ever, talked dirty to Edmund during sex. Actually, no one had. No one had bitten his lips or pulled on his cock as if she owned it, or told him that she was going to fuck his brains out, and he realized immediately, as his balls throbbed and tightened, that this was exactly what his entire adult life had been lacking. She was already ripping open a condom wrapper, rolling it onto his cock, and he felt like he might burst already: he reached up for her, closing his hands around her breasts for a wonderful moment, the skin so soft, the nipples so tight and hard at the centre, before she actually slapped his hands away.

"No touching me," she hissed. "Not yet. You haven't earned it. Fuck me good this time, and then maybe you can."

And the next thing he knew she was lowering herself onto him, so hot and wet that he groaned in utter pleasure, his arms thrown wide, his hands splayed and gripping the sheets and the mattress to hold on, just as she'd said, as she started to ride him so hard and fast that it hurt, and that hurt felt better than any sensation he'd ever had before in his life. She was grinding her arse down onto his balls, taking him in right to the root with every stroke, her strong, lean muscled legs making the movements seem effortless, and Edmund's fingers sank so deep into the mattress to get some purchase that he pulled a button loose with the force of his clutch.

"Oh God," Tamra panted above him, "fucking God, this is so good . . ."

His cock was considerably bigger than she'd felt it through his trousers, which was weird – maybe it had been the angle? – but definitely a positive thing. She'd driven down on it so hard as it entered her that she already felt bruised, but that was wonderful, just what she wanted, what she needed, extreme sensation: she wouldn't care if she woke up tomorrow morning covered in bruises, just as long as she left the same marks on him. And there was something about him that made her want to do that, to bite him, to spank him and have him spank her back, some wild energy that had sparked between them the moment she touched his cock. She felt him trying to rear his hips, to fuck her like she was fucking him, and she reached down and slapped the side of his bum so hard the slap resounded round the inside of the drawn curtains.

"I told you not to fucking move this time!" she hissed. "You dirty fucker, don't you dare!"

It was a power game, and so much fun; she drew that hand between her legs, starting to make herself come, knowing that he could tell what she was doing. His groans grew louder, his cock swelled inside her, and she was so excited that she came almost straight away, her pussy throbbing around him, came again and again just to torture him, knowing that he was doing his best to hold out, until finally she collapsed onto his chest, sunk her teeth into his lower lip and whispered: "Come on, you bastard, shoot inside me . . . come on, you dirty bastard, do it, shoot your load . . ."

She gasped as she felt his cock swell even more, as his hips did jerk now, pumping come so hot that she could feel it through the condom, his hands grabbing onto her hips and pulling her even further onto him: she screamed at how deep the tip of his cock drove for a split second before he arched his back, grunted and went limp beneath her.

His chest hair was already sweaty under her breasts. She loved it, the dampness, the coarse hair against her sensitive skin. She bent to lick the salty sweat from the pool between his collarbones.

"Well?" she said quietly, very aware of her daughter sleeping on the other side of the bedroom wall. "Did I fuck your brains out?"

"Uh-huh." He shifted her off him so that he could take off the condom. "So, um, is this what we're doing tonight? Fucking each other's brains out?"

Just saying the words sent a rush of such excitement through Edmund that he thought he might get hard all over again, with his cock still wet with come from the last fuck. *The last fuck.* He'd never dared use this language to a woman, had always felt that somehow it was disrespectful. But here was Brianna Jade, somehow transformed by the stress of the day, and maybe the utter darkness around them, into a total sex vixen, insulting him, biting him – God, his cock twitched just *thinking* about her biting him – and it had liberated something inside him he didn't even realize had been there all along.

"Have you been drinking?" he said, finding the gap in the curtains, tying the condom up by the faint firelight and managing, to his great satisfaction, to chuck it squarely into the bedside wastebasket. He was still trying to work out the reason for the metamorphosis of his fairly sexually modest fiancée into a full-blown porn fantasy woman.

She laughed deep in her throat. "No more than you," she said, which Edmund naturally took to mean "not much at all".

"So what happened to get you all—" he began, but at that point his arm was grabbed, he was pulled fully back into the darkness of the curtained bed, and Tamra's mouth closed on his.

"Stop talking,' she said, kissing him deeply. 'Finger me."

Edmund's cock surged again; her commands were delicious, her new-found confidence incredibly exciting. But whatever had taken control of her, he realized that he wanted not just to follow along with it, but to exert his own will too, and that this was the moment he needed to do it, or she would take over completely. And he needed to flex his own muscles too, to give his own commands. Without even thinking about what he was going to do, he slid his thumb into her mouth.

"Suck it," he said, wondering if she would get furious at his daring to order her around as she'd been ordering him.

When her warm wet lips folded over her teeth and she started to pull on his thumb, sucking it just as he'd told her, right up to the base of the second knuckle, he groaned loudly in surprise and pleasure, his balls tingling, growing fuller. His other hand slid down her body, squeezing each breast as he went, first tentatively, but then, as she arched wordlessly beneath him, he squeezed harder, his thumb flicking the nipples, his head lowering to close his teeth around each one in turn, hearing her moan around his thumb as he did so. She liked it as rough as he apparently did, and, realizing that, he narrowed three fingers together, parted her wet lower lips and drove the fingers inside her with barely any preliminaries.

She surged right up around his hand, fast and furious, pumping her hips against him. He rubbed his thumb against her, trying to feel what she wanted, what she needed, and apparently it was a series of steady quick strokes, making her pump her bottom right off the bed, reaching desperately for the orgasm that was just about to come, and did, and then the next one, and the next one, waves and waves, Edmund determined not to stop, although his hand was cramping, determined not to give up first to wear her out before she wore him out, not to give in. He found a rhythm of licking and biting her nipples, which finally made her head arch right back, his thumb slipping out of her mouth as she screamed a ragged series of "Fuck you!"s at the brocade tester overhead, her pussy contracting ever more tightly around his hand, the rush of moisture around his fingers, the scent of her sweat and come so intoxicating that he was hard as a rock again by the time she finally subsided, trembling with the aftershock, onto the mattress.

He wasn't sure if she was ready for him yet: probably not. He pulled himself back up to lie beside her, his own breath coming fast, but hers much louder, listening in utter happiness to the physical state to which he had reduced her. Never had she reacted like this to him before, nor him to her: tonight was some sort of alchemical reaction, a magic that had somehow sparked in the pitch-black of this bed. Maybe that was it, the fact that they were in neither of their bedrooms, that this bed was neutral ground: maybe that was why she felt so free to let go in a way that she had never done before? He assumed, of course, that she'd gone to his room first, found Dominic doubtless passed out and snoring on the fish-stained bed, and realized what must have happened. Maybe the fact that she'd come to find him in the night, something she'd never done before, added to finding him in an unfamiliar place, had set this connection between them fizzing like an electric cable?

He wanted to ask her, but his cock was demanding some sort of attention more urgently than his brain, and he heard himself say: "Can I—are you ready to, um . . ."

"Oh hey," she said drowsily, "don't pussy out on me now, boy! Say what you want!"

She rolled over, reached down, closed her hand around his stiff cock. He felt like wailing with pleasure, but somehow managed to keep it to a more manly groan.

Her voice was smug as she said, "Well, *you*'re good to go again, aren't you?"

"I'm gagging for it," Edmund said, leaning forward, finding her mouth, plunging his tongue into it deeply, exactly what he wanted to do with his cock.

Her hands came up and twined in his sweat-curled hair, pulling him closer, kissing him back, their tongues battling for supremacy, their teeth biting each other's lips, his hands now buried in her long hair, pulling it, hearing her moan as he did that, pulling it harder, twisting it into a rope, really dragging it now, feeling her pressing even tighter against him. Obviously she liked this, wanted it, and he was hugely grateful because he absolutely loved it, was horrified how much he did love it, how it made him even harder, even keener to fuck her as hard as she'd fucked him—

"Fuck me up the ass and pull my hair!" she said, managing to wrest her mouth from his. "Do it, fuck me up the ass, now, do it."

Edmund had never done this before in his life, and her words made his balls tighten in soaring anticipation.

"Go slow at first," she said, turning over and pushing up her bottom. "That's a big cock you've got there. Take your time and then fuck me with everything you've got."

He didn't need to be told twice: he was already behind her, finding the condoms scattered over the mattress and pulling one on his throbbing cock, reaching between her legs for her own moisture, working it into the cleft of her arse, again and again, making it a series of caresses, hearing her wail and push against his hand, her face, he assumed, buried in a pillow, because her pleas of "Fuck me, fuck me, do it, please fuck me now" were muffled, taking his time until he thought he had enough lubrication not to hurt her too much, and, to be honest, enjoying torturing her, making her beg for it until she was screaming in frustration into the pillow, and then, finally, when he couldn't bear it any more himself, dipping the tip of his cock for a second into her pussy for extra wetness and then dragging it up to where she wanted it, easing it in.

"Oh Jesus fuck!" he said as her body closed around him, the sensation of entering the tight ring of muscle incredibly intense. He could feel how snug the fit was, understood what she'd meant, did his absolute best to go as slowly as he could, feeling as if his head was going to explode with the sheer excitement of doing something this taboo, of fucking his fiancée in the arse. He leant forward, felt for her mane of hair, grabbed it and pulled back – *Jesus*, burying his cock in his fiancée's tight arse while tugging on her hair, starting to fuck her like she'd said, with everything he had—

She was screaming her head off into the pillow now, a stream of filthy encouraging curses, calling him a dirty bastard, a fucking dirty animal, her arse pumping back against his balls, clearly loving what he was doing to her. Emboldened, he twined her hair around one of his wrists, pulled harder, forcing her to arch up off the pillow and, with his other hand, he landed a hard slap on her arse cheek.

It sent her even more wild. She bucked beneath him frantically, and it sounded as if she'd stuffed one hand into her mouth to keep her from shrieking.

"Yes, yes, fuck yes, oh fuck yes, do it, fucking do it!" he heard her crying into her knuckles, and he lifted his palm and spanked her again, a whole series of spanks, her firm flesh quivering every time, his cock pounding inside her, finding a rhythm where he drove deep, pulled out almost to the tip, landed a slap and then thrust inside her again. It was ecstasy, it was the most intense thing he'd ever done, it was actually going to burst the top of his head right off if he didn't tell himself he could come almost immediately, his balls were so tight it was agony—

He managed, somehow, to reach around, to grab her mound in his palm and find her clit with his finger and bring her off. She went absolutely limp as she came, as if all the bones in her body had dissolved, and once he knew she was done, he let go and came like a runaway train hitting the buffers at full blast. It was as if his cock actually blew up, exploded inside her for good, like a bomb detonating. He knew exactly how she'd felt, coming, because he went limp too, collapsing on top of her with his entire weight, something he would never normally do because it was so ungentlemanly to crush a woman like that, as if she were the mattress . . .

But then, nothing I've done with her has been remotely gentlemanly. And the more I acted like an animal, the more she liked it – and God, the more she acted like an animal, the more I bloody loved it . . .

They were both running with sweat, her back wet with it, his chest plastered to her shoulder blades. His heart was pumping out of his chest, and beneath him he could hear her panting, feel her body heaving as she also struggled to catch her breath. His head was resting on her upper back, and he licked her sweat, tasting it, her salt and his, and he felt her tremble beneath him just at this touch of his tongue.

"I have to pull out," he said into her back, and heard her moan erotically in denial, not wanting him to leave her body.

"No, I have to . . . the condom's slipping . . ."

He had never been so reluctant to slide his cock out of a woman in his life. He disposed of it as fast as he could, racing back to press himself against her; her back was turned, and he spooned her, trying to get as much of himself as he could against her smooth skin, her wonderful round arse, wrapping an arm over her and closing his hand over her equally wonderfully round and heavy breast. He was going to kiss the back of her neck, but then he thought better of it, opening his mouth instead and sinking his teeth just fractionally into the damp skin, rewarded by the sensation of her whole body trembling in response.

"I need to sleep, tiger," she mumbled, already halfway there by the sound of her voice. "Give me a couple of hours and then I'll suck you off."

Edmund groaned. "Not fair, when we need to sleep . . ."

"Who said I was fair?" she mumbled.

He put his lips to her ear and whispered: "I bet you'll like it if I bite your pussy when I go down on you, won't you?" and this time it was she who moaned, unable to help herself writhing against him.

"*Fuck* yes," she sighed. "You *bastard.*"

And she did.

Breakfast at the Farmers' Market

Thomas S. Roche

When I saw the look the redhead gave her husband as she handled the cucumbers, I knew it wasn't just organic produce she loved. She looked nervous and excited and embarrassed and very much in love – all at once. He looked like he was thoroughly in charge, which I liked.

The exchange that really got me going was what I overheard while she was handling this particularly huge cucumber.

It was *big* – and I mean *big*. Something like twelve inches at least, and plenty of inches around. She looked at it like she was scared but thrilled. Her husband gave her this cruel little smile. Her eyes went big, as if to say, *I couldn't possibly!* His eyes narrowed, as if to say, *Oh, yes you will!* She stuck her lower lip out; she pouted. He cocked his head and gave her a stern little sneer. They never broke eye contact – not until she got all meek and lowered her eyes to the ground for a moment. When she raised them, slightly, a moment later, his were still there, and still ice cold. She nodded slightly, turned away a little; her pink lips twisted in a wicked little smile, just at the corner. I wasn't a hundred per cent sure her husband could see the smile, but I could, from quite a few feet away. She put the big cucumber in a clear bag of biodegradable plastic.

That was love, no question about it. How could I not want a piece of it?

I was not far away, milling in the tightly packed crowd sprawled in the shadow of the Bay Bridge. At a farmers' market, five feet is an eternity. I closed up the space between us, faster than fast, and made myself part of their world.

"Those are *excellent* cucumbers," I said. "Really amazing. My slave and I enjoyed some last weekend."

This was a lie, naturally, but did it matter? It got the couple's attention. It was San Francisco, and not really that far from the Castro, where you can sometimes get away with saying such things in the name of political visibility. I could have been talking about a male slave, right? I wasn't, but then, that wasn't the point. They both looked at me, sized me up, and exchanged a glance.

"You don't say?" the husband said. I realized for the first time that he had an accent – Britain, Commonwealth . . . somewhere.

"Yes," I said. "I can recommend the Armenian cucumbers, too. The ridges make all the difference." I grinned at them. "She really enjoyed those, as well."

"Excuse me?" asked the husband. British, I think.

"Trust me," I said. "The ridges add a certain flavour to the game." Not far from the table of cucumbers she'd selected hers out of was a pile of Armenian cucumbers. They were curved most provocatively, and covered with thick, deep ridges. I held one up at just the right angle to imply an erect cock. "It's spicy at once, but smooth. I can see you two know all about that."

Her eyes went bright and hungry. She looked at her husband and, I now presumed, her Master. He seemed amused. She looked back at me, shyly but excitedly.

"Where are you from?" I asked them.

"Is it that obvious?" the wife asked. She had the same accent, almost; hers was slightly more musical.

I shrugged and laughed. "Only this weekend," I said.

Her husband transformed into Master all in one moment, squaring his shoulders. "We're staying at the Pickford," he said. "Just a few blocks away. I'm Master Brock, this is Lady Sara."

"You're in town for Folsom," I said apologetically.

"Obviously. Otherwise, I wouldn't have volunteered my salad-making skills."

Brock seemed to like that. "Yes," he said. "We got in late last night from London. The airline lost our luggage."

"Ah," I said. "That explains the produce shopping."

"Yes," he said bitterly. "Floggers are quiet an investment . . ."

"But it's the other toys that are urgent right now," I said. "You must be morning people."

"Quite," he said. He smiled as his wife, distracted, handled the Armenian cucumbers. "Those look wonderful," he said. "How 'bout that big one? That looks perfect."

The wife was handling one ridged cucumber likely too large for her anatomy. She got big-eyed and mock-afraid, wiggling her butt back and forth in her practically see-through hippie skirt.

"But *Master*!" she said under her breath, protesting. Then, even more quietly, "It's too big." She glanced at me, obviously glad that I could hear.

"I said it looks perfect," he said roughly.

She had love in her eyes as she looked from me to him, then put the big Armenian cucumber in another plastic bag.

"Yes, Sir," she said softly as she did. Then she spoke to me, a little petulantly, pretending she was angry she'd have to fuck such a big hard vegetable cock. "You're a veg expert?" she asked. "A farmer?" Sarcastically, she added, "Food critic?"

"In a way," I said. "Let's just say I know my produce, and I'm getting hungry for breakfast."

The husband put his hand possessively at the back of his wife's neck. "We're not sure about breakfast just yet," he said. "But we'd like some coffee. Care to join us?"

"Yes, I'd like that," I said with a smile. I liked the way he spoke for both of them; it was hot. "Allow me?"

I paid for their cucumbers and the three of us went to get coffee.

* * *

The two of them were crazy for each other – that much was obvious as she did little things like put cream in his coffee, deferentially holding the creamer in place to pour more, if necessary, returning it to its place on the counter only after Master Brock had watched the cream swirl around in his coffee and decided it was the right amount. At a nod from Master Brock, she did the same for me. I ended up with a shit-ton more cream in my coffee than I usually liked, because it was so hot to stand there waiting for the cream to swirl in the darkness and then to tell her to add just another drop. She did, each time, until I was very well satisfied. Then the three of us sat down and talked.

It became even more evident that they were totally nuts for each other as we all sat there flirting and chatting. Sara's eyes flickered over to Brock now and then; his stern looks guided her closer to me as the three of us hit it off. Eventually, he smiled and ran one hand through her long red hair.

"Slave," said Brock, his voice firm. "Why don't you sit with Tom here?"

She looked scandalized, then scared, then excited. This was a game they were playing. Master Brock gave her a cruel, savage, nasty look, and then she meekly responded, "If it pleases you, Sir."

Then she sat with me. With a glance at Brock (who nodded), I let my hand rest on her thigh, gathering up the thin cotton of her hippie skirt. I made quite sure to do it where Brock could see – which meant that others could see, but I wasn't sure I cared about that. Sara did. She hated it, liked it and wanted and didn't want it, all at once. Sara looked at her Master; his eyes went from my hand to her eyes, and he smiled.

We kept talking, while I caressed Sara's thigh. Her legs spread open wider, till she was rubbing her knee against mine. Her breathing came quicker, more laboured, as her Master and I talked about their arrangement. Before long, Master Brock glanced down at my hand, then made eye contact with me. He nodded. I got the message. I moved my hand up further. Lady Sara responded with a soft little moan that she simply couldn't hide. Right there in the coffee shop, in the shadows under the table, my hand went up her skirt. If anyone saw, they didn't let on. It was just after eight in the morning; people were sleepy.

She wasn't wearing anything underneath the skirt. Her pussy was shaved, her clit pierced. She was wet as can be. She leaned forward and pushed herself onto my fingers.

Sara made eye contact with Master Brock the whole time as I fingered her – until, that is, he broke it so he could look at me.

"What do you say we go back to our hotel room," he said, "and feed Sara some breakfast?" As she worked her hips back and forth, pushing herself onto my hand, he asked, "Would you like that, slave?"

She nodded.

"Yes," she said. "If it please you, Master." Then she looked at me as I fingered her. "Does it pleases you, Sir?"

"It does," I told her, taking my hand out from between her legs so I could pick up our bag of cucumbers. "Let's go."

The Pickford is a tiny boutique hotel that's been there since the twenties; the rooms are small, which made things nice and cosy. Brock put out the DO NOT DISTURB sign.

At a soft but stern command from her Master, Sara lifted her filmy cotton top over her head the second we were in the door. She dropped her skirt; it pooled around her ankles.

She let me get a good look at her naked ass as she picked up the bag of cucumbers and bent over the bed, dumping them out and feeling them all over.

"Master," she said breathlessly. "These are too big!"

"Nonsense," said Master Brock, his hand on my shoulder. "Tom here says he's an expert in local produce. You say that these will fit, Tom?"

"It sure looks that way," I said, my eyes roving over Sara's pretty ass and exposed sex. "But either way, we'll have a great time finding out."

"You heard the man, slave," he said. "He'll make them fit. But why don't you give him some incentive?"

Sara dropped to her knees in front of me. "Yes, Master," she said.

Sara unbuckled my belt and unzipped my pants; she got my cock out and her tongue swirled in magic circles around my head. She had a stud through her tongue to match the ring in her clit. The smooth metal stroked the underside of my cock as she bobbed up and down with her eyes turned up towards me, obediently and worshipfully.

As she sucked my cock, she looked up at me with big bright green eyes and made little whimpering gulping noises. She slurped her way as noisily as possible. Her eyes fluttered closed and she stretched her neck a little, moaning softly as she worked it into the back of her throat and then silenced her moan with my cock, filling her throat and swallowing me to the hilt.

Master Brock was behind her, caressing her shoulders and running his hands through her hair. Suddenly, he seized her hair and pulled her face off my cock. This left her panting and gasping just a few inches away, strings of drool glistening between her pale pink lips and my cockhead.

"Put it away, now, slave," he growled sternly.

Obediently, Sara tucked my cock back into my pants and buttoned me, not bothering to zip or buckle. Master Brock pulled her halfway and then all the way back onto the bed.

"Spread," he ordered her. She did. "I'm going to wash our veg. Get her ready," he said to me.

"With pleasure," I told him, leaning over Sara on the bed. Her nipples were stiff and sensitive as I thumbed them. I started to pinch, and her back arched. I took one hand away from her breasts and brought it to her sex. I started caressing and found how wet she was – dripping. I slid two fingers in and felt the tightness, opening as I pushed, and felt the swell of her G-spot against the pads of my fingers. She let out a moan.

Brock returned with the cucumbers, wet from the hotel room sink. He knew what he was doing; he'd used warm water, so they were almost up to room temperature. Still thumbing one of her nipples with one hand, I accepted a good-sized cuke from Brock in the other. It had a nice curve that was sure to hit her G-spot. Brock held another one ready – Armenian, ridged and even bigger. That one had an even more crooked curve to it. There was a third one with a swell in the middle and a fourth with a big bulb on the end that I was not at all sure she could take, but, as with all of them, I planned to have fun finding out. So did Brock.

Master Brock laid the cucumbers out on a towel on the bed next to Sara's spread thighs, within easy reach. He pulled up a chair for me; he preferred to stand. I sat down and leaned in between Sara's pretty, spread thighs, working the first cucumber up to her sex.

Leaning over her shoulders, Master Brock reached down and parted her lips with his fingers. He held Sara open for me as she squirmed, pinned between us. I looked into her bright green eyes as I fitted the cucumber into her opening and gently worked it in. It went in easy.

"Cold," she said, with a slight exhalation, as I pushed it in to her body.

"I used warm water, slave. It's warm enough. Besides, you're molten inside. Now, no more complaining."

"Yes, Master," she said with a thrill.

She gasped as I worked the first cucumber all the way in, tipping it at a generous angle to make sure it hit the swelling internal mound of her G-spot. I let my thumb settle into the cleft between her clit hood and the top of her pussy lips; her eyes rolled back into her head as I began to work thumb and cucumber back and forth. I pressed harder and began to fuck her. Her eyes still rolled back, she started making rhythmic whimpering noises. She breathed long and low and even through her nose, giving off obscene moans in time with my thrusts.

Master Brock pinched her nipples hard as I thrust into her. When I switched to the big, ridged Armenian cucumber, Sara's head went thrusting back into her Master's grasp, her back arched. He seized her hair with one hand and held her tight as her thighs wriggled closed around my hand. "Open, slave," he growled affectionately. Her eyes and legs opened wide at once, her knees parting smoothly as she leaned forward until I could get the ridged cucumber at least partially inside her.

She squealed a little when she felt the ridges filling her; she breathed quick and then slower as it sank in. Then her eyes rolled back as she felt the sensation of the cucumber fucking her; as big as it was, I knew it wasn't yet the biggest she'd take. I worked her clit and fucked her rhythmically, sensing that she was not yet close to orgasm. The thrill of exhibitionism was countered by the nervousness of performing in front of a stranger.

"Fuck," she gasped. "Oh fucking oh my God FUCK—"

She continued her string of profane exclamations as I worked the cucumber as deep into her as it would go – which, with its ridges, was just a few inches. That was plenty, though; I worked it down like a lever and watched Sara's back arch.

Her Master tipped her head back and cradled it in his arms as I fucked the ridged cucumber into her. He held her there in the crook of his arm and stared into her eyes as she moaned. His other hand pinched one nipple harder and harder as Sara surrendered to the thrust of the Armenian cucumber.

Her eyes were wide now, and she squirmed between Master Brock and me. Now and then, he would growl commandingly: "Stay open, slave. Open your legs." When he did, she would obediently open her legs and let me fuck her harder, her hands hanging limp at her sides.

"Thank you, Sir," she cooed obediently, between whimpers and moans of pleasure. She worked her hips onto my strokes as I fucked her with the Armenian cucumber; she took it a little more with every few thrusts, and soon it was sunk into her as deep as she could take it.

Master Brock moved away from Sara just enough to let him unfasten his pants and pull his cock out. He guided her hand onto his cock as he cradled her in his lap. This required her to tuck her hand awkwardly under her head, but she managed it. "Help Tom out, too" said Master Brock commandingly. Sara obeyed, reaching out to pull my cock out as I leaned over, fucking her. I looked into her eyes. Even if her hands trembled, she seemed to be an expert at unfastening men's pants. She got my cock out, spat on her hand, and started to stroke me off, jerking me quickly towards an orgasm.

Her Master and I both came before she did; how could we not, with that performance to fuel us. He was thrusting his hips underneath her when he let out a soft murmur of pleasure; I saw a wet slick streak down her shoulder and onto her breast, then a few more soaking her hair. That set me off, as Sara's hand tightened on my cock; I exploded all over her tits while I kept thrusting the cucumber rhythmically into her body. She fucked herself onto me as I sighed with wet pleasure.

Her orgasm revealed itself in stages; first there was the slowing of her thrusts, then a pause in them, then a violent rapid jerking as the spasms overtook her naked body. Then the sounds began: a great high wail as she surrendered to her orgasm, and a series of visible waves going through her body as she undulated in the wake of the pleasure. She twisted back and forth as she finished climaxing, and I left the vibe tight against her clit until she was good and finished.

Gingerly, I slid the cucumber out of her.

"Thank you, Sir," she said – to me. Then, "Thank you, Master," she said to him, with a much deeper tone to her voice.

"I think I've worked up an appetite," said Master Brock. "For *real* breakfast."

"I think we all have," I said, tossing the Armenian cucumber on the towel. We called up room service and made a day of it.

With the help of Brock and Sara, it proved my best Folsom Fair since at least 1993 . . . maybe earlier.

The Trespass

K. D. Grace

It was never my intention to trespass. Honestly I'm not that kind of person. I came to Lyme Regis in an attempt to throw off my growing depression. I walk when I'm depressed. It's one of the few things that balances me and helps me see more clearly.

I'd been walking since dawn. I was only a half an hour out from Lyme, on the homeward stretch, looking for a nice spot to have lunch.

I had the sea and the cliffs to one side of me and a long stretch of wooden privacy fence on the other. I wondered what kind of idiot would block off his view of the sea just to keep out the riff-raff. I'm a firm believer in the right to ramble, and I already had the picture in my head of some old rich fart, who couldn't bear the sight of the unwashed masses traipsing past his manicured lawn while Fifi served tea on the veranda.

As I walked along the path, the wood of the fence became more weathered and in some cases rotted and downright dilapidated. Apparently whoever was on the other side wasn't too concerned about the view we riff-raff got. When I came to a place where a couple of slats were actually missing, I just had to take a peek. I mean really, how could I not want to see what was so precious that the owner would erect such a monstrosity on such a beautiful stretch of coast?

I hadn't planned to do more than peek, but it rained. Hard. One of those summer showers that came out of nowhere. I was pretty sure it would pass, but there was a big oak with lush foliage only a few metres beyond the fence, a perfect place to wait out the rain and have my sandwich. As I took shelter beneath the densest part of the foliage, I got a glimpse of a sculpture peeking from behind a rhododendron thicket.

All I could see was a tantalizing thigh and a nicely sculpted stone buttock. It was enough to make me curious, but not enough to move me until after I finished my sandwich and the rain subsided. Then I stood, wiped my hands on my walking shorts and stepped forward onto the grassy path.

I expected some sort of Greek statuary like I'd seen in formal gardens on great estates. But there was nothing formal about the sculpture's surroundings. It stood in an area that looked as wild and overgrown as the woodlands I'd walked through on some of my wanderings. In the syrupy light that penetrated the storm clouds, the pale marble took on a golden suppleness that was almost the colour of sun-kissed flesh. So much so that had I not been speculating about the piece of statuary for the last fifteen minutes, I'd have thought I'd just surprised some guy having an alfresco frolic in the buff. Even knowing, I might have turned and fled but for the quick flit of a robin on the sculpture's shoulder and then its head. The statue was only a few inches taller than I, which made the whole situation even more disconcerting.

As the bird flew, I stepped cautiously around to the front of the piece and found that the man was having way more than a naked frolic, and he wasn't having it alone. He held his rather urgent erection in a grasp that was clearly an act of presentation to the second statue: a woman on her knees. Her hands, behind her back, were crossed at the wrists. Her eyes were closed; her lips parted to receive his offering.

I felt a moist tremor against the crotch of my walking shorts as I circled round behind to view her raised bottom. Her thighs were parted so I could admire the detailed folds and the hungry gape of her pussy. I glanced around to make sure no one was looking then I leaned closer. What I saw made me forget that I was trespassing. Heart galloping in my chest, I dropped to my knees for a better look. The sculptor had missed no details – from the ripe berry bulge of her clit to the gathering sheen of moisture between her labia, which looked so real I reached out and stroked it before I caught myself. I gave a little moan of surprise at the cool feel of the stone, a sound that seemed disturbingly loud in the quiet copse, and yet I couldn't hold back a startled response to my own pussy's reaction as I caressed the statue.

By that time my trespass had completely fled my mind and, in my imagination, I was there to help the stone couple come. I wanted to wrap my fingers in the wild flow of the woman's hair and guide her head forward onto the man's needy cock, or I wanted to push my mouth in next to hers to take his offering for myself. As I leaned close, still stroking between the woman's marble folds I could see the pre-come on the tip of the man's penis. The plum-swell of his balls resting tightly in the thatch of pubic hair looked positively strokeable. And, before I knew it, my other hand snaked in for a grope; tentatively at first, thumb and forefinger, and then my entire fist; a perfect fit around his girth. It was as though I had just completed a circuit, one hand fingering the woman's pout the other fisting the man's engorged cock. My pussy felt electric, gripping and tensing against the gusset of my panties. I wished like hell I had a third hand to slip into my own wet snatch.

A sudden clap of thunder made me yelp and, as I stepped away from the pair to flee back for the fence, I tripped over an exposed root and sprawled on my back, knocking the air from my lungs. A few harsh gulps for breath and I scrambled to my feet, but, as I did so, I realized with a start that the marble couple weren't alone in the woods.

There, next to the unkempt remains of a hawthorn hedge, overgrown with ivy to create a natural bower, was another sculpture of a man, this one spreadeagled on a white marble bed, his erection pointing skyward. Both his fisted hands and the outward turn of his ankles rested against the bedposts as though he were bound, unable to move amid the disarray of bedding. His partner squatted over his face, her knees wide apart to show the puckered bud of her anus and the swollen arousal of her cunt as she lowered herself onto his open mouth. Her hands rested on her thighs; her eyes were locked on his begging penis. I could imagine her next move. She would arch over the tensed muscles of his belly and take his stretched cock into her mouth. Or I would beat her to it. I would slip out of my shorts and panties and straddle him and kiss her and nurse at her hard nipples while I settled down onto his penis. Archaeologists have found stone dildos in Neolithic digs. Clean, rain-washed stone; how could I not want to know what it felt like?

At the thought, I jerked opened my shorts and shoved a hand deep into my knickers, convulsing against my fingers at first contact, catching my breath with a hard tug of my lungs. I was wet and slick and the smell of me, aroused, suddenly dominated the rain-washed air. I brought my slippery fingers to my lips to taste, then thought better of it and wiped my wetness all over the man's cock, an act that made me drench myself, made me stroke him all the more, made me reach to fondle and tweak the woman's erect nipples. I could imagine that the look of arousal on her face was because of me as much as him, because she wanted to see me ride his cock while she rode his mouth, because she wanted me to play with her tits while she returned the favour. The view in my head was vivid, and for what my imagination couldn't fill in, the sculptor had furnished every minute detail in luscious, caress-able 3D. The tableau was all so real, and the wet grip of my pussy at the thought of riding that hefty stone cock sent me convulsing into an orgasm, clenching and quivering out my release until I doubled over the bed, my head resting on the man's sculpted belly. And there I half lay, gasping for breath, revelling in the aftershocks. When I rose, my cheek was wet from the rain on the stone so I took the cotton scarf from around my neck and wiped my face, resisting the urge to wipe down below where I had completely soaked my panties.

But I did wipe my sticky fingers, planning to wear my horny scent home around my throat, close to my face, and then I'd have another good wank when I got back to the cottage. As I turned to go, I caught a glimpse of other sculptures nestled in the heavy foliage along the length of the overgrown path. I couldn't tell how many. As I squinted to see, there was a loud snap of a twig, and the spell was broken. I yanked my zipper up and gave a wild look around. Another snap and a rustle low in the dense thicket had me grabbing for my rucksack and running for the gap in the fence. Once safely back on the path, I hoofed it hard all the way home to the cottage.

I had no intention of returning. Really! Just your basic trespassing was as much a walk on the wild side as I was up for. But then I dreamed that night. I dreamed that the statues had all been brought to life by my sexual attentions, by the touch of my aroused juices against the stone. When the moon came up, they followed me back to the cottage. I, being a good hostess, invited them in to do very naughty things to me. I've never had an orgasm wake me up before, but as I lay there in the bed trembling out my release, fingering my wet pussy, spurring myself on to another one, I kept wondering about the man's cock. He was all tied there to the bed just waiting for me to mount him. He was big enough that I'd have to work to sheath him, but as I rode four fingers to another orgasm before falling back into a sated sleep, I was pretty sure I was up for the challenge.

Even after the dream, I wasn't going to go back. I'm simply not a rule breaker. But somehow in my hurried exit, I'd lost my good luck scarf. It was just a cheap paisley neckerchief I wore when I walked. It was bright and cheery. I bought it from a shop in Tintagel as a reward for finishing a particularly challenging leg of the Southwest Coast Path. It had been a personal triumph, something there'd been way too few of in the past two years. Back then I was just beginning to realize what walking could do to ease my depression.

When I woke up the next morning, I masturbated to thoughts of eating out the woman in the first set of sculptures, who was poised to suck the man's cock. I masturbated a lot in those days. It was my escape from the thoughts that dragged me down, it was the one place where I had control, in the pleasuring of my flesh, in the exploration of my great unknown that was almost as varied in its offering as my walking was.

But all discussion aside, my reasons for returning to the breach in the fence were just excuses. The truth was I couldn't resist a proper look around. Who could have under the circumstances?

My cottage wasn't far from the hole in the fence. I had already convinced myself over breakfast that I was just flighty from trespassing, that I really hadn't heard anything the day before that couldn't be explained away easily if I had stayed around to investigate. In thirty minutes, I stood at the breach once more, heart hammering, sweat dripping down between my breasts from the unusually intense sun. This time I squeezed through the gap in the fence without a second thought. Honestly, it was just a little look-see. And besides, I really wanted my scarf back.

The shade of the trees was a relief from the heat and, as I made my way around the rhododendrons and hawthorn anticipating a little exploration, I stopped short in my tracks. There was my scarf folded neatly and tied over the eyes of the statue about to fellate the marble erection of her male counterpart.

I was just going to grab the scarf and run and never come back. Really, that was my plan. But as I approached I caught a whiff of sandalwood, and there was a rustling behind the rhodies. I froze, nostrils flaring, ears and eyes straining. Maybe I'd imagined the sandalwood. I stepped forward cautiously, and there it was again. It was coming from my scarf! I glanced around quickly. The wood was silent, not even the whisper of a breeze. Cautiously, I bent to sniff the scarf, and my insides stirred, low and humid. Could I recognize the scent of a man mixed with the sandalwood and with my own picante smell? Surely it was my imagination, but my pussy clenched in muscle memory, and there I was bending down close to the woman's bound wrists and her parted pussy, sniffing like a bitch looking for a mate. Something in the scent, something more than just sandalwood, made everything down below my belly tight and heavy. I hadn't been with a man in a long time. The roller-coaster ride of trying to find someone and build a relationship was just too much for me. But the scent still haunted me; the smell of maleness, the smell of masculine pheromones rubbing up against my own, stimulating the biological urge that left me aching, itching, needing to fuck. And I was certain it was there. I could feel it way down where my pussy pouted, slick and tetchy.

With awkward hands I undid the scarf from the sculpture's eyes and placed it around my neck, close to where I could feel my pulse beat, beat, beating in my throat. I walked to the sculpture of the man on the bed. The urge to interact was overwhelming and, for some unbelievable reason, even more so with the possibility of being watched. I lay down on the stone bed and threw one booted leg over the man's waist just above his hips. I lay my head on his chest where I had a perfect view of the marble pussy he was about to eat. It was a position that allowed me to rub against his hip, to get that hardness right where I needed it. I still wasn't brave enough to slide down my shorts and panties and mount his thick cock. The feel of the stone was warm against my thighs, against my bare arms, and I wanted more. I undid my bra and lifted my shirt and felt a surge of wet pleasure in my panties as my nipples raked the sun-drenched marble.

There was rustling in the trees. I could hear it. I was sure I could, as I pumped against the man's hip, sliding more on top of him with each gyration, wriggling my fingers down so they could get into my shorts where I was hot and hungry. I was certain I could hear heavy breathing, but then I wanted to hear heavy breathing, I wanted to make someone come by watching me come. I lifted myself just enough to slide my top up and slip my arms out of the sleeves. I didn't take it completely off, just in case I had to leave in a hurry. It bunched around my neck next to the scarf, allowing me to wriggle free of the bra so that my whole chest and belly pressed against rock. My nipples plumped and beaded until they felt like the stone against which they chafed.

I was completely on top of the sculpture by the time I came, spread-legged, driving my hips up and down his torso, still not brave enough to mount his ever-taunting cock, but brazen enough to wipe my pussy-soaked fingers up over his chest, down around his penis and even rub them against his parted lips. Then I collapsed in a pheromonal heap where I lay.

I couldn't believe that I actually slept. Okay, I sleep a lot when I'm depressed, but this was an in and out sort of place. Whether I was being watched or not, someone knew I'd been there, and that I shouldn't be. Nevertheless, I slept, soundly and deeply. It was the slight chill that woke me, that alerted me to the growing shadows, to the passage of way more time than I'd intended to spend.

I slid off the man and off the stone bed and was about to put on my bra when I thought better of it. I pulled the shirt down over my bare tits, then took the bra and tied one of the man's wrists to the headboard with it. I thought about taking off my panties for the other, but I couldn't bring myself to leave something so intimate and so soaked with my essence. Instead, I removed the scarf and bound the other wrist. That done, I straightened, tucked and turned to go. I might not have even noticed in my rush to get home before dark, had the first set of sculptures not been right in my line of sight when I turned. And there, bound around the wrists of the woman about to suck cock, was a bright blue silk tie.

I swallowed back a little whimper and tried to will my feet to run. But, I swear, they wouldn't. They would only carry me as far as the sculpture where they dropped me on my knees just behind the bound hands and the raised pussy of the woman. This time there was no mistaking, the air was heavy with the smell of sandalwood and male heat.

With fingers now cold from nerves, fingers still smelling of my cunt, I reached out and stroked the clearly expensive silk. It was soft against my caress and still warm from the waning sun or perhaps still warm from its owner's body. It was bound around the sculpture's wrists in a series of knots that were beautiful to look at, and would have held her securely if they had been a little tighter. Carefully, barely breathing, half expecting whoever had done this while I slept to pounce from behind a tree and grab me, I slipped the tie from the woman's wrist and tucked it, still knotted, into my rucksack. Then I hurried back through the fence.

I walked home with my tits bouncing and my pussy wet from making love to a statue while some unseen stranger watched. I barely got in the door to the cottage before I stripped. Then I carefully pulled the knotted tie from my backpack and hurried into my bedroom. It took some doing, but I was able to slide my hands into the little wrist-shaped noose. Not behind my back, though. I wanted it in front of me so I could see it while I touched myself, so I could feel it resting against my pubic curls while my fingers shoved and scissored into my cunt.

I fell asleep with the tie binding my wrists. That night in my dreams, I wandered among the sculptures in a heavy glaze of moonlight, and the one who watched me, the one who left the tie, took me from behind, yanking the scarf from my neck and tying it over my eyes with rough hands. He never spoke. His breath was heavy, his body scented with sandalwood and desire, his touch strangely impersonal.

In my dreams, he tied me to the marble bed, now vacated by the amorous couple. He tied me there, spreadeagled, my pussy exposed and begging and my breasts peaking towards the moon. In my dream I feared he'd left me there as punishment for going where I wasn't invited. He didn't touch me; he didn't kiss me; he didn't speak. And just when the panic rose to a near fever pitch, he mounted me without warning. In my dream I screamed and tried to struggle, but I couldn't. I was bound. The world morphed from shades of silver and slate to bright bursts of colour, blood and roses, heat and fire, sex that seared and burned and left its after-image on every cell of my flesh. There was only my cunt and his cock to fill the vast dreamscape, to burn the woods down around us and mark again and again the trespass.

I woke up aching and tender as though I had been so ravaged, aching and tender as though I desperately needed to be so ravaged. My wrists were still bound, my fingers were still nestled in the slick of me.

I didn't go back to the breach that day. My mind buzzed with all that had happened. I needed to think through the strange space in my head that had opened up, a space that hadn't been there before. I wandered the narrow steep streets of Lyme and walked on the Cobb and the Ammonite Pavement amid the flurry of tourists and fossil hunters. I wandered through Mill Green, even walked the beach to Charmouth while the tide was out. When I returned to my cottage in the fading light, I knew that tomorrow I'd go back through the breach. And I knew I'd keep doing so until the mysterious sculptor showed himself or until it was time for me to return home. Strange how even then I assumed that it was the sculptor who watched me. Of course I had a vivid imagination. For all I knew it could have been the janitor or the groundskeeper. For all I knew the sculptor was long gone, dead before I was born. Perhaps the unkempt state of the sculpture garden was because the present owner was embarrassed by it, or perhaps he was the one who sneaked away for a wank periodically. Perhaps I was an unexpected treat for him to perv on. But in my fevered imagination, the sculptor was already my lover by virtue of my intimacy with his work. I was resolved that whether I ever saw him or not, in my next visit, I would consummate our relationship in the company of his creations.

In my fantasies I'm often bolder and braver than I am in reality. Such was the case the next day when I arrived at the breach. My nerves had settled in the pit of my stomach like a coiled snake, and I had convinced myself I'd just return the tie, take back my bra and scarf, have a look around at the rest of the sculptures and leave. I mean really, it was simple. I had trespassed. I had a very active imagination, and what I was doing could become very dangerous if I escalated the situation.

My heart felt like a huge gong beating against my sternum as I moved cautiously past the big oak, anticipating . . . anticipating what?

The first set of sculptures stood in a pale wash of sunlight, as though they had never been touched. No tie, no scarf. Nothing. I hurried past to the couple on the stone bed, my disappointment bottoming as I saw that they too were completely unadorned. My bra and my scarf were gone, and nothing had been left in their place. Was that it then? Had we two had a wank, exchanged trophies and that was all there was to be? I stood staring at the sculpture with its accusing erection pointing at me, no longer in the mood to mount it, no longer in the mood to leave another memento. I was no longer able to remember why I thought that I had connected, on some level, with the mystery man in the thicket. He was probably the rich old fart who owned the place. I was nothing more than a trespasser allowed to transgress because I was entertaining.

I was hardly aware that I had begun to move again, to walk, to put one foot in front of the other. Nor did it seem to matter that my feet were following the overgrown path deeper into the woods, further from the fence. My descent was witnessed only by the stone glimpses of the sculptor's work, a veritable orgy of breasts presented, penises demanding, cunts displayed. And yet in the lustful abandon carved in rock, not one cock penetrated, not one pussy was filled, and in the wild eyes of the statues, not one face was sated or satisfied or at ease. There was raw burning need, there was aching and longing and frustration, but there was no satisfaction on those faces.

Each set of sculptures along the path was like a new page in an erotic novel, ripe with possibilities, but yet disturbingly without resolution. In breathless fascination, I studied each one. Each one took me a little further into the shadowy depths of the wood and into the darker corners of my imagination. Each one took me a little further from the breach in the fence. One at a time I inspected them, tried to memorize them. I seriously considered taking photos on my iPhone, but that seemed like a violation somehow. As I walked, the beating of my heart felt magnified, moving through me with a thunderous rhythm and then moving beyond me, out to each statue, out to each unsatisfied work in marble, moving over them, beat, beat, beat. Passing through them, beat, beat, beat. And then returning, not to the confines of my ribcage, but to the juncture between my legs, beat, beat, beat; settling with urgent force right behind my clit at the place where all that was flesh and bone and solid opened and expanded and gave way to emptiness seeking to be filled, aching for the same satisfaction for which the statues seemed to ache. But the statues were solid and substantial and impenetrable, while my flesh was open and vulnerable and empty.

And then I saw her in a web of black rope. I think I cried out. I might have even screamed. The play of light and shadows made her seem so real, bound there, arms extended between two birch trees, extended and stretched until every marble muscle, every sinew in her biceps and shoulders bulged. Her eyes were wild; her mouth was open, perhaps to gasp, perhaps to plead for her release. She knelt on the ground, knees spread wide to display lust that defied the binding of her thighs bent tightly against her calves. The woman was stone, but the rope was real. And so was the perfect red rose caught up in the knots that bound the woman's chest, pressed thorn-tight to her left breast.

"You're trespassing," came a sharp voice behind me.

I yelped ungracefully and nearly fell back against the sculpture as I spun to see who spoke.

Immediately I recognized his face. His was the face of every male sculpted there in the overgrown wood, and yet, I hadn't noticed until I saw him, sun-kissed like my first view of his sculptures. His hair was dark, nearly as black as the rope that bound the woman. It fell to the collar of his white shirt, which he wore unbuttoned and untucked. It was thick and heavy and my fingers twitched with the urge to touch it. In spite of the dark hair, his eyes were deep-ocean blue. Unlike the sculptures, there was a long scar snaking the length of the left side of his face, barely missing his eye before disappearing below his ear. There was another puckered trail of scarring visible from his open shirt. It ran from his collarbone over the swell of his left pectoral muscle, stopping just before it reached the golden apricot erection of his nipple. He wore faded jeans that rode low on his hips, revealing the tensing and relaxing of his muscles as he breathed, while only just managing to conceal the erection pressing tight against the zipper. His hands were relaxed at his sides and his feet were bare.

"You're the sculptor? You made them?" My voice was a tremor of nerves.

"You know that I did." He stepped towards me in an olfactory wave of sandalwood and male lust, pulling a Swiss Army knife from his pocket, and opening it.

I gasped and stumbled backward, landing on my butt between the spread of the woman's legs. He offered a bemused smile as he moved to one of the birch trees, selected a supple young branch about the circumference of his finger and roughly the length of his arm. He sliced it free with a single arc of the knife, which brought another involuntary gasp from my throat.

"Don't be ridiculous," he said, as he removed the leaves, all but a few at the very tip. "The knife's not for you, but the switch is. You were trespassing."

"There's a huge ugly hole in your fence. In fact your entire fence is ugly. It's an eyesore," I shot back, as though that vindicated me for coming right on in. Three times.

"Thank you for bringing that to my attention. I'll have it fixed," he said. "Now take off your shorts."

"What?" Before I could protest, he brought the switch down hard across the stone thigh of the bound woman only inches from my own leg and I yelped, then cursed.

"Do it!" he said.

"What, so you can hit me with that?"

He dropped to his knees in front of me, so close I could feel his breath on my face, I could see the dilation of his pupils. "There are lots of things I can do with this lovely switch, darling, besides warm your bottom, now take off your shorts."

Strangely it never occurred to me that I was wearing shoes, and he wasn't. I could have probably outrun him and made it back to the breach. Instead, I took off my shorts, struggling to get them down over my walking boots.

"And your panties," he added. "Oh, don't play coy with me, this is what you've wanted from the beginning, from the very first moment you suspected you were being watched, isn't it? Isn't it?" He raised the tip of the switch beneath my chin and lifted it so I had little choice but to meet his gaze.

"Yes," I whispered, and I eased my knickers down over my hips, feeling the tickle of grass against my bare buttocks as I settled back onto the ground.

From where I'd laid them on top of my shorts, he picked up my panties and stuffed them into the pocket of his jeans.

And suddenly I was shy, even though I had fantasized about meeting the sculptor, about him commanding me the way he did the stone he'd shaped so evocatively. I shrunk back against the statue, my arms wrapped tightly around my knees. But with the flick of the birch he thwacked my hands, and I winced. "Lift your arms onto hers." He gestured to the statue at my back.

Trembling slightly, I did as he asked, pressing my arms up and out along the length of the woman's, feeling as though I were being prepared for some obscene crucifixion. Then he eased the tip of the switch in between my knees like the brush of a feather, and yet demanding enough that I grudgingly opened.

"Wider," he said. "Let me see your cunt. You want me to see, don't you? You've wanted to show me, but you weren't brave enough." He tap, tap, tapped the switch against the inside of my thighs, and I had little choice but to comply. He kept tapping, and I kept opening until my thighs rested against the spread legs of the sculpture at my back.

The catch of his breath and the jerk of his cock against the restraint of his fly were the first signs that he might be moved in any way by me, the first signs that he was anything other than upset about the trespass. A wash of emotion crossed his face so quickly that I almost missed it, and then his expression was unreadable again, but his voice was tight, breathless.

"I've imagined what you looked like down there. And every time you come here, I wait and watch, but you keep it from me." He nodded down to my pussy. "You tease me by touching it, by playing with it, by filling the whole glade with the scent of it, but you keep it from me." Without warning, he brought the end of the switch up between my labia and I jerked and gasped at the parting of my lips with something other than my fingers, the parting of my pussy for the pleasure of someone else. With the very tip of the branch, he probed me, and I shifted my hips and quivered, feeling my slickness sheen the remaining leaves.

"You left me your scarf and your bra," he said. "But this is what I want." With an artist's flourish, he tapped the springy birch against my clit, and I caught my breath at the shock of it. I sucked my lip and rocked and lifted my ass to get closer to it. The next flick stung enough to make my eyes water, and damn near enough to make me come. That I hadn't expected.

"This is what I need." His voice was nearly crushed by the weight of his breath. With the hand not wielding the switch against my snatch, he undid his fly and released his engorged penis, watching it for a second as though he didn't completely trust it to its new freedom. And I watched it too. Was this the source of his inspiration, the never completely sated lust that worked its way out in such demanding, moving art? When I was most my creative self, my pussy drove me, always slick, always heavy, always demanding more of me, more of my head, more of my heart, more of my imagination. The fire never left me when I was there in that place. I was never sated, and I never wanted to be. I only wanted more of the lust that led me deeper into myself.

Like the sculpture on her knees to receive her counterpart's cock, I wanted the cock of their creator in my mouth. But as I took the position and crawled forwards on my hands and knees, the sharp smack of the birch came down on my bare arm and I yelped and pulled away.

He crab-walked back beyond my reach. "Don't touch me!" His eyes were wild, his breathing fast and furious. Sweat sheened his brow, and his cock was suddenly flaccid. "Don't ever, ever touch me."

"I'm sorry! I'm sorry," I managed, rubbing my stinging arm.

He scrambled to his feet and paced in front of me. "I don't . . ." He half turned his back to me and I heard his fly zip as he retucked himself. "I don't like to be touched. I . . . I can't stand it." He spat the words into the thicket, and I couldn't see his face. I could only see the rapid rise and fall of his shoulders, but I know distress when I see it. I know the sudden, unwelcome invasion of personal demons, and a quick glance around me at the sculptures, at the lack of satisfaction amid such an orgy of sexual want, suddenly made my heart ache. For the first time it hit me, not only was there no satisfaction, but not one of the sculptures was actually touching any of the others.

"All right." I barely recognized my own voice, calmer than it felt. "I won't touch you. I promise." Carefully I lowered my hand to my mons and began to stroke the wetness he had elicited. "Tell me what you want me to do."

The lash of the switch came so quickly across my hand that I bit my lip, tasted blood and cursed.

He stood once again facing me. "I don't want you to touch yourself until I say."

"Okay," I said, running the tip of my tongue over my wounded lip. I could see his cock beginning to strain once more at the half-closed zipper.

"Get up," he said. He nodded back down the path towards the fence. For a second I was afraid my punishment was to be sent home with no satisfaction and no shorts. But he stopped me next to the stone bed. "Suck his cock," he said. When I offered him a shocked look, he added, "I know you want to. You've wanted to from the beginning."

I stood beside the bed, and leaned in, touching the tip of the stone phallus cautiously with my tongue. The taste was earthy, slightly salty, not totally unlike pre-come. The threat of the switch against my bare bottom spurred me on. I lowered the O of my lips down over the stone, careful to protect my teeth from the unforgiving marble, feeling the sting where I'd bitten myself as I sheathed it. The resulting groan from behind me and the catch of breath urged me on. I took the penis deep into my throat and gagged. My eyes watered, I knocked my teeth, and pulled back wiping my lips. I glanced over my shoulder at the sculptor's once again free erection bobbing in his hand. Wanting to please him, I tried again, this time opening my throat, breathing deeply through my nose.

"Yes," he hissed. "That's it, just like I imagined. Now spread your legs. I want to see your pussy." He slipped the switch between my thighs and I spread for him. "I want to see how slippery it makes you, to suck cock." He guided the switch up to stroke between my folds and my pussy gripped desperately, wetly.

Then he moved so he could see my mouth working up and down the stone. I noticed he'd lost his shirt. He brushed the switch, which now smelled of my heat, along the side of my cheek, while his other hand pumped furiously at his hard-on. "This is what you want, isn't it? What we both want." He leaned so close that I felt his breath, and I thought he might actually kiss me. But instead he spoke in a whisper. "It's not all we want, though, is it?"

I pulled away and wiped my mouth on the back of my hand, knowing with a little skitter in my belly what would come next.

"Your shirt and bra. Lose them." The urgency in his voice was mirrored in the anxious jut of his cock liberally crowned in pre-come.

As I took off my shirt and bra, he moved to cup and caress the breasts of the female counterpart who squatted, poised to ride the man's face, and I swear I felt his touch on my own heavy nipples. As his hand slid down her belly, as his fingers circled her clit, I drenched myself and whimpered like a baby, gripping my legs together, barely able to contain my lust.

He slicked his fingers with saliva and stroked harder at the woman's splayed cunt, but his eyes were locked on mine. "You know what to do next. You've known since the first time you came here."

I nodded slowly. Holding his gaze, I mounted the stone bed and positioned myself above the man's marble cock, the sculptor's cock, I reminded myself, and that thought made me even wetter. As I lowered myself, I shifted so that he got a view of the whole of me. And then slowly, deliciously, I squatted onto the cock still slick from my mouth, feeling it stretch me and shove at me and fill me until I cried out in some insane blend of pleasure and pain.

"Oh God," the sculptor gasped. "I've wanted this. I've needed this so badly. Now fuck me," he said. "Fuck me like the filthy little trespasser you are."

And I did. I rode him hard, feeling myself abraded and bruised and not caring, feeling a river of lust flow from me and down onto the stone cock; feeling as bruised by the groans and grunts of the sculptor as from the stone of his creation. He knew. He had long ago internalized the lack of satisfaction, the lack of release, the lack of human contact that drove him to carve stone. "You want to taste me," I managed in a breathless rush. "I know you do." I lifted myself from the cock, and wiped the flat of my hand up between my folds where the heat of me gathered salty sweet and thick. His eyes widened as I stretched forward across the stone torso and wiped my juices over the woman's marble cunt. "Taste me. It's you I'm wet for. I'm yours to taste."

He rose onto the bed in front of me, as I settled back on the cock, placing my hands against the stone thighs behind me, careful not to touch the sculptor as he manoeuvred his way in to lick and suck my wetness from the rock. The powerful muscles of his back expanded and contracted and moved in an exquisite dance of flesh and sinew. And, God, I wanted to touch him, to lay my face against him, to feel the pounding of his heart through his ribs while I came. Instead, I rode his cock, touching him vicariously, just as he licked my pussy until the lust in both of us built to the point of no return, until it could no longer be contained by stone. It started with a rake of my clit against his unforgiving art and expanded up my spine through the crown of my head. I growled it, I screamed it, I wailed it. The sculptor repositioned himself to face me, tugging at his erection in desperate dragging strokes, his face dark, the muscles along his neck corded as though they would snap. And he came, shooting the warm, viscous essence of himself in an arc to the hollow of my throat, to the valley between my breasts, to the tightened muscles of my belly. He never blinked, he never looked away, but he held me in a gaze as steady as marble as blue as the sky above us, and the lines of his face were as hard edged as the stone he'd sculpted. And just when I was sure they'd shatter, they relaxed, softened and curved into a look that might have been the look of a satisfied man.

"You can't come back," he said. We lay on either side of the man on the stone bed, as close to a post-coital snuggle as he would allow.

"Why not?" I asked.

"Because you're trespassing."

"You could give me the keys to the front door," I said.

"Why would you even come back. You can't touch me." He rolled onto his side and turned his back to me, already brooding a loss that hadn't yet happened.

"But you can touch me. You have touched me." I slid my hand across the marble aching to comfort him. "In fact, I'm sure we touched each other."

"I have to go." He stood and began to dress. "You should go too. It'll be dark soon."

He walked me as far as the first set of sculptures; the uncertainty of what was to come already tightening my chest. He caressed my cheek with the birch switch. "You shouldn't come back," he said, holding me in that deep blue gaze.

"I know," I replied. Honestly, I knew. This couldn't be good for me. I had enough of my own demons, I really didn't need someone who was even more neurotic than I was. I even contemplated not going back. But of course I couldn't stay away.

* * *

The next day there were workmen at the fence and the breach had been closed with pristine new boards. My heart plummeted. I didn't even know the sculptor's name, and he didn't know mine. He never asked. He just shut me out because we couldn't touch. But I had touched him and he me. Didn't he understand? What we shared happened in places where people *really* touch each other, deeper places than flesh and bone. How could he not know?

I swallowed back tears that I wouldn't allow, reminding myself I was only the trespasser. I deserved what I got. And if things had been different, I'd have had enough wank material for ages to come. I'd have filed it all away with my best memories, and I'd have smiled and wriggled in my wet panties every time I thought about it. But then I never could let things be what they were. I always had to make everything personal. I always had to want more.

As I turned to go, one of the workmen called after me. "You the woman who's been trespassing here?" My pulse raced. I shielded my eyes to the sun and nodded. He handed me a manila envelope. "I'm supposed to give this to you." Then he went back to work on the fence and left me standing with the sea at my back and the ugly fence in front of me.

Back in my cottage, I poured a glass of wine and settled on the sofa. I drank for courage, then I opened the envelope. Inside was my scarf washed, pressed and neatly folded.

This time, I didn't fight back the tears. I let them come in racking sobs. I cried for my poor untouched sculptor, whose name I didn't even know, as alone in his isolation as I was in mine. I went to bed and cried myself into the soft oblivion of dreamless sleep.

It was late morning when I awoke, aching all over, but clear-headed. If ever I needed a walk, it was now. I dressed and grabbed my rucksack. I'd pick up a sandwich at the local shop. I needed to go before I changed my mind. I couldn't deal with this loss if I were depressed. I needed to face it from a position of strength. Just before I left, I grabbed my scarf. It was a symbol of my victories, something I really needed to be reminded of right now. I would wear it, and I would heal. As I shook it open to tie it around my neck, a note fell from between the folds of fabric. It read: *If you want your bra and panties, you'll have to come get them. No trespassing. This time you'll have to come through the front door like a civilized person.*

There was an email address and a mobile number.

Laughing out loud, I texted a response*: I'm fine with the front door, but don't expect me to return your tie. I'm not that civilized.*

And then I went for a nice long walk.

Tell Me

Donna George Storey

You ask me for a bedtime story.

Remember the rules: I tell the tale; you make it real. So snuggle up close because I like to feel it when my story makes you hard.

Shall we begin?

Once upon a time, in a great City of Commerce and Dreams, there was a Secretary named Margaret and Her Boss.

It was just after Christmas, the season when the light is thin and a pitiless wind blows through the City's canyons. On this fateful January day, Her Boss – we'll call him Walter Grey – requested that Margaret come into his office to take dictation.

Early dusk had fallen, and Margaret instinctively caught her breath as she entered the room. Mr Grey's corner office looked straight into the bellies of similar soaring skyscrapers, each of a thousand windows now glowing in the darkness like golden tapestries adorning a lord's great hall. It reminded her of a banquet hall suspended in mid-air, like the evil giant's in "Jack and the Beanstalk". Margaret was predisposed to see beauty and magic wherever she could find it. The City and Mr Grey had, in the six months since she'd graduated from Katharine Gibbs, provided her an abundance of both.

Mr Grey gestured for her to sit on the sofa and offered her a drink, which didn't quite fit with dictation, but Margaret had yet to question Her Boss's judgement. She raised her whiskey dutifully when Mr Grey proposed they toast the prospect of signing up a certain Mr Hill as a new client before the end of the week.

"I know I can rely on you to help me seal this deal, Margaret," he said with a smile.

"You can count on me, sir." She beamed back.

"Hill and I had an interesting discussion at lunch today, and I'd like you to take down some notes for future reference."

Margaret crossed her legs and held her shorthand pad at the ready.

Mr Grey cleared his throat. "This is not exactly official business, but you'll see this information gives us valuable insight into our client's needs. Shall we begin? Now Hill and I had finished our steaks and were having one last martini for the road, when he casually asked me about the quality of the company's support staff – in particular, my secretary, Miss Peabody. He was curious if you were as competent as you were pretty."

Margaret's eyebrows shot up at the mention of her name, but she continued sliding her pencil over the page with professional *sang froid*.

"I assured him you were the most trustworthy assistant I'd had in all my years in the business, but that your sweet face belied a passionate nature that was frankly a torment to me."

At this the Secretary stopped short and regarded Mr Grey with wounded brown eyes. How could he reveal their affair to a business acquaintance? For indeed, Her Boss – or "Walt" as she called him in private – was making love to her on a regular basis after work in his divorcé apartment in the Upper West Side and occasionally on this very sofa when they stayed late to work on a "special project".

Mr Grey waved his hand as if he were giving her shoulder a reassuring pat from across the room. "Of course, he assumed you and I were having relations, but I quickly told him this was not true, as much as I wished it were."

Margaret exhaled quietly and bent over her notebook, although her stomach was still twisted in consternation. Whatever was Her Boss's purpose with this tale of half-truths?

He continued, "However, I did tell him that I'd been privy to the confession of another client, over a cocktail or two, and from this I'd become aware the young lady had an adventuring spirit that would make a beatnik girl blush. This man, whose name I naturally could not divulge, claimed he'd asked Miss Peabody out for a drink, which led to dinner and then a tryst in a hotel room involving a variety of sexual acts, most of them unspeakable in the company of gentlemen."

Margaret slapped her notebook down on her lap. "There's no such client. That's a complete fabrication, Walt."

"But you did exactly that with me, Meg," Mr Grey reminded her with a wink.

The young woman pressed her Cupid's bow lips together. Her Boss was indeed giving an accurate description of their first date. His mischievous tone and twinkling eyes told her, too, that like a father coming home from a business trip, Walter Grey's story was but a teasing prelude to a gift he had hidden away for her in his pocket. His trousers' pocket, if the past was any teacher.

"May I continue?" Mr Grey asked, one eyebrow arched.

Her curiosity piqued, Margaret nodded.

"I went on to tell Mr Hill that this fortunate client – who was alas, no gentleman – related the nature of these acts to me in detail. Miss Peabody had explained to him that although she was officially engaged to her high-school sweetheart, an upright, God-fearing boy, she occasionally indulged in a flirtation with a distinguished older man 'who knew what he was doing in bed but wouldn't expect anything long-term'. To this client's shock and delight, the first thing she did once they got to his room was fall down on her knees and pleasure him with her mouth, stimulating him orally to the point of release, which she then swallowed with a great show of enthusiasm, as a thirsty girl might slurp down a root beer float. The young lady proceeded to enjoy several spirited releases of her own during intercourse in a variety of positions. The client confessed that at the time, he was concerned, and I quote, 'she was so insatiable that she'd wear out my dick so I couldn't get it up for my wife for a week'."

By now Margaret had stopped taking dictation. She merely listened to Her Boss's words, her lips parted, her shapely chest heaving beneath her prim white blouse.

"Mr Hill found my tale of great interest, to judge by the eager light in his eyes and the way he wiped his lips repeatedly with his napkin. He then asked me why I had not been able to take advantage of my secretary's penchant for hotel romps with older men. I admitted that I'd tried to invite you for a drink, but you immediately put me in my place by pointing out that the president of the company would not look favourably on a workplace romance. I took that as a sly hint you were banging my boss and retreated."

A strange smile played over Margaret's lips. Her own role in Mr Grey's narrative was as fanciful as a fairy tale. Yet, as always, his deep, soothing voice was having a most enchanting effect on her body. Her panties, in particular, had become noticeably damp.

Mr Grey returned her smile. "You might want to take this next part down, Margaret."

As she picked up her dictation pad, her hands trembled.

"Hill laughed at my thwarted efforts, but I told him that my loss was likely his gain. For I'd seen Miss Peabody eyeing him with the same interest she'd shown my other very satisfied client. I mentioned that my secretary would be working late this evening with me on the presentation for him, but tomorrow night I'd bet good money she'd happily join him for a drink. And doubtless more."

Margaret felt a shameful flutter deep in her belly, a sensation she often experienced in the company of Mr Grey. Ambitious and restless, her lover was always proposing some new depravity for their amorous delight, acts so lewd that her dear mother back in Cleveland hadn't even thought to warn her against them. Yet, each time she lost more of her innocence to him, Margaret discovered a thrilling truth. Being bad felt very, very good. It was the most soaring pleasure she'd experienced in all of her twenty-one years. Until now, however, she'd told herself she did these sinful things for the higher purpose of pleasing the Man She Loved. But the faithless, and decidedly lustful, young woman in Her Boss's story was a very different character indeed.

She gulped. "Are you telling me you want me to go out for a drink with Mr Hill tomorrow? For real?"

Mr Grey nodded.

"And then go to his hotel room with him?"

"You always were a smart girl."

No words could get past the knot in her throat.

Brow furrowed in tender concern, Mr Grey sat next to her on the sofa and held the whiskey to her lips as if it were medicine. She drank deeply, then dabbed at her mouth with her handkerchief.

"But I love you, Walt," she said softly.

"I love you, too, darling. But you know Helen's lawyer took me to the cleaners. I need to bring in a big client to give you the life you deserve. Hill will be a huge step in that direction."

"I could never cheat on you with another man."

"If I tell you to do it for us, Meg, it's not cheating." Mr Grey's voice dropped to a murmur. "I'll be there with you in spirit every step of the way. Remember that you're my apprentice, a woman of uncommon instinct and sensuality. You can make this happen for us with your gift – your unique feminine sorcery."

Mr Grey ran his fingertip over the sensitive skin exposed by the modest V-neck of Margaret's blouse. She shivered.

"Make love to me, Walt. Right now."

"As much as I want to, my darling, I think you need to save your strength for tomorrow evening." Mr Grey squeezed her arm encouragingly. "By the way, I have something for you."

He pulled a small velvet jeweller's case from his jacket pocket. Through the swirl of confusion – and yes, arousal – Margaret secretly marvelled that she'd been right about the hidden gift.

"Isn't this exactly the kind of puny little rock an earnest young man would buy his virgin fiancée? It will make Hill all the harder to think he's stealing you away from a callow youth.

Ah, the deceitful hearts of men!" Chuckling at his own machinations, Mr Grey took the ring from the box.

Margaret extended her hand instinctively. As she inserted her slender finger into the golden band, a strange thought flitted through her brain – this timeless ritual was exactly the opposite of what a man and woman did with their bodies in bed.

"One more thing. I told Hill 'the client' mentioned you had no hair down there, the prettiest pink clamshell he'd ever seen. Hill practically jumped out of his chair at that piece of news. So you'll want to shave your privates when you have your bath." He slapped her thigh lightly, as if to send a high-strung filly trotting back to her stall. "Now, best be on your way home to get your beauty sleep."

Margaret rose and walked unsteadily to the door, dictation pad in hand.

"Oh, and Meg?"

She paused obediently.

"If you do a spanking good job on Hill, I just might get you a real ring next time."

His deep laughter coiled around her until she pulled the door closed with the lewd click of the latch fitting into the strike plate.

The next afternoon, Margaret was still feeling distracted by the unfamiliar sensation of shaved flesh between her legs when Mr Hill stopped by her desk to ask her out for a drink at his hotel. Her heart skipped a beat, and her secret muscles clenched. It was happening just as Her Boss had told her it would. But with a day to prepare herself, she knew just how to play her part. She accepted the invitation with a blush, then tossed him a coy glance that promised so very much more.

Just before she was to go off to meet Mr Hill at the cocktail lounge, Her Boss called her into his office. He had Margaret raise her skirt so he could check that she had complied with his intimate grooming request, then gave her a light kiss on the cheek so as not to disturb her make-up.

"Come over to my place afterward with a full report."

"Shall I bring my steno pad and take down minutes of the meeting with Mr Hill for your reference, sir?" she asked, pursing her lips saucily.

For once Mr Grey was taken aback, but he quickly recovered his composure. "Of course not, my dear. You'll whisper every dirty detail in my ear, like a Russian spy."

Margaret decided to walk to the Roosevelt, which was but a few blocks from the office building where she worked each day and some nights. To the click-clack of her high heels on the frosty pavement, she reminded herself how her lover had suggested she get through this "date". Mr Hill's genial red face and silver hair would become Walt's chiselled, Scandinavian good looks. Hill's round belly and thin legs would redistribute themselves into Walt's athletic physique. And Hill's manhood? Margaret's steady boyfriend back in high school had taught her how to satisfy him with her hand, but she could barely recall those back-seat gropings. But the pulsing heat, the musky scent, the salt-and-vinegar flavour of Walt's *thing* was burned into her memory. She'd lick this stranger's maleness and ride him to a lather as if he were her beloved. So would she work her "feminine sorcery" and earn Her Boss's approval for a job well done.

Thus fortified, she managed to be perfectly charming and flirtatious as she sat perched on a stool beside Mr Hill – "please, honey, call me 'Bob'" – at the hotel bar, nursing her whiskey sour.

"I know your name is Margaret, but I'm sure your friends call you something prettier."

She admitted she preferred "Meg", and so did he address her with an unflagging smile as the cocktail hour slipped into a duckling *à l'orange* dinner in the hotel restaurant. Margaret realized she did enjoy the company of this older man with his avuncular interest in her Ohio girlhood and his animated, almost giddy manner, as if he'd suddenly been paroled from a dour life sentence – at least for one evening.

Tipsy on wine and Bob Hill's obvious infatuation,

Margaret found it easy to follow him up to his room to fetch a book he was set on lending her, Robert Traver's *Anatomy of a Murder*. The novel wasn't for the faint of heart, he told her, but she struck him as unusually sophisticated for her age.

She accepted the book and then his kiss, with but a faint protest, "I'm engaged."

"Not tonight, honey," Bob Hill said, taking her in his arms. "Not tonight."

She kissed him back then, savouring the masculine taste of him: wine, cigarettes, the lingering note of citrus and Parisian decadence. She was equally beguiled by her own fiery response: the way her nipples hardened against his soft chest, the shudder rippling down her spine as his fingers found her zipper, the way her secret place tightened when he pulled down her panties and gazed upon her smooth cleft.

"Oh, my dear girl, what have you done to yourself down there?"

Margaret blushed. "I can feel a man ... *it* ... more this way," she stuttered, making it up on the spot, yet knowing somewhere inside that what she said was true.

Then Bob Hill fell to his knees and put his lips to her there, and although Walt had done this many times, it did feel different when she was bare. Hill's tongue burned deliciously, her own tortured flesh more sensitive to its sinuous movements. As she accepted his ultimate tribute to her feminine charms, Margaret felt the room dissolve around her so that she was floating high above the City, suspended in her own ecstasy. She'd thought this pulsing, electric sensation was a gift only Her Boss could give at his whim. But in fact she didn't need him at all. It was her own body, with its dizzying and marvellous response, that made this sweet, dark Magic possible.

Thighs shaking, she clutched at the side of the bed to steady herself against her impending release. That's when the setting of her diamond ring caught on the nubby surface of the bedspread, tugging her back to herself, the real reason she was here. And so she stopped Bob Hill, saying she preferred to have him inside for her finish. She then offered to pleasure him with her mouth.

He did not refuse.

His *thing* jutted straight out from his body rather than rearing skyward like Walt's, but his response made her feel just as powerful and daring. He called her mouth "hot, wet satin" and pawed her hair murmuring over and over like a prayer, "Such a sweet young thing and so very, very wicked."

He insisted they both gargle with mouthwash before he would kiss her again, and perhaps it was the sight of his paunchy stomach under the glare of the bathroom lights, but Margaret no longer feared she would lose control. She feigned one orgasm as she lay beneath him on the narrow twin bed and was about to run through her act again as he took her on her hands and knees, but suddenly he pulled out and rested between her legs, panting like a dog.

"I've heard about trollops like you. I heard you like to take it in the back door, too." Without waiting for her reply, he fumbled at her other hole, the one Walt had entered for the first time just a few weeks before.

Margaret's first impulse was to protest, but she was too distracted to recall the particulars of her alleged romp with the anonymous client. By all means, she had to stay on script, preserve Her Boss's credibility. If he had told Hill she was depraved enough to do this, too, then do it she must. Still she had enough wits about her to ask in a sultry voice, "You dirty old man, haven't you taken a lady back there before?"

"Hell, no," he growled. "And you're no lady. You're more wicked than any whore. Because you love it so much you do it for free."

Margaret's cheeks burned as if she'd been slapped. And yet, this insult, delivered in the madness of lust, was not far off target. She did love it. Not the physical act so much as the way her surrender transformed this worldly older man into someone so very different. She had brought him – literally – to his knees.

"You guessed my naughty secret, Bob," she cooed. "There's nothing I love more than getting screwed in the bum. So stick it in. Shoot your hot seed in my bunghole."

These were words Walt had taught her, words that had made her blush in bed with him, but now gave her the means to bring this interlude to a quicker conclusion. Bob Hill let out a groan and plunged into her rear entrance with abandon. Margaret braced herself against the headboard, grateful that Walt had initiated her more gently into this exotic form of coupling. Fortunately, her temporary lover took but a few thrusts to discharge with a guttural cry, "Oh, God, your ass is so fucking tight."

Mr Hill seemed genuinely disappointed when she said she couldn't spend the night. Her roommate was like a worrying mother, she told him, and would wait up until she returned. It wasn't quite a lie. Someone was waiting for her – most impatiently, she hoped.

Besides, something told her it was always best to leave a sucker wanting more.

In the cab on the way to Walt's apartment, Margaret wrinkled her nose at the smell of Bob Hill on her skin – the now acrid tang of his sweat, the faintly feral scent of his saliva. Her whole bottom tingled so fiercely, she could barely sit still. Tonight she'd been fucked and sodomized by a man for whom she had but the most passing affection. Yet that only seemed to make her all the hungrier for Walt inside her.

Her lover answered the door in his red plaid bathrobe, a tumbler of whiskey in his hand. His eyes leaped out at her, a wildcat pouncing on prey.

She threw herself against him. He hugged her tight, kissed her hair.

"Shall I tell you all about it?" she murmured into his shoulder. She sounded too breathless to be a Russian spy.

"Of course," he said, but his voice was curiously tight.

He sat on his leather recliner and pulled her onto his lap. She curled into his embrace, glancing around the sparsely furnished room, unrelieved by a single touch of feminine softness. She felt elated yet deliciously disgraced. She had once been such a good girl. Now she was the mistress of a divorced man – one who lent her out to other men for his own financial gain. She could only imagine what her mother would say about that.

"I did everything you told me to do," she said in a low, quick voice, thinking, perversely of slumber parties with her friends. "I complained about my dull fiancé. I let him lure me up to his room with the promise of some scary crime novel about a loose woman and her jealous husband. He just about had a heart attack when he saw me smooth down there. And he called me 'wicked' when I took him in my mouth, but I think he liked it very much. He really went wild, though, when I let him in the back way. I didn't remember you saying anything about doing *that* with the other client, but Bob, I mean Mr Hill, seemed to expect it."

Margaret felt her lover's body tense. "I mentioned no such thing, Meg. What did he tell you?"

The anger in his voice made her stomach turn to ice.

"He just said he'd heard I did that, so I assumed you wanted me to," she said, hoping a dutiful spirit would smooth over her apparent mistake. "He couldn't get it in right away, so I asked if it was his first time, and he said yes. That's good for us, isn't it? He'll be more grateful."

"I suppose." Walt's voice warmed, but only a degree or two.

Her chest tight with panic, Margaret knew she had to say something quickly to make it right again. "I have something else to tell you. About me. Us." She brushed her lips against her lover's cheek and pressed her thigh against his hardness, a promising sign that feminine sorcery might indeed save the evening from disaster. "I didn't climax with him, Walt. I didn't even get close. Everything he did to me made me long for you. So what you said last night was true. You *were* there with me every step of the way."

He sighed. "I know. Damn my overactive imagination, I couldn't stop thinking about you with him all evening. It was torture, Meg. Torture. I was crazy to make you part of this deal. And tomorrow I have to get that bastard drunk and listen to him crow about having you. It won't be a phony story this time. Every goddamned word will be true."

Margaret slipped her hand under the collar of his robe, marvelling at how meltingly soft his skin was over the hard muscle. Why did she find his suffering so sweet? "Just remember that everything he tells you will be a lie."

"Will it?"

"You'll believe my side of the story over his, won't you?"

In the dim light, Walt searched her face. "Let me buy you a real ring, Meg."

"Now? All the stores are closed, silly," she laughed, nuzzling his neck. She felt too restless, too hungry for such romantic talk.

He tightened his arms around her. "Tell me what you want then."

She paused as if deep in thought. But she'd already plotted out in the cab exactly what she wanted to happen next.

"You must do everything he did to me. But this time will be different. Your kiss will taste familiar, whiskey sweet, not strange and spicy like his. When you undress me and see my bare, pink cleft, you won't cry out in surprise, because you'll know I did it at your command. And when you kiss me down there, I won't have to hold back because I'm saving myself for the man I love. I'll let myself really feel your wet tongue lapping and swirling until my insides turn to syrup. Then, when I lie under you in bed, I'll move my hips against your belly so that I reach a real climax. After that, I'll get on my hands and knees like a bitch in heat and let you mount me, overlay his scent on my body with yours, like an animal."

Walt whimpered and arched up against her. His face was moist with sweat.

"When you take me the back way, I'll shout out as I did for him, 'Shoot your hot seed in my bunghole.' But you won't be rough and desperate like he was. You'll be as gentle as when you first taught me those filthy words, that forbidden Greek pleasure. Do all these things for me, my love, and then I will be yours again."

With a soft moan of acquiescence, Walt helped her up from his lap. He fell to his knees before her.

Margaret smiled down at him. This was the real Magic of the City. By day she was a humble secretary, serving every whim of an arrogant, world-weary man she called Her Boss. But when the neon winked on and the ribbons of sky above the canyons turned to blue velvet, she was no longer the apprentice. Night transformed her into this – a Great Sorceress of formidable powers.

Because the man kneeling at her feet would do everything she told him to do, until the sun rose, and the story began anew of a Secretary named Margaret and Her Boss.

That's my bedtime story. Who doesn't love a happy ending? It's obvious you do. Now remember the rules: I tell the story. You make it real.

Shall we begin?

Saving Sage

Michael Hemmingson

1.

Never been much of a ladykiller. I am a man killer. That is what I do now. Never considered myself a "hit man," but I have killed men, back when I was a sniper in the Army Rangers, stationed in Iraq and Afghanistan.

I was good with a rifle, but never that good with the girls. In high school, I was one of the straight-arrow good guys that always got the dreaded "I like you as a friend, but . . ." Maybe that's why I joined the Army, got buff, and was recruited into the Special Ops: so I would never be that geeky kid again, and get fooled the way Nancy Ellen Crow fooled me. She was the town slut but I was not wise to that stuff and when I went out with her and she wanted to fuck in the back seat of my father's car, she laughed at me because I came too fast. "You'll never please a woman, you nerd," Nancy Ellen Crow said over and over and laughed and laughed.

"You have a good shooting eye, Private," I was told by a certain lieutenant colonel who was observing the new grunts on the firing range. "I could use a man like you on my team," he said, and then I was made a killer.

That's what I'm good at: aiming through the scope and getting the shot to the head. That's why I was on the roof of an apartment building that night I saved Sage, lying flat on my belly, a McMillan Tac-50 rifle nestled on a tripod and pressed against my arm, my right eye resting on the scope like my eye had been made for it.

Waiting.

Waiting three hours.

Tick-tock . . . time means nothing to a sniper. They teach you to compartmentalize the idea of time so that hours are like minutes, minutes like seconds.

They teach you infinite patience in the Rangers. You could sit for ten, thirteen hours waiting for a mark, out in the cold desert, alone with your thoughts.

Keep your thoughts simple, they told us, keep your thoughts on the job and the kill, not home, the past or the future.

Thinking: *I am doing this for her, because she asked me to.*

She convinced me.

We made a deal.

She said he came here every Thursday night to see his mistress, and he usually left at eleven to go home.

Eleven: he emerged from the apartment building, just as I was told.

A tall man, six-foot-three, in his early sixties, with a big head of shaggy silver hair: an easy target.

Followed him via the scope to his car, a black SUV.

Waited until he got into the driver's seat.

Pulled the trigger.

No need to leave a mess of brains and blood on the street.

The CSI guys could clean up the car. Keep them all busy for a few weeks trying to find his killer, trying to figure out why he was the target of a professional hit.

But I'm not a hit man.

I'm just a guy who knows how to use a rifle, and I did it for the promise of sex and servitude.

I'm a lonely guy. I need things like any man.

It's not easy for me to meet women. I take what I can get.

Now I got it.

Maybe love.

2.

Stopped in the strip club for a drink, to watch the girls. Stayed at the bar counter, not the seats around the stage, what I call Peeper's Row. I never like getting close to the stage, where you can see too much of a girl: the shaved pubes, the small pimples, the lines on the face under the lights. That always takes the spiciness out of it all.

She came onstage.

Nordic features, blonde hair in a ponytail, wasp waist, about five foot eight or so with legs that went all the way up to her lungs.

She strutted like a true torrid harlot in a schoolgirl outfit with book bag, blue blazer, tight white blouse filled to bursting by C-cup breasts, grey pleated miniskirt six inches shorter than any schoolgirl would ever wear in public, white fishnet stockings, black patent leather pumps with stiletto heels that enhanced those already remarkable gams.

She went into her routine, shedding first the book bag, then the blazer, her blue eyes and pouting red lips teasing the audience. Gyrating to the beat of her music, she slowly unbuttoned the blouse and worked the sides of the stage, the men seated there caressing her thighs as they stuffed bills into the fishnets – a switch from the usual garter, I noted. The last button came undone, and she danced backwards almost out of the spotlight.

Whipped off the blouse, spun it over her head and threw it backwards. She wasn't wearing a bra. They never do here. High-stepped forward into the light again, shimmying, those magnificent, sturdy tits with deep cleavage exposed like a Taliban fighter poking his head out of a dune; the pink, erect nipples poking proudly forward, inviting kisses and caresses that would have put Marilyn Monroe, in her prime, to shame.

Dropping into a crouch, she crawled her way across the front of the stage like a submissive slave girl, presenting herself for the attentions of the lust-eye males sitting close to the stage, tormenting the peepers by keeping just out of reach until they stuffed money into the stockings, then permitting them to squeeze her boobs and kiss them.

That surprised me; usually, it's "look but don't touch". I saw one black-haired, balding man, bolder than the rest, catch her pebble-hard right nipple between his teeth and bite down while cruelly pinching the left.

Expected a scream from the blonde and a slap to the pervert's face followed by the bouncer giving him the bum's rush. Instead, she threw her head back, moaned dramatically and moved on to the next creep, his hands already up and waiting eagerly. Very odd, that the manager would permit this to go on. What if the vice cops came in? They could lose both cabaret and alcohol licences. Plus, the audience hadn't acted like this with any of the other dancers.

When she got to the end of the line of groping men, she came back to her feet and swayed for a moment as the music changed from driving rock to a sensual samba. Picking up the tempo, she swayed back to centre stage, slipped most of the bills crammed into her stockings into the book bag and began to move to the samba beat. Every man in the room had their eyes glued to her as, ever so slowly, she toyed with the waistband of her miniskirt, easing it up, down, running her fingers beneath it, her hips bucking and churning. Without warning, she ripped it off and tossed it behind her. She wore no panties. They usually don't here. Then this marvellous female animal glided to the edge of the stage where waving hands clutching greenbacks awaited.

Even from the bar, I could glimpse the juices that glistened on her pussy lips as she worked the line, the eager hands fondling and probing her pubis, coming back wet. Her head thrashed on the slender column of her white neck without ever dislodging the choker she wore, apart from the heels and fishnets her only adornment. This girl was a real exhibitionist; the real deal.

The greedy apes were satisfied for the moment and she moved to the pole that some of the other dancers used in their routines. The samba beat faded as the lights darkened to a single spotlight on the pole. The dancer bent to her book bag, swiftly shedding her stockings and their loot, then stepping back into the pumps while withdrawing two objects. One she left on the floor; the other she held in her right hand as a modern rendition of "I Got the Fever" began pulsing from the speakers, the bass shaking the bar counter – it was that thick and loud and deep.

Standing with her back to the audience, her legs spread wide, she grabbed the pole, then brought the limber cane she held in her right hand down onto her small, round buttocks, lashing them to the beat and throwing her head back in time to the singer's moaning. By the end of the song, her perfect ass glowed red in the spotlight.

A new number came on, the generic fuck-music you hear in a pro porno video. The spot focused on the object she had placed on the floor: a dildo, one of those big, realistically moulded rubber ones that tend to put any man to shame by comparison. The torrid wench began sucking on it, on hands and knees, her ass elevated, her head bobbing to the music. No man in that club could have taken their eyes off her even if they had wanted to. As the tempo sped up, so did her strokes. When the piece reached its climax, her head came up and liquid spurted from the tip of the dildo, splattering her face as she screamed in "orgasm".

The watching crowd split the air with applause, whistles and howls as the stripper, white fluid dripping down her face, stood up, made a slow, hip-swinging circuit of the stage to collect still more money – ones, fives, tens – smiling at the audience, then grabbed her costume and props and disappeared through the same door by which she'd entered.

Waved the bartender over, laying a couple of hundreds from my money clip on the counter. "Another one, a double; and I'd like to ask if you can do something for me," tapping the bills.

"If I can," said the bartender, noticing that these weren't tens as he'd first thought.

"Will this cover your sending a bottle of champagne to that dancer who just finished? With my compliments."

The bartender disappeared.

Sipped my drink, looked at the stage. The oiled, sleekly toned body of the black stripper working the crowd should have commanded my undivided attention, but after that blonde's schoolgirl-slut act she just didn't attract me. I turned away and contemplated my snifter. A gentle touch on my arm turned my head to the right. The luscious dancer who had changed a club full of men into a mob of would-be rapists was standing at my elbow.

Up close, in a low-cut, short white silk dress that looked as if the silkworms had spun it onto her flesh, she was even more stunning than onstage. She'd changed into a pair of white stiletto heels, not as extreme as the pair she'd worn onstage. A black leather belt emphasized the narrow span of her waist and her flaring hips. Her beautifully shaped legs were tanned and bare. I could see that the choker I had noticed onstage wasn't a piece of jewellery. About half an inch wide, it featured a pattern of steel lozenges, with four letters centred on the front:

SLUT.

She held a tray with a pair of glasses and a bottle of champagne.

Her light blue eyes were wary as she studied me with the same intensity I apparently was focusing on her. My confidence waned. Here is what she eyed: an average-looking guy, six feet tall with light brown hair cut military short; carefully trimmed beard, in good shape but no bodybuilder god, casually dressed in khaki slacks, Hawaiian shirt and plain, spit-shined black cowboy boots, my one concession to vanity.

"Please forgive me for staring," I said, "but it is seldom that a woman as beautiful as you materializes next to me, like Scotty beamed you right here."

She did not understand the reference. She must have never watched *Star Trek*.

"May I join you, sir?" she asked.

She made no move to do so. I stood and motioned to an

empty table behind us, walked to it and held a chair for her. She followed and sat gracefully. Every movement she made with that body was easy on the eye.

I reached for the bottle and she grabbed it. "Permit me, sir," she said, working the cork free with a pop, and expertly filling our two glasses without spilling a drop. She set the bottle down and handed me my glass; made no move to pick up her own.

"Please join me in a glass. And please feel free to speak," I told her.

"What should I say, sir?"

"First, your name."

"My name is Sage, sir," the blonde said, picking up her glass.

We raised our glasses for a toast.

"To all the ones who weren't as lucky," I said, offering my all-purpose toast, thinking of the man I had just murdered. To my surprise, those lovely eyes filled with tears because she knew what I meant: *the job was done.*

"Is he . . . ?"

"Yes."

I covered my concern by drinking half the glass. She gulped down the whole thing and poured herself more, her hand trembling like a frightened child.

"I still have an owner, sir," she said.

"He's not here," I said, "and he won't be. It'll be all right."

"You really think so, sir?"

"I'm quite certain of it, Sage."

We sat there, drinking the champagne and talking as two people in a bar tend to do, like we were anybody but a woman who had just hired an assassin.

I noticed the bartender eyeing us and frowning and thought nothing of it. After we'd worked most of our way down the bottle, Sage looked up at me with half-lidded eyes.

"Would you care to dance with me, sir?"

I'm not much of a dancer, but for a chance like this I'd have walked a mile in bare feet on broken glass.

"Yes," I said, standing up and helping her with one hand from her chair, which action earned me a startled glance, swiftly concealed, from Sage. She indicated a small side room, to which I led her. Just as we were about to pass the threshold, a slight pressure from her fingers stopped me. Although in those heels she was only an inch or two shorter than I, she still looked up at me.

"Sir, I am afraid I must explain to you the rule of the house for this room. Men must pay to play."

She hesitated, not meaningfully, but what seemed out of fear.

I followed her gaze. The bartender was glaring at us, disapproval in every line of his fat ugly face.

I removed the money clip in my front pocket and extracted a couple of bills. "Will this be sufficient, my dear?" I showed her the cash.

She nodded, relieved.

She said, "Kindly place your deposit in the First Valley Bank, sir. Nothing but the best for our customers," thrusting her chest forward to bring her bounties into even greater prominence.

I placed the folded bills into the cleavage of those lovely breasts, stopping when my hand just grazed her flesh.

Sage reached up with her free hand and pressed mine to her, guiding it down across her exposed boob to rest on the hardened pebble that was her left nipple beneath the dress. I instinctively squeezed gently; she sighed and pushed forward, tightening her hand over mine, tipping her head back, eyes closed, clearly enjoying the sensations my hand was evoking. With a shiver of pleasure, I led her into the room and onto the dance floor. She flowed into my arms.

I knew that if a dancer chose to dance with a customer, she was likely to close-dance, but Sage was much closer than I expected. She pressed tight against me, swaying her hips and rubbing her crotch against mine. Well, it was obvious that I was interested. The heat from her suffused me. I could just feel her nipples through the clothing separating us, and as her breathing quickened I could feel her nails as she dropped her hand to my butt to pull me closer.

I responded by sliding my hands down to her ass. I tightened my grip, took a chance based on what I suspected and whispered in her ear, "Come for me."

I felt her shuddering against my body as she dropped her head to my shoulder, muffling her cries in my neck as I daringly slipped my hand under her dress and inserted a finger into her. Her shudders slacked off and I brought the finger to her lips. Without prompting, she took the finger into her mouth, tongue flicking over it as she sucked it clean. I guided her to a loveseat in a dark corner of the room and we sat down. Her legs weren't the only ones that were shaky. She huddled against my chest as I stroked her hair.

"He's *definitely* not going to like this," she whispered.

Whispered back: "Don't care."

She wouldn't meet my eyes. I took her chin gently between thumb and finger and forced her to look at me.

"Sage, you are a marvellous, giving, sensuous woman. How could anyone *not* like anything you do?"

"He will be displeased when I get home tonight, sir." Fear in her voice.

She didn't say anything more, content to rest next to me, not displaying herself as she had onstage, but still open for inspection to my eyes. My caresses seemed to soothe her and she did not object to my eyes devouring her beauty like a desert plant sucking up rain after a drought. After one of those indeterminate periods had passed where time seems to have no meaning, she stirred, rubbing against me like a friendly cat, the feral type of pussy that always comes to the killer breed.

"Sir, you are too kind, to be gentle with one such as I," she said. "I hope your lady appreciates you."

She pulled herself up to lean against the arm of the loveseat, stretched across my lap, those creamy breasts with their lustful nipples inches from my mouth.

"No lady," I said. "I am alone."

Sage settled back on me, pinning me where I sat and holding herself in that position with her right arm behind my back.

"No man ever has a woman in his life when he's in this club," she said, sounding hurt. Obviously she had heard this line before and had expected better of me. I could see disappointment and reproach on her face.

"I'm telling the truth. I'm not in any kind of relationship at the moment. Nor have I been, for longer than I care to remember."

Looked away, feeling a combination of self-loathing for my inability to attract women and anger at this wench for rubbing my nose in the fact that women would only spend time with me if they were paid for it. She shifted on my lap, and a tentative hand on my cheek brought my attention back to her.

"I'm sorry, sir, I did not mean to hurt you. Please forgive me."

She popped her breasts out of the dress's confinement, like prisoners released for the day in the sun. She took my hand and squeezed it tight on her nipple, as if seeking atonement through pain. I caught the nipple in my fingers and twisted, offering what she wanted. A mixture of pain and pleasure washed over her face, followed by remorse as I changed my grip to a gentle squeezing of her stupendous tits, teasing the erect nipples with my thumb.

I said with gentle firmness: "I imagine in this job you probably hear all sorts of rude comments and come-ons from the men that come to watch you dance, especially the wannabe studs that sit down front. But there are those like me that come to admire your beauty and wanton sluthood, wishing they had a magnificent woman like you, thankful for your merciful calling that offers us the illusion of hope."

We stayed like that, Sage watching me, her breathing frayed, my hand teasing her to arousal. The feeling of her buttocks grinding against my leg was pleasant.

She said, "I have to dress for the finale."

She caught my hand, brought it to her lips and kissed the

palm lingeringly, before using me as a fulcrum to get to her feet and rearrange her clothes. I stood as well, noticing that we were alone in the room.

She stood, head down, and without warning threw her arms around my neck, kissed my cheek and whispered, "I wish I deserved someone as nice as you."

The bartender gave me another hard look as I left.

I was sure he could see the smear of lipstick on my face.

3.

Outside, in the club's parking lot, it was easy to find her car. I took care of business and did it fast.

I climbed into the truck I used for business trips (that is, kills). Getting behind the wheel, I locked the door and settled in for a nap to sleep off the alcohol I'd consumed.

Tapping on my window interrupted my very pleasant dreams some time later. I seldom dream of anything good. I usually dream of Afghanistan and killing Hadjees.

I opened my eyes and sat up, looking out the driver's window, expecting the bartender or a cop ready to tell me how I couldn't sleep here.

Sage was standing there in the same white dress she'd worn when dancing with me. She visibly shivered.

I opened the door and got out. "Not that I'm not glad to see you, Sage, but what are you doing here?"

She stepped closer to me, as if seeking protection.

"Sir, it's the car. All the tyres are slashed, and I have no way to get home. He won't be happy if I'm late."

I looked at the only other car left in the parking lot. Even from here, the two tyres I could see were flat, and nobody carries more than one spare. I looked down at her.

"This isn't the golden coach you deserve, Cinderella, but I would be happy to take you wherever you like."

I led her around to the passenger door, unlocked it, and handed her in as if she was a queen. I got back behind the wheel and started up. Sage slid across the bench seat and wrapped both hands around my right arm, sitting very close and whispering directions to me as we went.

We ended up on a country road where the houses were not very close together, a mixture of post-war construction and ticky-tacky eighties developments. I gently detached her hands and put my arm around her to draw her close and she didn't resist. She leaned into the embrace and laid her head on my shoulder, seeming to draw comfort from the contact. I could feel her trembling; why, I didn't know. A twenty-minute drive brought us to a fifties house on a couple of acres set well back from the road, a gravel driveway leading up to it, with no neighbours within 2,000 feet and a dilapidated pole fence defining the property. I turned off the road and went up the driveway, the crunch of the gravel announcing our approach.

As we neared the house, Sage said softly, "Please stop here, sir. He'll be angry at my late return as it is. No need for you to be part of it."

"Maybe I should do it tonight."

"Not tonight."

"Why not?"

"You already took care of one."

"Two in a single night is not an issue."

"Not tonight."

"When?"

"Soon," she said, "I'll tell you soon."

"You'll be free."

"I'll never be free," she said, "women like me are not free."

She took my hand, squeezed it tightly for a moment, and then kissed my palm as she had done before, sending a thrill straight to my groin. She opened the door and got out. I could see her clearly in the headlights. Every step she took was filled with apprehension. Waiting as any good taxi driver would to see her safely enter the house, I cranked down the window to better observe. Something didn't feel right here.

Sage opened the front door and I noticed a man's hand flash out and grab her by the V of her neckline.

A fist punched her squarely between the eyes.

She screamed and she was dragged inside.

The door slammed.

I was out of the car and at the door in an instant. I could hear the high, thin whistle of a whip and the sickening crack as it landed.

Sage yelled: "*Pickles!*"

Had no idea what that was all about, but I didn't hesitate.

The door wasn't locked.

I twisted the knob and went in like a banshee with haunted intent.

"Sage?" I said.

She lay face down on the rug, sobbing in pain. The back of her dress wasn't white any more; it was red, wet, split and torn.

The cause was instantly clear.

A black-haired, balding man with a satanic beard. He was dressed in the white silk jabot shirt, skintight trousers and black riding boots of a Regency dandy.

He was holding a bullwhip.

His dark eyes glittered nastily, the pupils contracted to pinpoints. From my time in the battlefield, I remembered the symptoms of drug use. Lots of soldiers got high to stave off boredom and fear, the sun and the dirt. This guy certainly had the look.

I stepped between Sage and this dandy with the whip.

"Don't hurt him, Master!" Sage pleaded through tears.

I looked at her master with the steady look of warning. "Hit her with that whip again, and you will regret it," I said, flatly.

He grinned like the devil he was and flung the whip, the tip cracking an inch from my head.

I noted with detached analysis that this whip was no toy for someone with delusions of Indiana Jones grandeur. It had a metal tip and at intervals down its length barbs were knitted into the leather. It was a weapon for inflicting maximum pain and physical damage in minimum time. We had used similar things on Iraqi soldiers that were "interrogated".

"Get out of my way," he ordered me. "I'll discipline my slave as I see fit!"

"I don't think so."

The whip lashed out and hit my face. Red exploded across my sight, and time ceased to have meaning. My memory went on hiatus. My Ranger training kicked into automatic . . .

When I returned to the present moment and myself, the whip was clenched in my right hand.

Sage's master lay on the floor, curled in a foetal position, gasping for breath. His dandy's outfit was in shredded ruins, the cuts and welts inflicted by that torturer's implement visible through the torn cloth trying to absorb the blood oozing from them.

Sage was up on hands and knees. Her sobs had stopped, and she was staring at me with something like wonder on her bruised face.

"Sage, do you want to continue to be with this—this—*animal*?" My words were harsh in a dry throat.

She looked up from underneath dishevelled hair, wet with pain sweat, tears and drops of blood.

She mumbled, "No."

"Say it again, louder!" I demanded.

She looked me square in the face for the first time. I don't know what she read there, but she repeated, clearly: "No. No, sir, I don't."

"Good. You have one minute to gather anything you absolutely can't live without and get back here. *Move!*"

She staggered to her feet and went up the stairs that came down into the living room where we were. The monster at my feet groaned and started to get up. Without a thought, my boot slammed into his gut, knocking the wind out of him again.

"Move without my permission, you miserable sack of shit, and I'll cut your cock off with this whip!"

Was this me? I seemed to be standing behind and to the right of my body. Part of me knew this for dissociation. The rest, enraged, simply didn't care.

How many times had this happened when I was in battle?

Sage came back down the stairs clutching a lumpy

pillowcase and an athletic bag trailing a couple of sleeves from its unzipped top. She had taken me at my word about one minute. She was moving better now but still painfully.

"Set that stuff down and come here," I commanded.

Obediently, Sage set the bag and the pillowcase by the front door and came to stand next to me, head down, hands clasped neatly in front of her.

Looked at her beautiful face, disfigured by raccoon-eyes from the punch she'd taken, then down at the man who had done it to her.

I tossed the whip behind me and slid the fingers of my left hand under her collar. My right fished in my back pocket and came out with my pocket knife. Its razor-sharp, serrated blade is tough enough to cut through a car door. I flicked it open with my thumb, and carefully slipped the knife between her neck and the collar. Ignoring the lock set into the collar at the back, I picked a spot between two of the steel diamonds. The blade cut through the leather like soft butter. I folded the knife and put it back into my pocket.

Drawing the collar from Sage's neck with my right hand, I reached down with my left, hauled her master up by the throat and held him against the wall with his feet off the floor. He seemed weightless. I glared at him and spoke, my voice cold and distant in my ears, trying to keep my rage under control.

"Listen very carefully. As of now, Sage is free of you. This is her choice. She is lost to you, now and forever. You abused the most precious thing a woman can offer, *her trust*. When you broke that trust you broke the bond that bound her to you. Do not try to find her. Do not try to speak to her if you ever see her. She no longer exists for you. Do you understand me?"

He said nothing. I slashed the broken collar across his face, rocking his head, the raised letters gouging his cheek.

"*Answer me, you fuck!*"

"Yes," he croaked through the windpipe that I had started to choke shut.

Let go of him and he fell to the floor.

"Let's go," I said to Sage.

Without a second look, she started for the door. Took a look around the room, for the first time, taking in the glass table in front of the couch. I could see a pill bottle on its side, a couple of capsules lying loose on the tabletop, a half-empty bottle of whiskey and a glass.

I looked down at the man who, until moments before, had been Sage's master, and owner of the strip club where she worked.

"Don't know what your scene is, but pills and booze sure as hell don't mix with it. Get some help before you kill yourself or someone else."

He'd managed to get up onto his hands and knees. Didn't want him trying to reopen the issue so I dropkicked him square in the balls, lifting him and dropping him back to the floor in a foetal position, hands clutching his groin and eyes squeezed shut in agony.

Partial repayment for what he'd done to Sage.

I walked over to the door, picking up the whip as I passed, motioned for her to open it and went through. She closed it behind us. We went to the truck, its motor still running, got in, backed out of the driveway, and headed down the road. I was running on autopilot, adrenaline still flooding my system, heterodyning with the anger I felt over what he'd done to Sage to produce a towering rage. I was peripherally aware she was in the cab with me, sitting close, her legs almost but not quite touching mine, as we reached the highway and got up to speed.

For fifteen minutes or so, time seemed to move at a crawl. As the anger and the adrenaline bled off along with the endorphins they produced, the world seemed to speed back up and return to normal. I became aware of my throbbing hands with their white-knuckled grasp on the steering wheel. Had to consciously ease my grip, letting the right go from the wheel and shaking it to get the blood flowing again. Sage caught it in both of her hands.

She looked at me with bowed head and said, "If you'll permit me, sir?" and began to massage it. Working her way outward with her thumbs from the middle of the palm, she took the pain away, leaving a feeling of ease behind.

She turned my hand over and worked on the tendons for a bit, flexing the fingers and watching my face for signs of discomfort. She replaced my hand on the wheel and wordlessly reached for my left.

She slid closer and repeated the process. I was able to hold the wheel without pain. She made no move to pull away from me. I lifted my right arm to hold her as she seemed to want. As I laid my arm across her shoulders, she whimpered. I released her at once.

"It's nothing," she said.

I wasn't buying that.

"Turn and let me see your back," I ordered.

Sage slid away on the bench seat as I switched on the cab light. I winced at what I saw. There were four bloody rips in the back of her dress, and I had put my arm down right on one of them. The pain must have been agonizing. I turned the light off.

"I'm sorry," I said, embarrassed at what I had done. "I didn't mean to hurt you."

She slid back next to me so our thighs touched again and leaned on my shoulder, holding my right arm gently in both hands, leaning forward so her back didn't touch the back of the seat. Could feel her warmth through the reaction chills that always accompany the end of an adrenaline rush.

"Don't be sorry, sir," she said. "I know you'd never hurt me unless I deserved it. You'll be a good master, not a bad one."

She reached out, took my right hand, and continued to massage, starting up my forearm, apparently content just to be next to me.

Say what? I couldn't have heard right. *Me*, her master?

The first thing to do was to treat her injuries. From past trips over this highway I knew of a small picnic area with permanent bathrooms and running water. At this hour of the night, it would probably be deserted. When we reached it no one was there, for which I was grateful. I pulled in so that the headlights lit one of the picnic tables.

I turned to Sage, said, "Take off your belt and go lie across that table. I'm going to take care of you."

She obediently did so. I opened the rear doors and took my medic's kit, something any hit man has besides a gun and knife, and went into the bathroom to get water. Carried everything out to the table where my beautiful patient waited. Setting up to do what had to be done, I selected what I'd need and laid everything out on the bench, the instruments soaking in antiseptic.

As I prepared, I talked to Sage, explaining what I was about to do.

"Brandy or morphine would make this easier, but you'll just have to endure it. We have to get that dress off you and treat those cuts before they get infected. Bite on this if it gets too bad."

I put a bitestick, normally used for epileptic seizures, into her mouth.

"Scream if you must, but don't let go of that stick."

"Where did you learn to do this?"

"Doesn't matter," I said. She didn't need to know about Afghanistan and Iraq. "Are you ready?"

She looked at me trustfully and nodded.

Reached out and gently brushed her eyelids, indicating that she should close them. Then I gritted my teeth and began.

The blood had clotted and stuck the silk to the wounds. Took the antique pitcher I had filled and soaked the back of the dress. Sage's head came up, her jaw clenching on the bitestick. I gently pressed her head back down and stroked her hair to soothe her. After a minute, I poured on some more water, took the dress at the hem and eased it up over her hips, past that narrow waist and up to the gashes. She lifted herself cooperatively.

Knowing what this was going to feel like, I took a deep breath, grasped the fabric and yanked sharply. The dress tore free of her back, up over her head and onto her arms. Sage reared up, eyes wide with pain, the cry she made muffled by the bitestick. I finished skinning the dress off her, as tears trickled down her bruised face from the pain I was inflicting.

It tore at me, so I said harshly, "Lie flat on the table and spread your legs and arms out. I still have things to do."

She obediently assumed the position. Caressed her for a moment to reassure her. Went back to the truck and brought out the digital camera I carried in my "just in case" box. I shot half a dozen pictures from various angles and set it aside. Insurance for later, but there was work to do now.

Got to it.

Had to pick bits of cloth out of all four gashes. The cuts those horrible barbs had made were ragged and likely to knit without leaving scars on her silken skin. From time to time she whimpered as I probed deeply to make sure everything was out, but I ignored it, as I had to. When I was satisfied the wounds were clean, I swabbed them out with antiseptic. Sage groaned at the antiseptic's bite and squirmed.

To take her mind off her back, I slapped her buttocks sharply and growled, "Hold still, strumpet!"

Her head went down again and the groan that she made wasn't one of pain.

Squeezed antibiotic ointment into the cuts and used butterfly closures on the worst ones, following up with a topical anesthetic to dull the pain before applying adhesive gauze pads and Band-Aids. Finally, it was done. I reached around and took the bitestick out of her mouth.

"Are you all right?"

"Please, sir, I was disobedient, moving when you wanted me to lie still. Please punish me. I deserve it. Please . . ." Her voice trailed off as her buttocks wriggled enticingly.

The trick of overlying pain with something pleasant is an old animal training trick. If this was her idea of pleasure, I'd oblige her. I hauled off and spanked her, gently at first, then up to strokes that stung my palm. Sage cried out in pleasure, her hips bucking. With one last slap, I stepped in behind her, reached around and pinched her clitoris gently. She pressed back against me, her climax wetting my hand as she collapsed onto the table, moaning sensuously.

As her breathing returned to normal, I said, "Now clean up every bit of paper trash. I don't want anyone to know we were here." She went to work, naked except for her high heels.

I went back to the truck and brought out my black leather coat. It came to mid-thigh on me; on her, it would do for a mini-dress. Ordering her over, I told her to put the trash in the back of the truck and come to me. When she returned, I held the coat out for her and helped her into it, tying it tightly at the waist.

She took my hand, kissed the palm, and said timidly, "Sir, may I serve you by tending your own wound?" Gently touched my left cheek.

It was the first time I remembered the lash I had taken in her defence, despite the blood that had dribbled down my face and ruined my shirt. The bolt of pain that shot through my head wiped out any endorphins that might have been left in my bloodstream. I reeled away from her.

When I could talk again, I said, "I think you'll have to. But before you start, take a couple of pictures of it."

I handed her my cell phone, with a camera feature.

Walked with her to our impromptu operating room and sat down, closing my eyes against the glare of the headlights. Obediently, Sage snapped three photos.

Took the bitestick and bit down, anticipating the pain and not welcoming it. What happened next didn't qualify as agony only because I expected worse. Sage didn't help by flinching away each time she had to touch the welted slash.

Took out the stick and snapped: "Dammit, don't try to be gentle! Just do what you have to and get this over with!"

Biting down again, I held still while she cleaned and bandaged the cut. Cleaning up the debris without being told, she wouldn't meet my eyes. Finally, I caught her arm and pulled her into an embrace, tipping her head up to look at me.

"You did fine," I said.

She huddled against my chest apparently reassured by my words.

We finished up quickly. I handed her a cold pack to hold against her face to slow the bruising and ease the pain.

In the darkness and silence between us, I wondered what might come next.

4.

With a throbbing gash on my face that would probably leave a scar, a drop-dead-gorgeous blonde snuggled into my arm on the seat next to me that I didn't even know, whom I had rescued from an abusive bastard and a relationship I couldn't even begin to guess about, whose history was a mystery, my life had surely taken a strange turn.

Sage set the cold pack down on the seat. The black eyes didn't show in the low dashboard lighting. She had to be in even more discomfort than I was. Home was still a ways away.

"How do you feel?" I asked, the beast of this tale.

"Safe, sir," the beauty replied. "For the first time in a long while, I feel safe."

"Good. That's good."

"If I may be so bold, sir, don't concern yourself with Mas— him. He dares not call the police. He has beaten me badly enough to send me to the hospital before. Three times in the last fourteen weeks, with his fists twice and a paddle once – that was the time he cracked two ribs. And I think that—what he takes is illegal. With those photos you took, he would not come off well in court. Knights in shining armour who rescue the maiden from danger are respected."

Her smile was reassuring; she at least believed it. I wasn't so sure.

"I should have killed him," I said.

"Didn't want that," she said, "not like . . . no, he was a bad man, but he didn't deserve to die."

"The other did."

"Yes," softly.

"I'd rather he's *dead.* So when we get home here is what we will do. Your dress, my clothes, that whip and your old collar will be put in plastic bags and sealed with tape, which we will sign and date to show we put them there. After I print out copies of the photos, the chip with the data on it goes into another bag. You'll make a tape telling the story, a verbal affidavit. I'll do the same. We put everything into a box and have my lawyer lock it up. If that swine does try anything, he'll get it right in the neck."

The venom in my voice when I thought about what he'd done to her startled me. In that moment, I would have strangled him and enjoyed his trip to hell. Sage must have felt my anger.

"Please, sir, even if he were to try, you'd defeat him. I know it. I can tell you take care of what is yours."

She untied the belt on the car coat, allowing it to fall open. She reached into my lap, feeling me through my slacks.

"Let me ease your mind, sir," she whispered, fingers on the zipper. Hating to do it, I took my left hand off the wheel for a moment and removed her hand from my lap.

"Baby, not just now. We'd end up in the ditch. What are you thinking?"

Alarm flared in Sage's face at this rebuke. I tempered it with a squeeze of my right arm around her and dropped my hand to her breast. Finding a nipple, I tickled it to erection.

Her eyes closed as she enjoyed the sensation, realizing I was neither upset nor offended. Allowing my hand to slide down her body, I began to gently finger her. Her breathing quickened and her hips began to flex under my tormenting ministrations. I could feel her clitoris swelling as my hand dampened with her juices. Little moans of pleasure, nipples hard as pink marble and panting breath indicated an approaching orgasm.

Was in unknown territory here. My best guess was that she was trying to bond with me. I didn't object, but after the emotional fucking-over that I had received at the hands of my ex-fiancée and the disdain with which my romantic overtures had been received in the past, any bond with a woman would be on my terms or not at all.

Pulled my fingers back and lightly grasped her clit.

Sage cried out.

"You may not climax until I permit it, wench," I said calmly. She beat her heels against the floor. Instantly, I withdrew my hand and snapped my fingers sharply against her nipples. She groaned in a combination of frustration and pain.

Putting my hand back on her mound, I said, "Sage, you must learn the pleasure of anticipation."

She started to move her hand over mine, but stopped as I shot her a look of warning.

I said, "Caress your boobs. Flaunt yourself for me. Tease yourself, especially your nipples."

Her hands rose obediently to those spectacular breasts, stroking them, squeezing, pulling and twisting the nipples. As she began to whimper with lust and the pleasurable pain produced by her nipples being pinched between her long nails, I again began to stroke her clitoris, first with a fingertip, then, as her whimpers began to turn to little squeals of pleasure, with the sharp corner of my thumbnail. She gasped at the exquisite agony, hanging on the very cusp of climax but unable to finish without permission. I alternated looks between the road and her face contorted in the dashboard lights, head back, eyes squeezed shut, tears leaking from the corners of her eyes, tortured whines coming from her throat.

"Please, sir . . . please, oh," she pleaded, so wet, so hot, her nipples, clit and pussy swollen . . .

I looked into the mirrors and saw we were alone on the road. I thrust two fingers into her, cruelly pinching her clit shaft between fingers and thumb and pubic bone.

I said into her ear, "Come for me, girl."

Her orgasm brought her off the seat. Her hands tightened on her breasts mercilessly as she gasped joyously. I could see the tendons in her neck outlined against the skin. Her pussy clamped down hard on my fingers and a flood inundated my hand. Involuntarily I pinched harder and she came again, a small scream escaping her as her hand came down on mine, trying to drive it deeper. The pain in my hand forced me to pull over and stop. I half turned her to face me. Sage cried out as I pulled my right hand free. Then I was holding her close, enjoying her panting sobs with satisfaction. I stroked her as she fell down the far side of her climax. When she was back, I sat back from her and caressed her face, careful of the swelling there. I gently kissed her cheek.

"You will find one way to please me is to respond to me like that," I said softly. "Pain and delight is a wonderful mixture."

Sage brought my right hand to her lips and kissed it, then, without being told, began to sensuously tongue-wash it clean, sipping her own juices. She removed the car coat completely and nestled into me. Holding her tightly, we set off down the road again. I moved my hand over her body, caressing, feather-stroking, lightly pinching, softly probing. Eyes closed, a smile on her face, she accepted my ministrations humbly, reading in them a tacit acceptance of her. I knew we had much to settle, but for the moment, her complaisance was enough.

We arrived at my place just before morning twilight, when the day is darkest. I backed the truck into the garage and brought Sage out of her semi-doze with a firm cupping of her breast and a gentle pinch of a lovely pink nipple.

"Wake up, pet. We're home."

She stretched sensuously, smiled sleepily and reached for the car coat. I stopped her.

"No. Leave it off. Take off your shoes, too. Leave your bag and the pillowcase here," I ordered. "I will bring them in later. Come with me."

I got out of the truck, went around to her side and helped her down onto the concrete floor. Nude, she stood there, a vision of loveliness. I took her by the hand and led her across the stone yard as the overhead door ground closed behind us. Isolated and set back from the road as the farmhouse was, we could have done this at high noon on the Fourth of July without anyone noticing, but I was still glad of the darkness.

Sensors switched the door light on as we stepped onto the wraparound porch. Sage found herself facing an oak door with black iron hardware that would have not been out of place in a castle. I unlocked it with its remote, shut down the security system, swung it partly open and stepped into the gap, turning to face her. She looked at me. Even with the dark bruises around her eyes, a man could lose himself in their depths.

"Sage, we don't know really each other. You may be having second thoughts about how we've been thrown together and what happened this night. If you are, all you have to do is walk past me, turn left and go into the first room on the right at the top of the stairs. You can be my house guest while you heal and arrange to get well away from that abusive bastard, and I will remember you as that glorious blonde who made me happy for a little while. However, if you meant what you said as we drove here, cross the threshold, close the door behind you and come to me because you wish to. The choice is yours."

I stepped backward into the foyer and waited. I hoped she understood symbolism as well as I.

Sage looked at me through the open door, backlit by the light. She raised her head, stepped through the door and pushed it shut. She walked to me, head up, reached out and took my left hand. She laid it over her heart, holding it there with her right hand. I could feel it rapidly beating under my palm.

"I come to you freely, sir, of my own will. I offer myself to you in perfect trust. Take or leave me, as you wish."

She bowed her head and would have knelt, but I stopped her. Taking her hand, I kissed her palm, enjoying the thrill that ran through her. I drew her into my arms where I had longed to have her. Tilting her face up, there in the darkness I kissed her for the first time. Her lips opened under mine like a rare flower. Our tongues touched. She pressed herself fully against me as our embrace tightened, her hands hooking under my arms to lock into my shoulders, flattening her fabulous breasts against my chest as my hands found her buttocks and pulled her hard against my erection. She moaned in her throat and I thrust my tongue deep into her mouth, symbolically taking her. She accepted me eagerly, lightly sucking my tongue and rocking her hips against me as I dug my fingers into her ass. We were both ready, but this wasn't the place. I broke our kiss and pulled her head to my shoulder, stroking her hair. She sighed in mixed frustration and contentment as we eased apart. I looked down at her.

"Want our first coupling to be perfect," I said. "That means we should be rested, bathed and settled in our minds. We have things to do before we can sleep. Shall we get started?"

"Yes, Mas—"

I stopped her lips with my finger. "Don't call me that. *That* is not just a title. It is an accolade that must be earned. I assume the beast that whipped you called you his 'slave', didn't he?"

She nodded, head down.

"If my slave is what you want to be, you will have to earn it. When we are ready to take on those roles, it will seem perfectly natural to both of us. Would you have it any other way?"

She shook her head and whispered, "No, sir. I feel so lucky, to be with you now."

"As do I, to have you," I said, continuing to stroke her hair. "Come with me and I will show you your new home."

Keeping hold of her hand, I walked to a switch panel and turned on the lights in the room beyond. Sage gasped in surprise.

An irreverent friend once described my house as being decorated in Early Terran Arsenal. I began collecting bayonets and daggers as a kid, and graduated to swords, armour and unusual weapons, many of them souvenirs from trips. The collection covers much of the wall space in the house.

Also had the necessary assortment of rifles. The guns were locked in a cabinet, not for display.

Led Sage through the parlour, across the hall to the dining room, and through the serving pantry into a country kitchen. We passed through another door into a sunroom I had redone as a gym. Turning left and crossing another hall, I opened the door into my study. Inspired by Henry Higgins's sanctum in *My Fair Lady*, it is a huge double level room lined with book-cases. The second level has a glass floor laid in an iron frame, with wrought iron and brass rails bordering the open space, with a spiral staircase salvaged from a demolished library in one corner. Velvet curtains opened to show the outside or insulate me from it as I wished.

Going up the spiral stairs, we came out in the upstairs hall. I pointed to the next door across the hall on the right, by the stairs from the foyer.

"Had you not chosen to give yourself to me, that guest room is where you would have stayed. As you have chosen to serve me, you will sleep elsewhere."

Crossed the hall, passed a bathroom and opened the door beyond it.

"This is your room, Sage. We will return to it."

I explained that the rooms opposite hers were unused at present. The door next to hers led into my bedroom, over the exercise room.

We entered. There was a fireplace on one inner wall. It backed onto the one in her room. A large mirror spanned it. Opposite the mirror was a large mahogany Renaissance Revival carved four-poster bed, complete with flat canopy and velvet bed curtains. With the curtains drawn, the bed was a self-enclosed universe. A walk-in closet was to the left of it, a highboy next to it and a bureau opposite. Two leather wing chairs and footstools were in front of the fireplace. Thick silk Persian carpets covered the floor. I led her to the door to the left of the fireplace. It led into the master bath, walled and floored in white marble with black accents. The bath contained a shower and a tub big enough for four that doubled as a Jacuzzi.

I led her back to her room.

Sage's room was furnished with a brass double bed, a bureau, a vanity, a nightstand with a reading light, a leather club chair and ottoman. I showed her the closet near the window. It contained a selection of bathrobes and slippers.

"Choose the ones that please you. Tomorrow you will store the rest. The bath is through here," I said, pointing to the far corner.

Its most prominent feature was a huge claw foot bathtub. A cabinet behind the showerhead held towels and terrycloth bathrobes. An Oriental rug covered the floor of the bedroom from wall to wall. Sage let go of my hand and turned, taking it all in.

"Sir, all this is too good for the likes of me. Do you not have servants' quarters and simple clothing for one like me?"

Putting a touch of mock severity in my voice, I said, "What is it to you, wench, if I choose to dress you in silks and fine leather? It pleases me to house you here and dress you as I like a woman to look." She reacted by quickly crossing the room to kneel at my feet, forehead touching the floor.

"Sir, I meant no disrespect. I am yours to use as you like. Please punish my insolence, sir."

I looked down at her. "Rest assured that when you have been *insolent*, I know what to do about it."

I helped her up and led her to the bed, sweeping the covers back with one hand while sitting her on the sheets with the other. I actually wasn't sure what to do, but knew I urgently needed to find out what she wanted.

"Wait here. I will bring you a tape recorder and you will make that tape we spoke of." Leaving her there, I trotted down to the study and brought a recorder back. I showed her how it worked.

"I will be in the study. Put on a robe and slippers and come to me when you are done."

I closed the door as I left.

Returning to my desk, I turned my swivel chair to look out the windows. The sun was just beginning to rise. A new day indeed was dawning for me – for us.

Having responded as a true knight would for the damsel in distress, I was going to have to accept the consequences.

I recalled the old saying about adopting a stray kitten, but on second thought realized it was not on point. Maybe Sage was not normal as the average citizen thought of such things, but I had never identified with the great unwashed and cared not what they thought about anything. To me, she was everything I had ever dreamed of in a woman: beautiful, willing, responsive, sensuous, eager to please. She also seemed perceptive. I remembered a study that showed beautiful women were often more intelligent than their plainer sisters. The "gorgeous ditz" is a cultural phenomenon, not a genetic one.

But what about love? You don't know a thing about her and you're letting her into your life? Have you lost your mind or has it just been so long since a chick paid attention to you that you'll grasp at any straw?

Well, what *about* love? I had little enough experience with the emotion; had never felt anything like the attraction Sage had for me. If she was missing emotional pieces, well, so was I, an adult male with a record of exactly zero successful relationships with females. I realized that she was offering me everything I wanted, and it was clear she thought I could give her what she needed.

I concluded that I would do whatever it took to forge a bond so complete that no other male would be able to take her from me. Having settled that in my mind, I turned the computer on and began typing my record of how this newfound female had come into my life.

I was just finishing when I heard the second floor door open. I looked up and watched Sage descend the spiral stairs, those long legs flashing in and out of the cream silk Jean Harlow-type robe she had selected, her feet in the bedroom pumps that complemented them. I raised my eyebrows in approval and was warmed by the dazzling smile I received in return. She came to the desk and gracefully knelt there, settling back on her heels like a geisha, content to wait until I should deign to notice her. Satisfied with my account, I copied the file to the CD burner and waited for it to finish. I turned to her, simply enjoying looking at her.

With her head bowed and her blonde hair partly forward, her black eyes were concealed. The silk clung to her curves, stimulating my imagination even though I had already seen what lay under the robe. I reached over and helped her to her feet as I stood. Keeping her hand, I led her to the stairs and motioned her to precede me so I could enjoy the flexing of her buttocks under the silk.

At the top of the stairs, I reached out and laid a hand on her shoulder. She stopped instantly. Stepping close, I reached around her and cupped her breasts through the silk. I pressed hard against her, my rigid erection nestling between her buttocks while I fondled her boobs. Sage tipped her head back against my shoulder, eyes closed, little noises indicating her enjoyment. I took her by the hand again and led her to her bed.

"Disrobe," I ordered.

The robe slithered to the floor in a whisper of silk. I motioned her to me. Lips parted, she kissed me softly but eagerly.

"Lie on the bed, face down."

Sage pouted, seeing that sex was not the immediate goal. I instantly sat on the bed, seized her, pulled her across my knees and spanked her hard as rapidly as I could, ten fast whacks. She cried out in surprise and pain. I sat her back up and held her by the shoulders.

"I want you as much as you want me, trollop, but there is much I have to do before I will be free to give you my undivided attention. You aren't some cheap beer to be swilled for drunkenness. You are like fine brandy. You intoxicate my senses with sensual pleasure. Like that brandy, I intend to present you properly, with my hands heating you so I may savour you before I taste your glowing charms. Don't ever behave like a cheap whore unless I order you to, Sage. Do you understand?"

"Yes, sir," she whispered. "Whatever you wish, sir, I will be for you. I want you to be proud of me, sir."

"For the moment, *this* is what I wish. Get some sleep. I must go into town to deliver our evidence to my lawyer. You may go anywhere in the house you like, but don't open the doors or windows. I will be setting the alarms before I go.

Setting one off will bring the police in short order. Some doors and cabinets are locked. Respect them. Otherwise, you may do as you like. Eat if you feel like eating; drink if you wish, but don't get drunk. I don't like drunken sluts. Any questions?"

"Yes, sir. Would it be presumptuous to offer to dress you before you go to town? I would serve you ill if I let you leave in the same clothes you've worn since we met at the club, stained with the blood of the blow you took for me. Please, sir?"

She was right. I had been so concerned for her needs I hadn't taken the time to change. I stood up, picked up her robe and held it for her. She slipped into it, and followed me to the master bedroom.

I opened the closet door and motioned for her to choose, curious to see what her taste was. While she studied my wardrobe, I took underwear from the highboy and laid it on the bed. Sage selected a silky blue shirt, pale sand slacks, black ankle boots and a black blazer for me. I sat on the bed and allowed her to undress me. As she helped me out of my shirt, I saw her kiss the bloodstains on the collar and shoulder. She expertly skinned me out of pants and underwear so I stood there naked before her.

Looking at me unclothed for the first time, she said huskily, "Sir, you have a beautiful body. So smooth, with its strength hidden."

She stepped closer and ran her hand over my chest, feeling my nipples stiffen at her touch. She continued, "May I ask that you take the edge off her before you leave?"

Replied by reaching out and pulling the tie on her robe loose. She shrugged out of it and knelt before me, taking my penis in her hand and kissing the head. I reached down and pulled her to her feet.

Her eyes widened, but she said nothing as I sat down on the bed and pulled her to me, kissing her breasts, then without warning biting a nipple, not hard enough to hurt but hard enough to startle. She gasped and I stood, catching her with her mouth open and kissing her hard. She whimpered deep in her throat and rubbed herself against me, trying to mount my cock. I didn't let her. I spun her about, grabbing a breast with my left hand and penetrating her with my right.

I growled in her ear, "Come, slut!" as I closed my hand hard on her mound with no attempt at tenderness.

Sage shrieked with mixed pleasure, pain and humiliation as her body responded to my command. Letting go of her, I turned her to face me again, grabbing her by the hair and kissing her hard as I tripped her and let her down to the rug. She lay there, eyes slightly glazed, as I stood, waiting for her.

As her breathing slowed, without a word, I pointed to the clothes on the bed. She obediently dressed me. I motioned her into my arms and held her lovingly, stroking her, careful to avoid her stripes and bruises. She sighed, a little smile on her lips.

"Better?"

Eyes closed, she nodded, her hair caressing my chest. I tipped her face up and she met my eyes.

"Tonight we will both give and receive pleasure. Some time today, I require you to write for me what your limits are. I have no wish to drive you from me by accidentally breaking one. It is my intention to formally bind you to me tonight, but before we make that commitment both of us must agree if you want it to work."

Sage took my right hand and again laid my palm over her heart, holding it there as she looked me in the face.

"Sir, this woman is not one who promises by night to repudiate by day. I have been yours since you rescued me. I wanted you as my master after we danced at the club. Your presence struck me like a thunderbolt. The Italian poets say love hits people that way sometimes. I sensed you could give me what I need and take all I have to offer. Punish me if you wish for using the word, Sir, but this woman is your devoted love-slave. I belong to you. I am your round-bed toy."

That made me laugh. "My what?"

"I'm a round-bed slut," she said with a smile.

"My round-bed chick," I said.

"Yours, yes, sir."

She laid her head against me and I held her for a long time as I considered what she had said. I led Sage back to her room, and lay her on the bed face down.

Stroked her arms and hair and said softly, "Sleep, my pet. Wait for me. I will return to you."

She caught my hand and brought it to her lips, then fell asleep with her lips still brushing it. I took hers and kissed it in return; she smiled in her sleep.

5.

A delicious odour awakened me. I had no idea how long I'd been asleep, but it was dark outside. I sat up and looked around in the light spilling from the fireplace. A fire had been lit there, the flames providing the only light in the room. My clothes and Sage's robe were nowhere to be seen.

"Would you care to eat, sir?" a voice said from the foot of the bed.

Sage, freshly bathed, perfumed and dressed as a French maid, was standing there with my silver coffee service and a cup. I surmised that the outfit was one of her stripper's costumes. I motioned her to come to me.

"Just milk," I said.

Sage set the tray down on a portable butler's table brought up from the dining room and prepared the cup. She leaned in as she gave it to me, the better for me to admire the breasts straining to escape their confinement. I took the coffee with one hand and cupped a breast with the other.

"Sir!" she said in mock outrage, playing her part to the hilt as I kissed her mouth slowly, enjoying the feeling. When we broke the kiss, I could see a flush on her chest, though not on her face. She had applied heavy make-up to hide the black eyes.

"Do your talents extend to an omelette, wench?" I asked.

Sage nodded. "I can have one here in five minutes, sir."

She swayed her way out of the room, the micro skirt, six-inch stilettos and black sheer stockings giving me an enhanced view of her taut dancer's legs.

I sipped my coffee and thought happy thoughts. All my life, I had been someone females confided in and came to for advice. A non-threatening, asexual male. A confidante, a trustworthy friend, yes. But not a romantic lover or a lusty male animal, never someone to whom a woman would surrender herself – *until now.*

My French maid came back from the kitchen with a covered plate. It held a cheese omelette. Sage wouldn't permit me to feed myself. She fed me one bite at a time, using the food as a sensual substitute for her lips, breasts and pussy. When I had finished eating, she leaned close with a napkin to wipe my mouth. I allowed it, then traced her lips with my finger, watching her eyes close as she savoured my touch.

Continued my tracing along the line of her jaw, down the side of her throat and along the curve of her breast, around the areola, then back as her breathing deepened. Reaching behind her neck, I pulled her lightly towards me. Her mouth opened as it touched mine, anticipating my kiss and anxious to receive it. Our tongues danced. She started to climb onto the bed, but stopped as she felt the warning pressure of my hand on her breastbone. I drew my mouth away from hers with more reluctance than I allowed to show.

"Run a tub, Sage. I wish to bathe."

Could see hints of frustration as she obediently went into the master bath, and smiled to myself. I was learning the truth of the old joke that the ultimate in sadism was the submissive pleading to be beaten while the Dominant said, "No." I swung my feet out of bed, opened the closet door and selected a wine-red silk dressing gown, a find I'd made when clearing out an estate three years ago. More Hollywood than practical, it was perfect for tonight. I joined Sage in the bathroom.

The splash of water into the bathtub masked my entrance. Sage was bent over, testing the water temperature. She jumped as I caressed her ass, those firm globes only partly concealed by her costume. She pressed back against my hand as I gently kneaded her rump. I eased my hand under her panties and introduced a finger into her slit. She was already moist and her muscles clasped it, grabbing and releasing in promise of what lay ahead. She moaned as I withdrew my finger.

"Help me into the tub, whore," I ordered.

Sage turned to remove my robe and for the first time got a clear look at the wound in my cheek. "Oh, sir, I am so sorry!"

I held her at arm's length.

"Take off your top," I commanded. She immediately did.

"Turn around."

The bandages I had put on her earlier that day covered half her back. I reached out and pulled them off her. She made no sound. I examined them. No sign of infection, though the welts were inflamed. The edges of the cuts were tight to each other, bound close by the butterflies and the beginning of the healing process. I led her to the big mirror by the sink.

"Look over your shoulder, dear."

She could see the gashes the whip had made.

"Now look at my face."

The silk sutures were dark against my skin.

"These are part of what binds us. They are part of what we are to each other. Your stripes will heal and leave no visible mark. Mine, I am told, will leave a scar. When you look at me, you will see a badge of honour and know that the man to whom you have given yourself is proud of the pain he ended for you by taking it. Do you see that, Sage?"

She looked at the scar for another moment, then whispered, "Yes, sir. I understand. May I please touch it?"

She stepped close and delicately touched her lips to the stitches as if to consecrate them. I turned her about and did the same to the four worst marks on her back and saw her happy smile reflected back at me.

I entered the tub and Sage took on the role of bath girl, shampooing my hair, washing me, rinsing me off and even shaving me as I lounged in the warm water. Before it could cool, she took a fluffy bath sheet and dried me. I donned the dressing gown again and led her, still nude from the waist up, back into the master bedroom. I sat in the chair by the fire and she settled beside me, her head leaning on my thigh, content as a cat. I looked down at her and felt her hair, corn silk in my fingers.

"Did you make that list, pet?" I asked.

"Yes, sir. It is in your study on your desk. Shall I fetch it here?" She looked up enquiringly at me, ready to spring up at my command.

"Is there anything on it so far out that I would have no way of knowing it might trigger you?"

"Sir, may I speak freely?"

I nodded.

"Trust is my greatest issue. It always has been. I have been used in the past, and abused, as you saw yourself. I do know this: I need to be owned by a dominant male. I am driven by sex; I have to belong to someone.

"I long to be the property of a master who will give me the discipline I need. Who will care for me, but will not allow transgression without punishment. Who understands me better than I do myself. I want to surrender my will to yours. I want to be your slave. I want to please you, for you are strong in spirit and will care for me and will permit me to care for you and serve you in every way. I will do anything to satisfy you, but I must know that you will respect my needs as well. One like me has no rights, only privileges permitted by her owner. I must know you will set guidelines and make your submissive abide by them, so I can feel secure."

I considered this before I answered her. "The only thing we need between us is for you to know that if you say 'STOP!' whatever is happening stops instantly and we discuss it right away until we solve the problem. Does my word that I will do this suffice, or must we have something more elaborate?"

Sage sat up, leaning against my legs, and studied my face carefully. I was painfully aware of her closeness, wanting nothing more than to grab the lovely slut, throw her on the floor and take her, remembering her wantonness onstage. I was sure she could sense my urge even as I strove to keep my mask of calm in place, even as I could sense her readiness to yield if I decided to rape her.

"I believe you, sir," she said. "I remember what you said to me at the club, about telling the truth. Your word is your honour. You would not break it, even to one like me. You said you would take care of my problems for me, and I said I would be yours if you did. Now here we are."

As she spoke, she rubbed her breasts against my thigh and her hand crept under the dressing gown, seeking my cock. Her fingers closed on it and she began to slowly stroke me, each motion sensual torment. I reached down and indicated she was to sit on my knee. I drew her to me, caressing her breasts, making the self-imposed torture mutual. Her grip tightened as she conveyed her willingness to me. I turned her head, kissed her, and stood, nearly dumping her on her delicious derrière. Eyes wide, she stared at me.

"Sage, go to your room and prepare. I like a woman who is properly depilated. No hair on your body, save your eyebrows and your lovely blonde tresses. Make yourself up as you like. I have a fondness for blood-red nails and lipstick. You will find a black robe in the closet. Put it on. Those stilts you are wearing will do. When you are finished, wait for me to come for you."

"Yes, sir," she said.

I was once more treated to the sight of that perfect ass and those long legs doing a slow strut out of the room, hips seesawing in invitation.

I listened for her door to click closed, then began making preparations. These included two stops in the basement, one at the safe concealed in the study, another at my desk to examine Sage's list, and the moving of a few things into my bedroom. After an hour, I stood back, put on the dressing gown, donned a pair of black leather slippers and walked to her room. Psyching myself up, I opened the door.

Sage was sitting in the leather chair by her fireplace. Her shining hair was freshly brushed and hung free to the middle of her shoulder blades. The black silk robe she wore was just a little too small for her and barely closed in the front. Its two short ties and sash strained to conceal her with only limited success. She held her legs together, bent at the knee, showing a good amount of thigh despite the fact the robe was ankle length. The six-inch heels brought out the curve of her calves. When she saw me, she stood. I remained in the door, waiting.

"This is the last chance to change your mind. Do not join me unless you are sure that this is what you desire with your whole heart and soul. Choose."

Sage did not hesitate. She walked across the room, head up, and took my hands in hers. "You are what I want, sir. I am sure. I am in good health. I have no diseases. I do not use drugs. My tubes are tied. You need not fear that I will betray your trust, and I know you will not betray mine. Bind me to you, sir, I beg you." She bowed her head and kissed my hands.

"Very well."

I produced a satin sleep mask and blindfolded her. I led her into my bedroom and locked the door behind us. Leading her forward, I positioned her in front of a cushion I had placed in the firelight, the only light in the room, and pressed on her shoulders. She knelt on both knees, hands down at her sides, head erect.

Using the remote that controlled the in-house sound system, I activated the CD player to provide appropriate background music at low volume to heighten the occasion. I took my position in front of her next to a low table that held a goblet, a couple of folded napkins, a lancet used for taking blood for test strips, and a necklace. I reached down and removed her blindfold.

"Sage, is it your desire to become my submissive? To have no rights save those I grant you? To surrender without reservation? To obey without question any order I give you? To accept any punishment without resentment, complaint or explanation? To be whatever I may choose to make of you?"

"Yes," she whispered, voice humid.

"Do you accept that you are no longer free, but bound to me?"

"Yes," she repeated, as if in a dream. "It is my dearest wish."

I stepped closer.

"Put your hands between mine," I ordered, holding my hands up as if praying, but held apart. Sage raised her hands in the same position. I pressed hers between mine in the way of a medieval lord taking the oath of fealty from a vassal.

"Promise in your own words, Sage."

She swallowed and looked up at me with devotion.

"By all I am, I swear myself to you. I will be whatever you want me to be, at any time. Your servant, slut, sex toy, stripper, submissive slave, sweet girl, dancer, wanton nymph, masseuse, model, whore, lover. Whatever you want me to be, whatever you need me to be, I shall be for you. I am yours, completely, to be used as you see fit. Everything I have, I freely give to you. Your lightest wish shall be as a command to me. By the bond of pain between us, I will not leave you. This I swear until I die, or until you die, or until you order me to go."

Sage leaned against our joined hands, eyes closed. I looked down at her and responded.

"I accept you as my bond-maid. I swear to protect you. To give you firm discipline. To cherish you as mine. Never to cause lasting harm to you or violate your trust. Your pleasure shall be my concern, as mine is yours. I accept your submission. I will help you perfect it until, if all goes well, you are ready to wear my collar as my slave and I consent to become your master. This do I swear until death parts us or you ask me to release you from your vow."

Sage looked radiant as a bride before the altar, her eyes sparkling, joy on her face in the firelight. I released her hands and turned to the table, picking up the goblet and the lancet.

"Hold this," I said, putting it into her right hand.

I took her left hand and held it over the goblet. The lancet pierced her third finger. Blood welled out, formed a drop, and fell into the wine the goblet contained. I watched as five drops of blood fell from her finger before I took one of the napkins and staunched the bleeding. I held my left hand over the silver cup and applied the lancet to my own ring finger. I too let five drops of blood splash into the thick, sweet wine. It took but a moment for the bleeding to stop. I took the cup from her and held it in both hands, swirling the wine gently.

"Our blood is now one. I drink in token of this."

I held the shining goblet up and slowly, savouring the taste, drank half of it. I offered Sage the cup. Mimicking me, she solemnly accepted it.

Looking me in the eyes, she repeated, "Our blood is now one," and drained the goblet without haste, ceremoniously.

I took the empty cup from her and set it back on the table. Picked up the necklace that waited there and showed it to her. It was a gold herringbone chain a quarter-inch wide, so cunningly crafted you could wrap it around your fingers without hurting it. Its quality was evident in the workmanship and weight. Foreign made, its clasp involved a spring pin that worked by pressure. Easily closed, it was hard to open, which had influenced my choice.

"This is your mark of servitude, Sage. The weight of this necklace will remind you how much further you have to go before you are worthy to become my slave. It does not broadcast your status to the world, but *you* will know. Do you choose to wear it, knowing what it means?"

"Of my own choice I choose to wear it, as the visible symbol of my bond to you. Please, sir, place it on me, as one day I hope to receive your collar."

She gathered her hair up in her right hand and first raised her chin, then lowered it as I stepped behind her and passed the necklace around her neck. Then, with a click, it was done. The chain rode just below her collarbone at its deepest point. It went well with her skin and hair. I stepped back in front of her.

"Now you are mine," I said. "I think you will find that necklace the lightest of burdens."

I helped her to her feet and held her in my arms.

The ceremony was over.

6.

"Are you happy?"

"*So* happy, sir. Now I am truly *yours.* I will care for you and make myself worthy of you, obeying you in all ways, pleasing you, loving you," she said in a whisper, her hand moving on the dressing gown, seeking the overlap of the open front.

Knew what she sought; knew what she needed.

"We will prove your submission, pet."

I led her to the foot of the four-poster. Spare silk rope curtain ties hung down from the crossbeam, their loops waiting for her hands. She did not resist as I slipped first the left, then the right into position, took up the slack and tied them off, leaving her hands extended in a broad V over her head, her hands grasping the cord above the loops.

"Spread your legs," I told her.

Her stance changed to an X.

I picked up the sleep mask and approached her. "Do you trust me?"

"With my life, sir," she said softly, seriously.

I put the mask back on her. She waited, not knowing what I had in mind for her. Although I was new to the Dominant/submissive game, I was not unread in the field. It was time to put what I had read to work. Whispered in her ear, "Tonight, my sweet, you may climax as often as you like as well as at my command," and lightly nibbled her ear lobe. She shivered deliciously.

I moved to the butler's table that waited in the shadows. On it was an old-style razor strop, a feather, a section of an old bamboo fly rod with the guides removed, and three clip clothespins. I picked up the feather and the clothespins and knee-walked across the foot of the bed until I was in front of her. I took a moment to examine her beautiful body, her nipples already puckered with excitement. I had the feeling this could turn into a night neither of us would ever forget.

Reaching out with the stiff goose feather, I tickled her right nipple, watching it lengthen as blood hardened the pliant flesh. I shifted the feather to the left, enjoying the sight while I leaned in and blew a thin stream of air across the right, making her moan and shiver with excitement. I switched back and forth between them randomly. A look at her mound revealed Sage's labia as puffy.

Her breathing began to be ragged and I pinched the two clothespins open and let them close on her lustful pink nipples. She cried with the sudden pain; I ignored it and began to stroke the feather across her clitoris.

Her cries of pain changed to whispers. "*Yes . . . yes . . .*"

Slipped off the bed, never interrupting my teasing of her clit for more than a second or two, as I gauged her reactions.

Not quite yet.

Stepping in behind her, I replaced the feather's touch with my finger.

I caressed the length of her labia and the clit shaft, slowly at first, then faster. Her pussy lips reminded me of an orchid, wide open and inviting at the bottom and narrowing as they reached the un-hooded clitoris at their apex. Swollen on the end of its shaft, it resembled the stamen of an exotic flower. The oils starting to ooze down the labia put me in mind of the nectar a hummingbird sips. Her hips rocked as far as they could with her legs spread, and everything I had seen of her so far told me she was about to come. She reached her peak and I reached out and clipped the third clothespin onto her clit. Sage screamed in mixed delight and agony as the orgasm ripped through her. I had no intention of allowing her to fall down the other side. I reached out, grabbed the razor strop, doubled it so only leather would touch her, and began to slap her ass with it, conscious of the rampant erection inside my dressing gown. She wasn't the only one getting off on this!

The first stroke chopped her moans of satisfaction off in mid-squeal. She cried in surprise and hurt at first, her cries quickly changing to something that sounded more like enjoyment as I first eased off, then increased the tempo and the impact of the blows. A minute or two brought her back up towards climax, as the pain somehow transmuted into pleasure for her.

She was hit simultaneously front and back as I flicked one hand into her crotch, lightly striking the clothespin, and delivered a hard whack with the strop onto her glowing buttocks.

The effect was electric.

She thrust her groin into my hand and climaxed again, and then again, panting, unable to speak, sounds I'd never heard coming from her mouth. I dropped the strop and seized the bamboo, taking a second to slide my hand up her open pussy lips, feeling the wetness.

She was starting to flow now, fully aroused by my harsh and loving treatment. I stepped back, measured the distance by eye, and swung the bamboo across her ass cheeks with a sharp smack.

She bucked and screamed, trying to get away from the red-hot burn of the improvised cane. I struck her with it twice more and felt compelled to step close and say, "How are you?"

"Please," she whimpered, twisting in her bonds. "Sir . . . please . . . oh, don't stop . . . *hurt me so good* . . ."

I resumed the caning, varying the impact from barely touching to just short of breaking the skin. My slut whipped her head back and forth, her hips thrusting back to meet the bamboo, urging me to beat her. She was something I had never seen before, a woman caught in an orgasmic loop, only to find a new pleasure peak rising beyond this one. This went on for maybe fifteen minutes before I decided it was time.

After dropping the bamboo, I pulled the small tags of curtain rope that undid the quick-release knot on the bedposts, first on the left and then on the right. As Sage started to collapse to the floor, I caught her and laid her on her back on the bed, her legs spread and her feet just touching the floor in her patent leather pumps, her thighs wide apart, her hair-free pussy wide open and inviting. I knelt between her legs, removed the clothespin from her clit, and settled in to tongue her to orgasm.

She responded, her moans rising in intensity and volume as I used tongue, teeth, fingers and the stiff bristles of my moustache on her. Her hips rocked up to meet my tongue and questing fingers as she came again and again, the frequency between climaxes shortening. My face was sticky with her juices as I sought to drive her out of her mind. Her hands, still trailing the silk ropes that had held her to the bedposts, kneaded her breasts. Any sensory input was pleasurable to her now. I knelt there performing cunnilingus for half an hour, listening with satisfaction to her cries of hedonistic rapture when I realized that she was saying something.

"Take me . . . use me . . . fuck me . . ." over and over.

She protested as I pulled my fingers out of her, trying to hold them in her vagina. I stood, grabbed her thighs and pushed them even wider. With one stroke I rammed my swollen, ready cock deep into her.

Our coupling could not be called lovemaking. It had been too long since I'd had a woman and this one wordlessly urged me to prove my dominance over her in bed. Both of us were too aroused, no longer human but the embodiment of lingam and yoni.

I fucked her brutally with no concern for her pleasure, only my own needs. She met each thrust with eager lust, taking me in up to the root, bucking and twisting like a horse with a burr under the saddle. She started to reach for me. I caught her wrists and pinned them to the bed, leaning forward to hold them down, reinforcing her helplessness and inability to resist my taking her like this. The incoherent noises she was making goaded me to drive ever harder, reducing her to a receptacle for my sperm and nothing more.

Neared my own climax, watched her face: a portrait in pleasure beyond pleasure. I knew it would be only moments before I came. Reaching down with my teeth, I unclipped first one, then the other of those pink nipples, darkly swollen now from constricted blood flow, and spat the clothespins aside.

With a roar, I came like Godzilla destroying Tokyo, Sage's hypersonic shriek telling me we'd reached the magic moment together. Her spasms almost threw me off as I latched onto a nipple and sucked for all I was worth as my semen flooded the inside of her vagina like an invasion force marching into Baghdad.

In that moment, I felt I was a god as I collapsed onto her and almost passed out from the greatest climax of my life. Her pussy muscles clenched and loosened spasmodically, obviously out of her control, still responding to my cock inside her. As my penis gradually went flaccid and slipped out of her, I picked myself up and looked at my submissive.

She lay on my bed, her body, built for sex, slack, sweat-slicked and pale. I removed the blindfold. Her eyes were rolled back in her head and her mouth hung open. I had to press my ear to her chest and hear the reassuring "lub-dub, lub-dub" of her heart to assure myself that she had only fainted dead away, that I hadn't actually fucked her to death.

Moving to the side of the bed I gently tipped her up onto her side to check her back.

Two small breaks in the whip slashes seeped tiny droplets of blood.

I took a minute to clean myself and returned with bandages and ointment. It took only a minute to repair the reopened cuts. I looked at her with immense tenderness and pride, realizing that now I owned her, and she wanted it that way.

I carefully moved her until her head was on a pillow at the head of the bed. I closed the bed curtains, shutting out the world so it could not reach in and disturb our privacy. I pulled a silk satin coverlet over us and settled next to this wonderful, sensuous, desirable submissive who had chosen me as her Dominant and drifted off to nap in the dark pool that was our world in this bed.

A tickling feeling brought me back to the surface. I opened my eyes. Sage had turned on the reading lamp on the headboard, its low illumination giving just enough light to see her. Her head was resting on my chest listening to my heart as a short while before I had listened to hers. I could feel her arm wrapping around my shoulder, while her other hand caressed me with her nails. She looked satisfied, happy and content, serene with the proof I had indeed taken her as my own.

"Oh, sir, *thank you*," she said. "I did not know anything could feel as good as that without drugs or booze. I do not know where I have been, but I beg you to take me there again soon."

"Thank you for the most intense experience I have ever known, my sweet," I replied, taking her in my arms and kissing her hair. "No woman has honoured me by climaxing under me before. You, my darling pet, are the first."

Sage sat partly up and I looked into those blue eyes of hers, unafraid now of falling into them, as she realized I meant it. Hookers rarely come with their johns; and my unlamented ex-fiancée had been not only unskilled at sex but frigid to boot. Sage wriggled up so her head lay beside mine on the pillows, within easy kissing reach if I wanted her and at intimate closeness for conversation.

"Where are we?" she asked. "Did you transport us somewhere while I was away? Some other world where there are only the two of us, sir?"

"No, I just closed the bed curtains. But no one can disturb us until I will it so."

She sighed and snuggled close to me as I began to caress her, using just as light a feather-touch as she had. I was sure she could feel my cock erecting against her, for her complaisance and sensuality acted on me like a dose of cantharides on a prize bull. I wasn't ready to take her again just yet. I wanted to talk to her a bit and enjoy the feelings as I indulged in foreplay. Her own hands with those nails she had painted bright red for me gently ran along my spine and buttocks.

"What are you?"

Sage pressed my hand firmly to her breast and looked pleased. "I am your thrall, my lord." She pushed me onto my back and began to kiss her way down my body, murmuring,

"My lord, please let me fellate thee. Please let me feel thy cock in my mouth."

I sat up, the better to watch her. Sage reached my cock and began licking the head, her hand softly squeezing the shaft. She looked surprised and pleased as she gently stretched the foreskin, discovering I was not circumcised. She opened her mouth and took the head between her lips, licking the frenulum as she stroked the shaft slowly, tightening and loosening her fingers as they moved. I knew from what she had written that she enjoyed giving and receiving oral sex. The moans deep in her throat told me she was excited by what she was doing. Sage took me all the way into her mouth and began to bob the full length of my shaft, sucking and flicking with her tongue. I closed my eyes and gave in to the sensations, feeling my prick swell. I could feel my climax building. So could she. She sucked harder, eager to receive my sperm.

I felt myself losing the ability to restrain my climax; reached down to grab her hair, intending to shoot straight down her throat. She caught my hands and held them away, doing something with her teeth and tongue that kicked me over the edge. She held me off, my cockhead just behind her teeth as I spurted into her waiting mouth. She held that position until the spasms subsided. Shifting to one hand, Sage held up her head so I could clearly see the satisfied expression on her face, and swallowed, smiling as she ran her tongue over her lips in satisfaction before bending her head to clean my cock.

When she was finished, she slid back up along me and said, "Your come is sweet, my lord. Your little slut would drink it by the bottle if she could. Are you pleased with me, sir?"

"No," I said. "The piano does not write the concerto. You displease me, slut. On your hands and knees, *now*!"

She immediately assumed the position of a penitent: hands and forearms flat on the bed, head down between them, her rump elevated, legs together and bent at the knees, toes pointed. I rummaged beneath the coverlet and came up with one of the clothespins I had used earlier.

"Lift your head," I ordered. Her head snapped up. "You *see* this?" I said, brandishing it in her face.

"Yes, my lord," she whispered.

"Kiss it," I ordered, "and thank me for the lesson I am about to teach you."

She kissed the wood and mumbled in a fearful voice, "Thank you, my lord, for this lesson in obedience. Please punish me."

I ignored her whimper as the jaws closed.

"Head down and watch it," I ordered.

Her lovely blonde head dropped. I got behind her, took aim, and began to spank her, setting a pace of about one blow per second, hearing the sharp reports as my hand struck her already sore ass, not alternating cheeks but striking at random. I paid no heed to her tears or her cries.

After fifty strokes of shaded intention, I slid my free hand under her and caressed her mound. As I had anticipated, it came back wet with her secretions.

My cock had regained its stance. The combination of her submission and the knowledge that she was getting off on what I was doing to her acted like a drug on me. I rubbed her juices over my cock, going back again for more to anoint the head. When I was ready, I forced my cock into her ass.

She screamed. She pressed back against me, crying from the pleasure she was receiving in the heat in her bowels, as I grasped her hips and used her. The squeals Sage made triggered me as well, and I came just after her, barely managing to hold off long enough to unclip the clothespin. She cried again, surprised by a second small climax as the blood flowed more fully into her clit and I rubbed it roughly.

Done.

I withdrew from her. It took more control than I thought I had to grab a handful of that silky hair and tip her face up.

"Do you think you will remember your lesson?"

"Yes, my lord."

I dropped her head and slipped outside the curtains to the bathroom for a fast wash. On my return, I saw with approval that she had not moved. I motioned for her to come to me and held her close, using my fingers to gently feather-touch her glowing buttocks and take the pain away. She looked at me, saw I was not angry with her any longer, smiled and snuggled contentedly onto my chest.

She felt very good resting there.

For the rest of the night I used her for my pleasure, purging myself of resentments I hadn't realized ran so deep, unburied from the sands of Afghanistan and Iraq. We fucked in every position we could fit ourselves into. She drew off psychic poisons that had accumulated over the years, wanting only to please me by any means, taking pride in my use of her.

I spanked her ass with my hands and her inner thighs with the bamboo, tying her to a convenient bedpost, ignoring her pleading and begging, paying more attention to the juices that soaked the bed and her thighs before taking her yet again than to any protests of hers. I pumped myself dry. What a glorious sex machine my submissive turned out to be!

Later, Sage was tight against me, holding my cock in her aching cunt, accepting the pain as the price for keeping her lord and future master inside her as we drifted off to sleep. I marvelled at my incredible good fortune in finding this woman, an assassination job leading to the strangest of love.

Tomorrow Never Comes

Vanessa de Sade

Night descends on the city in a welter of neon and exhaust smoke as Sexy Lexie puts on her happy face. Nobody knows exactly how old Lexie is. Some say older than Methuselah, but that's never been proven.

And tonight the night is ripe with dyke bars where the pussy hangs ready to be plucked like ripe fruit in September, but Lexie cares little for checked shirts and scarlet Aids ribbons. Instead, walking like a panther in the blood-red glow of neon signs on the wet pavement, Sexy Lexie teeters townwards on six-inch spikes, the shiny PVC of her boots gleaming in the gloaming. Tiger, tiger, burning bright, Lexie is a deadly predator with sharp white teeth and a hungry mouth tonight.

Men whistle and call out ribald remarks, but she turns a deaf ear to their appetites. She's done cock before and found it wanting, far prefers the intricate folds of labia and the sticky tropical sap of an excited pussy. And Lexie surely knows how to dress to turn a girl. She's clad tonight in a black Lycra mini that barely covers her crotch, sheer black tights like the finest membrane of the skinniest condom and killer boots in PVC that's as obsidian as wet tarmac, zips and buckles everywhere.

But it's already well past midnight and the girlies are getting unsteady on their feet as they flow from bar to bar like the ebb tide, a giggling, surging froth of them in their glitter slippers and little black numbers, eyes full of promise. But Lexie simply sips her drink and watches and waits, knowing that her hour is not yet come.

She's marked a little brunette as a possible, small and chubby with big brown eyes that make Lexie's sad heart sing. Girlie has been downing Bacardi Breezers all night, her lush lips getting pinker by the minute with all that potent watermelon colouring. Lexie visualizes just how pink her nipples will be when she sucks them, plus the pink of all those hidden places beneath her little pink panties.

But like an antelope that's being stalked by a lion, this particular little filly has been sheltered by the herd all night and a brittle bottle blonde with eyes like acid drops keeps a protective arm linked with Girlie's, her dead-fish peepers alert for wolves in sheep's clothing. But Lexie knows her kind and stays well away, sneering at the curly boys, who proffer drinks and innuendo, only to be rebuffed. Instead she eyes the clock, watching, waiting, tick-tock, tick-tock.

The bar they're in has an aquatic theme. Faux fish tanks bubble soundlessly on the walls and marine ephemera decorates the old wood panels of the bar, posters for the fantastic voyages of Captain Nemo and his ilk. But Lexie sees them not and keeps her sharp chicken-hawk's eyes on the doors instead. Heavy dark wood with worn brass finger plates and porthole windows glazed in thick greenish bottle-glass filled with little trapped bubbles, perfect smokescreens for dastardly deeds.

Girlie normally pees with the herd, but by now their drinking is getting ragged and they're splitting into splinter groups, the calls of insistent bladders overriding popular protocol. And, a little after one in the bleary morning, she teeters off through the door marked "Ladies" alone, the portal swallowing her up into a whirlpool of dryer noise and women's chatter.

Lexie follows, quick as a flash, her spiked heels like glass slippers as she streaks across the groaning old floorboards, rat-a-tat-tat. She fears the watchdog will see her with her looking-glass eyes, but Blondie has let her guard down and is flirting with a barman laden down with used receptacles, so Lexie makes her move, ever the tiger.

Inside the ladies' room there are girls everywhere, repainting their faces for the final round of tonight's bout with carnality. And at first Lexie thinks that she has been too slow and that Girlie's already in a cubicle, but then she spots her gliding into a tiny cabinet packed with porcelain and obscene graffiti, chubby little fingers pulling the door shut behind her.

"Excuse me, can I share with you, I can't wait," Lexie wheedles, slithering into the confined space with her, more intimate than the confessional. It's an old ploy but it's worked many times before and it works again tonight. Girlie's not shy about peeing in company, it seems. Probably quite likes it, Lexie reckons, and her cunt gives a little twinge of anticipation, licking its lips at the very thought of the candy in store.

The girl giggles, embarrassed, and flattens herself against the polished coffin wood of the inner wall, raising her skirt a little. "Do you want to go first," she proffers, indicating the toilet seat like a flight attendant. Lexie nods and squats, sliding her panties down and her skirt up just enough, her big cunt like a midnight panther with its sleek dark fur.

She pees, letting it trickle slowly at first and then build up to a gush. She keeps her eyes front, but allows herself a momentary flick at the end to see if Girlie's watching. She is.

Lexie feels a heat pass through her. Stays where she is. Doesn't attempt to pull her panties up or wipe. She feels the girl blush and turns to meet her gaze.

Girlie has her skirt raised and is fiddling tipsily with the buttons on the crotch of a tight black all-in-one, trying, unsuccessfully, to get them undone. Lexie's heart skips a beat.

"Need a hand?" she asks. Words of the temptress.

Girlie nods. "Please," says she, inviting the vampire in. Lexie doesn't hesitate and fingers fly like insects, busy little bees, unbuttoning, liberating, covertly stroking, her rings like iridescent scarab beetles scrabbling all over the tender white flesh.

Girlie's cunt is waxed clean and smooth as silk. Lexie imagines her rubbing scented lotion into it each night and almost groans out loud. Girlie does it for her.

"I like how you're touching me," she purrs, all kittenish and willing to play.

"I like touching you," Lexie replies, pulling the open flap of the flimsy underwear to one side and taking in the full beauty of the bare pussy in front of her. Fat puffy mound, deep slit, shy labia nervously poking out like the first snowdrops, everything all pinkie-white like a strawberry-flavoured white chocolate mouse.

The girl makes her purring sound again and Lexie grows bolder, running an exploratory finger down the underside and then mounting a reconnaissance mission within to check for wetness, which she finds in plenty. Lexie doesn't believe in straight women, anyway, thinks they can all be turned. Lexie's probably right.

This one's grinding her ass against the toilet wall, thrusting her hips and fanny into Lexie's face and moaning, "Fuck me, fuck me." And Lexie's perfectly happy to oblige. She plants a trial kiss on Girlie's pudenda then goes to work seriously on her slit, delighting in the taste of the girl's arousal, quickly finding her clit and sucking on it, her hands up and digging into Girlie's plump butt cheeks as they bump and grind together.

And in the next cubicle a very drunk girl pees loudly like a horse letting fly by the roadside and bangs on the wall. "Get a room, you dirty cow," she shouts, laughing, thinking that Girlie's smuggled a man into the sanctuary of all femaleness and Girlie's in no state to contradict her. Or care.

"I think I'm going to come," she whispers, her hands in Lexie's lacquered hair, pushing the older woman's face into her fanny, desperate to be eaten. "I am. I'm going to come. I'm going to come. I'm . . . I'm coming. Oh fuck, I'm coming. Oh fuck. Oh fuck. Oh fuck . . ."

Lexie feels the orgasm sweep over her and sucks hard on an engorged clit that's already as stiff as a slippery pecan nut, pulling it out from under its hood and making Girlie tug her hair some more as she writhes and twists in the divine agony of her *petite mort.* That's our Lexie. Satisfaction guaranteed or your money refunded. Often imitated but never redundant.

* * *

Girlie pushes Lexie to one side, flops down on the toilet and lets fly, her pee like a stream in full spate. Sexy Lexie sighs, not feeling particularly sexy any more, and stands, hauling her knickers up and fixing her clothing.

Hell, it happens. And this is not the first time that a fuck has ended in an awkward silence, so she quickly makes to leave as the cistern flushes, but Girlie calls her back. "Don't you want to take me home?" she asks, sounding disappointed. "I haven't eaten you yet."

Talk about turn again, Whittington, Lexie thinks.

They kiss, there and then, always a good sign, and several times on the way home, Girlie dragging Lexie into the shadows of shop doorways and Frenching her passionately, rubbing her cunt insistently on the older woman's thigh, almost coming again as Lexie kneads her pert little breasts.

"I've never done it with a girl before," she confesses, as they fall through the leaded door of Lexie's old house on a tree-lined street in the outskirts of the city, kissing and touching, desperate for fulfilment.

"I only ever do it with girls," Lexie confides, fumbling for the zip on Girlie's dress and yanking it down, unpeeling her like the horny little banana that she is. She's practically nude already, the clingy all-in-one still flapping unfastened at the gusset, and Lexie quickly pulls it up over her head leaving her lover completely naked and exposed.

Girlie's nipples are huge, soft and brown, not pink and perky as Lexie had imagined, but twice as sexy. "Come here," she whispers, enveloping the other's chubby nakedness in her arms, physically restraining herself from pushing two fingers up her slit.

Girlie groans, kicking off her shoes. "Hurry, take your boots off, I want to see you naked . . ."

"Are you sure you're ready for my big hairy cunt?" Lexie asks, unbuckling and unzipping furiously.

"I've been fantasizing about your hot and hairy cunt all the way here," Girlie counters, turning Lexie round and unzipping her.

"Then kiss me again." Lexie gasps as the other clutches her from behind and cups her breasts, their lips meeting as Girlie grinds her hips into her elder's ass. The narrow hall is painted a dark grocer's shop green and festooned with Art Deco plaster heads, a winking Marlene Dietrich leering down on them as Lexie gets her cunt groped.

"I have to go down on you, *now*," Girlie finally pants, clawing at the waistband of Lexie's tights and pulling them and her slinky black thong down in one. "Fuck, you've got a sexy bum."

"Play your cards right and I might let you spank it," Lexie purrs, but Girlie's already spun her round and is kissing her big pussy, tongue quickly finding her hot wet crevice amidst the thick tropical jungle of her lush and hairy bush.

She's obviously an amateur, Lexie thinks, as Girlie laps away down there like she's licking an ice-cream cone, but something about her very ineptness turns the temptress on and Lexie's astounded to realize that she's more than ready to come at any second. My reputation's ruined if this story ever gets out down at the dyke bar, she thinks, vainly trying to remember the names of the dwarves in "Snow White" to help delay the inevitable, but then Girlie goes and reaches up for her tits, pushing her bra up and releasing them like quivering jellies from a whetted mould, and Sexy Lexie's quite lost.

Girlie's up on her feet and kissing her again before she can even draw breath, and Lexie can taste her own cunt as she's consumed. Fuck, this girl knows just what buttons to push, Sexy Lexie thinks. "Can you bring yourself off on my leg?" she manages to gasp, her pussy still throbbing and convulsing with the aftershock.

"Can a bear shit in a wood?" Girlie replies, humping her like a bitch in season, the smooth white flesh of her honeypot gliding up and down Lexie's thigh like a potter's hands in wet clay.

"I fucking love this, I'm done with men for ever," she gasps, hovering on the brink, "and I'll have no more of knobbly cocks that smell of cheese and sweaty socks . . ."

Lexie wants to cry but holds her feelings in check. "I can't fuck you like they can," the cautious Mama Bear replies. Also, she's heard promises like these before and doesn't believe in happily-ever-after anyway. "What happens when you want that beautiful cunt of yours filled right up to the brim? What happens then, my fickle little dove?"

"Just shut the fuck up and fill 'my beautiful little cunt' with your fingers," Girlie groans, moans, shouts, as Lexie finds her hot wet hole and roughly finger-fucks her. "Oh fuck, fuck, fuckity-fuck, I'm coming again!"

"Let's go to bed," Lexie sighs, pointing upwards. "It's that way."

"You just want to look at my bum as I go up the stairs," Girlie giggles as she mounts the first riser and then the second. Then: "Do you like it?"

"Totally fuckable," Lexie confesses, planting kisses. "I want to bend you over and tongue-fuck you right here and now."

"Patience, Moriarty," Girlie teases, leading Lexie by the hand into her own Bluebeard's chamber. "I've got plans for you and your fat furry cunt."

"You're certainly a bold one for a beginner," Lexie sighs, allowing herself to be led to bed nevertheless. Her room smells of a myriad of old colognes, summer scents of violet and lavender on an evening breeze. There's a sea-green embroidered satin coverlet on the bed and cabbage rose paper on the walls, an old bear watching them from the pillow with one glassy eye.

"You live here alone?"

"Just me and my memories . . ."

"That's the Marx Brothers. I'm not as young as you might think, you know."

"So, you want to fuck or play Trivial Pursuits?"

Girlie pushes her onto the bed in reply. "What do *you* think?"

Sexy Lexie shakes her head, lies back down upon her bed. "If you're done with fucking boys, Mama Bear has lots of toys . . ."

"I've no use for rubber cocks, keep them in your sex toy box."

"Then tell me how we'll fuck tonight?"

Girlie smiles with sly delight.

"I think I've been bad," Girlie whispers, turning over to lie on her tummy and offering up her plump little butt, all soft and shadowed in the half-light. "I think I need to be punished."

Lexie runs a thin fingernail over the proffered chubby cheeks. "And do you have a punishment in mind?" she asks, trying hard to keep the excitement out of her voice.

Girlie gives a little shudder. "Streak my lily white ass with some strokes of crimson, make me smart and tingle . . ."

Lexie swallows long and hard. "Kneel on the floor and drape yourself over the bed," is all she says.

Lexie keeps an old leather belt tucked under all the pale green silk in her top drawer. It's thin as a whip and cracked from years of use, but it still has a viper's bite.

"You're sure you want this?" she asks, slicing experimentally through the empty air.

Girlie's humping against the bed and desperate to be dominated, her ass voluptuous and inviting. "Yes, yes, yes," she moans, then gasps as the first kiss of leather makes a neat red stripe across the perfect white of her snowy derrière. "More," she says through gritted teeth.

A second swish, a third, a fourth. Girlie's almost coming where she kneels. And Lexie's in the same place.

"That's enough for now," she says in a choked voice, laying down the belt.

"Fuck, don't leave me up here," Girlie begs, biting back the tears.

Lexie smiles and plants a kiss on the first red streak. "Don't worry, Mama Bear's going to kiss it all better," she promises, turning out the light.

* * *

"Could you love me, even a little?" Girlie's voice creeps, treacle-like, from the velvet darkness.

"Isn't it a little too early to be talking about love?"

"Not when you've turned my life around and made me into one of your kind. Tell me there's going to be a tomorrow."

"There's never a tomorrow. Tomorrow's always coming but it never arrives. There's only today . . ."

"That's a Christmas cracker riddle. Why won't you answer?"

"Because."

"Because why?"

"Just because . . ."

There's a silence for a moment and then the sound of a warm body moving on the cool satin of the bedspread and then the reading lamp snaps on. It's an old-style one, with a – predictably – green metal shade. An anglepoise, it was called when Lexie bought it all those years ago. It casts a warm circle of light onto the bed and the two white bodies lying there. No faces or feet or even tits. Just two bellies, two pairs of thighs and two very happy cunts.

Girlie's hand strokes Lexie's face in the dark, like brushing a fine gossamer thread of cobweb in a bluebell wood. Lexie lets out a little sigh.

"Want to watch a dirty movie?" says Girlie with a suggestive grin in her voice.

"Who's in it?"

"Just our fingers and our cunts."

Lexie doesn't reply but makes a little noise of acquiescence, watching in fascination as Girlie's hand sidles out of the dark and crawls Incy Wincy Spider-like up the inside of her thigh.

"What are you thinking about?"

"My first time . . ."

"Which was?"

"When my college professor did what you're doing to me now . . ."

Girlie lets out a little groan, seeing it all in her head. "You liked?"

"Feel and see . . ."

"Mmmmm! Oh yes, you liked. Fuck, you're wet."

Lexie arches her back just a little. Doesn't want to appear too Mills and Boon, but a little arching can't hurt, can it?

Girlie has two fingers in there by now and splits her open like a peach, gasping at all the hot pinks and fiery reds, everything wet and sticky with juice and sap. "My, what a big clit you have, Mama Bear," whispers Goldilocks's voice.

"Pull me right open and make it really stand out!" Lexie manages to gasp, quite sure that she's going to regret this in the morning.

"Like this? Oh fuck, that's big. So big . . ."

"No, do it harder, like this!" Lexie's hand snakes over and her fingers grip Girlie's chubby little fanny and pull the waxy soft-pillow lips apart, making her love button pop up from under its little pink hood. Girlie almost comes on the spot.

"I love it when you expose me like this," she pants. "I want to be naked for you all the time, show you everything . . ."

"And so you shall, so you shall," promises Sexy Lexie, finally throwing caution to the winds. "Tomorrow and tomorrow and tomorrow . . ."

And Girlie smiles to herself in the dark as her little doll-like fingers coax Lexie to orgasm, feeling her lover's wetness pouring over her hands and surrendering herself to her own lusts, as outside the sun rises cautiously over the towers of the city, announcing a new day and the fact that tomorrow has, finally, arrived.

"I love you, Sexy Lexie," she whispers, lying her head down on the satin pillow beside the other, their lips meeting tenderly.

"And I love you too," Lexie finally concedes, as, outside, the morning sun begins to shine . . .

A Very Desirable Property

Elizabeth Coldwell

Simon should have gone to view the Morgan property. As senior manager at the branch, he usually went out to price up the new listings. With over a dozen years' experience in the field, he was more adept than anyone at Palace and Winter at sizing up what a house would fetch on the open market, and advising clients how best to present their home so potential buyers wouldn't notice the rickety guttering and the lingering smell of damp in the utility room.

But Simon was ill, laid low with a bout of food poisoning, or what Darren, looking up from a half-completed mortgage application form, laughingly referred to as "manthrax". "Not that I think he's putting it on or anything, Gina," Darren continued, "but I reckon it'll clear up in time for him to go see the Arsenal play tomorrow . . ."

Gina tuned Darren out before he could start droning on about football, bringing up the address of the Morgan home on an online mapping service, and finding it just off Highgate Hill. In Simon's absence, she was the most senior member of staff, and the task of viewing the house fell to her. Not that she minded too much. She'd never known the property market as slow as it was now, and too much of her time over the last few weeks had been spent fantasizing about the builders renovating the pub over the road, in particular the dark-haired guy with the tribal tattoo on his left biceps who liked to work shirtless in the late August heat. Dragging her mind away from thoughts of that brawny, tattooed arm pinning her wrists together above her head while his big cock ploughed into her pussy with rough, unyielding strokes, Gina gathered up her bag, car keys and smartphone.

"Right, so if anyone needs me, I'll be over at Chantenay Street,. meeting a—" she consulted the notes scrawled on the manila file detailing potential listings "—Finlay Morgan.'

Darren glanced at the clock on the wall. "Well, I'll probably be nipping out for a sandwich at one . . ." His tone gave the impression he wasn't intending to hurry back. Gina wasn't surprised.

"OK, see you later." Leaving him to his paperwork, Gina stepped out into the high street, hoping for once, she'd be viewing a property that could legitimately be described as something special.

At first viewing, there was nothing to distinguish Finlay Morgan's home from any of the others on the street. A three-storey terraced house with an arresting gabled roof and neat, white-painted windows and front door, its guide price was around eight hundred thousand pounds. A couple of years ago, that price would have been closer to a million, and it would have been snapped up within days of appearing on the market. Now, who knew how long Morgan might have to wait before someone put in an offer he found even halfway acceptable?

Gina would be nothing less than optimistic in her valuation and estimate on how long it would take the property to sell, or run the risk of Morgan choosing to let another agency handle the sale. Running a hand through her caramel-blonde hair, a nervous habit she'd never quite managed to shake, she stabbed the doorbell with a freshly manicured finger.

The man who answered the door drove all thoughts of a stagnant housing market, and rough-and-ready builders, from Gina's mind. To her lust-dazzled eyes, Finlay Morgan appeared to fill the entire doorframe. Well over six feet tall, he had a broad, athletic frame that his sober outfit of black roll-neck sweater and dark jeans did nothing to diminish. Thick, midnight-black hair fell appealingly into his blue eyes, and when he smiled, Gina felt her belly give an excited little flip.

"Mr Morgan? I'm Gina Carson, from Palace and Winter. My colleague was supposed to come and view your house, but he's been laid low by a dodgy seafood salad." Aware she was babbling, she simply couldn't stop herself. Morgan cut her short by taking her hand in a firm grip.

"Lovely to meet you, Gina. Do come in. And please, call me Fin. The place is in a bit of a mess, I'm afraid."

Stepping over the threshold, Gina found herself in a hallway piled high with cardboard boxes. Morgan guided her through to the living room.

"I run a business from home, buying and selling academic textbooks," he explained, as she took a seat on a comfortable black leather sofa. "Had a new shipment delivered yesterday and I haven't had the chance to sort everything out properly. It completely slipped my mind you were coming, or I'd have done more to tidy up."

"Don't worry about it, Mr—er, Fin. We'll give you plenty of advance warning when we start sending clients round."

"Excellent. Now, can I get you something to drink?"

While Morgan busied himself making coffee for the two of them, Gina mentally appraised the room, in advance of the sales description she'd write when she got back to the office. It was standard practice to bill a house such as this as "a very desirable property", though in this case it was no cliché. Its size and location would make it a perfect family home, and even though Morgan would be taking the furniture with him, whoever moved in would need to do very little in terms of redecoration.

When he returned with their drinks, handing a mug of strong, sugared black coffee to Gina, she suggested, "Why don't you give me a tour of the place? I'd like to get on with some measuring up."

"Of course. I think the kitchen might be a good place to start. It's a little tidier than some of the other rooms."

As they moved from room to room, Gina measuring the dimensions of each one in turn and writing down the details on a notepad, they made small talk. More accurately, Morgan talked and Gina listened. His voice had a gravelled quality to it that was almost hypnotic; a voice, she thought, before wondering where such a thought might have come from, designed to give instructions that couldn't be disobeyed on pain of punishment.

Her mind must have been running on a particularly kinky track this morning, for when they walked into the master bedroom, she thought the iron rail at the head of the king-sized bed was perfectly suited for bondage games. She pictured herself cuffed to the bed, naked, while Morgan, still clad all in black, ran a sliver of ice along the length of her body, causing her to shudder in erotic torment and her nipples to pebble with anticipation. Even though she begged for mercy, her pleas would be half-hearted and he'd simply ignore her, trailing the ice ever lower till it hovered above her sensitive pussy lips . . .

She'd never analysed why so many of her fantasies saw her taking the submissive role, whether that involved letting the tattooed builder grip a fistful of her hair and plunge her sucking mouth hard down on to his cock, or finding herself at the mercy of Morgan and his ice cubes. All she knew was the thought of being bound and made to do whatever her lover chose never failed to get her hot and bothered. Indeed, there was a definite stickiness in her panties as she crouched down by the bedroom's bay window, laying her tape measure out along the wall.

"The largest bedroom has a south-facing aspect," she muttered to herself, imagining long strands of afternoon sun slanting through the drapes, striping her body as she writhed in her bonds, just as Morgan might later choose to stripe it with some implement of punishment: a crop, or maybe a whip. She'd never been cropped, never even had her bottom spanked, but the thought of it sent a shivery excitement through her as she wondered how much it might hurt, and how many blows her punisher might give her before deciding she'd suffered enough.

When she looked back over her shoulder, she saw Morgan regarding her with an amused expression. "Oh, I was talking to myself again, wasn't I? Sorry. It's one of my many bad habits."

"Don't worry about it," he assured her. "I'm far from being a paragon of virtue myself."

"Well, we're all done in here," Gina said, rising to her feet and crossing the room to where Morgan stood in the doorway. He'd been careful to keep out of her way as she measured and made her notes, and she respected the manner in which he'd let her get on with her job, even though he took a clear interest in everything she did. "I just need to check the room across the landing and then we're finished—"

"Oh, I'd rather you didn't go in there," Morgan said hurriedly. "Like I said, I haven't had time to tidy everything away."

But Gina's hand was already on the door handle, turning it and pushing the door open before he could stop her.

She'd expected to see more of the clutter that littered the hallway downstairs, boxes of books, the tools of Morgan's trade. Instead, she took an astonished step back at the sight that greeted her eyes. He had tools in this small black-painted room, all right, but ones that chimed in uncanny fashion with the fantasies she'd been weaving about the man. A wooden cross in the shape of an X stood in one corner, while the centre of the room was dominated by a high stool with a padded leather top. In racks on the walls hung canes, paddles, whips and other implements whose names she could only guess at. She'd heard of rooms like this, but never had she imagined she'd find herself standing in one.

"It's – it's a dungeon," she breathed.

"I prefer to use the term playroom," Morgan replied, "but yes, you're right."

"I've never seen anything quite like this before. It's amazing," she told him. Now she was over the initial shock, she couldn't resist walking into the room, running her hand over the top of what she knew to be a whipping stool and wondering how it would feel to be tied in place over it, waiting for the first stripe of the cane across her bare backside. Or maybe he'd prefer to have her fastened to the cross, so he could whip the whole length of her back and the sensitive tops of her thighs.

Why am I thinking about him doing this to me? she asked herself. And why is it turning me on so much? Her panties clung to the lips of her pussy, soaked through with her juices, and, as she moved, she caught the strong, truffled scent of her arousal.

"Maybe you ought to leave this room now," Morgan said. "I think you've seen enough to make an assessment of this place."

Gina's voice took on a bratty quality she'd never known it might possess, until now. "And what if I don't? What if I decide I want to stay and take a look at all those whips and canes and . . . and other things?" She moved closer to the wall, reaching out a hand and flicking the soft suede tails of a pretty purple flogger.

"Well, then I might just have to show you what happens to naughty girls who don't do as they're told."

Had he really just said that? Had he really implied that unless she did as he asked, he would punish her? Gina couldn't help feeling this was all a dream, that boredom had caused her to nod off at her desk in the Palace and Winter office, and any moment now Darren would come back with his sandwiches and wake her up. One of the items hanging on the wall was a cruel-looking spiked pinwheel with a long metal handle. She recognized it as some kind of surgical tool. Gina touched a finger to one of the spikes. Feeling a sharp pricking in her finger, she knew she wasn't dreaming.

"Don't play with that," Morgan ordered her, his tone almost compelling her to disobey him, just to see what might happen. She spun the wheel, listening to its metallic tinkle with a satisfied smile on her lips.

Morgan caught hold of her wrist, his grip surprisingly strong. She assumed hefting heavy boxes of books was a good way to build up muscles. Turning her to face him and pushing her up against the wall, he murmured, "I did warn you."

"But I told you I had a lot of bad habits," Gina replied. Her body was crushed tight against his. She could feel the hard length of Morgan's erection pressing against her body, and knew he was just as turned on as she was. If she'd had any doubts that she could trust him, given that they barely knew each other, they were slowly but surely melting away. "And one of them is not doing what I'm told."

"Well, I'll have to make sure you learn what happens when you disobey me and see if you don't modify your habits, won't I?" As he spoke, Morgan snaked his hand up under Gina's skirt, fingers brushing against the soaking crotch of her underwear. "Hm, it seems you really are a bad girl, aren't you, Gina? I can tell from just how wet your knickers are." His breath was warm in her ear, and she couldn't fail to appreciate the broad muscularity of his body. She felt weak and helpless in his grip, and the thought of all the many ways in which he might discipline her awoke the deeply buried, submissive heart of her. Never had she believed being in this position could be quite so exciting.

"I'm sorry, sir," she said, her tone making it perfectly clear she was anything but.

"Oh, you will be," he told her, "because bad girls don't get to keep their knickers on." He took a firm grasp of her panties, tugging them down in slightly awkward fashion till the waistband was around her knees. Gina felt foolish, but even more aroused than before.

Morgan relaxed his hold on her, so she could step all the way out of her underwear. He smiled at the sight of the scrap of damp white lace, lying forlornly on the black, varnished floorboards.

"In fact," he continued, "bad girls don't get to wear any clothes at all. So take them off."

Gina couldn't quite work out how things had moved so quickly. One moment, or so it seemed, she'd been measuring the dimensions of the master bedroom; the next, she was shrugging out of her neat checked jacket, and dropping it on the floor alongside her panties. Reaching behind her, aware that Morgan's appraising blue gaze never left her body for a moment, she unzipped her black dress and let that fall, too. Now she stood in only her bra and knee-length boots, fighting the urge to cover her pussy with her hands.

"You can leave the boots on," Morgan told her. "What are those – three-inch heels? They'll give you the extra height you need to make yourself comfortable over the whipping stool."

As if anything could make me comfortable there, she thought, looking over at the stool and feeling her stomach clench with sick anticipation at the thought of being stretched over it. But the fact he appreciated she was a novice when it came to these matters made her trust that he wouldn't do anything she really didn't want. Unclipping her bra and letting it slip from her shoulders, she took a pace towards the whipping stool.

"Stay where you are for a moment," Morgan ordered her. "Let me take a good look at you."

This was one instruction she was happy to obey; it delayed the moment when she'd have to get into position over the stool. His eyes raked over her from head to toe, lingering on the full swell of her breasts and the smudge of dark hair on her mound.

"See, sometimes you can do as you're told," he said. "And it feels good, doesn't it?"

She nodded, unable to deny the truth of his words. Obeying him felt good; more than that, it felt right.

He gestured to the stool. "Over you go, girl."

For a moment, she hesitated. Then the bold, curious part of her – the part that had marched straight into his playroom, rather than shutting the door and walking away – took over. She draped herself over the stool, her hair falling into her face as she lowered her head. Moving to brush it away, she felt Morgan catch her wrist, securing it to one of the legs of the stool with the broad Velcro strap designed for that purpose. Quickly, he did the same thing with her other limbs, immobilizing her. She tugged at the straps, but they were secure; not so tight as to be uncomfortable, but not allowing her to wriggle free of the stool. She wasn't going anywhere until Morgan decided, she knew that.

"Now, every sub needs a safeword, and yours is—" Morgan cast around for the perfect word, plucking it from memories of their earlier conversation with a grin. "'South-facing'. If it all gets too much for you, you only have to say that and I'll stop at once. OK . . . All we need is to choose the right implement for your punishment."

He'd carefully positioned her so she couldn't see the rack of tools. Gina had no idea which one he reached for, out of the many on display. She heard the tinkling of the surgical tool, and prayed it wouldn't be that; it was too harsh, too intimidating to her untutored eyes. To her relief, Morgan seemed to seize on something else, muttering, "Aha. Just the thing!" as he did.

When he came to stand in front of her, she saw he held the purple flogger she'd admired earlier. That she felt she could take.

"So, why am I punishing you?" Morgan asked.

Because you want to, and because I want you to, Gina thought. Aloud, she said, "Because I'm a bad, disobedient girl, sir."

"Very good. I do love a quick learner . . ."

With that, Morgan moved to stand so that he was behind her, to the left of the stool. Letting the soft tails of the whip trail over the bare skin of her arse, he chuckled at the moan he drew from her, the pure need in its tone unmistakable.

For an agonizing moment, nothing more happened. Then she felt the flogger land with some force, its tails spreading out over the surface of her backside, each one stinging where it touched. Brief flares of pain died away to almost nothing, but as he continued to flay her arse with the suede whip, layering blow upon blow, the throbbing in her nerve endings gradually became too insistent to ignore.

"You should see this, Gina," Morgan crooned. "Your skin

is turning such a delicious shade of red. Oh, you need this, don't you, baby?"

His tone was tender, almost reverent, and she wished she could look behind herself, to see not only the marks he was leaving on her arse but the look on his face as he did so. Yes, this was painful, but for him she'd endure it. For him, she would surrender the part of her she'd kept hidden away for so long, the part that yearned to call a man "sir" and kiss his whip when he'd finished using it on her skin.

On and on Morgan flogged, making sure to catch the sensitive crease where her buttocks joined her thighs, and occasionally swiping the tails dangerously close to her wet, vulnerable pussy lips, so that she wriggled and moaned, almost afraid she wanted him to carry out the threat of punishing her there.

At last, he dropped the flogger, telling her how beautifully she'd taken her punishment. She heard rustling, but couldn't turn her head enough to see what he was doing. Only when he came to her again, parting her swollen nether lips with his fingers, did she realize he was about to fuck her. He'd found a condom from somewhere – she had no idea where – but the pulsing heat of him was obvious even through the thin latex, as he slowly pushed into her hole. Her tight walls parted, welcoming him in, allowing her master to claim her as his own.

Beautifully in proportion to his big frame, his cock filled her utterly, his groin pressed so close to her that she could feel the rough denim of his jeans against her hot, sore arse.

"Mine," he murmured, as he began to fuck her, taking her with harsh but oh-so thrilling jerks of his hips, and she could only sigh in agreement. Moving like a well-maintained engine, he powered into her slick depths, waking the nerves in her punished backside, his thumbs gripping at her flanks and her senses alive with him, only him.

Almost before she knew it, she was tumbling headlong into orgasm, crying out as he pushed her through one peak and into another, so close behind it was like a delicious echo of the first. Vaguely, she heard him call her name as he came, but the pleasure was too much and she closed her eyes till her world stopped spinning.

"So, do you think you'll be able to sell this place for me?" Morgan asked as she dressed, stepping back into the role of client once more.

"Well, my initial assessment of the property is favourable, and we should be able to get plenty of interest, even given the current slow market conditions," she replied, "but I may need to come back and look at its more unique features again."

"Oh, I'm sure that could be arranged."

Morgan smiled, and Gina knew then she hadn't seen the last of the house on Chantenay Street, or its enigmatic owner, a man even more desirable than his unique property. Blessing the illness that had stricken down her boss, she gave Morgan a soft kiss on the cheek and headed back to the office.

No Good Deed

James Desborough

There's no air conditioning in these big old trucks and, with the sun beating down on the steel box of the cab, it's like some punishment cell from an old war movie, only without the cruel, Japanese camp commander. I'm built for Europe, not for the Middle East. The sweat trickles down my back and mingles with the dust under my shirt, it turns to mud and stains my skin yellow and brown in salty streaks. I love what I do here, but I hate it too. It's too hot, too violent, too alien – but people still need help and people are people the world over.

Zach is out at the checkpoint, showing the raggedy-arsed policeman our papers and arguing our case in his halting Farsi. There's a lot of gesticulation, pointing and laughing – which is a hopeful sign at least. The truck's got food, books, anything we could scrape together. The fighting's still ongoing, there are still refugees and radicals and all the corruption in the government means if you want something done right, you really do have to do it yourself.

There's a clanking of bells and what sounds like a party of Young Conservatives out for a drink in Winchester of a Friday night. Then a herd of hungry-looking goats meanders past, herded – with a great deal of disinterest – by a young boy who doesn't even glance at the truck.

Coming the other way is one of the local women, swathed – almost entirely – in a big black circus-tent of a dress. I can't help but see it as a shame. She passes close by me and glances into the cabin. All I can see are her eyes, but after months out here even that amount of female contact hits like a hammer blow. Beautiful, almond eyes. Deep and rich and brown. Defiant, proud, not beaten down or fearful like so many people's eyes here – even mine. It's a country and a people ground down to a nub.

I'm snapped away from her eyes, and my thoughts, by the miraculous. My phone, deep in the thigh pocket of my combats, bleeps loudly for attention. I blink the sweat from my eyes and haul it out. There's signal, barely, and a threadbare charge. In the time I've been sitting here the connection has somehow managed to tease the bits and bytes out of the ether and to grant me one of the few things that makes life tolerable here.

A picture of my Rose.

I can hear my heartbeat in my ears as I get sight of her. My girl, my woman, my love. Naked as the morning I left, she's a gift from across the sea, from another world. Wicked eyes look at me from a rumpled mess of dirty-blonde hair and there's just a hint of hesitancy to them. One heavy, pale breast lifted in her hand, the nipple pinched, teased and presented. The other indented, the plastic shape of that toy, the one she doesn't like but that I love to fuck her with, pressed against the curve of her chest.

The camera phone doesn't do her justice. It makes her look washed out, but I can still see the flush of her cheeks. She doesn't like to take pictures for me, but she does it for me when I'm away. She thinks she's getting fatter, she thinks she looks bad no matter how often I tell her she's beautiful. No matter how eagerly I take her in my hands and kiss every curve swell, she stubbornly refuses to believe me and wastes her time on fad diets, pining for her days as a dancer.

She does this for me though. This and more. All I ask for, she gives me. All I can take from her, she accepts willingly. She bites back her reservations and her modesty and she sends me these gifts that make me yearn to return to her, that make being here the sweetest torture imaginable.

I lick my lips and I glance up again as a shadow falls across me. The woman with the almond eyes is right by the dusty window of the truck. She sees the phone. She sees Rose. Her bold and prideful stare becomes one of disgust and then . . .

It doesn't hurt. That's the strange thing about it. I'm aware of no pain, I'm barely aware of myself. Disembodied almost, like the first moments of wakefulness.

I'm not in the cab any more and somehow I feel cool, refreshed, even cold. The blue sky stretches above me in every direction, punctuated by little, wistful attempts at cloud. My ears ring. I smell smoke. A poppy sways in a breeze I do not feel and sheds a petal at the boundaries of my vision.

My phone. Where is my phone? Rose will be upset if anyone else sees her.

I try to reach for it, but I have no hands.

I try to stand, but I have no legs.

Zach leans over me, his face sooty and bloodied. He is shouting something but I cannot hear him. Cannot make the shapes of his lips into anything that makes sense. I just smile at him and tell him I'm fine, but I can't even hear myself.

I'm tired.

I'll have a little nap.

Morphine is a hell of a drug. It almost makes me not mind that I'll never touch or hold anything ever again. It dulls the incomprehensible ache of my arms and legs, arms and legs I no longer have, to something manageable. It makes everything seem like a dream and the great thing about dreams is that you wake up. I hope I wake up soon. I need to go for a run.

How much time has passed? I have no idea. I think there was a helicopter, perhaps a plane. This isn't a local hospital. Am I home?

I don't say anything to anyone. What would be the point?

They don't bother to watch me, how would I even go about hurting myself?

Days and nights are meaningless, one day after another of glass-eyed staring at the ceiling, listening to the hum of the light and counting the divots in the ceiling tiles. There's about five-hundred in each, I think.

They bring a shrink of some kind to talk to me.

At me.

I tell him nothing, of course. I almost think I've forgotten how to speak. He adds some drugs to the daily cocktail they are giving me but I barely notice thanks to the painkillers. They wheel me in and out of surgery and I let them do their work without a word.

When Rose comes to visit no amount of drugs can dull that pain.

I refuse to look at her. I don't want to see her disgust. I don't want to even look at her. I couldn't bear her pity. I don't want to be reminded that I will never again lift her in my arms, spin her around, throw her, squealing, over my shoulder or pin her down and pepper her with kisses.

I don't want to see the hurt in her eyes when she sees me broken, weak and useless.

I don't want to see her nostrils flare and her mouth set, determined not to upset me.

I don't want to see her long neck taut and tense when I can't even lean up to kiss it and feel her arch into my mouth.

I don't want to see her body, which I will never again touch and hold, that I will never bend and turn and shape to our passions.

I don't want to see any tears.

I don't want to see this beautiful, brilliant woman weighed down by the need to stay with me, just because it's what everyone expects.

She tries to speak to me. I refuse to hear her. I simply don't let the words penetrate. I make myself forget how language works. I turn my head and stare at the wall until I hear her leave. Then I cry for her sake, because the man she loved is dead.

* * *

The surgeries come to an end, but they cannot give back what was taken. They can only take what was given. Several pockets' worth of spare change in shrapnel and pieces of truck. They tell me they took someone's tooth out of my shoulder. I never even saw her smile.

They can, and do, take away the drugs though. Pain is going to be a constant companion now, but I can't take any more of the "good" stuff without even more problems.

Now, unlike before, I feel the passage of time and I'm bored. I'm bored out of my mind. I've been here weeks or months already and this is just days, but without the blessed haze of opiates, I feel the passage of every second like an eternity. I'm just waiting to die.

A nurse dresses me, though I hardly see the point. Rose is talking to a doctor just outside the room, earnest and organized and intent. She used to leave everything to me. I would take care of her. Now she has to take charge, at least until I make her leave. We're not married, she didn't choose to be with a cripple. I will drive her away with my silence and indifference so she can be happy again somewhere else, with someone else.

They load me into a wheelchair like a side of meat into a shopping trolley. I can't even push myself around with the useless stumps I've been left with and they haven't gotten one of those fancy wheelchairs you can control with your eyes or your mouth for me yet. It's Rose who has to wheel the ghost of her dead lover out of the hospital and into a special taxi, made just for crips.

Home.

Our home.

She moved in with me about a month before I left on my "do-gooder" mission. The place is more hers than mine now. It's no longer familiar to me. She wheels me into the lounge, the seats pushed back or taken elsewhere to make room for this bloody chair. I sit there, impassive, staring at the carpet, ignoring her with every fibre of my being. In my mind I'm willing her to go away, to leave, to find someone better, someone whole. I want her to just leave me alone so I can die with some dignity.

"Look at me."

I don't.

"Look at me goddamnit. Say something. Anything."

I still don't. Her voice tickles at my ear, teases at my memory. Low and husky with pained emotion it echoes other, better times between us.

She grabs my head in her hands and tries to twist my face to look at her. I set the muscles and refuse to move. Her nails dig into my cheek, rasp against the stubble, but I am stone, I am iron. She cannot move me despite her efforts and the pain is nothing to me. Not any more.

"You're still stronger than me," her voice quieter now, weaker, lower. She's kneeling on the floor in front of me, I can tell, even though I don't look. Those words though, they anger me. Errant bullshit. She's just lying to me to make me feel better.

"No." The first word in months and that's what I choose to say – "No".

I look at her, finally. She looks tired and angry but still beautiful to me. She's lost weight, worrying over me, it pains me to see it, though she's likely perversely happy to have done so. I meet her eyes and then turn my head left and right, glancing to the ugly stumps where my arms and legs used to be.

"I am not."

She slaps me, hard, across the face, and makes me snarl with impotent rage. "Hitting a fucking cripple, Rose? Very brave, very helpful. You wouldn't dare fucking do that if I were whole."

"You wouldn't stand for it. You shouldn't stand for it now." She hisses the words out so viciously I feel her spittle speckle my chin.

"What am I going to do? Hit you?" I snort at her and roll my eyes to the heavens. "I might be able to bite if you get close enough."

"You don't need to hit me. You don't even need to touch me. You're already hurting me." She shakes her hair down over her face to hide her tears. More bashful now than she ever was when I was away.

"I can't touch you." I mean to spit it out angrily, but it comes out as a near sob because . . . Christ . . . I want to touch her. I want to feel the soft give of her body. I want to taste her. I want to breathe the scent of her in from my fingers and bury my face in her hair. But I don't have fingers any more, or hands. My flesh is scarred and burnt even more intimately in ways I daren't even contemplate. I'm a broken horror.

She tugs her hair in her hands and silently sobs, shoulders shaking. I try not to look, but even in anguish she's beautiful to me. So much time passes like this, both of us silent, then her back stiffens and she lifts red-rimmed eyes to meet mine again.

"You don't need hands to touch me. You don't need to force me to do what you want. You touched me with a handful of words from a world away. I showed myself to you, I did what you asked because of . . . because of your soul and that hasn't gone anywhere."

"It is." I shake my head again, more firmly. "Dead and gone. I can't be who I was. I'm not who I was. I can't even touch you."

"I slapped you." She leans closer to me. God, her breath smells sweet. "Hurt me back." Her lips are a tiny space from mine as she says it; her voice tickles at my spine.

"I can't."

"Try."

"I can't. You'd have to slap your . . ."

I don't even finish the word. She slaps herself hard across the face, her cheek blossoming like her namesake. She whimpers at it, lifts her hand to her cheek and holds it, cradles herself in her hand and stares at me. "Whatever you want of me, it's yours. It always was."

"Again." I test her, angry, fierce. I feel tricked somehow,

betrayed. There's no hesitation on her part. She slaps herself, hard, across the other cheek, snapping her own head to the side.

"Again!"

Am I being cruel? She only slapped me once, but this is making me feel strong, powerful. Even whole. She lifts her hand and smacks herself back and forth, once on each cheek, so hard the sound rings off the walls. Wide dark eyes stare into mine, challenging, hopeful.

"Strip," I hiss and suddenly I ache with frustration. I need her. I've needed her since the day I landed in that godforsaken country. And after, lying in that hospital bed night after night where I couldn't even masturbate? Even more so. Though I wouldn't admit it to myself.

She writhes out of her blue jeans and striped top. Out of her mismatched and over-washed bra and panties and she kneels before me in supplication. Offering herself to my frustration, my hurt, my need and my pain.

"Arch your fucking back." Why am I so angry at her? Am I angry at her? Why do I want to see her hurt? She arches her back and thrusts out those gorgeous breasts, tipped candy pink. The nipples are stiff and eager but I cannot even lean to take them in my mouth, I would fall. "Slap them." I nod to her breasts, taunting me with their inaccessibility.

She whimpers as she does it, but she does it. I see her body tense, I watch as the soft flesh bounces, sways and reddens. Everything seems hyper-real to me. Every sight, every sound, the scent of her wetness, surprising me as I am so cruel to her.

I cannot touch, so everything else seems stronger, more significant.

"Harder," I whisper, and she obeys, fresh tears tracking down her cheek.

"Again." She does, and again, as often as I ask. I ask many times.

"Come closer." She shuffles forward on her hands and knees, a reluctant child being dragged around a supermarket, but she does it. All it takes is the word.

"Stand. Lean over me." I bark it out and she does so. It amazes me that I can still feel this way, this powerful, that she will do as I ask when I have no way to make her.

She leans forward and sets her hands on the arms of the chair, bracing. Her scarlet tits so close, so wonderfully close. I risk it, I lean, somehow. I press my face into the embrace of her warm bosom and suckle at her. I catch that stiff swollen nipple in my lips and roll it between my teeth. It is heaven.

And then I bite.

Slowly at first, lightly, then firmer, and tighter. She tenses, shifts her weight from foot to foot and then gasps as I bite down harder. "Please . . . not so hard." A hand lifts and curls in my hair, too tight, trying to pull my head back.

"Please . . . what?" I speak, freeing her for a moment. Then bite into the ripeness of her, behind the areola, teeth digging into tender flesh, suckling her deeper into my mouth.

"Please. Oh please, Sir. Please, Daddy. Please . . . M-Master."

She always hates calling me that. To hear it come from her so easily sends a shudder of desire down my spine and tightens my jaw. It was not what I wanted to hear though. Not quite. I tighten my jaw further, harder, even as her fist tears strands of hair from my head.

"Yellow, Master. Yellow. It's too much."

I release her breast with a lick and a kiss, a whisper against the angry bruise already rising. "I love you, Rose, but this is all I can do."

Her hand touches me, firm, daring, between my legs. She could feel how hard I was but . . .

"You can do more, my Master." There's a hungry edge to her voice now. She's broken me down and built me up, but some things are impossible to explain. I'll have to let her see for herself.

She strips me gently, carefully, reverentially almost until I snap at her to hurry up. I am crippled, not a totem, not some object of religious fetish. I'm already broken, I'll break no further than this. I let her strip me and I let her see me. The burns around my belly. The scars where torn flesh was sewn back together over days and weeks.

A cock isn't the prettiest thing in the world at the best of times but one that has been torn and rent and stitched back together? Doctor Frankenstein would reject such a thing from being sewn onto his monster and the scars are tight and painful from me getting hard. Swollen flesh draws scarred skin paper thin and taut, threatening to tear.

"Can I?"

"Why would you want to?" I blurt, flushing and looking away from her again. The shame and sense of weakness comes back, overwhelming. "I can't fuck you."

"Not yet. You're still healing, but you're still you and I still want you, Master."

I shake my head, I don't believe her, won't believe her. In spite of all she's said and shown me. There must be a limit to what she can take. She cannot want to be with this, with me, not this way. It's impossible.

She is determined to prove me wrong.

How can the touch of lips feel so intense and so gentle at the same time?

She makes me groan with the hot-wet hunger of her mouth. I've felt it before but never, ever like this. I cannot hold her. I cannot set the pace. I cannot pull her deeper onto me, but she doesn't need me to.

A kiss for every scar, the trail of a tongue over every line, every crevice, every stitched-together piece of torn meat. She leaves me wet and dripping from her mouth and tongue and suckles at my stitched sac, teasing me with a flash of teeth.

"More than enough," she murmurs and suckles me deeper, wetter, stopping just short of her throat, that completeness that I crave but will have to wait for. She gently, teasingly, tauntingly rocks her head, playing at the scarred and ragged head of me.

It hurts – almost – raw nerves and twisted flesh. The pleasure is there, but distant, almost out of my reach but it slowly builds. With patience and adoration, she works her lips and her fingers over me. She moans for me, she looks at me, she lets her breasts stroke against what is left of my legs and, moment by moment, impossibly, she brings me to that explosive and needful apex. All I can do is arch my back and howl in joy as the proof I'm still a man fills her mouth and coats her tongue and the distant promise of satisfaction becomes something true, something real.

She swallows once, making sure I see her do it. She strokes her bottom lip with a fingertip and shifts to sit her bare, warm body in the ruins of my lap, slippery with my sweat and come and her spittle. She twines her arms around me and presses soft kisses to my jaw as she straddles and presses her body to me.

"I am still yours, if you want me. Master."

I feel her tense against me. She's worried I will say no. This is genuine, not pity. She's afraid.

"Always and forever, mine. Held closer than any arms could."

A Breath of Peace

Jacqueline Applebee

Violence is relative. A slap to my face could be viewed as a terrible thing to some. Whereas others won't be satisfied until their palms are stained crimson, and the smell of copper consumes them.

Violence is a relative. Eddie had been a friend of my parents for as long as I'd known. He had been a soldier, like my dad. Unlike my dad, Eddie was timeless, never seeming to change or age in all my years. Sometimes I wondered if he were an alien for whom the passage of time meant nothing. I liked the idea of having an eternal man as a family friend.

Eddie and I were not connected by the blood in our veins, at least not when I was younger. When my dad served in Afghanistan, Eddie had fought right alongside him. I'd seen plenty of photographs of the two men standing with an arm slung around the other's shoulder. I also remembered the glint of metal that reflected the light and dazzled my eyes as my dad angled his medal this way and that. He told me to call his friend *Uncle Eddie*, and that he would be staying with us for a while. Blood brothers didn't begin to cover it.

Uncle Eddie was a constant from that point on. He didn't seem to have a family of his own. I didn't know what he used to do or where he used to live before he came to our house. He was just always around. I was grateful for that. When my dad would grow silent and sad at times, Eddie always had a smile ready for me. He would sit out in the yard, polishing his boots with vigour. Even the instep didn't escape his attention.

One night, not long after Dad and Uncle Eddie had returned, a loud cry made me sit up in bed. I knew that sound; it spoke of the mean boys pushing me against the wall of the schoolyard as they bundled past. I felt the rough scratch of concrete even as I rolled out of my little bed. The sound had stopped, but the echoes of pain drew me forward. Ours was an old house, complete with floorboards that creaked beneath my tentative feet. I rounded a corner, and came face to face with Uncle Eddie, standing outside my parents' room like a sentry guard.

"Bad dream, Jenny?" His voice was breathless. I saw his clenched fists even in the low light. I saw how his usually smart hair was wild, but it was his voice that stayed with me as he placed a hand on my shoulder, turning me around in a smooth movement. I wondered if he'd been in a fight with my dad, but I dismissed that. Eddie and he never said a cross word to each other. My dad was more likely to speak in sharp tones to me or my mum. Even at my young age, it was plain to see that the two men cared for each other. But I still wondered what he had been doing outside my parents' room.

Eddie kissed me on the forehead. "You don't have to be afraid," he'd said. "Your dad has nightmares. He feels better if I'm close by."

I wished that Eddie could scare away the monsters that lurked in silent shadows beneath my bed; the ones that would threaten to take my dad away once more.

I stretched my wings and left home at eighteen to study history at York University. I moved into an apartment with two other girls. The sound of squeals, loud music and their belligerent boyfriends seemed to surround me. But sometimes I was left alone to the groan of the wind as it moved and twirled around the building. I'd think of my parents; of Eddie and his polished boots. I'd imagine him running into battle, rocked by explosions, but ultimately unstoppable. He would rescue me from an unknown evil force, and then he'd bring me home. It was a fantasy, nothing more, but one that persisted over time.

"Sounds like you've got a crush on your soldier boy," my boyfriend, Howard would say. Howard was a gentle man with curly brown hair and deep blue eyes. He loved to suck on my nipples for hours on end. Time didn't mean too much when the world went spiralling out of my tits. He was so good at this that I almost came a few times just from his mouth on me. It wasn't just the delicious sex that made me appreciate my lover. I could talk to him about absolutely anything. I doubted I could ever shock him with my secrets.

"Do you love Eddie?" Howard asked. He didn't sound jealous, but I was still afraid to look him in the eye as he spoke. "Fantasy isn't the same as reality," he said with a gentle voice. Howard helped me into my warm coat, and held open the door as my taxicab pulled up outside. "Don't be so hard on yourself." He kissed me on the cheek and then he went back indoors.

Howard liked his space; I respected that. He lived in an attic room in an isolated spot outside of town. I'd only been there twice, but it left me cold and desperate. I wished we were closer sometimes; that he would stay the night more often. I longed to be held as I fell asleep. The nightmares had mostly disappeared, but there was still a part of me that felt afraid when the lights went out.

I returned home for the Christmas holidays. Eddie opened the front door to my home. He drew me into an incredibly firm hug. He held on for just a little longer than necessary. His bulk was solid, warm and reassuring. And it was then that I knew something would happen between us. Eddie moved a fraction. I squeezed past him; his hard chest was like a wall against me. I practically ran up to my room. A surge of need assaulted me. I flung my bags to the floor, threw myself down on my bed, and stuck a hand into my knickers. I masturbated hard and fast with the image of Eddie in my mind. I pictured him in full uniform, those damn boots gleaming as he bent me over his knees to finger my cunt and slap my bare arse. It was safe to say that my crush on him had moved up a notch.

I could barely eat that evening. The others sat around watching the television after our meal, but it was nothing but static to me. Eddie sat between my mum and dad on the sofa, his arm slung over both of their shoulders. It was as it had always been – the three of them suspended in a beautiful bubble of affection. I felt suddenly bad for even thinking of Eddie in a sexual way. I made an excuse and went to bed.

I pulled my plain nightdress over my head, shivering as the winter chill touched my skin. I considered phoning Howard, but a knock at my bedroom door made me drop the phone to the bed. Eddie stepped inside as if it was his room, his domain and not mine. I looked down to see his boots, shiny and black. My clitoris throbbed from out of nowhere.

Eddie was close, but he still waved me closer. "Come here, Jenny."

I made a tiny step towards him.

"Closer."

I shook my head. "Why?"

"Come here right now." Eddie's eyes were vibrant blue and unblinking as he stared at me. I couldn't help myself. I moved until my chest was touching his. For several long moments he did nothing but look at me. The breath in my throat refused to come out.

"Good girl." Eddie's voice was low. I trembled. I knew he could feel me trembling too.

"What do you want?" I asked, my own voice a bare whisper.

Eddie gripped my hand. "I want you to tell me to stop." He brought my hand to his mouth, but then he angled himself and bit down on my wrist. I hissed at the flare of pain. I tried to jerk away, but in truth I was spellbound. I could hardly move at all. "Tell me to stop." This time his voice was gravel hard. He swept the strap of my nightdress aside. He bent to bite down on my shoulder. Fire raced from his lips right down to my clitoris. I whimpered like a wounded animal, but yet I wanted more. I wobbled as the world around me broke apart. My legs could barely sustain me.

"Please, Eddie." I didn't understand what was happening. None of my fantasies had included anything like this.

"On your knees, girl." Eddie gazed down at me with a look of certainty. "Get on your knees or tell me to stop."

My legs folded beneath me in submission. The only thing I could see was his shiny black boots. Did Eddie expect me to kiss them? As soon as I thought that, I couldn't think of anything else. I could smell the faint scent of boot polish as I bent lower. I didn't kiss his boots, but I just pressed my face to the dark leather. When my skin made contact, it was as if a weight had just slid from my shoulders. It was unlike anything I'd experienced before. I felt a blanket of safety all around me. I was amazed.

"Good girl." Eddie's voice was soft.

I moved to the other boot. I never wanted to rise up from that place. Eddie's hand moved to my hair. He crouched down low to my level, crooned nonsense words in my ear as he petted me. Finally, he stood.

"Off to bed with you."

I stood with shaky legs. Eddie pulled back the covers and helped me to bed. He leaned over to kiss me on the cheek.

"Goodnight, Jenny." He switched off the light, and with that he was gone. I closed my eyes and slept better than I'd done in years.

It carried on that way for a while. Every night, Eddie would come to my room. He would make me kneel and scurry after him on my hands and knees before he'd put his mouth on me. Each bite he inflicted released a stream of sensation from within. I was relaxed and aroused all in the same moment. Our encounters would always end with me kissing his boots. And it really was kissing by then; my tongue swiped all over the leather with reverence.

Eddie never asked me to do something I didn't want. He never touched me in a sexual way. I became aware of his crotch whenever I was on my knees, but he only pressed me back down to the floor if my hopeful gaze lingered on the bulge in his trousers. My life had truly turned upside down.

New Year's Eve saw me sitting on my bed, trying to decide what to wear to a party I had been invited to. A firework went off outside, even though it was only nine in the evening. When the noise and sparkle died away, another sound caught my attention. Experience and the passage of time made me realize just how sexual the noise was. I leapt off my bed in moments. I stepped carefully out into the hallway, half expecting to see Eddie standing there just as he'd done when I was a little girl.

The door to my parents' room faced me. The sounds were even louder when I pressed my ear to the wooden barrier. The keyhole sat at waist height. I could not bring myself to look through it.

I heard my dad's voice cry out. I stumbled backward, tripping on my feet in my haste. I half ran back to my room, my heart pounding. I'd barely got inside and under the blanket, when I heard a quiet knock on the door. My dad stood there in a rumpled pair of pyjamas. His face was creased with worry.

"I think we need to talk, sweetie."

I released my blanket from the death grip I'd had on it. "What's going on? Are you okay?"

My dad sighed, and then he sat perched on the edge of my dressing table. "It's not what you think. Eddie was just helping us out."

"Us?"

"Me and your mum." He smiled briefly. "Ever since you were little I've had trouble sleeping. When I was in the Army, well, you were too young to understand. But, Jenny, you can't imagine what it was like."

"In the war?"

Dad nodded and looked away for a moment.

"What happened?"

"I had a rough time. We all did. And now the sound of these bloody fireworks, they stir up all sorts inside me. I just want to hide sometimes. The noise is too much." Dad looked embarrassed, but I didn't know what to do or say. "Eddie helped me out years ago, just like he helps me out now. Me and your mum, well, of course, we got closer to him than we thought we would, but it's a good thing, sweetie. Eddie is a good man."

The penny dropped. "You're both sleeping with him?" I snapped my mouth shut the moment the words came out. I never wanted to have this kind of conversation with my dad.

"We both owe him so much. Without Eddie, well I don't think I'd be here now."

I looked up to see Eddie at the door. Dad held out his hand, waving him inside. Eddie pressed himself to my dad's back. He wrapped his arms around my dad's chest, making a sound like a hum of pleasure. It was the last thing I'd expected, even with all the new information at hand.

"I made a promise." Eddie's voice filled up the entire room, even though he spoke in a whisper. "I promised I'd look after this family if anything happened."

"But you were okay, dad," I began. You came home. You . . ."

Dad shook his head. "Part of me is still out there, love. Part of me never made it back from Afghanistan."

Eddie squeezed my dad in his embrace. "Let it go, love. Let it go."

"And how about you?" I turned my gaze to Eddie. "What did you leave behind?"

Eddie grinned at me. "I didn't lose a thing. I gained a family."

"You don't have sex with your family," I snapped, feeling frustrated.

"And I never had sex with you." Eddie's voice was calm and serene.

My dad stood. "Please don't be angry." He looked at Eddie. "We all do what we have to in order to survive." They both left without another word.

* * *

I dressed for the party with shaking hands. I caught a cab to my friend's place on the other side of town. There were so many people in her home I could barely squeeze inside. I felt like a ghost as I sat at the top of the stairs, sipping on punch that had been spiked to hell and back. At midnight we all moved to the big garden. The sky exploded in colour and noise. Fireworks filled the night with sparkling detonations. I suddenly thought of my dad and how awful he must be feeling with his post-traumatic terrors. I edged my way out of the house and made my way back home. Once inside I ran upstairs and pounded on my parents' bedroom door.

Mum answered, looking harried. "Jenny, what's the matter?"

I scooted past her, to where Eddie and my dad sat huddled on the floor. I knelt and then spread my arms around them both. "Thank you," I said to Eddie. "Thanks for loving my dad."

I met up with Howard the first evening after I returned to university. I told him all the things that had happened over the holidays, keeping nothing back. He was silent as I spoke, but when I was done, he simply stood and held my hand. He pulled me onwards to his room. He didn't have to say a thing. I undressed, standing naked before him in the cold space. Howard kissed all the half-healed bite marks on my skin, tonguing the angry circles of pain and pleasure. I arched to him, undone by emotion, and then I dropped to my knees. Howard smiled down at me with gentle affection. I kissed his scuffed shoes, working my way up his legs and thighs with presses of my mouth. My hands went behind my back as Howard unzipped his fly. He was hard and ready for me. I kissed the head of his cock, silently giving thanks as my tongue swirled all over. I drew him deeper into my mouth, welcomed him home. Howard thrust in deep, strong enough to almost knock me over, but not quite. I wanted to split myself wide open on him. I felt his firm hand curl around the base of my neck, holding me in place as I kept on sucking and kissing. My breath didn't matter. My past didn't matter. The only thing that made any sense was my lover's cock inside me. Howard came in my mouth with a roar. He jerked out and splattered my face and shoulders with his cum.

I remained on my knees for some time after. Streaks of white cooled on my skin until Howard wiped it away with a wet cloth. My mouth felt slack. Words tumbled out with no thought on my part.

"Will you bite me?" My voice sounded as if it were coming from a faraway place.

Howard's eyes went wide for a moment. "Are you certain?"

I nodded. Howard kissed my throat. He was hesitant. I couldn't blame him for it. But in time his kiss became harder. I felt the sharp burn of sensation as he nipped the flesh of my neck. Howard moved lower, biting a path to my breasts. I ached for the feel of his teeth there. He suckled, bit and chewed on me until I clutched at him. Each bite made me pulse with need. I was on fire.

Howard held me when my orgasm struck. I shook and rocked against him until my tremors ceased.

"Stay tonight?" Howard's voice was rough and ragged. I nodded just once, bumping my head on his shoulder. And then we hugged each other, holding on so tight. The only sound was our heartbeats. I felt more alive than ever, like a survivor who had made it through a war. Peacetime was a wonderful thing.

Tied Noon

Victoria Janssen

Outside the barn, rain sheeted down, so heavily it looked like twilight instead of morning. Sarah Jane Austin made the rounds of their horses, seeing they were all securely hobbled; thunder might spook them, and then they would be in serious trouble, instead of just wet. They'd had quite enough trouble lately. Though they'd made it through all right, she wanted to avoid nasty surprises for a while.

A crack of thunder made her jump. Virgil's flashy chestnut didn't even flinch, intent as he was on nosing her pockets for treats. They hadn't encountered civilization in several days; she was right out of everything at the moment, but took a few moments to scratch his favourite spot, before she joined her two companions, engaged in spreading out the contents of their saddlebags and packs to make sure everything dried.

She'd been travelling with Virgil DeVille and Aaron Harcourt for a few weeks now, leaving behind a settled if unfulfilling life spent in male disguise, her only way of making a living. She last worked as a wrangler for a widow, who'd hired the two men to ward off a passing gang of ruffians. Soon after, her disguise revealed, Virgil had cheerfully seduced both her and an initially reluctant Aaron.

Sarah had been desperately lonely, but the men were moving on, heading to California. So she decided to go with them. The opportunity to travel across America with two men whom she found so entertaining was too serendipitous to pass up, and aside from all that, after years of abstinence forced by her disguise, she was desperate for sexual affection as well. She'd fallen easily into the bantering and easy camaraderie of their long friendship, and had hopes that their feelings for her would deepen, as well.

She had yet to regret her decision.

"You need to get out of those wet clothes," Virgil was saying to Aaron. This was true, but the way he said it, rich with sexy suggestion, made Aaron bluster.

"It isn't even ten o'clock in the morning!"

Sarah grinned. "I'll help," she said, advancing on him. Aaron was tall, dark-skinned, and menacing with his twin pistols and scarred cheek. He hardly looked the type to back away slowly from a slender woman like her and an overdressed fop like Virgil, but back away he did.

"You two are only ever thinking of one thing," he protested. "Since we met Sarah, we've already—"

"Are you a maiden lady?" Virgil asked silkily, appearing at Aaron's side and swiping his hat.

"We're hardly finished with the gear—"

"I took care of the tack already," Sarah said. "We're going to be here until this storm passes, and we don't have any entertainment in this leaky barn, except for tormenting you." She pulled his head down to hers and kissed him, to cover her actions as she swiftly unbuttoned his shirt. She was surprised anew by the gentleness of his calloused hand as he cupped her cheek and kissed her in return. Though he was considerably more reticent than Virgil, she never doubted Aaron wanted her as well, with a tenderness she'd rarely experienced in her life.

Something poked her in the belly and she pulled back. "Damn it, Virgil."

He'd reached between them to unbuckle Aaron's gun belt. "You don't want anything going off untimely." Aaron batted at his hands, but it was too late; Virgil stepped back, pistols held aloft in one hand, Aaron's sheathed knife in the other. "I'll just put these over there while Sarah finishes getting you undressed. Since it takes you forever to do on your own."

Aaron evaded Sarah's reach and crossed his arms over his impressive chest. "Why am I always the one you two go after?"

"It's hardly *always*," Virgil said. "We've only been together for—has it been a whole month yet?"

Sarah asked, "What's your thought, Aaron?" For the merest hint of a grin at the corner of his shapely mouth belied the belligerence of his posture. She hadn't seen much of his playful side so far.

Virgil put down the guns and stripped off his gold waistcoat, arranging it carefully next to his deep red coat. "Don't tell me you don't *like* being gone after, as you call it. Because otherwise, you'd never get your pants off."

"Not true," Aaron said. "There was that time in Maryland—"

"Doesn't count," Virgil said airily. "I introduced you to her."

Sarah leaned against Aaron's muscular back and wrapped her arms around his waist. "Don't let him distract you. What're you thinking?"

Aaron closed his hands over hers, squeezing them with easy affection that melted her heart. "I was thinking maybe we ought to go after Virgil instead."

Virgil paused in the midst of unbuttoning his shirt. "Fine. Consider me at your disposal. In fact, you may hurry it up as much as you like."

"Truly?" Aaron asked. Sarah felt a sudden tension in him, but what it implied, she didn't know.

Virgil's hands fell to his sides as he met Aaron's gaze. "Truly. Did you think I could refuse you anything?"

Sarah felt Aaron relax. "Good. Maybe we should get out of these wet clothes first then."

None of them were that wet; Sarah had her long sourdough coat that fell past the tops of her boots, Aaron had a black duster, and Virgil had covered his elegant duds with a sort of poncho-shaped tarpaulin. It still felt good to get out of clothing she'd been wearing for two days straight while they rode through land reportedly rife with outlaws. This abandoned barn was their first shelter in quite a while.

While she and Virgil finished undressing, Aaron dragged the barn doors shut and barred them against the wind and rain. It became much quieter and darker inside, but warmer as well. Sarah discovered one of their bedrolls was damp, but the others were fine; she spread them out on a scratchy cushion of musty straw and sat there, cross-legged. It felt decadent to be naked at this time of the morning, even more so when they might have still been miserably pushing on, rain pouring off their hat brims.

Virgil sprawled next to her on the blankets. She edged closer, rubbing her hand up and down his thigh and stroking the old shrapnel scars across his stomach. She said, "I'm curious what he'll want." She kissed the top of Virgil's shoulder, then the back of his neck.

"I don't dare to hazard a guess, but I welcome any forwardness on his part," Virgil said. He leaned back on his elbows, accepting her petting like a cat. "Perhaps I shouldn't have shown him my naughty playing cards. No decent man will ever marry him now."

"I'd like another look at those cards one day," Sarah said. "Tell me more about Aaron."

Virgil shook his head and mock-sighed. "Women like him best and ignore my amazing talents. Aaron's the quiet one, and that makes them curious. It worked on me, too. I teased him something awful when we were little ones, trying to get him to talk or, failing that, to hit me or fight or . . . well, anything at all. I thought he just didn't care what I did, and it drove me wild."

"So why Aaron?"

"Everyone else either beat me up or chased me away," he said, wryly. "We neither of us were popular in our town; our families didn't offer any advantages, you see. Mr Harcourt was a lawyer and had a bit of position, but being a coloured man took away some of the respect he was due. And me, well, my father was the town drunk."

"So how—"

"That's a story for another day," Aaron said. He'd taken off his shirts and boots, but left on his snug buckskins. Sarah's eyes settled on the dip below his hip bones and imagined unbuttoning his pants and peeling the leather down, so that very spot would be exposed to her mouth.

Echoing her thoughts, Virgil said, "You're looking mighty fine today, Aaron. If you could unbutton just two or three of those buttons—"

"Hush," he said. "None of your ridiculousness. You said that Sarah and I could have our way with you, didn't you?"

"Did I?" Virgil's looks of innocence were normally frighteningly convincing, but batting his eyelashes went a touch too far.

"Close enough," Aaron said. "A historic occasion." He grinned, his flash of white teeth like a bolt of lightning to Sarah's belly. Then he dug into their piles of saddlebags and produced a scrap of rope. "I can make sure you don't get away from us."

It was *soft* rope, and the implication struck her immediately. Shocked and mesmerized, she gaped as staid Aaron Harcourt wound the length around his hands, giving experimental yanks to test its strength. Virgil, for once, was speechless.

Aaron dropped to his knees next to Virgil. "I know how your mind works, Virgil DeVille," he said. His tone was tender. "You like all sorts of things I never would have thought of, or even imagined. There was that time down in Delaware, when you made me go with you to the Cunning Cat, and you had your two ladies, plus the one you tried to send over to me until she went off with you, too. Madame Stovall took pity on me because there wasn't a single thing to read in that parlour of theirs, and brought me upstairs to a special viewing area. You thought I wasn't watching, but I was. That was one of the more unusual experiences I've had."

Virgil was grinning now, and he grabbed Sarah's hand in his as he sat up. "You *weasel*! She didn't charge you for it, either, did she? You always manage to charm the older ones."

"Hush, now." Aaron grasped Virgil by the forearm, his thumb sliding in an absent caress. It always gave Sarah a warm thrill to see them touch each other so sweetly. Aaron said, contemplatively, "I tried not to think about it afterwards, but sometimes you try my patience sorely, and that night would come to mind."

"It's my intent to try your patience," Virgil assured him. "It's good for you." Aaron glanced at Sarah meaningfully, and she placed her hand firmly over Virgil's mouth, his moustache tickling her palm.

She said, "Go on, Aaron."

He said, "I know it's not right, in the general run of things, to impede a man's freedom."

Sarah said, "But when he gives his permission, that's acceptable, ain't it?"

Virgil was nodding vigorously; the motion dislodged Sarah's hand and he said, "Don't you two dare to disappoint me now." He thrust out his hands to Aaron.

"Patience," Aaron said. "I'd like your hands over your head. And no untying yourself, or we will stop right there, won't we, Sarah?"

She nodded. "That would be a sad ending." She could see Virgil's pulse jumping in his throat as he stretched his arms over his head. Aaron loosely tied his wrists together, then straightened slowly, his hands stroking the underside of Virgil's arms thoughtfully, as if he'd never done so before; Sarah realized then that he probably hadn't. The two men had never had any kind of sexual encounter together until they'd met her and, so far as she knew, Aaron had only ever been interested in women before. She liked that, as if it was not only their long friendship but her presence that helped them to express their affection for each other.

Aaron was kneeling next to Virgil's torso, studying his face; Virgil met his gaze, his expression unusually solemn. Then Virgil's eyes flicked to Sarah's face. "You've never tried this before, have you, Sarah? You'll like it, I promise."

"Hush," she said. She leaned down and kissed him.

Aaron appeared frozen; he blinked and whispered, "I'm not sure I can—"

Virgil went limp. "Do you want to stop?"

"No," Sarah said. "Aaron, kiss him."

Virgil said, "I like how you—mmph."

Sarah sat up, so she could see what they were doing more clearly. It was still new to her, being so close to two other people while they kissed, and men at that, but the newness and strangeness aroused her. Aaron's eyes closed as he deepened the kiss, his fingers trailing along Virgil's jawline; Virgil's shoulders shifted and strained as if he wanted to embrace his friend. Sarah stroked Aaron's close-cropped curls, tracing the tidy shape of his ear with her fingertip, pleased at the small murmur of pleasure he made into Virgil's mouth. Then she began to please herself by taking the opportunity to lightly scratch her way along Aaron's muscular arm and shoulder, alternately teasing at Virgil's nipple, which she knew he liked.

Aaron drew back from the kiss, breathing hard, his eyes vague. He cupped his hand over Virgil's cheek, looking at him for a long moment before releasing him and sitting up. "Sarah," he said, his voice even more gravelly than usual. "Since I know from personal experience how good you can make a man feel with your mouth, I would appreciate it if you could show me how best to make him come undone. That seems fair, doesn't it? Quiet, Virgil. I don't want to hear a word out of you."

Sarah leaned over and kissed him. "You're a very fair man, Aaron Harcourt." She looped her thumb and forefinger around Virgil's cock, pulling back his foreskin just a bit. "Watch me."

Instead of immediately taking Virgil's cockhead in her mouth, she took time to stroke her lips along his soft foreskin, occasionally clasping skin between her lips in almost-bites. This was more successful than she'd imagined it would be; she had to clasp her hands on his thighs to hold him still, while Aaron pinned his hips. She kept this up as long as she could, then teased the very tip of his cock, not swirling her tongue until Aaron said, "He wants more." Then she slipped her tongue-tip beneath his foreskin, tasting there, and using her hand to help bring him to full hardness.

"Do you want to have a try?" she asked. "Wait, let me do this first." She seized one of Aaron's belt loops and tugged him closer so she could unbutton his buckskins and shove them down over his hips. She gave his ass a squeeze. "And here, taste." She kissed Aaron, making sure Virgil could see her enthusiasm. Aaron took the chance to massage her breasts and nibble at the crook of her neck.

Virgil growled impatiently. Aaron said, "Quiet. I don't want to hear any complaining when I do this wrong." After he'd shucked his buckskins, he grasped Virgil's cock, gently pulling back the foreskin and studying the head. Then he licked, wetting it more thoroughly, before closing his lips around it.

Virgil arched. "Christ, Christ, I didn't think you really would. Oh, Aaron. Don't stop."

Aaron sat up and glared. "Did I not tell you to be quiet? *And* you took the Lord's name in vain."

"Shit," Virgil said. "Sorry." He opened his eyes wide, pleading, and Aaron relented, returning to nuzzle Virgil's ball sac and slowly lick up the length of his cock. His expression was pensive, but his breathing had sped up; Virgil was tense as a bowstring.

Sarah settled in at Virgil's side, nuzzling his throat and ear, murmuring as if she was gentling a skittish horse; at the same time, she eased the ache in her breasts by pressing into the tense muscles of his side. It was affecting to see all Virgil's clever remarks left behind. Aaron was surely leaving fingermarks on his hips as he teased with both hand and mouth. She hooked her leg over Virgil's, sliding her cunny up his leg; the sensation wasn't as intense as she was beginning to want, but it was enough to keep her where she was. She didn't want to interrupt Aaron until one or both of them had reached a peak. This time was for the two of them.

"Harder," Virgil said, hoarsely. Aaron complied, so Sarah set to biting Virgil's nipple, sucking it into her mouth with a force that likely would have been painful had he not been so close to coming. The dual sensations sparked something off in him. She heard Aaron's startled cough just as Virgil jerked violently beneath her mouth, bruising her lip against her teeth. She sat up quickly and nursed the small pain while she watched them come, Aaron quickly following on Virgil's crisis.

When at last Virgil's head fell back against the blanket, Aaron sprawled across his legs, she untied Virgil's wrists. "Your arms must be hurting," she said.

"Nothing hurts," he murmured, stretching luxuriously before resting his hands on Aaron's shoulders. "Need a nap. See to you when I'm awake."

"I'll hold you to that," Sarah said, sighing. She settled in against him, trying to calm her breathing. It moved her inexpressibly to see the two men limp with satisfaction, though she herself was still restless and aroused. She was content to wait for them, though, rather than take care of herself. So far they had shown they cared for her feelings, more than Sarah was used to experiencing. She had no fear she would be left hungry.

She let them sleep for a while, stroking the smooth curve of Aaron's arm, marvelling at his satiny skin. She drifted for a time herself, until another explosion of thunder brought all three of them abruptly awake. The rain pounded on the roof like galloping horses. She nuzzled at the tender spot beneath Virgil's arm until he whined. "Enough rest," she said. "You're going to get numb unless Aaron gets off your crotch."

Aaron's hand clamped over her wrist, his thumb sliding over the knobby bone. "I could stay here," he mumbled.

"No, you can't," Virgil said, groaning as he tried to sit up. "I can't feel my leg."

Between Virgil's undignified hopping about to alleviate his pins and needles, Aaron's smothered laughter at the sight, and one of the packhorses getting snappy, it looked as if Sarah was not going to find her satisfaction as quickly as she'd hoped. Walking gingerly on the prickly dry straw, she unbarred the barn doors and had a look outside: it was still raining in sheets, but showed no signs of flooding. She held a cloth out in the rain until it was soaked, tossed it to Aaron so the men could clean up, then closed and barred the doors again. Virgil came up behind her and wrapped her in his arms, snugging his naked front up against her naked back and luxuriously nuzzling the back of her neck.

"I was wanting to do that earlier," he said. "Except that one over there wanted to tie me up and ravish me."

"I liked you tied up," Sarah said, leaning into his embrace. "You were so nice and quiet. Mostly." She reached backwards, grabbing his hips. "We should tie you up more often."

"Next time, it's his turn," Virgil said. "Did you hear that, Aaron?"

"I'll think about allowing it," Aaron said. He kissed Sarah, his hands closing on her breasts; she abandoned her awkward grip on Virgil and dragged Aaron closer, until she was snugged tightly between them.

That was cosy and sexy all at once. She hummed into Aaron's mouth, grabbed his ass and rubbed into him. In her ear, Virgil said, "Do that again. The look on his face—"

Sarah did it again, then, to be fair, ground back against Virgil's front. She drew back from the kiss to say, "I can't decide which one of you I want. Maybe both. How can I have both of you?"

Virgil said, "Well, you won't be having my cock for a half-hour, at least. Somebody wore it out already. But I think I would like to see how many times I can make you come with my mouth, and Aaron can watch and get inspired to be inside you after that."

"We could take turns doing that," Aaron said, mildly. "Or . . ."

"Or?" Sarah asked, then squeaked when Virgil squeezed her ass.

"Or we could tie Virgil's hands again, and see how many times he can make you come." Aaron paused. "You'd like that, wouldn't you?"

"Yes," Virgil said, even as Sarah tried to decide if she would like it or not. She supposed she could give it a try. Where was the harm?

Virgil's warmth disappeared from her back and she turned – he had gone to get the rope. "Think of it, Sarah," he said. "I won't be able to touch myself, only you. You can tell me exactly what you want. This will be all for you. I like it when I can make a woman happy. You're so beautiful with your cheeks all rosy, your lips swollen from kisses, your eyes glassy while you think on how good you're feeling. And I'm doing it, I'm making you feel that way."

Sarah asked, "And what do you like about this idea, Aaron? Tell me."

He drew a long, deep breath before he answered. "I don't know." He paused. "No, I . . . I think it's sort of what Virgil said. Only . . . only I like to see him that way. I like to see him feeling pleasure. That gives pleasure to me."

Sarah noticed he hadn't explained how having Virgil's hands tied was part of that, but she didn't push. Maybe he didn't know. Maybe Virgil knew, but if he did he wasn't saying.

Well, she hoped they would all be together long enough for her to find out. She sat cross-legged on the blankets while Virgil flung himself down next to her. He held out his hands in front of him. "Tie me," he said.

Sarah found the discarded rope and carefully knotted it around his wrists, leaving a long tail that she could hold on to. He studied her work. "I like that," he said. "Aaron, get over here. You're not getting out of any work."

"You'll be running your mouth to Saint Peter at the gates, won't you?" Aaron said.

"Damned straight. Lie back, Sarah, honey."

The endearment startled her, then warmed her. She stretched out on her back, shifting to get comfortable. Aaron took her head onto his lap; she smiled up at him and said, "Virgil wants me to tell him what to do. At least I think that was what he said. He don't seem to be sticking to it."

"I just wanted us to get started!" Virgil protested. "We haven't got all—well, I suppose we do have all day. Go on, Sarah."

"I want you to kiss me first. Get that tongue of yours warmed up."

Virgil's tongue was clever at more than just speech; contrasted with the soft scratchiness of his moustache, his kiss warmed and softened her all over. Every once in a while, she tugged at the loose end of the rope, and he would shift his kisses from her mouth to her ear or throat. She was unexpectedly stirred by directing his attentions this way. She was also aware of the warmth of Aaron's muscular thighs and his half-hard cock; he petted her hair with one hand and Virgil's loose curls with the other.

When she needed a breath, she said against Virgil's mouth, "Now I want you to kiss my belly. Aaron's going to hold on to my shoulders, so he can't touch his cock." She paused. "I'm going to play with my breasts, so you can both see what I'm doing."

Virgil flashed a grin at her. He brushed his moustache down the middle of her chest and nibbled just above her belly button, grinning again when she jumped. "No tickling," she said, sternly, and cupped her breasts in her hands. They'd had some stimulation earlier, but not nearly enough. She squeezed gently, rubbing her tender nipples with her thumbs. It felt so good, she sighed.

The kisses on her belly had stopped. She said, "You can watch, but keep at it!" Above her, Aaron snorted with laughter. He trailed his fingertips over her face and combed them through her hair before returning to her shoulders.

Virgil's talented mouth made a leisurely meal of her belly, her sides, her hip bones, and finally the top edges of her mound. Soon, she was lost in a state of half-dreaming, her hands clenching and releasing her aching breasts, but her focus on Virgil's brushing and sucking and nibbling all around her cunny. It was growing harder to breathe; she pressed her legs together and arched up, bumping into Virgil's nose. "Lick my cunny," she said. "I need to come. Lick me until I come. Then . . . then I'm going to kneel over Virgil, and I want Aaron to take me from behind."

The hands on her shoulders abruptly tightened; Aaron murmured an apology as he let go. Instead, he stroked feather-light brushes down her nose, across her forehead, out from her mouth, and along her jawline. Virgil's tongue strokes on her cunny lips were firm, and soon she was whimpering, begging for more. He pressed her open with the flat of his tongue, scrubbed her sensitized skin with his moustache, fastened his lips around her clit and sucked, more firmly, as she demanded more.

She came with no warning, one moment shaking from head to toe with desperation, the next her pleasure stretching her out like a tense wire. The men changed position, and then Aaron was licking her, soothing but also slowly, slowly building her up to another climax while Virgil whispered filthy encouragement. This time, she cried out with each contraction; Aaron kissed her feverishly, and she tasted herself on his tongue.

They were all quiet for a time, after that. Rain still pounded on the barn's roof, and the horses occasionally shifted their stance. She moved her head, once, to allow Virgil's cock a little more space next to her cheek, but couldn't be bothered to let go of Aaron's hair. Eventually, though, the scant padding on which they lay began to reveal the hardness of the wood floor beneath, and they sat up to stretch.

Aaron cupped her cheek in his palm. She smiled at him. "We ain't done. I want you to fuck me fast and deep. You go so deep from behind."

"How romantic," Virgil said. He flopped over on his back. "You wanted me under you."

"Yes," she said, languidly. "Suck my nipples. Don't talk."

On hands and knees, she had to rest on her elbows so Virgil could reach her with his mouth, but the awkwardness was worth it to hear Aaron's breathing as he stroked and massaged her rear. He laid a kiss on the small of her back and said, "I want to be inside of you so badly."

"Fuck me," she said. "Please."

She was already soaking wet, her clit feeling huge and tender. Aaron slid all the way into her cunny on the first thrust, then grasped her hips and trembled. Sarah groaned at the feel of his hips snugged up against her ass. "Hard," she said.

Aaron's thrusts jolted her forward; she rocked back into him, moaning, while Virgil, beneath her, sucked first one nipple and then the other. This proved to be a bit too awkward, and she gasped, "Hold me."

Virgil shucked the rope and wrapped his arms around her shoulders, holding her painfully tight. Aaron's hands stroked her back, brushing over Virgil's arms, then grabbing her hips firmly when she cried, "Harder! Your cock feels so good. So deep. Harder. Please. Please. Please."

Her skin slid hot and sweaty against Virgil's beneath her; Aaron's hands skidded as he tried to grab her hips, then dug in firmly, yanking her back onto his cock. She gasped as he jolted more deeply with her. "More," she said. "Like that . . . like—" Then she was coming, every last scrap of strength being wrung from her one convulsion at a time.

"Sarah," Aaron gasped, following her into pleasure.

They collapsed on the blanket, Aaron in the middle this time. Virgil murmured, "That was awe-inspiring . . . but . . . enough even for me."

"Thank God," Aaron slurred.

Sarah thought about making a joke, but could only smile sleepily. She cushioned her head on Aaron's chest and closed her eyes.

They slept away most of the afternoon, waking occasionally to chew on venison jerky and the last of the caramels Virgil had hidden in his coat pocket. By evening, the rain finally slowed. By then all three of them were restless, and when Virgil said, "I'm for a bath," not even Aaron argued, though he took care to make sure his pistols were handy before they went outside. Without a care they cavorted naked in the rain, trading off a single bar of soap and washing each other's hair. Laughing crazily, Virgil and Sarah attacked Aaron, bringing all three of them down in the mud, so they had it all to do over again. They were lucky the rain lasted long enough so they could end up clean.

It was, bar none, the best day Sarah had ever spent in her life. She wondered what tomorrow would bring.

Juliett 222

O'Neil de Noux

READAND DESTROY
THIS IS COPY #____2____

CODE RED
Eyes Only
001 through 0059 authorized
Transcription of recording and descriptions

TO: Alpha 003
FROM: Bravo 114
RE: 04-00066-2013 – Cotte

Tuesday, 2 July 2013
1612 hours

Briefing at Dobbs House. Present: Bravo 114 (case agent) Alpha 003 (supervisor), Echo 047 (recording agent) and Juliett 222 (operations agent).

Juliett 222 entered wearing a blue skirt suit with a fitted jacket, white blouse, slimming skirt about five inches above her knees, pantyhose and black high heels. She carried a black purse with a shoulder strap and a black portfolio. Her long blonde hair, parted down the centre, hung straight, six inches past her shoulders. Her large blue eyes stood out on her small face, along with her sculptured lips and slightly pointed chin. A petite woman at five foot three, she was twenty-four years old, born and raised at the geographic centre of the contiguous United States, Lebanon, Kansas. She sat at the table, opened her portfolio, took out a Parker t-ball jotter ballpoint pen, clicked it and was ready.

Bravo 114, the case agent, sat up in the chair directly across from Juliett 222, straightened his blood-red tie that stood in bright contrast to his navy-blue suit. Bravo 114 was fifty-two, stood five foot eight on the heavy side, with green eyes, grey-white hair he had to keep short as it had become too unruly to wear it longer as he did as a young man. He opened his portfolio and took out a gold Cross pen.

On the left side of the table sat recording agent Echo 047, an Asian male in his late twenties, wearing a white polo shirt and khaki pants. He turned on the digital video device and announced, "Recording."

The mission supervisor, Alpha 003 nodded to Bravo 114 to begin. Having an Alpha at a briefing was rare, having one as high as 003 was unheard of.

"This is the final briefing," Bravo 114 began. "We have confirmation this morning that target Malinski Cotte is in the Casbah and his response to our email is in front of each of you."

Juliett 222 picked up the lone sheet in front of her. It was a simple email message from Bravo 114's alias – Cuck Henry – to one of Malinski's known aliases – Malarge. It confirmed their "rendezvous" Friday.

"Any hesitation?" Alpha 003 asked.

"None." Juliett 222's blue eyes were so innocent looking. She gave the case agent a knowing smile.

"I have to put it plainly," Alpha 003 continued. "You're about to get gang-banged. Have you had sex with more than one man at a time?"

"Yes. I have. Wasn't a lot to do in rural Kansas on a Friday night, Saturday night, any Sunday. I grew up pretty and the boys liked me and I liked them and I started with the Tarleton twins and often did several boys at a time. The weekend before I went off to UCLA we had what the boys called a 'fuck-athon'. Banged all weekend, including a couple of their daddies. Never counted exactly but there must have been two dozen and many of them fucked me more than once."

Damn. Bravo 114 resisted reaching down to readjust his growing cock. This Barbie-doll-looking sweetheart talking dirty made his neck grow hot and palms grow moist. As she spoke, her face remained expressionless, but her eyes, focused on his, made the connection that raised his heartbeat. He was going to screw this cutie pie agent.

What a man, and a woman, must do for their country in times like these.

"OK, let's go over the details again," Alpha 003 said and they all opened the plan and went to it.

Friday, 5 July 2013
0900 hours

Preparation at Hotel Addington. Present: Juliett 222 and Bravo 114.

Juliett 222 worked an hour on her make-up until her face was subtly radiant with just enough blush, just the right amount of eyeliner, just enough mascara and shadow to give her eyes a sultry look. Three layers of lipstick began with a brownish-red base, then scarlet, then shiny crimson, resulting in candy-apple red lips. The undercoat of russet drew down the sparkle, but kept the gleam. She'd moved the part in her hair to the right side, giving her a Veronica Lake, peekaboo look. The spaghetti straps gave her black minidress the look of a slip. Beneath, she wore sheer white panties. No bra. When in doubt, always wear a little black dress. No need for a purse.

She'd carefully checked the implants, each under the fingernail of the middle fingers of each hand. The attachable implant, one of the most sophisticated listening and GPS devices on the planet, would be imbedded in the world's more dangerous man. A simple plan. All she had to do was get him naked and brush him with a nail. Simple. Dangerous.

Juliett 222 felt eyes on her as she crossed the small lobby to the couch where Bravo 114 sat. Hotel Addington, built in

1924, the last year of British rule, was an Art Deco gem that had somehow maintained some of its lustre.

"You look great," Bravo 114 said as he stood.

She did a slow pirouette for him and the dress was so short he caught a hint of white panties when she twisted around.

"You don't look bad yourself."

Bravo 114 had the casual look down, gauzy off-white shirt, khaki trousers, brown loafers. The ultra-thin, eighteen-carat gold Piaget watch on his left wrist screamed "money", as did the Hasselblad Limited "Ferrari" Edition camera dangling in its strap from his neck.

This should work. The plan carefully laid out by the Alphas. Two years researching and locating terrorist-financier Malinski Cotte drew them here. Twenty thousand dollars in bribes revealed Cotte's weakness. It was all orchestrated for this meeting of exhibitionist wife, her cuckold husband, and Cotte's secret identity – Malarge, the man who arranged parties for men who wanted to watch their wives get fucked by strangers.

This should work. All it took was the right girl and Juliett 222 sure looked the part.

Bravo 114 snickered and she said, "What?"

"When you assured Alpha 003 how you would do it, did you see him trying to keep his face stony?"

She snickered now. "What? When I said like sucking cock? Or when I said they are going to want pussy and, to tell the truth, a hard dick pounding followed by another hard dick is very, very nice."

"That and how you don't actually swallow the come."

"Just come in my mouth and I spit out after you're done."

Damn!

Friday, 5 July 2013
1122 hours

The Casbah. Present: Juliett 222 and Bravo 114. Cover team remained at Hotel Addington.

The café sat off the main Kocin Road in the centre of the

Casbah. Nestled among clothing shops and antique shops of used furniture and fake ancient Egyptian artifacts, it was a narrow place with two tables outside. As indicated in Malinski's last email, three red camels were painted above the doorway and Bravo 114 led Juliett 222 in. The line of small boys who had followed the short dress and swaying hips of the blonde American woman, as the couple perused shops since leaving the hotel, were shooed outside by one of the men sitting at a small table just in the doorway. No doubt the boys had been getting a nice view of Juliett 222's sheer panties when she bent over while looking at merchandise outside shops before reaching the café.

Bravo 114 removed his sunglasses immediately and paused for his eyes to adjust to the dimness. Juliett 222 continued a few paces, stopped, took off her sunglasses, folded them, raised her arms as she ran her hands through her long hair. Only half of the twelve tables in the place were occupied, by men exclusively. Mostly middle-aged, in casual clothes. Every pair of eyes ogling the blonde woman with her arms up, her dress so short it crawled halfway up her panties.

A pudgy man shuffled from a back room separated from the main café by a latticework wall. Bravo 114 recognized the man immediately – the director of French avant-garde films such as *The Mole Catcher's Wrath*, *Pride of the Gregorians* and *The Oyster Glutton*.

"*Bonjour*. Hello. Hello." He went straight to Juliett 222, took her hands and kissed them, said, "You must be Elvira and Jonathan Whitney. I am Samuel Bonaparte and I shall be directing our little adventure today."

No relation to anyone in Napoleon's family – Samuel had depicted three of the seven deadly sins on film and was about to film lust in its purest form, which would cause envy in any man. All he needed was to include a little avarice and sloth to get all the deadly sins in. A skinny black man and an Arab came out of the back room, both in their twenties, and Samuel introduced them. Both had French names and were his cameramen.

The place smelled of coffee and sugar and Juliett 222 stood in its centre, feeling the eyes of the men on her. She'd counted fourteen in the café, before the three came out of the back. Through the latticework she spied a small waterfall and a huge bed, two large cameras on rolling tripods and a man in all white, the top buttons of his shirt unfastened to show a hairy chest, his pants baggy with cuffs. There was a three-day growth on the face, but she recognized it, the face they'd been searching for all these months.

Samuel extended a hand to Bravo 114 and smiled. "The envelope please."

The man exchanged an envelope and the case agent thought again, Damn, *men actually pay this much to have their beautiful wives fucked by other men.*

The plan should work, Juliett 222 thought, as the man behind the lattice came around and into the café. He moved up to her and stood close. The man was forty-two, black-haired, with chiselled features, thick, soft-looking lips, a square jaw. Good-looking except the look in his eyes. Brown eyes were usually warm, especially large eyes with long eyelashes any woman would envy. But the eyes of Malinski Cotte were cold, like empty pools, like a shark's eyes. They sent a shiver through Juliett 222.

The cold eyes examined her face up close and then he took her hand and led her through the café, through a door and past the cameras and they were behind the latticework now. He stopped her next to the bed. The bed sheet glowed bright white and she looked up and saw they were in an open-air patio.

Malinski moved behind her and reached up, took the spaghetti straps from her shoulders and her dress pooled at her feet. The eagle eye of a video camera closed in, the operator recording as the strobe light of Bravo 114's Hasselblad flashed. Juliett 222 felt her heart thumping as she stood there in panties and high heels. Eyes peered at her through the latticework.

My God, thought Bravo 114. Her breasts were gorgeous, perfectly formed with creamy, light pink areolae and small pointed nipples. Malinski sat on the bed and worked her panties down. Juliet 222 raised her arms again, brushed her hair from her face and looked up at the sunlight.

The Hasselblad's strobe bathed her momentarily, as the sun caressed her breasts and highlighted her close-cropped blonde pubic hair. Damn, she's gorgeous, with those red lips glistening. A sound turned Bravo 114 to his right, as two young Arabs brought in chains and leather straps and moved to either side of the bed.

Malinski turned Juliett 222 to face him and began to knead her breasts. He kissed them, licked her nipples, back and forth, as both video cameras were in action now. Samuel directed Bravo 114 to remain behind the up-close camera. The other camera was back and videoing the entire scene. The Arabs fastened the chains and leather straps to poles Bravo 114 had not noticed at the head of the bed.

Malinski's right hand moved between Juliett 222's legs as he brushed her bush with his fingers. His other hand reached around and squeezed her ass. She moved her feet apart and his fingers found her pussy lips. He was gentle and she felt a shudder race through her as he fingered her. She was wet already.

It was as he was turning her around to the bed that she noticed the two men with the straps and chains and thought fast. She reached around Malinski's head and moaned loudly as her left hand gripped the back of his neck. She tapped her fingernail against his neck and hoped the dot implanted itself as it should.

Malinski lifted her and deposited her on her back on the bed, as the two men with the chains and straps quickly cuffed them to her wrists and worked her up into the centre of the bed. She was able to glance at her left hand and saw the nearly invisible dot was still under her fingernail and she knew she had failed.

The leather straps were tightened and most of the slack in the chains taken up. She could move her arms a little so there was no pain in them opened like this, but the chance of her fixing the dots to Malinski was impossible now. She looked down past her spread knees and the man was removing his shirt and pants as he stared at her open pussy.

Bravo 114 stood behind the large camera and focused his lens on her and snapped a picture. She took in a deep breath as a naked Malinski crawled up on the bed. His cock was hard and stood straight up, as he climbed on her, rubbed the thick tip of his cock against her pussy lips, found them lubricated enough and worked that thick cock into her.

He slow-fucked her in long, deep strokes and she felt the pleasure shoot through her. He was atop her, but his weight was not on her. Muscular arms held him above her in a push-up position and he looked down at her bush as he fucked her. He pulled his cock almost all the way out and pushed it back in slowly, then not so slowly and soon he was pumping her, pile-driving her into the bed. His body came down on her as he piped her good now and she felt a quick climax shoot through her.

He came in long, hot spurts and got right off. Another man climbed on the bed and impaled her. This man was thick bodied and older and he smiled at her as he banged her. Bravo 114 stood on the left side of the bed and took pictures. She looked to the right and saw more faces beyond the latticework as the men watched this blonde American get screwed.

When the thick-bodied man was finished, a man with dark-brown skin took his place, while an older man with olive skin brought his swollen cock around to her head and pressed it against her mouth and Juliett 222 had two cocks in her.

Bravo 114 moved back to get the entire scene in the shot, the two video cameras moving around the bed like circling vultures, the dark-skinned man atop Juliett 222, her mouth wrapped around another cock as a second man pumped his hips and fucked her in the mouth. The sound of slapping bodies and wet plunging was mated with grunts from the men and high-pitched squeals from Juliett 222 as the men filled her with cum.

A line of men from the café stood beyond the foot of the bed now, most of them naked or half-naked, each stroking their cocks in anticipation of fucking the blonde American. One looked at Bravo 114 with a cold smile, another looked at him with disgust as a man who whored out his wife to other men.

Juliett 222 let the come roll out of her mouth when the man finished, spit and gasped as another man plunged his cock into her sopping pussy. She reached for the pleasure shooting through her body. She would think of a way to stick the dots on Malinski after, but for the moment she would let it unfold. It had been a long time since she had hard cock after hard cock in her and it was *delicious*.

Cocks came in like lions and left like lambs, while her pussy took it all and sent wave after wave of pleasure through her. The men were Arabs, some Africans with skin almost blue-back. She spied the cameramen being relieved to take their turn with her. She lost count but was sure Bravo 114 would keep count. A towel was brought to wipe her down before two more men came at her. They smelled of coffee breath and tobacco, some actually wore cologne, but the most prevalent scent was the chlorophyll smell of semen. And Juliett 222 let it flow over her and into her, the scintillating sex and the powerless feeling of being trapped and used by these men like such a complete whore.

Bravo 114 had never seen anything like this, as it went on and on, man after man climbing on her. He'd checked out porn sites on the internet before they started this operation – gang-bang sites – and saw snippets of women getting gang-fucked, but seeing it live, knowing it was an *agent*, knowing it was Juliett 222 getting fucked like this, made his cock so hard he thought he would do something he hadn't done since he was fifteen. Have a spontaneous ejaculation.

He had lost sight of Malinski Cotte until the man came back in the room, still naked, and moved to him. He tapped Bravo 114's shoulder and nodded to the man's wife. No need to speak. Bravo 114 should take a turn.

Bravo 114 stepped to the end of the line, noticed no one move behind him. They had all had her. Most were back in the café now with their coffee and cigarettes. A couple of youngsters peered in through the latticework now. He put his camera next to Juliett 222's body as he climbed atop and he slid his cock into her and she gasped up at him and smiled.

Damn she was hot. He started slowly, but she would have no part of that and gyrated those sexy hips against him.

He kissed her lips and kissed her cheek and whispered in her ear, "You all right?"

"Oh, yes," she gasped and he fucked her and came in her and she let out another squeal.

More towels were brought as two men unfastened the straps on Juliett 222's wrists. Including himself, Bravo 114 counted forty-eight men had fucked her. Malinski stood next to him at the foot of the bed. The man was putting his shirt on, still watching Juliett 222 as she ass-crawled to them, her legs still wide open, the pink slit of her pussy seeping white come.

"I like fucking another man's wife," Malinski said.

"I like watching," said Bravo 114.

"I like taking pretty blonde American girls and making them whores. Some of the men who fucked your wife live on the street. What you call 'bums'."

Juliett 222 saw Malinski starting to pull up his trousers and reached out as she came to the edge of the bed.

"I want to suck your cock."

"You have had my cock, whore."

"I want it in my mouth." She grabbed his half-swollen cock and drew it to her. Juliett 222 kissed the shaft, caressing his balls. Cupped in her left hand, she tapped the fingernail against his ball sac and kept it pressed there a second. She took his stiffening cock in her right hand and pressed her middle fingernail against his skin just above the shaft.

Bravo 114 stood back and took photos of this, full lengths, then close-ups of the cock in her mouth until Malinski came with a grunt. Samuel Bonaparte was there, naked now and speaking to the cameras.

"This is Samuel Bonaparte." He reached down and guided Juliett 222 to stand up next to him, facing the cameras, one in close, one back to show all of her body. He waved Bravo 114 to stand with them. "And this is Jonathan Whitney and his beautiful wife Elvira who has just been gang-banged by fifty Arabs and Africans. How did it feel?"

Juliett 222 looked into the lens of the closest camera and said, "Wonderful. And filling."

Samuel laughed and asked Bravo 114 what it was like seeing his wife used like a whore, fucking all those men and Bravo 114 said it was stimulating.

The director put his hands on Juliett 222's hip and turned her around, said, "I like it doggie-style." She had to help him get his cock up with some sucking first, turned her ass to the cameras, hands on the bed and Samuel fucked her. It did not take long. He talked the whole way through it. "Nice, clean, young American housewife. I love fucking another man's wife in front of him. Such a tight little pussy."

Juliet 222 was a little rubber-legged as they walked back to their hotel. She hung on to Bravo 114's arm. They'd put her dress back on her, but kept her panties and the breeze flapped her dress. She liked the coolness on her pussy and realized the show she was putting on as people gawked at her in passing.

As soon as they stepped into their hotel room, Juliett 222 headed for a nice, long, warm bath, while Bravo 114 checked in on the secure cell phone. He took the good news into the bathroom as Juliett 222 soaked.

"Both dots are working perfectly. We'll know everything he says and where he goes for at least a year."

She looked up at him dreamily and said, "You have one more thing to do for me."

"What?"

"Dry me off after and take me to bed and snuggle with me. We girls do like to be held after."

END OF REPORT

READ AND DESTROY
THIS IS COPY #____2____

CODE RED
Eyes Only
001 through 0059 authorized
Memorandum

TO: Bravo 114
FROM: Alpha 003
RE: 04-00066-2013 – Cotte

Monday, 8 July 2013
1222 hours

Real fucking funny, Jack. You know you cannot use "Fuck" in a report. Additionally, this reads like porn, rather than a government memo. Redo this and get it to me by 1600 tomorrow.

FYI: I got nine erections reading this tripe. Can't wait to see the pictures.

10 a.m. – A Dull Creature, or The Art of Ugly Romance

Kelly Jameson

The morning was heavy with that twisted rope of fresh, quiet newness that I can't stand.

10 a.m. I swung my legs over the side of my bed, stared out the window for a while, stared at my feet. Swung my legs back into bed and huddled beneath the blankets.

10.03 a.m. What reasons did I have to get out of bed, really, with the sun shining like that? With the yawning cacophony of people in cars going the same places they always went, doing the same things they always did, thinking and saying the same things they always thought and said?

10.05 a.m. I began to masturbate. But the mood was killed by the fact that Shemp of Three Stooges's fame was staring at me from a poster on the wall. I made a mental note to move that poster to the bathroom. I got up, showered, got dressed, put my socks and sneakers on, started the coffee pot brewing, and went into the living room of my small apartment, where I sat on my custard-coloured couch and stared at my feet some more.

10.30 a.m. I'd lived through times where everyone was throwing money around. And now they weren't. Now I was living in the times where horribly inept managers spent their days figuring out how to out-source their entire departments and cut office supply budgets and make a nice big, fat bonus doing it, while scratching their asses and sniffing their fingers.

Now I was living in the time of mass layoffs, strange bird flu, anthrax, 24/7 media stupidity, genital wart treatments, Snooki, and *Dancing with the Stars*. What the fuck.

I drank a cup of coffee. Stared at the pile of dirty clothing on the floor. Thought about moving it to the hamper, but I couldn't fit it into my day.

I decided to head to the bar, a place where people lived and tipped atrociously in the semi-darkness. A place where hijacked, pissed off, scared, defeated, deadened people with just the tiniest bit of hope for getting laid by some dark, prothrombotic creature that had splashed a little bit of lipstick over its sour lips dwelled, with hardly a heartbeat.

As I entered the sprawling cave of a bar I thought about how the train had replaced the horse-drawn carriage, pulling people west, how the car and airplane had replaced the train, how the computer and cell phone and iPad had replaced human connection.

I was poorly dressed, except for my shoes. New running shoes adorned my feet despite the fact that I never ran anywhere, unless there was a Pabst Blue Ribbon or Entenmann's truck driving down the street. Ripped denim shorts revealed my muscled, hairy thighs, which were my best feature; a rumpled aqua blue T-shirt with Cher's face on it graced my chest. I sat next to some overly made-up savage at the bar. "Scotch and water, with a beer chaser," I said to the bartender.

He gave me a look that said, "OK, fuckface, coming right up."

He brought me my drinks and I forgave him his subtle sarcasm and overt apathy.

I turned to the savage, the dull creature on my right, and stared at her mountainous breasts, the kind that inexplicably made me think of cowboys and Indians fighting it out on the plains of the Wild, Wild West. She wasn't under forty. Her waist and her ass spilled from her clothes like gobs of raw pie crust. She was on the edge of beauty, had probably once been sort of good-looking, you know, back when the internet had been invented.

I studied her profile. Big nose, bigger lips. Shoulder-length curly hair that was dyed very dark red.

"Captain America saved my life," I said into my Scotch and laughed. She looked at me for the first time.

"I'm not a very good housekeeper," I said. Then, "Where do you think I ought to go? Portland? Miami? The Jersey Shore? 'Cause 'shore' ain't shit happening here."

"I think you should go home with me, honey."

I nearly spit out my Scotch. She got up from her bar stool and nearly tripped. She knew how to *move*.

I stared at her dumbly.

"Well?" she said, clutching her bag as the barkeeper waved his bar rag.

Something about her made me think of an opera singer, and not just any opera singer, but the one Tchaikovsky married. Later Tchaikovsky had stood like a douche bag in a freezing river hoping to catch pneumonia and die while his opera-singer wife went mad. Now that's how a marriage should be.

"F. Scott Fitzgerald couldn't write worth shit," I said, finishing the last of my Scotch and downing my beer while she studied my hard, hairy thighs.

"Look, you look like someone who'd put a jockstrap on backwards. But you have nice legs. Do you want me to suck your cock or what?"

I stood up, my motivation renewed. "Zelda Fitzgerald spent the last days of her life in an insane asylum," I barked.

"You're a beefy man, aren't you, sweetheart?"

As we walked out into that defecating sunshine again, I thought, I'm not a man of Catholic tastes. I'm not a sweetheart. But I am certainly beefy.

We walked along the sidewalk, the jerks in business suits and bitches in skirts and heels passing us, yapping away on their cell phones, not seeing the watery blue sky or smelling the smell of delicious, fatty burgers frying at nearby burger joints, or feeling the spring wind on their faces, but drinking their black coffee and silently passing gas and bad business advice on to their publics.

We passed a liquor store and then a doughnut store and then a quarter-operated laundramat where people stood circus-still while their bright clothes danced round and round. I thought about how Van Gogh was an Aries, an ugly, oil-on-canvas, French-fried fuck with shock-orange hair who wanted to fuck his cousin, a man who lived in pooling misery and staggered from one failure to the next. Lost jobs, failed careers, failed relationships, obsessions he couldn't tame. Sunflowers and wilting whores and starry nights and probably constipation, brought on maybe because in extremes of madness, he ate paint directly from the paint tubes. I wondered what colours were his favourites.

"Isn't art supposed to have a message?" I asked the prothrombotic bar creature. We'd walked up two flights of stairs to her dull apartment. She unlocked and opened her door, her keys jangling. Then she grabbed my crotch. "I have a message for you, buddy."

I got hard, because that's what generally happens when a woman grabs your crotch. "Have you suffered any side effects or complications from transvaginal mesh?" I asked. It was the only thing I could think to ask.

She pulled me inside her apartment and slammed the door shut, pushing me up against it and undoing my jean shorts, sliding them and my underwear down to my ankles. My dick stood straight-up-hard. She bent down and sucked the knob, rubbing my thighs, her manicured, eggplant-purple fingernails digging into my flesh. "Ooh, baby, oooh," she said.

"Van Gogh followed Gauguin around like a puppy," I said, gasping as her sloppy red lips sucked at my root and her dull tongue swirled around my balls and then up my shaft.

I grabbed the top of her head and pushed at it, pulling at her dyed red hair, seeing an inch of grey at the roots. "There are poems in your hair," I breathed.

She started to bob over my dick like an empty milk carton floating on a river and I rolled my hips. The sucking noises were God awful, and beautiful as hell.

"Yeah, baby, yeah." I grunted. "Hemingway, Baudelaire, Verlaine, Rimbaud, oh yes! Toulouse-Lautrec! Van Gogh, oh my God, you're wild. Oscar Wilde! They all drank absinthe . . . oh yeah, baby, oh yeah yeah, suck it good, that's good . . . Wilde described the phantom sensation of having tulips brush against his legs after leaving a bar at closing time. But absinthe doesn't cause hallucinations, really. Uh, that's good . . ."

She rammed her finger up my asshole.

"Rossetti!" I screamed. "He blamed himself for spending too much time on his work, and at his wife Lizzie Siddal's funeral, he put all his poems in her casket and buried them too." I came almost immediately.

The dull creature got up and went into the bathroom off the hall. I heard water running from a faucet as my veins throbbed and sang and pumped with leftover pleasure.

I waddled into her kitchen, found some paper towels, and cleaned myself up. Pulled my shorts and underwear back over my hips. Thought about how seven years after he buried his art with his dead wife, Rossetti exhumed Lizzie's coffin and disentangled his poems from the corpse's hair. He published them in his first book, *House of Life*.

I turned at the sound of footsteps. The dull creature stood there in all her glorious, pale, doughy nudeness, pinching her own gigantic rosy nipples. "Now you're going to bend me over and fuck me hard. And tie me up." She walked to a cabinet, reached up and opened it, and pulled something out that had apparently been hidden behind some cereal bowls. It was a man's striped work tie. Red and blue.

My dick got hard again. Generally that's what happens when a woman says, "Now you're going to bend me over and fuck me hard. And tie me up."

I followed her big, shapely, swaying ass to the living room and was surprised to see a custard-coloured couch very much like my own. Was Ikea having a sale on them when I'd bought mine? I put my hand on her back and pushed her forward over one end of it.

I pulled her arms behind her, tied her wrists with the man's tie.

"Tighter," she said.

I tied them tighter. I wondered briefly who the tie had belonged to, but I didn't care very much. It smelled like smoke.

"I don't smoke," I said, pushing my cock right inside her big, wet pussy, "but if I did, I wouldn't smoke Camels because of the stupid picture of a camel on the front of the package." I slammed myself inside her quivering flesh, which was pungent with her desire, a sudden assault on my nostrils, like something out of Coney Island. I realized I'd brought all kinds of hunger to this room. Also, I wasn't good at dirty talk.

"Oh!" she cried out. "You shouldn't be spreading my legs and fucking me like this, making me so wet and horny. You're a naughty man with a big cock."

I tried not to think about how later, when she was older, she wouldn't be one who defied age and rheumatism with any kind of grace. For now she was a big, hot dripping, wet mess of fucking and I slammed her over and over until she moaned and whimpered and begged for more, her voluptuous ass twisted up against me.

I reached around and grabbed a mountainous breast. It was then I noticed the set of six coloured prints of military men hanging above the wall.

"Look at my pussy, lick it, finger it, and then fuck me some more," she demanded. "I like it, I like your big, fat cock pounding me . . ."

I pulled out, bent down, spread her wide with my fingers. She was a dripping mess. I fingered her as requested. Then I fucked her harder, liking the fact that she was run-down at the heels, just past her bloom, dripping with neediness and surrender.

"Spank me! Spank me hard and talk dirty to me! My cunt's dripping for you! My cunt's dripping for your cock!"

I smacked that lovely, large moon-ass and smacked it hard. It was some of the ugliest art I'd ever seen. "Pythagoras the

Greek mathematician," I said. "Uh, oh yeah, baby . . . the one who came up with the Pythagorean theorem . . . shit that *feels good* . . . thought beans were evil." I thrust inside her and came hard and she screamed and creamed, that dull mouth biting custard-coloured cushion as she came around my cock, pulsing in her middle-aged absurdity and sex stench.

"Smack my ass again and tell me I'm a bad girl . . . say something dirty."

I did. I improvised. "Henri Matisse was so bored when he worked as a law clerk that he sat in his window and shot spitballs at random people who walked by. *Dirty* spitballs." Her flesh trembled in response. "Matisse had a nervous breakdown and was in the hospital when he was first introduced to painting. If he hadn't had that breakdown, he might never have smeared paint on anything. You know, I could probably love you, baby, but I'd love painting more."

Then she took a shower. Then I took a shower, using her strawberry-scented shampoo in my hair and to wash my balls.

When we were both dressed, she demanded I take her to a local diner for a big breakfast of ham and eggs, flapjacks, fried potatoes, toast with strawberry jam and coffee. So I did.

I was salting my eggs when I looked up at her face. The dull creature was staring out the diner window at the passing people and traffic, and for just a second I saw horror, compassion, sadness, recognition, surprise and resignation. Maybe also a love of free, butter-coated flapjacks swimming in syrup on a Tuesday when everyone else was working away at their dull, meaningless lives. It was as close as we both got to love that day.

"Picasso survived the Occupation, you know, and the Liberation of Paris marked the start of his incredible fame. He became the first art celebrity. Some critics say his work suffered as a result. But critics are constipated fuckwads."

She poured more syrup on her flapjacks. "Why is it that whenever you eat flapjacks, no matter how much syrup you pour over them, they always need more?" she said. "It's like they suck it all up or something."

I settled back against the booth back, watching her sloppy red lips close over her fork while I sipped my diarrhoea-inducing load of diner coffee. When she pulled the fork away, there was nothing left on it, every morsel, every drop of syrup gone, every tong stripped bare and shining with her saliva.

"In 1923, Duchamp abandoned his art for chess," I said. "In 1968, he died of a sudden heart attack after a pleasant dinner with friends."

"Were they having flapjacks for dinner?" she said, syrup now dribbling down her chin, her fingers greasy from clenching fatty bacon strips and lifting them to her mouth.

"He left a surprise though. A year after he died, they unveiled a new artwork of his at the Philadelphia Museum of Art. A huge pair of wooden doors pierced by two small peep-holes. When you looked through the holes, you saw a shattered brick wall, and through that you glimpsed a life-size nude mannequin, sprawled on a bed of twigs, with her legs spread right open, holding a gas lamp in one hand. This from a man who had officially given up art forty-five years before."

The waitress hurried by and left the bill on the table, mumbled some thanks without looking at us too closely. I looked at the slip of paper. Thought about how much I liked waffles with butter on a warm, spring morning.

"Should art be beautiful, meaningful, understandable?" I asked. "Should it always have a purpose? Or should it be disturbing, ugly, dripping, disquieting, offensive, raw, twisted and shocking?"

She stood up, her mountainous breasts bobbing, and wiped her wide mouth with a paper napkin. She sucked her fingers, one by one. "I want you to think about me and my pussy all day," she said loudly.

"Believe me, honey, I won't forget."

"You might."

She reached beneath her sundress, wiggled, and pulled off her panties, tossing them on the table. The panties were very large.

"I want you to wear my panties. It'll feel like it's me squeezing your balls down there." She made a motion with her hands like she was squeezing my balls. A balding, elderly gentleman at the diner counter gaped at her, grinning like a fool behind his thick bifocals, his eyes roving her up and down.

I gripped the dull creature's panties in my hand, staring at them. "Salvador Dali said those who do not want to imitate anything produce nothing. At Dali's Night in a Surrealist Forest Ball, a dinner benefit in California for European artists displaced by World War II, Dali's wife Gala wore a unicorn head and presided over the event from a giant bed. Distinguished guests were served such delicacies as live frogs." I looked up, but the dull creature had started to move towards the doors. The old man frowned at me and shook his head, turning back to his eggs. He adjusted his bifocals, stuck a fork in his egg yolks, and swirled the cheery yellow, broken egg goo around his scratched, white plate, a plate that hundreds before him had eaten from.

I stood up, pressing the panties to my nose as the dull creature hesitated before the door and looked back at me, her eyes gold-brown unreadable. I said in a loud voice, "Don't forget! Frida Kahlo was riding in a bus in downtown Mexico City when it was rammed by an out-of-control electric trolley. She had many broken bones and a shattered pelvis. The collision had unfastened her clothes so she was nude, and a packet of powdered gold that someone had been carrying on the bus broke . . . it dusted her bleeding body. She was also impaled by a steel handrail that went in through her left hip and exited through her vagina. Before the ambulance came, her boyfriend picked her up and put her gently in the display window of a billiard room and put his coat over her. Kahlo said later that the accident took her virginity."

The old man was back to staring at me while he chewed his food.

The dull creature still held the door open and stared at the floor.

"Frida recuperated for two years but never fully recovered," I said. "While she was confined to bed, she learned to paint. She hung a mirror overhead in the canopy of her bed so she could use her reflection as a starting point for painting portraits of other people. If she hadn't been on that bus, maybe she never would've smeared paint on anything . . ."

The dull creature left me then, a gust of warm wind dancing inside, leaving a quilt of dead leaves in her place. I paid the bill and stepped outside, my hard, hairy thighs trying to determine which way to walk, a pair of 3X pink women's panties balled up in my shorts pocket. Duchamp had had the last laugh. Who needed a peephole when the world gave it all away for free?

Nothing much happened the rest of the day, or the next, as the sun squeezed its rays of hope all over a city that had stopped dancing towards anything long ago.

Spanish Fly

Ian Watson

Ricardo lay upon Zahra, fucking. His penis felt like some big chilli pepper, stiff as wood, sweating fiery capsaicin. The head must be choked scarlet with engorgement – yet he couldn't burst with an orgasm, as if string was tied tight to delay him. If only her juices would soothe him more as she shrilled, fingernails raking his back. The fierce itching increased whenever he slacked.

From time to time, Zahra's heels drummed at his buttocks. His heart thudded in response.

Who was the confined one? Who was the slave? Zahra? Or himself?

The bed was heavy old oak such as a fat village priest or a local *cacique* despot may have lolled upon. Slanted mirrors set into the headboard showed Ricardo the angled mirrors of the ceiling, and thus the stinging progress of the emerald beetle across his back.

He must be hallucinating to some degree, imagining the beetle's wanderings as intentional. The human brain sought for patterns. He thought of the arrays of mirror segments that resolve close binary stars by interferometry, fractured images which a computer combines into greater clarity than any one telescope can see on its own. Ricardo wasn't a professional astronomer like those other scientists at Yerbes, north-east of Madrid, but as a visitor guide in the pavilion that popularized astronomy he must understand in order to explain. Every other weekend he drove back to his mother's flat in Madrid. Apart from Mother and his job, he had no ties, as it were.

No need to twist his neck to watch himself fucking, in a compound vision, fly's-eye way, nor to follow the journey of Zahra's sharp fingernails across his back. Shouldn't the beetle slip in his sweat? Mightn't she crush it?

He realized how intensely her gaze was concentrating, as if the motion of her heels and her outcries belonged to a different person.

It was very hot that day in Granada, even in the shade of vines overhanging the tiny courtyard pebbled like a maze. Oleanders with their long thin leaves bloomed pinkly around the walls. Invisible cicadas were rubbing their legs together shrilly in the heat. Zahra had led Ricardo here from the tea house through the twisting narrow medieval alleyways, but instead of taking him straight up to a room, which he anticipated, sat upon a stone bench, as if he must prove himself further. Perhaps a black-clad crone would come to question him or simply take more money from him. He had little idea if he was actually in a brothel, or whether Zahra was a whore pretending not to be so. "Submission" was what "Islam" meant, although the voluntary submission was to God, not to a woman. Zahra was a Moor, one of those who had ruled the whole South of Iberia for hundreds of years. Moors might be second-class citizens since then, though once they had ruled the roost. Ricardo was certainly seeking submission, but to what extent?

Zahra waved a hand at the oleanders. "The most poisonous of plants," she remarked. "A deadly beauty. But the first plant to blossom after the atom bomb fell on Hiroshima."

The taste of the minted, honeyed tea was still in his mouth. He was effectively lost in the Albayzín district sprawling on the hillside opposite the Alhambra Palace. True, he only needed to walk downhill constantly, whatever the twists and turns, to emerge into a more normal modern world, but that wasn't his desire; not yet.

"My name," she said, "means flower. Or—" and she smiled slyly "—beauty. Would you taste a little poison, so as to discover . . . ?" Though she didn't specify what. "You must accept my judgement about the amount of poison."

"I accept," he told her. "I submit." Ricardo was certain that this was no scheme to kill and rob him. On the contrary, failure to comply with a desire of hers might see him back on the alleyway outside the gate, excluded due to unsuitability, even though he had already presented her with two fifty euro notes, to be allowed to accompany her.

From her bag she took a big twist of paper and unwrapped a small green cake. A heady aroma arose to his nostrils.

Earlier, in the tea house, the *tetería*, his eyes had strayed frequently to her tits, her *tetas*. The black rope of her hair, passed over one shoulder, hung between them. Black as the pupils of her eyes. She wore a purple kaftan embroidered with golden crescent moons. On her wrists were no bangles, and her manicured, violet-varnished fingers lacked rings, which suggested to him potential nakedness, availability. Skin, only dusky skin. Yet at the same time her black sandals, their high heels rising almost from a pencil-width, clasped her calves with a lavishness of studded leather – how much more such was hidden beneath her long clothing? Those sandals might have been specially made for her by a local Moroccan craftsman. Moroccan, for sure. She must be from Morocco. Briefly he felt as if the south of Iberia had never been purged of the Moors, as if al-Andalus survived.

A comment on the internet had mentioned this particular tea house in the street of the tea houses as a rendezvous for a certain sort of person; consequently he came here the day following his business visit to the Sierra Nevada Observatory up in the huge mountains where some snow still clung.

She was sitting alone at a little low octagonal table of carved wood, on a many-coloured leather pouffe, reading a magazine about fate and fortune. A floppy bag lay by her feet. Other customers were a couple of old men, playing some card game, and a group of giggling students passing round a hubble-bubble pipe.

Nothing ventured . . .

"Would it disturb you if I sit here?"

She seemed provoked, in more than one sense, by his intrusion – offended initially by his presumption, as well as by his assumption about her, yet at the same time mischievously excited. As though she was, and also was not, what he hoped. She didn't actively discourage him, yet he realized that he must offer more, of *himself*, irrespective of whatever might await her in his wallet.

Eyeing her magazine, he said, "Some people think that the stars in the sky show our destinies, but when I look through a telescope there's so much more than meets the naked eye . . ."

Zahra stared up at the mirrors on the ceiling. "Now you're perfect," she whispered in his ear, and added, "and now I think you must love me . . .

". . . and must use the map to find me again."

The map.

What she had drawn upon his back, the trail that the stinging emerald beetle followed, was all of a sudden clear to him as the plan of a city district

. . . *somewhere else*. He was fairly sure the district wasn't the Albayzín of Granada, where he was now.

When he did eventually come, his semen burned, and he cried out as much in pain as in relief. He began to roll aside.

"Be very careful not to crush the beetle, or you release its full dose, which will surely destroy your kidneys."

Afterwards, a robe around her, she helped him resume his shirt and trousers. His back was aflame, and his penis throbbed hotly, still half erect; had there been Viagra in that little cake? His legs wobbled; the room oscillated softly. Flutterings of light and twinklings affected his vision.

When she led him down into the tiny, leafy courtyard, where leaves fractured sunlight confusingly, he gasped, "Zahra, when may I see you again?"

"You would risk your body once more?"

"Yes, yes!" He must be mad. Whatever aphrodisiac he had swallowed had warped his mind, filled him with yearning. He craved. He adored.

She opened the gate to the alleyway.

"You'll not be able to find your way back to this Carmen, because the map shows otherwise."

Carmen, Carmen ... the fiery seductive manipulative gypsy woman of the opera, who destroys a man ... No, surely Zahra had said *this* Carmen. You won't find your way back to *this Carmen*. Not referring to herself, but to a location.

"Remember," she said, "when you consult your flesh in a mirror, the image will be reversed." And she pushed him gently enough on his way, although her touch, her parting caress, felt almost like a whiplash.

A few alleyways later and lower, nausea overtook him. He stooped over, palms clutching his knees, but he couldn't vomit on to the cobbles.

Next morning Ricardo's back still stung all over, though the inflammation was less. He pissed blood painfully in the cramped bathroom of his hotel, as if the tube in his penis was raw. Initially this terrified him, but then he drank a lot of water direct from the tap to dilute what afflicted him, and felt better. If he shut his eyes, he could see the dark-nippled plums of Zahra's breasts, her shallow bowl of a belly, the black bush beneath so slicked with moisture that it no longer concealed her cleft. If another man had been coming to meet her in the *tetería*, Ricardo had displaced that fellow, had become him.

In the *tetería* the same couple of old men were playing cards; and the same big-bellied Moroccan served him mint tea again.

"May I ask you? Do you sell little green cakes here? This size?" Ricardo demonstrated with thumb and forefinger.

The proprietor looked offended.

"Certainly *not*, Señor."

"You know what I mean?"

The Moroccan said nothing.

"Someone told me ... though not regarding your own establishment. Not here at all. I only want to know *what* those cakes contain. Supposing that you happen to know." Feeling naive, Ricardo slid a twenty euro note on to the table.

"You'll not find those cakes in here, nor in any Arab cake shop nearby, nor even on sale in the souk of Marrakesh. The true Dawamesk cake is banned since the nineties of last century. So what is the value in knowing?"

A reasonable value seemed to be ten euros extra, and the proprietor conceded that the cake contained cannabis along with almond paste, ground pistachios, cloves and other spices.

Cannabis, yes that would be true. The smell.

"One of the spices makes the mouth burn?"

"Not a spice, no. Cantharides, which smells unpleasant on its own, thus it needs masking. From a green beetle which causes blisters ... and other dramatic effects in the body."

Ricardo knew those dramatic effects very well. He had been simultaneously stoned and highly stimulated.

"One other thing," he said. "What is a Carmen?"

"I don't know if you're a journalist, pretending ignorance, but I think, Señor, you should leave as soon as you finish your tea. It's a house, large or tiny, with a courtyard garden. Garden is *karm* in Arabic. Many Carmens are in the oldest districts of this city."

Ricardo dared say, "I might wait for the woman who was here yesterday."

"Which woman?"

"Her name is Zahra. You served us both."

"It may be so. I never saw her before." The man sketched in the air what may have been an eye. "You went with a witch, not a whore."

So, on that one and only occasion in her life, Zahra had been waiting for him in that particular *tetería* out of a dozen more in the same street because she believed she had seen in the stars that her destiny and his was to meet at that special time and place.

No, no, *her* destiny – and that of a *man* who might be himself or who might be another. His desire to submit had led him to one of the few possible places where such an encounter might occur – maybe to the only place, if that hint on the internet was accurate. The chances of their meeting weren't astronomical.

Which other man, wondered Ricardo, might have changed his mind that afternoon without quite understanding why, and walked off elsewhere?

That bedroom in the Carmen where he had submitted to Zahra, even while on top of her, that bedroom with mirrors in the ceiling and in the antique headboard, had been so well equipped for her purpose of inscribing his back. The Carmen must have been a brothel, where Zahra could come and go as she pleased, as she chose.

With months between visits? Or even years?

As Ricardo walked back from the *tetería* to his hotel to check out, his gaze darted as if he might catch sight of her. Several times he stopped suddenly and spun round.

How foolish to think she might be following him! For he was her follower.

In the hotel bedroom, his cock stiffened hotly at the very thought of her. If only she were lying on the bed. No way could he relieve himself without her. Provided that she commanded him to.

Back in Yerbes, concentration warred with impatience as Ricardo took photos with his phone of his red-scored back as seen in the bathroom mirror. Only after half an hour was he satisfied with the completeness and clarity of the map. Only then could obsession fully unrein itself.

What district of what city might the map most closely correspond with? Where, where? He would Google maps of Barcelona, Venice, Marrakesh. If need be, of a hundred cities which surely must be in southern Europe or North Africa or the nearby Middle East. Cheap flights and hostels existed for him. When he found a correspondence, he must go wherever.

Zahra had become his Mistress, whom no other woman could now displace, and he was her underling, her knight errant who must search. She had given him a quest, to find her again. Find her he must, for Zahra had loved him in a special way beyond his wildest expectations even though they had both just met. She had known his needs exactly, or perhaps for the first time she had given full form to those needs, embodying them. Now she controlled those, from wherever she had gone to.

His mundane astronomy job was incompatible with his quest. He had some savings; he could borrow from his mother. He must follow the itch in his back as if the Spanish fly beetle had burrowed under his skin to take up residence.

Or else he would choke, he would burn. Choke like the victim of bee stings, burn like a heretic on a bonfire.

Damned Love

Lynn Lake

Rebecca first spotted the man of her demented dreams when she was working the Saturday shift at the used bookstore. He pushed his way into the small shop and glanced around, strode over to the classics section.

Rebecca's heart leapt into her mouth and her small hands shook on the book she'd been inputting behind the glass front counter. The man was in his early twenties, tall and slim, with short glossy black hair and a pale aristocratic face, dark eyes with long lashes. He was dressed in a fashionable blue peacoat and black pants, polished black shoes.

Rebecca stared at him as he browsed through the bookshelves, admiring the way he popped out a volume, flipped through it, snapped it shut and re-slotted it. His every movement and gesture, the way he held his well-formed head tilted slightly upwards, denoted decisiveness and arrogance, and domination.

She rose from her chair behind the computer. Her legs quivered and lips trembled, nipples stiffening beneath her peasant blouse and pussy surging in her white cotton panties beneath her jeans. "Is—Is there anything I can help you with – particularly?" she stammered, her voice thin and cracking.

The man turned his head briefly towards her, gave her a perfunctory smile, and then went back to perusing a leather-bound volume of Virgil. "I can find what I'm looking for on my own, thank you."

Rebecca gripped the counter to steady herself. His voice was clear and cold, as obviously cultured as the rest of him.

She eased back down into her chair, watching him over the counter, her breasts and clit tingling with barely hidden desire. She felt that this was a man who could dominate her, humiliate her, would be quite capable of abusing her for his own personal amusement (and her pleasure). Doing what came naturally to him, and (some would say) unnaturally to her. She wanted it so badly she could hardly contain herself.

When he left the shop after fifteen minutes, without buying anything, Rebecca rushed around the counter and raced down the book-lined aisles to the small bathroom at the rear of the store. She plunged one hand into her jeans and panties, the other up into her blouse. She came almost immediately, desperately rubbing her swollen clit and moistened pussy lips, frantically squeezing her shimmering breasts and rolling her rigid nipples. Staring at her reflection in the cracked mirror, and picturing the man doing whatever he wanted to her.

He came into the store about once a week; usually, but not always, on the weekend. Rebecca worked extra hours during the week, hung around the shop unpaid, to be sure she didn't miss him. She applied make-up and perfume, visited the hairdresser's, wore skirts and stockings and high heels.

Malcolm, the runty nerd who managed the store's website and accounting, gaped at her from behind his thick lenses. And Gladys, the huge old woman who owned the shop, also noticed the difference, complimenting Rebecca by wheezing, "You can catch more flies with honey than vinegar, that's for sure." Meaning sales, not sex, of course.

Finally, the man actually approached Rebecca where she stood quivering behind the counter, on a Sunday. "Do you have any Céline anywhere? I heard *Journey to the End of the Night* is an interesting read."

Rebecca gulped, batted her eyelashes, looking as meek as possible (which wasn't difficult for her). She felt weak in the knees and the heart. "Um, I—I think so. In the French section, under D, for Destouches."

"Ah." The man wheeled and walked off, without a word of thanks.

Rebecca stared at his haughty butt cheeks clenching in his tight pants, her mouth dry and pussy wet. The fact he hadn't appeared to be the least bit impressed by her literary knowledge pleased her immensely. And when he didn't buy the book, gave her only a tight smile and pushed his way out the door of the store, she almost ran over Malcolm in the back hallway in her sprint to the bathroom.

The relationship soon stalemated, in Rebecca's fervent mind. She was just too shy to suggest anything to the man other than the possible location of a book. And he was just too good (looks and status-wise) for a mildly attractive used bookshop girl. It became clear to Rebecca, then, that if he was too good for her, she had to become *bad* for him, to attract his attention.

So, when Malcolm reported one day that her "book lover" had given him his email address, so that Malcolm could let the man know when a certain book had finally been priced by fat Gladys, Rebecca leapt at the opportunity to put her humiliating plan of seduction into action. Desperate times called for depraved measures.

The place was called Dungeons & Dragons. A BDSM sex club on the seedy side of town. Rebecca had learned about it online when surfing for similarly themed websites, images, videos and literature on the subjugating subject that was so near and dear to her heart and pussy.

It was located in the basement of a crumbling building on a darkened street. Rebecca clutched her purse tight to her trembling body and took a deep breath of the chill night air. Then she gripped the rusty iron railing and descended the cracked cement stairs, slipped through the battered red metal door and into the club.

It was darker inside than out. Heavy metal music growled deep and angry, and the cloying scent of leather and sex hung in the humid air. The walls were painted black and the carpeting was crimson. Men and women, wearing chains and chaps and emblazoned with tattoos and piercings, prowled the bar/lounge area. Rebecca staggered to the rear of the throbbing room, pushed through a padded black door, and then stumbled down another flight of dimly lit stairs.

Cries rang out, screams; the crack of a whip; the frenzied smacking of flesh against flesh. Six red doors lined the gloom-laden hallway, the heavy air now dripping with perspiration and sex. Rebecca opened the second door on the right, entered. Six men and three women wearing only black leather masks stood inside the violet-lit room, as if waiting just for Rebecca. Fresh meat to feed the beasts.

The men removed Rebecca's clothing, their long, hard cocks bobbing dangerously close. Then the women led her over to a black padded bench, their large, thick-nippled breasts swaying lasciviously. They set Rebecca up on all fours on the bench, chained her ankles and wrists to the bench's metal railings. She'd only just managed to set up her purse, with the pinhole camera peeking out, against the near wall of the room, before they'd grabbed her, stripped her and secured her.

She trembled up on the bench, naked, exposed, shackled – in a position of obvious sadistic sexual disadvantage. A man picked up a cat-o'-nine-tails from the scarlet-carpeted floor and got in behind Rebecca. A woman picked up a riding crop and stood next to the man.

Rebecca swallowed hard and fought back tears, goose-bumps prickling her chocolate flesh, her liquorice nipples seized up rigid, her pussy sodden. She pushed her bum out higher into the air, gripping the bench.

The man lashed the cat-o'-nine-tails across Rebecca's buttocks. She jumped, and screamed. The woman slashed Rebecca's bottom with the riding crop, and Rebecca jerked and groaned.

The blows came fast and furious, singeing across Rebecca's rippling butt cheeks. She shuddered with every jolt to her bum and body, her teeth gritted and eyes gaping, knuckles burning light on the bench. She thrust her stung bottom out even higher, arching her back and tilting her head up, meeting the wicked leather crashing against her ass, and begging for more, harder.

The whips cracked into her flesh, streaking her being with pain and pleasure, searing her bum and shimmering through the rest of her body. And then a man stepped forward and grabbed onto her dark hair, stuck his huge cock into her open mouth. Rebecca gasped, gagged. A slash across her butt jumped her forward on the bench again, and the man's cock leapt deep into her mouth. He grunted and pulled on her hair, pumping her head and his hips back and forth in rhythm to her wild rocking.

Rebecca sucked on the man's cock, her bum and body blazing with passion. He was heavy set, his cock a wedge of veined meat that stuffed her mouth and ballooned her cheeks. Her eyes bleared with tears and snot bubbled out of her flared nostrils, the whips whaling her ass and the cock ramming her mouth. She ate it up, at both ends.

They whipped her bottom until she could hardly feel it any more, the raw, bloated flesh beaten numb. Her butt cheeks gyrated wantonly out of control. More cocks filled her mouth and fucked her face, one pulling out and another plugging in, fingers clawing at her hair, balls slapping against her chin. Tears streaked her cheeks and drool strung out of her mouth. Her clit was as swollen numb as her ass.

After one cock pulled out of her mouth, one of the women jammed her damp cunt up against Rebecca's mouth, rubbed her wet, engorged lips all over Rebecca's face. Rebecca shot out her tongue as far as it would go, panting, into the woman's moist bush. She fucked herself on Rebecca's outthrust tongue, undulating urgently, riding Rebecca's head with her clutching hands. The beat continued on Rebecca's bum, blasting off her blistered cheeks.

Finally, they freed her, helped her up off the bench. Her legs buckled, her head swimming. Pussy juice streaked her quivering thighs. Her mouth felt gapingly empty after all of the cock and cunt. Her buttocks clenched red-hot needles, the skin vibrating fire.

They led Rebecca over to a giant black padded X that filled part of the room, out from a wall. Then they turned her around and lifted her arms and spread her legs. They clamped her wrists to the tops of the X, her ankles to the bottom. Her beaten bum stuck out back in the opening built into the middle of the X.

Rebecca squirmed against the metal clamps, but there was no breaking free. The ends of the X were bolted to the floor and ceiling. A masked woman stepped close and slapped one of Rebecca's breasts, hard. Rebecca jerked. Another woman slapped her butt from behind. Rebecca screamed and arched forward, into another slap on her other breast.

The two women smacked Rebecca's tits and ass, sending electric arcs shocking through Rebecca's body. The third woman kneeled down and parted Rebecca's swollen pussy lips and smacked Rebecca's swelled-up clit. Rebecca shuddered and moaned.

The women abused her, front and back. Then it was the men's turn.

A hard cock speared up into Rebecca's pussy. She jumped to her toes. A thick cock ploughed into her ass from behind. She snapped forward bow-like, a charged cable, her cunt and anus stuffed with meat.

The men fucked her front and back, sawing in rhythm, their cocks brutally churning her pussy and ass, almost rubbing together inside of her, bodies banging against. Then another set of men. And another.

Rebecca was savagely reamed. She screamed and writhed, desperately undulating to the powerful pistoning strokes of the cocks fucking her pussy and anus. Until the pounded-in pressure built and built and became too much, and she exploded with orgasm.

Burst after burst of white-hot ecstasy tore through her flaming body, the cocks relentlessly pumping into her. She almost ripped the X loose with her violent shuddering, her shrieks of depraved joy piercing the thickened air. Rebecca came so hard and so long and so wet, she barely felt the cocks going off inside of her; the men jetting their own scorching orgasms into her burning cunt and chute.

Until she was left hanging and dripping from the X, utterly wasted. Her head hung down, her body tremoring, bum and pussy steaming; a small smile flickering at the corners of Rebecca's fucked-over mouth.

She emailed the video to the man.

She received no response. And he stopped coming to the store.

Angered, Rebecca begged Malcolm to hack into the man's email account. It cost her more of her dignity, and earned Malcolm a blowjob. But Rebecca got the man's name, phone number and home address.

His name was Brock James, and he lived in a condominium complex in the high-rent district. Rebecca slipped inside his building by helping an old lady loaded down with groceries. Then she knocked on the door of Brock's twenty-second floor condo.

"Yes? Who are you? And how did you get inside?" he said, sniffily, cracking the door open.

"Don't you recognize me!? I work at Booked. I served you once." Rebecca shyly glanced down. "I want to serve you again."

Brock started to shut the door. "I'm busy."

Rebecca burst into tears and shoved the door open, sending Brock staggering backwards.

"Why didn't you answer my email? Didn't you see what I'm willing to do for you?" She stormed into the condo, an emotional outburst born of months and months of frustration taking hold of her.

"I—I-I . . . You can't just . . ."

Rebecca swiped away tears and glared at the stammering man. Then she slapped him across the face.

He stumbled another couple of steps back, holding his

inflamed cheek, his eyes wide and mouth hanging open. And then Rebecca *really* got mad, when Brock suddenly collapsed to his knees and gazed pleadingly up at her, his thin handsome face drained of all its arrogance and aloofness. He wasn't the *man* Rebecca had thought he was, at all.

"Get up! Take off your clothes!" she gritted through clenched teeth. She hadn't come this far, undergone so much, to let him off the hook now. He owed her something.

Brock scrambled back up to his feet and stripped off his clothes. His body was smooth and slender; without the expensive, flattering clothing, almost effeminate. His cock, though, rose strong and hard up from his shaven balls, the man obviously excited about what Rebecca was doing to *him*. She stepped forward and slapped his cock, one way, then the other.

Rebecca unzipped her black silk dress, shrugged it off and let it fall. She stepped out naked in her high heels. Then she spilled her purse out on the white shag carpeting. They both looked down at the metal and wooden rulers, the paddles and whips, the purple velvet ties and blue stretchable cords, the thick pink dildos, and the metal nipple and clit clamps and handcuffs.

Rebecca had come prepared for submission. Only now, the situation was reversed, and she was the dominant one. She was just furious and disgusted enough to go with the flow.

She sat down on the edge of Brock's black leather couch and spread her legs, ordered the man onto his knees. He crawled forward in compliance with her crooked finger, in between her legs. She lashed his thin neck and his thick cock with some cord, took hold of both ends. Then she jerked his head down and his cock up, clutched his soft hair and slammed his anxious face into her cunt.

He obediently licked her, like a heeled dog, down on all fours, lapping her shimmering slit. She clasped his head tight between her thighs and thrust her mound into his face, almost suffocating the man in the heated wet swamp of her pussy. He tongued her deep and quick and compliant.

Rebecca lifted her legs around his head and dug her high heels into his upraised ass. He whimpered into her pussy, his voice vibrating through her glowing body. She kicked at his soft, white buttocks, leaving red heel-marks, spurring him on.

Until she yanked his head up by the hair and the cord around his neck. Her thighs glistened with her juices, like his nose and lips and chin. She stood up and led him by the neck and cock down the hall of his condo, into his spacious, well-appointed bedroom. He had to crawl rapidly to keep up with her, his watery eyes fastened on her clutching, shifting, welted butt cheeks.

"Get on your bed, on your back!" Rebecca ordered. "I'm going to fuck you!"

He scrambled up onto the bed and rolled over onto his back. She lashed his wrists and ankles to the four dark wooden bedposts with the velvet ties, then stepped onto the bed and stood over him.

She thought about pissing on the disappointment of a man, to really show her disapproval. But her pussy was too brimming with other, hotter juices. So she tugged his cock upright into a towering pole. And then she abruptly sat down, on Brock's trussed-up erection. The mushroomed hood of his prick split her pussy lips and his swollen shaft speared into her tunnel – inches and inches and inches. Until she sat down flat on his trembling legs, his cock buried up to the lashed base in her cunt.

He groaned and arched upwards. She bounced up and down, pulling on the cord around his neck, like reins. The bed creaked and her beaten buttocks smacked against his quivering thighs, her breasts shivering to her fucking canter.

Rebecca rode harder, higher, glaring down at the gaping-mouthed man; her sweat-sheened body burning as hot as her anger and her cock-churned pussy. Brock twisted his arms and legs against the ties that bound him, in pleasure, not pain.

Rebecca fucked herself on his cock in a frenzy. Then she threw back her head and screamed, orgasm crashing through her body in wet, wicked waves, her hair flying and breasts jumping, her squirting pussy sucking on Brock's rigid pole. Until she had expended all of her lust and disgust.

She swung her legs off the laid-out man, her pussy spitting out his stiff cock. Rebecca stood at Brock's bedside, looking down into his agonized eyes, at his gleaming, twitching, tied-up cock. And she took even more mercy on the pathetic man, unleashing his bound erection.

The bloated tool surged with blood and semen, and Brock bucked on the bed, spraying into the air. She left him to wallow in his own sticky juices.

Despite the crushing failure with Brock, Rebecca wasn't defeated.

In fact, only two weeks later, she spotted a well-dressed, distinguished-looking, older man browsing through the religion section of the bookstore. The type of stern, experienced man Rebecca was just certain could dominate her as she so mightily deserved.

She asked in a quaking voice if she could help the man.

He arched his white eyebrows, turning his lion's head to study Rebecca. His thin, red lips formed a cold, cruel smile that made Rebecca weak in the knees and wet in the pussy.

The Crop

Jeff Cott

1

We met on the day after Christmas. I was protesting against fox hunting, which is supposed to be illegal in England but still happens. She was on horseback, one of many milling around at the meeting point. The hungry barking call of the dogs, the blood atmosphere all swirled in the air as I grabbed hold of her reins, looked up and saw her face for the first time. She whipped my face with her crop not once but twice. Beautiful green eyes said "sorry" as she took in my pain and I the beauty of her face.

She urged her horse on and galloped off. I ran to my car as all the other protestors did to theirs.

We were all networked, fellow protestors at vantage points all over, up trees, on hilltops, telling us the direction of the hunt. I was told to go to Ashley Wood and to wait there for the next call. I parked up and in the quiet knew the hunt was moving away from me.

I'm disappointed. They'll be trying to drive the fox out into open ground. But not here. I look in the mirror, see the blood on my cheek and grin. It's a trophy. I use a tissue but the wound still bleeds.

I get out of the car and walk up the hill, the presence of the trees calms me. I know these woods, played here as a kid.

I know if I strike east a little and follow the rise of the ground I'll come to a clearing. I'll be able to see the whole scene, might even meet one of my mates up there on recce . . .

But I meet her instead. She's been unhorsed, is walking through the woods her jacket unbuttoned. She's carrying her helmet, has wonderful red hair, I just can't tell you how red. We walk towards each other and stop together as if both knowing the perfect distance to leave between us.

As far as I'm concerned, the hunt is over. The chaotic sounds of horses, dogs and the horn recede further.

She takes in my bloodied cheeks and then logs on to my gaze.

She undoes the black cravat round her neck and holds it out for me to take together with the riding crop. A breeze combs through the trees and her hair and then is gone. All is still.

She says quietly, "You can tie me up, punish me. I deserve it. I never meant to mark such a handsome face . . ." I'm in a rush. There's nothing I'd like more than to take the whip to her arse in revenge and the thought arouses me . . . But next I'm speaking out loud with no idea what I'm going to say until I've said it. I hear myself say, "If you want to pay, you pay my way."

She nods.

"Here's what's going to happen. You're gonna put those things down, back yourself against a tree with your hands behind and I'm going to kiss you. Then we're quits."

She does everything exactly as instructed and is just about to put her hands behind her when I add, "Take off your jacket first."

There's a pausc but she obeys. Her jacket falls on the leaves with a warm-scented rustle. She stands against the tree, hands behind, eyes large and expectant – her lips slightly parted and as my lips find hers, I find myself thinking, *With this kiss I will break your heart.*

Until today I never knew I could kiss that tenderly. But in

contrast I grip her upper arms tight to keep her hands behind and press her against the tree whilst my lips are talking to hers in whispers, as if in isolation and complete privacy.

My mouth has always got me into trouble.

Our kiss hardens gradually, music growing in tempo, and I so love the way she dances. I am pressing against her, between her legs, harder and harder, even as her returning kiss is savage with passion.

And then – an unexpected, odd silence invades the woods. It's eerie. We stop kissing. All we can hear is the pant of our breath and somewhere in the distance something which I recognize as my mobile phone. I must have left it in the car.

An unstoppable rolling thunder approaches.

I let go of her arms. "We've got to keep still."

A scorching trail of sound rockets past us.

It's the fox, hacking, breathless, desperate.

I take her face in my hands and seal her lips with mine. I begin to count just as if between lightning's flash and the inevitable thunder to judge the distance.

The cheese-wire slice of the horn slashes through next.

I've reached a count of two hundred before the dog chorus penetrates the woods, squabbling up the air until there is nothing but their row receding.

The fox has a chance. She'll cross the road where my car is parked, go on further into the woods on the other side and head for the river.

Thunder shakes the ground long before it smashes through the woods. I hold her head still and kiss her again with all the passion of the thunder as the entire mounted hunt charges blindly through the woods.

We are invisible to them.

I am shaking.

I have never kissed a woman like this before.

I have never been kissed by a woman like this before.

And now I'm wondering whose heart is going to be broken by all of this.

In the aftermath silence, bird sounds blip back onto the

radar. I feel the race of her heart pressed close to mine and the rise and fall of her breasts.

I let go of her, step back. Her wondrous lips have that temporary, post-kiss passion pout which is so sexy.

She has blood on her cheeks, mine. "You've been bloodied. We're quits," I say. "Get dressed."

I can see the "do I or don't I obey?" argument in her eyes. She picks up the jacket, puts it on, buttoning it with care. There is no eye contact.

"I'm parked just down there," I say, "I'll give you a lift back to the pub."

She snatches up riding crop, helmet and cravat and we make our way down through the trees. The woods are singing again as if nothing has happened or else chattering with the news.

When we get near to the car and I press the unlock tab on the key, I hear a tiny groan of defeat.

She hears it too. I get down to look under the car and the fox's eyes and bared teeth greet me.

"What is it?"

"It's your fox, the one you are so keen to kill."

I see the quick set of her jaw as a feisty streak disturbs her green eyes.

But I stare her down and say, "Here's what's going to happen. I'm gonna give you a blanket. I'm gonna let the handbrake off. Everything has to be quiet and slow. I'll push the car forwards and you will throw the blanket over her."

"How do you know it's a she?"

"How do you know it's a he?"

Her curt nod grants me a point

I hand her the blanket. As quietly as possible, I open the car door, put key in ignition, release the steering lock and then the handbrake. I encourage the car to roll.

She casts the blanket beautifully, not too soon, not too late.

The blanket takes on the shape of a fox-sized animal, struggling, growling but weak and exhausted.

I scoop up the blanket, cuddling it still as she goes after the car.

I can't help but watch her bum. She gains control with grace and elegance, getting in, braking, starting the engine and reversing the car back to us. She gets out and opens the hatchback.

One-handed, I open the cage I keep in the back of the car and the fox is a reluctant prisoner but safe.

She's watching. We exchange glances. I want to kiss but that possibility has fled down the road and we'd have to run faster than time to catch up with it. There's a resentful glint in her eyes and I guess it's because she didn't get her own way in the woods.

"Get in," I say bluntly.

Driving, we hear the laboured breathing of the fox. I'm working out where the nearest rescue centre is but utterly aware of the woman's presence, of the very smell of her and my desperate wanting of her.

At the pub she gets out without a word. I call her back. "You forgot your crop!"

She dips back into the car, her eyes on mine and her lips shaping incredible words. "Did I? It's yours," she says, "as I am – if you ever learn how to use it."

With that she tosses a card at me with a hint of contempt and slams the door loud enough to make the caged fox groan. I watch her walk away, tight jodhpurs and subtle watch-me attitude in motion. My hand grasps the crop. A coulda-shoulda-woulda argument begins its chasing orbit round planet-me.

I thought about joining her in the pub, of course I did, but head instead for the rescue centre, putting twenty miles of safety between me and her.

I didn't want to get involved with some hunt-loving posh woman.

But I'd done that already and I wanted more.

The coulda-shoulda-woulda song has a fast tempo, its orbit is short, because planet-me isn't a big place.

The fox is welcomed at the rescue centre.

As I drive away, my song is stuck on the shoulda verse. I shoulda tied her hands, like she wanted. I shoulda bent her over and whipped her arse.

The coulda verse starts up.

I coulda stripped her, got her out of those jodhpurs.

To me jodhpurs are ugly, *were* ugly, because of the hunting connection, but she'd made them beautiful.

When she was nothing less than naked I coulda got her to the ground and loved her in the leaves with the smell of the earth and the passionate leafy sound of a dead autumn beneath us disturbing the thin cold air. And the splash of her red hair would've been a living pool of autumn in winter. Shoulda. Coulda. Woulda!

And I woulda tied her up . . . but for the kiss. Why did I mess with that break-your-heart kiss stuff?

I pull the car over as if this will stop the song.

I don't know if I'm whip-angry or kiss-in-love with her. We're worlds apart. Arguments bark and squabble through my head. The frightening, inviting leap into madness seems just a moment away, but, in the next moment, *quiet*, nothing but the sound of the engine cooling off and the music of birds in distant trees.

Calm again, I notice the riding crop, the cravat and her card on the passenger seat.

With a deep breath, I reach for the card knowing that I'm picking up her identity, her address.

I expect a posh name like Jocelyn or Pippa but it turns out to be Debbie.

She lives in posh London, that's great and that's crap.

It's crap because she's way out of my reach.

I recall our words as if quoting from an Oscar-winning film.

You forgot your crop

Did I? It's yours– as am I – if you ever learn how to use it.

It's great because it gives me time to learn.

2

Her card gives only a landline number. When the moment comes to make the call, I'm teen-nervous and grown-up wise together. I have every possible variation the conversation might take covered including the worst of all possibilities – that she wouldn't even remember me. But it doesn't go as expected simply because I never expected it to go so perfectly.

I hear her breathy voice say, "Hello."

I reply, "It's me . . ."

The purr of her giggle tells me we are connected again. She says, "Hello, I thought you'd never ring – on bad days, that is. On good days I always knew you would."

We share a breathy silence.

"I still have your crop," I say, trying to sound businesslike, "and I wondered what you'd like me to do with it. I could post it or . . ."

". . . or you could bring it here, on Sunday, early, and use it, we'd have all day long then."

The lightness of her voice rides the thunder of my heart. The casual, ordinary words "and use it" plume in echoes behind every new phone-call moment.

"Oh, by the way—" she says, a harsh slice to her voice.

I interrupt. "Don't worry, I've learnt—"

"I was going to ask," she interrupts back, "what happened to the fox?"

I'm impressed. "I took her to the rescue centre and, when she was strong enough, they invited me to go there and take her back home, release her."

She leaves enough silence to soak up the words before saying quietly, "It was a she then. Good."

I say, "I'll see you on Sunday morning, at ten?"

"I'll expect you from eight—" she giggles, "—and I predict your first words will be: *Here's what's going to happen.*" She mocks my accent and laughing cuts me off.

I smile.

When Sunday comes I pick up the overnight bag I'd so carefully packed so many times over and leave to catch the earliest train. I hate London traffic and won't drive in it even on a Sunday. From the station, I take a short taxi ride into her posh world.

The door pass security code she gave me over the phone purrs in the quiet. I enter the building. Ring her doorbell.

After only moments of delay, she opens the door . . . there's a strip of black tape across her lips. She's in full riding gear, boots and all, and I love that her eyes are awash with uncertainty as mine must be.

The tape tells me she won't talk and that I mustn't kiss.

Even before I set foot in her apartment I say, "First, you're going to take off that hat, shake out your hair."

It's only now I realize how much I've yearned to see that colour again. The stupid hat is discarded and her hair dawns with a shake, as her hands rise automatically to shape and improve perfection but I say, "Don't. Take off your jacket."

She unbuttons it then takes it off provocatively, the action emphasizing her breasts briefly beneath the tightened white blouse. She tosses the jacket aside and again goes to tidy the wildness of her hair but again I say, "Don't. Give me your hands."

I unzip the overnight bag and pull out her cravat from that day and tie her wrists with it.

I glimpse her eyes within the tousled red forest, relieved to find excitement and yearning and uncertainty there.

"One step back."

She obeys.

I enter her apartment, drop the bag inside and back-kick the door shut. Gripping her arms, I walk her backwards until we reach some anonymous wooden door, it might just as well be a tree. I press her against it, pull her arms above her head and she keeps them there. I part the curtain of hair from her face and rest my lips against her taped mouth. I can't help but kiss her and when I've finished the tape is tighter, revealing the shape of her lips. She is breathless.

Now I arrange her hair properly because I want her to see. I go to the bag, fetch the crop, put it down on the carpet by her feet and then quickly, before I can have second thoughts, I rip open her blouse, muttering, "I'll buy you a new one."

She gives a little whelp of shock and then a barely audible moan when I touch her nipples so clearly defined beneath the thin white cotton bra.

I tug the blouse up from the tight waistband of the jodhpurs and say, "Now turn round. Keep your hands high."

She obeys.

I gather the blouse up and tuck it under the straps of her bra – her back is revealed. My hands find her breasts. I kiss the warm flesh of her back. Goosebumps rash over her.

As I pick up the crop and begin to use it on her, I'm nervous.

A pitter-pat pattern of gentle flicks cover her back.

I'm nervous, because I'm unsure. Am I doing this right? Should I ask? For once, being stubborn helps and I persist, as her skin begins to blush pink and then she lets her head bow with a moan of approval and it's all I need.

"That's enough for now," I say, surprised at the husk in my voice. "You can put your hands down and turn around."

She obeys.

There is a bloom of pleasure on her cheeks and desire in her eyes.

I rip the tape off her mouth. She lets out a gasp of pain and the merest flick of a wry smile before I kiss her lips, encouraging her bound hands between my legs. Her fingers explore me. Her breath whispers into mine, "Let me show you where the bedroom is."

In a rush of confidence, I untie her hands, strip off her blouse, but hesitate when it comes to the bra. She reaches behind to unfasten it. I can't decode her smile.

Bare-breasted, she is so achingly beautiful I reach out to touch her, but she grabs my hand, turns and leads me into the bedroom in triumph.

I realize I've lost the initiative. In the sexiest voice I've ever heard she says, "I can undress for you or you can strip me . . ."

The jodhpurs are the all that separate us.

I say, "Here's what's going to happen . . ."

A neutral stillness clouds her eyes.

I keep my voice steady. "In the woods, you said, 'Punish me. I deserve it.' I've dealt lightly with your back, but who told you it was over? You're about to learn what my hand thinks your bum deserves. You're going to bend over."

There's a long pause before she nods.

I say, "Stand back from the bed, put your hands on the bedrail so you're bent over. I want your legs together."

She obeys, making a beautiful shape. The jodhpurs are a good barrier so I smack her hard, left and right, until at last she moans and then I stop.

I step away, waiting for her breathing to quieten. "I can strip you or you can undress."

"Strip me."

I force jodhpurs and panties down together as far as the tops of her boots. "Face me," and then say, "Now you can undress."

She gets herself out of the boots, jodhpurs and panties with impressive elegance.

When she is naked, I say, "Bend over."

Surprise lights in her eyes but she obeys.

Her beautiful bottom is pink.

I start to spank her saying, "This message is from the fox," and continue until she whispers, "Please, stop now."

I obey and she turns and we're kissing.

My hands move over her bum as she undresses me.

We tumble onto her bed; it might as well be a forest floor. The urgent splash of her hair onto searing white sheets is the last thing I remember seeing before feelings overwhelm me.

It's Monday morning before we talk, face to face, in bed, in a twilight we both wish could belong to sunset rather than dawn.

"You warmed my back exquisitely, but a few sharp lashes would have been welcome. Your hand, however, is a thing of beauty."

I touch her cheek. "When I go, I'm taking the crop with me. I'll leave it on the train with a message attached: *This whip is for domestic use only; unsuitable for hunting*." I love her smile and whisper, "So if you want me to whip you again, lady, you'll have to buy a new one. At least then I'll know it's never been used on a horse—"

She interrupts, "Or a protester." Despite the gloom, her fingertip unerringly finds the faintest scar on my cheek as my fingertip finds her again and she closes her eyes.

Later, in the undeniable goodbye of daylight, she's cloaked in a winter robe more silver than black and we're standing at her door again.

I walk away saying, "It's your turn to ring me."

"But I won't," she says.

I turn. Stop.

"Because I don't have your number."

I smile.

"It's under your pillow, my lady."

She smiles.

Later, on the train, thinking back, there's nothing I coulda, shoulda or woulda have done different.

I leave the crop on the train.

I’m Waiting for My Mail

Vina Green

It was his coyness that first attracted me to him. A naivety in his manner that was like a slow-creeping vine, with tendrils that appeared so gradually that by the time I noticed the web which had imperceptibly gathered around me, I was powerless to extract myself, even if I had wanted to.

Our first meeting occurred entirely by chance.

His voice on the intercom was breathy and came out in a squeak at the end. Pleading lifted his tone an octave and made him seem younger than he was.

“I have a package for number twenty-one,” he said. “But they’re not in. Will you take it?” I was number forty-six. He must have pressed nearly every button on the intercom before finding me home.

The security camera was set too low and so instead of framing his face I could see only the bottom half of his throat, a triangle of pale bare flesh delineated by the thick seam of his grey T-shirt cut in a V-neck, which pointed down like an arrow to the parts of him that remained hidden from view. It was raining, and I paused before I replied, distracted by a thick rivulet of water wending its way from the base of his jaw and along the curve of his throat until it managed to climb the small hill of his collarbone before gravity pulled it further downward and out of sight.

“Sure,” I replied, pressing the button that caused the heavy metal security gates to lumber open and swallow him up.

I was dressed, and had been for hours, in Lee Capri jeans

and a soft cotton T-shirt, but when the doorbell whined to signal his arrival I wrapped the silk kimono, usually reserved for straight after bath-time, over the top of my clothes and tied it tightly at the waist. It was white with a cherry blossom pattern, which my husband had once remarked made me look as though I had been shot in the side. My hair hung like a lead weight sandwiched between the kimono and my cotton top. I opened the door with one hand, and slid the other around the back of my neck, freeing my long locks with one swift motion, hair-commercial-esque.

He stood with his toes an inch or two from the threshold, carefully observing the invisible boundary that separated our forthcoming transaction from my private life. His eyes travelled over my silk robe without settling anywhere in particular and then he blinked and looked away.

His reticence roused something in me. Curiosity, I suppose, and, with it, something darker. I wanted to make him uncomfortable, just to see what he would do, in the same way that a child might prod at a cornered spider to observe its response.

I pointed to the piano at the far end of the kitchen. The lid was closed and covered in stray pages of notepaper, the top used as a shelf for keys, pens, stray hairbands.

We spoke at the same time.

"Thank you," he said, extending his arm. "You can leave it inside, over there," I interrupted, ignoring the package in his outstretched hand.

We stood in silence for a moment, engaged in a stand-off between my demand and his obvious desire to remain on the other side of the doorway. I loosened the tie around my waist and then pulled it tighter, knowing that he believed me to be naked beneath my robe and this fact was contributing to his discomfort.

"Over there," I repeated.

His brow furrowed, but he followed my instruction without question, stepping gingerly inside, careful not to bump against the doorway or knock the frame of the baroque mirror that hung on the passageway wall. The sole of his trainers squeaked against the polished wooden floors and he seemed embarrassed by the sound.

He deposited the package, turned to leave and paused at the door again. I leaned against it so that he would need to pass by me closely to slip through. It was a tactic that had been used against me many times in West End nightclubs by groups of men who crowded the path to the ladies' bathrooms, intent on enjoying the press of breasts, thighs and arse as women were forced to squeeze through the tunnels of masculine flesh that trapped them in search of a sly grope. My conscience barely prickled as I used the same manoeuvre against my own quarry.

I watched the almost imperceptible movement of his chest. His heart was beating quickly, as though he'd ignored the elevator and run up the stairs, two at a time. We were about the same height. He was slim, but had the look of a person who had been in their high-school athletics team. Swift, nimble, firm of thigh, someone who flew over footpaths and fields with nimble feet. I imagined how his chest would move when he ran. In out, in out, in out, an exertion measured in deliberate breaths, with the metronomic precision of a person blessed with both youth and fitness. He shook his head slightly and ran his hand over his brow, wiping away drips of moisture. His eyes were the improbable blue of the lead singer in a boy band, his eyebrows twin bridges over top. Did he pluck them? He didn't seem like the sort of person who would.

I knew that he wanted to leave. I was trapping him inside, if only for a few moments. I didn't care. He was a trespasser in my home, though admittedly not of his own accord. I turned and looked out of the window. The steady drizzle outside had become a torrent. He would be soaked through in seconds.

"Don't they give you a van?" I asked him.

"No," he replied, "I cycle."

That explained the improbably firm upward curve of his arse. He must cover a lot of hills in his daily mail round.

His hair, damp, was brown, though might have been blonder dry. He ran his hand through it, impatient.

"Thanks again," he said, with a nod so slight I nearly missed it. I nodded back, a quick, sharp motion of chin to jaw, and he ducked beneath my arm and slipped past me without brushing so much as his T-shirt against my robe.

The package was addressed to a Mr. A. Abrahams, another neighbour who I didn't know and didn't care to. The name irritated me, in the unnecessary formality of a title and initial preceding a surname that ought to have been a first name, were it not for the "s" clinging onto the end like a poor excuse for a spelling mistake. I ran the sharp point of my thumbnail under the envelope's seal and extracted the contents, an illustrated book about ancient Rome. The subject didn't interest me particularly, but the pictures did, and the images that my mind created when inspired by thoughts of muscled gladiators baking under a hot sun and oiled slave boys taken advantage of by their rich masters. Yes, it would do, nicely. I took the book to the couch by the window and fell backwards with a whump, and lay with my back flat and my feet over the sofa's arm, crossed at the ankles.

I tried to read, but couldn't. My mind kept returning to the postman, and in particular the beads of moisture that had gathered on the back of his neck and might have been rain, or sweat, or both. I had wanted to grab him by the scruff of his neck like a kitten, drag him backwards through the doorway and run my tongue along his shoulder blades, just to see how he tasted. I imagined him coated in a washed-out saltiness, like the sea-salt tang of a fresh oyster. I let the book slip from my hands and fall to the floor and then arced my back over the other end of the sofa so my head hung down and the blood rushed into it creating the sort of dizziness that I imagined auto-asphyxiation might produce but without the corresponding risk. I flattened my hand and wriggled my palm from side to side to gain access to my knickers, trapped beneath the tight denim waistband of my jeans.

* * *

Masturbation was my secret pleasure, and also how I passed the time. I enjoyed it beyond the simple joy, and the physical release of an orgasm. My mons and lips are permanently bare, the result of laser hair removal treatment. Not, as Mark, my husband, believes, for his benefit, but for my own. I love the feeling of my soft smooth skin, particularly when I'm wet, and I like the look of my naked cunt, the way the V shape sits so proudly visible at the top of my thighs. Bold, inviting, perverse.

When we had worked together – Mark my employer, me his PA – I had taken regular breaks to sneak into the disabled toilets and finger myself to orgasm before carefully repositioning my skirt, straightening my stockings and modestly buttoning an extra button on my blouse. I would then enter his office with some spurious excuse – to deliver a letter that had arrived for him hours earlier, a cup of tea or an urgent message – and sashay near him until he finally draped me over his desk and fucked me from behind.

"God," he would say, "you're so wet. And tight."

I had never admitted that was because I had made myself come minutes earlier.

Of course, he thought that he had seduced me, never the reverse. I simply went along with it, although I wasn't in love with him. Like a cork bobbing along in the sea, carried by invisible currents to directions unknown. We had been married five years and I had stopped working partly as he seemed to prefer it that way. He liked to act the caveman, going out each morning to make a living and leaving his wife at home to play house. He wanted children. I kept my birth control pills hidden beneath the kitchen sink and took them after he left for the office.

Sometimes I spent entire days wanking.

I masturbated according to my mood. If I was feeling particularly rebellious or filthy, I would watch pornography. The sort that I guessed Mark would be horrified to find me watching. Not your run-of-the-mill, fake-titted blonde gyrating against a cock large enough to split a woman in two, or the porn pedalled as woman-friendly erotica, black and white and arty and often featuring a chubby brunette touching herself while an equally atypical female friend watches in a show of feminist solidarity. No, I watched fat, old men grinding against young co-eds, their fat bellies jiggling like sausage meat jello, or fake-rape scenarios that featured angry jilted husbands and cheating wives. I regularly got off on the sort of thing that would have me forever barred from the sisterhood.

When I was feeling more indulgent, I ran baths, lit candles and slowly massaged myself to climax. At times I was more imaginative. I clamped my own nipples, painstakingly tied myself to a kitchen chair and ground my clit against the thick length of rope I held between my teeth. I had come on every flat surface in each room of the house. It was either that or spend my days doing housework and watching television, and I preferred wanking. I was supposed to be practising music, with the aim to advertise around the local area for students and become a piano teacher. The perfect career, Mark thought, for a stay-at-home mum. But instead I used the instrument as a shelf to stack unopened mail on.

That day, he came home from work to find me asleep on the sofa with my hand down my pants.

"Did you miss me, baby?" he joked, waking me with a wet kiss on the lips. He did not, as I thought he might, remark on the fact that I had not started dinner despite being home all day. I felt a pang of guilt, and so ignored the fact that he tasted of cigarette smoke masked with peppermints although he had supposedly given up smoking.

"Like a hole in the head," I replied, covering my mouth as the last word turned into a yawn.

It had begun as a joke between us, this eschewing of what we both saw as saccharine romance that pervaded modern romantic life. Mark refused to celebrate Valentine's Day, thought flowers and chocolates were pointless and claimed that we had never dated, merely gotten used to each other, like wearing in a new pair of shoes. There was some truth in that fact. We had never dated, just had sex in his office regularly until he proposed.

"I'm making spaghetti," he called from the kitchen. "With tomato and red wine sauce."

"I'll just have the red wine," I yelled back.

I stretched out on the couch, easing the cramp in my legs. The gap between the denim waistband of my jeans and my skin that had seemed so tight earlier now felt like a yawning, empty cavern. All of the muscles in my pelvis were alive and itching with the need to be touched. I considered joining Mark in the kitchen and surreptitiously giving him a hard-on so we could fuck, but discarded the option as too time consuming. He was the type of man who liked to think that he was the horny one and me the unwitting object of his desire, so working him into the mood was always an elaborate game that took both time and subtlety and right now I couldn't be bothered.

Instead, I pretended to fall back asleep until the twilight outside had turned to the thick darkness of night and Mark had long ago drifted upstairs to bed alone, leaving a mess of pots decorated with sticky globs of spaghetti, and a bowlful of pasta out on the bench.

While I was dozing, I let my mind run amok. Thoughts of the mailman consumed me. I smiled as I daydreamed, remembering some of the more clichéd adult video clips that had often fuelled my masturbatory sessions. Plumbers seduced by their middle-aged female clientele, electricians who find themselves creating a spark more than they planned for. I picked up the book he had delivered again and ran my forefinger along its spine.

Then I reached for my laptop.

First, there was the matter of deciding what to purchase. A book? A DVD? I considered the options in my mind as if they were stones, each of them carrying the weight of possibility. Finally, I opted for a boyish pyjama set. Sexy, in an understated way. Blue and white cotton short shorts, a baby-blue vest with a thin line of white lace bordering a V-neck, spaghetti straps.

At the online checkout I selected "gift wrap" and "express order" although I knew that the package itself, as per the website's delivery policy, would be wrapped in discreet brown paper, surely advertising to all that the parcel within must be either lingerie or a sex toy. The "gift wrap" option would ensure that the pyjamas arrived in a box, which would be too thick for the mail slot, so he would need to buzz. Delivery was scheduled for the day after tomorrow.

It was near 1 a.m. by the time I entered the bedroom, slipped off my robe, jeans, and blouse and slid into bed next to Mark. He was lying on his back, snoring softly. I brushed my lips softly against his and he stirred briefly but didn't wake. Whether motivated by guilt or by arousal, I'm not sure, but instead of settling into sleep next to him, I slid down his body, kissing the length of his torso until I reached the loose drawstring on his pyjama pants. I reached inside and flopped out his cock. It was soft, warm and small in the palm of my hand but beginning to twitch into life. His breathing changed, becoming less regular as he shifted to wakefulness. He didn't acknowledge me. Perhaps he thought he was dreaming. I took the nub of his flaccid penis, no bigger than my thumb, into my mouth and sucked with the desperation of a hungry baby attached to a nipple until his cock grew into fullness and his breath became fast and ragged. His hands found the top of my head and he knotted his fingers in my hair and guided my head up and down as if he was correcting the movement of the steering wheel on a car. He came within a minute or two, and I held his come in my mouth for a few moments before I swallowed, savouring the bittersweet tang of him.

Mark maintained the embarrassed silence of a man who has come to soon and has no intention of returning the favour, and I shuffled up the bed and fell asleep alongside him with the taste of his semen lingering in my mouth as I dreamed.

The following day drifted by slowly though not unpleasantly, as I spent most of it in a post-orgasmic blur, watching film clips of older women seducing younger men. Muscled pool-boys and vulnerable stepsons, or the beefy brawn of high school quarterbacks. Each of them seemed modestly delighted by the interest taken in them, as I hoped the object of my attentions would be.

When the appointed delivery date arrived, I carefully washed and blow-dried my hair, so it settled around my shoulders in gentle waves. I considered wearing the silk robe again, or a negligée, but not wanting to look desperate or slovenly I opted for a tight white vest top and push-up bra over a pair of black knit leggings that I sometimes wore to yoga classes and knew highlighted the cleft of my ass cheeks perfectly. I had filed my nails short and painted them a rich shade of purple.

My nipples hardened the moment I heard the buzz on the intercom.

"Package for you," he squeaked. Again I was rewarded with a brief triangle of bare flesh on the video screen. My finger trembled as I pressed the button that opened the gate.

The minute or so I had to wait as he crossed the paved driveway and made his way up the steps to our apartment gave me time to think about what I would do next. Thus far my fantasies had only included his appearance on the intercom and then our sexual exploits, conveniently overlooking the crucial exchange that would lead us from one point to the next.

Would I invite him in? Hope that he sustained some injury on the short walk to my front door that I could offer to bandage? Spill a drink over the crotch of his trousers that I would then enthusiastically dab with a cloth?

Everything was so simple in romance novels, and even simpler in pornography.

In the end though, his seduction was easier than I expected.

"Do you play?" he asked.

It took me a moment or two to realize that he meant the piano, which I had again indicated he should leave the parcel on.

"I teach, actually," I replied.

The words rolled off my tongue before I even realized they were a lie.

"Oh," he said. "How wonderful. I've just inherited a piano. From my grandmother."

I nodded, encouragingly. He spoke as though he had been born fifty years ago, somewhere posh, but rural. He had the voice of a landowning English countryman, someone who might play polo and spend weekends messing about near a boathouse.

"Do you play?" I asked him.

"No. I've been meaning to arrange piano lessons. But I've just been using it as a hallway table instead." He laughed awkwardly, and shifted from one foot to the other, waiting for a polite moment to end the conversation and leave.

"That's a shame," I said. "I could show you some scales. If you can spare the time."

He looked at his wrist and blushed when he realized he wasn't wearing a watch. His hands were large and his arms long. His limbs seemed almost slightly out of proportion for his body, as he was only slightly taller than me, but the effect was endearing rather than gangly.

"I have time," he said.

I sat down on the piano seat, lifted the burnished wooden lid and patted the small space alongside me, indicating that he should join me.

He lowered himself onto the stool slowly. I held my thigh firmly against his, not bothering to create any semblance of personal space.

"I'm Simona, by the way," I said as I ran my fingers gently over the keys.

"George," he said. "But everyone calls me Georgie."

He turned towards me as he introduced himself and I caught the scent of his breath. It was either coffee or chocolate, or a mixture of the two, I couldn't be sure. His mouth was wide and his lips unusually red, as though he had been bitten.

I touched his arm.

"Would you like a drink, before we start?" I asked him.

"I probably shouldn't stay too long," he replied.

His jaw was covered in the faintest hint of stubble.

I wanted to ask him how old he was, but it seemed too personal a question.

So I leaned forward and kissed him instead. First, just a soft, lingering kiss on the mouth, which it was clear that I had instigated. The second kiss followed almost immediately and this time we were like two lovers, each kissing the other. Our mouths opened and our tongues touched, a brief exchange of moisture. His arms remained firmly pinned to his sides and his body angled towards the piano, just his head turned to face me. He was following my lead, a confused but willing participant. I lifted my hands to his face and brushed my thumb against his lower lip and over his throat and he tilted his head to the side and moaned, softly. His neck was long, slim, graceful. My palms travelled over the fabric of his shirt, brushed across the tiny points of his nipples, squeezed the meaty flesh of his biceps, found the firm curve of his waist and the hard line of his hip bones.

He was holding my head in his hands now, his fingers tangled in my hair as he sucked my lower lip into his mouth, ran his tongue across my teeth. His breathing had the ragged, furious edge of an animal seeking a way out of a trap.

The piano stool creaked beneath us. It was narrow, and ill suited to carry even one person comfortably unless they were seated ramrod straight with knees bent at right angles. I lifted one leg over his in one swift motion and straddled him. His cock was rock hard beneath his shorts and I ground against it, but no matter how forcefully I moved my hips I could not achieve any more than a light rub of his tip against my clit. We were separated by geometry and the rustle of his shorts against my leggings.

I licked the curve of his ear and then pressed my mouth against him and whispered, "I want to fuck you." He uttered a noise somewhere between a growl and a groan and nodded his head, scraping the stubble on his cheek against my face as he did so.

Had I been seated as he was and blessed with extra human strength I would have risen with his legs still wrapped around me and carried him on my waist to the bedroom as men do. Instead, I slid my legs down onto the floor, my backside catching the piano keys in the process and then took his hand and pulled him to the couch. He nearly tripped as he hurried to follow me and then discovered the distance to the destination I was leading him to was just a few feet.

Our movements lacked the easy synchronicity of first-time fucks that I had experienced with other men. Then, I had felt assured in my role as the seduced rather than the seducer. A routine tune that I had danced to many times before. I would tilt my head to the side and laugh at all their jokes, run my forefinger around my wine glass, let my skirt slide up a little too high as I shimmied out of a booth seat to use the ladies' room. They would buy me too many drinks, lay a hand lightly on the small of my back as I exited the restaurant door, hail a cab with an air of authority usually reserved for policemen and the military. Pull me into their arms, lift me onto the bed, move my limbs into the desired position, let me nestle my head under their arm afterwards as we fell into post-coital slumber.

My first time with Georgie was different. We barely spoke. Given the unusual situation, conversation would have been awkward at best. It was easier to stave off any prospect of small talk by keeping our mouths full with each other's tongue. He waited for my implied permission before touching me in any new way at all. He kissed me back when I kissed him, lifted my T-shirt when I lifted his, slid his hands beneath my bra and groped my breasts after I had freed his cock. But it was obvious that by taking each of those steps he was crossing another Rubicon and he did so with brief hesitation followed by the great gusto that a starving man might apply when finally allowed access to a buffet, or an alcoholic who concedes defeat at a free bar.

Fucking him was like teaching a foal to walk, and I found that I liked it.

I liked it a great deal.

When I took his cock deep into my throat, he moaned and arched his back like a woman, like I did when I was beneath a man who had just hit the perfect spot. When I let his dick fall out of my mouth before he could come, he groaned in pain. When I crawled up his body, straddled his thighs and slid my cunt down over his cock, he gasped with pleasure. He exploded inside me the moment I wrapped my hands around his throat and choked him as I ground my body hard against his. After I then slid onto his face and had him lick my clit until I orgasmed, and dripped his semen back into his mouth in the process, he was hard again.

And that was when I decided that I would very much like to see Georgie again.

"I suppose you need to go. And deliver some other people's parcels," I said to him as I lifted myself up from his mouth, stood up from the couch and pulled on my knickers. I ignored the sight of his erect-again penis. I wanted him to want to come back for more.

He ran his tongue over his lips, stared at the ceiling, and then glanced at his watchless wrist. His eyes were wide, like a child who has just been given a present so big he doesn't know what to do with it.

"Shit," he said, "I have to go."

"No problem," I replied, slipping on my leggings and top. I left my bra lying on the floor, knowing that my nipples would be visible through the thin white fabric that covered my breasts. He stared at my chest as I dressed.

"Uhh . . . thank you," he said, as I held open the door. I leaned forward, took a fistful of his shirt into my hand and pulled him back towards me for another kiss.

"You're welcome," I replied, after I had extracted myself from his mouth.

I shut the door.

Caution persuaded me to shower, but I didn't want to. I wanted to let his scent linger on my skin, sleep with his fluid still inside me. Instead, I scrubbed myself carefully from head to toe, moved the scattered envelopes back onto the piano lid and straightened the cushions on the sofa to their usual positions. I tried to avoid acting too much out of character in case

Mark's suspicions were aroused, but I couldn't avoid being more cheerful than usual. Fucking the postman had filled me with an unmistakable inner glow. Not just a pleasant post-sex haze but the thrill of the seducer, like a young tiger who has successfully taken down her first prey.

That night, I ordered lingerie. A purple baby doll negligée with a deep red trim and tiny silk bows stitched to the base of each thin spaghetti strap. It came with matching panties. I chose the full briefs, not the G-string, and selected the complimentary gift box and nominated day delivery for the following Tuesday. Enough time for him to wonder whether he had dreamed the whole thing and for me to plan for his arrival with joyful anticipation.

It rained on Tuesday, and he arrived on my doorstep sodden from head to toe. I pulled him inside as he rang the doorbell, pushed him down onto the floor and fucked him almost fully clothed, just the button and zip on his shorts down far enough for me to get access to his cock. My thighs were red afterwards where our wet skin had chafed with the surprising dryness that water causes during sex. I didn't offer him a towel afterwards. He left the packet on the floor, buttoned his shorts again and left no later than ten minutes after he had arrived.

I continued ordering parcels, and we fucked like that for weeks. Very gradually though, Georgie began to change.

I first noticed it when he went down on me. We had been lying side by side, on the sofa, and he wriggled down my body and began to lap gently at my slit. He ran his tongue over my clit with the delicacy of an artist working in miniature and, as he did so, I forgot all sense of the way we had been together so far, the unspoken rules that I had created for us. His mouth transported me to some place where nothing mattered, besides pleasure. My limbs became weak and pliable and he grasped my thighs in his hands and held me down as he thrust his tongue inside my hole as if he were fucking me with his cock.

The next time, he flipped me over onto my belly and lifted me up onto my knees and ran his tongue over the full length of my cleft before concentrating on my arsehole. I gasped, and I knew that he now had the power that comes with being the first person to bestow a new pleasure on another. He pushed me back down onto my stomach, lifted my knee to a right angle and ploughed me from behind with so much of his weight in each thrust that the sofa bounced across the wooden floor and slammed into the wall with both of us on it.

And then one day he arrived at the doorbell without a delivery for me, when I hadn't ordered anything at all.

His eyes were alight with confidence and he met my gaze without any hesitation or downward glance. He held his shoulders back and stood straight, defiant.

"Hi," he said.

His voice still held its usual inflection, a slight falter, and a high note at the end that asked a question, although a question had not been asked, but one of his feet was already stepping through the doorway, and his mouth was on mine before I could reply.

Georgie knew that he had me then. I'd never told him so, but I knew that he knew he was the only one who ran his tongue over my arsehole, who could hold me hostage by the way he flicked my clit. He had made me a slave to his mouth.

Mark never found out. The lingerie remained hidden, still wrapped in the packaging it had arrived in, untouched in the back of my wardrobe. I stopped ordering parcels. And after that one last time, Georgie didn't return.

Perhaps he moved away, quit the postal service altogether, or transferred to another route. More likely though, he sensed that some of the magic between us was lost when he had taken over the reins, and sex between us became ordinary, banal, the stuff that other people did with predictable regularity and outcomes.

I saw him once, many months later. He was standing on a street corner with his arm draped over the shoulders of a girl.

She was petite, much shorter than he was and nestling her head against his chest. She looked through me as though I wasn't there. He met my eyes, glanced down, and looked away.

I never saw him again.

Autumn, Naked, Far from Paris

N. T. Morley

The live-work loft has a single window, floor to ceiling, dating to the twenties; the panes of glass are warped, some slightly, some more so; together they give a wicked cast to Autumn's actions, as if the world is split in two worlds, equally warped: as above, so below. The window shows the desk; it shows the loft. It shows the bed. It shows work and wank with equal clarity: always naked, far from Paris.

She spends one week and weekend, Monday to Sunday, framed thus – twelve, fifteen hours working downstairs at the desk, but with frequent trips upstairs, as she's been ordered. Downstairs, she gazes at the screen, sipping coffee in the mornings, spring water in the afternoons, tea-then-wine by evening. Estonian texts sprawl languidly about her. She is naked. It is not warm; it can't be warm inside that loft, because lofts do not grow warm in San Francisco, except when their residents do not wish them to.

The sky this time of year is predictably grey, and savagely disinterested; it hangs far above, not asking questions. But the residents of the building opposite their loft, in fact, do ask questions; were it a different neighbourhood, a different city, they might ask different questions, louder ones – even questions of the police, who would visit her with their close-cropped hair and embarrassed eyes and ask her to put some clothes on.

They would receive a tart response; what might happen then is, really, anybody's guess. Autumn – ironically – does not take orders well.

But those who live in lofts, in converted warehouses, in live-work spaces, occupy a tiny brotherhood, or like to think they do; of a certain age and very rarely blessed with children, they take the universe as it comes, as does the naked girl with a knack for Finno-Ugric languages. She sits there nude, tossing glances at her fellow city dwellers between struggling with memes and phrases; the arousal of their watching focuses her fiercely. It helps her know her place. A dozen neighbours, in a flow from 6 a.m. to midnight, sometimes longer, regard her curiously, approvingly. Several even wank; a few fuck. There is no negotiation; Autumn doesn't do that. She's a wicked, wicked girl, a very naughty one, earning a spanking or ten or a thousand, and prudent pervs now reading this may feel wrong, wrong, wrong for liking it, or self-righteous for disapproving, as is their wont. Self-righteous pervs: the cops don't visit. Numerous orgasms are had; it's a good week South of Market. It's San Francisco, dear, we do that sort of thing.

When Autumn's upstairs, framed in the top part of the great loft window for hours or minutes – once, on Friday, forty-five seconds start-to-finish – the texts scattered about her are different ones; forbidden, their titles would likely shock a Parisian, and would surely shock you. She lingers on them as she lingers on her language books – with relish, sometimes boredom, sometimes both. The upstairs being slightly warmer, she does not show as many goosebumps, but she feels them, always, in places wicked to contemplate.

As the week progresses, more is said than done, but much is done. The gay couple on the third floor has joked about breaking out their binoculars and counting the poor girl's goosebumps; one of them, graciously, admits he prefers her nipples, which leads to an interesting discussion between the long-term partners. The lesbians on four then fuck in front of her; graciously, she set down *Grammatiline Harjutused* and wanked back in return, face warm with arousal and embarrassment as they blew her kisses. The straight couple on two watches, wryly smiling, making out; the single yuppie woman walks upon her treadmill, staring mildly, for an hour more than usual – and smiles, wordless and glowing, when she and Autumn face each other across the marinated tofu and iced watercress at Orga(s)nix, the vegan restaurant six blocks away.

Not a single watcher calls the cops, and no one closes curtains. The loft grows warm when she runs the gas range. Sometimes the windows steam up. After that happens a couple of times, someone leaves a squeegee tucked into Autumn's security door. There's a happy face drawn in Sharpie on the handle.

She wanks openly for them, with dildos, wanting them to watch – because Julian wants them to watch.

Neighbours blow her kisses; SOMA! Quite a place. Prudent pervs there push the envelope, and feel bad and good at once; that, friends, is the idea.

Autumn and her lover Julian had evolved a rather curious exchange of authority and dominance: he owned her utterly, and she did not question.

Oh, to be sure, she pouted, glowed, inclined her head; she cocked her hips; she narrowed her eyes; she bit her lip every now and then, earning a hot pair of buns for her efforts.

But whine? Bitch? Moan? Say, "No, please, Sir, no, Sir, don't make me?" Fat chance; she's not the type. She merely trembles, and says, "Yes, Sir," deep eyes sparkling, diamonds.

This is not a recommended style of submission; in fact, in the absence of lightning striking, or explicit off-camera negotiating, it's almost guaranteed to bum you out, and probably your partner, too. But Autumn had been very lucky. Julian was in some ways luckier still.

Autumn had accepted, and never questioned, Julian's ownership despite his frequent orders that she do dangerous, wicked, even foolhardy things. In fact, she wildly craved it, practically bursting with excitement when she intuited, from the familiar if slight inclination of his jawline or the narrowing of his eyes that he was about to issue a proclamation she would find at best problematic, and at worst unacceptable – but would, nonetheless, obey.

Was she ever placed at risk? This is the question that you, readers, may be asking yourselves, or me; since I can't hear you, I shall only offer this, friends: Define "risk". Would Julian have hurt her? No. Allowed her to be hurt? He would have died, in fact, to prevent it. Allowed her to be arrested?

Well . . . you know, arrested isn't *hurt*, exactly. Maybe he's a bit of a scoundrel, but then, she rather goes for that.

Julian gave Autumn orders frequently. He commanded his plaything to be naked as much as possible during his work trip to Paris. It was the type of order that sent her spinning into tangled sensations of arousal and dismay. She found it – and, in finding it so, became fiercely wet and ravenous at knowing she would do it, and enjoy it; in fact, she'd love it.

The couple's long-term arrangement had been achieved in an improbable fashion. It was one that some prudent sexual epicures would consider unacceptable. Their power exchange had not been explicitly negotiated. It had not been established by contract or discussion or endless process of checking things off lists or writing memoirs about how it feels to be held down and spanked or to pull a lithe girl's hair or how a deep sense of desired violent dominance represented the profoundest sense of love. Had any such things been expected, Autumn and Julian – both dangerous romantics, and rabidly impatient in their calmest moments – would have rolled their eyes and moved on in interest, perhaps to watercolour painting or bug collecting. There lived in each of them the very real possibility that, required to behave in fashions intolerable to them – actually intolerable, as opposed to merely unacceptable – in order to achieve sexual congress and an acting-out of deeply held perversions with a "normal" person, either one of them might instead find solace in a shuttered life, with begged-for dates begged off with proclamations of hectic schedules, heterosexuality, homosexuality, or an unseen husband/wife in the attic/shed/basement, as the circumstances required.

But that was not to be, for they had found each other.

This had occurred during one of Julian's many forays into attempted "normalcy". His manufactured persona being wicked of interest and smarmy of character, he had invited Autumn to his fourth-floor loft to watch 1975's *Story of O.* When the explicit scenes of punishment failed to arouse any reaction in Autumn other than a sort of slit-lidded stare and pursed lips, he assumed he had been wrong in thinking that, with eyes like that, the girl had to be kinky. Or perhaps, as he had expected all along, Julian was merely too old for her. A difference of ten years can be a lifetime.

And so, when the girl suggested they view the DVD alongside *Story* on the shelf, which happened to be *9½ Half Weeks*, Julian was puzzled, shocked, and more than a little tormented. Autumn's rigid body language did not convey the sense of a woman wishing to view *9½ Weeks*, or just having viewed *Story of O.* The woman's perceived refusal to make eye contact with Julian convinced him that she had filed him in the category of, "Men with interesting shit at their houses", and, surely spurred by the opinion that he was too old, had decided never to go further.

It was thus that as he viewed *9½ Weeks*, a film countless straight men have used as an excuse to suggest their girlfriends consent to threesomes and an obligation to frequent anal sex, with a wispy grey coquette curled up on his couch, instead of suggesting rampant debauchery Julian sat politely on the far end of an Ikea futon, cradling his beetle-handled walking stick. He stared blankly at the screen, thinking, *How did I get her so wrong? She seemed like such a perv*, and considered whether, as he would surely rise early tomorrow without a naked vixen in his bed, he should devote the next morning to obtaining the Malaysian Stink Cricket or the Altaic Monarch, or possibly the Saharan Whirligig Beetle for his collection; he had the money to buy them all, but tried to limit himself to one bug a week so he could really savour them.

The credits rolled.

Autumn said tartly: "That girl was a cunt."

Julian, who had drifted off into the consideration of the Atlantic Death Moth as an alternative to either of the creatures thus far coveted, thought surely he had misheard her.

"What did you say?" he asked.

Autumn wheeled on him, her spindly frame nearly tucked into a ball with her bare feet under her ass; her battered combat boots sat stuffed with thigh-high horizontally striped socks beside the futon.

Her neck was flushed, slightly; she had unbuttoned a single button of her pale, thin hippie shirt, which was not long on buttons to begin with. At this time, perched ass-on-ankles with her knees pointed several directions, she toppled slightly and barely caught herself, resulting in a savage swirl of her long black crepe-cotton skirt.

The result was that Julian discovered three things in a great violent rush: she was not wearing a bra, she was not wearing panties, and her nipples were exceedingly hard.

She brushed her hair back. "I said, that woman was a *cunt*," she said, with fervent emphasis on the last word Julian expected to hear from her.

Julian reacted as if slapped hard in the face – which, if you knew what he'd had in mind for the girl when he'd scheduled this date, would seem rather ironic.

"Was she?"

"If she didn't want to do it," said Autumn, "why'd she do it?"

Julian groped after words.

Autumn gave a violent, improbable gesture, which consisted of her cocking her head and jerking it back and forth while bearing a wide-eyed expression of incredulity and outrage, all the while thrusting her splayed fingers towards the ceiling.

"I mean—" she said, and finished the sentence by flipping off the TV screen, with both fingers. "Just—" she said, and repeated the gesture. "I mean, seriously—" she said, and did it again. "Am I right?" She did it a fourth time.

"Well," said Julian gallantly. "The man was rather a cunt as well. They both were."

"She was bigger."

"Oh," said Julian. "Um. You don't think he was worse?"

"What the fuck?" she said, and flipped the screen off again and again, in savage, rolling hand-to-hand gestures that looked, at a distance of five feet, something vaguely like kneading invisible bread.

"Good point," said Julian weakly.

"I mean, she obviously totally got off on it," said Autumn, adding as an afterthought, "So—!" She flipped the screen off some more for a while.

His heart rather pounding, Julian took a deep breath and said, "Do *you* get off on it?"

Her hands dropped to her thinly clad thighs. "What the fuck?" said Autumn, with tangible outrage.

Julian shied away, expecting her next words to be those of reproach, rejection, the assigning of leper status.

He thought he'd go for the stink beetle when it came down to it, but there was still time to choose.

Instead, she said: "Christ, does a girl have to hit men with a mallet to get laid around here?"

It would be the closest thing to an explicit negotiation they would ever have, when Julian said softly, "No," and, hands trembling, came for her.

She fitted over his knee like she was *made* for it.

Between the time Julian first took her over his knee, and the time he left for a week abroad, there had been many incidences where Julian's assertions – orders – had been challenging or difficult for Autumn; she often objected in her mind. But she was not one of those girls who wished to whine and whimper about every command, only to be gagged or spanked or told she had to be a good girl. She wanted all those things, but had better ways of getting them. To say aloud, "No, please, I can't, don't make me," would be, for Autumn, dangerously close to an explicit negotiation, something that made her want to reach for her revolver.

Again, prudent perverts would drop dead of heart attacks

upon hearing this sentiment, and may even now across the nation be lying naked in bed inert with this book in their laps, fallen humming vibrators slowly overheating next to their cooling bodies as their souls limp, outraged, towards perv Valhalla.

We can dream.

But pouting? Glaring? Pursing her lips? Lord, the girl was an expert! The pouts on that girl! The glares! The gritted teeth! The politely angry passive-aggressive inclinations of the head, the narrowing of the eyes, the squaring of the shoulders! She was a genius! She simmered and seethed with the weapons of domestic terrorism; previous lovers, possessed of reasonable manipulability, had succumbed to a withering glance. Julian knew better – somewhat inexplicably, since he was rather a retiring man and, prior to Autumn's taking up residence across his lap, not well versed in the ways of the feminine gender. Julian treated Autumn with the firm hand her brilliant pouting deserved; not once did she mewl the word, "No," nor did she want to; she knew if she did, they'd have to talk about it, and if it came down to that she'd pack her bags first.

(Prudent perverts? Don't read on. You're in the belly of the beast; no, really, skip it.)

And so when Julian, one hand planted firmly on the beetle handle of his walking stick, the other stuffed firmly up Autumn's skirt as she writhed over his lap with her filmy, barely there black lace-mesh panties around her ankles, the pink embroidered "Sunday" tangled up around her combat boots. Julian had ordered her to begin wearing these panties daily for the sole reason that she had gone a dozen years without wearing anything of the sort. On her birthday, he'd unveiled the set of seven pairs as a gift to her; he'd seen in her eyes the violent flare of rebellion he expected – the same outrage he was very used to, of a brand that spelled sharp and sudden arousal.

"Yes, of course, Sir, thank you," she'd said coldly, and he'd spanked her for that coldness, until she came so hard she left furrows in his thighs, knees, calves, and ankles – all of this through his woollen suit pants. Christ, the claws on that girl!

The panties proceeded Monday to Sunday with each pair sluttier than the last, *Sunday* being the tartiest of the set. All day on Sunday ever since, Autumn radiated to acquaintances and strangers alike vast dangerous possibilities of misbehaviour, even if wearing coveralls. This was probably more about Autumn than the panties – but one works with the tools he is given.

Every time since that Julian had had cause or desire to draw down those panties, or to order Autumn to draw them down so he could see her, he'd been gratified by seeing the filmy crotches soaked and sticky – most of all each Sunday.

In this instance, however, on the Sunday evening not twelve hours before Julian's departure for Paris, the panties were not remotely soaked to his satisfaction. Autumn had experienced a frustrating day of copy-editing language books in the study Julian had built for her in the corner of their loft; far behind schedule, her employer had insisted she bust her ass – which was normally Julian's job – and rescue a disastrous Estonian textbook from the clutches of mediocrity. She had complied, but not without pouting, something for which Julian felt empowered but not inclined to spank her; asshat publishers deserve a pout or two now and then, and Autumn was well within her rights to pout so loud the jackasses could hear her three thousand miles away; Julian, in fact, so very much in love with her, owed his girl a round of applause, not a spanking.

And yet? He would also owe her a spanking, because he was groping for a reward.

"I think you'll go naked while I'm gone," he said, as he fingered her, her pussy dry, her G-spot soft and almost undetectable against the pads of his index and middle fingers. Her clit was not even, really, erect. She seemed bored.

"Yes, of course, Sir," she said with a sigh, as if humouring him. Going naked was de rigueur for her; she had lived without panties or bras for twelve years before meeting him, and shucked her clothes at the first opportunity – nowadays assuming she was permitted, of course, such indulgence by Julian.

But in this instance Julian quickly realized his misstep. Intending to provide a reward for her hard work and her taciturn acceptance of his upcoming absence, he had instead provided something she calmly accepted; it was familiar. As a result, the dark resistance Autumn craved could not be provided by the gift of simple nudity; had she worked in an office, sure, that would have been sensuously humiliating, but she translated at home, seven days a week, and rarely went out except to retrieve goodies from the salad bar at Orga(s)nix six blocks away, which also gave her the opportunity to show off her combat boots to the trio of foot fetishists in the cheese section – something she craved almost as much as she craves spankings and, conveniently enough, was often spanked for.

But it would not have been practical for Julian to have Autumn go naked down the street to Orga(s)nix – though their coop by-laws did, in fact, establish it rather belligerently as a Clothing Optional Fair Trade Organic Produce Market, the city Health Department would almost surely disagree were the dictum ever tested; furthermore, the six blocks there and six blocks back would be tacitly if not explicitly dangerous for her – and in any event would be probably more than Julian was going for, like killing a mosquito with a bazooka.

He needed a save.

That the opportunity for nudity had met with soft acceptance rather than the resistance Autumn craved was demonstrated by the fact that she was still not very wet; in fact, against his fingers, her sex was verging on dry. She did not, it seems, find Estonian as sensuous a language as did Julian, who had listened to all his beloved reading phrases aloud to check translations; it had driven him nearly to distraction. In fact, after a day of that lilting Finno-Ugric cadence, he was ready to erupt. The slightest jostle of her hips could probably send him off, and he knew at a command from him the girl would make short work of his belt and his suit pants, and give the shortest blowjob of her life; that would not do. Julian had made it a policy never to pop before Autumn; to do so, he felt, would be ungentlemanly.

And while Autumn would normally be gushing six minutes into an over-the-knee panties-around-ankles spank-jerk and finger-fuck, in this case she was dry, or almost so. The girl was stressed. She needed the big guns to get her going; Julian, thankfully, was wicked of nature and fearless of perv.

"With the windows open," he said.

Across his lap, she stiffened. She froze; she ceased breathing; she became, by his estimate, mildly anoxic.

Her pussy tightened so firmly around his fingers that he knew another instant would bring—well, more on that momentarily.

"What?" she said.

"Is that a question? Are you questioning me?"

"N-no, Sir. No, no, no, Sir." In another submissive, surely, the tremble in her voice, the sudden desperate wriggle of her bum, would come from fear of punishment for questioning; in Autumn's case, it came from the crash of two concomitant factors: acceptance and resistance.

"Of course, Sir, thank you, Sir, I will, Sir." She was now whimpering, even her whimpers laced with little tremors; her hips were gently starting to pivot, her thighs and belly to scissor against his thighs as little "ah-ah-ah-ah" sounds exited her mouth; in moments Julian's fingers, previously inserted shallowly in a tight, snug, disinterested and largely dry cunt, became deeply buried in a gushing one, as Autumn violently fucked herself onto his fingers, groping after his pants and tearing them open – earning, rapturously, a savage spanking for making him come before begging for the privilege.

But in the instants before that happened, he purred impetuously, "And wank all the time."

She let out a cry: "Sir, oh, all the time?"

His fingers worked; she humped against him, pushing herself onto his fingers as he worked her clit and felt her G-spot swell.

"Are you questioning me?"

"No, Sir, oh, never, Sir," she breathed.

He clarified "all the time": "Twice a day! Three times a day! Four times a day!" Each exclamation was punctuated by louder cries from Autumn, as she surged in his lap, threatening to tumble them off the big wooden chair and send them both to the floor. She gasped louder, muttering expletives; the number climbed until it was improbable.

Then she came; he was only a moment behind her. If he'd said, "Don't take my cock out," she would have stopped, but then, he was too busy moaning. And she was such a damn expert with a pair of suit pants – ten seconds from buckle to jerk, sometimes.

He soaked her skirt, her sleeve; it dribbled on her panties.

She looked up with big dark eyes and said, "Sir. Thank you, Sir."

Who knew the girl was such an exhibitionist? A million surprises, that one. A million surprises.

And so, from Monday noon to Sunday midnight, she wanks as much as she is able – in the window at her computer and in the window in the loft, sprawled sweaty or lube-sticky or freshly showered on the king-sized bed. She wanks with hands and vibe and dildos; she fucks herself silly. When she is not masturbating, she glides through the apartment, naked, barefoot; she sits at her computer, marks up books, even does some callisthenics, joyfully. She is watched more often than not; their eyes arouse her. She is fervent in her self-love when she can be.

But the frequency of her transgressions in the week does not approach the number he has named; after all, she has work to do, and the number he named was quite far from reasonable – it may have been physically and even temporally impossible. She came nowhere near it.

She's rather sure he'll spank her for that; in fact, she's counting on it.

She will not whine; she will not protest; she will not say, "No, Sir, please," or "That's not fair," or "Mercy, Sir." That would be dangerously close to a negotiation; while prudent pervs might in such case applaud the conversion of Autumn, they shouldn't get their hopes up.

She will not whine; to be honest, she won't even pout. She'll push her ass up in the air and spread her legs, and flood hungrily from the inside waiting for it.

Which, of note, is exactly what she does when she hears his cab outside; she does it slowly, savouring every millimetre of lift, till she's raised her ass so high the bed sheet slides to the floor.

She hears the jingle of his keys; she hears the lock go *click-ker-chunk*!; she hears his footsteps. She hears him mount the stairs and near her.

He sees her ass raised in the yellow, sickly street lights; every second or so there's a flicker, and sizzling sounds outside the great, vast planes of glass.

"Welcome home, Sir," she purrs softly, without opening her eyes. "Pleasant flight, Sir?"

He stands outlined in the window; she peeks with one eye slitted, sees him, catches her breath.

"Very. Pleasant week?"

Her flesh goosebumps.

"*Mais oui*," she says with breathless heat.

She hears the curtains close; she trembles slightly, hungrily.

"*Très bien*," he says, and comes to bed.

Briony Remastered

Justine Elyot

There are ghosts on the platform. Ghosts of me and ghosts of Max and all the times we met and parted here. But Max isn't here today, and no wonder, because I haven't told him I'm coming.

He will be expecting me all the same, after that tearful 2 a.m. phone call last week.

Five years have passed since our last conversation, but I needed to hear his voice and I poured out my heart, asking for his understanding and advice, yet all the time I was asking for something else, something more, without daring to say the words.

He knew what it was, though, because his last words to me were, "Why don't you come back?"

"I can't," I said, and then hung up and cried until dawn.

I really thought I couldn't, too. Yet here I am.

I decide against getting a cab. Instead, I choose to walk through the streets of the town, curious to see how much it has changed. I need this time to stop my heart from banging and my legs from wobbling, too, at the prospect of seeing Max again.

At the corner of his street, I stop and take stock. It's still a canyon of three-storey town houses, but gentrification is on the way, by the looks of things. Five years ago, most of these were split into bedsits, but now there are smart paint jobs and wooden blinds in the windows. Two have skips outside and scaffolding from basement to ceiling. Max is no longer the only outright owner-occupier here.

At the foot of his steps, I put my finger to my neck to straighten my collar before I remember that it's five years since I have worn it. The skin of my neck feels too exposed without it. I grab at a railing to steady myself, then ascend to the still-red door.

Perhaps, after all, he is out.

But it's Wednesday afternoon, and he always worked from home on a Wednesday. After all this time I still remember his schedule. Private consultations, Monday and Tuesday. Wednesday, working on his book at home. Thursday and Friday at the hospital. Saturday and Sunday only if urgently required.

I feel intrusive. I don't want to disturb his flow if he's having a good afternoon with the book. I turn around and think about coming back at the weekend, though there's no guarantee he'll be in then.

I'm still dithering, one foot on the lower step, when the door opens.

"Briony."

There is nothing else in the world but his eyes, so dark they are almost black in the dim hall light, locked on mine.

I can't speak, or move, until he opens the door wider, waving a hand.

"Come in."

"I didn't ring the bell," I say, looking around an unchanged hallway. Oh, but that plant is new. And that print.

I turn to him.

"I heard your footsteps," he said.

"You knew it was me from my footsteps?"

"Of course."

He stands a couple of feet away from me. I wonder if I ought to, I don't know, *do* something. Touch him.

I step towards him.

"I'm sorry," I start, but he shushes me.

"Go into the living room. I'll make tea."

It's more a command than an invitation and I realize, with a rush of heat to my cheeks, that it isn't for me to dictate the shape of this encounter. I am here as a supplicant.

Walking into the living room, I have to stop and grip the back of an armchair for support when the familiar smell of beeswax polish and old wood and leather settles around me like a sensual cloud. Once more I am kneeling on the hearth-rug, naked, my hands cuffed behind my back, my head bowed, waiting for him to finish his brandy and his book chapter. If the fire was lit, one side of me roasted while the other froze. He liked the way it sensitized my skin. The red side and the blue side. He performed comparative studies, using a riding crop.

I go to sit in one of the wing chairs, perching on the very edge of the buttoned leather. I smooth my hands over my skirt, down to where the hem rests just above my knee. I took a lot of care getting dressed this morning. I chose things I thought he would like. Ladylike things. And now I feel as if I'm about to be called in to a job interview, a horrible kind of job interview in which failure leads to execution.

The rattle of a tray warns me of his approach. The boss. The big boss. The man with the power to hire and fire.

My life is in the hands that set the tea tray on the table, so carefully, so deftly. Elegant hands with long, long fingers, belonging to a tall willowy tree of a man. I can't take my eyes off them. All I can think of is how they used to look, wrapped around the handle of the riding crop.

He pours the tea, remembering how I like it, and only looks at me when he hands me the cup.

"You don't take sugar now?" he says.

I shake my head and take a sip. It's too hot, of course. I do this every time and he smiles, seeing how little I've learned over the years.

"So," he says, taking his seat opposite me and steepling his fingers. Even on his "day off" he is wearing a suit waistcoat and trousers, of a killingly fine cut. Is it because he was expecting me? Did he strive to be prepared?

"So," I echo, looking into the tannic refuge of my teacup.

"The wild oats are sown," he says. His accent is the same as it ever was, subtle enough to pass almost unrecognized except for the odd slip with a "th" sound and the formal, old-fashioned enunciation. "And the prodigal returns."

My mind reaches out for some stupid, ice-breaking joke about a fatted calf but it can't quite make the connection. Instead, I just say, "I'm sorry."

"I see that you are," he says.

"You have every reason to hate me."

"Hate you?" He puts down his cup. "I can do a lot of things to you, Briony, but never that." He pauses, in the old way I remember, when he is putting his thoughts together into coherent order. Max never blurts, never blusters, never ums or ahs. He's the only person I know who can do this, but I guess it's a function of spending years translating your thoughts from one language to another. "You needed to grow up," he says. "And you needed to do it on your own."

"I was twenty-three, not some school kid."

"Maturity isn't commensurate with age."

No. No, that's a fair point and, if it feels like a slap in the face, that's probably fair too.

"You're right, though," I mumble. "I wasn't ready to settle down. I needed to live, go to festivals, get drunk, get stoned, and . . ." *And all that. Shag other men.*

He nods. "It's not unreasonable," he says. "You missed out on a regular adolescence when you spent those years caring for your mother. I expected it, in a way. I also knew you would come back, in the end."

"Did you?"

"Oh yes."

I can't believe he is letting me off the hook like this, after the way I treated him. I've been expecting harsh words, recriminations, even tears, although I never saw him cry in the two years we were together.

"If you love somebody, let them go," I say.

"Well, precisely. And wait for them to come back. I just hope it's for the right reasons," he said. "Is it?"

"I missed you," I say, my voice faltering. I never stopped missing him, never stopped feeling I'd made the most disastrous mistake of my life. But something had prevented me from admitting it – dull old pride, I suppose. I'm grateful, in a funny way, that he isn't being overtly emotional. This is the Max I remember and feel comfortable with – the man who never relinquishes control for a moment.

"You missed me?" he asks softly. "Or you missed all the comforts of our life together?"

"You," I insist, meaning it.

"Good." He takes a long draught from the teacup. Loose Earl Grey, from Twinings, strained. I missed that too. No more crappy soaked teabags left to stain the draining board in that skanky shared house for me. "Well, I'm glad you're back."

I can't shake the feeling that his calm hides a gathering storm. I want it to break before I can truly believe that I am allowed back in his life.

"Is that it?" I say, trying to hide the quiver in my voice. "Aren't you going to be angry? Aren't you going to make me . . . ?"

"Pay?" He smiles. "I think it cost you a lot to come here today. I wouldn't take you back if I thought you were just running away from something else. But I don't think you are."

"You're being so . . . reasonable."

He finishes his tea and puts the cup and saucer back on the tray, watching me through his dark crescents of eyes as he sits up in the chair again.

"Yes, I am," he says. "But, just because I'm a reasonable man, it doesn't mean I didn't get hurt by what you did."

Here it comes. Here is where the danger lies.

"Oh, Max." I half rise from my chair, wanting to go to him.

He gestures me back down. "No, stay where you are. I don't believe in broken hearts, but I suffered, Briony, and I have no intention of repeating the experience."

I shake my head, tense with building tears, and swallow. "I won't—"

"How can I be sure?"

"Test me. Any way you like. I'll prove it to you, over and over."

"All right. Do you remember where the canes are kept?"

The floor falls away beneath my feet. Now this is real. Now the payment is due. Madly, I want to laugh, but I merely nod.

"Go and fetch the one you liked the least," he says.

The one I liked the least.

His study is at the rear of the house, down some steps, looking out over the garden. It is small, but in perfect condition. I look over the gravel and watch the shrubs flitter in the breeze. Rain is on the way.

Rain is nothing compared to what will fall on me. There is the umbrella stand, and there, on the walls, are the photographs of me that I had assumed would be taken down. I stop and stare at them, tears gathering in my eyes now that Max isn't here and I'm able to indulge them.

Through the blur, I see myself in an outfit that is no more than some black leather webbing, hiding none of the most private parts of my body. I am kneeling up and holding a riding crop between my teeth. Between my spread knees is a thorny rose.

On another wall, the same outfit and posture, viewed from the back. The picture is black and white, apart from the welts on my exposed bottom, which have been touched up in vivid crimson.

On the desk is the only non-kinky photograph in the room. Max and I, heads leaning together, smiling at a mutual friend's wedding. It was the day we met. Best man and chief bridesmaid. The tears begin to roll and I brace myself against the desk chair until I am able to blot them and blow my nose. Even then, I can't tear my eyes from those two hopeful, carefree souls on a June day.

We flirted at the breakfast and danced together at the evening do. I had too much to drink and he delivered me home in a cab. The next day he turned up to scold me and take me out for fresh air and pancakes and gallons of coffee. Somehow, I ended up back here getting my bottom spanked. Best day of my life, hangover notwithstanding. I can still taste that blueberry sauce, feel that tender afterglow.

Why on earth, after all, did I leave?

"Because I'm stupid," I muttered to myself.

I select the second most vicious of the canes, not quite able to face my old rattan nemesis, and before I turn to go I think about what the still-displayed photographs tell me. They tell me that he has not had another woman here – at least, not in the way of a serious relationship. Five years.

I put back the second-worst cane and take out the worst. It is what I deserve.

It is like a slender snake in my hands and I almost imagine it might rear up and bite me. In past times, I used to carry it in my teeth, crawling to him with it on hands and knees. Should I do that now?

I don't feel properly dressed for crawling, though. I would be scantily dressed on those occasions, perhaps in a glossy black basque and stockings, no knickers. If I get down on all fours in this pencil skirt, the seam'll probably split.

Instead I bear it, rather formally, on both upraised palms.

He is expressionless as I go to him, even when I kneel down, back straight, and hold out the implement.

He picks it up.

"This was your least favourite?" he says. "You told me it was the lexan cane."

"I lied. I thought you might use this one less often if you didn't realize . . ."

He stares at me and my scalp crawls. This is not the best time for such a confession.

"You lied then, or you are lying now?" he asks, chips of ice in his voice.

"Then. I lied then. You know what I was like."

"Yes." He taps the tip of the cane under my chin, prompting me to crane my neck up at him. "You had many flaws, Briony, and the worst of them by far was dishonesty. With yourself as much as with me. If these last five years have taught you anything, I hope it is the value of being truthful with yourself."

"Yes, yes, sir, and that's why I'm here," I plead. The "sir" slipped out as naturally as my breath.

"Is it?"

"I couldn't lie to myself any more about what I needed. I've had it with pretending to be what I'm not."

"Then there has been no other master in your life?"

I shake my head. "Nobody could replace you," I say. "For the first three years I tried vanilla relationships, then I got too frustrated and joined a dating site for kinksters. But nobody came close to you. Two years of awkward dates that I never felt the urge to follow up. You cast the longest shadow in the world. I think it stretches to the end of my life."

There is a twitch of his cheek. I think he is moved.

"Yours is also quite impressive," he admits, tapping my chin a little harder. "I'm not going to talk about the last five years, but I've already told you I knew you would come back. I hoped it might be sooner."

"I'm sorry. I'm back now."

"Yes, and there is music for you to face. Stand up, Briony."

I stand, and it feels wrong to be taller than he is, but he soon remedies that by rising to his full height and turning me away from him by my shoulder.

He puts his hand on the seat of my skirt.

"This is rather tight," he observes.

"You used to like my tight skirts."

"I still do. But you must take it off. You can't bend in the way I will insist upon wearing that."

He hooks a finger into the waistband and pulls down the zip. The skirt is so well fitted that I have to push it down over my hips, the action one of submission, bringing me closer into the headspace I need to find if I am going to take this caning.

The crumpled fabric around my feet is a token of surrender.

"You wore stockings." He lays a palm on the bare expanse of my upper thigh. "That's good. Tights would have had to come off. Now go and stand in the corner, please, just there, by the window, and put your hands on your head."

The corner he has chosen is not visible from the street, but it is from the front doorstep. I will have to pray that the Jehovah's Witnesses aren't in the area today.

Placing my hands on my head makes my silk shirt rise over the top of my lacy knickers and pushes my breasts up too. I feel intensely conscious of this, even more so when Max comes to stand behind me.

There is a cold invasion at the top of my bottom, and I realize that he has placed the hooked handle of the cane inside the elastic waist so that the rest of its length hangs between my legs, a chilly reminder of what is to come.

I want to ask how long I will have to stand there, but not as much as I want to show him how good I can be. I want him to see that I have changed.

In the past, I would always sulk and huff when placed in the corner. I'd peek over my shoulder and shift positions when he wasn't looking. I'd ask what the time was, how much longer, could I have a drink of water?

He always extended the time I had to wait, of course, but I seemed incapable of absorbing that knowledge. I just couldn't relinquish my little traditional protest – it was the principle of the thing, I suppose.

Things are different now. I focus on quelling the urge to fidget and I hold my back straight so that the cane doesn't move from its central position between my cheeks.

I try to remember how it used to feel. Not that bad, was it? Not unbearable. Why am I kidding myself? It hurts like the fires of hell. I am all penitent bravado now, but once I hear that swoosh of air I will beg whatever powers might be above us to rewind time and let me take a different course.

But I know from experience that I will get through it. I've done it before and I'll do it again. I wish I didn't have to *wait*, though. I want it over with now, so we can move on to the next part: the forgiveness, the embraces, the return to a much-missed status quo.

I hear the creak of his leather armchair, then the tap of his fingers on his mobile phone.

"Hello, Brian." It is the manager at the clinic. "Yes. That week off we discussed? I'd like to take it from tomorrow, if you can manage it. I know that, but Lisa knows she might be called in at short notice. I spoke with her about it. That's good. Yes. Just the week. No, nowhere special, but something's come up and I have to deal with it now. Thank you. Goodbye."

Something's come up and I have to deal with it now.

He means me. I've come up. He has to deal with me now.

Delicious tremors radiate out from between my legs. It has only taken that relatively innocuous phrase to get me wet and wild for more of his disciplinary attention. I hope he will not be long, but he embarks on an interminable round of phone calls, cancelling appointments and redirecting his clients to another colleague.

By the time he finishes, my knees are trembling and the cane makes edgy little movements that cause the end of it to tap my calves. I want to stop looking at this wall. I want it done with, and I utter a silent prayer, *Please, God.*

"Well, Briony," he says, and I don't forget to whisper my *thank you*. "You have been in that corner for quite some time. What has been going through your mind, I wonder?"

I want to say something cheeky about not realizing this was a professional consultation, but it's not the time for breezy impertinence.

"How much I want to get this over with," I confess.

"Get this over with? The caning?"

"Yes."

"So you think everything can be cured by a few strokes of my rod? Hey presto, everything back to the way it was?"

"I . . . don't know," I say uncertainly. "But I'm looking forward to being yours again. Belonging to you."

"You think you stopped being mine?"

"N-no," I say, trying to be careful with my wording. He's a devil for tripping you up with unconscious subtext. "I was always yours, even when I tried not to be. I mean, I'm looking forward to being under your direct authority again."

"Well, so am I. But there is more to starting our lives together once more than an act of punishment followed by forgiveness, you know."

"Oh?" I feel stupid, talking to the wall, but I know I have to stay in this position until he directs otherwise.

"You will need to be retrained," he says. "We will have an intensive period of one week, and see how we go from there, I think. I'm not taking any more risks with my heart, Briony. I hope you appreciate that."

"Of course, sir," I whisper. This sounds frightening, but it's necessary and so I will accept it. Five years of pain will take some erasure.

"Well, then," he says, his tone brightening. "I think you should bring me the cane. On your knees, please."

I reach around to unhook the cane from my knickers, turn and drop to all fours. I put the cane between my teeth and crawl across the carpet to his waiting feet, so shiny black in their expensive leather.

"Up," he says softly, and I sit back on my heels, shoulders back, chin up, offering him the instrument of my discipline.

He doesn't take it for a moment or two, but simply looks at me, smiling. He is pleased with how naturally I have fallen back into this – so am I. He caresses me briefly under my chin then removes the cane from my teeth and lays it across his thighs.

"Pay your respects," he prompts.

I kiss his feet, giving the leather a loving lick. He has indoor and outdoor shoes and never the twain shall be mixed up.

"Enough," he says. "Now I want to hear your plea."

My plea. I had almost forgotten this part. Whenever he punished me, he made me beg for it first. It was part of the process, he said, a way of focusing me on what I was chastised for and how I expected it to change my behaviour.

"Sir, I need to be caned," I say falteringly. "Because I treated you badly. I left you without even telling you to your face. I emailed you because I didn't want to hear the truth, which was that I was making a mistake. I've been stupid and selfish and I want to show you how sorry I am."

He holds his grave expression, though his eyes seem a thousand miles away when I speak of what I have done, as if he doesn't want to hear it.

"Tell me what you deserve," he says. One finger strokes the length of the cane, making me want to shiver.

"I deserve a severe caning, sir. One that will make it painful for me to sit for a long time."

"How many strokes?"

"How many do *you* think, sir?"

"I don't know. Perhaps I won't cane you after all."

This is the really difficult bit, and the part he seems to enjoy the most, more even than the thrashing. I don't want to play along, but I owe him, so I do.

"Please don't say that, sir. Please cane me."

"I'm not in the mood, I don't think."

"Please, I beg you, please do it. I can't bear it if you don't."

"All right, if you insist. Show me how much you want it. Kiss the rod."

My lips touch the skinny barrel of the cane, pitilessly cold and smooth.

"Kiss it properly," he prompts. "Show it your love."

I shut my eyes, resisting the strong temptation to stand up and shake my head and say "Enough". I kiss the rod up and down, then put out my tongue and curl it around, licking the wood the way he likes, the way that will make it more painful when it falls.

"Good," he says, tugging it away from my craven mouth. "Now go and stand on the rug with your hands clasping your ankles."

One of my least favourite positions, to go with my least favourite cane – hell on the calves and hamstrings. I hope he won't make me hold it for long, recalling an occasion when I tottered, trembling, onto the floor halfway through a session.

I turn my back to him and bend. I am shaking already, highly conscious of my vulnerability in this position. He could do anything to me. He probably will.

My bottom is thrust out, cheeks slightly parted by the stringency of the position, and I know he can also see the cleft of my sex which I waxed so carefully this morning.

I hope the sight pleases him. I'm pretty sure it does because it's a few moments before anything else happens and I'm starting to feel the blood rush to my head.

"Yes," he says, and I hear his footsteps across the floorboards. "In some ways, you haven't changed at all, Briony."

In what ways have I? I want to ask, but the time and place could scarcely be more inappropriate.

"I'll give you only six," he says. "But you needn't think it's out of misguided leniency. It's because it is simply a first instalment."

I whisper a little "oh" of dismay, but don't question him.

"I mentioned retraining, and I was serious. You will get six strokes every day for this week. After that, we will rethink."

Oh God. A caning on top of a caning, seven days in a row. I'm not sure I can take it, but I suppose I'll find out. And I'll try. I'll prove to him that I'm here to stay, if that's what it takes.

"Now, I hope you remember our little ways?" he says, prodding my right bottom cheek with the tip of the cane as a prompt.

"Counting the strokes," I say. "And asking for the next."

"Precisely. I'll expect you to do it."

The thought of these little tasks soothes me, makes my situation something comforting and familiar rather than unknowable.

The soothing effect lasts about three seconds, which is the time between his last word and the fierce disturbance of air preceding his first stroke.

Despite everything that has built up to this, I am unprepared and I fall forwards, screaming and clutching the hot bar of pain across my bottom.

"It really has been a long time," he remarks, waiting for me to get back into position.

"One, sir. Please may I have another?"

The words come out all cracked and hectic, but at least they come out.

Doubled over once more, my legs ache already but I can't think about that – I can only think about the sheer impossibility of taking five more strokes.

Impossible.

"Two, sir. Please may I have another?"

Unlikely.

"Three, sir. Please may I have another, oh no, I don't want another, I can't."

I hear him take a breath.

"If you want to stop," he says, leaving the phrase hanging. The implication is clear. I wait for my senses to regroup after the three shocks they have endured. I need to think. Can I do it? I used to do it. Why can't I do it again?

"It hurts," I say, stupidly.

"You had forgotten?"

"Yes. I had."

"Perhaps, after all, too much water has run under the bridge. This is not for you any more."

I try to think straight. Is he right? I peer sideways and see him, holding the cane, looking like justice itself. The sight takes my recently recovered breath away. Then I feel the throb of my three welts and think, with greedy pleasure, of how they will make me wince when I try to sit down. I have missed that. I want that.

I can do this.

"I'm ready," I say. "Give me the last three, please."

"If you are sure?"

"Yes, I'm quite sure."

The fourth stroke falls and I'm not sure, and then I am, as the bloom of sweet pain takes me like wildfire. It is what I need and deserve and I know, with this thought, that I have achieved subspace.

The last two strokes are like gifts, precious tokens of forgiveness. Now we are renewed and we can start to live our lives again.

Six strokes mark my bottom, reminding me of what I have committed myself to. I glory in them. I could take more. I could take twice as many.

But Max puts aside the rod and I quiver, wondering what will come next.

He puts a hand in the small of my back.

"You are hot," he says.

He fetches a cold flannel and presses it to my brow. I hope he might do the same with my bottom, but he doesn't.

"I'm not going to touch you until this week has passed," he says. "And neither will you touch yourself. It will be a test of your commitment."

I can't say I'm delighted to hear this, but I accept it.

"Now, you can stay in that position like that until I say otherwise."

He goes to his desk and gets back to work, while I hold myself bent over the chair, keenly aware of my bare, striped bottom on display to the room.

But I don't want to complain. I don't want to do anything else, go anywhere else. Here, bent and compliant, made to do his will, I feel so calm I could almost drop off to sleep. I am home again.

Seven Stripes of Colour

Kristina Lloyd

Under a pale apricot sky, city buses looped in front of the railway station, their slow headlights weaving patterns in the dusk. Louise strode from cab to pub, her heart beating a little too fast. She loved doing this, meeting men in places where no one belonged, in stations, airports and motorway cafés. She imagined her grey, digitalized self on CCTV monitors as she made her way to another date.

The anonymity of these places appealed to the pessimist in her. She expected, at best, a short-lived affair. At worst, the two of them would part in relief after a sour coffee or nondescript wine. Then he and she would merge with the travellers around them, en route to elsewhere, confused and anxious, caught in the limbo of to-ing and fro-ing. Warp and weft. Yes and no.

Jason was different to the others, that much was obvious at once. His kindness and warmth were evident in his greeting: a broad grin and a kiss on the cheek. All too often, the dominants she met after "meeting" online were, if young, guarded and cocky or, if older, charmingly chivalric.

"I'll get this," he said when she'd selected her wine at the bar.

"OK, I'll get the next round," she replied, indicating that already she liked him enough to stay and wasn't expecting him to foot the bill. Establishing the importance of equality was, she felt, crucial if power-play negotiations were to be fair and mutual.

Fifteen minutes into their conversation she wondered what

the catch was. Married? Impotent? Deranged? Three hours later she knew, but by then it was too late.

"How's your hotel?" he asked, quickly filling a silence.

"Five minutes away."

He laughed but didn't take the bait. Well, it was still early in the game so fair enough. The photographs he'd emailed didn't do him justice. You wouldn't call him handsome but he was definitely striking. His face had a skew-whiff, battered quality and his dark eyes glittered, really glittered. They held the mad energy of a man whose zest for life has resulted in him seeing too much. He wore faded jeans, trainers, T-shirt and a suit jacket, which he hung over the back of his chair. His shoulders were wide, his arms muscular and darkly haired. Rogue strands of silver glinted in his short brown curls and flecked his neat sideburns.

As they talked, buses crawled beyond the long, low window behind him. Occasionally, headlights swept into the dark wooden bar, bathing the two of them in a shuddering glow or framing him in momentary halos.

"I haven't done this for over four years," he said after Louise returned from buying the next round. Wine for her, beer for him.

Uh-oh, she thought. Here's where it all goes pear-shaped. He's going to tell me he's just split up with someone and I've got a rebound on my hands. Or his ailing mother's about to die, or he's fresh out of jail.

"So how am I doing?" he added.

She laughed. "You're doing great. Nine out of ten. Clearly a natural."

"Damn, I dropped a point. How come?"

"Hey, no one gets ten. Ten would be perfection and a perfect person would automatically lose a point for being perfect, ergo insufferable."

Jason nodded thoughtfully then smiled. "Well, I got top marks. Go me!"

After a pause, she asked, "So tell me, what's the story?

Why've you been away from the joys of dating?" Nervous, she ran her thumb and fingers up and down the stem of her wine glass, desisting when she recalled a claim that it was indicative of a subconscious gesture to jerk a guy off. So much wishful thinking in pop psychology.

"Ah, this and that," he said. "Got out of the habit. Found myself continually disappointed. I was in a straight, you know, a vanilla relationship for around eighteen months but . . ." He trailed off with a shrug. "It's not for me. I tried, but the older I get, the more I . . . Anyway, that ended over a year ago. And since then, before then too, I've been trying . . . No, wondering how to realize my desires without, how shall I phrase it?" He inclined his head at a philosophical angle. "Without causing harm."

Her heart pumped harder. She found him simultaneously exciting and terrifying. She started to work the stem of her glass again, this time not stopping when she realized what she was doing.

"Should I be worried?" she asked. "I mean, if we decide we want to play together, would I be in danger? Because if so, I'm probably going to pass. Sorry." She took a large sip of wine as if to support her decisive words.

Jason shook his head. "I'm ninety-nine per cent certain you'd be safe with me."

He reached across the table, allowing his fingertips to drift over her hand. She returned the gesture, their contact tentative and fumbling like that of long-standing, melancholy lovers. The beam of headlights from outside crept across their table, casting glossy patches on the wood and rippling over their knuckles. When she looked up, his eyes were downcast, his curls briefly backlit. In that instant, she was irrationally afraid; not of him but for the two of them together. She felt as if they'd been caught in the arc of a searchlight and had nowhere left to run.

"And the missing one per cent?" she asked, as the bar's shadows settled around them again.

His smile was strained. Behind him, the buses kept huffing

and purring, their passengers silhouetted in halogen-white windows. She thought of Blanche DuBois at the start of her journey trilling, "Why, they told me to take a streetcar named Desire."

At length, he gave her a stern, serious look. "You," he said, "are fucking beautiful. And you're driving my cock insane. What's our safeword?"

The confident delivery of his sudden, dirty seduction was more than enough to arouse her. She loved knowing this new man was sitting opposite her in a pub, his cock secretly swelling as they talked. Adrenaline made her fingers tremble, and a beat throbbed between her thighs. For a moment, the world burned, the lights outside gleaming in tones of white gold, dark amber and bright cherry red. She experienced the slippage, the shift of the mundane into a spectrum of yellow-hued, fiery magic, the start of a rainbow. She recalled the schoolgirl mnemonic for remembering the order of colours in the spectrum. Richard of York gave battle in vain. Red orange yellow, and so on.

"Red," she replied, amusing herself by thinking, *A bus called lust.*

"We should drink up."

She grinned and touched her glass against his. "We should."

She was in Brighton for a conference on food-packaging design. At her hotel, eager to avoid being the source of gossip among industry colleagues, she asked him to take the stairs while she took the lift.

Alone in her room, she dimmed the lights, checked her make-up and began removing items from her luggage. She laid out on the bed four black leather restraints for wrists and ankles, a ten-metre length of hemp rope dyed a beautiful shade of indigo, clover clamps for nipples, half a dozen condoms and a wooden paddle. They were her travel basics: versatile, easy enough to pack, and a good starting point since they offered a range from which to select.

Over email, they'd discussed what they enjoyed in bed, how

they might please each other, the number of years they'd been practising BDSM, and so on. They seemed to be on a similar sexual wavelength, quickly establishing a connection they'd both thought worth pursuing. Of course, you could go through a checklist with anyone and it was meaningless if, once you met, that spark, that chemistry, that elusive something or other was absent. And checklists weren't shopping lists to be strictly adhered to. What worked with one person might bomb with another.

Jason, like Louise, had a diverse sexual history, which he'd sketched out only lightly. Twice married, twice divorced. Numerous shorter relationships. Some kinky, some not. The trajectory of being a sexual deviant hadn't been straightforward for either of them. You didn't decide one day to do this then get a handbook and membership to a club. Exploring was fraught, often confusing and occasionally delightful.

She gave herself a cursory inspection in the mirror again. He'd called her beautiful although in truth she was ordinary and her lips were too thin. Where was he? The stairs shouldn't take this long. Had he got cold feet? Got lost in the hotel?

She lifted one of the ankle cuffs to her nose and inhaled, the earthy scent of leather sending a charge to her groin. Her wetness throbbed, her anticipation connected to so many memories and associations. The cuffs she'd bought some years ago at a fetish market in Berlin where she'd been terrified someone might recognize her. Berlin! An attendee at a food and drinks fair! As if anyone would. But in those days she'd been anxious, paranoid, guilty. Married.

For almost three years, the new cuffs had languished in green tissue paper in a hatbox stashed among the shoes in her wardrobe, a mute reminder she wanted more from life and marriage. And in Berlin that time, she'd almost strayed. Almost. They'd got talking at the bar after supper. One flirtation led to another, and as the hour grew late, he began detailing the things he'd like to do to her involving manacles, crops, blindfolds and gags.

Balanced on her spindly bar stool, she'd listened and had felt afraid. Not of him, but of how he'd tapped into aspects of her self she could barely acknowledge. Staying loyal to her husband, she'd turned the man down, but two days later, she bought the leather cuffs even though she'd no intention of suggesting anything so outré to David. She knew he wouldn't be interested. She'd simply wanted to try being someone else, a woman who went to fetish markets alone in a foreign country.

Now, she was bolder, older and divorced. She sought out men online who might be able to fulfil her increasingly voracious sexual needs. Love and companionship would be nice, sure, but there was no rush. Her priority was to explore this fledgling sexual self after being blind to it for so long.

She checked her phone for messages. Nothing. Would it imply neediness if she texted to see where he'd got to?

She was taking a pee when he tapped softly on the door. Damn. Bad timing.

"It's me," he murmured.

She finished in a small panic. Didn't want to keep him waiting. Didn't want to spoil the mood by telling him she was on the loo.

When she opened, he was there with two glasses in one hand.

"I got us a couple of whiskies. Highland Park. Do you like whisky? I hope so."

"Yes, perfect. Thank you."

"Dutch courage," he said, following her into the room.

He handed her a glass. Smiling, they clinked a toast, watching each other all the time, knowing they were on the brink of intimacy. She sipped, trying to maintain eye contact. The liquor heated her mouth, its richness sliding into her throat. She couldn't help but think the whisky was warming a track for his cock. He sipped too, gold reflections swilling in his tumbler. He could barely drink for smiling.

"So . . ."

He removed the glass from her hand and set it down with his own. Swaying smoochily, they eased towards each other.

He placed a hand on her hip and she pressed her palm to his chest, stroking the hardness of him beneath his T-shirt. His nipple was a tiny bead below her fingers.

"So," she echoed, grinning. "Alone at last."

"You have some interesting objects on the bed."

"You want to check them out?"

His hand slid higher to follow the dip of her waist, thumb coming to a halt below her breast. He printed a couple of kisses on her neck. "Not yet," he said, voice firm. He began edging her back. "I want to check *you* out first."

He sandwiched her between his body and the wall, hips grinding gently. His erection rubbed against her, a bulkiness that nudged without imposing. They shared slight smiles, mischievous and ironic. Moving slowly, he clasped both her wrists, raised her arms and pinned them to the wall. A sudden weight of hunger plummeted to her groin, her face flushing as her senses spun. Her irony vanished, her entire body thrilling to what she regarded as the foundation of her desire: being held open by a man; being positioned by him and for him like a doll or a puppet.

So far, every kink she owned centred around that: doll, puppet, plaything, object, cumslut, fucktoy, and all the many different words that meant "his". Being his was so freeing. Well, assuming he was the right kind of guy. And so far, Jason seemed very right. Again, she wondered what the catch might be. There had to be one. Intelligent, attractive guy with a liberal conscience but comfortable with his dom side? Too good to be true, surely. Fogged by wanting, her concerns mattered less than they had done earlier.

He ground more firmly against her and she undulated her spine, cat-like in her pleasure. He brought his lips to hers and kissed with tender insistence, his touch moist and warm. At first, their mouths tasted of honey, smoke and high, heathery hillsides. But soon they'd kissed away the whisky and were tasting the pink, sweet succulence of themselves. Louise became weaker with every second, her legs scarcely able to support her. When Jason broke away, he looked down at her with mild amusement and a trace of irony. He'd retained his control while hers had been quickly defeated.

"You're almost too easy," he murmured. He drew her raised arms together and clasped her wrists with one hand, his gesture symbolic rather than restricting. With his free hand, he caressed her body, making her groan when he mashed her breasts through her blouse. He tried to hike up her skirt but it was too tight. Instead, he thrust a hand against her crotch, pushing inwards, wrinkling the fabric. Her clit pulsed, her labia swelled, and her cunt became hollow with need. Already she wanted him inside her but knew she wouldn't get satisfaction for some time.

"Are you wet?" he asked.

She nodded.

"Show me," he said.

She cringed, troubled by the instruction. "How do you mean?" she asked croakily.

He stepped away from her. She let her arms fall to her side, her back still flat to the wall, his request making her feel shy and stupid. Performance and display were not her forte, as he'd probably guessed. Using that detail, he'd found a swift route to making her suffer by humiliating her. No, worse than that. By making her humiliate herself.

"Remove your underwear," he said. "Then lift up your skirt and show me your cunt." He took his whisky then sat in the armchair, a low, black object that looked as if it had been cut from a cube. "And show me your tits as well. Don't get undressed. Just show me the most important parts of your body. Important to me, that is."

He sipped his drink and reclined sideways in the chair, one leg hooked over the arm, his bright gaze locked on her. Despite the T-shirt and jeans, he gave a successful impression of profligacy, a louche connoisseur of woman who always got what he wanted. His alert, gleaming eyes belied the aloofness of his affected pose, bringing an air of aggression to the scenario. If this man didn't get what he wanted, said those eyes, he would turn on you like a mad dog so best do as instructed.

Louise swallowed hard and stood before him, mentally doing a health-and-safety risk assessment. You were supposed to tell someone if you were meeting a stranger in a strange place but she never did. They'd think her crazy, and besides, she cherished her secrets. She was fairly sure she could trust Jason. They were both here to have a little fun together, that was all. So she wriggled her briefs from under her skirt and stepped free of the flimsy garment. With quivering fingers, she unbuttoned her blouse partway and knocked her bra straps aside. He smiled faintly and pressed a finger to his lips, watching as she scooped her flesh from the lacy cups. His eyes flicked left and right, assessing her breasts, their full swell perching awkwardly above the rumpled fabric, her nipples tight and dusky.

He nodded thoughtfully. "Good. Now lift up your skirt."

Louise closed her eyes in a heavy blink, summoning up the courage to comply. She could never explain to herself why she loved something which, during the moment of it happening, she loathed. How can you want what you don't want? She bunched the cotton around her hips, the skirt tight enough to stay raised without her assistance. Below the rucked-up hem, her triangle of hair was a neat patch against her pale skin, her labia peeking like a small, pink kiss.

"Step closer," he said. "Turn around."

She obeyed, presenting him with her naked buttocks. The armchair squeaked as he shifted position but he said nothing, nor did he touch her. The lengthening silence was torture to Louise, her anxiety and shame mounting as she waited for him to pass judgement. Was she acceptable to him? Did she even want to be when his assessment criteria were the merits or otherwise of her backside?

Just a game, she told herself. But she was playing the game, feeling it charge through her veins and pound in her heart, so the disclaimer brought no comfort.

When his cool fingers touched her rear, her intake of breath was audible. For the next few seconds, she forgot to exhale as he explored with a broad, roughened hand. He squeezed as if to test her plumpness then stroked across her contours before gliding down to the creases below each buttock.

"Nice." He rubbed a thumb into the fold where her flesh dipped, nudging towards her wet vulval split.

She released her breath on a gasp as he withdrew his touch.

"Seriously fucking nice." With an upswing, he cracked his hand on the underswell of one cheek, making its softness leap. She squealed and he repeated the action three times, each sting enhancing the last. With a bossy nudge, he adjusted her stance, making her tip forward a fraction, then he applied an equivalent series of blows to her other buttock.

Her breath raced and she tried not to holler, knowing only too well the thinness of hotel walls. He soothed a hand over the places of impact, but before she could relax he struck her several times again.

"Getting pink," he said. "Even nicer now. That feel good?"

"Yes," she whispered. "Thank you."

"Now I want you to get undressed, and quickly, mind you. No floor show. Shift all the gear off the bed apart from the paddle. Then stack the pillows in the centre but on the left-hand side. Make a mound with them so you can lean over it, head down, your arse raised and ready for me."

She faced him and hugged herself, nervous but thrumming with anticipation. He sprawled in the armchair, cocky and confident. In the dimly lit room, his weathered good looks gave him the air of a cynical crook, the smug tilt of his lips only adding to the effect.

"So I've got to do all that while you just sit there?"

He fought to repress a smile. "Damn right you do. Why? You got a problem with that?'"

"Depends on my reward. What are you going to do to me after that?"

He raised his brows, smirking. "Whatever the fuck I want. And if you don't get a wiggle on, I'm going to do it twice as hard."

She held still for a moment and smiled, reluctant to attempt bratty insolence but wanting to encourage the threat.

"Well?" he said.

Another deliberate pause to suggest she was gearing up for battle. Then she shrugged as if it were no big deal and stripped briskly. She followed his orders, moving this and that, heeding his request for speed while wishing she weren't naked. She couldn't have looked anything except inelegant. Finally, she clambered onto the bed and bent her body over the unstable heap of pillows. She placed her arms on the bedcover by her lowered head, waiting.

The floorboards gave a tiny creak as he approached. Her heart boomed in her ribcage and thundered in her ears, fear and excitement plucking at her nerves. His hand dusted her warmed, tingling buttocks.

"It makes me hard as rock to see how much you want this," he said. "Watching you scurry around the room like that. Seeing you so hungry for it. So deliciously, fucking hungry. You know what you're going to get now, don't you?"

She swallowed. "Yes, I think so."

"What?"

"Spanked."

His hand circled her flesh. "In email, you said you liked getting 'spanked to high heaven'. Do you remember that?"

In all honesty, she couldn't remember but she feigned familiarity. It sounded like the kind of thing she might say.

"And ever since then," he continued, "I've been itching to get at you and give you a good, solid, vicious walloping."

She whimpered, her juices churning.

"Are you ready? Braced for it?"

"Yes," she whispered.

Nothing happened and she feared he may not have heard her. Then disappointment fell as she realized he was about to run through the standard routine, the ritual of a snarly, "Yes, *what*?" and a hurried, "Yes, sir. Yes master," or whatever honorific of choice was being employed. Hadn't she mentioned those role-plays weren't really her thing? Ah well, too late, it seemed. May as well give him what he wanted.

"Yes—" she began.

"Good!" he cut in.

Their words collided and overlapped, a fraction of clumsiness to remind them they were practically strangers. In a different scenario, they might have become socially flustered with more verbal collisions. "Sorry", "Go on", "No, no, you first".

Instead, he hit her.

One blow followed another as he released a cascade of furious cracks that knocked the breath from her. When she attempted to raise herself from the pillows in defence, he gently and coolly pressed her back into position, his hand on the back of her head. The sureness of that touch, the subtle confident way he commandeered her body, sent a flood of sensation to her core. She groaned in blissed-out shock, the hand stilling her head having more impact on her arousal than the pounding he was delivering to her backside. It was one thing for a man to take over your body with restraints and pain, another thing entirely when he did it by adjusting your limbs to suit his needs. Doll, puppet, cumslut. Again, being his was at the heart of it.

The heat intensified as Jason continued with his pitiless onslaught. There was no punishment scenario, no cruel teasing, no counting out the thwacks or incorporating breathers. He unleashed himself, pure and simple. All Louise wanted to do was lose herself in the brutal pleasure. She gasped and cried, fists balled, feet banging on the mattress as she fought the gathering pain.

When Jason finally paused, panting for breath, her flesh was scorched to sensitivity. She held still, the fire rising even though he'd stopped swatting her. The flush of blood warmed her body several layers deep, her groin thumping and swollen. She whimpered as his hand stroked the soreness, unsure whether she could trust his touch. His caress might have been intended to calm but more likely he was admiring his burnished handiwork. Louise swore she could feel the whorls of his fingertips, the abrasion of his skin cells and the scouring lines on his palm as he swooped across her cheeks.

"Well done. That was a lot to start with. I'm pleased you could take it." His breath was ragged and eager although his tone was level. "We're going to take it up a notch now, OK?"

From the corner of her eye, she saw him reach for the wooden paddle. She made a tiny noise of complaint. The implement was shaped like a small, flat cricket bat, its mahogany polish gleaming in the half-light. Hell, this was going to hurt, especially if he was going to continue with his relentless force. She drew steadying breaths, trying to focus on the ebbing aspect of her pain, telling herself the next round would be bearable.

He touched the paddle to her sizzling skin. Its cool, smooth surface offered a moment's relief. He gave her several light, springy taps, getting the feel of the tool in his hands.

"Nice," he said, and she didn't know if he were referring to her arse or the paddle. He withdrew then slapped the nasty little bat hard on the fullest curve of one buttock. The contact brought sharp, high pain flooding to the surface of her cheek but the impact was less than she feared. After the thwack of his hand, the flat piece of wood seemed to bounce off resilient flesh. But no sooner had she thought that than the heat began to soar.

"Ah, ah, ah," she cried, trying to ride the intensity.

She steeled herself for another blow but for a while none came. She listened to him breathing, wondering what he was thinking. Then, without warning, another wedge of pain slammed into her hot cheek. She yelped in shock.

"I like that," he said. "Like hurting you. Physically hurting you."

Another crack detonated on her flesh, a neat hit spanning both cheeks.

"Count to ten," he said. "Out loud."

She did, slowly. When she'd finished, another blazing attack thumped into her soreness. His aim was lower, striping new pain across her upper thighs. Then again and again, until she was wailing in constant protest, old and new pain building indivisible layers of heat. She wasn't sure how much more she could take. What was he doing to her? Would she be marked and tender for days to come? Of course she would be. This wasn't a light spanking. Already, Jason was laying down memories in her body, deep memories that would blossom on her skin as blue-violet bruises pricked with hints of green.

Behind her, his breath pumped. He tossed the paddle aside, stripped off his T-shirt and chucked it to the floor. She caught a waft of fresh sweat and heard his belt buckle clink. It was over; he was going to fuck her. Well, thank God for that. Maybe she'd be able to sit down tomorrow after all.

He rubbed a gentle hand over her tenderized flesh. "I need to belt you." His voice was gravel, his words delivered in the banal, faux-apologetic tone of a psychopath.

She protested, twisting over her shoulder to see him fold the belt in two with luxurious, wanton leisure.

"Face forward," he said. Immediately, she returned to her demure, obedient position, her cunt throbbing, her pulses galloping. Even though she wanted him to push her, she dreaded the slash of his belt and feared the deadness in his voice. Pain came in different shapes and sizes. Louise liked solid thwacks of pain, the blocky sort that held and throbbed. Mean, pinching stripes of pain terrified her. The sting of crops and whips was outside her limit. A belt was right on the border. And an unknown man wielding a belt, a man oblivious to her fussiness, made that border hairline fine.

But at that moment, arse up, head to the bedcover, her psyche sinking into a state of submission, she was eager to test that border. Lazy reasoning would claim she was doing this for him. But she wasn't. She was doing it for herself. She craved surrender. She wanted to go deeper, wanted him to take her under so she was powerless and fully at his mercy.

The mattress bounced as he raised his arm. In her peripheral vision, a shadow leapt across the wall as he brought the looped belt crashing down on her rear. Pain burst across her crimson buttocks. She yelled and cursed, no longer caring about thin hotel room walls. Without waiting for her to recover, he landed another hit on her flesh, right on top of the last, or so it seemed. She banged one foot on the mattress.

"Fuckfuckfuck!" she said. "No more, please. No!"

A third agonizing stripe slashed at her rear.

"Please!" She hardly knew what she was begging for. More or less?

But he knew. He thrashed with all his might. The pain roared inside her, not just at the site of impact but everywhere. Even her ears were getting hot. Tears pricked her eyes.

The leather bit deep again, pushing her to the brink. Another blow followed, slicing into her skin. Too fast now. She was half-delirious.

"Red! Red!"

The safeword boomed in the room, cold and hard. A switch was flipped. Everything stopped. Show over. Red! But she didn't want to stop, wasn't near that point. Her flesh was zinging with excruciating bliss. She wanted to keep pushing this scene till she was in pieces, floating in subspace. And the pieces would be his, her shattered, unmoored self a gift to him, proof of how much she needed him to bring her to submission. Of how much she trusted him already.

Red!

Why was her mouth making this word in defiance of what she craved? Why had he stopped beating her?

Red! As if the buses from earlier had slammed to a stop, brake lights glaring, rays of rubies stuttering and flaring, fields of poppies. Red!

His voice cracked, splintering the sound. "Red." The word tumbled on a weak sob. The belt thudded in a far corner of the room. Louise swung around, the bank of pillows slipping and spilling from under her.

He was aghast, his hand clamped to his mouth, his eyes swimming with tears. He shook his head then snatched away his hand. "I'm sorry. I can't continue."

Louise gawped. *He* was safewording *her*? That made no earthly sense. He was the top, the one in control, the person who wasn't being subjected to a vicious barrage of pain.

"What?" She felt cheated, slightly angry. "What do you mean?"

"I can't continue."

"But I want to. Please!" She was too horny and frantic to be a decent human being.

"It's too much, I can't. I'm sorry."

The drop from arousal to reality left Louise reeling, her mind struggling to process the transition. Seconds ago he was her competent tormentor in a game of conflict and now he was broken and helpless, gazing at her in horror. Or was it fear?

"I don't understand," she said snappishly. Perhaps he wasn't dominant after all and was just trying it on for size, using her to better understand his tastes. What was the problem? Had he damaged her skin in some way? Drawn blood? She touched her bottom and twisted around, trying to examine herself. She checked her hand. Everything seemed to be in order. She frowned at him, baffled. He gazed back and his eyes seemed to have melted, the hard glitter of earlier dissolved into dark pools.

"What is it?" she asked, her compassion returning.

Jason raked his fingers through his brown curls. He offered a small smile intended to reassure.

"Phew," he said, forcing out a breath of a laugh. He sank onto the bed edge, sitting at a slant.

"You OK?" she asked.

He pressed his lips together, fighting back tears as he shook his head. "No. I need to stop."

"Hey, I know. That's fine. We've stopped." She cupped a hand to his upper arm, unsure how to touch him. Like a friend? A lover? "You want to tell me about it?"

He inhaled deeply, bringing himself under control. Louise felt bad for noting the muscular beauty of his torso. His shoulders were broad, his pecs defined but not sculpted, half hidden by his fur of dark hair. His abdomen was flat, a dark line running from his navel into the low-slung band of his jeans where black underwear peeked. He was hard, his angled shaft pushing at denim. She wondered if he felt bad for that.

"You mind if I get undressed?" he asked. "I could use some skin-on-skin contact."

"Be my guest."

Jason stood, shoved down his clothes and tossed them onto the cubed armchair. His cock was only semi-erect now but still handsome in the way it hung from his dark pubes. Guiltily, Louise eyed his pert, athletic arse as he strode across the room for their drinks. He returned, set down the glasses, and sprawled sidelong on the bed. Louise lay on her front, too sore to allow her buttocks contact with any surfaces. She ran a hand over his taut belly, wanting to be intimate without being inappropriately sexual. Jason edged closer so their bodies were touching and stroked along the dip of her spine. He traced a finger over one buttock, making patterns in the embers.

"Ouch," he said softly.

"It's OK. I liked it."

"I know. I'm not doubting you."

A silence passed. She took a sip of whisky, wondering whether she ought to wait for him to speak or encourage him to open up. What sort of person was he? Which approach would he prefer?

Eventually, he spoke. "I have some baggage."

"I think we all do once we're in our forties, if not before."

"Yeah, I know. But I'm carrying mine badly."

Her heart sank a little. She could now predict how this was going to pan out. He would start telling her about one of his exes, how his heart could never be mended. And he'd expect her to listen to his woes and bolster his ego, as he grew self-pitying and dull. She'd met them before, the lonely guys who didn't want a date but a therapy session. Such a shame because up until this point in the evening, she'd been liking Jason more and more. Clearly, desire had blinded her to the potential drawbacks. She was usually quick to pick up on the types who regarded intimacy as a chance to offload and get maudlin. Well, this was another one to chalk up to experience.

"When I'm domming someone," he began. He rolled onto his back and gazed at the ceiling, ankles crossed. "And it's getting good, really good, and I'm hurting her, I worry I might go over the edge. So I pull back. I'm scared that if I don't, the . . . the intensity, the pain and violence might . . ." He tailed off and drew a single deep breath, eyes fixed on the ceiling. "Might trigger flashbacks to my experiences in the Gulf War." He exhaled forcefully and twisted his head to look at her. "That's it, in a nutshell. I'm ex-military. I've got my own war going on." He tapped his temple then returned to staring at the ceiling. "I don't want to relive what I saw in Kuwait. And so sometimes, that stops me having the kind of sex I want to have."

Louise half wished he'd got cranky about an ex. So that's what he'd meant by not wanting to cause harm. Harm to himself. Mental harm. She struggled for a response and all she could come up with was a whispered, "Shit. I'm so sorry." She swept a hand over his chest, his body hair crisp and springy to her touch. He responded by rubbing her arm as if grateful.

"There's no aftercare in war," he went on. "You're on your own. I've no obvious physical scars or injuries so people assume I'm all right. Everything's healed, intact."

"You have PTSD."

He shook his head. "No, it's not that bad. I left the Army years ago, it's behind me. I'm OK for the most part. Jeez, better than a lot of vets. And compared to some guys, what I witnessed wasn't . . . I'm OK, I swear. I'm OK except when I have D/s sex with someone like you. Someone who's into it, whose safeword seems a long way off. I can't see where it's heading." He rolled his head to face her. "I'm sorry to disappoint. This hasn't happened for years. I thought maybe I'd got past it but . . ."

"Have you tried getting professional help?"

"Nah, no point. What do you do? How's anyone going to understand that? Hi, my name's Jason and I'm an inadequate pervert."

"You're not inadequate. You're suffering the consequences of war."

He scoffed without malice. "Hardly. This isn't suffering. It's nothing. Nothing important. It's a failure to access the full spectrum of pleasure available to me. So indulgent. Self-ish. I did terrible things as a soldier, monstrous. If you knew, you wouldn't want to be in the same room as me. Half the time, I don't want to be in the same room as me. They numb you to make you do it. And I did it. I did it. I saw the horror and futility of war, and I was part of that." His voice wavered, on the verge of a sob. He paused before continuing. "This now, not being able to go there, it feels like I got my just deserts. No, not even just. My penalty should be infinitely worse."

A murmur of voices passed outside the door, weirdly close and mundane.

"I'm a little out of my depth here," said Louise. "I'm a technologist working in food and drink packaging innovations. Today I've been discussing Squeezy Peasy – trademark, I'll have you know – sachets of spreads for children's lunch boxes. I'm no expert in war and psychological trauma. But I'd say, at the very least, you have a lot of guilt you're not dealing with."

Jason sighed heavily. "This date's not going too well, is it?"

For a long time, Louise said nothing. Jason reached for his whisky and downed the remainder in one.

"I'd like to see you again," said Louise. "I don't want us to stop here. But I don't want to be put in the role of fixer. Right now, I'm interested enough . . . I care enough even, to say, yes, I'm prepared to support you, to be patient and help if I can. But only if you do your part and start some kind of treatment or counselling. For my sake. Because I'm not equipped to deal with this. Nor are you. And I would like us to . . . to have access to this full spectrum of pleasure you mentioned. I don't think it's wrong to want that. I don't think we should spend our lives punishing ourselves for . . . for being human.'

He sighed and folded his arms back over his eyes as if shielding himself from a glare. His Adam's apple bobbed in his stubble-peppered neck. "Thank you."

Louise ran broad, comforting strokes over his torso, stretching to print a kiss by his armpit. "*De nada*," she said. "Maybe I'm just greedy. I enjoyed what we did together tonight, and I want more. I think we . . . I think this is promising. We're good together. And we only live an hour or so away from each other. I don't want to rush anything but, yeah, this is good. Nice. Sexy. I'm almost glad you had a little meltdown. I like a man confident enough to be vulnerable."

Jason smiled. "And I like a woman confident enough to tell me to sort out my own shit."

Louise laughed. "That isn't *quite* what I said."

He rolled towards her, sliding his arm across her back. "How's your arse?"

She turned onto her side, nudging closer to him. His cock bumped against her thigh, drawing tracks across her skin as it swelled.

"Good, thanks. How's your cock?"

"Excellent. Hard. Horny." He rocked against her. "Touch it. See for yourself."

She did, fingers curling around his warm, thick shaft. He twitched in her fist as she worked his length, his lips smearing kisses across her neck, his hand roving over her breasts. His jaw scratched her skin, his scent filling her nostrils.

"You OK?" she checked.

"Yes." His voice had that edge again, firm and harsh. His hand sped down to the juncture of her thighs and he hooked two fingers inside her with a ferocity that made her gasp. "Apologies if I'm too gentle with you," he growled.

Evidently, he was being ironic. He raised himself on one elbow and began slamming at the thick cushion of her G, his thumb bumping her clit. He watched her intently, studying her reactions and savouring the effect he had on her. Louise flopped onto her back, opening her legs as she groaned and writhed. The bedcover was cool and rough on her reddened buttocks, and she thrilled to recall how deliciously he'd hit her. She closed her eyes, discomfited by his focus on her face and wanting to abandon herself to unselfconscious joy.

"That's right," he cooed. "Relax into it. Let me make you come."

She bleated with nearness, tension bunching in her thighs.

"Let's see how greedy you really are." He eased a third finger inside her, filling her with knuckles and bulk, then twisted position to lower his mouth to her clit. Heat and wetness sloshed over her, his tongue flicking as he increased the pressure within her.

She cried out as her climax peaked. Ripples pulsed on his buried fingers, ecstasy gripping and flying.

"Fuck," he gasped. "Fuck, yes."

He withdrew briskly and lunged for a condom, tearing the foil with his teeth as if ravenous. He sheathed himself and shoved her legs aside, kneeling between her spread thighs. Inside, she was spongy and sensitive from coming, her breath still rushing. He drove into her tightness and they groaned in unison, her flesh clinging to his solid girth. She reached up to encircle him but he knocked her arms away, jamming them against the bed.

He fucked her like that, holding himself over her trapped, half-curled body. With her legs frogged back beneath his powering weight, she moaned greedily, wanting to come again but needing a touch on her clit.

"Come on me," she pleaded, hoping he would release her arms.

He grunted in eagerness and pulled away, tugging off his rubber with obvious satisfaction. He jerked his cock above her stomach and, her hands now free, Louise fretted her clit. His cries rose, his fist pumped, then he was spurting and groaning, his bliss jetting onto her skin.

The sound of his pleasure took her to the edge and she came for a second time, shivering and bucking beneath him. They paused, panting for breath, the world on hold. Then they collapsed together, his come sliding between them as they held each other tight.

Louise thought back to that moment in the bar when the swoop of bus headlights had reminded her of searchlights.

She'd imagined them caught out and guilty, nowhere left to run. The memory was young but it seemed like so many moons ago.

After a breathless while, they relaxed their embrace. With languorous affection, Jason stroked down Louise's spine. Teasing and testing, he clawed a slow, possessive scratch over one cheek, reigniting the heat of his frenzied spanking. He grinned, nails digging deeper, and she laughed gently.

Under the livid red surface of her buttocks, a storm of bruises was gathering, his marks formed of dark colours from the far side of the spectrum. Gave battle in vain.

She kissed him, determination and hope burning brightly inside her. She would fight with him to make this thing better.

The Subsequent State

M. Christian

The human intellect passes from its original state, in which it does not think, to a subsequent state, in which it does.

Aristotle

I don't know how to start this, so I guess I just have to. I hope you'll understand but this is something I have to do . . . I know it's wrong. Everything I've learned has taught me that.

But I also know that I can't live with myself until what happened to you will never happen to anyone ever again. Knowing that they are out there, and will come again, and possibly take more that they have already taken – I have to do something.

I love you – and until I knew you I never understood what that word meant, so I can say it in a way I could never say it before, to a person who has given me so much.

If I don't make it back . . . you have become love *for me – and it's because I cannot imagine life without you that I have to do this.*

Josh

The world – looking out at it through the night vision goggles – was green: the tall, wild grasses where he crouched, and slowly crawled through, were green; the trees on the distant hills, that swayed in the low wind he couldn't feel so close to the ground, were green. The stars in the sky were too bright – a wince there – pinholes of green stuck through a paler green canvas.

And there, between the hills, below him, were the rolling geometries of what he'd been told they called "environs": hexagonal panels joined together into organically rolling blisters. Through the plastic, fragmented by the interference of the structure, were the vividly dancing green of what he guessed were old flames – and, moving much more slowly, carefully, purposefully were the green illuminations of people.

No, he corrected himself, squeezing the polycarbonate grip of his father's gun tightly, feeling the grid pattern even through the material of his gloves. *Not people.*

There were cameras, why he was low in the tall grass, but he'd learned that there weren't that many of them, and the ones they did have more than likely wouldn't be able to pick him up.

Arrogant, he thought, relaxing his grip on the gun. A breath then, to steady himself: and, with the inhale and subsequent exhale, he closed his eyes against the green of the world. There were sensors – microphones and more – but they, too, shouldn't be able to pick him up . . . especially against the rustle of the trees, the sighing of the grass . . . so he allowed himself to move his lips, though he didn't speak the prayed: – *should we perish in the struggle, may God embrace us and find for us a place in His Kingdom.*

The hill he was on rolled down to an access road: an unpaved narrow ribbon that undulated around the edge of the structures. When he reached where the grass ended and it began, he turned and lowered himself down, taking the final inch between his boots and the dirt path cautiously slow. Both feet down, he dropped down, scanning left then right then left again, looking for any sign he'd been spotted, but all he saw was the road vanishing around one bend and then the other.

In front of him, between the hexagon-panelled roof of the environ and the ground, was a low wall of coarse-surfaced bricks. The wall, the plastic immensity of the structure, the dirt at his feet – everything he could see was still an artificially brilliant green.

When he turned the goggles off then flipped them off the world was dark, but only before his eyes adjusted: gradually his memory of the environ – its geometric panels, its organic bulge that now filled half the sky, blocking the intensity of the truly-white stars – the bare coarseness of the road, the almost-as-coarse bricks, was replaced by his actual vision.

A few yards away, he could see a break in the wall: a man-height indentation. Getting closer, his eyes had adjusted enough to see the hinges, and the handle.

There'd be an alarm the moment he turned it. He'd have five, maybe ten minutes maximum, before a patrol arrived and gunned him down. His best chance would be to get in and then move as far away from the door as he could – if he was lucky, buying him an extra few minutes.

Breath in, breath out, right hand on the gun, left hand a hovering inch above the handle. *Brave warriors, should fate find us in battle, May our cause be just. May our leaders have clear vision. May our courage not falter—*

He closed his eyes, and when he did he saw again their bodies . . . the blood, thick and brown on the carpet; their arms and legs turned and twisted clumsily where they fell. The smell of hot copper in the air.

On the wall – painted with the blood of his daughter or his wife, no one told him – was the Greek letter for *alpha*, the symbol of the Noos.

Five or ten minutes. Not much time. Turning the handle, pushing the door inwards, he prayed to Jesus Christ that he had enough time to kill at least that many of them—

From the door, he found himself on a narrow path, floored by planks: some kind of access way between the rest of the environ and the wall. The wood muffled his steps, a small miracle he was grateful for as he ran.

Earthly fertilizer, freshly cut wood, perfumed smoke, sickly-sweet flowers . . . an arboretum tickled his nose. Vision further adjusting, he saw the wall to his left, and the intertwined branches of trees on his right – bright and raw where someone had clipped them to keep the path free. Leaves swiped at his eyes, brushed against his uniform, but otherwise he trotted, hand on the butt of his gun, almost silently.

Silently . . . no alarm, no sirens. They must know; they had to be on the way. Five minutes, maybe ten, hopefully more.

Then the path turned sharply and vanished. Still being led by it, he was spilled out onto the edge of a small, ploughed field. When his boots kicked at one of the furrows, the scent of nature bloomed up his nose. In the distance were the golden glows of the fires that had been the green dancers in his goggles. Flickering in and out of darkness beyond them were more and more trees, but also the further distant forms of what looked like a four-tall step of square windows.

"Hello."

Down the sights of the gun, she was rosy . . . almost golden, intermittently lit, sporadically revealed, by the distant bonfires.

She was older than he was by five years or maybe even ten. Her hair was so red the fire made the curls and tumbles of it look like she was as much alight as the flames. Her face was lined, but each seam and wrinkle looked like the end, or the beginning, or maybe even the ending of a smile. Her eyes were bright, either orange from the far-off flames, or that colour under any light. Around her neck was a leather thong, tugged down between her breasts by what looked like stone charms and tiny brass bells. She was plump: a healthy weight in arms and legs that spoke of her nature, a comfort in that what she was . . . *she was.*

"It's all right. There's no reason to be afraid."

She was naked: not bare, not stripped, not exposed. She stood, still at the end of his pistol's sight, rich earth squished up between the toes on her bare feet; her heavy breasts, dark-nippled, and tanned were also . . . *what she was*. Between her heavy thighs was a triangular curl of also-red hair, as wild and unkempt as the hair that flowed and spilled down her back and arms. There was no clumsy dance of seduction, no loud arousal in her: the earth between her toes; the dark, tanned, richness of her skin; the freedom of her hair; the naturalness of her body; all of it was simple, honest, and earthy.

—and she, or her people, had killed his wife and daughter: slipping in at night and slitting their throats. *Brave warriors, should fate find us in battle, May our cause be just. May our leaders have clear vision. May our courage not falter. Jesus Christ, Our Lord And Saviour—*

"No one is going to hurt you."

She spread her arms. Down his sights, he saw her smile: a sign of calm, of peace, of welcome—

The shot was thunder, a crack of nightmare loud that matched and then beat the drumming of his heart. In his hands, the pistol bucked, wrenching his wrist and arm.

It fell from his hand, so heavy he felt its impact through the soil, through the soles of his boots. He followed it down, his knees plunging into the thick, soft darkness of the field.

The world wasn't green. It wasn't black. He couldn't see. He wouldn't see. Squeezed shut so tight he wanted it all, every leaf, tree, bit of dirt, star in the sky, man, woman, child to leave his sight. The tears came, and right behind them the sobbing, the screams. His fingers dug at his cheeks, wanting to rip it all away – rip everything away and just end.

Then she was touching him . . . no, that's not quite right. A handshake is a touch. A hand on the shoulder is a touch. She wasn't just touching him: kneeling down in the heady fertility of the field, she wrapped her arms around him and held him tightly, like she was trying to pull herself into him, push herself down into the pain that wracked his body.

"It's okay, it's all right. You didn't hurt me. You didn't hurt anyone. It's all right . . . everything is going to be all right . . . you're safe . . . I'm *safe . . . it's all going to be okay . . ."*

The way she spoke, the timbre of her voice, the tone of her words, the way they came – without suspicion or doubt – from within the honesty of her . . . he felt his body relax, his muscles release the fist they'd made of his arms and legs.

And when he was finally able to open his eyes the first thing he saw was her face: the joy and laughter of her lines, the dancing bonfires of her eyes; and her wide, beaming, and truly happy smile.

Then the tears came again, but this time they came from release, from relief, from light . . . and he wrapped himself around her just as she was wrapped around him, and just let them come.

Time . . . . . . broke.

He was aware, of course, of what happened, but only as it happened. Later, when he tried to piece it all together, it was as if the events, the happenings between pulling the trigger to when he opened his eyes to bright sunlight splintering, fragmenting through the distant, hexagonal ceiling: there was darkness, heaving sobs, hands on his body, her fingers entwined with his own, his feet stumbling over the furrows . . . growing closer to the fire, the soft music of low voices coming and going as he was led from the field and to a cement pathway, the flames revealing more and more of where he was . . . but he didn't care about that, or even where he was being taken. Her fingers were entwined with his, her body was next to his, and the other hands were gentle – forceful, guiding, but gentle.

His gun was gone: when it was taken he didn't care. The same with the grenades – both clipped to his web belt and in his backpack.

The cement pathway was smooth and hard under his feet, and he stumbled, almost falling, but her fingers were entwined in his and the other hands, how many he couldn't say and never did find out, caught him, supported him.

The bonfires' licking glow showed a staggered tier of repurposed shipping containers: a three-high step of rectangular boxes, windows where there'd previously been corrugated steel, doors where there'd previously been corrugated steel, miniature greenhouse blisters and boxes where there'd previously been corrugated steel.

They – whoever they were – and the woman, whose fingers

never left their firm mixing with his own, whose nude body never left his side, brought him up three flights of stairs, to a home that had previously been a shipping container.

His clothes were taken from him: how and in what order he didn't care. The same with his boots, and the rest of the gear he'd brought with him.

They – whoever they were – left him, fading away with soft murmurs of voices. One, though, stood out, a kind of marker in his memory: *"Are you sure?"*

"Yes," she'd answered, guiding him through a tiny house illuminated only by the heartbeat pulsing of the bonfire down below. *"We'll be fine."*

Then time . . . broke again: and all he remembered was her hand guiding him to a great bed, a shadowy ocean of quilt and comforter. Without releasing him, she took one corner and cast a triangle of it aside.

Without needing invitation or instruction, he sat on the exposed sheets – the coolness of the fabric a faint sensory shock against the heat of his bare skin. She lifted the cloth, lifted the quilt, and then guided him into the bed.

He remembered . . . he remember praying, though he was unsure if he spoke the words out loud or if they'd just been thundering through his mind: *Our Father in heaven, hallowed be Your name. Your kingdom come, Your will be done . . .*

He was committing a sin . . . he was committing *the* sin. There was nothing right about what he was doing: no justification existed or could even be argued. No priest back home in Liberty could absolve him. He had failed his community; he had failed his family; he had failed his wife; he had failed his daughter; he had failed Jesus Christ, His Lord and Saviour. He had failed everyone and everything that mattered to him . . .

She held him. That's all she did: just held him: her naked skin again his: the heat she generated like a stove, the thick texture of her skin – tanned with a calm and unashamed familiarity with the sun – against his. He felt her breathe – long, slow intakes that were held for the barest of moments before releasing in a similarly long, equally slow exhale, warmer (if possible) than her already hot skin.

In his broken memories, he remembered wanting to die – for the world to vanish, to absolve him of his failure and his sins, and then – with that further shame – he wanted to run, to escape . . . but with those feelings also came a weakness of his legs . . . his spirit.

The woman . . . he didn't even know her name . . . just held him, arm and legs next to and over his, her breathing against his neck and cheek, her arm stretched over his, her hand in his, her fingers knitted between his own.

His face felt warm . . . and wet. He was crying, the tears first then the shift, then wracking sobs that rippled and surged up and out of his lower body. Between the rasping gasps for air and the howling exhausts of sorrow and pain he heard her, a soft voice whispering in his ear, a warm song of presence, caring, and comfort: *"It's okay . . . it's okay . . . it's okay . . ."*

Her face was between her hot, heavy breasts: the earthy smell of her body, plus the equally rich early aroma of the soil she'd so recently been working. It was a smell he didn't know: his world had been clean, incensed, perfumed, and always so meticulously prepared to prevent offence, side-step blasphemy. This woman, who held him, his face between her large breasts, was only and just and pure was what she was: ground and dirt and warmth and she was holding him and telling him in a kind song of true caring that it was going to be okay . . . she was honest and true and, for the first time in his twenty-five years, he wasn't scared of doing the wrong thing.

His face was between her breasts, the heat and heaviness of her, the aroma of her body and the earth, becoming the only thing that he could – or want to – feel. A firmness grazed his cheek, a rubbery contact that drew his mouth to it without a care or a thought.

He nursed, he sucked, he suckled, and as he did he heard the softly, then throatily, moan – and as he did he felt the nipple in his mouth grow harder and harder . . . rising and expanding in his mouth – and as he did he felt his body, without thought or plan, respond with equal rising and expanding.

Her hand stroked the back of his shortly cut hair, a calming, caring motion that again brought tears to his eyes, that made his body wrack and surge with released pain and fear – but he didn't stop sucking and licking at her nipple. It was her, and she was here, with him, and she cared . . . she cared. For the first time in his life . . . she – anyone – honestly *cared*.

She moved, she changed how she lay on the bed. It wasn't a conscious thing, he felt – the same way his own body seemed to shift without thought of intention. They were simply together, in her big bed, she stroking his head, he sucking her nipple, and then his penis felt touched something hot and moist . . .

Time slowed, the world left. There was nothing but he and she and the bed. The rest of everything was unreal, a hazy domain beyond the darkness of her room . . . and none of it mattered.

Because time left, and the world slowed, he didn't know how long they were connected, his penis slowly, patently, sliding in and out of her . . . *region*. A voice whispered the word sin, and with it came another sob, but she spread her legs, pulled him deeper, and when his eyes flickered open for the briefest of moments and he saw her freckled, full and so-real face and then the beautiful, kind, sweet and kind – so kind – face lost to a kind of pleasure he'd never seen before, she ran her fingers over his cropped hair once again and she said, in a voice almost too low to hear, "It's okay . . ."

He ejaculated. It was something he had done before, of course. When he was younger it came with as much stabbing guilt and shame as any pleasure. Later, with his marriage, it had come as the sign of conclusion: a ritual performed for the purpose of the result . . . his daughter. But then, with the world gone, with time gone, it was nothing but a glowing, surging, roll of pure pleasure.

And with it, with the shaking release, the quivering that

raced up and down his body, he moaned – making a sound he'd never made before: a composition of happiness, bliss, relief, expansion and, for the first time ever, *safety*.

His collapse was into the swell of her breasts, his mouth's pursuit again for a nipple to fill his mouth with, was natural and comfortable: a progression that did not need thought or planning or concern for anything. He was there. She was there. Nothing else was.

In time, he slipped, tumbled, fell down and down and down into sleep: her arms curled around his body, his face pressed into the sweat and deep earthy relaxation of her breasts, her breath a slow, warm heartbeat on the top of his head.

He did not dream.

He awoke . . . when he awoke. It could have been morning, it could have been afternoon: he had no idea of the time – her room had no clocks. In the light of the next day, he could see more of what he couldn't the night before. The room was small and tight but didn't feel that way. Between everything was the distant history of a shipping container: ribbed steel walls, the bubbled stream of welds where what had been had been made into what was now.

The bed was the biggest thing there: a sea of quilt, a grid of symbols, some of which stabbed him in the heart with the ghostly memories of angry sermons of hellfire and sulphur, but others as simple as flowers, hearts, sheaves of wheat, corn, and – with a blush to his cheeks – naked men and women.

One wall was stepped, eccentrically placed shelves, each populated with earthen versions of what was on the quilt: handmade totems and icons of earth and men and women, plus glazed pottery, fabric structures he didn't understand. Some looked clumsy, like kindergarten exercises; others were elegant and . . . beautiful. But he frowned when he couldn't see a single cross.

Looking beyond the foot of the bed, he could see two glass doors, beyond them a shower and toilet. The walls of the bathroom tiered with the same kind of earthen humility, the same chaotic parade of symbols.

Light was coming from the right: the light from walls of sliding glass. Light from . . . he turned, twisted in the bed to look. He couldn't stop looking. Below was a field, the same one the night before had been technologically green in his goggles, but now he could see that the field was . . . the earth, the soil, as well as a few tentative stalks rising above the furrows. Above the ground was the sky: a geometric greenhouse dome that had seemed too clear and obvious through the enhancement of his goggles but then, there, looking out at it he could think of nothing . . . lost in the sparkling diamond faceted sun that broke into rainbows as it passed through it.

She came in, sliding one of the doors open, elegantly balancing a ceramic plate with one hand as she did so. "Good morning," she said, closing the door with the same smoothly practised movement.

In the light of the day through the great diamond dome high above them she was . . . *the same*, but there were differences. The light before – and with the recall a vertigo of shame and guilt that only abated, but did not vanish, with a few controlling breaths – she'd seemed . . . he wanted to say larger, like he'd laid with the world itself and not just this woman who sat down on the bed beside him.

His wife was dead, his daughter was dead: murdered by these people. The Fathers had given him tools, weapons, to go out and avenge them. He'd failed.

As he thought this, he looked, saw her in the light of their heretic sun and the only thing he could think was beautiful.

"You must be hungry," she said. The plate she put on the bed between them was a spiral of texture and colour, fruits and vegetables – many of which he couldn't identify.

She wore a simple, clearly handmade wrap that barely covered her ample, full body. Her face was freckled, her cheeks high and marked with comfortable smiles and rich laughter. Her hair was a cascade of brown curls. At first he thought she was much older than he'd first thought – then he realized he'd never seen a woman without make-up before.

Against the homespun and the natural, a tortoise-looking band curled behind one ear, across the bridge of her nose and then was hooked tentatively around her other ear. He thought nothing of it except that it might be an element of jewellery – a symbol he didn't understand.

The fruit she offered him was white, with tiny black seeds in it. She said something but he didn't hear what she said, his mind full of static and noise, flooded with serpents and apples and sin and hate . . . but then she smiled. The woman who was handing him a piece of fruit smiled and all he could think was . . . *nothing* and all he could do was take what she offered him and put it into his mouth.

It was different: a shock, a surprise.

But it was also good.

At first he thought there'd be a lot he had to learn, but after he'd begun he began to realize that, once he understood the direction, the rest came easily.

As the first day closed, night coming through the great dome of what he soon learned was called an environ, as easily as the sun had arrived, the woman – who held his hand gently, kissed his palm, and simply said "Petal" when he finally, clumsily asked her name – had invited him back into her bed. Beyond the speaking of her name she said nothing: they held each other as they had the night before and they soon were touching, caressing, and again his mouth found its way to her nipple and again he felt it swell warmly and richly in his mouth and she moaned and sighed in answer – and again he slid between her legs into a slow dance leading, when it came, to a release that was more than a release . . . and then sleep, heavy and comfortable.

The second day rolled by, a simple, slow predictability of fruits for breakfast, homemade breads and cheeses for lunch, strange and intimidating mixtures of spices and textures for dinner, leading again to Petal's huge bed. During the day she simply held him close and tight, stroking his head, and singing softly.

On the third day she left him, for how long he couldn't say. She explained that she had some work to do and, with a slow, gentle kiss on his cheek, she picked up the slender length of tortoise from a disc on a nightstand next to the bed, slipped it on as she'd worn it before and stepped out. At first he explored her little house, but found while much of it was familiar, the discordance of what he knew and what was different about it made him restless.

The home was the top of a staggered tier of three, the front of it – beyond the glass doors – forming a kind of porch but also the roof of the home below. Looking down the steps, Josh recalled, with the flickering poor memory of a child, lessons of heathen cultures, pyramids and sacrifices of still-beating human hearts.

"Welcome."

The man was . . . he couldn't say how old he was: there were lines around his eyes, a salt and pepper beard under, eyebrows that seemed far too wide and untamed, but there was a mixture to the elements of his face that confused him: his eyes, for instance, were very narrow, but the colour of his skin was far too dark for oriental. His hair was very long and very straight, pulled back and restrained by something Josh couldn't see. He was also very short, a fact that wasn't clear until he finished his climb up the wide stairs leading down from Petal's home towards the field in the center of the environ.

He bowed, a simple and fluid action. "You can call me Mwezi." Like Petal he wore a homespun wrap, though more of a *sarape* than her uncomplicated housedress. "Petal tells me you've been getting comfortable. That makes me happy." He gestured to a wooden chair that made up part of a set of three and a table in front of the house.

Josh nodded and the little man sat down. He gestured towards another chair and, because he simply had no idea what else to do, he sat down next to him.

Like Petal, he also sported an odd band from ear to ear, across the bridge of his nose. But his was warm copper, like sun-melted pennies.

"Excuse me," he said, turning away and looking out at the vastness of the domed environ. For a moment, he thought he might be swatting at flies, but if he was they were either too small or fast for Josh to see. Then, with an odd flourished gesture, he slowly brought his hands together. "Thanks," he said, "had a little work to do."

His laugh was musical and light, a chiming of bells – and not once from when it began to when it ended did Josh ever think that the humour was at his expense. "That must have looked odd to you. I apologize."

"No problem."

"This all must be so strange to you. I hope we've made you feel comfortable."

"It has . . . it is . . . yes, you have. She has . . ." Josh's words came, stumbling and tumbling out, changing meaning and reason between each vowel and syllable. It was like he hadn't spoken in years, had lost not just the ability but also the concept of doing it.

"That's all right. It's a lot to absorb. But you are welcome here – for as long as you want."

Josh nodded, the most simple and direct action he could make to reflect how he felt.

The afternoon felt long, as if the moment Mwezi sat down to when the sun began and Petal made her slow way up the steps, her arms wrapped around a great hand-woven basket of fruits and vegetables.

The lessons had, indeed, started with difficulty – words coming from the little man's lips that had not just no meaning but no context. But as he spoke, carefully, kindly, concept and ideas began to form around the terms until when he used them Josh not just knew their meaning but could begin to anticipate their belonging in the world around him.

Some of them were easy, right there in front of his eyes: a series of environs – climate-controlled greenhouses – gently parading down what was once a devastatingly polluted part of the landscape. Each one moister, cooler than the rest, as water flowed down from the top to the bottom, and warmer up from the ones at the bottom. Some of the details were less easy to comprehend – geothermal power and temperature regulation, bioreactors, passive solar – others as clear as the geometries of the dome and the gently turning wind turbines he could glimpse beyond.

"It's not perfect . . . but then nothing is. But our energy requirements are low so we get very close. The hard part is balancing so many ecosystems, that and keeping an eye on the reactive cultures. But different colonies have different specialties so if we can't handle something someone else out there can. Ours is genetic . . . I'm sorry, that must sound scary."

Josh hadn't realized his stiffening until Mwezi had apologized. At the word he had heard the volume, the thunder, the hell . . . even though the man who was sitting in front of him radiated nothing but quiet calm and tranquil reassurance.

"There's nothing to be scared of. Most of our work is virtual, and we follow the strictest protocols when – or, rather, if – we experiment."

The rest of the day was far smoother, Mwezi talking about their crops, the structure of the colony – that every member, without exception, was expected to perform three tasks: one of their own choosing . . . usually a craft, art, or field of study, one for the community picked from a list and another, also for the community, chosen at random based on their abilities. A laugh came with that, and after the chimes of his amusement: "There are always a few exceptions: doctors get a free pass, as do the folks who work on the bioreactor."

Then came the moment when the world vanished, when the real became the unreal and Josh felt as if he'd lost his anchor to the roughness of the wooden deck, the dirt between Petal's toes, the coarse stitches that held together Mwezi's *sarape*. It began innocently, simply, as the tiny man waved at another invisible insect. Seeing his gestures, he'd reached up and took off the narrow band and held it out. "You've never seen one before, right?"

Josh had shaken his head, accepting the thin copper ornament without thinking.

Standing, Mwezi moved behind Josh and after a softly spoken "Excuse me" he slipped it over Josh's ears and positioned a nearly invisible piece of plastic on the bridge of his nose. It was light, and slightly warm from Mwezi's own skin. It didn't seem to affect his vision at all, resting as it did near the tips of his eyelashes. "This is might be a bit . . . odd. I've set it for basic."

The band was off his face before he was even aware he'd removed it. Colours and shapes, floating letters and words, streams of symbols flowing and weaving in and out of the sky, information glowing from points of nothing but pinpoints of light into details of structure, stress, load, flow and tolerance.

"I'm so sorry," Mwezi said, the softness of his words undeniably sincere.

Josh rubbed his eyes, a prayer working his lips: the calming familiarity of God's wisdom slowing his stuttering heart.

". . . must have interfaces like that in Liberty. Guess not as intense. Oh, of course," Mwezi said, a rise in his voice. "Security . . . privacy. Misplaced logic of temptation being countered by constant dread of observation, eyes over shoulders the flesh and blood equal of content monitoring." The small man blinked. "Sorry," he said again with a wistful grin. "You got me on a tangent."

"It's . . ." Josh took in a slow breath. "I-I'm all right."

Everyone had them. Everyone. From children to adults, they all wore them. Information delivered directly into their eyes, received by optics, sensors, read and controlled by eye and hand gestures. A world of hand-fired pottery, looms, freshly baked bread, tilling the soil – yet a blink away was a world of visual information and imagination where any thought, any fantasy, any piece of information was available.

They were silent, the two of them, for a long time: slowly, the sun set, splintering into geometrics as it passed through each of the facets of the great environ over their heads – until, finally, Petal made her way up those stairs with her basket.

"You can see why they might be offended," Mwezi said, as he stood up and moved to help her with their dinner. "But that's not the only reason they sent you to kill us."

He saw an old man, his exact age a puzzle of grey and wrinkles, wearing nothing but a calm expression as he stood beneath the a massive tree, its leaves and branches broken into hard bright detail and dim shadows by the geometric light of the midday sun broken by the geometries of the dome high above. It wasn't his age, or his nudity, or the dark charcoal of his skin that tugged Josh's attention from the still strange world around him, but the expression of cool tranquility on his worn face. Looking at him, he knew that the man was . . . *there*, and that where he was, under the great branching arms of the tree, was not just a pause in a journey but an embracing of the experience of that exact moment.

He saw a flock of children, a giggling and laughing stream of bright expressions, musical joy, and dancing eyes, turn and stream and flow around and then past him: each one dusty, each one uniquely dressed in degrees of homespun simplicity, each one a different height, each one a different age, each one a different shade of skin, each one a different . . . each one different in too many ways he could measure, but all of them children, and all of them were running, each one was smiling, and each one was with the others – a happiness in their play that tugged at his heart . . . and his vision was blurred, clouded, until he wiped at his eyes and looked down with her clarity at the wetness on his fingers.

He saw a young woman, water cascading down onto her nudity from what, at first, he thought was a simply a decorative fall: the earth of whatever she had been, whatever she had been doing, contouring and winding down the valleys and peaks of her lithe body, the brownness of it just a little darker shade than her skin. She washed, running her hand over her body, with a calm, unhurried luxuriousness. With a turn and lift of her head, she looked at him – and with that same lift and turn of her head, he felt a knife turn and dig into his chest, a pounding weight of guilt and shame that made the air in that particular environ feel like it had been lit on fire. But, still, without a thought, he brought his head up a degree, or maybe two, and saw where he expected anger and shame, accusation and violation there was, instead, the simplest and sweetest of smiles.

He saw a man, tanned nearly to the brown of the stool he sat on, holding hands with a another man whose own colour was closer to that of the smoky small jar he was delicately examining – both dressed in what he had already become accustomed to seeing: clothing worn when protection was necessary, when the air might be cool, when a beautiful garment wanted to be shown . . . and no other reason. On the undulating shelves around them in that small niche pushed into the side of what smelled and felt like the side of a hill, were displayed a staggering in emotion and variety of pots and vases and dishes and urns and jugs and pitchers and . . . and the walls of the little space looked like they had been once cut from some tree, as carefully shaped as the ceramics on the also once-living tree. There was no one there to sell, no one there who seemed to be an owner: there was just the light from a high, frosted plastic or glass blister, the weaving and flowing shelves, the stone and clay items on them . . . and the man was holding hands with another man. They were holding hands. They were holding hands and even though there were no words that came to Josh's mind as sight came to him, he felt the calm casualness, the unrushed familiarity of . . . He saw a woman as she passed him as he walked through the momentary cool darkness of a short tunnel that connected one environ from other – in that case the descent from vampiric dryness in perfect balance with dancing waves of heat among the cacti sprouting green and needled from gravelly sand and parched stone to a new world of almost foggy humidity in a world of still hot but more abundantly verdant of some curling and some gently waving ferns and tall-reaching, wide-trunked, thick barked trees. As with all of them, he could not tell her age. As with all of them, she wore only what she wanted to wear. As with all of them, she moved with a graceful and relaxed purpose. As with all of them, her body was shaped by nature and worn without shame: heavy breasts topped by dark-circled nipples – pierced by bright steel rings – bounced and swayed as she walked, between her thickly muscled thighs she was smoothly shaved, the seam of her genitals rising up through a plush mons. Her hair was long and complex, woven into tight coils dotted with blue and red and yellow and green beads. As with all of them, she wore what Mwezi had called iglasses – and he did not know if she'd even seen him or was peering, as she strolled from a hot and wet world into a hot and dry world, into some unimaginable digital world.

Josh sat on the warm wood of a set of rising steps. The world in front of him was smaller than the others: just a great – if not majestic than at least noble – apple tree, a smattering of smaller bushes, a row of trellises that could have been holding up the coils of beans or berries . . . all ringed by triple-stepped repurposed shipping containers. The day was fading, the sun glowing redder and darker as it sank down behind the hills that he could still see through the hexagonal-panelled dome.

He felt . . . he didn't know how he felt. When he tried to think about it, to look down and understand all he felt was a broken cascade of emotion, a too-loud noise of shame and guilt, sadness, the tension of what could be a scream ready to burst out, the weight of what could be sobbing tears ready to pour – and keep pouring until there was nothing left of him but salty water on the wooden steps.

He didn't know he wasn't alone until the sun's descent was eclipsed and he looked up, and through himself to see Petal was standing a few steps below. "Hello," she simply said, a smile coming with the word.

He couldn't talk: he didn't know what words to use – so no words came.

"Let's go home," she said, reaching out to him.

He took her hand, and let her lead him down the stairs.

With the sun's sleep, the colony did not: lights grew in red and yellow brightness from where he hadn't noticed them into comforting, almost fiery, illumination. With their arrival, he knew the world actually didn't change, the people didn't actually change, but the flickering – as he was gently pulled along by Petal – seemed to pull back thousands of years: and each and every man or woman, old or young, child or adult, began step or move or dance from the walls of some ancient cave.

They stopped, and sat, on a bench by the beginnings of a fire. He may have visited this environ but if he did night and the glowing flames, the sparks rising high into the air and passing, he found himself noticing, through opened panels in the ceiling, had changed it all.

Petal held his hand – holding him there, holding him down. The cloth of the *serape* she wore pushed against his arm and thigh but he could feel, and he knew, that she wore nothing underneath. His arousal made him blush with shame, with him to be anywhere but there . . . but then Petal was holding his hand and even with the sharply broken glass of his mind cutting him, hurting him, he did not pull away, get up, run away . . . because Petal was holding his hand.

A drum began a beat, a flute began a chirping melody, a stringed instrument began to moan and soar, a voice – man or woman he didn't know – began to sing. The song wasn't in English . . . and that was the only language he knew . . . but he did know it was beautiful: a melody of earth and stars, wind and rain, and the joy that came from being a human being and being able to be in the world.

A circle began to spin around the growing fire: men and women, young and old . . . each one spinning past his eyes, twirling and laughing, everyone's eyes blazing with a beautiful bursts of what-could-be starlight. Bodies came and went: tight or not buttocks, large or small breasts, muscled or not legs, swaying or not genitals . . . the dance felt new, like it had just happened; the dance felt old, like it had been happening forever.

The drumbeat began to match the pulsing thunder of his heart, the flute started to complement his in-and-out-of breath, the stringed instrument imitated the song growing in his mind, the voice wove its way down and down and down to where there was a storm of glass shards . . . and then a hand came, a hand reached out from the turning, twirling dancers and he felt a pull, a tug, and then he hadn't let go of Petal's hand but she had simply, lovingly released him.

He spun, he kicked, he danced, he even sang – he held hands with someone, he didn't know who, on his right, and he held hands with someone, he didn't know who, on his left, and it didn't matter. Dust and sand clouded his feet, the fire spat and crackled and snapped up hot embers that tumbled up through the grey smoke smudging the night sky. He saw bodies, naked and raw and beautiful. He saw men and women, joyous and free and beautiful. He saw smiles, pure and bright and beautiful—

—and he saw them – in the starlight of their eyes – seeing him . . . with nothing but affection, caring, love . . . and welcome.

That night, Petal led him back to her little home. There, his feet still dusty from the earth of the dancing circle, his face muddy from the tears that had come, she gently, unhurriedly, undressed him.

Again, they moved to her big bed. Again, they curled together: arms and legs weaving together, lips seeking lips, hands moving where they wanted to go – without thought, without shame, without guilt: as natural as the smell of the dust that still lingered on their bodies.

They kissed: lips and tongues following the same unthinking, unconscious, unhurried pursuit. Time, as he was beginning to not just accept to welcome, stopped for them in her little home, her big bed. The world beyond, too, shrank until it was just the two of them, together.

"Do you trust me?" she whispered.

He nodded, the action transmitted into the soft plumpness of her warm, tanned shoulder, and then to the swell and plushness of her left breast – his head having fallen, naturally and calmly, into the tender valley of her armpit.

"We . . . we don't have a usual way of thinking about the world here. But many of us . . . like me . . . we see the earth, the universe, as being a loving, strong . . . a woman. A Goddess. She cares for us, gives us life, gives us love . . . and so we care for her, listen to her, let her guide us in all things."

He lifted his head. The room was dim but not dark: a dull yellow glow from an ornately decorated shade on one side of the bed, the distant orange of a few still burning bonfires outside the window. Looking at her, at Petal, he saw her as if she were carved from ancient wood, hewn from deeply excavated stone. For a moment, the glow from that simple light reminded him of candles – and candles pulled from the seemingly-so-far-away past sitting in the cold, stiff, discomfort of his family's church. None of the words returned with the memory, but flickering in and out, here and away with the recall of the candles – and matched with the golden glow of Petal's light – he remembered nothing but fear, nothing but guilt, nothing but shame.

There, then, resting his chin on the earthy valley of where her arm met the rise of her shoulder, he felt . . . buoyant, lifted, released. Without a single thought, he pushed himself down, pressed his nose into her armpit and smelled the reality of her, the naturalness of her. Still undirected, he put an arm across the gentle lift of her belly and hugged her – not tightly . . . just enough to hold himself down.

No fear, no guilt, no shame – that world, the one he had left behind, was far behind him, far below him. This world . . . this world, with half-naked men and women, with sex and love, with dirt and knowledge, with kindness and the beauty of learning, with looking forward and not backward . . . it was the only place he wanted to be, the only place that mattered.

On those cold, wooden pews, listening to the thunder and

sulphur of why he was damned, why he was nothing but a sinner – and those who didn't feel the same were even worse – back then he hadn't felt anything but that bitter, cramping trinity of fear, guilt and shame.

But tucked against Petal, smelling her, feeling her sun-baked skin, listening to the music of her voice, he felt it – a lifting, a rising, a soaring. He began to cry again: slow, heavy drops of tears that slickened her arm, the side of that one breast.

She stroked his head, cooing and murmuring not words but the sounds of presence, kindness and love.

He'd never used the word before – in fact even thinking had been considered a great sin – but then and there the word was what he wanted to say, needed to say, because it was right and true and this woman, Petal, had become that and more to him: "My Goddess."

She gently lifted his head from where he'd sought refuge and, in the soft lift of the single lamp, she kissed him on the lips. Not a hot kiss of their lovemaking but, instead, a kiss of sacrament, of blessing, of healing.

"It is an honour," she whispered, "to be your Goddess."

Slowly, as if time had been left behind with those hard wooden pews along with hell and damnation, they moved: her hand stroked his head as his kissed, then licked, then gently sucked on her nipple, feeling it rise and swell in his mouth . . . and with his the sounds from her lowering in tone, coming from down deeper insider her natural self.

The night became a dance of their own, a music of their own: moans and sighs, laughter and little groans: as primal and beautiful as the one Josh had just joined in – but this time the rhythms, the celebration was a timeless two-step for just the two of them: a movement, a celebration of a man and a Goddess.

A movement of arms, of legs, a shifting of hips, a sliding with and then without the remarkably smooth sheets, and she was above him, head resting on the homespun pillows, the bedclothes pushed to one side, and her legs . . . her legs were spread before him.

There she was: not exposed but revealed, not ugly but beautiful, not sinful but human, not damnation but . . . Petal. He'd seen pictures, ones that could cost him chores, beatings, more shame, more guilt, and painful and tedious redemptions. Even his wife's had all but remained a mystery save for moisture and pressure when they performed their expected duties. But here, there, before his eyes, was Petal: curly dark hairs framing an oval of softly glistening lips.

Without a word, she reached down between her legs and parted her lips, revealing to him what was, to her, herself, but what to him were mysteries.

"My Goddess," he whispered at the revelation of her. The glory of her. He would do anything for her. He was hers, and it made him very happy – for the first time in his life.

Even in the soft light he could see her wide smile. "My beautiful worshipper," she said. "My adoring devotee." A laugh then: bright and sparking and beautiful: "My sweet supplicant."

Her hands went down, sliding gently past his face and to the sparkling moisture between her legs.

Patiently, kindly, caringly, she showed him her divinity: "Labia," "urethra," "clitoris," she said, fingers touching as she gently whispered each and every one. As she did, he noticed the texture change, the moisture of her growing more reflective, the perfume of her becoming deeper.

Her fingers moved to the last, the tiny bead at the top of the oval of her intimacy. Slowly, patiently, she began to rub it: and, with each circular stroke of that small point, her voice dropped, her hips swung outwards towards him, her legs moved further apart. As she rubbed, she removed one hand and brought it to her left breast where she plucked but then began to earnestly pull at her nipple.

As with the two of them, she began to make noises by herself: moans and sighs, laughter and little groans . . . and as she did he felt his member, his manhood, what had been his shame and guilt, what he'd wished so many times to be free of, grow firmer and firmer, requesting then demanding that he touch it, stroke himself, as he watched Petal's hand between her legs, pulling at her nipple.

Spreading her lips – the *majora* she called it – she revealed to him the growth of – the clitoris she'd called it – where she'd been rubbing, and as she did a slow, leisurely drop of sweet, slick fluid descended from the depths of her and rolled down between the dim, barely seen, almost unseen curves of her buttocks.

"This," she said of herself, of the slick, hot folds between her legs, "is *life*. It is where we all come from, where every man or woman or—" she stopped for a moment, as if the word meant more to her than most, had connections down deep, entwined around a part of her he couldn't see "—child comes from. It is pleasure, and pleasure is life. My devotee, my worshipper, my lover, my supplicant. I give to you my special gift . . . because you have earned it, and so much more," she said, with each word her voice growing deeper, stronger.

"Now kiss your Goddess—" she said, but as she did, her voice throaty and hoarse, she did not finish – if there was anything she'd intended to speak – because without thought, without any feeling, without anything but a need to touch her, this special woman who smelled of nothing but herself and the earth, who'd opened her life and her arms for him – for the first and only time in his life – he pulled himself up the sheets, rubbing his almost painfully erect penis along the fabric and kissed her gently, reverently, on that small, intimate spot.

No spark, no burst, no roar, no scream, no stars tumbling down from heaven, no cracks yawning open from below, no sulphur, no pain, no suffering, no tears from Jesus, no slap from God . . . there was just the music of her, the throaty, deep, and glorious sound of her pleasure as it rolled and surged through her body, arching and pulling her hands away from her clitoris and nipple to grip, grab, and almost tear at the sheets.

When she calmed, when it had passed to gentle heaves and quakes, Josh pulled himself up and moved – patiently, slowly, naturally – up her full body to where he could wrap his arms around her, her breasts moving against his chest, to where he could look down into her eyes, still unfocused and distant from her release. There, in the slightly remote starlight of her eyes, he saw her seeing him – with nothing but affection, caring, welcome . . . and love.

Petal . . . his lover. Petal . . . who made him understand. Petal . . . who cared for him like no one else ever had. The woman he belonged to. The woman who was his entire world . . . his Goddess.

His Goddess

Time somehow passed. Sleep came, at some point, leading to a warm morning – when, again, they moved together: their pleasures mutual and unhurried, release arriving for them with no plan or purpose. Just he and she, she and he, touching and being touched, lips and tongue, clitoris and penis, until his stomach complained with grumble and she laughed, leaving the bed – but not after kiss after kiss after kiss (giggle) after kiss (giggle) after kiss (laughter) – to bring him something to eat.

Outside, the sun had passed a third row of hexagonal panels – a measurement he absently labelled as early morning. Sitting in one of the wooden chairs outside her little home, he watched it, for no other reason than not wanting to allow any thoughts, anything but what he was feeling, to enter his mind.

Josh saw Mwezi at the bottom of the stairs, the form of the little man, the way he stood, politely asking to ascend and join him. Still, without a thought, Josh nodded, bringing a bright smile to the other man's face.

"Good morning," Mwezi said, putting a hand on Josh's shoulder. The contact . . . *sometime* in the past, would have made Josh uncomfortable, made him pull away, but that was then, and in that moment, sitting and watching the sun inch from one dome panel to another, it was just his friend, just a greeting . . . and it felt good. They didn't say anything: not with a weight of silence but simply because they, the two of them, were sitting together in the sun.

"Thank you," Josh said, when the time was right.

Mwezi touched him again, his hand warmer on Josh's forearm than the sun high above. "There's no reason to."

"Still . . . I—thank you."

"You know now, don't you?"

Josh nodded, carefully, deliberately. There were only a few things to know, things that hadn't been said.

"You aren't the first, of course. Once every few years they send one . . . like you. We guess they have their way of choosing them . . . we don't understand how. They . . . arrange a motivation . . . like with you."

The view out across the environ began to blur, details hazing away until everything beyond was washed out, ill defined. Josh blinked, and clarity – for a moment – returned, but with the tears it all washed away again. He wanted to speak but couldn't, so he just nodded.

"They hate us . . . they *need* to hate us. But it's difficult to maintain that kind of hate, so they create an outrage. They create a man like you. A hero if they return, a martyr if they don't. Probably what you are now." Mwezi took a long, slow breath. "They'll create a suitable end for you: a sacrifice to a pagan god, no doubt. It says a lot about them . . . the shape they give their devils.

"We've debated about it, of course. We could . . . do some harm of our own. Nothing violent, of course; but we can access a lot of their systems, bring them to a halt. But then we'd just be as bad as they make us out to be: give them even more excuses to send men like you."

Mwezi stopped, his hand waved – for moment – out in the air, accessing no doubt some bit of information that only he could see. "It all began the same way, you know: with the death of huge infrastructures – it meant for the first time communities didn't need to be dependent on massive social or economic systems. Yours did the same thing . . . though not to our degree: bioreactors for power, water, and fertilizer; solar, wind, geothermal; more efficient transportation, living arrangements, computer use; 3D printers, so no massive manufacturing facilities—" He laughed. "Sorry, I shouldn't lecture."

Mwezi's hand had, once again, returned to Josh's arm. Josh, without a thought, placed his own on top of the old man's . . . and held it there.

After a long time – this time with the faint tension of an truly uncomfortable silence – Mwezi said, in a much lower, slower, voice, said: "You also . . . should know . . . about Petal."

He knew that Petal wouldn't be gone long. Each of her work shifts was only about three or four hours, and as Mwezi had walked down the steps, without ever turning his head to look back up at Josh, after spending what felt like – perhaps – an hour talking to him, it didn't give him a lot of time.

They'd given him clothes that were close to the ones he'd come in, but he'd seen where Petal had kept his originals. His gear, he found but also didn't expect to find, was gone. That would make things harder, but it didn't change his mind.

He didn't know what he was going to do, but for the first time . . . in what felt like his entire life, it felt right good. Not the way that used had been used before, with a lead weight of humiliation, disgrace, shame, and the unimaginable cruelties of hell and falling from the love of Jesus Christ. This time, as he changed, he felt good in that he was going to be – whatever it was he was going to do – because it was the right thing to do.

The story that Mwezi had told him lit and burned in his mind brighter than anything ever had. That night . . . the night he'd found his Goddess . . . had burned so much brighter in his soul the morning afterwards than the dull illumination that had actually been in his eyes. But now, with the old man's words, he had to blink and blink again. Both to try to hold back the tears he felt but at the brilliant light that streamed from his thoughts of Petal, the even more divine glow of his Goddess.

Beyond the truth that was Petal, Mwezi also told him, again, of when the earth was considered a woman, to be cherished and worshipped, and obeyed. Laughing, he'd said that, no doubt, most of the myths were far from true. Not that it made any difference: it was what the story said, what Petal had done. What so many of these people living their simple, honest and loving lives had done – that was what was important about the story.

He went back to where, he felt, it had all begun. This time, with the sun not high above, he felt more naked and exposed than he'd ever felt before. It was like being camouflaged in the hate and the lies he'd been told all his life, the lesson's beaten into him, the hate painted with the blood of his wife and child on the walls of his home, was a worse sin than any he'd ever been told never to commit. For the first time since he'd woken up in the tiny Noos colony, Josh felt shame.

The door was there, but this time he was looking at it just not in the harsh light of day but from the other side. Hurriedly, he cranked it open, rushed outside, and dogged the hatch shut.

The world was the same, but yet it wasn't. The sky was still blue, clouds still patently drifting across it; the sun remaining a painfully bright, hot point above it all; the friends beyond the colony buzzed and chirped with insects and animals calling to each other. Liberty was about twenty miles away – it would be dark by the time he got there. He could wait, of course. Try to walk in tomorrow, but he felt a tug in his chest that he wanted to at least try to get inside and not get shot approaching in broad daylight.

The story that Mwezi had told, the story that Petal had lived, was so simple, so pure: no contradictions of meaning, no confusion over definition. The old man said that many in the colony had different views, but that they all saw the world the same way.

Mwezi had laughed, despite the heavy air that had grown between them, saying that they had taken this to an extreme . . . sometimes painfully, but the rewards – when it went well – gave them some of their greatest gifts. Again, the old man's arm rested on Josh's – and, again, Josh did nothing to remove it.

The world, Mwezi had said, was how we allow it to be: anger gets nothing but anger . . . but if you – even suffering the deepest of wounds, the greatest of pains – answer with love then that is what you will receive.

Josh turned, for what he knew would be the last time, and looked back. Of the colony all he could see was the barest of pale blue of one of the environs rising above the hills. He wanted to do something, say something, but he couldn't think of anything, so he turned and kept walking. Again, he didn't know what he'd do when he got back to Liberty, or even if he'd have the chance to talk to anyone, but he had to try.

He hoped, too, as he slid down a dusty hillside and jarringly onto the fractured old highway, that Petal would understand the note he'd left—

—that he had to try, somehow, to stop it all from happening again . . . so that the death of her son, killed by a man from Liberty, would be the very last one.

Veiled Girl With Lute

Remittance Girl

Standing at her door in the grey-green evening light, he smells of ozone and sweat. Rain has plastered his hair to his face, his T-shirt and his pants to his body. Rivulets stream down the sides of his face. He blinks the drops from his eyelashes.

Nathaniel comes bearing paradox: rage and desire, hot blood and cold kerosene in equal measure. The iridescent mixture plays in prismatic patterns across his rain-slicked face.

How many miles has he run in an effort to expend the need that is consuming him? The sins lodged beneath his skin like locator beacons for a god who, it seems, has decided not to bother keeping track of his own. She knows the torturous route he's taken in a conscious effort not to end up here, at her door.

Were she a truly good woman she'd send him home to blaze in a solitary conflagration. Because, no matter how unbearable he believes it to be in this moment, it will burn itself out in his airless solitude. If she lets him in he will, despite her complicity, leave convinced he has added to the mountain of trespasses he already carries.

She steps aside and motions him in, feels the heat coming off his skin as he passes her, sees the hunted, haunted look in the eyes that won't meet hers. This is no measured thing, no barbarous pastime made harmless by consent.

The hand that flashes out to seize the hair at the nape of her neck does so with uncanny precision. He drags her to him. Kisses her with a resolute cruelty. Her lip splits on the corner of his tooth. Livid and instinctual fear pumps billows of adrenaline into her bloodstream. The most primitive part of her brain urges her to either fight or flight, but the gravity well of his desire makes flight unthinkable, and experience has taught her that fighting it leads to darker places.

None of those things, however, are the reasons she lets him in or allows him do the things he does to her. To her shame and incomprehension, it is the ugly ache between her legs and the screaming rush that threatens to close her throat. She cannot bring herself to ask him to come to her. But when he does, she cannot turn him away.

The first time they'd met it was here, at her door. He arrived as an expert in something quite different.

The small porcelain figure of a veiled woman playing a lute stood on her deep windowsill; it seemed the safest place to keep the arcane and, to her eyes, gaudy piece of antique frippery. Bequeathed to her by a recently deceased and not particularly beloved uncle, the solicitor representing the executors had suggested that, should she not care to keep it, they could arrange for someone to come and give her a valuation for auction. Having no tolerance at all for knick-knacks, she accepted their offer.

She had expected someone small and delicate in a hand-knitted sweater with wire-rimmed glasses. The man who arrived three days later was much bigger, dark, and suited.

"Nathaniel Bennett. I'm here on behalf of Taylor and Lyons," he said. He had a worn sort of grammar-school accent, with a hint of Belfast in it.

When she led him into the living room and showed him the figure, he picked it up confidently but with focused care in one enormous hand. These weren't the hands of a porcelain expert. They would have looked more at home on a builder or a gardener. He upended the piece, and examined the blue marks on the base: a pair of crossed swords and single blurred dot. He ran his thumbnail over the rough outer edge of the base and made a soft noise in his throat.

"You have a very nice piece of porcelain here, Ms . . ."

"Gennie."

He turned the figure upright and, stepping a little closer to the recessed window, examined the form in the natural light. Made another small noise, and put the piece back on the sill but did not release it.

"You don't have any pets, do you?"

"A cat, why?"

"Then I wouldn't leave it here in the open," he said removing his hand and stepping away.

She eyed the figure again and shrugged.

"Can we sit?" he asked.

"Sure. Of course," she said, shoving a pile of books off the sofa and onto the floor.

Despite his size, he was fastidious in the way he sat down, pinching the thighs of his suit trousers and hitching them a fraction to save the crease at the knee. The armchair was similarly piled with books so Gennie took a seat on the floor. Then, suddenly remembering her manners, offered him some tea.

"That's not necessary." He regarded her in silence for a while.

"Okay, so . . . give me the news," she said, unaccountably nervous.

"It's a piece of Meissen. Very fine. Modelled by Kandler. In about 1743, I believe."

"That means very little to me, Mr Bennett."

"So I see. Don't leave it where your cat can knock it over. That would be a great pity."

She looked up at the figure and the around the room, thinking of somewhere else she could store it for the present. In a drawer, somewhere, perhaps. The sideboard cabinet?

"All right. So . . . Do you think anyone would want it?"

He sat back, interlaced his hands in his lap and peered up at the ceiling. "I imagine there would be many people who want it. It's rare. In perfect condition. Museum quality. German eighteenth-century porcelain is not fetching as much as it used to at auction these days, but there's always a market for the best pieces."

"Oh," she said, unable to think of what else to say.

"I think it would fetch about £5,000 at auction. But if you were to keep it, I'd insure it for a good deal more than that."

Gennie was stunned. "£5,000?" That was no small sum to her. She wasn't impoverished. Her work at the institute paid her some and the odd editing job brought in a little more, but this was an unexpected windfall. "I had no idea."

"There are, of course, private collectors. That would save you the auction fees." He hesitated for a moment. "I could ask around, if you like."

"Would it make much of a difference?"

He shrugged. It was a tense, irritable gesture and showed up the tendons that stretched from his jaw down his neck. Handsome man, thought Gennie. Too bad he's such an asshole.

"Perhaps."

"Look, as I said, I know nothing about stuff like this. So, what do you suggest?"

"It's not 'stuff', Ms . . ."

"Gennie."

"Ms Gennie."

"Just Gennie, actually." Meeting his gaze, there was irritation and weariness in his eyes. She stared back, willing him to thaw a little. What a shame he was so patronizing. He had wonderful eyes. In the slanting light of the afternoon, they were a rich olive colour – not like the usual watery green – but darker and warmed with brown flecks. Silvery threads shot through the dark hair at his temples and he had beautifully sharp, high cheekbones. There was a thin, pale scar that rounded the corner of his jaw and a similar one just above his right eyebrow that dented the skin and interrupted the developing frown lines on his forehead.

He gave her a curt, dismissive shake of the head and stood up. It was like a dismissal. His great frame loomed over her in the small room. Gennie scrambled to her feet, and then felt vaguely annoyed at herself for letting the prat intimidate her in her own house.

"If you're not in a hurry, I will see what I can do."

Standing up didn't help. "I'm not in a hurry," she said, more defensively than she intended. "Just let me know."

At the door, she watched him walk back up the path to his car. It was an immaculately preserved E-type Jaguar. She watched him fold his massive body into the low-slung car and drive away.

A week later, as she was rushing to get out the door and catch the train into London, he phoned her.

"It's Nathaniel Bennett."

No *Hello, no how are you?* Prat.

"Hi, what's up Nathaniel?"

"I've found a buyer for your beautiful little lute player."

The last of the sentence was said with such affection that Gennie realized she was speaking to a man who hated people but loved porcelain. Again, it struck her as ironic that he had been, in his physical presence, and most especially in his manner, the perfect bull in a china shop.

"That's wonderful. Thank you."

"May I come round?"

"I'm sorry. I'm just headed out to work. But I'll be back around five, if that suits you."

"It does."

He was waiting for her under the overhang of her porch when she let herself in at her gate, soaked from the rain, at 5.15.

"I'm sorry I'm late. Fucking trains," she said, hurrying up the path. But she wasn't truly sorry. She was angry for being late and looking like a flake. She was irritated that he was perfectly dry; his massive black umbrella leaned up against the porch trellis. She was especially irked with herself for giving a shit, even as she made an attempt to push the rat's tails of wet hair off her face.

Gennie looked back over the gate, at the lane. "Where's your lovely Jag?"

"I walked."

She fumbled in her purse until she found her keys, slid the right one in the lock and then struggled a bit with the old, warped door. She gave it a tug and an unnecessarily sharp kick to open it.

"Come in," she muttered, without looking back, as she let her satchel slide off her shoulder and shrugged out of her sodden coat, draping it over the banister in the hall. "Want some tea?"

"No."

Walking into her decrepit kitchen, she glanced back at him and flicked on the kettle. "Wine?"

He stood in the doorway, plastic bag dangling from his meaty fingers. "No."

Clearly, he just wanted to get on with this and leave. "You're busy. Of course," she said, snatching the dishtowel from its hook. She rubbed it through her sodden hair, trying to squeeze out the excess. "Let's go through to the living room and we'll get this sorted."

She paused at the kitchen threshold, waited for him to move, unable to get by him. "Shall we?"

"I'm not busy," he said, in a soft, absent way. But he didn't move.

It brought her up short, physically close to him, and she stepped back. The body rush came on so fast and so acutely, it shocked her. She smelled something on him: an acrid, chemical scent, like the smoke after fireworks. Her nipples, already peaked from the rain and the chill of the under-heated house, seized and stung. Suddenly, she couldn't look him in the eye. Gennie was inexplicably convinced he was going to touch her, kiss her and, for a fraction of a second, she saw it vividly in her head.

"You're the torture woman, aren't you?" he said, and stepped back into the hall to let her through.

It was over. Just like that.

She took her a moment to process the question, and laughed. "That's not a very flattering way to put it," she said, leading him into the living room.

"You write about it. I saw an article in the paper."

She raised her eyebrow and grimaced. "The piece on Jordan in the *FT*? Not the nicest of topics, is it?"

Unlatching the cabinet door on her second-hand sideboard, she reached in and took out the figurine. It felt poignantly delicate in her hand. She set it down on the stone mantel of her fireplace.

"No." He didn't move to pick it up. Instead, he set the bulging shopping bag down on the sofa and pulled out a roll of bubble wrap, a roll of sticky tape and a sturdy cardboard box.

"Sorry," she muttered.

"I've found a buyer in Germany. The Germans tend to pay the best prices for Meissen. Although there are a few very dedicated Japanese collectors. He's willing to pay £5,500 for the piece. Is that acceptable to you?"

"Absolutely. That's wonderful."

He reached into the inner breast pocket of his overcoat and pulled out an envelope. Opening it, he drew out the contents. "I have a bill of sale here, which will require your signature on one copy, and a bank draft for the amount."

"Oh, that's . . . that's just great," she said, taking the proffered papers. It was indeed two copies of a private bill of sale, with her named as seller, and the buyer identified as a Markus G. Verner, and a stern-looking draft from the London branch of Deutsche Bank.

Picking out a pen from the bristling cup on the sideboard, she signed one copy in the space provided and dated below it. When she turned back to hand him the letter, he was carefully rolling the piece of porcelain in what seemed like a bizarre amount of bubble wrap. She watched him secure the padding with tape and nestle the bundle into the open box. It fitted perfectly. When he was satisfied, he put the box back into the shopping bag, set in on the sofa and turned to her.

"What drew you to that field?" he asked, taking the letter, folding it, and slipping it into his coat pocket.

"Sorry?"

"Torture. Why torture?"

"Oh, I just sort of drifted into it, really," she said, trying to sound casual. "I took a degree in international law. Human rights issues."

"Really?" He said it as if he didn't believe her.

She shivered, felt cold again and remembered the kettle she'd set to boil in the kitchen. Suddenly she just wanted him out of her house. "No. Actually it was prurient fascination," she snapped.

He was on her in a fraction of a second. She felt the back of her head hit the plaster wall and slide upwards as he hitched his hands under the curve of her buttocks and lifted her off her feet. But the kiss frightened her more. It was nothing like the kiss she had imagined earlier. Not passionate or feral like the rest of his body, it had the eerie quality of a surgeon's knife. Careful, measured, he kissed her as if he were opening up her brain and tasting what lay inside.

It was manipulative and expert. He didn't thrust his tongue into her mouth, or devour her face. It was a stepped, concerted pressure on her senses. He sucked at her lips, pressed into them softly, trailed the tip of his tongue across them until she was kissing him back without having ever made the decision to do so. Her body had decided on its own to wrap an arm around his neck, to hook a leg around his hip. The wiser, rational part of her witnessed this with utter disgust.

"Thank you," he said, pulling away from her mouth.

"For what?"

"For telling the truth."

Gennie blinked. "What truth?"

"Don't do that." He wore the hint of a smile and beneath it a hum of a threat, despite the good humour in his voice.

"Put me down." She used as calm and firm a tone as she could manage, letting her arm slip from his shoulder. "Now, please."

"Aw, don't take it back." The grip on the back of her thighs tightened. He leaned into her, intentionally crushing her against the wall.

"Take what back?"

"The prurient fascination. That," he said, grinding his hips into hers, making his arousal plain, "interests me. Tell me about it."

"What?" Gennie glared at him. Wedging her hands between their chests, she pushed. "Get off me."

"Shush." Nathaniel rolled his hips again, and then again, and again. Even through his clothes and hers, the motion was obscene, bruising, arousing. "Don't lie to me, darlin'," he said, pressing his lips to her temple. The Irish in his accent leaked through the grammar school veneer. "I fucking hate lies."

It didn't matter that the wetness at her crotch made the fabric slip as he dry-fucked her against the wall, or that every bruising grind only intensified the arousal, or that the acrid, gunpowder scent of him, now that he was so close, made her salivate. He was sick: sick like the people she'd spent so much of her life studying from a distance. She knew it in her bones. So why wasn't she kicking and screaming her fucking head off?

"Look," she said in a studied, steady voice. "I mean it. Stop."

"Haven't you ever wondered what it feels like?"

"What 'what' feels like?"

"To be tortured? To be the one who tortures?"

Images, phrases, trial transcripts, military manuals, first-person accounts all crowded her brain. How long had she lived with this mental archive of atrocities? Disgusted, Gennie shook her head to push the thoughts away. "God, no."

Quite abruptly, Nathaniel released his grip on her legs and stepped back, easing her to the floor. His tie was askew. The immaculately crisp shirt now creased. "Another expert who has no idea what they're talking about. Well, that's not news, is it?"

She was cold again, her pelvic bone ached and unexpectedly very, very angry. "What the fuck would you know about it? You're a . . . porcelain expert?" she sneered.

"Among other things." His accent was now full-on Northern Ireland.

"Let's wrap this up, shall we? What kind of commission do I owe you?" she asked, turning and stalking towards the kitchen to get the chequebook in her purse. Behind her she heard the rustle as he picked up the shopping bag and heard his steps behind her in the hall.

"You don't owe me anything."

She was cool now – in control of herself and itching to be rid of him. A glass of wine and a hot bath was what she needed. "No. I don't want to owe you any favours. Ten per cent? Fifteen? Twenty?"

Fishing out her chequebook and a pen, she clicked it efficiently and dated a blank cheque on her kitchen island.

"Really, I'm not a dealer. I'm just a consultant. The love of porcelain goes back a long way in my family. I'm glad I could find a good home for it."

Gennie sighed and looked up at him. It was as if she were talking to an entirely different person. "You're sure?"

"Absolutely."

She was about to see him to the door, but her curiosity got the better of her. "'Among other things'. That's what you said."

"Yes."

"What other things?"

He lowered the box in the shopping bag on the floor and leant his large frame on the worn wood top of the island. Then he levelled his gaze at her. "I think you know, sweet Gennie."

A curious sensation crept up her spine – hot and cold at the same time. She inclined her head. "Do I?"

"Oh, yes. I think you do." He reached across the surface and slid his large hand over hers. "But the question is, do you want to know that you know?"

She should have pulled her hand away, but she couldn't. She should have pulled her eyes away from his, but she didn't. "I'm not sure."

"Well, if you ever get sure, phone me." Nathaniel nodded and stood up, withdrawing his hand. He used it to fish in his coat pocket and pull out a card, which he laid on the table. "And I'm sorry about . . . before." Then, without another word, he picked up the package and saw himself out.

It was dark outside and still raining.

The white linen business card remained exactly where he'd left it for three weeks.

Gennie wasn't much of a cook, but each morning she crawled into the kitchen in search of coffee and on the countless occasions she made herself tea or poured a glass of wine, there it was like an accusation.

By the end of a fortnight, it had acquired a red wine stain on its corner and she was compelled to ask herself why she hadn't chucked it out or at least shoved it in a drawer somewhere.

Nathaniel H. Bennett
International Security Services

Beneath was a mobile number and an email address set in smaller type, but the answer to her question lay in the innocuous language under his name.

There had always been something wrong with the original picture. The incongruity of Nathaniel cradling the delicate china figure in the massive meat hook of his hand kept haunting her. There were, she imagined, a few passionate porcelain experts built like brick shit houses in the world, but the statistical chances of her running into one were, she felt, pretty slim. After spending longer pondering the porcelain expert than she was proud of, she wondered why the name on the card had not been appended with some retired use of rank. Only a few possible reasons for that: either he'd been dishonourably discharged, he was reluctant to state – up front – what his rank had been, or he'd been in a part of the service whose members didn't normally reveal their rank.

At first she told herself her reluctance to be rid of the card was simply that she loved a mystery. True as that was, there was more to it. By the end of the third week, she had to admit to a less morally defensible motivation.

In all the years she'd spent awash in a sea of information of man's inhumanity to man, of war criminals and the silent, sociopathic men employed by governments to maintain their power by less than fastidious means, she had never come face to face with one.

Her database on governments, individuals and victims of torture was extensive and information rich, but her knowledge of the men – very occasionally women – who perpetrated those atrocities was sterile and impersonal. When she'd finally, tentatively asked herself the question Nathaniel had posed as he ground his cock against her crotch, she had to admit, however unwillingly, to a fascination with the men who did this.

Did they tell themselves comforting patriotic lies? Did they find ways to inure themselves to the screams and the pain of their victims? How did they distance themselves from the humans they were destroying? Or perhaps they didn't? Perhaps that was the most frightening prospect of all: that they enjoyed doing what they did – took pleasure in their work. These men who did unspeakable things, not in the red rage of battle or from the cockpit of long-range bombers, but in such personal, intimate settings lived with the stench of urine and faeces and blood and the agonies of their subjects so close at hand.

Nathaniel Bennett was not on any list of human rights' violators, that much Gennie knew. There were thousands who never made those lists, who flew below the radar of international authorities: the lesser demons of the torture world, the officially sanctioned, if usually unacknowledged, executors of state will.

She didn't consider her interest in the psychological dynamics of these people to be prurient. Understanding why people gave themselves permission to do this was important to finding ways to stop them.

What frightened her, when she finally forced herself to confront her feelings, was that she found Nathaniel Bennett excruciatingly attractive.

It was not his physical beauty, although he was a very handsome man; that had never been the mechanism of her attraction. She could appreciate aesthetic male beauty when she saw it and walk right by without regret. Nor was it his charm, which – on the rare occasions he'd turned it on – was considerable.

There was something at a level far deeper than the visual or the social that called to her in him. Something chemical. Something visceral. Something that both pulled her in and scared the living shit out of her.

After three large glasses of merlot, on a cold Thursday evening, she went into the kitchen, picked up the card, and dialled his number.

He answered on the second ring. "Good evening, Gennie."

"How did you know it was me?"

"I'm organized."

She paused for a moment, then pushed on. "Is everything okay with the figurine? Did the buyer get it?"

"I'm thinking that's not why you've called."

"No. Not really." Come on, she thought to herself. Don't be such a fucking coward. But her mind was racing and she couldn't think how to formulate what she wanted to say. "I . . . um . . ."

"I'd rather not talk on the phone, Gennie. Are you free now?"

The old kitchen clock stood at ten thirty, but she decided that she'd given him enough mixed messages already. "Yes, I am."

"Good. Then I'll be with you in about . . . let's see . . . five miles . . . thirty minutes? If you'll excuse the sweat."

"Sure. If you'll excuse the mess."

Nathaniel was nothing if not punctual; the bell rang at exactly eleven. Gennie had spent the preceding thirty minutes fighting the desire to fix her hair, put on make-up and tidy her living room. She had done none of these, but expended her energy trying to restrain herself from doing it. He was dressed in a black hoodie, white T-shirt and jogging pants and was, as promised, very sweaty. When she motioned him in, he walked past her smelling of musk, bonfires and damp autumn leaves.

"Would you like some wine?"

"I'd prefer water, if you don't mind."

"And a towel?"

He grimaced, skin flushed, dark hair plastered to his forehead. "A towel would be good."

"Go through," she said. "I'll be along."

In the kitchen she fished the pitcher of filtered water out of the fridge and found the one tall glass she knew didn't have a chip in it. She poured herself another glass of wine and then, rummaging in her drier, pulled out the only towel she was absolutely sure was clean and wedged it under her arm.

Nathaniel sat on the floor, legs bent, arms balanced on his knees, and back propped up against the book-and-file-strewn sofa.

"I'm sorry. Let me make some room there," Gennie said, dropping the towel beside him and then handing him the jug and the glass.

"No, I'm good here."

She settled on the floor opposite him, realizing with disgust that she was still wearing a ridiculous pair of orange fuzzy socks. Taking them off would look – something, something not good – so she knelt and sat on them instead. She took another deep swig of her merlot and watched him chug water instead.

The longer the silence grew, the more unsure she became about how to start the conversation. When he'd finished half the jug of water, he began to towel his hair.

"I served in Iraq and Afghanistan," he muttered, rubbing his head vigorously, "I did a couple of freelance stints in Africa, one in Thailand with the Yanks. I did some of the stuff you've written about. Is that what you wanted to know?"

Gennie swallowed. "Yes."

"Well, that's sorted then. Is that it?"

"No."

"You want know how, why? That sort of thing?"

"Something like that."

"You want to know if I liked it."

She took another sip of the wine and then put it down. Was she even sober enough to be having this discussion? "Yes, I guess I do."

He folded the towel and draped it on one of his knees. Beneath his rolled-up pants, his legs were tanned, dark haired, muscled. There was an ugly scar stretching from just below the hem to the top of his sock. When Gennie looked up, he was staring at her. The ghost of a grin played on his lips.

"That has a more complicated answer. One that would require you getting to know me better," he said, his smile broadening. "And you aren't sure you want to do that, are you, Gennie?"

"I . . ."

"Don't lie, Gennie. I fuckin' hate lies. They bring out the bastard in me."

"I'm not sure. No," she said, rushed and definite.

He nodded. "That's understandable. But here's the thing. I like you. I like that you know at least a bit of who I am. I'm tired of fucking women I have to lie to. I don't like the man I am, but trying to be someone else is worse."

She opened her mouth to speak but he cut her off. "And you could say that those are just the wages of sin," he went on, "and that might be true enough. But I figure I'd give it a try anyway. So, whatever it is I can do to change your mind, I'm gonna do. Understood?'

There was a tingling, an eerie surge that started at her buttocks and crept up the sides of her back. Only when it reached her shoulders did she realize her cheeks were flaming. She nodded.

"I'm not going to change your mind with words. So, are you going to come over here and kiss me, or do I have to come to you?"

"No," she said quickly, confused. "It's not like that."

He smiled and lay the towel aside. Carefully he moved the glass and the pitcher aside and pulled off his hoodie. "Yeah, darlin'. It is like that." He said it soft and low. "It is."

On his hands and knees he moved slowly towards her. It felt like a strange, electric paralysis; she couldn't move – just watched him close the gap between them.

"Because I can smell you, Gennie. It is exactly like that."

He kissed her the way he had before. A studied, careful kiss. It prised at her senses, pulled all her focus down to the inexorable sensation of his mouth on hers. While he kissed her, his hands rounded her hips and covered her ass, pulling her up onto his lap until she was straddling him. And just like before, her body cared nothing for her mind's hesitations. It would be so easy to just surrender. It frightened her, this strange and unfamiliar war.

When he broke the kiss, cocked his head and engaged her eyes. "Let me offer you the first piece of goodwill."

His hands slid beneath her jumper and lifted it upward, following the contours of her body. Pulling it over her head. He stroked her bare back and curled his fingers around her shoulders, then pushed her down until she could feel the hardness of his cock against her.

"It's not about pain, Gennie. It's about fear."

He kissed her again and, as he did, his hands travelled from her shoulders to enclose her neck. His thumbs edged under her jaw. Not hard but there. Gennie stiffened.

"Hush," he whispered, and pressed his cheek against hers. "Feel it? Can you feel it?"

"Yes, I can."

"You've such a pretty neck, pretty Gennie. And there," he said, easing his thumbs until they were poised above her carotid arteries, pressing just enough so she could feel the throb against them, "right there is your pulse. Feel that?"

All the rush of arousal began to knot into fear. Her thoughts were racing. Jesus fucking Christ, was she out of her mind? How had she fantasized that she would ever be in control of this? He was twice her size, he could snap her neck with a single hand. She'd be some obit in the papers.

"Yes. Please, stop," she said softly. Her voice trembled. "I don't think . . . I don't think I can do this."

"'Course you can, girl." The thumbs rubbed at her skin, ribbed over the tunnels of blood beneath the surface. "Because you want to know, don't you?"

"Oh . . . um . . . fuck," she stuttered. "God, I . . . I . . ."

"Sh-shush." It was a soporific sound, hypnotizing, which only frightened her more. Nathaniel pushed his hips up, not rough, sinuously. "I could end your life in three minutes. I know it. You know it. And it frightens you. Doesn't it?"

"Yes."

"Good. Because I like it when you're frightened." He pulled back his head, looked straight into her eyes, and gave her a chilling, charming grin. "You can feel that, too."

His eyes were not the olive of before, but black holes in the lamplight. Or perhaps they were all pupil. It wasn't that he was detached or unengaged, but horrifyingly, monstrously there. He had killed people like this. In that moment, she was sure of it. Her body shivered violently, and although she tensed her muscles to quell it, it wouldn't stop.

"It's a good way to die," said Nathaniel, tilting his head, putting the tiniest bit more pressure on her throat. "A peaceful way. Painless. Would you like to go, Gennie?"

"No!" she whimpered. Her breathing was shallow and fast,

ragged with the tremors that shot through her frame. "No, no. Please."

"Well, that's good. Because you're no use to me dead." The grin grew into a wide smile. "So touch me."

"What?"

"You heard me. Show me you're of use to me." Again, he pressed his thumbs a little deeper. "Reach inside and stroke my cock."

"But . . . Christ." The smile was gone. She began to feel slightly dizzy. Her pulse hammered against her inner ears.

"Do it!" His voice was low, dry, brittle, suddenly cold.

Gennie scrabbled with the hem of his damp T-shirt. The waistband beneath was soaked with perspiration. It felt wretched as she tugged at the elastic webbing and burrowed her hand inside his hot, humid sweats and curled her fingers around his cock. It was turgid, veined and circumcised, viscous with pre-come, difficult to fully encompass with her hand.

"Stroke me. Slowly."

She did, the roll of his hips setting her pace.

He gave her the smallest of nods, and his eyelids fluttered. "Now this . . . this is going to keep you alive."

"Will it?" She asked.

His lips parted, he raised his jaw in a small gesture of arousal. On his breath, which was coming slightly faster now, she detected the tang of cloves below the now familiar smell of spent fireworks. Between her legs, her hand made slick, obscene sounds with each stroke of his cock. It would have turned her on had she not been so aware of the pressure at her neck.

"Your hand is trembling, Gennie." He smirked.

She gave him a stricken look. "I'm . . . I'm sorry."

"So you should be," he said. There was a dry, bored tone to his voice, completely at odds with the cock swelling and sliding in her hand. "You're not really very good at this, are you?"

Before she could answer, he changed the angle of his hands. His thumbs dug into the underside of her jaw, forcing her head up. She made a miserable sound, one she'd never heard herself make before.

"Is this how you've touched your boyfriends, Gennie? Is this why you don't have one? I'd rather have your cunt. It's got to be better than your manual efforts. You don't need a brain to use your cunt, do you, Gennie?"

"For God's sake. That hurts," she whimpered, trying to pull away from his bruising hands. The fear was bad enough, but there was something about the words – no matter how ridiculous – that cut. It didn't matter that he was throbbing in her hand and obviously aroused. It didn't matter that she didn't pride herself on delivering quality hand-jobs while being threatened with strangulation. He had managed to make her feel like nothing. A terrified, wretched loser.

"Come on. Don't make me wait."

Tears prickled at the corners of her eyes. "What the fuck do you want?" she whined.

"You know exactly what I want."

"I can't."

Nathaniel adjusted his grip on her. One hand encircled her throat almost completely. The other fisted the hair at the back of her head. He gave her a short, sharp jerk and forced her to look at him. "Say that again and I'll snap your neck, you stupid cunt."

Gennie opened her mouth but there was nothing.

"I want you on my cock. Do I have to explain how?"

"No," she whispered. She was crying silently, her breath hitching in her chest as she inhaled.

"Good. Don't make me wait."

All she could think was how lucky it was she'd worn a skirt. Had she been in trousers, in this position, the logistics would have been harder.

She didn't realize she'd stopped stroking him, but she released him now and fumbled with her skirt. It was a faded cotton thing – too full to be fashionable – she wore around the house, and she fought to pull it up enough to get the fabric out of the way to reach her panties. Having hooked her thumbs under the hips, she tried to squirm her way out of them with only partial success. She finally got one leg free and heard a seam rip in the process.

Only when she began to tug at the waist of his sweats again did it strike her that, not once, had it occurred to her to refuse him, to tell him she didn't want to fuck. The fear had completely eclipsed any arousal she had felt at first. As she struggled to get the wadded fabric over his hips without being able to look down and see what she was doing, she started to panic. Not because she was about to have intercourse with someone who was terrifying her, but because he was so obviously amused at her inept attempts to get his pants down.

His face changed. Nathaniel relinquished his grip on her neck and her hair. "Okay. Okay," he whispered, as if to a child. He wrapped his arms around her shoulders and, bending forward, lowered her onto the floor.

Perhaps it was his tone, or the change of position, but suddenly Gennie was drowning in sorrow and a choking sense of relief. She turned her head to the side and cried.

"Oh, Gennie, Gennie," he soothed, pressing his mouth to her salt-wet cheek. "It's over. Done. Finished."

She fought for breath between monstrous sobs and, for a while, he simply made hushing sounds and stroked her hair. Cupping her face, he kissed her with all the terrible gentleness of a total stranger. Then he entered her.

Her first disembodied thought was that it shouldn't have been so easy. How could she be wet? Even as she canted her hips in response to that first delicious violation, even as she spread her legs wider, and bent her knees, even as she groaned at the meaty, visceral sensation of his cockhead hitting the end of her passage, a drone of self-disgust settled into her spinal column.

He fucked her with the slow deliberation of restrained violence. His sinews were taut, his mouth was open, at her throat his teeth rasped against her skin. And she knew these weren't two different men. Just one that could switch modes with an ease born of years of practice.

Pausing for a moment, he reached back, tugged his damp

T-shirt over his head, and groaned at the meeting of skin as he lowered himself onto her.

"Tell me to fuck you, Gennie."

That's when the sense of relief obliterated everything else. When the muscles of her cunt spasmed around him, and she began to come, she begged him to fuck her.

After he'd finished, in the awkward stillness that followed, Gennie felt the bizarre disorientation that comes with having done something she'd never thought herself capable of doing. With it came a swell of revulsion. At herself. At him.

On her back, on the floor, the light from the floor lamp above her burned a painful hole into her brain. The two painful spots under her jaw acted as a mnemonic. She had never been in any danger of dying at all. Now she was sure of that. How had she so thoroughly convinced herself otherwise? She had slipped so easily, so willingly into the mindset of a victim. The shame of it knotted her stomach and she felt the first cramp.

"Off. Get off me," she said, panicked, pushing him as the first wave of nausea hit her.

Gennie scrambled out from beneath his lethargic body, got to her feet and, clamping one hand to her mouth and an arm across her bare breasts, rushed down the hall. In the small, old-fashioned bathroom, she sank to her knees and retched into the toilet.

It seemed as if there were no end to what she could bring up and, in the weak moonlight streaming through the high window, the regurgitated wine looked like blood as it splashed onto the white porcelain. Like a monumental act of refusal – one she seemed incapable of only minutes before – her body convulsed and attempted to expel all the fear, the arousal, the sense of self-disgust, the weakness of the previous hour. Between her bare legs, the same convulsions forced the blood-warm remnants of his seed down her inner thighs.

The hand on her head made her flinch.

"No! Don't," she croaked into the echo of the toilet bowl.

But Nathaniel did not retreat. He caught a curtain of hair and smoothed it away from her face. "Shush, darlin'. Get it all out. It's normal."

He was crouched next to her, his T-shirt back on, his face in deep shadow. Reaching above her, he pulled the towel off the rail next to the sink and draped it over her bare shoulders as another volley of retching overtook her.

When she thought it was over, when she was panting into the void and assuring herself that her legs would hold her if she tried to stand, she sat back on her heels and wiped her mouth with a corner of the towel. She couldn't look at him.

"I think you need to go now." Her tone was flat.

"That's the one thing I'm afraid I cannot do, sweet Gennie."

"Why?" she asked the darkness.

"Because if I go now, you're going to remember only that other man, and not this one.

"Yes and no," he said. His knees cricked in the shadows as he got to his feet. She felt him slip his hands beneath her arms and pulled her upright. "You want it to be simple, but it's more complicated than that. I assume you have a bathroom with an actual bath somewhere?"

"At the end of the hall, through my bedroom."

He lifted her easily, as if she were something entirely portable. And that was, in a way, what she felt like: something that had been taken to atrocious places, into unsolvable mazes, and then been carried back.

She expected him to simply plop her down on the bed, but he carried her through it and into her bathroom instead. He lowered her onto the side of her tub and switched on the light.

"I just want to sleep," she said miserably.

But he was already turning the creaky taps on, playing his fingers beneath the flow until the old boiler grudgingly gave him a stream of hot water. Satisfied with the temperature, he tugged the little stopper and rerouted the water through to the shower head.

"Come on. Get in," he said, stripping off his shirt and stepping out of his sweats.

When she hesitated, he pulled her to her feet again and reached around her waist, hunting for the closure on her skirt.

"I can do it," she said waspishly.

He stepped away from her. "Then do it, Gennie."

He stood naked, his arms crossed over his chest. There was, she thought, a flurry of tangled things simmering beneath the kindness in his voice. The tendons of his neck were rigid, his shoulders tense. It didn't show on his face, but she was almost sure, as she stepped out of her skirt and kicked it aside, that he was, perhaps, nervous.

He looked down her legs to the obnoxious, fuzzy orange socks that puddled sadly around her ankles. "Now that . . . is very sexy."

"They're warm," she snapped, tugging at them furiously to get them off.

Without waiting, he picked her up and stepped over the lip of the tub, lifting her into the shower. The water was far too hot. She yelped and tried to pull away, but he had her.

"I thought you said it was over!" she sobbed, suddenly frantic again.

"It is. It is."

She was beyond the point of control. There was nothing left to be rational with. "Fuck off. Get out, you bastard." She was yelling, struggling, her hands skidded over his chest as she tried to push away from him.

Still, he wouldn't let her go. He locked his arms behind her back and let her rage. When, after several minutes of panicked frenzy, she'd exhausted herself, the water didn't seem quite so unbearable, and she resorted to weeping against him.

"Stuff like this, Gennie, you have to wash it off. You can't sleep with all that fear stinking up your dreams. Trust me about this. I really do know. It's like a ritual." Nathaniel pressed a kiss to the top of her wet head. "Now, if let you go and reach for the soap, do I have to worry about you kicking me in the balls?"

* * *

Gennie was sure she would not sleep with him lying beside her, but exhaustion took her nonetheless. Despite the shower, she dreamed of suffocating and woke up gasping, flailing blindly in the darkness. A large arm surrounded her waist and pulled her tight into the bowed warmth of Nathaniel's body, and she slept again. When she awoke, it was to an insistent tap on her shoulder.

"I have a day full of shite, and I need to talk to you before I go." He was crouched by the side of the bed, holding a blurry cup of something in front of her face.

Gennie struggled to sit up and took the mug. It was tea. Insanely strong tea. "I'm not sure I'm conscious enough for this," she muttered, pulling the sheet around herself. "But, okay."

Nathaniel prodded her a little to give him room, and sat on the side of the bed. He was wearing the same clothes. The smell of rank, stale sweat. In her hazy morning mental state, all she could think was how disgusting they must have felt to get back into. But, having been in the military, he was probably used to it. He sat with his elbows on his knees, looking away from her, a cracked china cup cradled in his hands.

Those hands. She tensed her jaw, felt the two spots of dull, bruised ache beneath it.

"I know it's likely you'll decide you never want to see me again. Fuck all I can do about that. But I'm tired of hiding who I am from almost everyone. I have a few mates, from the old days, who know me well." He gave a bitter laugh. "It would be easier if I were gay."

The silence stretched on into the dull light that filtered through the curtains, and Gennie let it. The clock beside her bed blinked 6.40. She pushed the mass of tangled hair off her face.

"Of all the women in the world you could have chosen to—" she hunted for the right word "—reveal yourself to, why me?"

He inhaled and let it out slowly. "After coming to take a

look at the Meissen figure, I found out who you are and what you do. It seemed ironic that our paths should cross. I guess I took it for a sign."

Gennie cocked her head. "But didn't you think that I, more than most people, would be unsympathetic?"

He turned and looked at her. There was a frightening vulnerability in his face. All of a sudden she realized what he was looking for, and she had no idea if it was possible to give it to him.

"Intelligent, educated people usually get to choose the world they immerse themselves in, Gennie. I think you did."

It was a cryptic answer but before she could say so he went on.

"I'm sure there is a large part of you that is full of condemnation, and rightly so. But I think there's a part of you that is fascinated by it, too. That's usually the way of it. Maybe you just don't want to admit it."

He was right. She didn't. Two sides of the same coin. Two edges of the same knife. But this was an invitation to cut herself on one of them. She'd left objective interest behind last night. Perhaps she'd never get it back.

"I'm willing to be honest about it if you are," she began, shocked at what she knew was coming out of her mouth. "I'll admit to an unhealthy interest in torture if you'll admit to a desire for absolution."

Nathaniel stroked her cheek with a finger. "I will. But I'll not get it. And you can't give it to me."

"No," she whispered.

When he kissed her, it was the way she had imagined it might be that first time. There was no precision to it. It was a raw, feral, desperate kiss. All hunger and taking and it tasted of sadness. He pushed her back into the pillows and fed on her.

She let him, not because she was scared, but because it made her blood sing. Because he tasted like everything she'd ever wanted a man to taste like. And for a moment, she didn't want to think about anything else.

He left her hungry, wet, her cunt aching. When she heard

her front door close, she curled onto her side, slid her hand between her thighs and masturbated. The images that took her to orgasm were horrific.

In the early afternoon, Gennie worked on tagging the summaries of testimony in the Khmer Rouge tribunals dragging on in Phnom Penh. This was the second co-prosecutor to resign from the post, and it meant that the hearings would stretch on past the end of the year. Her mobile chimed to alert her to a message.

"Did you have a wank after I left, sweet Gennie?"

Witty? Snarky? Truthful? It took her a minute to decide how to respond.

"Yes."

"Tell me what you thought about."

She stood up, deliberately putting distance between herself and material at the desk. It was not possible for her to be truthful about that.

"I just did it. "

"You're a filthy liar. Tell me."

"Mind your own business!" She tapped it out with a spurt of anger, then relented. "I can't put that in a text."

"That's better. Thank you. How are you fixed for Saturday night?"

She put down her phone on the counter, switched on the kettle, and made tea. All the images flooded back. They made her feel queasy. Queasy and aroused.

Finally, thirty minutes later, she texted him back.

"Saturday night is fine."

Nathaniel arrived looking like a man who'd never perspired in his life: in a charcoal suit, demure silk tie and his date-smile. Gennie struggled into her only pair of high heels and walked down to the gate with him. The waiting car wasn't his: a sleek, black sedan with tinted windows.

"What happened to your lovely old Jag?" she asked, as she watched a massive man with close-cropped blond hair get out of the driver's seat and open the rear door.

"This is my mate, Karol. He's playing chauffeur for us."

Gennie cocked her head at the over-muscled man. "Hello, Karol."

"Good evening, madam," the man replied, words sludgy with an Eastern European accent. Polish, she thought.

She threw Nathaniel an inquisitive look.

"He's been practising that all day," said Nathaniel, helping her into the car. When he slid in beside her, he grinned.

"This isn't his usual job, I gather."

"Not buying the driver persona?"

"Not really, no."

"You've been blown, Karol," he said, addressing himself to the back of the other man's round, close-shaved head. The driver shrugged his massive shoulders, grunted and started the car. "What gave him away?"

"Most chauffeurs don't look like they can bench press the car they're driving."

Nathanial smirked. "Fair enough."

She'd never been to the restaurant although it was in the small, rather quaint village of Bray, less than twenty minutes from her house. They ate and drank and talked of things in the news. Looking around at the other guests, Gennie felt underdressed in her plain black silk shift, but it was the only evening wear she had, purchased in an emergency from a store in Kowloon on a trip for the Institute.

Nathaniel noticed and furrowed his brow. "You look very sexy," he said, swirling burgundy in an oversized wine glass. "Elegant."

"Thank you for the lie." She tucked inanely at a stray wisp of hair. "Kind of you."

His smile was bland. "I'm not a kind man, Gennie. Believe me."

Sitting back as the waiter took away her plate, she considered for a moment. "Yes, strange as it sounds, I think you are."

He turned his head, as if easing the muscles in his neck. "And that's hard to process?"

"No, not really."

"Ah, I forgot. You have files on people like me." He reached across the table and wound another stray strand of her hair around his finger. "They're nice to their children. Faithful to their wives. Attached to their pets."

To the restaurant's guests, it looked like an affectionate gesture, but Gennie could feel just how firmly he had the curl anchored around his digit. There was no sitting back without a painful tug of war.

"That's not what I said," she hissed.

"Yes, essentially it was." He offered her his most boyish, winning smile. "I forgive you, since it's true."

"Then let go of my hair."

Nathaniel leaned in closer and whispered: "Beg me. Quietly."

At first she thought he was joking, but she saw his pupils dilate in the subdued lighting and reconsidered.

"Don't be ridiculous."

He licked it lips, quickly, unconsciously. The smile went from open to teasing. "Beg me, darlin'."

"I'm not going to beg you."

"Oh, you will. Now, later, but you will."

Gennie glanced around the restaurant, exhaled, swallowed and muttered, "Please let go of my hair."

"Mmm. Again. Try sayin' it like you mean it."

Then it struck her like thunder: the sheer simplicity of it. All it took was her reluctance to make a fuss in a public place to have control over her. How pathetic. And yet she still couldn't pull herself to even raise her voice.

"Please," she said and took another breath. "Please let go of my hair."

The smile, far more of a threat than an expression of benevolence, disappeared. "You're so easy, Gennie," he replied, unwinding the tendril on his finger. "You make me hard."

She sat back and took an unladylike gulp of her wine. "You're an evil bastard."

"Undeniably. But I do believe your panties are wet anyway."

They were. As if him saying it made it true. *Fuck you*, she mouthed silently.

Karol was leaning against the car, smoking, when they walked out into the parking court. He rushed around to open her side door, but not, Gennie thought with quite the efficiency he'd managed earlier. In the darkness of the car, the smell of new leather was intense. The chill made Gennie shiver and she pulled her velvet wrap tighter.

Nathaniel settled in next to her and snaked an arm around her shoulders. "Cold?"

"I'm fine."

The car began to move and, without ceremony, Nathaniel slid his free hand between her wrap and her dress and palmed her right breast. Gennie stiffened.

"Don't," she whispered, clutching his wrist and pushing his hand off her. The idea having a stranger glance in the rear-view mirror and see her like this didn't feature in any of her sexual fantasies.

Nathaniel curled his arm tighter, pulling her ear to his mouth. "If you make a fuss, he'll look and he'll see. I'm guessing you don't want that. So don't make a fuss."

There was a cruel humour in his voice, and the touch that followed, on her thigh, sliding the hem of her dress up her thighs. In that moment, Gennie pledged to never, ever wear stockings again. She felt the warmth of his fingers on the bare skin above the stocking top and squirmed. And this time, when she tried to push his hand away, he simply didn't respond.

It was the same strange, trapped feeling she'd had in the restaurant. Only worse. When she turned her head to whisper a plea to him to stop, he cupped the back of her head and kissed her.

She had come to understand that he gave two kinds of kisses. This was the deliberate, manipulative type. It was controlling, muting. So that when his fingers curled around the leg of her panties and pushed between the wet folds of her cunt, all she could do was stifle on the whimper.

God, she was wet. Why was she so wet? Something inside her broke as she heard the slick, liquid noises his moistened fingers made as they moved between the lips of her cunt. All of a sudden, she was complicit. He'd made her complicit because she was wet and he wouldn't stop, and he was using her shame, her fear, and her arousal against her. His tongue was just like his fingers, probing and prying and forcing her open. Until she had to clench her fists to stop herself from arching her hips and hold her breath to stop herself from moaning. But he was in her: in her mouth, and her cunt and her head. Her muscles fluttered and convulsed. The sounds were loud and lewd and now it didn't matter any more who heard them, because she was coming. Her thighs drenched in her fluids, trapping his hand. Having forgotten how to kiss or even whom she was kissing. Her body twitched and arched as if plugged in to a live outlet.

When she thought it was over, and the violence of her spasms had died, he withdrew his fingers, fumbled in his pocket, and, with a kiss on her forehead, pulled a hood over her head.

He let her scream for what seemed like a very long time. In the darkness it was easy to scream. Now Gennie knew why the need for a driver, why not Nathaniel's car. There was no offer of comfort, physical or otherwise, just the crushing pressure of a single hand around her wrists. Through the fabric of hood, she could smell her spent arousal – a choking, cloying scent. Trapped in the dark with the reek of her own stupidity and a thousand fragmented images she stored in her head.

Two stood out more than all the others: an old black and white photograph taken in Buenos Aires during Argentina's Dirty War. The precise date was never identified, nor was the hooded woman under a street lamp being pushed into a car. The other was a more recent colour picture of shackled and hooded Afghan prisoners in the back of a cargo plane, bound for Guantanamo Bay.

When she finally quieted down, Nathaniel spoke.

"I figured you'd want to know what this feels like. Taking someone off a battlefield is a hit or miss proposition; their blood's up, they were all set on dyin' for the cause. But take them in the middle of the night, from the place they feel the safest – especially if you can get their family screaming, too – and you've got a far better chance of success. Disorientation is useful."

"Don't you quote from some fucking HUMINT interrogation manual to me!" she roared from inside her darkness. "How fucking could you? You needed to scare me to death to show me this? Why the fuck didn't you just tell me?"

He laughed. "Oh, you already knew all the facts, Gennie. You're just a filing cabinet full of facts. But that tells you nothing, really. You've got to feel it."

"Right. I've felt it now. So, take the hood off."

Something pushed against the left side of her head. She flinched. "Not yet, darlin'. The ride's not over," he whispered, and pressed a kiss to the side of her covered face.

She heard the high hissing sound of material being drawn out, and felt her wrists released only to have them bound together. Then a clink, and another, softer hiss, and she felt something tighten around her neck, over the hood. It was – she was almost certain – his belt.

Although there are many instructional documents on how to treat and interrogate prisoners, there are very few on how to resist it. The US has put a number of its officers through mock capture and torture scenarios, believing that forewarned is forearmed, but Gennie knew that, to a certain extent, resistance was futile. Eventually, a tortured prisoner will not only tell you everything you want to know, but a great deal of crap, as well. One of the many problems with non-humane interrogation techniques was that it took considerable human resources just sorting out the wheat from the chaff.

The civil authorities – police and national intelligence organizations like the FBI – who interrogated people on a daily basis came to this conclusion long ago. Torture is a very poor way of producing actionable intelligence, but it's an excellent way to terrorize a larger population into meek acquiescence.

Thinking this way calmed Gennie. It was the subject in the abstract. So when the car finally drew to a stop and hands reached in and pulled her from the back of the car and onto her feet on a gravel surface, she did not resist. Nathaniel was right, fear of small things – embarrassment in a public place, sexual exposure – served the purpose of the controller. Fear, in essence, made her complicit.

Not that she wasn't scared. She was. So as the large hand curled around her upper arm and led her, feet crunching on stone, across an expanse and up the stairs to what she assumed was the entrance to some sort of building, she decided that hiding her fear was the best defence she had. Not because it would enable her to resist anything, but because it would simply make her harder to read.

When he pulled the hood off her head, it was in a plain, bare concrete basement. He'd seated her on a chair, re-secured her hands behind her back and tied her ankles to the chair legs. In some very clear, very analytical part of her brain, she noted that he hadn't taken her heels off. Men, she thought bitterly, it's all about the visuals.

"You're quiet, Gennie. What's going on in that pretty little head of yours, I wonder?"

The chair back dug into her spine when she tried to move her arms. "I'm all screamed out," she said quietly, eyeing him through the strands of her dishevelled hair.

He looked older and tired in the harsh light of the ceiling's bare fluorescent strip. Stepping towards her, looking down at her, she was shielded from its glare, but it set his expression in shadow. He touched her cheek with the tips of his fingers. "So you've decided not to play, have you?"

Gennie's first instinct was to pull away from the caress, but she resisted the temptation and, instead, leaned her cheek into it. "Is this a game?"

Nathaniel exhaled. "In a way, Gennie, love." He traced his fingers over her lips, pinching the bottom one with a curious gentleness. "You can learn a lot from games."

He drew his hand away and, so fast she had no time to see it coming, backhanded her across the face with a force that snapped her head sideways and robbed her of breath and, for a moment, sight.

She saw stars. Until that moment, she'd always thought the expression a bad cliché. But now she knew it was entirely accurate. Sparkling phosphenes flared and died, flared and died in the dimness of the room. Her cheek throbbed as the blood rushed into it and she tasted copper in her mouth from where her cheek had cut against her teeth.

"The danger in not playing the game, sweet Gennie, is that it forces me to up the ante until I have you convinced that I will, without much hesitation, hurt you very badly."

It took her time to order her thoughts enough to say anything. She tried to remember if she'd ever been hit like this before. Spanked as a child, certainly but, no, no one had every done this to her. The cut inside her mouth was stinging; the side of her face, hot and swelling.

This time, when he extended his hand to touch her lips, she flinched and pulled her head back. He smiled and reached instead for the loose end of the belt that dangled from where it was looped around her neck. The smile stayed fixed as he slowly wrapped the leather around his fist.

Despite all her best intentions, Gennie let out a whimper. As it escaped her, she hated herself for it. Despised her heart for racing, her muscles for trembling, the tears that erupted and flooded over her face – all the bastard parts of her that wouldn't be reined in by her intellect. There was simply no forcing them to obey her as she felt him pull the strap tighter and tighter.

"Look at me," Nathaniel said, pulling the short end of the belt upwards. "Up, look up!" As if he spoke to some wayward puppy.

In the angle of the light, his eyes were two black holes. His free hand cradled the back of her head, then pulled it to his suited groin, pressing her face into it, against the hardness of a rampant erection beneath the fabric.

"This," he said softly, "is truth. Feel it?"

Gennie sobbed once into the wool of his trousers.

"I'm so hard for you now, I could unzip, shove my cock down your throat and come in under a minute." His hips rolled once, and she felt it twitch against her face.

"There, I've just told you something absolutely true." Threading his fingers into her hair, caressing her head, he went on: "And I want you to tell me something absolutely true. Do you understand?"

The stuff of his trousers felt coarse against her bruised skin. It smelled of steam ironing and the acrid scent of dry-cleaning solution, as if the thing she had her faced pressed to was not human. "I . . . I don't know what you want me to say."

"Something true. Like this: when I was in Thailand, I attached electrodes to the testicles of some poor bastard from Yemen and sent thousands of volts through him. Not much amperage but it hurts like sin."

"Oh, God," she gasped. "I've never . . . I've never done anything. Not like that. Never."

She'd begun to babble, to sob. She couldn't breathe, couldn't take in enough air. And still the hand cupping her head stroked her hair, pressed her cheek to his groin, rubbed himself against her.

"He screamed like a woman. Screamed and screamed. At first, it made me sick to do it. Then I felt cold, nothing. But after a while . . ." He paused for a moment, took a breath. "After a while it got me hard. Just like this. And I hated that."

"Stop it," she cried. "I don't want to hear this. Fuck."

"I hated it, but I did it. Because . . . that was my job. And good men – real men – do their jobs. Don't they, Gennie?"

"Shut up!" she yelped. "Fuck, shut up!"

Suddenly, he stepped away and jerked the belt back. The

loop slid taut against her throat and cut off her sobs. He bent over her until his face was inches from hers.

"Now it's your turn. Tell me something true."

"Oh, Jesus . . . I . . . don't know what you want." The words came out like staggered steps. She really didn't know: sifting through a thousand petty transgression she thought significant at the time but, which now, seemed laughable.

"Think, Gennie. Think." He gave her sore face a hard tap for every word.

She remembered a dim hallway, the sensation of fraying carpet under her bare knees, and the rank taste of an unwashed cock that made her gag.

"I . . . I paid my rent in sex. As a student—" the words rushed out "—a long time ago. I couldn't come up with the money and he—"

The slap cut her off. Sharp, not as hard as the first, but it still took her breath away.

"Really, Gennie? You tellin' me you're a whore?" He crouched in front of her, one huge hand on her stockinged knee. "Cos I already know that. I could have fucked you the first time I met you. I did you on your living room floor, remember? You came so fuckin' hard. So hard. I felt you."

The knee beneath his hand began to tremble and she couldn't stop it. It made her strangely angry with herself. "Not my finest moment," she muttered.

"Don't insult the millions of women on this planet who have to sell themselves to feed their babies by feeling guilty for sucking off your landlord. It's a waste of time. We're all whores, darlin', one way or another."

"Then . . . Then I don't know what to tell you."

Nathaniel tilted his head, as if in sympathy, and wrapped another few inches of belt around his fist. The leather slid, the buckle clinked and pinched her skin, the choke tightened.

"I stole," she gasped, nodded franticly. "I stole something."

The belt loosened, the smile widened. "Really? What did ya take?"

"A ring. His dead mother's ring."

"Whose?"

"A lover. I took it. Took it."

A dark eyebrow rose. "Really," he whispered in mock awe, sliding his hand further up her thigh, pulling the silk with it. "I hadn't pegged you as a girl who's overly fond of jewellery."

"I'm . . . I'm not. No." Her leg was shaking so badly now the trembling spread to the other. The heels forced her feet at such an angle to make controlling her muscles almost impossible. "He fucked . . . he fucked around on me. He hurt me. So . . ." Gennie's breath hitched in her chest. "I took the thing I knew would hurt him. It was all he had left of his mother."

"And it did warm you, your revenge?" His hand gripped the meatiest part of her thigh and began to dig his fingers into the muscle of it.

"It did!" she sobbed. "It fucking did."

"You bitch," he whispered. "More."

"There is no more!" Gennie bellowed at him. "There's no bloody more."

It was the most curious sensation. Just pressure. Then, in the blink of an eye, she was screaming, trying to lift her body out of the chair to get away from the pain. And then it was gone. Her stomach cramped at the nausea that rose once the pain had stopped.

"Christ, I'm going to be sick."

"Breathe, Gennie. Breathe through it." He was up on his feet, loosening the belt from around her neck. He clasped her face in both hands and looked into her eyes. "Come on, big breath! You can do it."

She took a huge, wheezing gulp through a throat constricted in panic. She took another, then another.

"Please, Nathaniel. Stop. It's enough. Please."

His thumbs caressed her cheeks, wiping away the tears. "But you haven't told me what I want to know."

It was in the softest, kindest voice. As if it were breaking his heart to do this to her. As if she needed to be reasonable and understand that all this was only for her own good. He nodded again and kissed her once, gently, on the lips. In that moment, she would have given him anything. Anything. Even as part of her mind registered the thought as insane, all she wanted in the world was for him to release her and gather her up in his arms and tell her she was forgiven, and that everything would be all right.

"Tell me, darlin'. Because you're going to tell me anyway. And you'll feel so much better when you get it out, won't you?"

She caught her lips between her teeth and whimpered. Tears streamed down her cheeks and she sniffled, knowing her nose was running. "Yes."

"Yes?"

Shaking, weeping, she lowered her eyes and nodded. "Yes."

He took his hands away from her face and affectionately tucked a tangled lock of hair behind her ear, his eyes locked on hers. "Then get it out and shame the devil, Gennie."

"I was ten. My sister was—oh, God, maybe eight? I can't remember. She had this lovely little Siamese kitten named Annie. What a stupid name for a cat, isn't it?"

Nathaniel nodded. "Stupid."

"She got it as a present. Not me. Just her. But I played with it anyway, just to make her angry. And one day . . . I was playing with it and it scratched me. Hard. It made me bleed. So I grabbed it roughly and shook it. I shook it to teach it, you know?"

His eyes willed her to go on.

"It bit me. With it's awful little needle sharp teeth. It bit and it wouldn't let go. So I hit it. Really hit it. To make it let go. I didn't mean to hit it so hard. But I did. And I heard something snap, like a twig or a toothpick breaking."

"You're doing fine."

She wasn't sobbing any more, but the tears were blinding her. "It just lay limp for a moment. Then it started quivering.

Its back legs were moving and it was making the most horrible sound. And I watched it for a while. I thought: *Serve you right, you nasty little beastly cat.* But it didn't stop, and I got scared that someone would come and hear it, and see it, and know what I'd done."

There was a tender, awful warmth in Nathaniel's eyes. "What did you do?" he whispered.

"I . . . I put my hand around its little throat. It was warm, I could feel the noises it was making through the skin. So I squeezed." Gennie was shaking again, as if she were cold and never be warm ever. "And I squeezed. And I squeezed. It felt so good to do it, to stop its dreadful noises. Until it stopped making the sound."

"What happened?"

"I took it to the bottom of the garden, and I hid it. Under a huge pile of leaves. Two days later, they burned the leaves. No one ever found out."

"And your sister?"

"She thought it had run away. She cried for days."

"But?"

"But I was glad. We were even again."

Gennie sat in a docile haze, watching as Nathaniel undid the straps around her ankles. When he untied her wrists, he had to prise her interlaced fingers apart. All she could think about was that evil, demonic little girl she had been. And that that little girl was still inside her somewhere. She'd never be rid of her, because she'd never been punished, and she'd grown into the fabric of who she was, like one of those terrible parasites that slowly devours a tree from the inside.

Nathaniel helped her up the stairs from the basement and down a dimly lit hallway. He led her into a very neat, masculine living room, with an old fashion oxblood leather sofa, in front of a large fireplace. The fire crackled, and the flames licked upwards as he sat down, and pulled her into his lap.

She couldn't take her eyes off the fire, although she felt his fingers trace the raw abrasion the belt had made around her neck and winced as he drew his hand over the bruise on her cheek.

He made shushing sounds and kissed her, at first gently and then with more and more hunger. Until, at last, he pressed her back into the sofa, pushed up her dress, and fucked her.

As she strained beneath him, arching her hips up to meet his thrusts, every time his cock filled her, it felt like forgiveness. And when it felt like she'd had enough of it, she bowed her back, cried out, and came. Then, with one hard plunge that made her cervix ache, he flooded her.

It wasn't until she was lying still, feeling his weight on top of her, that she turned her head back to the fire and saw, on the mantelpiece, the figure. The little veiled girl with the lute.

She came awake in a strange bed and could not remember how she got there. Beside her, Nathaniel was still sleeping, on his side with a proprietary arm flung across her chest. Light filtered through a trio of slatted wooden blinds. The room was very plain, as if it were only ever used to sleep in.

Her cheek was tender, the inside of her mouth sore. It tasted of stale blood. When she went to move her legs, her right thigh ached and, edging it out from beneath the neutral coloured sheets, it was banded in a livid, dark red bruise on the cusp of going purple.

Sliding carefully out of bed, she limped to the equally sparse en-suite bathroom. She switched on the light and gasped at her reflection in the mirror above the sink counter. The side of her face was darkened and swollen, as was her bottom lip. Around her neck, a lighter red abrasion and a darker, broader bruise around one upper arm.

She looked, for all the world, like a battered woman. Someone she didn't recognize – frightening. Not because any of the marks were disfiguring, but because of what each of them meant. Sane women didn't let people do this to them. A sane woman would be angry. And in her heart, she could find absolutely no anger towards him for the bruises. No, that wasn't why she was angry. She was angry because she'd told him the truth – her truths, all her terrible truths.

But he had lied to her.

"Morning," said Nathaniel.

Gennie startled and froze. "Where are my clothes?"

He glanced back into the room. "On the chair, over there," he said, indicating with a toss of his dishevelled head. "Counting your war wounds, were you?"

She gave him a tight, slightly painful smile and pushed passed him into the bedroom, fighting the urge to cover herself. The clothes were draped over the chair. Facing away from him, she grabbed her panties and pulled them on, grimacing at the sensation of the wetness that had dried stiff at the crotch. She did the same with her bra and then pulled the black shift dress over her head.

"Gennie?"

Wadding up her stockings into a ball, she stuffed them into her purse and stepped into her shoes.

"Where's my wrap?"

"It's downstairs."

"Can you call me a taxi?"

"No need. I'll drive you."

She turned to look at him. He'd pulled on a pair of soft grey sweats while she'd been dressing. "Just call me a taxi, okay?"

"Is it the bruises?" he asked, in a soft voice.

Shooting him another tight smile, one that hurt considerably more than the last one, she strode past him, heels clicking on the polished wooden floor.

There was a set of stairs off the corridor, and now she thought she remembered coming up this way. Behind her, the wood creaked under the weight of his bare feet as he followed.

He caught her halfway down the stairs, a hand on her shoulder. "Gennie, come on. Stop."

"I want to go home. Please call me a taxi or I'll walk until I find something."

"Have some tea. Then I'll call you a taxi. Promise."

She was right on the edge of losing it, not certain whether

she was going to scream or break down and cry again. It didn't matter; it was the same feeling inside. Like lava setting fire to her insides. Like those people they discover three days later in a chair, totally incinerated with pair of perfectly unblemished feet.

"I don't drink tea for breakfast! I hate tea for breakfast!"

It came out like a proclamation of war.

"Fine. I've got some coffee somewhere. Maybe," he said, stepping ahead of her and trotting down the stairs to the hall below. He stood at the bottom with his hand out. "Come on."

The tragedy of high heels is that, no matter how fast you can race upstairs in them, you have to descend with a certain amount of fanfare, whether you want to or not. When she reached the last step, she ignored the hand and glared at him. "Promise you will call me a taxi? Fucking promise."

The kitchen was at the back of the house. It was, like the bedroom, very neat and clean. Terribly modern. Not much in it, though. "So this is what you get paid for doing your country's dirty work," she said, knowing just how cruel it was to say so. But she needed to be cruel then.

He had his broad, naked back to her, scooping coffee out of a tin into a French press. The kettle beside it was coming to the boil, and she felt the same. Nowhere to put all the lava that filled her. He poured the scalding liquid into the beaker.

"Are you angry about the bruises, Gennie?" The question was offered to the air in the sort of measured voice they used to show you they weren't upset when, in fact, they were.

"At you? No. I knew what you'd do."

Silence filled the room as he pushed the filter down through the dark brown liquid, then took two cups from hooks and filled them with the brew.

"Sugar? Milk?"

"No." He slid her coffee across the central counter. She put down the purse she'd been clutching onto like grim death, and picked up the cup.

"So what is it?"

Gennie took a sip of the coffee, holding it with both hands, letting it warm her fingers. She waited until he looked up to get his answer.

"'I fucking hate lies'," she spat, in a fair imitation of his unpolished accent. "Isn't that what you said? Remember? Do you?"

"Yes," he answered quietly.

"The truth, Gennie, you said. That's what you said. The truth, the whole fucking ugly, sick unforgivable truth." She cut herself off, her cheeks flaming, waiting for a reaction from him.

But he said nothing, simply took a sip of his own coffee and stared at her.

It was as if once she opened her mouth, she'd never be able to stop and there was no violence she would not do with her words. "Nathaniel. Honourable, damaged, loyal Nathaniel. The man who did his job, who let it turn him to shit, who did the things that no one else would do. Poor suffering, tortured Nathaniel the fucking torturer, with his guts all knotted up with rage and his head full of pain."

She stood back and pitched the cup at him with all the force she had. It hit him full in the chest, the liquid splattering all over him. The vessel didn't break but bounced off and onto the counter, splintering white shards of china back at him.

"You're a fucking liar. I trusted you. I trusted you with my life, I trusted you with things I've never told anyone. I let you hurt me, humiliate me. I let you terrify me. And you, you twisted cunt, you lied to me!"

Nathaniel stared at her, open mouthed, horrified. He shook the coffee off his arms and, with it, shards of pottery tinkled to the stone floor. In several places the shrapnel had ricocheted. There were white flecks and small cuts in his stomach and chest, just starting to bleed.

"What the hell are you talking about," he demanded.

"The girl!"

"What fucking girl? There is no girl."

"The piece of Meissen, you prick. The one on your mantelpiece."

He shut his mouth, flinched as if he'd been struck.

"You didn't sell it to some German. You bought it for yourself." Gennie let out her breath and picked up her purse. "Now, call me a taxi."

His teeth worried at his lower lip for a second, then he straightened. "Sure," he said, put his own cup down and felt in the pockets of his sweats. "My phone's in the sitting room. Let me get it."

As he passed her, Gennie closed her eyes, not wanting to look at him, not wanting, if she had to admit it, say goodbye.

The tug at her hair almost pulled her off her feet. She whipped around, despite the pain, but he was already in motion, dragging her behind him as he stalked down the hallway towards the front of the house and into the darkened sitting room. It had the charcoal smell of a long-dead fire and leather and polish.

"This," he said, yanking her in front of him and wrapping his arms around her body so tight she could hardly expand her chest, "this is a beautiful thing. It has survived three hundred years, in perfect condition. It was modelled by a master, painted with loving hands, made to do nothing more than delight the eyes. She's a pure, pure thing, Gennie. Not like us. Not like any of us. Not corrupted with age, not cracked. Flawless."

Nathaniel pressed his lips against Gennie's bruised cheek. "She was stuff to you. You'd have happily chucked her out. But I wanted her. I wanted her, like I wanted you."

Quiet for a moment, there was only the sound of his agitated breathing. He pressed his cheek against hers and rubbed. She felt the stubble of his unshaven face against her skin.

"So, yes. I lied to you. And I don't regret it."

"Why?" It was all she could get out at first. "Why couldn't you just tell me it was you buying it?"

Gennie heard his swallow, felt it. Then his heart thundering against her back. The arms around her moved, and his hand slid up her stomach, closing over a breast. He cupped it through her dress, squeezed it, caught the nipple between to fingers and pressed. "Let's play the truth game. All right? You know the rules."

She knew them now, even as she felt the pressure of the pinch, her eyes began to water before the pinch became the pain that streaked through her breast and up the side of her neck. "Okay," she gasped.

"Would you have kept my card, would you have phoned me if I had bought it?"

"No." It was a bleat. A whimper.

And then the pressure was gone. "That's my girl," he cooed, rocking her, stroking her breast. He buried his face into the side of her neck and kissed her, speaking against her skin. "That's my girl."

"There was something in you, Gennie. That very first time we met." With one arm, still firmly around her waist, Nathaniel grabbed a handful of her dress, lifting it, sliding his hand over the bare thigh he'd exposed. "Something wrong, deep inside you. They say you can smell your own kind, I know. But I think it's in the eyes." Cupping her mound, he squeezed hard once and released, then wedged his fingers beneath her panties.

They slipped into the swollen, wet valley of her cunt so easily, it made her weep. Or perhaps it was something else. He shuffled back, still holding her, still with his hands between her legs, and pulled her down onto the couch with him.

She felt him beneath her, hard and pressing between the cheeks of her ass, through the silk. It was impossible not to move, not to spread her legs, not to grind her ass against him, not to raise her arms and reach back, grasping his head and straining upwards to kiss him. She thrashed and fed on his lips, on his tongue, until he pushed two fingers deep into her cunt and she came, sobbing into his mouth.

Even before her spasms had died, before he pulled his fingers out of her, cupped her jaw and forced her to look at him. "Do you want me to call you a taxi?"

"No."

"Good, because I can't send you home like this. You're filthy."

The hot torrent drenched her the moment she entered the shower, and yet she shivered as he stepped in behind her. Gennie didn't want to analyse what had made her stay, why she had let him touch her. She wanted to believe she'd had no choice, but knew that wasn't true at all. That she could have told him to stop, then, in front of the little porcelain figurine, and he would have.

It didn't seem to matter now. He was pulling her to him, bending to kiss her under the flow, and it felt like whatever terrible thing she carried inside her, he could make it better. Perhaps because he carried something so much worse. She knew then, that he would never stop hurting her, and she didn't want him to, because it was a cycle of light and dark that obscured everything else.

The tile was hot against her back as he lifted her and pinned her to the wall. Wrapping her legs around his waist, he paused, trapping her in that moment of strange breathless possibility before he entered her. Like the wait before the jump, like a hanged man before the drop, like the time you can never take back.

He entered her in one brutal thrust. It made her keen and throw her head back against the wall. The water streamed over her, into her eyes, her mouth, her nose. When she tried to move her head, she felt him bury his face in the crook of her neck. His hand encircled her throat, forcing her to fight for air in the plummeting torrent, struggling in his grip, as he thrust into her again and again until he pressed his teeth into the meat of her shoulder. She screamed as he came.

"Oh, Gennie," he panted, pushing her wet hair out of her face. "It's never going to be over."

He lowered them both to the floor of the shower, and began to weep.

* * *

This is what it would always be like for them. Always the terrible rage followed by even more frightening tendernesses. That is why, when he stood at her door and rang her bell, she answered.